WORLDWAR: IN THE BALANCE

By Harry Turtledove
Published by Ballantine Books:

The Videssos Cycle:
THE MISPLACED LEGION
AN EMPEROR FOR THE LEGION
THE LEGION OF VIDESSOS
SWORDS OF THE LEGION

The Tale of Krispos:
KRISPOS RISING
KRISPOS OF VIDESSOS
KRISPOS THE EMPEROR*

NONINTERFERENCE
A WORLD OF DIFFERENCE
KALEIDOSCIPE
EARTHGRIP
DEPARTURES

THE GUNS OF THE SOUTH

WORLDWAR: IN THE BALANCE

*Forthcoming

WORLDWAR: IN THE BALANCE

Harry Turtledove

DEL
REY

A Del Rey Book

Ballantine Books • New York

A Del Rey Book
Published by Ballantine Books

Copyright © 1994 by Harry Turtledove

All rights reserved under International and Pan-American
Copyright Conventions. Published in the United States by
Ballantine Books, a division of Random House, Inc., New
York, and simultaneously in Canada by Random House of
Canada Limited, Toronto.

Turtledove, Harry.
    Worldwar: in the balance / Harry Turtledove. — 1st ed.
        p.   cm — (Worldwar series)
    "A Del Rey book."
    ISBN 0-345-38241-2
    1. Imaginary wars and battles—Fiction. I. Title. II. Series.
PS3570.U76I5 1993
813'.54—dc20   93-22133
                                                          CIP

Text design by Alexander J. Klapwald

Manufactured in the United States of America

First Edition: January 1994

10   9   8   7   6   5   4   3   2   1

WORLDWAR: IN THE BALANCE

1

Fleetlord Atvar strode briskly into the command station of the invasion fleet bannership *127th Emperor Hetto*. Officers stiffened in their seats as he came in. But for the way his eye turrets swiveled in their sockets, one to the left, the other to the right, he ignored them. Yet had any been so foolish as to omit the proper respect, he would have noticed—and remembered.

Shiplord Kirel, his body paint less elaborate only than Atvar's, joined him at the projector. As Atvar did every morning, he said, "Let us examine the target." Kirel served the fleetlord by touching the control with his own index claw. A blue and gray and white sphere sprang into being, a perfect representation of a life-bearing world floating in space.

All the officers turned both eyes toward the hologram. Atvar, as was his custom, walked around the projector to view it from all sides. Kirel followed him. When they were back where they had begun, Atvar ran out a bifurcated tongue. "Cold-looking place," the fleetlord said, as he usually did. "Cold and wet."

"Yet it will serve the Race and the Emperor," Kirel replied. When he spoke those words, the rest of the officers returned to their assigned tasks; the morning ritual was over. Kirel went on, "Pity such a hot white star as Tosev has hatched so chilly an egg."

"Pity indeed," Atvar agreed. That chilly world revolved around a star more than twice as bright as the sun under which he'd been raised. Unfortunately, it did so toward the outer edge of the biosphere. Not only did Tosev 3 have too much free water, it even had frozen water on the ground here and there. In the Empire's three current worlds, frozen water was rare outside the laboratory.

Kirel said, "Even if Tosev 3 is colder on average than what we're used to, Fleetlord, we won't have any real trouble living there, and parts will be very pleasant." He opened his jaws slightly to display small, sharp, even teeth. "And the natives should give us no difficulty."

"By the Emperor, that's true." Though his sovereign was light-years away, Atvar automatically cast both eyes down to the floor for a moment. So did Kirel. Then Atvar opened his jaws, too, sharing the shiplord's amusement. "Show me the picture sequence from the probe once more."

"It shall be done." Kirel poked delicately at the projector controls. Tosev 3 vanished, to be replaced by a typical inhabitant: a biped with a red-brown skin, rather taller than a typical male of the Race. The biped wore a strip of cloth round its midsection and carried a bow and several stone-tipped arrows. Black fur sprouted from the top of its head.

The biped vanished. Another took its place, this one swaddled from head to foot in robes of dirty grayish tan. A curved iron sword hung from a leather belt at its waist. Beside it stood a brown-furred riding animal with a long neck and a hump on its back.

Atvar pointed to the furry animal, then to the biped's robes. "Even the native creatures have to protect themselves from Tosev 3's atrocious climate." He ran a hand down the smooth, glistening scales of his arm.

More bipeds appeared in holographic projection, some with black skins, some golden brown, some a reddish color so light it was almost pink. As the sequence moved on, Kirel opened his jaws in amusement once more. He pointed to the projector. "Behold—now!—the fearsome warrior of Tosev 3."

"Hold that image. Let everyone look closely at it," Atvar commanded.

"It shall be done." Kirel stopped the flow of images. Every officer in the command station swiveled one eye toward the image, though most kept the other on the tasks before them.

Atvar laughed silently as he studied the Tosevite fighter. This native belonged to the pinkish race, though only one hand and his face were visible to testify to that. Protective gear covered the rest of him almost as comprehensively as had the earlier biped's robes. A pointed iron helmet with several dents sat on top of his head. He wore a suit of rather rusty mail that reached almost to his knees, and heavy leather boots below them. A flimsy coat of bluish stuff helped keep the sun off the mail.

The animal the biped rode, a somewhat more graceful relative of the humped creature, looked bored with the whole business. An iron-headed spear projected upward from the biped's seat. His other armament included a straight sword, a knife, and a shield with a cross painted on it.

"How well do you think his kind is likely to stand up to bullets, armored fighting vehicles, aircraft?" Atvar asked rhetorically. The officers all laughed, looking forward to an easy conquest, to adding a fourth planet and solar system to the dominions of the Emperor.

Not to be outdone in enthusiasm by his commander, Kirel added, "These are recent images, too: they date back only about sixteen hundred years." He paused to poke at a calculator. "That would be about eight hundred of Tosev 3's revolutions. And how much, my fellow warriors, how much can a world change in a mere eight hundred revolutions?"

The officers laughed again, more widely this time. Atvar laughed with them. The history of the Race was more than a hundred thousand years deep; the Ssumaz dynasty had held the throne for almost half that time, ever since techniques for ensuring male heirs were worked out. Under the Ssumaz Emperors, the Race took Rabotev 2 twenty-eight thousand years ago, and seized Halless 1 eighteen thousand years after that. Now it was Tosev 3's turn. The pace of conquest was quickening, Atvar thought.

"Carry on, servants of the Emperor," the fleetlord said. The officers stiffened once more as he left the command station.

He was back in his suite, busy with the infinite minutiae that accompanied command, when his door buzzer squawked. He looked up from the computer screen with a start. No one was scheduled to interrupt him at this time, and the Race did not lightly break routine. Emergency in space was improbable in the extreme, but who would dare disturb him for anything less?

"Enter," he growled.

The junior officer who came into the suite looked nervous; his tail stump twitched and his eyes swiveled quickly, now this way, now that, as if he were scanning the room for danger. "Exalted Fleetlord, kinsmale of the Emperor, as you know, we draw very near the Tosev system," he said, his voice hardly louder than a whisper.

"I had better know that," Atvar said with heavy sarcasm.

"Y-yes, Exalted Fleetlord." The junior officer, almost on the point of bolting, visibly gathered himself before continuing: "Exalted Fleetlord, I am Subleader Erewlo, in the communications section. For the past few ship's days, I have detected unusual radio transmissions coming from that system. These appear to be artificial in nature, and, and"—now he had to force himself to go on and face Atvar's certain wrath—"from tiny doppler shifts in the signal frequency, appear to be emanating from Tosev 3."

In fact, the fleetlord was too startled to be furious. "That is ridiculous," he said. "How dare you presume to tell me that the animal-riding savages our probes photographed have moved in the historic swivel of an eye turret up to electronics when we required tens of millennia for the same advance?"

"Exalted Fleetlord, I presume nothing," Erewlo quavered. "I merely report to you anomalous data which may be of import to our mission and therefore to the Race."

"Get out," Atvar said, his voice flat and deadly dangerous. Erewlo fled.

The fleetlord glared after him. The report was ridiculous, on the face of it. The Race changed but slowly, in tiny, sensible increments. Though both the Rabotevs and the Hallessi were conquered before they developed radio, they had had comparably long, comparably leisurely developments. Surely that was the norm among intelligent races.

Atvar spoke to his computer. The data the subleader had mentioned

came up on his screen. He studied them, asked the machine for their implications. The implications were as Erewlo had said: with a probability
that approached one, those were artificial radio signals coming from Tosev 3.

The fleetlord snarled a command the computer was not anatomically
equipped to obey. If the natives of Tosev 3 had somehow stumbled across
radio, what else did they know?

Just as the hologram of Tosev 3 had looked like a world floating in
space, so the world itself, seen through an armorglass window, resembled
nothing so much as a holographic image. But to get round to its other side
now, Atvar would have to wait for the *127th Emperor Hetto* to finish half
an orbit.

The fleetlord glared down at the planet below. He had been glaring at
it ever since the fleet arrived, one of his own years before. No one in all
the vast history of the Race had ever been handed such a poisonous di-
lemma. The assembled shiplords stood waiting for Atvar to give them
their orders. His the responsibility, his the rewards—and the risks.

"The natives of Tosev 3 are more technologically advanced than we
believed they would be when we undertook this expedition," he said, seeing if gross understatement would pry a reaction from them.

As one, they dipped their heads slightly in assent. Atvar tightened his
jaws—would that he might bite down on his officers' necks. They were going to give him no help at all. *His* the responsibility. He could not even
ask the Emperor for instructions. A message Home would take twenty-
four Home years to arrive, the reply another twenty-four. The invasion
force could go back into cold sleep and wait—but who could say what the
Tosevites would have invented by then?

Atvar said, "The Tosevites appear at the moment to be fighting several wars among themselves. History tells us their disunity will work to
our advantage." *Ancient history,* he thought; the Empire had had a single
rule so long that no one had any practice playing on the politics of dis-
union. But the manuals said such a thing was possible, and the manuals
generally knew what they were talking about.

Kirel assumed the stooping posture of respect, a polite way to show he
wished to speak. Atvar turned both eyes on him, relieved someone would
say at least part of what he thought. The shiplord of the *127th Emperor
Hetto* said, "Is it certain we *can* successfully overcome the Tosevites,
Fleetlord? Along with radio and radar, they have aircraft of their own, as
well as armored fighting vehicles—our probes have shown them clearly."

"But these weapons are far inferior to ours of similar types. The probes
also show this clearly." That was Straha, shiplord of the *206th Emperor
Yower*. He ranked next highest among the shiplords after Kirel, and
wanted to surpass him one day.

Kirel knew of Straha's ambitions, too. He abandoned the posture of respect to scowl at his rival. "A great many of these weapons are in action, however, and more being manufactured all the time. Our supplies are limited to those we have fetched across the light-years."

"Have the Tosevites atomics?" Straha jeered. "If other measures fail, we can batter them into submission."

"Thereby reducing the value of the planet to the colonists who will follow us," Kirel said.

"What would you have us do?" Straha said. "Boost for home, having accomplished nothing?"

"It is within the fleetlord's power," Kirel said stubbornly.

He was right; abandoning the invasion was within Atvar's power. No censure would fall on him if he started back—no *official* censure. But instead of being remembered through all the ages as Atvar Worldconqueror, an epithet only two in the long history of the Race had borne before him, he would go down in the annals as Atvar Worldfleer, a title he would be the first to assume, but hardly one he craved.

His the responsibility. In the end, his choice was no choice. "The awakening and orientation of the troops has proceeded satisfactorily?" he asked the shiplords. He did not need their hisses of assent to know the answer to his question; he had been following computer reports since before the fleet took up orbit around Tosev 3. The Emperor's weapons and warriors were ready.

"We proceed," he said. The shiplords hissed again.

"Come on, Joe!" Sam Yeager yelled in from left toward his pitcher. "One more to go. You can do it." *I hope,* Yeager added to himself.

On the mound, Joe Sullivan rocked into his motion, wound up, delivered. Some days, Sullivan couldn't find the plate with a map. *What do you expect from a seventeen-year-old kid?* Yeager thought. Today, though, the big curve bit the outside corner. The umpire's right hand came up. A couple of people in the crowd of a couple of hundred cheered.

Sullivan fired again. The batter, a big left-handed-hitting first baseman named Kobeski, swung late, lifted a lazy fly ball to left. "Shit!" he said loudly, and threw down his bat in disgust. Yeager drifted back a few steps. The ball smacked his glove; his other hand instantly covered it. He trotted in toward the visitors' dugout. So did the rest of the Decatur Commodores.

"Final score, Decatur 4, Madison 2," the announcer said over a scratchy, tinny microphone. "Winner, Sullivan. Loser, Kovacs. The Springfield Brownies start a series with the Blues here at Breese Stephens Field tomorrow. Game time will be noon. Hope to see you then."

As soon as he got into the dugout, Yeager pulled a pack of Camels from the hip pocket of his wool flannel uniform. He lit up, sucked in a deep drag, blew out a contented cloud of smoke. "That's the way to do it,

Joe," he called to Sullivan, who was ahead of him in the tunnel that led to the visitors' locker room. "Keep the ball down and away from a big ox like Kobeski and he'll never put one over that short right field they have here."

"Uh, yeah. Thanks, Sam," the winning pitcher said over his shoulder. He took off his cap, wiped his sweaty forehead with a sleeve. Then he started unbuttoning his shirt.

Yeager stared at Sullivan's back, slowly shook his head in wonder. The kid hadn't even known what he was up to; he'd just happened to do the right thing. *He's only seventeen*, the left fielder reminded himself again. Most of the Commodores were just like Joe, kids too young for the draft. They made Yeager feel even older than the thirty-five years he actually carried.

His "locker" was a nail driven into the wall. He sat down on a milking stool in front of it, began to peel off his uniform.

Bobby Fiore landed heavily on the stool beside him. The second baseman was a veteran, too, and Yeager's roommate. "I'm getting too old for this," he said with a grimace.

"You're what? Two years younger than I am?" Yeager said.

"I guess so. Something like that." Fiore's dark, heavily bearded face, full of angles and shadows, was made to be a mask of gloom. It also made him a perfect contrast to Yeager, whose blond, ruddy features shouted *farmboy!* to the world. Gloomy now, Fiore went on, "What the hell's the use of playing in a lousy Class B league when you're as old as we are? You still think you're gonna be a big leaguer, Sam?"

"The war goes on long enough, who can say? They may draft everybody ahead of me, and they don't want to give me a rifle. I tried volunteering six months ago, right after Pearl Harbor."

"You got store-bought teeth, for Christ's sake," Fiore said.

"Doesn't mean I can't eat, or shoot, either," Yeager said. He'd almost died in the influenza epidemic of 1918. His teeth, weakened by fever, rotted in his head and came out over the next few years; he'd worn full upper and lower plates since before he started shaving. Ironically, the only teeth of his own he had now were his four wisdom teeth, the ones that gave everyone else trouble. They'd come in fine, long after the rest were gone.

Fiore just snorted and walked naked to the shower. Yeager followed. He washed quickly; the shower was cold. It could have been worse, he thought as he toweled himself dry. A couple of Three-I League parks didn't even have showers for the visiting team. Walking back to the hotel in a sticky, smelly uniform was a pleasure of bush-league ball he could do without.

He tossed his uniform into a canvas duffel bag, along with his spikes and glove. As he started getting into his street clothes, he picked up the conversation with Fiore: "What am I supposed to do, Bobby, quit? I've been going too long for that. Besides, I don't know a lot besides playing ball."

"What do you need to know to get a job at a defense plant that pays better'n this?" Fiore asked. But he was slinging his jock into his duffel bag, too.

"Why don't you, if you're so fed up?" Yeager said.

Fiore grunted. "Ask me on a day when I didn't get any hits. Today I went two for four." He slung the blue bag over his shoulder, picked his way out of the crowded locker room.

Yeager went with him. The cop at the players' entrance tipped his cap to them as they walked past; by his white mustache, he might have tried volunteering for the Spanish-American War.

Both ballplayers took a long, deep breath at the same time. They smiled at each other. The air was sweet with the smell of the rolls and bread baking at Gardner's Bakery across the street from the park. Fiore said, "I got a cousin who runs a little bakery in Pittsburgh. His place don't smell half as good as this."

"Next time I'm in Pittsburgh, I'll tell your cousin you said that," Yeager said.

"You ain't going to Pittsburgh, or any other big league town, not even if the war goes on till 1955," Fiore retorted. "What's the best league you ever played in?"

"I put in half a season for Birmingham in 1933," Yeager said. "The Southern Association's Class A-1 ball. Broke my ankle the second game of a Fourth of July doubleheader and I was out for the rest of the year." He knew he'd lost a step, maybe a step and a half, when he came back the next season. He also knew any real chance he'd had of making the majors had snapped along with the bone in his ankle.

"You're ahead of me after all. I put in three weeks at Albany—the Eastern League's Class A—but when I made three errors in one game they shipped me right on out of there. Bastards." Fiore spoke the word without much heat. If you screwed up, another ballplayer was always ready to grab your place. Anybody who didn't understand that had no business playing the game for money.

Yeager stopped at a newsstand around the corner from the hotel and bought a magazine. "Something to look at on the train back to Decatur," he said, handing the fellow at the stand a quarter. The year before, he would have got a nickel back. Now he didn't. When you got a Three-I league salary, every nickel counted. He didn't think going from digest size up to bedsheet was worth the extra five cents.

Fiore's lip curled at his choice of reading matter. "How can you stand that Buck Rogers stuff?"

"I like it." Yeager hung onto the new *Astounding*. He added, "Ten years ago, who would have believed the blitz or aircraft carriers or tanks? They were talking about all that kind of stuff in here then."

"Yeah, well, I wish they'd been wrong," Fiore said, to which Yeager had no good reply.

They came into the hotel lobby a couple of minutes later. The desk clerk had a radio on to catch the afternoon news. H. V. Kaltenborn's rich, authoritative voice told of fighting in North Africa near Gazala, of fighting in Russia south of Kharkov, of an American landing on the island of Espíritu Santo in the New Hebrides.

Yeager gathered Espíritu Santo lay somewhere in the South Pacific. He had no idea just where. He couldn't have found Gazala or Kharkov without a big atlas and patience, either. The war had a way of throwing up name after name he'd never learned about in school.

Kaltenborn went on, "Daring Czech patriots have struck at the *Reichsprotektor* for occupied Bohemia, Nazi butcher Reinhard Heydrich, in Prague. They say they have slain him. German radio blames the assault on the 'treacherous British,' and maintains Heydrich still lives. Time will tell."

"Nice to hear we're movin' forward somewhere, even if I can't pronounce the name of the place," Yeager said.

"Means 'Holy Spirit,' " Fiore told him. "Must be Spanish, but it sounds enough like Italian for me to understand it."

"Okay," Yeager said, glad to be enlightened. He walked over to the stairs, Fiore trailing after him. The elevator man sneered at them. That always made Yeager feel like a cheapskate, but he was too used to the feeling to let it worry him much. For that matter, the hotel was cheap, too, with a single bathroom down at the end of the hall on each floor.

He used the room key, tossed his duffel onto the bed, picked up suitcases and tossed them beside the duffel, started transferring clothes from the duffel and the closet to the bags as automatically as he hit the cutoff man on a throw from the outfield. If he'd thought about what he was doing, he would have taken twice as long for a worse job. But after half a lifetime checking out of small-town hotels, where was the need for thought?

On the other bed, Fiore was packing with the same effortless skill. They finished within a few seconds of each other, closed their bags, and hauled them downstairs. They were the first ones back to the lobby; for most of their teammates, packing didn't come so easy yet.

"Another road trip done," Yeager said. "Wonder how many miles on the train I've put in over the years."

"I dunno," Fiore answered. "But if I found a secondhand car with that many miles on it, I sure as hell wouldn't buy it."

"You go to the devil." But Yeager had to laugh. A secondhand car with that many miles on it probably wouldn't even run.

The rest of the Commodores straggled down by ones and twos. A few came over to shoot the breeze, but most formed their own, bigger group; the bonds of youth were stronger than those of the team. That saddened Yeager, but he understood it. Back when he started playing pro ball in the long-dead days of 1925, he hadn't dared go up to the veterans either. The war only made things worse by taking away just about everybody between him and Fiore on the one hand and the kids on the other.

The manager, Pete Daniels (universally called "Mutt"), settled accounts with the desk clerk, then turned to his troops and declared, "Come on, boys, we got us a five o'clock train to catch." His drawl was as thick and sticky as the Mississippi mud he'd grown up farming. He'd caught for part of two seasons with the Cardinals thirty years before, back in the days when they were always near the bottom of the pack, and then a long time in the minors.

Yeager wondered if Mutt still dreamed of a big-league manager's job. He'd never had the nerve to ask, but he doubted it: the war hadn't opened those slots. Most likely, Daniels was here because he didn't know anything better to do. It gave the two of them something in common.

"Well, let's go," Daniels said as soon as the clerk presented him with a receipt. He marched out onto the street, a parade of one. The Decatur Commodores tromped after him. The year before, they would have piled into three or four taxis and gone to the station that way. But with gas and tires in short supply, taxis might as well have been swept off the street. The ballplayers waited on the corner for the crosstown bus, then plopped their nickels into the fare box as they climbed aboard.

The bus rolled west down Washington Avenue. At the intersections with north-south streets, Yeager could see water looking either way; Madison sat on a narrow neck of land between lakes Mendota and Monona. The bus went around Capitol Park before returning to Washington to get to the Illinois Central station. The capitol itself, a granite-domed white marble building in the shape of a Greek cross, dominated the low skyline of the city.

The bus stopped right in front of the station. Mutt Daniels waved train tickets. He'd kept track of things in a four-city swing through Illinois, Iowa, and Wisconsin; now the Commodores would spend the next month back at Fan's Field, so he'd only have to worry about lineups for a while.

A colored porter wheeled up a baggage cart. He tipped his cap, grinned to show off a mouthful of gold teeth. "Heah you go, gentlemen," he said, his accent even richer than the manager's. Yeager let the fellow heave his bags onto the cart, tipped him a nickel. The gleaming grin got wider.

Sitting beside Yeager in the passenger car, Fiore said, "When my dad first got to New York from the old country, he took the train from there to Pittsburgh, where my uncle Joe already was. First smoke he's ever seen in his life is the steward, and he's got gold teeth just like the porter here. For months, my dad thought all colored folks came that way."

Yeager laughed, then said, "Hell, I grew up between Lincoln and Omaha, and I never saw anybody who wasn't white till I went off to play ball. I've barnstormed against colored teams a couple of times, make some extra money during the winter. Some of those boys, if they were white, they could play anywhere."

"That's probably true," Fiore said. "But they ain't white." The train started to roll. Fiore twisted in his seat, trying to get comfortable. "I'm gonna sleep for a while, then head back to the dining car after the crowd thins out."

"If you aren't awake by eight, I'll give you a shot in the ribs," Yeager said. Fiore nodded with his eyes closed. He was good at sleeping on trains, better than Yeager, who got out his *Astounding* and started to read. The newest Heinlein serial had ended the month before, but stories by Asimov, Robert Moore Williams, del Rey, Hubbard, and Clement were plenty to keep him entertained. In minutes, he was millions of miles and thousands of years from the mundane reality of an Illinois Central train rolling south over flat prairie fields between one Midwestern town and another.

A field kitchen rolled up to the tank company somewhere south of Kharkov. After a couple of weeks of motoring this way and that, first to halt a Russian attack and then to trap the attackers, Major Heinrich Jäger couldn't have said where he was more precisely than that without a call to Sixteenth Panzer's signal detachment.

The field kitchen didn't properly belong to the company. Like the other two units that made up the Second Panzer Regiment, it had a motorized kitchen that was supposed to stay with it, while this one was horse-drawn. Jäger didn't care. He waved the driver to a halt, shouted to rout out his tank crews.

Some of the men kept on sleeping, in their Panzer IIIs or under them. But the magic word "food" and the savory smell that wafted from the stew kettle got a good many up and moving. "What have you got for us?" Jäger asked the driver and the cook.

"Boiled kasha, sir, with onions and meat," the cook answered.

Jäger had never tasted buckwheat groats till the panzer division smashed its way into southern Russia the July before. They still weren't his top choice, or anywhere close to it, but they filled the belly nicely. He knew better than to ask about the meat—horse, donkey, maybe dog? He didn't want to know. Had it been beef or mutton, the cook would have bragged about it.

He dug out his mess tin, got in line. The cook ladled out a big dollop of steaming stew. He attacked it with gusto. His stomach complained for a moment; it wasn't used to taking on a heavy load in the wee small hours. Then it decided it liked being full, and shut up.

Somewhere off in the distance, a machine gun started chattering, and a few seconds later another one. A frown twisted Jäger's stubbly face as he ate. The Russians were supposed to have been kaput around these parts for most of a week. But then, nobody lived to grow old by counting Russians out too soon. The previous winter had proved that.

As if drawn by a magnet, Jäger peered through the darkness toward the hulk of a T-34 that sat, turret all askew, perhaps fifty meters away. The killed tank was only a vague shape in the darkness, but even a glimpse could make fearful sweat start under his arms.

"If only we had panzers like that," he murmured. He stuck his spoon into the stew still on his tin plate, stroked the black ribbon of his wound badge. Thanks to a T-34, he would have a furrow in his calf till the day he died. The rest of the crew of the Panzer III he'd been in at the time hadn't been so lucky; only one other man had bailed out, and he was back in Germany getting pieced together one operation at a time.

Simply measured tank against tank, a Panzer III, even one with the new, long 50mm gun, had no business taking on a T-34. The Russian tank boasted a cannon half again as big, thicker armor cleverly sloped to deflect shells, and an engine that was not only more powerful than a Panzer III's but a diesel to boot, so it wouldn't go up in flames the way the German machine's petrol-powered Maybach so often did.

"It's not so bad as all that, sir." The cheerful voice at his shoulder belonged to Captain Ernst Riecke, his second-in-command.

"Ha. You heard me muttering to myself, did you?" Jäger said.

"Yes, sir. You ask me, it's the same in tanks as it is in screwing, sir." Jäger raised an eyebrow. "This I have to hear."

"Well, in both cases knowing what to do with what you've got counts for more than how big it is."

The company commander snorted. Still, no doubt Riecke had a point. Even after almost a year of painful instruction at the hands of the Germans, the Bolsheviks were still in the habit of committing their armor by dribs and drabs instead of massing it for maximum effect. That was how the dead T-34 had come to grief: rumbling along without support, it had been set upon and destroyed by three Panzer IIIs.

Still . . . "Think how fine it would be to have a big one *and* know what to do with it."

"It *is* enjoyable, sir," Riecke said complacently. "Or were you talking about panzers again?"

"You're incorrigible," Jäger said, and then wondered if it was just that the captain was still on the sunny side of thirty. Promotion came quickly on the Russian front. Good officers *led* their troops forward rather than sending up orders from the rear. That meant good officers died in larger numbers, a twisted sort of natural selection that worried Jäger.

He felt every one of his own forty-three years. He'd fought in the trenches in France in 1918, in the last push toward Paris and then in the grinding retreat to the Rhine. He'd first seen tanks then, the clumsy monsters the British used, and knew at once that if he ever went to war again, he wanted them on his side for a change. But they were forbidden to the postwar *Reichswehr*. As soon as Hitler took the gloves off and started rearming Germany, Jäger went straight into armor.

He took another couple of mouthfuls of stew, then asked, "How many panzers do we have up and running?"

"Eleven," Riecke answered. "Maybe we'll be able to get another one going in the morning, if we scrounge around for some fuel line."

"Not bad," Jäger said, as much to console himself as to reassure Riecke. On paper, his company should have had twenty-two Panzer IIIs. In fact, it had had nineteen when the Russians launched their attack. On the eastern front, getting that close to paper strength was no small accomplishment.

"The Reds can't be in good shape, either," Riecke said. His voice turned worried, just for a moment: "Can they?"

"We've bagged enough of them, the last three weeks," Jäger said. That was true enough; a couple of hundred thousand Russians had trudged off into captivity when the Germans pinched off the opening through which they'd poured. The enemy threw away more than a thousand tanks and two thousand artillery pieces. Bolshevik losses the summer before had been on an even more colossal scale.

But before he crossed from Romania into Russia, he'd never imagined how immense the country was; how the plains seemed to stretch on and on forever; how thin a division, a corps, an army, could spread just to hold a front, let alone advance. And from those limitless plains sprang seemingly limitless streams of men and tanks. And they all fought, ferociously if without much skill. Jäger knew too well the *Wehrmacht* was anything but limitless. If every German soldier slew two Red Army men, if every panzer knocked out two T-34s or KVs, the Russians had a net gain.

Riecke lit a cigarette. The flare of the match briefly showed the dirt ground into fatigue lines he'd not had a month before. Yet somehow he still looked boyish. Jäger envied him that; at the rate he himself was going gray, he'd look like a grandfather any day now.

The captain passed him the pack. He took a cigarette, leaned closer to light it from Riecke's. "Thanks," he said, shielding the glowing coal with one hand: no point giving a sniper a free target. Riecke also hid his smoke.

After they'd crushed out the cigarettes under their bootheels, Riecke said suddenly, "*Are* we going to get new models anytime soon, sir? What does your brother say?"

"Nothing he shouldn't, which means I don't know for certain," Jäger answered. His brother Johann worked as an engineer for Henschel. His letters were always censored with special zeal, lest they fall into enemy hands on the long road between Germany and somewhere south of Kharkov. But brothers had ways with words that censors could not follow. After a moment, Jäger added, "It might be possible, though I thought size didn't concern you . . . ?"

"Oh, I'll carry on with what we have," the younger man said breezily. *Not that there's any choice in the matter,* Jäger thought. Riecke went on, "Still, as you say, it would be nice to be better and bigger at the same time."

"So it would." Jäger splashed a little water onto his mess tin from his water bottle, pulled out some fresh spring grass to wipe it more or less clean. Then he yawned. "I'm going to try to sleep till sunup. Don't be afraid to wake me if there's any sign of trouble." He'd given Riecke that order at least a hundred times. As he always did, the captain nodded.

The drone of the four Merlins made every filling in Flight Lieutenant George Bagnall's head feel as if it were shaking loose from its tooth. The Lancaster jounced in the air as 88mm flak burst all around it, filling the night with puffs of smoke that absurdly reminded the flight engineer of dumplings.

Searchlights stabbed up from the ground, seeking to impale a bomber like a bug on a collector's pin. The Lancaster's belly was a flat matte black, but not black enough to make it safe if one of those skewers of light happened to catch it. Fortunately, Bagnall was too busy monitoring engine temperature and revolutions, fuel consumption, oil pressure, hydraulic lines, and all the other complex systems that had to work if the Lancaster was to keep flying, to be as frightened as he would have been as a mere passenger.

But not even the most mechanically attentive man could have stared at his dials and meters to the exclusion of the spectacle outside the thick Perspex window. Even as Bagnall watched, more flames started in Cologne, some the almost blue-white glare of incendiaries, others spreading red blisters of ordinary fire.

Perhaps half a mile away from Bagnall's plane and a little lower in the sky, a bomber heeled over and plunged groundward, one wing a sheet of flame. The flight engineer's shiver had nothing to do with the frigid air through which his Lanc flew.

Ken Embry grunted beside him. "We may have flown a thousand bloody bombers *to* Cologne," the pilot said. "Now we have to see how bloody many fly back *from* it." His voice rang metallically in the intercom earphones.

"Jerry doesn't seem very pleased with us tonight, does he?" Bagnall answered, not about to let his friend outdo him in cynicism and under-statement.

Below them in the nose, Douglas Bell let out a whoop like a red Indian. "There's the train station! Hold her steady, steady— Now!" the bomb-aimer shouted. The Lancaster shuddered again, in a new way this time, as destruction tumbled down on the German city by the Rhine.

"That's for Coventry," Embry said quietly. He'd lost a sister in the German raid on the English town a year and a half before.

"Coventry and then some," Bagnall agreed. "The Germans didn't throw nearly so many aircraft at us, and they don't have a bomber that can touch the Lanc." He set an affectionate gloved hand on the instrument panel in front of him.

The pilot grunted again. "They slaughter our civilians and we slaughter theirs. The same with the soldiers in the desert, the same in Russia. The Japanese are still moving against the Yanks in the Pacific, and Jerry is sinking too many ships in the Atlantic. If I didn't know better, I'd say we were losing the bloody war."

"I wouldn't go that far," Bagnall said after a few seconds of judicious consideration. "But it does rather seem to hang in the balance, doesn't it? Sooner or later, one side or the other will do something monumentally stupid, and that will tell the tale."

"Good Lord, we're doomed if that's so," Embry exclaimed. "Can you imagine anyone more monumentally stupid than an Englishman with his blood up?"

Bagnall scratched at his cheek below the bottom edge of his goggles; those few square inches were the only ones not covered by one or more— usually more—layers of clothing. They were also quite numb. He flogged his brain for some sort of comeback, but nothing occurred to him; this time he'd have to yield the palm of cynicism to the pilot.

He had only a few seconds in which to feel rueful. Then shouts from the rear gunner and the top turret rang in his ears, almost deafening him: "Enemy fighter to starboard and low! Bandit! Bandit! *Bloody fucking bandit!*" Machine guns began to hammer, although the .303 rounds were not likely to do much good.

Ken Embry heeled the Lancaster over on its side and dove away from the menace, flying his big, unwieldy aircraft as much like a fighter as he could. The frame groaned in protest. Like any sensible pilot, Embry ignored it. The German up there was more likely to kill him than he was to tear off the Lanc's wings. He piled power onto the engines of one wing, cut it from those of the other. The Lancaster fell through the air like a stone. Bagnall clapped a hand to his mouth, as if to catch the stomach that was trying to crawl up his throat.

The shouts from the gunners rose to a crescendo. All at once drenched in sweat despite the icy air outside, Bagnall felt shells slam—one, two, three—into the wing and side of the fuselage. A twin-engine plane roared above the windscreen and vanished into the blackness, pursued by tracers from the Lanc's guns.

"Messerschmitt-110," Bagnall said shakily.

"Good of you to tell me," Embry answered. "I was rather too occupied to notice." He raised his voice. "Everyone present and accounted for?" The seven-man crew's answers came back high and shrill, but they all came back. Embry turned to Bagnall. "And how did our humble chariot fare?"

Bagnall studied the gauges. "Everything appears—normal," he said, surprised at how surprised he sounded. He rallied gamely: "We might have been a bit more embarrassed had Jerry chosen to shoot us up *before* we disposed of our cargo."

"Indeed," the pilot said. "Having disposed of it, I see no urgent reason to tarry over the scene any longer. Mr. Whyte, will you give us a course for home?"

"With pleasure, sir," Alf Whyte answered from behind the black curtain that protected his night vision. "I thought for a moment there you were trying to fling me over the side. Fly course two-eight-three, I say again two-eight-three. That should put us on the ground back at Swinderby in about four and a half hours."

"Or somewhere in England, at any rate," Embry remarked, long-range navigation at night was anything but an exact science. When Whyte let out an indignant sniff, the pilot added, "Maybe I should have flung you over the side; we'd likely do just as well following a trail of bread crumbs back from Hansel and Gretel Land."

Despite his ragging, Embry swung the bomber onto the course the navigator had given him. Bagnall kept a close eye on the instrument panel, still worried lest a line had been broken. But all the pointers stayed where they should have; the four Merlins steadily drove the Lancaster through the air at above two hundred miles an hour. The Lanc was a tough bird, especially compared to the Blenheims in which he'd started the war. And—they'd been lucky.

He peered through the windscreen. Other Lancasters, Stirlings, and Manchesters showed up as blacker shapes against the dark sky; engine exhausts glowed red. As burning Cologne receded behind him, he felt the first easing of fear. The worst was over, and he was likely to live to fly another mission—and be terrified again.

The crew's chatter, full of the same relief he knew himself, rang in his earphones. "Bloody good hiding we gave Jerry," somebody said. Bagnall found himself nodding. There had been flak and there had been fighters (that Me-110 filled his mind's eye for a moment), but he'd seen worse with both—the massive bomber force had half paralyzed Cologne's defenses. Most of his friends—with a little luck, all his friends—would be coming home to Swinderby. He wriggled in his seat, trying to get more comfortable. *Downhill now*, he thought.

Ludmila Gorbunova bounced through the air less than a hundred meters off the ground. Her U-2 biplane seemed hardly more than a toy; any fighter from the last two years of the previous war could have hacked the *Kukuruznik* from the sky with ease. But the Wheatcutter was not just a trainer—it had proved itself as a military plane since the first days of the Great Patriotic War. Tiny and quiet, it was made for slipping undetected past German lines.

She pulled the stick back to gain more altitude. It failed to help. No flashes of artillery came from what had been first the Russian assault position, then the Russian defensive position, and finally, humiliatingly, the Russian pocket trapped inside a fascist ring.

No one had reported artillery fire from within the pocket the night before, or the night before that. Sixth Army was surely dead. But, as if unwilling to believe it, Frontal Aviation kept sending out planes in the hope the corpse might somehow miraculously revive.

Ludmila went gladly. Behind her goggles, tears stung her eyes. The offensive had begun with such promise. Even the fascist radio admitted fear that the Soviets would retake Kharkov. But then—Ludmila was vague on what had happened then, although she'd flown reconnaissance all through the campaign. The Germans managed to pinch off the salient the Soviet forces had driven into their position, and then the battle became one of annihilation.

Her gloved hand tightened on the stick as if it were a fascist invader's neck. She'd got out of Kiev with her mother bare days before the Germans surrounded the city. Both of her brothers and her father were in the army; no letters had come from any of them for months. Sometimes, though it was no proper thought for a Soviet woman born five years after the October Revolution, she wished she knew how to pray. A fire glowed, off in the distance. She turned the plane toward it. From all she had seen, anyone showing lights in the night had to be German. Whatever Soviet troops were still unbagged within the pocket would not dare draw attention to themselves. She brought the *Kukuruznik* down to treetop height. Time to remind the fascists they did not belong here.

As the fire brightened ahead of her, her gut clenched. She bit down hard on the inside of her lower lip, using pain to fight fear. "I am not afraid, I am not afraid, I am not afraid," she said. But she was afraid, every time she flew.

No time for the luxury of fear, not any more. The men lounging in the circle of light round the fire swelled in a moment from ant-sized to big as life. Germans sure enough, in dirty field-gray with coal-scuttle helmets.

They started to scatter an instant before she thumbed the firing button mounted on top of her stick.

The two ShVAK machine guns attached under the lower wing of the biplane added their roar to the racket of the five-cylinder radial engine. Ludmila let the guns chatter as she zoomed low above the fire. As it dimmed behind her, she looked back over her shoulder to see what she had accomplished.

A couple of Germans lay sprawled in the dirt, one motionless, the other writhing like a fence lizard in the grasp of a cat. *"Khorosho,"* Ludmila said softly. Triumph drowned terror. *"Ochen khorosho."* It *was* very good. Every blow against the fascists helped drive them back—or at least hindered them from coming farther forward.

Flashes from out of the darkness, from two places, then three—not fire, firearms. Terror came roaring back. Ludmila gave the *Kukuruznik* all the meager power it had. A rifle bullet cracked past her head, horridly close. The muzzle flashes continued behind her, but after a few seconds she was out of range.

She let the biplane climb so she could look for another target. The breeze that whistled in over the windscreen of the open cockpit dried the stinking, fear-filled sweat on her forehead and under her arms. The trouble with the Germans was that they were too good at their trade of murder and destruction. They could have had only a few seconds' warning before her plane swooped on them out of the night, but instead of running and hiding, they'd run and then fought back—and almost killed her. She shuddered again, though they were kilometers behind her now.

When they'd first betrayed the treaty of peace and friendship and invaded the Soviet Union, she'd been confident the Red Army would quickly throw them back. But defeat and retreat followed retreat and defeat. Bombers appeared over Kiev, broad-winged Heinkels, Dorniers skinny as flying pencils, graceful Junkers-88s, Stukas that screamed like damned souls as they stooped, hawklike, on their targets. They roamed as they would. No Soviet fighters came up to challenge them.

Once in Rossosh, out of the German grasp, Ludmila happened to mention to a harried clerk that she'd gone through *Osoaviakhim* flight training. Two days later, she found herself enrolled in the Soviet Air Force. She still wondered whether the man did it for the sake of the country or to save himself the trouble of finding her someplace to sleep.

Too late to worry about that now. Whole regiments of women pilots flew night-harassment missions against the fascist invaders. *One day,* Ludmila thought, *I will graduate to a real fighter instead of my U-2.* Several women had become aces, downing more than five German planes apiece.

For now, though, the reliable old Wheatcutter would do well enough.

She spotted another fire, off in the distance. The *Kukuruznik* banked, swung toward it.

Planes roared low overhead. The red suns under their wings and on the sides of their fuselages might have been painted from blood. Machine guns spat flame. The bullets kicked up dust and splashed in the water like the first big drops of a rainstorm.

Liu Han had been swimming and bathing when she heard the Japanese fighters. With a moan of terror, she thrust herself all the way under, until her toes sank deep into the slimy mud bottom of the stream. She held her breath until the need for air drove her to the surface once more, gasped in a quick breath, sank.

When she had to come up again, she tossed her head to get the long, straight black hair out of her eyes, then quickly looked around. The fighters had vanished as quickly as they appeared. But she knew the Japanese soldiers would not be far behind. Chinese troops had retreated through her village the day before, falling back toward Hankow.

A few swift strokes and she was at the bank of the stream. She scrambled up, dried herself with a few quick strokes of a rough cotton towel, put on her robe and sandals, and took a couple of steps away from the water.

Another drone of motors, this one higher and farther away than the fighters, a whistle in the air that belonged to no bird . . . The bomb exploded less than a hundred yards from Liu. The blast lifted her like a toy and flung her back into the stream.

Stunned, half-deafened, she thrashed in the water. She breathed in a great gulp of it. Coughing, choking, retching, she thrust her head up into the precious air, gasped out a prayer to the Buddha: "Amituofo, help me!"

More bombs fell all around. Earth leapt into the air in fountains so perfect and beautiful and transient, they almost made her forget the destruction they represented. The noise of each explosion slapped her in the face, more like a blow, physically felt, than a sound. Metal fragments of bomb casing squealed wildly as they flew. A couple of them splashed into the stream not far from Liu. She moaned again. The year before, a bomb fragment had torn her father in two.

The explosions moved farther away, on toward the village. Awkwardly, robe clinging to her arms and legs and hindering her every motion, she swam back to the bank, staggered out onto land once more. No point drying herself now, not when her damp towel was covered with earth. She automatically picked it up and started home, praying again to the Amida Buddha that her home still stood.

Bomb craters pocked the fields. Here and there, men and women lay beside them, torn and twisted in death. The dirt road, Liu saw, was untouched; the bombers had left it intact for the Japanese army to use.

She wished for a cigarette. She'd had a pack of Babies in her pocket, but they were soaked now. Water dripped from her hair into her eyes. When she saw columns of smoke rising into the sky, she began to run. Her sandals went *flap-squelch, flap-squelch* against her feet. Ahead, in the direction of the village, she heard shouts and screams, but with her ears still ringing she could not make out words.

People stared as she ran up. Even in the midst of disaster, her first thought was embarrassment at the way the wet cloth of her robe molded itself to her body. Even the small swellings of her nipples were plainly visible. "Paying to see a woman's body" was a euphemism for visiting a whore. No one so much as had to pay to see Liu's.

But in the chaos that followed the Japanese air attack, a mere woman's body proved a small concern. Absurdly, some of the people in the village, instead of being terrified and filled with dread like Liu, capered about as if in celebration. She called, "Has everyone here gone crazy, Old Sun?"

"No, no," the tailor shouted back. "Do you know what the eastern devils' bombs did? Can you guess?" An enormous grin showed his almost-toothless gums.

"I would say they missed everything, but . . ." Liu paused, gestured at the rising smoke. "I see that cannot be so."

"Almost as good." Old Sun hugged himself with glee. "No, even better—nearly all their bombs fell right on the yamen."

"The yamen?" Liu gaped, then started to laugh herself. "Oh, what a pity!" The walled enclosure of the yamen housed the county head's residence, his audience hall, the jail, the court that sent people there, the treasury, and other government departments. Tang Wen Lan, the county head, was notoriously corrupt, as were most of his clerks, secretaries, and servants.

"Isn't it sad. I think I'll go home and put on white for Tang's funeral," Old Sun said.

"He's dead?" Liu exclaimed. "I thought a man as wicked as that would live forever."

"He's dead," Old Sun said positively. "The ghost Life-Is-Transient is taking him to the next world right now—if death's messenger can find enough pieces to carry. One bomb landed square on the office where he was taking bribes. No one will squeeze us any more. How sad, how terrible!" His elastic features twisted into a mask of mirthful mourning that belonged in a pantomime show.

Yi Min, the local apothecary, was less sanguine than Old Sun. "Wait until the eastern dwarfs come. The Japanese will make stupid dead Tang Wen Lan seem like a prince of generosity. He had to leave us enough rice to get through to next year so he could squeeze us again. The Japanese will keep it all for themselves. They don't care whether we live or die."

Too much of China had learned that, to its sorrow. However rapacious and inept the government of Chiang Kai-shek had proved itself, places under Japanese rule suffered worse. For one thing, as Yi Min had said, the invaders took for themselves first and left only what they did not want to the Chinese they controlled. For another, while they were rapacious, they were not inept. Like locusts, when they swept a province clean of rice, they swept it *clean.*

Liu said, "Shall we run away, then?"

"A peasant without his plot is nothing," Old Sun said. "If I am to starve, I would sooner starve at home than somewhere on the road far from my ancestors' graves."

Several other villagers agreed. Yi Min said, "But what if it is a choice between living on the road and dying by the graves of your ancestors? What then, Old Sun?"

While the two men argued, Liu Han walked on into the village. Sure enough, it was as Old Sun had said. The yamen was a smoking ruin, its walls smashed down here and there as if by a giant's kicks. The flagpole had been broken like a broomstraw; the Kuomintang flag, white star in a blue field on red, lay crumpled in the dirt.

Through a gap in the wrecked wall, Liu Han stared in at Tang Wen Lan's office. If the county head had been in there when the bomb landed, Old Sun was surely right in thinking him dead. Nothing was left of the building but a hole in the ground and some thatch blown off the roof.

Another bomb had landed on the jail. Whatever the crimes for which the prisoners had been confined, they'd suffered the maximum penalty. Shrieks said some were suffering still. Villagers were already going through the yamen, scavenging what they could and dragging out bodies and pieces of bodies. The thick, meaty smell of blood fought with those of smoke and freshly upturned earth. Liu Han shuddered, thinking how easily others might have been smelling her blood right now.

Her own house stood a couple of blocks beyond the yamen. She saw smoke rising from that direction, but thought nothing of it. No one willingly believes disaster can befall her. Not even when she rounded the last corner and saw the bomb crater where the house had stood did she credit her own eyes. Less was left here than at the county head's office.

I have no home. The thought took several seconds to register, and hardly seemed to mean anything even after Liu formed it. She stared down at the ground, dully wondering what to do next. Something small and dirty lay by her left foot. She recognized it in the same slow, sluggish way she had realized her house was gone. It was her little son's hand. No sign of the rest of him remained.

She stooped and picked up the hand, just as if he were there, not merely a mutilated fragment. The flesh was still warm against hers. She heard a loud cry, and needed a little while to know it came from her own throat. The cry went on and on, seemingly without her: when she tried to stop, she found she couldn't.

Slowly, slowly, it stopped being the only sound in her universe. Other noises penetrated, cheerful *pop-pop-pop*s like strings of firecrackers going off. But they were not firecrackers. They were rifles. Japanese soldiers were on the way.

David Goldfarb watched the green glow of the radar screen at Dover Station, waiting for the swarm of moving blips that would herald the return of the British bomber armada. He turned to the fellow technician beside him. "I'm sure as hell gladder to be looking for our planes coming back than I was year before last, watching every German in the whole wide world heading straight for London."

"You can say that again." Jerome Jones rubbed his weary eyes. "It was a bit diccy there for a while, wasn't it?"

"Just a bit, yes." Goldfarb leaned back in his uncomfortable chair, hunched his shoulders. Something in his neck went *snap*. He grunted with relief, then grunted again as he thought about Jones' reply. He'd lived surrounded by British reserve all his twenty-three years, even learned to imitate it, but it still seemed unnatural to him.

His newlywed parents had fled to London to escape Polish pogroms a little before the start of the first World War. A stiff upper lip was not part of the scanty baggage they'd brought with them; they shouted at each other, and eventually at David and his brothers and sister, sometimes angrily, more often lovingly, but always at full throttle. He'd never learned at home to hold back, which made the trick all the harder anywhere else.

The reminiscent smile he'd worn for a moment quickly faded. By the news dribbling out, pogroms rolled through Poland again, worse under the Nazis than ever under the tsars. When Hitler swallowed Czechoslovakia, Saul Goldfarb had written to his own brothers and sisters and cousins in Warsaw, urging them to get out of Poland while they could. No one left. A few months later, it was too late to leave.

A blip on the screen snapped him out of his unhappy reverie. "Blimey," Jones breathed, King's English cast aside in surprise, "lookit that bugger go."

"I'm looking," Goldfarb said. He kept on looking, too, until the target disappeared again. It didn't take long. He sighed. "Now we'll have to fill out a pixie report."

"Third one this week," Jones observed. "Bloody pixies're getting busier, whatever the hell they are."

"Whatever," Goldfarb echoed. For the past several months, radars in England—and, he gathered unofficially, the United States as well—had been showing phantom aircraft flying impossibly high and even more impossibly fast; 90,000 feet and better than 2,000 miles an hour were the numbers he'd heard most often. He said, "I used to think they came from something wrong in the circuits somewhere. I've seen enough now, though, that I have trouble believing it."

"What else could they be?" Jones still belonged to the circuitry-problem school. He fired off the big guns of its argument: "They aren't ours. They don't belong to the Yanks. And if they were Jerry's, they'd be dropping things on our heads. What does that leave? Men from Mars?"

"Laugh all you like," Goldfarb said stubbornly. "If there's something wrong in the machinery's guts, why can't the boffins find it and fix it?"

"Crikey, I don't think even the blokes who invented this beast know what all it can and can't do," Jones retorted.

Since that was unquestionably true, Goldfarb didn't respond to it directly. Instead, he said, "So why has the machinery only started finding pixies now? Why didn't they show up on the screens from the first day?"

"If the boffins can't figure it out, how do you expect me to know?" Jones said. "Pull out a bloody pixie report form, will you? With luck, we can get it done before we spot the bombers. Then we won't have to worry about it tomorrow."

"Right." Goldfarb sometimes thought that if the Germans had managed to cross the Channel and invade England, the British could have penned them behind walls of paper and then buried them in more. The pigeonholes under the console at which he sat held enough requisitions, directives, and reports to baffle the most subtle bureaucrat for years.

Nor was the pixie report, blurrily printed on coarse, shoddy paper, properly called by a name anywhere near so simple. The RAF had instead produced a document titled INCIDENT OF APPARENT ANOMALOUS DETECTION OF HIGH-SPEED, HIGH-ALTITUDE TARGET. Lest the form fall into German hands, it nowhere mentioned that the anomalous detections (apparent detections, Goldfarb corrected himself) took place by means of radar. As if Jerry doesn't know we've got it, he thought.

He found a stub of pencil, filled in the name of the station, the date, time, and bearing and perceived velocity of the contact, then stuck the form in a manila folder taped to the side of the radar screen. The folder, stuck there by the base CO, was labeled PIXIE REPORTS. With an attitude like that, the CO would never see promotion again.

Jones grunted in satisfaction, as if he'd filled out the form himself. He said, "Off it goes to London tomorrow."

"Yes, so they can compare it to others they've got and work out altitude and such from the figures," Goldfarb said. "They wouldn't bother with that if it were just in the circuits, now, would they?"

"Don't ask me what they'll do in London," Jones said, an attitude Goldfarb also found sensible. Jones went on, "I'd be happier believing the pixies were real if anyone ever saw one anywhere but there." He pointed at the radar screen.

"So would I," Goldfarb admitted, "but look at the trouble we've had even with the Ju-86." The wide-span reconnaissance bombers had been flying over southern England for months, usually above 40,000 feet—so high that Spitfires had enormous trouble climbing up to intercept them.

Jerome Jones remained unconvinced. "The Junkers 86 is just a Jerry crate. It's got a good ceiling, yes, but it's slow and easy to shoot down once we get to it. It's not like that Superman bloke in the Yank funny books, faster than a speeding bullet."

"I know. I'm just saying we can't see a plane that high up even if it's there—and if it's going that fast, even a spotter with binoculars doesn't have long to search before it's gone. What we need are binoculars slaved to the radar, so one could know precisely where to look." As he spoke, Goldfarb wondered if that was practical, and how to go about setting it up if it was.

He got so lost in his own scheme that he didn't really notice the blip on the radar screen for a moment. Then Jones said, "Pixies again." Sure enough, the radar was reporting more of the mysterious targets. Jones's voice changed. "They're acting peculiar."

"Too right they are." Goldfarb stared at the screen, mentally translating its picture into aircraft (he wondered if Jones, who thought of pixies as something peculiar going on inside the radar set, did the same). "They're showing up as slower than they ever did before."

"And there are more of them," Jones said. "Lots more." He turned to Goldfarb. No one looked healthy by the green glow of the cathode-ray tube, but now he seemed especially pale; the line of his David Niven mustache was the sole color in his thin, sharp-featured face. "David, I think— they must be real." Goldfarb recognized what was in his voice. It was fear.

Hunger crackled like fire in Moishe Russie's belly. He'd thought lean times and High Holy Days fasts had taught him what hunger meant, but they'd no more prepared him for the Warsaw ghetto than a picture of a lake taught a man to swim.

Long black coat flapping about him like a moving piece of the night, he scurried from one patch of deep shadow to the next. It was long past curfew, which had begun at nine. If a German saw him, he would live only so long as he still amused his tormentor. Fear dilated his nostrils at every breath, made him suck in great draughts of the fetid ghetto air.

But hunger drove harder than fear—and after all, he could become the object of a German's sport at any hour of the day or night, for any reason or none. Only four days before, the Nazis had fallen on the Jews who came to the Leszno Street courthouse to pay their taxes—taxes the Nazis themselves imposed. They robbed the Jews not only of what they claimed was owed, but also of anything else they happened to have on their persons. With the robbery came blows and kicks, as if to remind the Jews in whose clawed grip they lay.

"Not that I needed reminding," Russie whispered aloud. He was a native of Wolynska Street, and had been in the ghetto since Warsaw surrendered to the Germans. Not many had lasted through two and a half years of hell.

He wondered how much longer he would last. He'd been a medical student before September 1939; he could diagnose his own symptoms easily enough. Loose teeth and tender gums warned of the onset of scurvy; poor night vision meant vitamin A deficiency. The diarrhea could have had a dozen fathers. And starvation needed no doctor to give it a name. The hundreds of thousands of Jews packed into four square kilometers had all too intimate an acquaintance with it.

The one advantage of being so thin was that his coat went round him nearly twice. He'd liked it better when it was a proper fit.

His furtive movements became even more cautious as he drew near the wall. The red bricks went up twice as high as a man, with barbed wire strung above them to keep the boldest adventurer from climbing over. However much he wanted to, Russie did not aim to try that. Instead, he whirled the sack he carried around and around like an Olympic hammer-thrower, then flung it toward the Polish side of the wall.

The sack flew up and over. Heart pounding, Russie listened to it land. He had padded the silver candlestick with rags, so it hit with a soft, dull thump instead of a clatter. He strained to catch the sound of footfalls on the other side. He was at the Pole's mercy now. If the fellow simply wanted to steal the candlestick, he could. If he had hope of more, he'd keep the bargain they'd made in Leszno Street.

Waiting stretched like the lengths of wire on the wall, and had as many spikes. Try as he would, Russie could hear nothing from the other side. Maybe the Germans had arrested the Pole. Then the precious candlestick would lie abandoned till some passerby came upon it . . . and Russie would have squandered one of his last remaining resources for nothing.

A soft *plop* on the cobblestones not far away. Russie sprinted over. The rags that bound up the tattered remnants of his shoes made hardly a sound. He held his hat on with one hand; as he grew thinner, even his head seemed to have shrunk.

He snatched up the bag, dashed back toward darkness. Even as he ran, the rich, intoxicating odor of meat flooded his senses, made his mouth gush with saliva. He fumbled at the drawstring, reached inside. His spidery fingers closed round the chunk, gauged its size and weight. Not the half a kilo he'd been promised, but not far from it. He'd expected the Pole to cheat worse: what recourse did a Jew have? Perhaps he could complain to the SS. Sick and starving though he was, the thought raised black laughter in him.

He drew out his hand, licked the salt and fat that clung to it. Water filled his eyes as well as his mouth. His wife, Rivka, and their son, Reuven (and, incidentally, himself), might live a little longer. Too late for their little Sarah, too late for his wife's parents and his own father. But the three of them might go on.

He smacked his lips. Part of the sweetness on his tongue came from the meat's being spoiled (but only slightly; he'd eaten far worse), the rest because it was pork. The rabbis in the ghetto had long since relaxed the prohibitions against forbidden food, but Russie still felt guilty every time it passed his lips. Some Jews chose to starve sooner than break the Law. Had he been alone in the ghetto, Russie might have followed that way. But while he had others to care for, he would live if he could. He'd talk it over with God when he got the chance.

How best to use the meat? he wondered. Soup was the only answer: it would last for several days that way, and make rotten potatoes and moldy cabbage tolerable (only a tiny part of him remembered the dim dead days before the war, when he would have turned aside in scorn from rotten potatoes and moldy cabbage instead of wolfing them down and wishing for more).

He reached into a coat pocket. Now his spit-wet fist closed on a wad of zlotys, enough to bribe a Jewish policeman if he had to. The banknotes were good for little else; mere money was rarely enough to buy food, not in the ghetto.

"I have to get back," he reminded himself under his breath. If he was not at his sewing machine in the factory fifteen minutes after curfew lifted, some other scrawny Jew would praise God for having the chance to take his place. And if he was there but too worn to meet his quota of German uniform trousers, he would not keep his sewing machine long. His narrow, clever hands were made for taking a pulse or removing an appendix, but their agility with bobbin and cloth was what kept him and part of his family alive.

He wondered how long he would be allowed to maintain even the hellish life he led. He did not so much fear the random murder that stalked the ghetto on German jackboots. But just that day, whispers had slithered from bench to bench at the factory. The Lublin ghetto, they said, had ceased to be: thousands of Jews taken away and— Everyone filled in his own *and*, according to his nightmares.

Russie's *and* was something like a meat-packing plant, with people going through instead of cattle. He prayed that he was wrong, that God would never allow such an abomination. But too many prayers had fallen on deaf ears, too many Jews lay dead on sidewalks until at last, like cordwood, they were piled up and hauled away.

"Lord of Abraham, Isaac, and Jacob," he murmured softly, "I beg You, give me a sign that You have not forsaken Your chosen people."

Like tens of thousands of his fellow sufferers, he sent up that prayer at all hours of the day and night, sent it up because it was the only thing he could do to affect his horrid fate.

"I beg You, Lord," he murmured again, "give me a sign."

All at once, noon came to the Warsaw ghetto in the middle of the night. Moishe Russie stared in disbelieving wonder at the sun-hot point of light blazing in the still-black sky. *Parachute flare*, he thought, remembering the German bombardment of his city.

But it was no flare. Whatever it was, it was bigger and brighter than any flare, by itself lighting the whole of the ghetto—maybe the whole of Warsaw, or the whole of Poland—bright as day. It hung unmoving in the sky, as no flare could. Slowly, slowly, slowly, the point of light became a smudge, began to fade from eye-searing, actinic violet to white and yellow and orange. The brilliance of noon gave way little by little to sunset and then to twilight. The two or three startled birds that burst into song fell silent again, as if embarrassed at being fooled.

Their sweet notes were in any case all but drowned by the cries from the ghetto and beyond, cries of wonder and fear. Russie heard German voices with fear in them. He had not heard German voices with fear in them since the Nazis forced the Jews into the ghetto. He had not imagined he could hear such voices. Somehow that made them all the sweeter.

Tears poured from his dazzled eyes, ran down his dirty, hollow cheeks into the curls of his beard. He sagged against a torn poster that said *Piwo*. He wondered how long it had been since beer came into the ghetto.

But none of that mattered, not in any real sense of the word. He had asked God for a sign, and God gave him one. He did not know how he could pay God back, but he promised to spend the rest of his life finding out.

Fleetlord Atvar stood before the holographic projection of Tosev 3. As he watched, points of light blinked into being here and there above the world's ridiculously small landmasses. He wondered if, once Tosev 3 came under the dominion of the Race, manipulation of plate tectonics might bring up more usable territory.

That was a question for the future, though, for five hundred years hence, or five thousand, or twenty-five thousand. Eventually, when everything was decided and planned down to the last detail, the Race would act. That way had served it well for centuries piled on centuries.

Atvar was uneasily aware he lacked the luxury of time. He'd expected to enjoy it, but the Tosevites, having somehow developed with indecent haste the rudiments of an industrial civilization, posed a greater challenge to his forces than he or anyone else back Home had anticipated. If he failed to meet the challenge, only his failure would be remembered.

Accordingly, it was with some concern that he turned to Shiplord Kirel and said, "These devices were properly placed?"

"It is so, Fleetlord," Kirel replied. "All placing vessels report success and have returned safely to the fleet; instruments confirm proper targeting of the thermonuclear devices and their simultaneous ignition above the principal radio communications centers of Tosev 3."

"Excellent." Atvar knew the Tosevites had no way to reach even a fraction of the altitude of the placing vessels. Nevertheless, actually hearing that matters had proceeded as designed was always a relief. "Their systems should be thoroughly scrambled, then."

"As the exalted fleetlord says," Kirel agreed. "Better still, many parts of those systems should be permanently destroyed. Unshielded transistors and microprocessors are extremely vulnerable to electromagnetic pulse and, since the Tosevites have no nuclear power of their own, they will never have seen the necessity for shielding."

"Excellent," Atvar repeated. "Our own shielded aircraft, meanwhile, should have rare sport against them while they writhe like roadscuttlers with fractured vertebrae. We should have no problem clearing areas for landing, and once our troops are on the ground, conquest becomes inevitable." Saying the words brought fresh confidence to the commander. Nothing reassured the Race more than a plan that was going well.

Kirel said, "May it please the exalted fleetlord, as we land, shall we broadcast demands for surrender to be picked up by whatever receivers remain intact down below?"

That was not part of the plan as formulated. Of course, the plan as formulated went back in its essentials to the days when no one thought the Tosevites had any technology worth mentioning. Nevertheless, Atvar felt an almost instinctive reluctance to deviate from it. He said, "No, let them come to us. They will surrender soon enough when they feel the weight of our metal."

"It shall be done as the fleetlord wishes," Kirel said formally. Atvar knew the shiplord had ambition of his own, and that Kirel would make careful note of any and all mistakes and failures, especially those he had argued against. Let Kirel do as he would. Atvar felt sure this was no mistake.

Flight Leader Teerts stared in disbelieving wonder at the head-up display reflected against the inside of his windshield. Never in training had he imagined sorties in such a target-rich environment. The great herd of Tosevite aircraft crawled along below and ahead of him, blissfully unaware he was so much as in their solar system.

The voice of one of the other two pilots in the flight rang in the audio button taped to his hearing diaphragm: "Pity we have no more killers to assign to this area. They'd enjoy themselves."

Before he answered, Teerts checked the radio frequency. As ordered, it wasn't one the Tosevites used. Relaxing, he answered, "We're taking on an entire world, Rolvar; we don't have enough killers to knock down all the native junk at once. We'll just have to do the best we can with what we have."

That best gave every sign of being spectacular. All six of his missiles had already selected targets from the herd. He ripple-fired them, one after another. His killercraft bucked slightly under him as the missiles dropped away. Their motors kicked in and spat orange flame; they sprinted downward toward the ungainly Tosevite flying machines.

Even had the locals known they were under attack, they could have done little, not when his missiles had ten times the speed of their aircraft. The head-up display showed his salvo and those of his wingmates streaking home. Then, suddenly, Teerts needed no head-up display to gauge what was happening: gouts of fire suddenly filled the darkness below as aircraft tumbled out of the sky.

Rolvar yowled in Teerts' audio button. "Look at them fall! Every shot a clean hit!"

Killercraft pilots were chosen for aggressiveness. Teerts had won flight-leader paint because he also kept track of details. After a glance at the display, he said, "I show only seventeen kills. Either a missile was defective or two went after the same target."

"Who cares?" said Gefron, the other member of the flight. Gefron would not make flight leader if he lived to be a thousand, even counting by double-length Tosevite years. He was a good pilot, though. He went on, "We still have our cannon. Let's use them."

"Right." Teerts led the flight down into gun range. The natives still didn't know what had happened to them, but they knew something horrible had. Like a flock of frenni beset by wild botor, they were scattering, doing their feeble best to get out of harm's way. Teerts' jaws opened in mirth. Their best would not suffice.

His engines changed pitch as they breathed thicker air. Servos squealed, adjusting the sweep of his wings. His speed dropped to little more than that of sound. A target filled his windshield. He stabbed the firing button with the thumbclaw of his stick hand. The nose of his plane disappeared for a moment in the glare of the muzzle blast. When his vision cleared, the Tosevite aircraft, one wing sheared away, was already spinning out of control toward the ground.

He'd never been among so many aircraft in his life. He bled off still more speed, to avoid collision. Another target, another burst, another kill. A few moments later, another, and another.

Off to one side, he saw brief spurts of flame. He turned one eye that way. A Tosevite aircraft was shooting back at him. He abstractly admired the natives' courage. Once pacified, they would serve the Race well. They weren't even bad pilots, given the limitations of the lumbering aircraft they flew. They were maneuvering with everything they had, trying to break contact and escape. But that was his choice, not theirs.

He shot out the front of the aircraft pack, began to circle back toward it for another run. As he did so, a flash on the head-up display made him slew both eyes toward it. Somewhere out there in the night, a native aircraft with better performance than those of the herd was turning in his direction and away from it.

An escorting killercraft? An enemy who thought him a better target? Teerts neither knew nor cared. Whoever the native was, he'd pay for his presumption.

Teerts' cannon was radar-controlled. He fired a burst. Flames sprang from the Tosevite killercraft. At the same moment, it shot back at him. The shells fell short. The native, all afire now, plunged out of the sky.

Teerts raked the stampeding herd of aircraft twice more before his ammunition ran low. Rolvar and Gefron had also done all the damage they could. They streaked for low orbital pickup; soon enough, the Race would have landing strips on the ground. Then the slaughter of Tosevite aircraft would be great indeed.

"Easy as a female in the middle of her season," Gefron exulted.

"They're brave enough, though," Rolvar said. "A couple of their killercraft came right for me; I might even have a hole or two. I'm not so sure I got both of them, either; they're so little and slow, they're a lot more maneuverable than I am."

"I know I got mine," Teerts said. "We'll snatch some sleep and then come down and do it again." His flightmates hissed approval.

One second, the Lancaster below and to the right of George Bagnall's was flying along serenely as you please. The next, it exploded in midair. For a moment, Bagnall saw men and pieces of machine hang suspended, as if on strings from heaven. Then they were gone.

"Jesus!" he said fervently. "I think the whole ruddy world's gone mad. First that great light in the sky—"

"Lit us up like a milliard star shells all at once, didn't it?" Ken Embry agreed. "I wonder how the devil Jerry managed that? If it had stayed lit much longer, every bloody Nazi fighter in the world would have been able to spy us up here."

Another Lanc blew up, not far away. "What was that?" Bagnall demanded. "Anybody see a Jerry plane?"

None of the gunners answered. Neither did the bomb-aimer. Embry spoke to the radioman: "Any better luck there, Ted?"

"Not a bit of it," Edward Lane answered. "Ever since that light, I'm getting nothing but hash on every frequency."

"Bloody balls-up, that's what it is," Embry said. As if to italicize his words, two more bombers went up in flames. His voice rose to near a scream: "What's doing that? It's not flak and it's not planes, so what the hell is it?"

Next to the pilot, Bagnall shivered in his seat. Flying missions over Germany was frightening enough in and of itself, but when Lancs started getting blown out of the sky for no reason at all . . . His heart shrank to a small, frozen lump in his chest. His head turned this way and that, trying to see what the devil was murdering his friends. Beyond the polished Perspex, the night remained inscrutable.

Then the big, heavy Lancaster shook in the air for an instant like a leaf on a rippling stream. Even through the growl of the plane's four Merlins, he heard a shrieking roar that made every hair on his body try to stand erect. A lean shark-shape swept past, impossibly swift, impossibly graceful. Two huge exhausts glared like the red eyes of a beast of prey. One gunner had enough presence of mind to fire at it, but it vanished ahead of the Lanc in the blink of an eye.

"Did you—see that?" Ken Embry asked in a tiny voice.

"I—think so," Bagnall answered as cautiously. He wasn't quite sure he believed in the terrible apparition himself. "Where did the Germans come up with it?"

"Can't be German," the pilot said. "We know what they have, same as they know about us. My dad in a Spitfire above the Somme is likelier than a Jerry in—that."

"Well, if he's not a German, who the devil is he?" Bagnall asked.

"Damned if I know, and I don't care to hang about and learn, in case he decides to come back." Embry banked away from the track of the impossible fighter.

"Ground flak—" Bagnall said as he watched the altimeter unwind. Embry ignored him. He shut up, feeling foolish. When set against this monster that swept bombers from the sky like a charwoman wielding her broom against spilled salt, ground flak was hardly worth worrying about.

Jens Larssen's thumb throbbed fiercely. The nail was already turning black; he suspected he'd lose it. He scowled as darkly as his fair, sunny features allowed. He was a physicist, damn it, not a carpenter. What hurt worse than his maimed digit was the snickers from the young punks who made up most of the work crew that was building strange things in the west stands of Stagg Field.

The evening sun at his back, he tramped along Fifty-seventh Street toward the Quadrangle Club. His appetite wasn't what it had been before he'd tried driving his thumbnail into a two-by-four, but food and coffee kept him going in place of sleep. As soon as he'd gulped his meal, he'd be back at the pile again, hammering away—this time, with luck, a little more carefully.

He sucked in a lungful of muggy Chicago air. Having been born and raised in San Francisco, he wondered why three million people chose to live in a place that was too hot and sticky half the time and too damned cold most of the rest.

"They have to be crazy," he said aloud.

A student going the other way gave him an odd look. He felt himself flush. Dressed as he was in a dirty undershirt and a pair of chinos, he didn't look like anyone who belonged on the University of Chicago campus, let alone a faculty member. He'd draw more looks in the Quadrangle Club. *Too bad for the Latin professors in their moth-eaten Harris tweeds,* he thought.

He walked past Cobb Gate; the grotesques carved on the big stone pile that was the northern entrance to Hull Court always made him smile. Botany Pond, surrounded on three sides by the Hull Biological Laboratories, was a nice place to sit and read when he had the time. Lately, he hadn't had the time very often.

He was coming up to Mitchell Tower when his shadow disappeared. One second it stretched out ahead of him, all fine and proper, the next it was gone. The tower, modeled after that of Magdalen College at Oxford, was suddenly bathed in harsh white light.

Larssen stared up into the sky. The glowing spot there grew and faded and changed color as he watched. Everyone around was pointing at it and exclaiming: "What's that?" "What could it be?" "Have you ever seen anything like that in all your life?" People stuck their heads out of windows and came running outside to see.

The physicist watched and gaped with everyone else. Little by little, the new light dimmed and his old, familiar shadow reasserted itself. Before it had fully recovered, Larssen wheeled and began running back the way he had come. He dodged past dozens of people who were still just standing and gawking. "Where's the fire, buddy?" one of them yelled.

He didn't answer. He just ran harder toward Stagg Field. The fire was in the sky. He knew what sort of fire it had to be, too: the fire he and his colleagues were seeking to call forth from the uranium atom. So far, no atomic pile in the United States had even managed a self-sustaining chain reaction. The crew in the west stands was trying to put together one that would.

No one in his most horrid nightmares imagined the Germans had already devised not just a pile but a bomb, even if the uranium atom had first been split in Germany in 1938. As he ran, Larssen wondered how the Nazis had exploded a bomb over Chicago. So far as he knew, their planes couldn't reach even New York.

For that matter, he wondered why the Germans had set off their bomb so high overhead—too high, really, for it to do any damage. Maybe, he thought, they had it aboard some ocean-bestriding rocket like the ones the pulp magazines talked about. But no one had dreamed the Germans could do that, either.

Nothing about the bomb made any rational sense. The dreadful thing was up there, though, and had to be German. It surely wasn't American or English.

Larssen had an even more horrid thought. What if it was Japanese? He didn't think the Japs had the know-how to build an atomic bomb, but he hadn't thought they had the know-how to bomb Pearl Harbor so devastatingly well, or to take the Philippines, or Guam, or Wake, or Hong Kong and Singapore and Burma from the British, or practically drive the Royal Navy out of the Indian Ocean, or . . . The further he went, the longer the melancholy list in his head grew.

"Maybe it *is* the goddamn Japs," he said, and ran harder than ever.

■

Sam Yeager had the curtain closed over the train window by his seat, to keep the westering sun out of Bobby Fiore's eyes while his roommate slept. In his younger days, he would have resented that: having grown up without traveling more than a couple of days' ride from his folks' farm, he was wild to see as much of the country as he could when he started playing ball. Train and bus windows were his openings on a wider world.

"I've seen the country, all right," he muttered. He'd rolled through just about every piece of it, with swings into Canada and Mexico to boot. Rubbernecking for one more swing through the staid flatlands of Illinois no longer meant as much as it once had.

He remembered the sun rising over the arid mountains near Salt Lake City, shining off the lake and the white salt flats straight into his dazzled eyes. Now that had been scenery worth looking at; he'd carry the picture to his grave with him. Fields and barns and ponds just couldn't compete, though he wouldn't have lived in Salt Lake City for Joe DiMaggio's salary. *Well, maybe for DiMaggio's salary,* he thought.

A lot of the Commodores had headed off to the dining car. Across the aisle, Joe Sullivan was staring out the window with the same avidity Yeager had known in his early days. The pitcher's lips moved as he softly read a Burma Shave sign to himself. That made Yeager smile. Sullivan needed to lather up maybe twice a week.

Suddenly, bright light streamed in through the windows on the pitcher's side of the car. He craned his neck. "Funny thing in the sky," he reported. "Looks like a Fourth of July firework, but it's an awful damn bright one."

Mutt Daniels was sitting on that side of the train, too. "Awful damn bright one is right," the manager said. "Never seen one like that in all my born days. It just keeps hangin' up there, don't seem to move a-tall. Kind of pretty, matter of fact."

The light went from white to yellow to orange to red, fading little by little over several minutes. Yeager thought about getting up and having a look at where it was coming from. He might have done it if Sullivan hadn't compared it to something you'd see on the Fourth of July. Ever since the Fourth when he broke his ankle, he'd had no use for fireworks. He stuck his nose back into his *Astounding.*

The rising sun snuck under Heinrich Jäger's eyelids, pried his eyes open. He groaned, shook a few of the cobwebs out of his head, got slowly to his feet. Moving as if every joint in his body were rusty, he got in line for breakfast. More kasha stew, his nose told him. He shrugged. It would keep him full.

"No more lights in the sky?" he asked Ernst Riecke, who looked as tired as he felt.

"No, sir," the captain answered. "I don't know if I should have bothered you, but—"

"You did the right thing," Jäger said, mentally adding, *even if it did cost me another hour in my blanket.* "I don't know what the devil that was. It looked like one of our recognition flares, but it was a million times as big and bright. And it didn't fall, either. It stayed in one place till it went out. I wonder what it was."

"One of Ivan's tricks, maybe," Riecke suggested.

"Maybe." But Jäger didn't believe it. "If it was, though, he should have followed it up. No bombers, no artillery . . . If the Russians were trying something, it didn't work."

Like the rest of the tankmen, Jäger gulped down his stew. When everyone was fed, he reluctantly sent the field kitchen on its way. He hated to part with it, but it wouldn't be able to keep up with the tanks.

One after another, the Panzer IIIs rumbled into life. The whole company let out a cheer when the motor of the twelfth tank caught. Jäger shouted as loud as anybody. He didn't think they'd be facing enemy armor today, but you never could tell in Russia. And if not today, then one day before too long.

He clambered up into the turret of the tank he personally commanded, radioed division headquarters to see if orders had changed since yesterday. "No, we still want you to shift to map square B-9," the signal lieutenant answered. "How do you read my transmission, by the way?"

"Well enough," Jäger said. "Why?"

"We had some trouble earlier," the signalman answered. "After that explosion in the sky, reception went into the toilet for a while. Glad it didn't trouble you."

"Me, too," Jäger said. "Out." He unfolded his map, studied it. If he was where he thought he was, he and his panzers needed to make about twenty kilometers to get to where they were supposed to be. He leaned down into the crew compartment of the tank, called to the driver. "Let's go. East."

"East it is." Dieter Schmidt put the Panzer III into gear. The roar of the Maybach HL120TR engine changed pitch. The tank began to roll ahead, chewing two lines through the grass and dirt of the steppe. The engine went up the scale and down, up and down, as Schmidt worked his way through the six forward speeds of the gearbox.

The dustbin cupola at the back of the turret gave a decent view even when closed down. Like any tank commander worth his black coveralls, Jäger left it open and stood up in it whenever he could. Not only could he see more than even through good periscopes, the air was fresher and cooler and the racket less—or at least different. He traded being surrounded by engine rumble for the iron clash and rattle of the spare wheels and tracks lashed to the tank's rear deck.

He frowned a little. If the German logistics train were better run, he wouldn't have had to carry his own spares to make sure they were there when he needed them. But the eastern front ran more than three thousand kilometers from the Baltic to the Black Sea. Expecting the high foreheads who were out of harm's way to care what happened to any one tank commander was too much to hope for.

The panzers rolled through the detritus of battle, past graves hastily dug in the rich dark soil of the Ukraine; past stinking, bloated Russian corpses still unburied; past wrecked trucks and tanks of both the *Wehrmacht* and the Red Army. German engineers swarmed over those like flies over the corpses, salvaging whatever they could.

The gently rolling country stretched in all directions as far as the eye could see. Not even war's wounds scarred it too severely. Sometimes when Jäger looked out across that sea of green, his dozen tanks seemed all alone. He grinned when, off in the distance, he spied a German infantry company.

Once or twice, planes buzzed by overhead. That made him grin more widely. Somewhere east of Izyum, Ivan was going to catch hell.

A noise like the end of the world—the panzer a couple of hundred meters to his right went up in a fireball. One second it was there, the next nothing but red and yellow flame and a column of black, greasy smoke mounting to the sky. A moment later came the barks of secondary explosions as the tank's ammunition began going off. The five-man crew couldn't have known what hit them. Jäger told himself that, anyhow, as he dove down inside the turret.

"What the fuck was that?" asked Georg Schultz. The gunner had heard the blast through thick steel and through the racket of his own tank's motor.

"Joachim's tank just went up," Jäger answered. "Must have hit a mine—but the Ivans aren't supposed to have laid any mines around here." His voice showed his doubt; the explosion had been very violent for a mine. *Maybe if the blast went up into the gas tank,* the captain thought. No sooner had the idea crossed his mind then another panzer went up with an even louder detonation than the first.

"Jesus!" Schultz shouted. He stared fearfully at the metal floor of the tank, as if wondering when a white-hot jet of flame would burst through it.

Jäger grabbed for the radio that linked him with the rest of the company, hit the all-hands frequency. "All halt!" he bawled. "We're hitting mines." He shouted the order forward to Dieter Schmidt, then stood up in the cupola to make sure it was being obeyed.

The ten surviving tanks of the company did stop. The rest of the commanders bounced up just like Jäger, each of them trying to see what was going on. But for two blazing hulks, nothing seemed out of the ordinary.

Jäger was about to call divisional headquarters to ask for a sapper detachment when a lance of fire tore across the sky and blew the turret clean off one of the stopped panzers. The oily chassis promptly began to burn.

Cursing his own mistake, Jäger let himself fall back into the turret. He grabbed the radio, screamed, "Get moving! They're rockets from the air, not mines! The Ivans must have found some way to mount *Katyushas* on their ground-attack planes. If we stay where we are, we're sitting ducks." He didn't need to relay the order to Schmidt this time; his Panzer III was already lurching ahead, the engine roaring flat out.

Only as the captain went up into the cupola again did he consciously realize the trail of fire in the sky had come from the west, from behind him. "Turn the turret around!" he yelled, and cursed the hydraulics as the heavy dome of metal ever so slowly began to traverse. A couple of the other commanders had been more alert. Their tanks' turrets were already slewing to the rear.

Jäger turned that way himself. As he did so, a fourth panzer was hit in the engine compartment. Flames began to spurt. Turret doors flew open; men started bailing out. One, two, three . . . commander, gunner, loader. Fire washed over the whole tank. The driver and hull gunner never had a chance.

The company commander frantically scanned the sky. Where was the Stormovik, the armored Russian attack plane that was likeliest to be carrying *Katyusha* rockets? His heart leapt when he spotted a flying shape. The coaxial 7.92mm machine guns of the company's faster-reacting panzers spat flame at it. They weren't likely to hurt it, but might keep the pilot from making a low firing run.

They didn't. Here he came. Jäger got ready to throw himself behind the turret's armor the instant the Stormovik's guns started shooting back. Then, as the plane drew swiftly nearer, he noticed it wasn't a Stormovik. And when it fired, its whole blunt nose went yellow-white with the muzzle blast. Dust fountained around two more panzers. Both of them stopped dead. Smoke poured from them. Along with the reek of flaming gas and oil and cordite, Jäger's nose caught the roast-pork stink of burning human flesh.

The airplane passed overhead, almost close enough to touch. In spite of everything, Jäger stared at it in disbelief. It was almost the size of a medium bomber, and had no propeller he could see. It bore neither the German cross and swastika nor the Soviet star; in fact, it bore no device at all on its camouflaged wings and body. And it did not roar like every other airplane he had ever known—it shrieked, as if its motive power came from damned souls.

Then it was gone, vanishing into the east more swiftly than any fighter Jäger knew. He gaped after it, mouth fallen open in most unofficerlike fashion. One pass, and half his company was flaming wreckage.

Like his own, Ernst Riecke's panzer had survived the onslaught. It came rattling over. Riecke was standing up in his cupola. The captain's face bore the same expression of stunned disbelief Jäger knew his own did. "What—" Riecke had to try twice before he could get the words out. "What the devil was that?"

"I don't know." Jäger found an even worse question: "What if it comes back?"

The Japanese were looting the village. They'd already shot a couple of people for protesting when their possessions were hauled away. The bodies lay as mute warnings in the square beside the ruined wall of the yamen. As if they did not suffice, the invading soldiers swaggered around with fixed bayonets, ready to spit anyone who gave them so much as a hard look.

Liu Han had done her best to make herself invisible to the Japanese. She knew how they recruited their pleasure battalions. Ashes grayed her hair; charcoal added not just filth but also lines to her face, giving her the look of a much older woman. Grief made it easy for her to assume the stooped posture of the elderly. She wandered aimlessly around the edges of the village, in part to keep away from the soldiers, in part because, with home and family gone, she had nothing better to do.

Because she kept away from the noisy chaos that engulfed invaders and townsfolk alike, she might have been the first to hear the thuttering in the air. Her head came up in fright—more bombers on the way? But surely not, not when the village already lay under the Japanese boot.

Or could they be Chinese planes? If the Kuomintang government wanted to hold Hankow, it would need to fight back with everything it had. And the noise was growing from the south! Fear and excitement warred within Liu Han. She wanted the Japanese dead, but did she wish to die with them?

In spite of her anguish, she decided she wanted to live. Stoop forgotten, she ran for the woods—the farther from the village when bombs began to fall, the better. The drone of approaching aircraft swelled in her ears.

She threw herself down in a tangle of bushes and ferns. By then the planes were almost overhead. She stared up at them through tree branches. Despite anguish and terror, her eyes went wide. The planes she was used to had graceful, birdlike bodies. These flying—things—looked more like dragonflies. They were angular, awkward-seeming, with landing gear projecting from their bodies like insect legs. And they had no wings! If anything save magic kept them in the air, it was the whirling disk above each of them.

They hovered in midair like dragonflies, too. Liu Han had never heard

of an airplane that could do such a thing, but then, all she knew of airplanes was the death and devastation they brought.

There these dragonfly planes proved no exception. As they hung in the
sky, they fired machine guns and rockets into Liu Han's poor bleeding village.
Screams pierced the rattle of gunfire and the crash of explosions. So did the
deep, harsh cries of the Japanese soldiers. Liu shuddered to hear them; they
reminded her of the baying of wolves. Seeing the invaders lashed with such
pitiless fire almost made her forget the ruination of her village.

Then a machine gun began to chatter inside the ruins of the yamen.
The Japanese were doing their best to fight back. Tracer bullets drew fiery
lines up toward the dragonfly planes. Two rockets snarled groundward. A
roar, a flash of light, and the machine gun fell silent. Forgetting she was
supposed to be in hiding, Liu Han let out a delighted screech. With chaos
all around, who was likely to hear one more screech?

A couple of dragonfly planes settled toward the ground, floating through
the air as light as windborne snow. Doors opened in their sides as they
touched down. Liu Han saw motion inside them. Holding her breath, she
waited for soldiers to leap out and finish slaughtering the Japanese.

Could they really be men of the Kuomintang? Liu Han hadn't imagined that her country boasted such marvelous airplanes. Maybe they came
from America! The Americans were supposed to be the most clever of all
the foreign devils when it came to machines—and they were fighting the
Japanese, too. Liu Han had seen an American once, a big, fat Christian
missionary who spoke bad Chinese. He'd sounded very fierce, she remembered. She imagined big, fierce American soldiers springing out of the dragonfly planes, each with a sparkling bayonet half as long as he was tall. She
hugged herself with glee at the delicious thought.

Helmeted soldiers began springing out of the dragonfly plane. They
were not big, fierce Americans. They were not Chinese troops, either. Liu
Han's glee turned to horror in the space of a single breath. The Chinese
commonly called foreigners "devils"; just a moment before, Liu Han had
been thinking about American devils. But here were devils in truth!

They were shorter than people, and skinnier. Their green-brown hides
glistened in the afternoon sun like snakeskin. They had no noses; instead,
the bottom parts of their faces were pulled out in short muzzles—Liu Han
thought first of cats, then of lizards. The devils had tails, too, short blunt
ones that hung a third of the way down to their knees. Liu Han rubbed her
eyes, hard, but when she opened them again, the devils were still there.
She moaned, deep in her throat.

The devils did not move like people, either. Liu Han thought of lizards
again; the devils' motion had something of that same loose-joined skitter
to it. And when they were still, they were absolutely still, in a way no human save a meditating monk could match.

They did not act like monks. They had things that looked like guns in their hands. The things were guns—they started firing into the village. And what guns! Instead of the *bang, bang, bang* of ordinary rifles, the devils' weapons spat streams of bullets like machine guns.

Despite their barrage, despite the rockets and gunfire from the dragonfly planes, Japanese soldiers in the village kept shooting. The devils on the ground advanced against the invaders, some rushing forward while others covered them. Had she been attacked by such monsters, Liu Han knew she would have either given up at once or fled. The Japanese did neither. They fought on until they were all killed. It did not take long.

By the time the little battle ended, the whole village was on fire. Peering through a screen of brush, Liu Han saw the townsfolk, those who still lived, scattering in all directions save toward her (the dragonfly planes on the ground were a potent argument against running that way).

After a few minutes, a couple of villagers did come toward the dragonfly planes, chivvied along by the devils with guns. One of those devils lay on the grass just outside the houses. The blood that splashed its scaly hide was red as a man's. Liu Han rubbed her eyes again. She hadn't thought devils could bleed.

Some of the hovering dragonfly planes flew off to the north. Before long, they began firing again. *Good,* Liu Han thought. *They're killing more Japanese.*

With resistance in the village —and the village itself—destroyed, the little scaly devils on the ground began prowling about, as if to make sure no more enemies lurked nearby. When one came in her direction, Liu Han frantically tried to bury herself under leaves and branches. If the Amida Buddha was kind, the devil would not see her.

The compassionate Buddha must have been looking somewhere else. The scaly devil yelled something in whatever language devils used among themselves. Liu Han shivered under her makeshift shelter, but did not come out. Then the devil's gun roared. Bullets snarled through the branches around her.

The devil yelled again. She knew it could have killed her had it cared to, so maybe it was ordering her to give up. She stood up, raised her hands above her head. "P-please don't shoot me, master devil," she quavered.

When the devil spoke once more, she saw it had lots of small pointed teeth and a long forked tongue like a lizard's. One of its eyes kept looking at her. The other, unnervingly, swiveled this way and that. When Liu Han took a step toward the devil, it sprang backward and raised its gun in clear warning.

She realized it barely came to her shoulder. "Are you afraid of me?" she said. The idea of a devil's knowing fear was so absurd that she wanted to laugh in spite of all the disasters of this dreadful day.

The little scaly devil didn't act as if it was funny. It gestured with the gun, pointing back toward the dragonfly planes. Some other villagers were already being marched aboard them. Liu Han knew she had no choice but to go in that direction. As she walked past the devil, it stepped back to make sure she didn't come within arm's length. If it wasn't afraid of her, Liu Han couldn't figure out why it was so cautious.

Before she climbed up the ramp into the dragonfly plane, another devil tied her hands together in front of her. It followed her inside, then motioned her into a seat with its gun.

The seat was uncomfortable, being both the wrong shape for her backside and too small; she had to draw her knees up to her chin to fit her legs into a space that would have been fine for one of the little scaly devils. In the seat beside her sat Yi Min, who looked even more cramped than she felt.

The apothecary looked up dully as she joined him. His face was bloody from a cut by one eye. "So they got you, too, did they?" he said.

"Yes," Liu Han answered. By village standards, Yi Min was an educated man, so she asked him, "What sort of devils are these? I've never seen or heard of anything like them."

"Neither have I," he said. "In fact, I hardly believed in devils—I thought they were superstitious rubbish. They—"

The little scaly devil with the gun said something. It put one hand over its muzzle, holding its toothy mouth closed. Then it pointed to Liu Han and Yi Min. After it did that two or three times, she figured out that it didn't want them to talk. She set a hand over her own mouth. The devil made a noise like a bubbling pot and sat down. Liu Han decided she'd satisfied it.

The dragonfly plane's engine began to roar. The blades that sprouted from the top of it started spinning, first slowly, then faster and faster until they looked like one of the flickering disks she'd noticed above the dragonfly planes when she was still out in the woods.

Without warning, the machine climbed into the air. Liu Han's stomach lurched. She let out a frightened, involuntary squeak. The little scaly devil swung both its turreted eyes toward her. "Sorry, master devil," she said. It kept on glaring. She realized she'd made a new mistake, clapped a hand to her mouth to try to set it right. The devil made that boiling noise again, let its eyes wander away. Had she room, she would have sagged with relief.

She looked out the little window by Yi Min. Through it she could see, frighteningly far below, the burning ruins of her village. Then the dragonfly plane spun in the air and flew off, taking her away from everything she had ever known.

The train had just rolled south past Dixon when everything went to hell. Sam Yeager read the last letter in his *Astounding*, set the magazine down on the seat beside him—Bobby Fiore had woken up and was back in the dining car. Yeager hoped he'd finish soon. He was getting sleepy himself, but how could he doze off when his roommate was going to step over him—or on him—any time now?

Stymied by a complete lack of facts, the Decatur Commodores had given up arguing about what the light in the sky had been. Several of them were sleeping, some with caps or hats over their eyes to keep out the overhead lights. Yeager yawned, stretched, thought about doing the same thing. Maybe he'd be out by the time Bobby got back.

He'd just decided he would go to sleep when something roared past overhead, so loud it woke up everyone who had been resting. Yeager leaned over and jammed his face against the window, wondering if he'd see an airplane go down in flames. That roar sounded as if it had come from just above the train, and he'd never heard a healthy engine sound anything like it.

Sure enough, a moment later a tremendous bang came from in front of the train, and then another one, even louder. "Jesus," Yeager said softly. On the other side of the aisle, Joe Sullivan crossed himself.

While Yeager's head was still ringing from the explosions, the train hit the brakes for all they were worth. He slammed into the seat in front of him. Iron screamed as wheels clenched track. Sparks shot up high enough for him to see them through the window.

The brakes were not worth enough. The passenger car suddenly flipped onto its side. Yeager dropped like a stone, landed on top of Sullivan. The pitcher yelled. Yeager yelled, too, as his head hit what had been the far wall of the car and was now abruptly the floor. His teeth dug into his lip. The hot, metallic taste of blood filled his mouth. He ran his tongue around in there. Luckily, his dentures hadn't broken.

Through the cries of his teammates and the other people in the car, he listened to the rest of the train derailing. The receding string of crashes and bumps made him think of an earthquake bought on the installment plan.

He tested each limb as he untangled himself from Joe Sullivan. "You all right, kid?" he asked.

"I don't know. My shoulder—" Sullivan clutched the injured part. His eyes were wide with fear as well as pain—it was his throwing arm.

"I think maybe we'd better get out of here if we can. Come on." In the darkness, Yeager walked back toward the rear of the car across what had been window frames. Sullivan didn't follow. Yeager hardly noticed; he was stepping as carefully as he could. Some of the windows were broken, and he didn't want to slice his leg on jagged glass.

"That you, Sam?" Mutt Daniels asked as he went by. It took more than a derailment to make him sound anything but slow and relaxed.

"Yeah, it's me." Yeager listened to the moans, and to one woman who kept letting out little screams every few seconds. "I think we got some hurt people here, Mutt."

"Reckon you're right," the manager said. "How the hell we supposed to put a team together tomorrow when shit like this happens to us?"

"You're a baseball man, Mutt," Yeager said. The crash had driven all thoughts of tomorrow's game out of his head. He decided not to tell Daniels about Joe Sullivan's shoulder. Poor Mutt would find out soon enough.

The sliding door to the next car back had sprung off its track when the train went sideways. It gaped open. Yeager pulled himself up into the doorway. He sniffed the outside air, didn't smell smoke. He didn't see any fire, either. *One thing to be thankful for, anyway,* he thought, especially when a man at the front of the car yelled, "Somebody here hurt his neck bad!"

"Don't move him," three people said at once.

Mutt Daniels scrambled up beside Yeager. The manager had a tougher time of it, being both shorter and rounder than his ballplayer. He said, "Wonder what the hell we hit."

"If it was that plane, there'd be burning." Yeager cocked his head. That screaming roar was still in the sky, which meant the plane hadn't crashed after all. But in that case, where had the explosions come from?

The scream got louder, as if the crazy-sounding airplane was coming back. Just when it made Yeager want to scream, too, a new noise joined it, a deep, rapidly repeated bark. The derailed train shook under Yeager and Daniels as shells slammed into it. Glass tinkled. Screams redoubled.

"Holy Jesus God, it's the Gerps shootin' us up!" the manager shouted. He hadn't known whether to say Germans or Japs, and came out with both at once.

Through the railing of the little platform between cars, Yeager watched the airplane—whosoever it was—flash past overhead. It went by so fast, it was just an unidentifiable streak in the sky. The roar of its engines beat at him, faded . . . then began to grow again.

"It's coming back," he said. With all the screaming and yelling up and down the length of the train, that should have come out as a bellow. Instead, it was hardly more than a whisper, as if the louder he said it, the more likely it was to be true.

He said it loud enough to convince Mutt Daniels. The manager paused to stick his head back into the passenger car and yell, "Y'all better git out while y'can!" Then he took his own advice and jumped off the train. His shoes scraped on the graveled roadbed, then clumped more quietly as he reached the soft dirt of the fields.

Yeager hesitated a moment more, but the rising shriek in the sky got him moving. He leapt down, landed heavily. For an instant, he thought he was going to take another fall on that ankle of his, but he managed to catch his balance and stay upright. Young corn plants beat against his legs as he ran between the rows. Their sweet, moist smell took him back to his boyhood.

Mutt Daniels tackled him, lay on top of him in the dirt. "What the hell you doin', Mutt?" he demanded indignantly.

"If he's comin' back for another pass, you don't want to give him no movin' target to shoot at," Daniels said. "Learned that in France back in nineteen an' eighteen. Hadn't thought about it in twenty-odd years, but the stink of blood and shit in that there car brought it right back up to the top o' my mind."

"Oh." So Yeager wasn't the only one who'd had an odor jog his memory. His dredged-up piece of past seemed happier than Mutt's, though.

The plane's gun cut loose just then, lashing the derailed train with another whip of fire. Yeager buried his face in the cool, damp earth. Beside him, Daniels did the same thing. The enemy airplane streaked away. This time, it did not sound as if it was coming back.

"Jesus," Mutt said, cautiously getting up on hands and knees. "Never thought I'd be under artillery fire again, though that's just a squirrel gun if you set it alongside what the Germans threw at us."

Yeager gaped at his manager. He hadn't imagined there could be anything worse than what he'd just been through. He tried to pull himself together. "We've got to get the people out of there, Mutt," he said. His legs wobbled under him when he stood up. That made him angry; he'd never been shot at before, and didn't understand what reaction could do.

"Reckon you're right," Daniels said. "Good Lord's own miracle the whole train's not on fire." He looked at his hands. "Son of a bitch—I got the shakes. Ain't done that since nineteen an' eighteen, neither."

Yeager looked at his hands, too. Now they were steady enough, but that wasn't what he noticed about them: though night had come, he could see them clearly. The train might not have been set afire, but the northern horizon was ablaze. Two big cement plants in Dixon were going up in flames, and most of the rest of the town seemed to be burning, too.

The red flickering light showed Yeager more people scrambling out of the derailed train, and others standing in the cornfield like him and Mutt. He looked down toward the locomotive, and saw at once why the train had overturned: the engine and the coal car behind it had tumbled into a bomb crater.

Mutt Daniels' head made that same slow, incredulous traverse from north to south. "Saw this so't of thing plenty of times in France. My grandpappy talked about what it was like in the States War. I never reckoned the U.S. of A. would get it like this, though."

Yeager hadn't started thinking about the whole United States yet. The ruined train in front of him was disaster enough to fill his mind for the moment. He started toward it, repeating, "We got to help those people, Mutt."

Daniels took a couple of steps with him, then grabbed him by the sleeve and held him back. "I hear more planes comin'. Mebbe we don't wanna get too close to a big target."

Sure enough, a new drone was in the air, or rather several drones, like a swarm of deep-voice bees. They didn't sound like the screaming monster that had bombed the track and shot up the train. "Maybe they're ours," Yeager said hopefully.

"Mebbe." The drones got louder. Daniels went on, "Y'all can do what you want, Sam, but I ain't gonna get out in the open till I see the stars painted on their sides. You get shot at from the air oncet or twice, you plumb lose the taste for it." The manager squatted, ducked under the corn.

Yeager walked a little closer to the train, more slowly with each stride. He still wanted to rescue the people there, but Daniels' caution made a solid kind of sense . . . and the closer those droning engines got, the less they sounded like the airplanes with which Yeager was familiar. He got down on his belly. If he was wrong to take cover, he'd cost himself and the injured people on the train a minute or two. But if he was right . . .

He rolled onto his side so he could look up through the cornstalks' bent green leaves. By the sound, the approaching airplanes were hardly moving: in fact, by the sound they weren't moving at all, just hanging in midair. *But that's impossible,* Yeager thought. Then he saw one of the aircraft, lit up against the night by Dixon's burning cement factories.

The briefest glimpse told him it was no American plane. It hardly looked like a plane at all—more like a flying polliwog. Then Yeager noticed the spinning disk above it. His mind seized on the hovering gyros in Heinlein's "If This Goes On—". But what were those flying marvels from a story set far in the future doing in here-and-now Illinois?

He found the answer a moment later, when they opened fire. The noise of the automatic guns sounded like a giant ripping endless sheets of canvas. He didn't stick his head up to find out what had happened to the people standing in the cornfield. He just thanked his lucky stars—and Mutt Daniels—that he hadn't been one of them.

Staying as low as he could, he crawled backwards through the plants. He hoped their waving above him as he moved wouldn't give him away. If it did, he hoped the end would be quick and clean.

He kept backing up, wondering all the while when he'd bump into Mutt. Surely he'd retreated past where the manager had ducked down. "Idiot," he muttered under his breath. If Mutt had an ounce of sense—and Mutt had a lot more than an ounce—he was getting away from the derailed train, too.

A couple of the gyros settled to earth, one on either side of the train. The one that landed on the eastern side happened to be directly in front of Yeager. His curiosity wrestled down his own good sense, and he stuck out his head far enough to peer out between the rows of corn: he had to know who was attacking the United States. Germans or Japanese, they'd regret it.

His vision path was so narrow that he needed most of a minute to get his first glimpse of an invader. When he did, he thought the soldier had to be a Jap—he was too little to be a German. Then Yeager got a better look at the way the figure by the train moved, the shape of its head . . .

He turned around and crawled through the corn as fast as he could go. He wanted to get up and run, but that would have drawn the invaders' attention for certain. He didn't dare do that, not now.

He almost crawled right over Mutt Daniels, who was still retreating slowly and carefully, head toward the front. "Watch it, boy," Daniels hissed. "You want to get the both of us killed?"

"I saw them, Mutt." Yeager needed all the willpower he possessed to keep his voice low—to keep from screaming, as a matter of fact. He made himself take a deep breath, let it out slowly. Then he continued, "I saw who got down from those hoverplanes of theirs."

"Well, who?" the manager demanded when Yeager went no further. "Was it the Boches"—he pronounced it *Boash*—"or the goddamn Japs?"

"Neither one," Yeager said.

"Got to be one or the other," Daniels said. Then he let out a wheezy laugh. "You ain't gonna tell me it's the Eyetalians, are you?"

Yeager shook his head. He wished he hadn't left his *Astounding* on the train. "Remember that Orson Welles Halloween radio show three, four years ago, the one about Martians that scared the country half out of its shoes?"

"Sure, I remember. Didn't hear it myself, mind, but I sure heard about it later. But what's that got to do with—" Daniels broke off, stared. "You expect me to believe—?"

"Mutt, I swear to God it's true. The Martians have landed, for real this time."

One second, Bobby Fiore was spooning up thin vegetable soup in the dining car of the train. He'd already spent some time thinking disparaging thoughts about it. All right, there was a war on, so you really couldn't expect much in the way of meat or chicken. But vegetable soup didn't have to be dishwater and limp celery. Give his mother some zucchini, carrots, maybe a potato or two, and just a few spices—mind you, just a few—and she'd make you a soup worth eating, now. The cook here was cheap or lazy or both.

The next second, everything went to pieces. Fiore heard the same roaring wail in the sky Yeager had, the same twin blasts. Then the train slammed on the brakes, and then it went off the track. Fiore flew through the air. The side of his head fetched up against the side of a table. A silver light flared behind his eyes before everything spiraled down into darkness.

When he woke up, he thought he'd died and gone to hell. He felt like it; his head pounded like a drum in a swing band, and his vision was blurry and distorted. Blurry or no, the face he saw looked more like a devil than anything else he could think of. It sure (*as hell* whispered through his mind) didn't belong to any human being he'd ever set eyes on.

The thing had sharper teeth, and more of them, than a person had any business having, and a forked tongue like a snake's to go with them. It also had eyes that reminded him of those he'd seen on a chameleon in the Pittsburgh zoo when he was a kid: each in its own little conical mounting, with one quite capable of looking north while the other looked south.

Remembering the chameleon was the first thing that made Fiore wonder if he truly had ended up in Satan's country. The devil—or even *a* devil—should have looked more supernatural and less like a lizard, even an African lizard.

Then he noticed he was still in the flipped dining car; for that matter, he had a butter knife lying on his stomach and a sesame-seed roll by one shoe. He was certain hell had to have worse pangs than a dining car, no matter how bad the soup in this one was. *Had been,* he corrected himself.

The—well, if it wasn't a *devil*, it had to be a *thing*—the thing, then, pointed what looked like a gun at the butter knife near Fiore's belly button. If he wasn't in hell at the moment, he realized, he could get there in a hurry. He smiled the smile a dog smiles after it's lost a fight. "You want to be careful with that," he said, and hoped he was right.

The thing hissed something in reply. Fourteen years of playing ball all over the United States and with and against players with parents from all over Europe and Latin America left Fiore able to recognize a double handful of languages, and swear in several of them. This wasn't any he knew, or anything close.

The thing spoke again, and jerked the barrel of the gun. That Fiore understood. He staggered to his feet, wondering as he did so whether his abused head would fall off. The thing made no effort to help him while he swayed. Indeed, it skittered back to make sure he couldn't reach it.

"If you think I'm bluffing, you're outta your mind," he said. It ignored him. Considering that it came up only to the middle of his chest (and he needed shoes to make the five-eight he always claimed), maybe it had reason to be nervous of him, although he doubted he could have squashed a slug if you gave it a running start.

At another motion of the gun barrel, he started walking forward. After three or four steps, he came to the body of the colored steward. The fellow had a hole in the back of his white mess jacket big enough to throw a cat through. Pieces of him poked through the hole. Fiore's stomach did a flip-flop. The gun at his back concentrated his mind remarkably, however. Gulping, he walked on.

Only a few people had been in the dining car when it derailed. So far as Fiore could tell, he was the only person left alive (he did not count his captor as qualifying). The side of the car—actually, it served as the roof just now—was pierced in a dozen places by bullet holes that let in the warm night air. Fiore shivered. Only dumb luck had kept him from stopping a round, or more than one, while he lay unconscious.

The thing made him scramble out of the dining car. More creatures just like it waited outside. For no good reason, that startled the ballplayer—he hadn't imagined there could be more than one of them.

He saw he wasn't the only person being hustled toward some peculiar gadgets that sat on the ground by the train. Not until another of them thundered past overhead did he realize they were flying machines. They didn't look like any flying machines he'd seen before.

One of the captured people tried to run. Fiore had also been thinking about that. He was glad he'd only thought about it when the things—he still didn't know what else to call them—shot the fleeing man in the back. Just as their flying machines didn't look like airplanes, their guns didn't sound like rifles. They sounded like machine guns; he'd heard machine guns once or twice, at fairs after the first World War.

Running away from somebody—or even something—carrying a machine gun wasn't smart. So Fiore let himself be herded onto the flying machine and into a too-small seat. A good many of the scaly things joined him, but no people. The machine took off. His stomach gave a lurch different from the one he'd felt when he stepped over the dead steward. He'd never been off the ground before.

The things chattered among themselves as they flew through the night. Fiore had no idea which way they were going. He kept sneaking glances at his watch. After about two hours, the darkness outside the little window turned light, not with daytime but with spots like the ones at a ballpark.

These spots didn't show bleachers, though. They showed—Fiore gaped for the right word. Spaceships? Rockets? They had to be something like that. *Sam Yeager would know for sure,* he thought, and suddenly felt ashamed at teasing his friend over that stupid science-fiction magazine . . . which turned out not to have been so stupid after all.

Then he wondered if Yeager was still alive. If he was, he'd have found out about the Martians, too.

3

The *Kukuruznik*'s engine complained about the thin air it was breathing; at four thousand meters, it was way over its proper cruising altitude—up near its ceiling, as a matter of fact. Ludmila Gorbunova's lungs complained, too. The little biplane was not equipped with oxygen, and even sitting in the cockpit made her feel as if she'd just finished a twenty-kilometer run.

She would have gone higher if she could, though. At such a height, the U-2 was hardly more than a speck in the sky—but the Lizards were proving even more skilled than the fascists at spotting such specks and knocking them down.

Ludmila did not even try to fly directly over the new invaders' base. Planes that did that quite simply never came back. The base, a giant ringworm on the smooth skin of the steppe, was visible enough even at the greater distance an oblique view gave.

She counted the huge flying towers that formed the perimeter of the base, shook her head, counted them again. She still got twenty-seven. That was four more than she'd spotted on her last flight, the day before yesterday. From four thousand meters, most things on the ground looked tiny as ants. The towers, though, still bulked large, their shadows darkening great strips of grassland.

They were large, too; from them poured the impossibly deadly planes and tanks that were wresting great tracts of land not only from the Russians who owned it but from the Germans as well. Ludmila still did not know how to feel about that. She hated the Germans with all her soul, but against them one could contend with hope of victory. How could mere men fight the Lizards and their marvels?

Mere men kept trying. Even now, if the radio was to be believed, Soviet tank columns were engaging the Lizards' armor and pushing it back in disarray. Ludmila wondered if anyone believed the radio any more. The year before, the radio had said the Germans were being pushed back from Minsk, then from Kiev, then from Smolensk . . .

Such thoughts were dangerous. Ludmila knew that, too. The purges of the thirties had swept through Kiev as they had everywhere else in the Soviet Union. One day a teacher would be there, the next day vanished. You learned not to ask where he'd gone, not unless you wanted to join him there.

Ludmila shook her head, as if to drive the worries out of it. She peered down at the ground again, squinted to sharpen her vision as much as she could. That plume of dust there in the distance—she squinted harder. "Yes, those are tanks down at the bottom of it, may the Devil's grandmother run away with them," she said.

The *Kukuruznik* had had a radio fitted when Ludmila went from night harassment to reconnaissance. She did not use it. Aircraft that used radio around the Lizards generally did not last long afterward; her information, while she thought it important, didn't seem worth dying for.

She banked away from the Lizards' base. She wondered if her own base would still be there when she landed. The new invaders, like the old, pounded every airstrip they could find. But the so-called strip had been only a length of smooth steppe, and she could find another such strip at need. The U-2 didn't need much room in which to set down.

Even when she got to the airstrip, she had to circle twice to be sure it was there. Camouflage nettings and sod roofs disguised the few buildings. A couple of kilometers away stood a strip camouflaged not quite so well. The Lizards had already bombed it twice. That was all right, or better than all right. The planes there were dummies, the buildings repaired every night but uninhabited.

Her teeth clicked together as the Wheatcutter bounced to a halt. Ludmila scrambled down to the ground while the prop was still spinning. The instant it stopped, groundcrew men threw grass-covered nets over the biplane and hauled it away to hide under still more nets which concealed earthen blast barriers.

Ludmila pulled up a corner of the command shack's camouflage net, hurried through the doorless entrance, let the net fall behind her. With netting over all the windows, the interior of the shack was gloomy. "I return, Comrade Major," she announced.

"So you do, Comrade Pilot," Major Yelena Popova said, returning her salute. "You are most skilled, or most fortunate, or both." In the space of a sentence, she went from mild greeting to pure business: "Tell me at once what you saw."

Ludmila obeyed. Major Popova scowled when she mentioned the four new flying towers on the ground. "These—creatures—swarm onto the soil of the *rodina*—the motherland—like locusts."

"Yes, Comrade Major, and they consume all before them like locusts, too." Ludmila described the column of tanks she'd observed.

The squadron commander's frown, never pleasant, grew downright fearsome. "This is vital information. Those above us must learn of it at once. I shall use the radio. Repeat your statement to me, that I may be sure to report it accurately."

As Ludmila obeyed, Major Popova wrote down what she said, then repeated it back. When Ludmila nodded to show it was right, the major went over to the radio. It and its battery were stowed in a wheelbarrow and covered with hay. Yelena took the wheelbarrow out through the door, started in the direction of the dummy airstrip. To anyone—say, a Lizard—in a plane, she looked like a peasant shambling along.

Ludmila watched her slow progress across the plain. Then the tiny shape that was she disappeared into one of the Potemkin sheds. She emerged a bare minute later, moving much faster than she had on the way over.

Seemingly out of nowhere, a rocket slammed into the empty shed. Flames leapt up from it. The deception team would have a lot of work to do tonight, Ludmila thought. After the rocket hit, Major Popova slowed down again. Ludmila did not blame her. Weighted down by radio and battery, the wheelbarrow was heavy.

"The Lizards are *very* good at picking up radio signals," the major said as she arrived at the real airstrip. She wiped her forehead. Her sleeve came away dark with sweat. But her eyes, narrow and black like a Tatar's, gleamed in triumph.

Even though the breeze was chilly against his muzzle, landcruiser driver Ussmak preferred moving along unbuttoned when he could. The periscopes didn't give him nearly the view he enjoyed with his head out. Besides, being cooped up in the driver's compartment reminded him too much of the cold-sleep coffin in which he'd hibernated away the years between Home and Tosev 3.

He had an audio button taped to one hearing diaphragm. "Better get down, Ussmak," said Votal, the landcruiser commander. "Airscouts report Big Ugly landcruisers ahead."

"It shall be done," Ussmak said, and slid back down into his compartment. Even as he dogged the hatch over his head, he wondered why he was bothering. The Big Uglies, especially this set that used a red star as its emblem, had lots of landcruisers, but they weren't very good ones or used very well. But his commander had given the order, so he obeyed. That had been ingrained in him since his hatching day.

Gunner Telerep said, "What do you want to bet we don't even get in on the fun? Our air will probably take them out before they're in range for us."

"We may have some work," Votal said. "The farther away from base we move, the thinner our air cover gets. And—" His voice rose to a sudden shout. "Big Ugly airplane!" In his audio button, Ussmak heard the commander dive down in the landcruiser's turret. A roar overhead, a couple of shells bouncing off metal and ceramic armor, and the natives' craft sped away, its belly almost scraping the grass.

Two landcruisers in the formation fired missiles after it. However fast it was, they were faster. It tumbled to the ground; dust flew from the brown track it plowed through the green. *Brave,* Ussmak thought, *brave but stupid.* The Tosevites seemed like that.

"Tosevite landcruisers!" Telerep said. "Looks like you were right, commander."

"I see them," Votal answered. Ussmak still didn't, being down low in the hull rather than up in the turret. That didn't matter. Votal told him what to do: "Steer 22, Ussmak."

Ussmak started turning from north to west. Yes, there they were. Being big and clumsy themselves, the Tosevites built big and clumsy, though these landcruisers didn't have a bad ballistic shape compared to some others the crews had been briefed about. At least their turret armor sloped . . . not that that would help them now.

"Gunner!" Votal said loudly. He'd picked a target, then, one from among the several that sought to bar his path. A moment later, he added, "Sabot!"

"Sabot!" Telerep repeated. The automatic loader cranked a round into the breech of the cannon. Ussmak heard it not only in his audio button but also through his whole body—clang-*clang!* Another metallic noise announced that the breech had closed. Telerep said, "Up and ready."

"Landcruiser—front!" That meant Votal had the target Tosevite in his sights.

"Identified." Telerep saw it, too. Over Ussmak's head, the gun tube swung slightly as it moved toward the enemy's center of mass.

"Fire!"

Through his periscopes, Ussmak saw flame leap from the muzzle of the gun. Armor shielded him from the roar of the report. Recoil made the landcruiser seem to hesitate for an instant. The aluminum sabots fell away from the tungsten penetrator arrow. Ussmak did not see that, of course. A heartbeat later, he did see the turret leap off a Tosevite landcruiser. "Hit!" he yelled, along with Votal and Telerep.

Another Tosevite was killed, this one in a pyrotechnic display of exploding ammunition. The Big Uglies lost whatever formation they were trying to keep. Some of them stopped, as they had to if they hoped to fire accurately. *Their eggs are broken now,* Ussmak thought with cold glee. They were easy enough to kill on the move. Stopped . . . "Landcruiser—front!" Votal said.

"Identified," Telerep answered.

As the automatic loader clattered into action, a Tosevite landcruiser spat fire. Ussmak's jaw opened in a laugh. *Another one down,* he thought, and wondered which of the other landcruisers in his unit had scored the kill. Then—*wham!* Something smote the glacis plate like a kick in the teeth.

"Ussmak!" Votal said. "You all right?"

"Y-yes," the driver answered, still more than a little shaken. "Didn't penetrate, the Emperor be praised." *Or I'd be splashed all over the inside of the compartment,* he added to himself. The Big Uglies were doing their best to fight back. Their best, fortunately for Ussmak, was not good enough.

He must have been too stunned to listen to the whole command sequence, for the big gun fired then. He had the satisfaction of watching the landcruiser that had almost killed him start to burn. He wondered if any of the crew got out. In a way, they were guildsmates of his, and so deserving of respect. On the other hand, they were only Big Uglies, and knew not the Emperor's name.

When most of the Tosevite landcruisers were dead, some of the survivors turned tailstump and started to run. Ussmak laughed again. They couldn't outrun cannon shells.

A funny noise in his audio button, sort of a wet splat. Then a cry of disbelief and rage from Telerep: "Votal! Vo— They've killed the commander!"

Ussmak's belly went strange and empty, as if he'd suddenly been dropped into free-fall. "How could they?" he demanded of the gunner. "We're slaughtering their landcruisers. They're hardly fighting back any more."

"Sniper, or I miss my guess," Telerep said. "They can't meet us in honest battle, so they lie in wait instead."

"We'll make them pay," Ussmak said fiercely. "The past Emperors have learned Votal's name. He is with them now."

"Of course he is," the gunner answered. "Now shut up and drive, will you? I'm going to conn this landcruiser and run the gun, too, so I'm too busy to chatter. I'm going to be busier than a one-handed male with the underscale itch, as a matter of fact."

Ussmak drove. When he'd stepped into the starship and slung his gear down beside his cold-sleep coffin, he'd expected the Race to overrun Tosev 3 without losing a male. It wasn't turning out to be so simple, not with the Big Uglies knowing more than anyone had suspected they did. But they didn't know enough. The Race could still drive them as easily as Ussmak drove his landcruiser.

A *pinng* off the turret—"Steer 25, Ussmak!" Telerep shouted. "I saw the flash!"

The driver obediently turned due west. Another *pinng,* this one off the glacis plate. After taking a hit from a landcruiser cannon, Ussmak ignored the tiny nuisance. He tramped down hard on the accelerator. This time, he'd spotted the muzzle flash, too. He drove straight toward it. The Big Ugly fired again, uselessly, then turned and tried to run.

Telerep cut him down with machine-gun fire. Ussmak ran over the carcass, smashing it into the grass and dirt. His jaws opened wide. Votal was avenged. The landcruiser formation rolled on across the steppe.

Even the smallest noise or flicker of motion in the sky drew Heinrich Jäger's complete and concerned—he was too stubborn to admit to a word like *fearful*—attention. This time, it was just a linnet flitting past, chirping as it went. This time.

He had three tanks left, three tanks and a combat group of infantry. "Combat group" was the *Wehrmacht* way of describing odds and ends of military meat pressed together in the hope of turning out a sausage. Sometimes it even worked—but when it did, the sausage went right back into the meat grinder again.

Another motion across the sky turned out to be another bird. Jäger shook his head. He could feel how jumpy he was getting. But the Lizards' aircraft didn't have to be right overhead to kill. The company had learned that, too, to its sorrow.

He managed something halfway between a laugh and a cough, leaned down into the turret. "I wonder if the Ivans felt this naked after we smashed so many of their planes on the ground last year," he said.

"If they did, they hid it damned well," his gunner answered. Georg Schultz wore the ribbon for a wound badge, too.

"So do we—I hope," Jäger said.

A squad of infantry was posted on a swell of ground a few hundred meters in front of the tanks. One of the foot soldiers turned and waved urgently. The signal meant only one thing—Lizard panzers, heading across the steppe. Jäger's testicles tried to crawl up into his belly. Schultz looked up at him. The gunner was dirty and unshaven. "We must try," he said. "For the Fatherland."

"For the Fatherland," Jäger echoed. Given that the alternative was bailing out of his tank and trying to foot it across the Ukraine through Lizards and partisans both, fighting for the Fatherland looked like the best bet he had. He leaned down into the turret, called to Dieter Schmidt: "To the prepared position."

The Panzer III slowly rumbled forward. So did the other two survivors of the tank company. In slots dug into the reverse slope of the rise, they exposed only the tops of their turrets to the enemy. Jäger stood up in the cupola, peered ahead with field glasses. He took even fewer chances than he had against the Russians. Shrubs tied to his leather headgear broke up his outline; he used his free hand to shield the binoculars so no sun reflected off their lenses.

Sure enough, there were the Lizards, eight or ten tanks' worth, with more vehicles scurrying along behind to support them. Jäger recognized the ones with small turrets as troop carriers, on the order of the German SdKfz 251 but far more dangerous—they could fight his panzers on largely even terms. And the Lizards' tanks . . .

"You know what's the funny thing, Georg?" he said as he lowered himself once more.

"Tell me anything funny about the Lizards, *Herr* Major," the gunner grunted. "I will laugh, I promise you."

"They're lousy tankers," Jäger said. He was a lousy tankman himself, but only in the literal sense of the word. No one who was lousy in the metaphorical sense could have lasted almost a year on the eastern front.

Sure enough, Schultz laughed. "They've been good enough to kick our ass."

"It's the panzers, not the crews," Jäger insisted. "They have better guns than ours, better armor, and God only knows how they make engines that don't smoke. But tactics—*pfui!*" He curled his lip in disdain. "The Russians have better sense. They just motor along shooting at anything that happens to cross their path. They aren't even looking this way, though it's an obvious place for trouble. Stupid!"

"No doubt a run through the *Panzer Lehr* training division would improve their skill, *Herr* Major," Schultz said dryly. "But if the tanks themselves are good enough, how good do the tankers have to be?"

Jäger grunted. It was a cogent question. In Panzer IIIs, little *Pimpfs* from the Hitler Youth, boys too young to shave, could have taken out whole divisions of British tanks from the Great War: the rhomboidal monsters were too slow to run and too lightly armed to fight. He'd thought the Panzer III a great tank until he ran up against his first Russian T-34, and a good tank even afterward. Now—now he might as well have been in one of those obsolete rhomboids himself.

"We do what we can, Georg," he said. The gunner nodded.

Jäger stuck his head out of the cupola again. The Lizards were trundling happily past his strongpoint, no more than five hundred meters away, without the slightest idea he was there. He glanced over to Ernst Riecke and Uwe Tannenwald, his other surviving tank commanders, and held up one finger. Both men waved to show they understood. Hanging around for more than one shot against the Lizards was an invitation to a funeral.

The company commander pointed to one of the troop carriers. "That one, Georg," he said quietly.

"*Ja,*" the gunner said. He spoke to the loader. "Armor-piercing."

"Armor-piercing," Stefan Fuchs echoed. He pulled the black-tipped round out of the ammunition rack, loaded it into the five-centimeter gun, closed the breech.

The gunner traversed the turret a few degrees so it bore on the troop carrier. He took his eyes away from the gunsight for an instant to make sure Fuchs was clear of the recoil, then looked back and squeezed the trigger at almost the same time.

The cannon roared. Through his field glasses, Jäger saw a hole appear in the troop carrier's flank. "Hit!" he shrieked. The carrier slewed sideways, stopped. It was burning. A hatch came down in the rear. Lizards started bailing out. German foot soldiers opened up on them, picking them off as they emerged.

"Back!" Jäger shouted. If he waited around to see how the foot soldiers did, one of those Lizard panzers would blow him to bits. Already, with terrifying speed, their turrets were traversing to bear on his position. Dieter Schmidt jammed the tank into reverse. It jounced down the low slope. So did Sergeant Tannenwald's. Ernst Riecke was a split second too slow. Jäger watched in dismay as the turret flew off his panzer and crushed an infantryman who was scrambling to get out of the way.

Later, Jäger told himself, *I'll grieve.* That assumed there would be a *later* for him. At the moment, the assumption looked bad. One of the things he'd learned fighting the Russians was to have more than one firing position available whenever he could. His second one was at the base of the rise.

"Maybe we'll give 'em a surprise, Major," Schultz said. He and Fuchs already had another AP round loaded and ready. The gun bore on the place where the Lizard panzers were likeliest to breast the rise.

A couple of foot soldiers dashed forward with satchel charges. That meant the tanks were close, then. Machine guns chattered furiously. An explosion sent up smoke and dirt, then another. Jäger hoped the brave men hadn't thrown away their lives for nothing.

Then he had no time for hope or fear, for a Lizard panzer nosed over the horizon right where he'd thought it would—the Lizards really were lousy tankmen. The Panzer III's cannon roared as he drew in breath to yell, "Fire!"

Schultz was an artist with the long gun. He put the AP round right in the middle of the tiny bit of belly plate the enemy tank exposed as it came over the rise. The glacis plate laughed at even high-velocity five-centimeter shells. The belly plate, as on merely human panzers, was thinner. The shell pierced it. The tank stopped. *They'll have to take the driver out of there with a spoon,* Jäger thought.

Two Lizards popped out of the turret, one after the other. The hull machine gun from Jäger's tank cut them down.

Tannenwald's tank had done almost as well as the company commander's. Its first shot knocked the track off a Lizard panzer's road wheels. The hit tank swerved, out of control. A foot soldier ran up to it, tossed a potato-masher grenade into the open cupola. Its small blast was followed an instant later by a big one as the panzer's ammunition went off.

"Back again!" Jäger told Schmidt. Already they'd hurt the Lizards worse in this engagement than ever before. That was important, but it would matter only so much if he wound up dead . . . as he probably would as soon as a Lizard panzer made it onto the reverse slope of that little rise.

A scream in the sky— Death would come even without the Lizards' tanks, then. Their aircraft were just as deadly. Jäger resigned himself. Bombs burst all around—the other side of the rise, the side the Lizards were still climbing.

"Stuka!" Georg Schultz screamed in the voice of a man who knows himself reprieved.

"By God, it is," Jäger said. He, by contrast, spoke softly, for he could scarcely believe he might yet live a while longer. The Lizards had taken as dreadful a toll on the *Luftwaffe* as on the *Wehrmacht*. But this pilot, somehow, had still got his dive-bomber into the air and still had the nerve to fly it straight down the Lizards' throats.

More bombs went off in quick succession—he'd loosed the whole stick. Only a direct hit would take out a panzer, but even experienced tankers had to hesitate before advancing through that sudden storm of explosives.

The Stuka pilot couldn't have been more than a hundred meters off the ground when he pulled out of his dive. Two of the Lizard panzers fired their guided rockets at him, but the missiles shot harmlessly past his plane. He skimmed away, his landing gear just above the waving grass of the steppe.

"Get us out of here," Jäger told Dieter Schmidt. The Panzer III's engine roared as the driver obeyed. Jäger felt an itch between his shoulder blades. He knew that was stupid. If one of the Lizards' shells got him, he'd be dead too fast to know it.

He looked back toward the rise. If his tank could make it over the next one before the Lizards climbed this one and spotted him, he really did have a chance to get away. He wouldn't have believed it when the engagement started, but it was true. He felt a surge of pride. His troops had hurt the Lizards, and not many units could boast of that. *Gott mit uns*, he thought, *we might even do it again.*

Two Lizard panzers came over the rise. His own tank was only halfway up the next slope. A turret swung his way. His eyes went up to the sky, seeking, praying for, another Stuka. But God lives in only so many machines. The Lizards didn't even need to slow down to fire.

Less than a heartbeat after the big cannon spat smoke and flame, Jäger felt the mother of all kicks in the arse. His trusty panzer, which had served so well for so long, died under him. Smoke poured up through the engine vents of the rear deck.

"Out, out, out!" he screamed. He had almost been thrown out, on his head. Only two armored walls and the full weight of the engine had kept the enemy shell out of the fighting compartment. Once the fire got going, nothing would hold that at bay.

Machine-gun bullets stitched the air around him as he pulled himself out of the cupola and dove into the tall grass. Other hatches came open. His crew began bailing out with him. A bullet struck home with a noise like a slap on a bare, wet back. Somebody shrieked.

The clean green smell of the weeds through which Jäger scrambled filled his nostrils. He had two somewhat contradictory goals. He wanted to put the hulk of the killed tank between himself and the oncoming Liz-ards, but he also wanted to get as far away from that hulk—and from the Lizards—as he could. The ammunition in the Panzer III was going to start cooking off any minute now, maybe any second, and the Lizards were not likely to be well-disposed toward German tankmen, especially a crew that had managed to destroy one of their fancy machines.

Another shell slammed into the Panzer III. It went up with a roar. *Stu-pid*, Jäger thought, *stupid and wasteful*. That tank was already dead meat. Meanwhile, though, machine-gun bullets probed the grass. They made tiny, whispering *tic-tic-tic* sounds as they clipped the leaves. Jäger won-dered what kind of sounds he would make if they clipped him.

The Lizards' tank rolled majestically past, fewer than fifty meters off. Jäger lay facedown and unmoving. If the enemy saw him, maybe they'd think he was already dead. Not only was it faster than both his Panzer III and a T-34, it was ghost-quiet to boot.

Somewhere a few hundred meters away, an MG-34 began to bark. Bul-lets ricocheted off the armor of the Lizard panzer. Its machine gun re-turned fire. The panzer itself turned toward the German machine-gun position.

As he crawled in the opposite direction, Jäger almost bumped into Georg Schultz. After an instant of fright, the two men grinned at each other. "Good to see you, sir," the gunner said, grin broad and white in his dirty face.

"And you," Jäger answered. "Have you seen Fuchs?"

Schultz's grin slipped. "He didn't make it out."

"That was the shriek, then," Jäger said. The gunner nodded. Jäger went on, "What about the two up front?"

"Don't know."

They found Dieter Schmidt a few minutes later. Klaus Bauer, the hull gunner, remained missing. "We both got out," Schmidt insisted. "I don't know what happened to him afterward." He didn't say *nothing good*, but the words hung in the air.

"Lucky we didn't blow up when we were hit," Jäger said.

Schmidt surprised him by laughing. "Luck, hell, sir. We were just about dry of petrol, that's all. We had maybe enough for another kilometer or two, no more."

"Oh," Jäger said. He started to laugh himself, though it wasn't really funny. Here he'd just fought what had to be one of the most successful small-unit actions ever against the Lizards, and to what result? Only the final destruction of his tank company. How many actions like that could the *Wehrmacht* take before there wasn't any *Wehrmacht* any more?

For that matter, even this action wasn't over yet. Lizard infantry had been moving up along with their armor. Jäger had a pistol in his holster that he hadn't fired in months. Schultz and Schmidt were both clutching their personal Schmeissers. Submachine guns were better than nothing, but they didn't have the range to make proper infantry weapons.

"What now, sir?" Schultz asked.

"Now we get out of the sack," Jäger said. "If we can."

Moishe Russie held up the Bible, read from the Book of Joshua in a loud voice: " 'And it came to pass, when the people heard the sound of the trumpet, and the people shouted with a great shout, that the wall fell down flat, so that the people went up into the city.' "

The crowd of Jews behind him cheered. At his side, his wife, Rivka, beamed at him, her sweet brown eyes enormous in her thin face. Their son, Reuven, was even thinner, his eyes, so like his mother's, even bigger. A starving child could not help rousing horror and pity in any adult who saw him—save perhaps in the Warsaw ghetto, where the sight had grown so common that even horror and pity failed at last.

"What now, *Reb* Moishe?" someone called.

"I'm no *reb*," he said, looking modestly down at the ground.

"No *reb*?" several people exclaimed together in tones of disbelief. One added, "Who but you asked the Lord for a sign and was answered?" That tale had run through the ghetto almost before the miraculous light in the sky faded. Every tale with hope in it spread even faster than typhus. With only hope to live on, the Jews made of it a banquet.

Someone else, a woman, said, "He's no *reb*; he's a prophet. Like Joshua whose Book he reads, he made the walls fall down."

The Jews cheered again. Russie felt his ears grow hot. *He* hadn't made the ghetto walls fall down, and he knew it. But the bombs that screamed out of the sky and smashed brick to powder seemed to have come from the same—people? monsters?—who'd touched off the light in the sky he'd taken for a signal from On High.

The only accounts of them in the ghetto came from garbled shortwave reports. By the rumors he'd heard, Russie knew the Lizards (a name he wondered about) were bombing fortifications all over the world. Nowhere, though, had their explosives done more than in Warsaw.

He wondered whether the Lizards thought the Nazis had an enemy under siege in the heart of the city (if so, they'd been right, though perhaps not in the way they'd believed). Whatever their reasons, they'd attacked the wall less than a week after they revealed their presence.

Russie remembered the German bombers dropping their endless loads of death almost randomly over Warsaw (although they had paid special attention to the Jewish districts). The Lizards' raid was different. Even though they'd come at night, their bombs hit the wall and only the wall, almost as if they were aimed not by men—or even Lizards—but by the hand of the Almighty.

Rivka smiled at him. "Remember how we shivered under our blankets when the explosions started going off?"

"I'm not likely to forget," Russie answered. Since Warsaw surrendered, the ghetto hadn't known the sounds of real warfare. The dreaded *crummp* of bombs reminded everyone who had managed to endure since 1939 that more straightforward means of death than starvation, disease, and beatings were loose in the world. Russie went on, "And then, when the curfew lifted . . . Oh, when the curfew lifted!"

Bombs or no bombs, if he didn't get to his sewing machine, he'd lose his job. He knew it, and sallied forth at the usual time. The streets had seemed to fill with amazing speed that morning. People moved along at their usual pace; no one who had work would risk losing it, and no one without would throw away a chance to find some. But somehow everyone managed to stop for a few seconds and gape at one—or more than one—of the holes torn in the wall that sundered the ghetto from the rest of Warsaw.

Russie stood in front of one of those holes now, a three-meter stretch where there was no wall. As he stepped into the bomb crater, the soles of his feet felt every sharp brick fragment through the rags that wrapped them. He did not care. Still holding the Holy Scriptures before him, he walked through the shallow crater and out of the ghetto.

Turning, he said, "Jericho's walls could not hold the Hebrews out, nor can Warsaw's hold us in. The Lord has set us free!"

The crowd of Jews cheered once more. He drank in the shouts of "*Reb* Moishe! *Reb* Moishe!" The more he heard them, the better they sounded in his ears. God *had* given him the sign, after all.

Someone in the crowd, though, called, "The Lord may have set us free, but has He bothered to tell the Nazis?"

The word itself was enough to make people look this way and that in alarm, Russie among them. Even without walls, the Germans could have kept the ghetto sealed by posting machine guns in the streets around it. They hadn't done so, which seemed to Russie another sign of divine intervention.

He took a short, fearful breath. As if thinking of Germans was enough to conjure them up, here came two. The crowd behind him started to melt away. "Moishe, get back here!" his wife said urgently.

Too late. One of the Germans, an officer by his peaked cap, pointed to Russie. "You, Jew, come here," he said in peremptory tones. His companion, an enlisted man, had a rifle. If Russie ran, the fellow might shoot, and wasn't likely to care whether he hit the man he was aiming for or some other fleeing Jew.

Russie took off his hat to the officer—an army man, he saw with relief, not a member of the SS. Some army men were decent. Still, omitting the gesture of respect the Nazis demanded was too dangerous to risk. If he'd been on the sidewalk, he would have stepped down into the street. As it was, he bent his head and said, "Yessir. How can I help you, sir?" in the pure German he'd learned in medical school: he also did not care to risk angering the man by making him try to follow Yiddish or Polish.

"What do you make of—this?" The officer—he was a major, Russie saw by his shoulder straps, which were embroidered but bore no pips—waved at the wreckage of the wall that had surrounded the ghetto.

Russie stayed silent for some time, considering the tone of the question. Germans were like any other folk in that some wanted to hear only that which agreed with what they already thought, while others asked in hope of learning something they did not yet know—and in that, the former type outnumbered the latter by a goodly margin. Safest to say nothing, and say it in a pleasing way.

Safest, yes, but he found all at once that he could not stomach simple safety, not any more, not with a German for once asking a question of a Jew and sounding as if the answer mattered to him. Russie held out the Bible he was carrying. "I take—this—to mean that God has not forgotten us after all."

Under the outthrust rim of his steel helmet, the enlisted man's ginger-colored eyebrows drew together in anger. The major, however, nodded slowly and thoughtfully. "You may be right. In truth, you would require the aid of God to escape from our hands."

"That I know." Russie did not bother to hide his bitterness. With the whole world turned topsy-turvy, somehow it did not seem wrong for the prisoner to speak his mind to his gaoler.

The German major nodded again, as if thinking along the same lines. He said, "Do you know, Jew, the Lizards who bombed these walls are not even human beings, but creatures from some other world?"

Russie shrugged. "How could it matter to us, trapped back in there?" He half-turned and pointed with his chin into the ghetto. "And why should it matter to you Germans, either? You named us *Untermenschen*— subhumans. What difference between subhumans and creatures from some other world?" He repeated the major's phrase without any real feeling for what it might imply.

"What difference? I'll tell you what. By all accounts, the Lizards are ugly enough to be *Untermenschen*, but they fight like *Übermenschen*, like supermen."

"So do the Russians, by all accounts," Russie said. Just standing on the far side of the ghetto wall was making him reckless.

He got away with it, too. The German enlisted man's scowl got deeper, but the major accepted the gibe. With almost British understatement, he said, "The problem with the Lizards is rather worse."

Good, Russie thought. If the mysterious Lizards ever showed up in person in Warsaw, the ghetto Jews would greet them with open arms. No matter how reckless he'd grown, though, he did not say that aloud. Instead, he asked, "And what, sir, do *you* make of this?"

"We are still deciding precisely what to make of it," the major answered. "I have as yet no orders."

"Ah," Russie said. In combat, a German without orders was as deadly as one who had them, for German soldiers were endlessly trained to react and seize the initiative when and as they could. In matters political, though, Germans without orders were as helpless as so many unweaned babes, fearing to take a step in any direction. *A strange folk,* Russie thought, *and all the more dangerous for their strangeness.* He asked, "Then you have no orders to keep us from coming out of the ghetto, *nicht wahr?*"

"That is so," the major admitted, in the hollow voice of a man who has had too much happen to him too quickly. "In any case, with the Lizards having established a base inside the Polish *Generalgouvernement*, the *Wehrmacht* has more to worry about at the moment than you Jews."

"Thank you, sir," Russie breathed. His own sincerity startled him. After a moment, it angered him as well: why should he thank this Nazi for deigning to allow him what should have been his by right?

And, indeed, the German tempered his own moderation: "You would likely do well to remember that the SS never has more to worry about than you Jews. Be careful." *Be very careful,* the cold gray eyes of the silent enlisted man seemed to add. *Be very careful . . . kike.*

"We have learned to be careful," Russie said. "Otherwise we would all be dead by now."

He wondered how the major would react to that. The man merely nodded, as at any statement of obvious fact. His arm shot up and out in the German salute. *"Heil Hitler!"*

Russie could not bring himself to answer with the Nazi farewell. But the officer had talked to him as man to man, not as master to slave. He said, "God keep you safe from the Lizards, Major."

The German nodded again, this time brusquely, did a military about-face, and strode away. The enlisted man stalked after him. They left Moishe Russie still standing in Polish Warsaw, outside the ghetto. "Moishe, are you all right?" his wife called from the other side of the fence. She had not fled, but Reuven was nowhere to be seen—a sensible precaution, for he was all they had left.

"I am all right," he answered, wonder in his own voice. He repeated the words, louder: "I *am* all right." Simply standing in broad daylight on what had been forbidden soil was as intoxicating as Purim vodka.

Timidly, Rivka picked her way across the bomb crater and joined him on the far side of the wall. "They spoke with you, and you took no harm." She sounded as amazed as he had. "Maybe even they felt God working through you."

"Maybe they did," Russie said as he slipped his arm around her shoulder. An hour earlier, he had scoffed at the idea that he—a medical student who ate pork if his need was desperate enough—might somehow be a prophet. Now he too began to wonder. God had not actively interfered in the affairs of His chosen people since the days of the Bible. But when since those days had His people been in such peril?

And why, Russie thought, would God choose *him*? He shook his head. "Who am I, to question Him?" he said. "His will be done."

"It is," Rivka said proudly. "Through you."

The lights were off in the auditorium of the Mills and Petrie Memorial Center; power had been erratic ever since the Lizards' airplanes started ranging over the Midwest. The gloomy auditorium was packed nonetheless, with youths and men from the village of Ashton and with refugees like Sam Yeager and Mutt Daniels.

Yeager was acutely aware that he'd been wearing the same clothes for several days, that he hadn't washed either them or himself any time lately, that he'd done a lot of walking and running and hiding in them. Seeing a good many men as grimy as he, and none of them taking any notice of it, was something of a relief.

A grim-faced, middle-aged man in khaki walked across the stage, stopped in the center. Crowd noises ceased, as abruptly as if cut off by a switch. "Thank you for being here this morning," the man said. "I want you all to stand and raise your right hands."

Yeager was already standing; the auditorium had more men in it than seats. He put up his right hand. The man in khaki said, "Repeat after me: 'I'—state your name—"

"I, Samuel William Yeager," Yeager repeated, "a citizen of the United States, do hereby acknowledge to have voluntarily enlisted the eighth day of June, 1942, as a soldier in the Regular Army of the United States of America for the period of four years or the duration of this war under the conditions prescribed by law, unless sooner discharged by proper authority; and do also agree to accept from the United States such bounty, pay, rations, and clothing as are or may be prescribed by law. And I do solemnly swear"—the echoing chorus grew ragged for a moment, as a few men said *affirm*—"that I will bear true faith and allegiance to the United States of America; that I will serve them honestly and faithfully against all their enemies whatsoever; and that I will obey the orders of the President of the United States, and the orders of the officers appointed over me, according to the Rules and Articles of War."

An enormous grin stretched across Yeager's face. It had taken an invasion from Mars or wherever the hell the Lizards came from, but he'd made it into the service after all.

"When do we get our guns?" somebody in the crowd shouted. Yeager quivered with that same hot eagerness; he hadn't yet been to war, unless having his train strafed counted. But he hadn't been able to shoot back then. Beside him, Mutt Daniels stood quietly. He wasn't eager—he'd done this before.

Up on the stage, the dour recruiting sergeant—Schneider, his name was—raised his eyebrows to the silent heavens. "Soldier, we don't have that many guns to give, or uniforms, or much of anything. We've been building an army to fight overseas since the Japs jumped us, and now all this shit lands in our own backyard—"

"Uh-huh," Mutt Daniels said softly. "They did the very same thing in the last war, grabbed the men 'fore there was anything for 'em to fight with."

"I want you to form two lines," Sergeant Schneider said. "One line for Great War veterans, over this way, the other for everybody else over there. Move it, people, and remember you're in the army now; lying isn't just a joke any more."

Daniels went "over this way," toward a table manned by a younger man in khaki, a corporal; along with most of the men in the auditorium, Yeager went "over there," a longer line toward a table behind which Schneider himself sat. He suspected that Mutt and the rest of the veterans would get first crack at whatever rifles became available. That was only fair. They had the best idea of what to do with them.

His own line moved much more slowly. He chatted with the men in front and in back of him. He'd come through the hamlet of Franklin Grove on his way to Ashton, and heard President Roosevelt's defiant speech "from somewhere in the United States of America." "He sure can turn a phrase," the fellow in front of Yeager said. " 'This Earth is ours, this nation is ours. No one shall take them from us, so help me God.' "

"That's just what he said," Yeager said admiringly. "How'd you remember it right on the button like that?"

"I'm a reporter—it's a trick of the trade," the man said. He was in his late twenties, with sharp foxy features, a hairline mustache, very blue eyes, and sandy hair combed down slick and close to his skull. He stuck out a hand. "Name's Pete Thomsen. I'm with the *Rockford Courier-Journal.*"

Yeager shook the proffered hand, then introduced himself. So did the fellow behind him, a bald, muscular man named Otto Chase. He said, "I was just heading to the cement works in Dixon when they blew up in front of me. That's when I got this here." He gingerly touched a gash on the top of his head with a blunt forefinger.

At last Yeager stood before Sergeant Schneider. The sergeant paused to sharpen his pencil with a pocket knife, then took Yeager's name and date of birth. "Married?" he asked.

"No, sir. Divorced," Yeager said, and made a sour face. Louise had finally gotten sick of his nomadic ways, and when he wouldn't settle down—

"Children?"

"No, sir," he said again.

Schneider made a checkmark, then said, "Occupation?"

"Ballplayer," he answered, which made Schneider look up from the form. He went on, "I play—played, I guess—for the Decatur Commodores. That's my manager over there." He pointed to Mutt Daniels, who'd already gone through his line and was jawing with several other First World War veterans.

The recruiting sergeant rubbed his chin. "What position you play? You a pitcher?"

"No, sir. Outfield—left, mostly."

"Hmm. You throw pretty good, though?"

"Yes, sir. Nothing wrong with my arm," Yeager said without false modesty. He wasn't fast, he wasn't the best fielder in the world, he was a sucker for a slow curve on the outside corner (or, worse yet, just off it), but by God he could throw.

"Okay," Schneider said. "You'll be able to chuck a grenade farther than most, I expect." He scribbled a note, then pointed in Mutt's direction himself. "You go over with those fellows. We've got some grenades and we'll be bringing more in—if the Lizards don't shoot up the trucks, anyhow. Go on, now." The sergeant raised his voice. "Next."

Rather hesitantly, Yeager walked over to the knot of men with Daniels. He was a rookie on this team; these men, many of them plump or balding or gray, had seen and done things he hadn't. Suddenly what they knew was in demand again. His own taste of combat had been solely on the receiving end, running away from death in the sky like the hordes of bombed-out refugees in Europe.

Mutt helped some by introducing him around. One of the plump gray men there, a fellow named Fred Walters, turned out to have played a few weeks of Class D ball back around 1912. "I couldn't cut the mustard, and they turned me loose," he said. "You been makin' a living at it seventeen years? That's pretty fine." His admiration also helped make Sam feel more at ease.

And, of course, they all had the war—or rather, the wars—to talk about. "With the Lizards here, are we still fighting the Germans and the Japs?" Yeager asked, adding, "But for Roosevelt's speech, I haven't heard much in the way of news till I got here yesterday."

"Me, neither." Mutt Daniels ran a hand over his ragged pants and filthy jacket. "We been on the move the last few days, you might say."

That got him a few wry chuckles. Several of the men standing there were a lot more bedraggled than he was. Fred Walters, by contrast, was clean and well-creased; he lived in Ashton. He said, "Fact of it is, nobody really knows what the hell is going on. I did hear tell, though, that a Jap fleet heading for Hawaii hightailed it back to the Land of the Rising Sun when the Lizards bombed Tokyo."

"They hit Tokyo," Yeager said. "First good thing I heard about 'em."

"They hit Berlin, too," Walters said, "and a lot of other places besides."

"One thing this does," said somebody whose name Yeager hadn't caught, "is shoot Lend-Lease right in the head. With the damned Lizards right here in the middle of the United States, we don't have enough for ourselves, let alone for anybody else."

"Gonna be hard on the Limies and the Russians," Daniels observed.

"We gotta worry about ourselves first," the other man said. Heads bobbed up and down, Yeager's among them. The fellow went on, "Plain fact is, we're short, too. If we weren't, we wouldn't be going through this folderol of separating out the ones who know how to fight to make sure they get guns first."

"Sergeant Schneider over there as much as told me we don't have enough guns for all the men who're joining up here," Yeager said.

"Plain fact is, gentlemen, we got trouble," Daniels said. "That's what the plain fact is, and nothing else but." Heads bobbed up and down again.

Something moving swiftly through the air— Alarm coursed through David Goldfarb as he caught the motion. He whipped his binoculars up to his eyes, took a longer look, relaxed. "Only a sea gull," he said, relief in his voice.

"Which kind?" Jerome Jones asked with interest. The events of the past few days had turned him into an avid bird-watcher.

"One of the black-headed ones," Goldfarb answered indifferently; his interest in birds began and ended with poultry.

He sat in a rickety folding chair of canvas and wood a few feet from the edge of the cliffs of Dover, where England dropped straight down into the sea. An observer might have sat thus a quarter of a century before, with the self-same binoculars, maybe even in the self-same folding chair, peering toward Europe in hope of spotting zeppelins. Only the field telephone by the chair was of a model impossible in 1917.

Jerome Jones laughed when he said that aloud. "Likely is the same folding chair; the forms for a new one won't have got to the proper office yet." He laughed again, this time mirthlessly. "Like the bloody Pixie Reports."

"I told you the flaw wasn't in the radar," Goldfarb said.

"That you did—and if you keep up with 'I told you so,' you'll make some nice girl very unhappy one day," Jones retorted. "Besides, don't you wish you'd been wrong?"

Having taken two solid hits in as many sentences, Goldfarb answered only with a grunt. His eyes traveled back to what had been the radar station that had superseded observers armed with nothing better than field glasses. Nothing there now but rubble and a faint stench, as of meat gone bad. The only reason Goldfarb could sit out here looking at those ruins was that he'd been off duty when the Lizard rockets struck home.

Up and down the English coast, the story was the same: wherever there'd been an active radar, a rocket came along and took it out. That meant only one thing: rockets able to home in on radar beams, even the new shortwave ones Jerry still hadn't figured out.

"Who'd have thought the Lizards could be so much smarter than the Germans?" Goldfarb said; no matter how much he loathed Hitler and the Nazis, he had a solid respect for the technical ability of the enemy across the Channel.

"Wireless says we knocked down a couple of their planes over London," Jones remarked hopefully.

"Good," Goldfarb said; any news of that sort was encouraging. "How many did we lose?"

"The commentator did not announce the full score of the match," Jones said. "Military security, don't you know?"

"Oh, indeed," Goldfarb said. "I wonder if their batsman made his century; no doubt it's a cricket score set against one footballers might make. God help us all."

"They've not tried a landing here," Jones said, still looking on the bright side.

"It's only a very small island." Goldfarb pictured a world globe in his mind, and realized all at once just how small England had to look from space.

"Not small enough to keep them from bombing us," Jones said bitterly. He and Goldfarb both shook their heads. They'd helped their country beat back the most savage air assault the world had ever known, then helped start paying the Germans back. Now they were under attack again. It hardly seemed fair.

"There's something!" Goldfarb exclaimed, pointing. He and Jones both swung their field glasses toward the moving specks in the sky. The specks—even through binoculars, they were little more than that—were southbound. "Ours, I think," Goldfarb said, "bound for the Lizards' lair in France."

"Lizards and Frogs." Jones laughed at his own wit, but quickly sobered. "I wonder how many of the poor brave buggers'll fly back north again after their run. Worse than the flak over Berlin, they say."

"I wonder if Jerry's hitting back at the Lizards, too." Something else occurred to Goldfarb. "If his planes and ours are both trying to hit them at the same time, do we shoot at each other, too?"

"I hope not," Jones exclaimed. "Wouldn't that be a balls-up?"

"It would indeed," Goldfarb said. "I hope not, too." He laughed, not altogether comfortably. "First time in donkey's years I've wished the Germans anything but a fast trip to the devil."

"The Germans, they're human beings. Stack 'em against things from Mars and I know where my choice lies," Jones said.

Goldfarb answered with a grunt. He was reluctant to concede anything to the Nazis; he agreed completely with Churchill's quip that, should Satan declare war on Hitler, he would at least give the Devil a favorable mention in the House of Commons. But quips came easy. Now the whole world faced devils it didn't know. Britain had allied with Red Russia when Germany invaded: Germany was worse. If the Lizards were worse than Germany, would alliances swing again?

He scowled. "I'm damned if I want to see us in bed with the Nazis." He wondered again at the fate of his cousins in Poland.

"Would you rather end up in bed with the Lizards?" Jones demanded. Before it could turn into an argument, he added, "Me, I'd rather end up in bed with the barmaid down at the White Horse Inn."

That sufficed to distract Goldfarb. "Which one?" he asked. "Daphne or Sylvia?"

"Daphne by choice. I'm rather keen on blondes, and she has more to hold on to." Jones's hands illustrated just which parts he had in mind. "But, of course, were Sylvia to smile at me in exactly the proper fashion— redheads are interesting because they're unusual, what?"

"They both fancy pilots," Goldfarb said morosely. Along with, no doubt, a great many other nonflying RAF men, he'd had his advances turned into retreats by both girls. For that matter, so had Jerome Jones.

The other radar man said, "Now there's something to say for the Lizards, at any rate." Goldfarb raised an interrogative eyebrow. Jones explained: "If they keep on as they've been doing, we'll soon have no pilots left."

"That's not funny," Goldfarb said. As if to contradict himself, he started laughing.

Then he choked on his laughter. Something screamed past overhead at just above treetop height. He grabbed for the field telephone, cranked as if his life depended on it while more Lizard planes streaked northwest above him. He shouted out his warning over the yowl of their engines.

"If it's London again, the bastards will be there in a minute," Jones yelled at the top of his lungs. He might as well have been whispering; Goldfarb had to read his lips.

Goldfarb did his best to sound hopeful: "Doesn't take long to scramble the Spitfire squadrons."

"Maybe not, but we can't catch their planes even if we do manage to get ours up."

"What's worked best is loitering alongside their return routes, then striking at them as they go past."

"Dogging and pouncing," Jones said, dropping his voice as the Lizard aircraft receded in the distance. Goldfarb raised that eyebrow again. His friend went on, "I did a bit of history at Cambridge along with the maths. The old Byzantines would let the Arabs into Asia Minor, you see, then wait at the passes for them to come out with their loot."

"Ah," Goldfarb said. "And did it work?"

"Sometimes. But even when it did, of course, Asia Minor took a bit of a hiding."

"Yes. Well, we've had hidings before. I hope we can ride out another one," Goldfarb said. "Not that we've much choice in the matter."

Neither of them said much after that. Goldfarb dug a finger into one ear, trying to make it stop ringing. He had little luck—the Lizards' engines were just too loud. He wondered if the RAF was having any luck, and wished he could be up in a Spitfire himself. His abilities didn't lie there, though. He consoled himself with the thought that he'd done what he could by spotting the flight of bombers.

He peered south, out over the English Channel. The springtime air— almost summer now, he reminded himself—was sweet and mild and clear. The French coast was a low, dark smear on the horizon. He raised the binoculars to his eyes. France leapt closer. Three years ago, that coast had been England's shield. Then, horribly, unexpectedly, the shield fell over, and it served as a base for a thrust at England's heart.

And now—what? Another thrust at England's heart, but one at Germany's as well. Goldfarb wished the Lizards would leave his country alone and go after the Nazis with everything they had. The wish changed the situation about as much as wishes commonly do.

He sighed. "It's a rum world, sure enough."

"Aye, it is." Jones looked at his watch. "Our reliefs should be here any minute now. When we're off, shall we head over to the White Horse? What they call best bitter's gone to the dogs since the war (gone through their kidneys, by the taste of it), but there's always Daphne to stare at, maybe even to chat up."

"Why not?" Goldfarb intended to try Sylvia again—his own taste ran to redheads. She wasn't a Jewish girl to bring home to his family (he'd thought a lot more about that since the war started), but he didn't aim to marry her—however attractive some of the concomitants of that relationship might be.

He laughed at himself. The next interest in him Sylvia showed would be her first. *Well,* he thought, *she can't very well show interest if I'm not there to be interesting.*

"Something else to thank the Lizards for," Jones said. "If they hadn't smashed up the radar set, we'd be spending all these idle hours fiddling with it instead of chasing skirt. Radar's all very well, but next to skirt—"

"Right," Goldfarb said. He pointed. "And here come Reg and Steven, so let's be off."

As Jones got up from his canvas chair, he asked, "Can you lend me ten bob?"

Goldfarb stared at him. He grinned back, cheekily confident. Goldfarb got out his wallet, passed over a note. "If you had the gall with Daphne that you do with me . . ."

"With ten bob in my pocket, maybe I will."

"Come on, then." There was a war on—there were, these last few crazed days, *two* wars on—but life went on, too. Goldfarb hurried through his report to the next watch crew, then hurried off with Jerome Jones toward the White Horse Inn.

I am flying toward my death. George Bagnall had had that thought every time the Lancaster made its ungainly leap off the tarmac for a run into Germany. Now, flying against the Lizards, it was much more tightly focused. Death lurked in the air over Germany, yes, but random death: a flak shell that happened to burst just where you were, or a night fighter coming close enough to spot your exhaust.

Going against the Lizards, death was not random. This was Bagnall's third sortie into France, and he had seen that for himself. If the Lizards chose your plane, you *would* go down. Their rockets came after you as if they knew your home address. You couldn't run; shooting at the missiles did no good to speak of; Bagnall wanted to hide.

He glanced over at Ken Embry. The pilot's face was set, the skin stretched tight across his cheekbones, his mouth nothing but a bloodless slash. They were coming in low tonight, too low to bother with oxygen, so Embry's whole face was visible. Going in high just made them better targets. The RAF had learned that lesson the hard way.

Bagnall sighed. "Pity we couldn't have come down with a case of magneto drop of some such, eh?"

"You're the engineer, Mr. Bagnall," Embry said. "Arranging a convenient mechanical failure should be your speciality."

"Pity I didn't think of it as we were running through the checklists,"

Bagnall murmured. Embry's answering grin stretched his mouth wider, but did nothing to banish the look of haunted determination from his features. Like Bagnall, he knew what the odds were. They'd been lucky twice—three times, if you counted the wild melee in the air over Cologne on what everyone was starting to call The Night the Martians Landed. But how long could luck hold?

Embry said, "Feels odd, flying out of formation."

"It did seem rather like lining up all the ducks to be knocked over one by one," Bagnall said. The first attack on the Lizards—in which, fortunately, his Lanc had not been involved—had been a failure horrific enough to make Bomber Command change tactics in a hurry, something the flight engineer hadn't previously imagined possible.

And attacking low and dispersed did work better than pouring in high and in formation, as if the Lizards were nothing but Germans to be overwhelmed by sheer numbers. Bagnall's bomber had made it back to England twice.

"Five miles to commencement of target area," the navigator announced over the intercom.

"Thank you, Alf," Ken Embry said. Ahead of them, streaks of fire began leaping up from the ground. Fully laden bombers exploded in midair, one after another, blazing through the night like great orange chrysanthemums of flame. They would have been even more beautiful had each one not meant the deaths of so many men.

Bagnall waited for one of those fiery streaks to burn straight for his Lanc. It hadn't happened yet, but—

Embry whooped, pounded his thigh with a fist. "Did you see that? Did you bloody *see* that? One of them missed. Somebody dodged it." Sure enough, one of the rockets kept flying up and up, then went off in a blast not much more impressive than a Guy Fawkes Day firework. Embry quickly sobered. "But there's so many that don't miss."

From his glassed-in window in the bottom front of the Lanc's nose, Douglas Bell said, "Coming up on something that looks like it belongs to the Lizards."

That was good enough for Embry. "Commencing bombing run under your direction, Bomb-Aimer."

"Very good," Bell said. "Steer slightly west, toward that—bloody hell, I don't know what it is, but it never came from Earth."

"Slightly west; straightening my course on the object ahead," the pilot acknowledged.

Peering ahead through the Perspex, Bagnall too saw against the horizon the great tower ahead. It looked more like a pregnant skyscraper than anything else he could think of, though even the Yankees' famous Empire State Building might have shrunk by comparison, for the tower was still miles ahead. It assuredly did not belong in the French countryside, a good long way south and east of Paris.

It was not the only tower—*spaceship*, Bagnall supposed the proper word was—in the neighborhood, either. The Lizards kept setting down more and more of them. And to attack the spaceships themselves was certain death. Nobody had succeeded in knocking one out; nobody had come back from trying, either.

The bomb-aimer, while as brave a man as could be hoped for—he was up here, after all, wasn't he? —was not actively trying to kill himself. He said, "Slightly more to the west, if you please, sir—three degrees or so. I think that's the tank park we were told of in the briefing, don't you?"

Embry and Bagnall both leaned forward to look now. Something big and orderly was going on down on the ground, that was certain. If it wasn't German, it had to belong to the Lizards. And if it was German, Bagnall thought, well, too bad for Jerry. His eyes flicked over to Embry's. The pilot nodded, said, "I think you're right, Bomb-Aimer. Carry on."

"Very good," Bell repeated. "Steady course, steady . . ." His voice rose to a shout. "Commence bombing!" The fuselage rattled and groaned as bombs rained down on the target. Bagnall took a moment to pity the poor French peasants below. They were, after all, his allies, now suffering under the double yoke of the Nazis and the Lizards, and some of them were only too likely to die in the bombardment that was at the moment the only hope of getting them free.

The Lanc staggered in the air. For a dreadful instant, Bagnall thought it was hit. But it was only plowing through the turbulence kicked up by exploding bombs—the plane was usually two or three miles higher above them when they went off.

"Let's get out of here." Embry heeled the bomber over and swung its nose toward England. "Give us a course for home, Mr. Whyte."

"Due north will do for now; I'll fine it up momentarily," the navigator said.

"Due north it is. I wonder how many will land with us," Embry said.

I wonder if we'll *be lucky enough to land,* Bagnall thought. He would not give the evil omen strength by speaking it aloud. Green-yellow tracers zipped past the windscreen, too close for comfort. Along with their rockets, the Lizards boasted formidable light flak. Embry threw the Lancaster into a series of evasive jinks and jerks that rattled everyone's teeth.

The rear gunner called, "We've a fighter to starboard, looking us over."

Whatever spit was left in Bagnall's mouth dried up as his eyes swung rightward. But the plane there, a deeper blackness against black night, was not a Lizard jet, only—only!—a Focke-Wulf 190. It waggled its wings at the Lanc and darted away at a speed the British bomber could not hope to match.

When he breathed again, Bagnall discovered he'd forgotten to for some time. Then another Lizard flak battery started up below. With a sound like a giant poking his fist through a tin roof, shells slammed into the Lancaster's left wing. Flames spurted from both engines there. To his subsequent amazement, the flight engineer performed exactly as he'd been trained. A glance at the gauges told him those Merlins would never fly again. He shut them down, shut down the fuel feed to them, feathered the props.

Embry flicked a toggle, made a face. "Flaps aren't responding on that side."

"No hydraulic pressure," Bagnall said after another check of his instruments. He watched the pilot fight the controls; already the Lanc was trying to swing in an anticlockwise circle. "Appears we have a bit of a problem."

"A bit, yes," Embry said, nodding. "Look for a field or a road. I'm going to try to set her down." Still sounding calm, he went on, "Sooner pick my time for it than have the aircraft choose for me, eh?"

"As you say," Bagnall agreed. The pilot's couple of sentences told the same story as his own bank of instruments: the aircraft would not make it back to England. He pointed. "There's as likely a stretch of highway as we're apt to find. One thing for the war—we're not likely to run over Uncle Pierre's Citroën."

"Right." Embry raised his voice. "Crew prepare for crash landing. Mr. Bagnall, lower the landing gear, if you please."

The right wheel descended smoothly; without hydraulics, the left refused to budge. Bagnall worked the hand crank. From the belly turret, a gunner said, "It's down. I can see it."

"One thing fewer to worry about," Embry remarked, with what seemed to Bagnall to be quite excessive good cheer. Then the pilot added, "That leaves only two or three hundred thousand, unless I miss my count."

"We could be trying this up in Normandy, where the hedgerows grow right alongside the roadbed," Bagnall said helpfully.

Embry corrected himself: "Two things fewer. You do so relieve my mind, George."

"Happy to be of service," Bagnall answered. Joking about what was going to happen was easier than just sitting back and watching it. A forced landing in a damaged aircraft on a French road in the middle of the night without lights was not easy to contemplate in cold blood.

As if to underscore that, Embry said, "Aircrew may bail out if they find that preferable to attempting a landing. I shall endeavor to remain airborne an extra minute or two to allow them to avail themselves of the opportunity. Had we suffered this misfortune a month ago, I would bail out myself and permit the aircraft to crash, thus denying it to the Germans. As you have seen this evening, however, that situation has for the moment changed. If you do intend to parachute, please so inform me at this time."

The intercom stayed silent until someone in the back of the plane said, "You'll get us down all right, sir."

"Let us hope such touching confidence is not misplaced," Embry said. "Thank you, gentlemen, one and all, and good luck to you." He brought the stick forward, reduced power to the two surviving Merlins.

"To us," Bagnall amended. The road, a dark gray line arrowing through black fields, was almost close enough to reach out and touch. Embry brought the Lanc's nose up a little, cut power still more. The bomber met the road with a bump, but Bagnall had been through worse landings at Swinderby. Cheers erupted in the intercom.

Then, just as the Lancaster slowed toward a stop, its right wing clipped a telegraph pole. It spun clockwise. The left landing gear went off the asphalt and into soft dirt. It buckled. The wing snapped off where the shells had chewed it. The stump dug into the ground. The aircraft's spars groaned like a man on the rack. Bagnall wondered if it would flip over. It didn't. Even as it was spinning, Embry had shut off the engines altogether.

Into sudden silence, a second round of cheers rang out. "Thank you, friends," Embry said. Now at last, when it no longer mattered, he let himself sound wrung out. He turned to Bagnall with a tired grin. "*Est-ce que vous parlez français, monsieur!*"

"Hell, no," Bagnall answered. They both laughed like schoolboys.

A metallic rumble echoed through *127th Emperor Hetto* as the transfer craft's airlock engaged with one of the bannership's docking collars. A speaker chimed softly in Fleetlord Atvar's office. "The Tosevite is here, Exalted Fleetlord," a junior officer announced.

"Fetch him hither," Atvar said.

"It shall be done."

Atvar hung in midair as he awaited the arrival of the Tosevite official. He'd ordered the spin taken off the bannership when he began receiving natives. He was used to free-fall; while he did not particularly enjoy it, he endured it without trouble, as did his crew. The Tosevites, however, were without space travel. Finding themselves weightless might fluster them and put them at a disadvantage. Atvar hoped so, at any rate.

He let his jaws fall open in amusement as he remembered the unfortunate native from the empire called Deutschland who had lost all his stomach contents, luckily while still in the transfer craft. That poor befuddled Ribbensomething had been in no state even to try to negotiate his empire's submission to *the* Empire.

The door to the office opened. An officer charged with learning the appropriate Tosevite dialect floated outside along with the native for whom he would interpret. The officer said, "Exalted Fleetlord, I present to you the emissary of the empire called the *Soyuz Sovietskikh Sotzialesticheskikh Respublik*—SSSR for short. His name is Vyacheslav Mikhailovich Molotov."

"Give him my polite greetings," Atvar answered, thinking the Tosevite empire was too small to deserve such a big name. Like most Tosevites, though, the emissary himself was substantially larger than the fleetlord.

The interpreter talked haltingly in Molotov's speech. Part of the problem was that Tosevite languages did not fit well in the mouths of the Race: to Atvar, all Tosevites sounded as if they had their mouths full of pap. Tosevite languages were also hard for the Race because they were so maddeningly irregular; they had not spent long millennia being smoothed into efficient rationality. And, even without those difficulties, the languages remained incompletely familiar to the officers assigned to learn them. Up until the actual landings on Tosev 3, they'd had only radio transmissions from which to work (the first convenient thing Atvar could see about the Tosevites' possessing radio), and comprehension had emerged slowly out of those, even with the help of computers programmed to deduce probable word meanings by statistics.

Molotov listened to the fleetlord's greeting, gave back one of his own. Unlike the Tosevite from Deutschland, he had sense enough to speak slowly so as not to overwhelm the interpreter. Also unlike that Tosevite, he gave no sign of discomfiture at being off his home planet and in free-fall for the first time in his life.

A viewscreen showed a hologram of Tosev 3 as it appeared from the *127th Emperor Hetto*, but Molotov did not even deign to glance at it. Through the corrective lenses hooked in front of his flat, immobile eyes, he stared straight toward Atvar. The fleetlord approved. He had not thought to find such singleness of purpose among these big barbarians.

Molotov spoke again, still slowly and without raising his voice. The interpreter turned both eye turrets toward Atvar in embarrassment; the fleetlord should have enjoyed the privilege of first address. But what could a Big Ugly know of proper protocol? Atvar said, "Never mind his manners. Just tell me what he says."

"It shall be done, Exalted Fleetlord. Vyacheslav Mikhailovich—this is the polite way to address the Tosevites who speak Ruskii: by their own name and that of their father—well, never mind that; the Tosevite demands the immediate unconditional withdrawal of all our forces from the land and air belonging to the empire of the SSSR."

"Oh, he does, does he?" The fleetlord let his jaws gape in a guffaw. "Remind him he is in no position to make demands. If he occupied Home, he might have the right to bend us to his will. But it is the surrender of the SSSR that is under discussion, not ours."

Molotov listened to the interpreter's translation without changing expression. To Atvar, the Tosevites he'd seen and met owned extraordinarily mobile features; his own facial hide and musculature were far less flexible. But this native might have been carved from stone. Still stubbornly ignoring his surroundings, he paused to think, then replied:

"We shall not yield. We have fought the Gitlerites ["By which he means the Deutsch Tosevites, exalted fleetlord," the interpreter explained] to a standstill when they expected us to collapse. Our land is vast, our resources widespread. We are not to be easily overcome."

"Tell him that his *vast* empire"—Atvar loaded the word with scorn—"would vanish almost without trace on any of the three worlds of *the* Empire."

Molotov again listened, thought, answered: "All three of your worlds are not here with you, and you seek to conquer not just the SSSR but the whole of this world. Consider if you have not overextended yourselves."

Atvar glared at the impassive Tosevite. The native might be barbarous, but he was no fool. A whole world—even a world with too much water like Tosev 3—was a big place, bigger than the fleetlord had truly understood until he began this campaign. He hadn't expected to face industrialized opposition, either.

Nevertheless, he and the Race had advantages, too. He bludgeoned Molotov with them: "We strike you as we please, but you come to grief whenever you try to hit us back. Once all your factories are in ruins, how do you propose to hit back at all? Yield now, and you will still have something left for your own people."

Molotov wore the same sort of bulky garments most Tosevites preferred. His face was damp and shiny with water exuded as a metabolic coolant; the *127th Emperor Hetto* was at a temperature comfortable to the Race, not for natives. But he still answered back boldly enough: "We have many factories. We have many men. You have won battles against us, but you are far from winning your war. We will fight on. Even the Gitlerites have more sense than to yield to you."

"As a matter of fact, I recently spoke with the foreign minister of Deutschland," Atvar said. That Tosevite had also been too stubborn to yield until his empire was pounded flat, but Molotov did not have to know it.

The native looked intently at the fleetlord. "And what had he to say?" Since the SSSR and Deutschland were at war before the Race reached Tosev 3, it stood to reason that they had little reason to trust each other.

"We discussed the feasibility of Deutschland's acknowledging the authority of the Emperor," Atvar answered. On speaking of his sovereign, he cast down his eyes for a moment. So did the interpreter.

"Emperor, you say? I want to be sure I understand you correctly," Molotov said. "Your—nation—is headed by a person who rules because he is a member of a family that has ruled for many years before him? Is that what you tell me?"

"Yes, that is correct," Atvar said, puzzled by the Tosevite's puzzlement. "Who else would rule an empire—*the* Empire—but the Emperor? The Tosevite named Stalin, I gather, is the emperor of your SSSR."

So far as the fleetlord could see, Molotov still did not change expression. Nor was his voice anything but its usual mushy monotone. But what he said made the interpreter hiss in rage and astonishment, and even lash his tail stump back and forth as if in mortal combat. The officer mastered himself, spoke in Molotov's language. Molotov answered. The interpreter trembled. Slowly, he mastered himself. Even more slowly, he turned to Atvar.

He still hesitated to speak. "What does the Big Ugly say?" Atvar demanded.

"Exalted Fleetlord," the interpreter stammered, "this—this thing of a Tosevite tells me to tell you that the people—the people of his SSSR—that they, they executed—murdered—their emperor and all his family twenty-five years ago. That would be about fifty of our years," he added, remembering his function as translator. "They murdered their emperor, and this Stalin, this leader of theirs, is no emperor at all, but the chief of the group of bandits that killed him."

Atvar was a mature, disciplined male, so he did not show his feelings with a hiss as the interpreter had. But he was shocked to the very core of his being. Imagining a government without an emperor at its head was almost beyond him. Home had been unified for scores of millennia, and even in the distant days before unity had seen only the struggle between one empire and another. Halless 1 was a single empire when the Race conquered it; Rabotev 2 had been divided, but also among competing empires. What other way was there to organize intelligent beings? The fleetlord could conceive of none.

Molotov said, "You should know, invader from another world, that Deutschland has no emperor either, nor does the United—" The interpreter went back and forth with him for a little while, then explained, "He means the empire—or not-empire, I should say in the northern part of the small landmass."

"These Tosevites are utterly mad," Atvar burst out. He added, "You need not translate that. But they are. By the Emperor"—just saying the name was a comfort—"it must have to do with the world's beastly climate and excess water."

"Yes, Exalted Fleetlord," the interpreter said. "It may be so. But what shall I tell the creature here?"

"I don't know." Atvar felt befouled at even contemplating speech with anyone, no matter how alien, who was involved in impericide—a crime whose existence he had not thought of until this moment. All at once, cratering the whole world of Tosev 3 with nuclear weapons looked much more attractive than it had. But the fleet had only a limited number of them—against the sort of fight the Tosevites were expected to put up, even a few would have been more than necessary. And with Tosev 3's land surface so limited, ruining any of it went against his grain.

He gathered himself. "Tell this Molotov that what he and his bandits did before the Race arrived will not concern us unless they refuse to yield and thereby force us to take notice of it. But if need be, we will avenge their murdered emperor." Thinking of a murdered emperor, the fleetlord knew the first pity he'd felt for any Tosevite.

If his threat frightened Molotov, the Big Ugly gave no sign of it; the native truly was as frozen of countenance as anyone of the Race. He said,

"It is true, then, that when you speak of an empire, you mean it in the exact and literal sense of the word, with an emperor and a court and all the trappings of the outworn past?"

"Of course that is true," Atvar answered. "How else would we mean it?"

"The enlightened people of the SSSR have cast the rule of despots onto the ash-heap of history," Molotov said.

Atvar laughed in his flat face. "The Race has flourished under its Emperors for a hundred thousand years. What do you know of history, when you were savages the last time we looked over your miserable pest-hole of a planet?" The fleetlord heartily wished the Tosevites had stayed savages, too.

"History may be slow, but it is certain," Molotov said stubbornly. "One day the inevitable revolution will come to your people, too, when their economic conditions dictate its necessity. I think that day will be soon. You are imperialists, and imperialism is the last phase of capitalism, as Marx and Lenin have shown."

The interpreter stumbled through the translation of that last sentence, and added, "I have trouble rendering the natives' religious terms into our language, Exalted Fleetlord. Marx and Lenin are gods or prophets in the SSSR." He spoke briefly with Molotov, then said, "Prophets. Vyacheslav Mikhailovich knew this Lenin himself."

Molotov said, "Lenin led the revolution which overthrew our emperor and established the rule of the people and workers of the SSSR. I am proud to say I assisted in this worthy task."

Atvar stared at the Tosevite in disgust. He spoke to the interpreter: "Tell the bandit I have nothing further to say to him. If he and his murderers will not yield themselves to us, their punishment shall only be the harsher."

The interpreter slowly, haltingly, turned the crisp words into the mushy native language. Molotov answered with one word. *"Nyet."* The fleetlord glanced with one quick flick of an eye at the interpreter to see if that meant what he thought. It did.

"Get him off this ship," Atvar snapped. "I am sorry he comes here under truce, or I would treat him as he deserves." The idea of wantonly slaughtering an emperor—even a Tosevite emperor—gave him an atavistic urge to bite something: Molotov by choice, though the Big Ugly looked anything but appetizing.

The doorway out of Atvar's office hissed open. The interpreter pushed off from the chair whose back he'd been holding and shot through it. Molotov followed more awkwardly, the graceless garments he wore flapping about him. As soon as he was gone, Atvar shut the door behind him. The rather sharp smell of his body remained, like a bad memory. The fleetlord turned up the air scrubbers to make it go away.

While it still lingered, he phoned Kirel. When the shiplord's face appeared in his screen, he said, "You will come to my quarters immediately."

"It shall be done, Exalted Fleetlord." Kirel blanked the screen. He was as good as his word. When he chimed for admittance, Atvar let him in, then closed the door again. Kirel asked, "How fare the talks with the Tosevites, Exalted Fleetlord?"

"Less well than I had hoped." Atvar let his breath hiss out in a long, frustrated sigh. "All their greatest empires still refuse to acknowledge the glory of the Emperor." He cast his eyes down in the ritual gesture. He would not tell Kirel what he'd learned from Molotov, not yet; his own pain remained too raw to permit it.

"This is altogether a more difficult task than we looked for when we set out from Home," Kirel said. The shiplord had tact. He forbore to remind Atvar that he had urged a surrender demand before actual ground combat got under way. After a moment, he went on, "It has been too many generations since the Race fought a real war."

"What do you mean?" Atvar tried to hold sudden suspicion from his voice. Tactful or not, Kirel coveted the ornate body paint the fleetlord wore. Atvar continued, "We are trained for this mission as well as we could possibly be."

"Indeed we are," Kirel agreed gravely, which only made Atvar more suspicious. "But the Tosevites are not merely trained; they are experienced. Weapon for weapon, we far surpass them. In craft on the battlefield, though, they exceed us. That has hurt us, again and again."

"I know. They are worse foes than I expected them to be even after we learned of their abnormal technological growth. Not only are they wily, as you say, they are stubborn. I was confident they would break when they realized the advantages we enjoyed over them. But they keep fighting, as best they can."

"It is so," Kirel said. "Perhaps already being locked in combat among themselves has given them the discipline they need to carry on against us. Along with being stubborn, they are well-trained and skilled. We can continue to smash them for a long time yet; one of our landcruisers, one of our aircraft, is worth anywhere from ten to twenty-five of theirs. But we have only so many munitions. If we cannot overawe them, we may face difficulties. In my coldest dreams, I see our last missile wrecking a clumsy Tosevite landcruiser—while another such landcruiser rolls out of a factory and toward us."

Of themselves, Atvar's clawed hands twitched as if to tear a foe in front of him. "That *is* a cold dream. You should have left it in your coffin when you awoke. We have set down our factory ships here and there, you know. As we gain raw materials, we shall be able to increase our stocks."

"As you say, Exalted Fleetlord," Kirel answered. He did not say—

presumably because he knew Atvar knew it as well as himself—that the factories, even at top output, could not produce in a day more than a small part of the supplies the Race's armed forces used during that day. Back on Home, no one had reckoned that the armada would use as much as it had.

As if to turn away from that unpleasant reflection, Atvar said, "For all the bluster the Big Ugly envoys show, they may yet prove tractable. The male from the empire called Deutschland, despite his sickness, showed some comprehension of our might." All at once, he remembered that Molotov had said Deutschland was a not-empire. He wondered queasily if its emperor had been murdered, too.

Shiplord Kirel said, "Deutschland? Interesting. May I use your screen to show you an image a reconnaissance satellite caught for us yesterday?" Atvar opened his hands wide to show assent. Kirel punched commands in the *127th Emperor Hetto*'s data storage system.

The screen lit to show green land and grayish sea. A spot of fire appeared in one corner of the land, not far from a clump of big wood buildings. The fire suddenly spread and got brighter, then went out more slowly. "One of our bombing runs?" Atvar asked.

"No. Let me show it to you again, this time in slow motion with maximum magnification and image processing."

The amplified image came up on the screen. Atvar stared at it, then at Kirel. "That is a missile," he said accusingly, as if it were the shiplord's fault. He did not want to believe what he had just seen.

But Kirel said, "Yes, Exalted Fleetlord, this is a missile, or at least was intended to be one. Since it exploded on its launching pad, we are unable to gain estimates of its range or guidance system, if any, but to judge from its size, it appears more likely to be strategic than tactical."

"I presume we have eradicated this site," Atvar said.

"It was done, Exalted Fleetlord," Kirel agreed.

The shiplord's doleful voice told Atvar what he already knew: even though this site was gone, the Race had no sure way of telling how many others the Deutsche possessed—until a missile roared toward them. And swatting missiles out of the sky was an order of magnitude harder than dealing with these slow, clumsy Tosevite airplanes. Even the airplanes were hurting his forces now and again, because the Big Uglies kept sending them out no matter how many got knocked down. As Kirel had said, their courage and skill went some of the way toward making up for their poor technology.

"We have to destroy the factories in which these weapons are produced," Atvar said.

"Yes, Exalted Fleetlord," Kirel answered.

Not, Atvar noted, *"It shall be done."* From the air, one factory looked like another. Destroying *all* the factories in Deutschland was a tall order. Compared to the size of the planet, Deutschland was a small empire, but even small empires, Atvar was learning, covered a lot of ground. The other Tosevite empires had factories, too. How close were they to making missiles?

The fleetlord did his best to look on the bright side. "Their failure gives us the warning we need. We shall not be taken unawares even if they succeed in launching missiles at us." *We had better not be,* his tone said.

"Our preparations are adequate," Kirel said. He did his best to keep on sounding businesslike and military, but his voice had an edge to it that Atvar understood perfectly well: if that was the bright side, it was hardly worth looking for.

The train chuffed to a halt somewhere on the south Russian steppe; men in field gray sprang down and went efficiently to work. They would have been more efficient still, Karl Becker thought, if they'd been allowed to proceed in their usual methodical fashion rather than at a dead run. But an order from the *Führer* was an order from the *Führer*. At the dead run they went.

"The ground will not be adequately prepared, Karl," Michael Arenswald said sadly. Both men were part of the engineering detachment of Heavy Artillery Battalion Dora.

"This is true, of course," Becker said with a fatalistic nod, "but how many shots are we likely to be able to fire before the Lizards descend on us?" They were sixty kilometers from the Lizard base. With aircraft, though, especially the ones the Lizards flew, sixty kilometers passed in the blink of an eye. Karl Becker was a long way from stupid; he recognized a suicide mission when he heard one.

If Arenswald did, too, he kept it to himself. "We might even get off half a dozen before they figure out what's happening to them."

"Oh, *quatsch!*" said Becker, a Berliner. He jabbed an index finger out at his friend. "You are a dead man, I am a dead man, we are all dead men, the whole battalion of us. The only question left unanswered is whether we can take enough Lizards with us to make our deaths worth something."

"Sooner or later, we are all dead men." Arenswald laughed. "We'll give them a surprise before we go, at any rate."

"With luck, we may manage that," Becker admitted. "We—" He broke off and started coughing. The battalion had a chemical unit attached to it, to send up smoke and hide it from view from the air while it was setting up for action. Some of the smoke came from nothing more sophisticated than flaming buckets of motor oil. Breathing it was probably doing Becker's lungs no good, but odds were it wouldn't kill him before he died of other causes. He coughed again, then ignored it.

Men swarmed over the train like ants. Special tracks had been laid for the heavy artillery battalion, four gently curved arcs, each always a constant distance from its neighbors. The inner two sets of rails were exactly twenty feet apart. Crews began moving specially built diesel construction cranes to the outer pair of tracks, for aid in the upcoming assembly process.

Looking at all the purposeful activity, Arenswald laughed again. "Not bad, considering how understrength we are." The smoke was already turning his face sooty.

"A lot of people we don't need, considering we won't be here long." When Heavy Artillery Battalion Dora came into Russia, it was accompanied by a security unit that included three hundred infantry and secret police with dogs, and by a four-hundred-man reinforced flak battalion. Neither the one nor the other mattered now. If the Lizards chose to come this way, German infantry could not hold them off, and the flak battalion could not keep their planes away. Dora's only hope of accomplishing anything was going into action before the enemy noticed it was there. And considering what Dora was . . .

Becker laughed, too. Arenswald gave him a curious look. He explained: "Keeping Dora a secret is like taking an elephant out of its enclosure at the Berlin *Tiergarten* and walking it out of the zoo without the keepers' paying you any mind."

"Something to that." Arenswald waved at the ever-denser smoke all around. "But you see, Karl, we have a very large pocket here."

"We have a very large elephant, too." Becker hopped down from the train and walked between the two center tracks, the ones that would have to bear Dora's weight. The tracks were laid with closely spaced cross ties to help strengthen the roadbed, but the ground was not nearly so stony as it should have been. That would matter a great deal if Dora stayed here a long while. For the few shots it was likely to get off, the ground was less important.

The next few days passed in a berserk blaze of work, with sleep snatched in odd moments, often under the train to give some protection in case Lizard aircraft did come by. The manuals said assembling Dora needed a week. Driven by the lash of fear for the fatherland, the heavy artillery battalion did it in four and a half days.

The two pieces of the bottom half of the gun carriage went onto the two central tracks and were aligned with each other. They rested on twenty rail trucks, again to distribute Dora's mass as widely as possible. Becker was part of the crew that hydraulically leveled the lower mount.

The diesel cranes lifted crossbeams onto the lower mount, then placed the two-piece upper mount where it belonged. The top of the carriage held Dora's loading assembly and the trunnion supports. It was joined to the lower mount by dozens of heavy bolts. Becker went down one side of the carriage and Arenswald down the other, checking that every one was in place.

They met at the rear, grinned, exchanged drawings, then went *up* the carriage to check each other's sides. Everything had to work once the shooting started; things would go wrong soon enough after that.

Assembly went faster once the carriage was together. The trunnions, the gun cradle, the breech, and the barrel sections all were raised to their proper positions. When Dora was at last complete, Becker admired the monster gun through blowing smoke. Carriage and all, the 80-centimeter cannon was fifty meters long and eleven meters tall; its barrel alone was thirty meters long. Somewhere far above the smoke, Becker heard a Lizard plane whine past. His shoulders slumped; his hands made futile fists. "No, God," he said, almost as a threat, "not now, not when we were so close."

Michael Arenswald clapped him on the shoulder. "They've flown over us before, Karl. It will be all right; you'll see."

No bombs fell on them; no guided rockets exploded by the gun carriage. A crane lifted from a freight car a seven-tonne shell, slowly swung the great projectile, more than five meters long and almost a meter thick, onto the loading assembly. It didn't look like an artillery shell, not to Becker. It looked like something more primeval, as if *Tyrannosaurus rex* had been reincarnated as artillery.

The breech received the shell, was closed with a clang that sounded like a factory noise. The whole battalion cheered as the gun barrel slowly rose, its tip no doubt projecting out of the smoke screen now. Laughing, Arenswald said, "It reminds me of the world's biggest prick getting hard."

"That's one hell of a hard-on, all right," Becker said.

The barrel reached an angle of almost forty-five degrees, stopped. Along with everyone else around, Becker turned away from it, covered his ears, opened his mouth.

The blast was like nothing he'd ever imagined. It sucked all the air out of his lungs, shook him like a terrier shaking a rat. Stunned, he staggered, stumbled, sat down hard on the ground. His head roared. He wondered if he would ever hear anything through that oceanic clamor again. But he could still see. Sprawled in the dirt beside him, Michael Arenswald gave a big thumbs-up.

A radar technician on the grounded transport ship *67th Emperor Sohrheb* stared at the screen in front of him, hissed in dismay. Automatic alarms began to yammer even before Breltan shrieked, "Missile incoming!" A warning had come down that the Big Uglies were playing with missiles, but he'd never expected to encounter one of their toys so soon. He raised both eye turrets to the ceiling in bemusement. The Big Uglies just weren't *like* the Race. They were always in a hurry.

Their missile was in a hurry, too, chewing away the distance to the grounded ships. Breltan's jaws opened again, this time in amusement. So the Tosevites had discovered missiles, had they? Well and good, but they hadn't yet discovered missiles too could be killed.

No sooner had that thought crossed his mind than the radars showed missiles leaping up to smash the intruder. Breltan laughed again, said, "You'll have to do better than that, Big Uglies."

A missile, as a rule, is a flimsy thing, no stronger than it has to be—any excess weight degrades performance. If another missile—or even a fragment hurled from an exploding warhead—hits it, odds are it will be wrecked.

The shell from Dora, however, had to be armored to withstand the monstrous force that had sent it on its way. A missile exploded a couple of meters from it. The fragments bounced off its brass sides. Another missile struck it a glancing blow before exploding and spun away, ruined.

The shell, undisturbed, flew on.

Breltan watched the radar screen in disbelief mixed with equal measures of horror and fascination. "It can't do that," he said. But it could—the Tosevite missile shrugged off everything the Race threw at it and kept coming. Coming right at Breltan.

"Emperor save me," he whimpered, and dove under his seat in the approved position for protection against attack from the air.

The shell landed about ten meters in front of the *67th Emperor Sohrheb.* Just under a tonne of its mass was high explosives. The rest, in a time measured in microseconds, turned to knife-edged, red-hot fragments of every shape and size.

Like all starships of the invasion fleet, the *67th Emperor Sohrheb* drew its primary power from an atomic pile. But, like most of the ships that landed on Tosev 3, it used a fair part of the energy from that pile to electrolyze water into oxygen and the hydrogen that fueled the Race's air and ground vehicles.

When it blew, it blew sky-high. No one ever found a trace of Breltan—or his seat.

The fireball was big enough to be visible across sixty kilometers. When it lit up the northern horizon, the men of Heavy Artillery Battalion Dora screamed with delight, loud enough for Karl Becker to hear them even with his abused ears. "Hit! Hit! Hit!" he shouted, and danced in a clumsy circle with Michael Arenswald.

"Now *that's* what I call an orgasm," Arenswald yelled.

The brigadier commanding the heavy artillery battalion climbed up onto the immense gun carriage, megaphone in hand. "Back to it!" he bawled to his capering crew. "We want to hit them again before they hit us."

Nothing could have been better calculated to send the battalion back to work at full speed. Unlike a tank gun, Dora could not traverse. A locomotive attached to the front end of the carriage moved forward a few meters, pulling nearly 1,500 tonnes of cannon and mounting along the curved track into its preplanned next firing position.

Even as the flagman brought the engine to a halt right at the mark painted on the track, Becker was dashing forward to make sure the gun carriage had remained level after the stress of the round and the move. The bubbles in the spirit levels at all four corners of the carriage hadn't stirred a millimeter. He waved up to the reloading gang. "All good here!"

The long barrel lifted a degree or two. A crane was already lifting the expended shell casing out of the breech. "Clear below!" the crane operator shouted. Men scattered. The casing thudded to the ground beside the gun carriage. That wasn't the way the manuals said to get rid of such casings, but it was the fastest way. The crane swung to pick up a new shell.

Karl Becker kept an eye on his watch. Twenty-nine minutes after Dora spoke for the first time, the great gun spoke again.

Krefak felt the heat from the burning *67th Emperor Sohrheb*, though his missile battery was posted a good ways away from the luckless starship. He was heartily glad of that; the blast when the ship went up had taken out several units closer to it.

Krefak also felt the heat from his own commander, who'd waxed eloquent over his failure to shoot down the Big Uglies' missile. He'd done everything right; he knew he had. The battery had intercepted the Tosevite projectile at least twice. Tapes from the radars proved it. But how was he supposed to say so, with only smoking rubble left where a proud starship had stood mere heartbeats before?

One of the males at a radar screen let out a frightened hiss. "The eggless creatures launched another one!" he exclaimed.

Krefak gaped in shocked surprise. Once was catastrophe enough, but twice— He couldn't imagine twice. He didn't *want* to imagine twice. His voice rose to a most-unofficerlike screech: "Shoot it down!"

Roars from the launchers showed him that the computers hadn't waited for his orders. He ran to the screen, watched the missiles fly. As they had before, they went straight to the mark, exploded . . . and were gone. So far as the Tosevite missile was concerned, they might as well never have been fired. It proceeded inexorably on its ordained course.

Below the radar screen that marked its track through the air was another that evaluated the ground target at which it was aimed. "No," he said softly. "By the Emperors, launch more missiles!"

"The battery has expended all the ones we had on launchers, superior

sir," the male answered helplessly. "More are coming." Then he too took
a look at where the Tosevite missile was heading. "Not the *56th Emperor
Jossano*." His eye turrets quivered with fright as he stared at Krefak.

"Yes, with most of our nuclear weapons on board. To treachery with
colonizing this stinking planet; we should have sterilized it to be rid of the
Tosevites once and for all. We—" His voice was lost in the roar of the exploding missile, and in the much, much bigger roar that subsumed it.

The *56th Emperor Jossano* went up in the same sort of blast as had
taken the *67th Emperor Sohrheb*. The fission and fusion weapons were
stored in the very heart of the ship, in a strongly armored chamber. It did
not save them. As the *56th Emperor Jossano* blew to pieces and burned,
the explosives that triggered the rapid joining of precisely machined
chunks of plutonium began going off, as if they were rounds of ammunition in a flaming tank.

The bombs themselves did not go off; the triggering charges did not ig-
nite in the precise order or at the precise rate that required. But the casings
were wrecked, the chunks of plutonium warped out of shape and broken
and, indeed, scattered over a goodly part of the Tosevite landscape as explosion after explosion wracked the *56th Emperor Jossano*.

They were very likely the most valuable pieces of metal on the face of
the Earth, or would have been had any human being known they were
there or what to do with them. No human being did, not then.

More screams of glee rose from Dora's firing crew. They did not waste
motion dancing at the sight of this new flame on the distant horizon, but
immediately set to work reloading the 80-centimeter cannon.

Michael Arenswald bellowed in Becker's ear. "Six! Didn't I tell you
we'd get off six?"

"We've been lucky twice," Becker said. "That's more than I expected
right there. Maybe we'll go again—third time's the charm, they say."

For an instant too long, he thought the scream in the sky was part of
the way his head rang after the second detonation of the monster gun. The
locomotive had just finished hauling Dora to its next marked firing position. Becker started over to the gun carriage to see if had stayed level yet
again.

The first bomb blast, a few meters behind him, hurled him facefirst
into that great mountain of metal. He felt things break—his nose, a cheek-
bone, several ribs, a hip. He opened his mouth to scream. Another bomb
went off, this one even closer.

Jens Larssen's apartment lay a few blocks west of the Union Stockyards. The neighborhood wasn't much, but he'd still been surprised at how
cheap he got the place. The incessant Chicago wind came from the west

that day. A couple of days later, it started blowing off Lake Michigan, and he understood. But it was too late by then—he'd already signed the lease.

The wind blew off the lake the day his wife, Barbara, got into town, too. He still remembered the way her eyes got wide. She put the smell into one raised eyebrow and four words: "Essence of terrified cow."

The wind was blowing off the lake tonight, but Larssen hardly noticed the rich manure stink. He could smell his own fear, and Barbara's. Lizard planes were over Chicago again. He'd listened to Edward R. Murrow on crackling shortwave from England, listened to that deep, raspy voice and its trademark opening: "This is London." Such was Murrow's magic that he'd imagined he understood what being a Londoner in the Blitz was like. Now he knew better.

More planes screeched past; more bombs fell, some, by the way the windows rattled, quite close by. He clung to Barbara, and she to him, under the kitchen table. Chicago had no shelters. "Hitting the stockyards again," she said into his ear.

He nodded. "Anything with rails." The Lizards were inhumanly methodical about pasting transportation hubs, and Chicago was nothing else but. It was also close to the landing zone they'd carved out for themselves in downstate Illinois, Missouri, and Kentucky. Thanks to both those things, the town was taking a heavy pounding.

Only a couple of candles lit the one-bedroom apartment. Their light did not get past the blankets tacked up to serve as blackout curtains. The blankets would not have contained electric lights, but the power had been off more often than it was on the past few days. It made Larssen glad for once that he had only an old-fashioned icebox, not a fancy electric refrigerator. As long as the ice man kept coming around—as long as the ice man still had ice—his food would stay fresh.

Antiaircraft guns, pitifully few and pitifully ineffective, added their barks to the cacophony. Shrapnel pattered down on rooftops like hot metal hail. Air-raid sirens wailed, lost souls in the night.

After a while, Larssen noticed he heard no more Lizard planes, though the rest of the fireworks display continued as gunners blazed away at their imaginations. "I think it's over," he said.

"This time," Barbara answered. He felt her tremble in his arms; for that matter, he felt pretty shaky himself. One by one, sirens fell silent. His wife went on, "I don't know how much more of this I can handle." Like a tight-stretched wire, her voice vibrated with hidden stress.

"The English stuck it out," he said, remembering Murrow again.

"God knows how," she said. "I don't." She squeezed him even tighter than she had when the bombs were falling.

Being a thoroughly rational young man, he opened his mouth to explain to her how bad a beating London had taken, and for how long, and how the Lizards seemed, for the moment anyhow, to be much more selective than the Nazis about hitting civilian targets. But however thoroughly rational he was, the springy firmness of her body locked against his reminded him that he was young. Instead of explaining, he kissed her.

Her mouth came open against his; she moaned a little, deep in her throat, whether from fear or desire or both commingled he never knew. She pressed the warm palm of her hand against his hair. He rolled on top of her, careful even then not to knock his head on the underside of the table. When at last their kiss broke, he whispered, "Shall we go in the bedroom?"

"No," she said, startling him. Then she giggled. "Let's do it right here, on the floor. It'll remind me of those times in the backseat of your old Chevy."

"All right," he said, by then too eager to care much where. He shifted his weight. "Raise up, just a little." When she moved, he undid the buttons on the back of her blouse and unhooked her bra with one hand. He hadn't tried that since they were married, but the ease with which he accomplished it said his hand remembered the backseat of the old Chevy, too.

He tossed the cotton blouse and bra aside. Presently, he said, "Lift up again." He slowly slid her panties down her legs. Instead of pulling off her skirt, he hiked it up. That made her laugh again. She kissed him, long and slow. His hands wandered where they would.

So did hers, unbuckling his belt, opening his trouser button, and, with several delicious pauses, lowering his zipper. He yanked down his pants and jockey shorts, just far enough. They were both laughing by then. Laughing still, he plunged into her, leaving behind for a little while the terror outside the blacked-out apartment.

"I should have taken off my shirt," he said when they were through. "Now it's all sweaty."

"It? What about me?" Barbara brought both hands up to his chest, made as if to push him vertically away from her. He raised up on his elbows and knees—and this time did catch the back of his head on the bottom of the kitchen table, hard enough to see stars. He swore, first in English, then in the fragments of Norwegian he'd picked up from his grandfather.

Barbara, whose maiden name was Baker and who had a couple of several-times-great-grandfathers who'd fought in the Revolution, always thought that was the funniest thing in the world. "You're in no position to laugh now, wench," he said, and tickled her conveniently bare ribs. The linoleum made moist squelching noises under her backside as she tried to wriggle away. That set him laughing, too. He grabbed her. They might have begun again, but the telephone chose that moment to ring.

Larssen jerked up in surprise—he hadn't thought the phone was working—and gave himself another crack in the head. This time he started out swearing in Norwegian. Trousers flopping around his ankles, he hobbled into the bedroom. "Hello?" he growled, annoyed as if it were the caller's fault he'd knocked his brains loose.

"That is you, Jens? You are all right, you and Barbara?"

The accented voice on the other end of the line threw ice water on his steam. "Yes, Dr. Fermi," he said, and made a hasty grab for his pants. Of course Fermi could not see him, but he was embarrassed even to be talking to the Italian physicist, a dignified man if ever there was one, with trousers at half-mast. "We came through safe again, thank you."

"Safe?" Fermi echoed bitterly. "This is a word without meaning in the world today. I thought it had one when Laura and I came here four years ago, but I am wrong. But never mind that. Here is the reason I call: Szilard says—and he is right—we must all meet tomorrow, and tomorrow early. Seven o'clock. He would say six if he could."

"I'll be there," Larssen promised. "What's up?"

"The Lizards, they are moving toward Chicago."

The words seemed to hang on the wire. "But they can't," Jens said, though he knew perfectly well they could. What the devil was there to stop them?

Fermi understood what he meant. "You are right—they must not. If they come here, everything we do since we begin is lost. Too much time lost, time we have not to waste even against Germany, to say nothing of these creatures."

"Germany." Larssen kept his voice flat. He'd been relieved past all measure when the atomic bomb that exploded above Chicago proved not to have a swastika painted on its casing. He once more had no idea how far along the Nazis were on their own bomb program. It would be a hell of a note, though, for humanity to have to depend on them alone for a weapon with which to do the Lizards some real damage. He wondered if he would sooner see Earth conquered than Adolf Hitler its savior. *Just maybe,* he thought. On the line, Fermi cleared his throat. That brought Larssen back to the here-and-now. "I'll be there," he said again.

"Good," Fermi said. "I go, then—many others to call while phones are working. I see you in the morning." He hung up without saying good-bye. Larssen sat down on the bed, thinking hard. His pants slid back down to his ankles. He didn't notice.

His wife walked into the bedroom. She carried a candle to light her way. Outside, fire-engine sirens rang through the night as their crews fought to douse the fires the Lizards had started. "What's up?" Barbara asked. She tossed her blouse and underwear into the wickerwork laundry hamper.

"Big meeting tomorrow," he answered, then repeated Fermi's grim news.

"That's not good," she said. She had no real notion of what he was working on under Stagg Field; she'd been studying medieval English literature when they met at Berkeley. But she knew the project was important. She asked, "How are we going to stop them?"

"You come up with the answer to that one and you win the sixty-four dollars."

She smiled at that, then set the candle in a silver stick—a wedding present Larssen had never thought they'd use—on top of the dresser. With both hands, she took off her skirt and threw it at the hamper. She glanced over to him. "You still haven't pulled up your pants."

"I did so," he said, then had to add lamely, "They must have fallen down again."

"Well, shall I put on a nightgown now, or not?"

He considered. The meeting in the morning was early, but if he poured down enough coffee, he'd get through it okay . . . and Barbara, naked in the candlelight, made him want to forget tomorrow anyhow. "Not," he said.

"Good. This time, take your shirt off, too."

Nothing was running the next morning when Larssen headed for the University of Chicago, not the buses, not the elevated, nothing. Only a few cars crawled cautiously along the street, inhibited not only by the gas shortage but also now by the risk of rubble.

A rifle-toting air-raid warden in a British-style tin hat and a Civil Defense armband nodded to Jens as he walked past. The wardens had flowered like weeds after a drought in the panicky weeks following Pearl Harbor, then disappeared almost as quickly when their services proved unnecessary. But these days, they really were needed. This one looked as though he hadn't slept in a month. His face was covered with graying stubble; an unlit cigarette dangled from the corner of his mouth. But he was going on as best he could, like everyone else.

An hour's brisk walk got Larssen onto the university campus. While he supposed that was good for him, he also gave some serious thought to trying to get his hands on a bicycle. The sooner the better, he decided, before everyone got the same idea and the price went sky-high. He didn't have two hours to spare every day going back and forth to work.

Eckhart Hall stood on the southeast corner of the Quadrangle. It was a new building, having opened in 1930. New or not, however, it didn't boast air conditioning; the windows to the commons room were open, allowing fresh warm muggy air to replace the stale warm muggy air already inside. In deference to the hour, someone had put out a big pot of coffee and a tray of sweet rolls on a table set under those windows.

Larssen made a beeline for that table, poured himself a paper cup of coffee, gulped it down hot and black, then grabbed a roll and got a second cup. With the caffeine jolt kicking in, he drank this one more slowly.

But as he carried the coffee and sweet roll to a chair, he wondered how long such things would continue to exist in Chicago. The coffee was imported, of course, and so were some of the ingredients in the roll—the cinnamon, certainly. How long could commerce continue at even its wartime level with Lizard bases scattered over the United States like growing tumors?

He nodded to Enrico Fermi, one of the two or three men who had beaten him to the meeting. The Italian physicist was wiping his mouth on a paper napkin (the pulp from which it was made was yet another import, Larssen thought). "We'd best enjoy life while we can," the younger man said, and explained his reasoning.

Fermi nodded. His receding hairline and oval face made him the literal embodiment of the word *egghead*, and also made him look older than his forty-one years. His smile now was sweet and rather sad. "My world has already turned upside down once of late. Another time seems somehow less distressing—and I doubt the Lizards concern themselves over my wife's religion."

Brought up comfortably Lutheran in a land where one could fairly comfortably be anything, Jens had never much concerned himself with religion. But Laura Fermi had been a Jew in fascist Italy. The Italians were not rabid on the subject like the Germans, but they had made matters sticky enough for the Fermis to be glad to get out.

"I wonder how far along this trail the Axis would be if Hitler only had the sense to leave some of his brightest people alone and let them work for him," Larssen said.

"I am not to any great degree a political man, but it has always seemed to me that fascism and sense do not mingle," Fermi said. He raised his voice to address a newcomer: "Is this not so, Leo?"

Leo Szilard was short and stocky, and wore a suit with padded shoulders which emphasized the fact. "What do you say, Enrico?" he asked. When Fermi repeated himself, he screwed up his broad, fleshy face in thought before answering, "Authoritarianism in any form makes for bad science, I believe, for its postulates are not rational. The Nazis are bad for this, yes, but anyone who thinks the American government—and hence its projects like our so-called Metallurgical Laboratory here—free of such preconceived idiocy is himself an idiot."

Larssen nodded vehemently at that. If Washington had really believed in what the Met Lab was doing, it would have poured in three times the research money and support from the day Einstein first suggested the violent release of atomic energy was possible.

Nodding also helped Jens keep a straight face. Szilard was both brilliant and cultured, and expressed himself so. But the Hungarian scientist's accent never failed to remind Larssen of Bela Lugosi's in *Dracula*. He wondered if Szilard had ever seen the movie, but lacked the nerve to ask.

More people drifted in, by ones and twos. Szilard looked pointedly at his watch every few minutes; his attitude declared that being bombarded by creatures from another planet wasn't a good enough excuse for missing an important meeting.

Finally, at about twenty-five after seven, he decided he could wait no more. He said loudly, "We have a question to face today: in light of the Lizards' move on Chicago, what is our proper course? Shall we abandon our research here, and seek some new and safer place to continue it, accepting all the loss of time and effort and probably also of material this would entail? Or shall we seek to persuade the government to defend this city with everything in its power for our sake, knowing the army may well fail and the Lizards succeed here as they have so many other places? Discussion, gentlemen?"

Gerald Sebring said, "God knows I want an excuse to get out of Chicago—" That occasioned general laughter. Sebring had been planning to go do some research back in Berkeley in early June—and, incidentally, to marry another physicist's secretary while he was out there. The arrival of the Lizards changed his plans, as it did so many others' (come to that, Laura Fermi was still back in New York).

Sebring waited for the chuckles to die down before he went on. "Everything we're doing here, though, feels like it's right on the point of coming to fruition. Isn't that so, people? We'd lose a year, maybe more, if we had to pull up stakes now. I don't think we can afford it. I don't think the world can afford it."

Several people nodded. Larssen stuck up a hand. Leo Szilard saw him, aimed a stubby forefinger in his direction. He said, "Strikes me this doesn't have to be an either-or proposition. We can go on with a lot of our work here at the same time as we get ready to pull out as fast as possible if we have to." He found he had trouble baldly saying, *if the Lizards take Chicago.*

"That is sensible, and practical for some of our projects," Szilard agreed. "The chemical extraction of plutonium, for instance, though it requires the most delicate balances, can proceed elsewhere—not least because we have as yet very little plutonium to extract. Other lines of research, however, the pile you are assembling among them—"

"Tearing it down now would be most unfortunate, the more so if that proves unnecessary," Fermi said. "Our k factor on this one should be above 1.00 at least, perhaps as high as 1.04. To break off work just when we are at last on the point of achieving a sustained chain reaction, that would be very bad." His wide, mobile mouth twisted to show just how bad he thought it would be.

"Besides," Sebring said, "where the heck are we likely to stay safe from the Lizards anyhow?" He was far from a handsome man, with a long face, heavy eyebrows, and buck teeth, but as usual spoke forcefully and seriously.

Szilard said, "Are we agreed, then, that while, as Jens says, we take what precautions we can, we ought to stay here in Chicago as long as that remains possible?" No one spoke. Szilard clicked his tongue between his teeth. When he continued, he sounded angry: "We are not authoritarians here. Anyone who thinks leaving wiser, tell us why this is so. Persuade us if you can—if you prove right, you will have done us great service."

Arthur Compton, who was in charge of the Metallurgical Laboratory, said, "I think Sebring put it best, Leo: where can we run that the Lizards will not follow?"

Again, no one disagreed. That was not because Compton headed the project, nor because of his formidable physical presence—he was tall and lean and sternly handsome, and looked more like a Barrymore than the Nobel prize-winning physicist he was. But the rest of the talented crew in the commons room were far too independent to follow a leader simply because he was the leader. Here, though, they had all reached the same conclusion.

Szilard saw that. He said, "If it is decided, then, that Chicago must be held, we must convince the army of the importance of this as well."

"They will fight to hold Chicago anyhow," Compton said. "It is the hinge upon which the United States pivots, and they know it."

"It is more important than that," Fermi said quietly. "With what we do here, Chicago is the hinge on which the world pivots, and the army, it does not know *that*. We must send someone to tell them."

"We must send some two," Szilard said, and all at once Larssen was certain he and Fermi had planned their strategy together ahead of time. "We must send two, and separately, in case one meets with misfortune along the way. The war is here among us now; this can happen."

Sure enough, Fermi spoke up again, as if with the next line of dialogue in an ancient Greek play: "We should send also native-born Americans; officers are more likely to hear them with attention than some foreigner, some enemy alien who is not fully to be trusted even now when the Lizards, true aliens, have come."

Larssen was nodding, impressed by Fermi's logic at the same time as he regretted the truths that underlay it, when Gerald Sebring raised a hand and said, "I'll go."

"So will I," Larssen heard himself saying. He blinked in surprise; he hadn't known he was going to volunteer until the words were out of his mouth. But speaking up turned out to make sense, even to him: "Walt Zinn can ride herd on the gang of hooligans working on the pile."

Zinn nodded. "As long as I can keep 'em out of jail, I'll get along all right." He gave away his Canadian origins by saying *oat* for *out*.

"Then it is settled." Szilard rubbed his hands in satisfaction. Fermi also looked pleased. Szilard went on, "You will leave as soon as possible. One of you will go by car—Larssen, that will be you, I think. Gerald, you will take the train. I hope both of you get to Washington safe and sound— and I hope Washington will still be in human hands when you arrive."

That sent a nasty chill through Larssen. He hadn't imagined Lizards marching up Pennsylvania Avenue past the White House. But if they could move on Chicago, they could surely move on Washington. He wondered if the invaders from another world had figured out it was the capital of the United States.

Looking at Szilard's smug expression, he realized the Hungarian had gotten exactly what he wanted. For all his devotion to democracy, Szilard had maneuvered the meeting like a Chicago wardheeler. Larssen chuckled. Well, if that wasn't democracy, what was it? A question better left unanswered in Chicago, perhaps.

The chuckle turned into a guffaw that Larssen fortunately managed to strangle before it got loose. If you played with the letters in Dr. Szilard's name just a little . . . Larssen wondered if Szilard himself had noticed, and how one said *lizard* in Magyar.

"I can report one riddle solved, Exalted Fleetlord," Kirel said.

"That will be a pleasant novelty," Atvar snapped; the longer he wrestled with Tosev 3, the testier he became. But he could not afford to irk Kirel excessively. All bowed to the Emperor, yes, but those below him competed. Even officers' cabals were not unknown. And so Atvar softened his tone: "What new things have you learned of the Big Uglies, then?"

"Our technicians have discovered why the high-burst nuclear weapons of our initial bombardment failed to completely disrupt their radio communications."

Kirel beckoned to one of those technicians, who floated up with a captured Tosevite radio set. Atvar opened his jaws in mocking laughter. "Big and ugly and clumsy, just like the Tosevites themselves," he said.

"You speak truth, Exalted Fleetlord," the technician said. "Also clumsy and primitive. The electronics are not even solid-state, as ours have been through almost all our recorded history. The Tosevites use as clumsy makeshifts these large vacuum-filled tubes here." He pulled off the back plate of the set to point to the parts he meant. "They are bulky, as you see, Exalted Fleetlord, and the amount of waste heat they produce is appalling—they are most inefficient. But exactly because they are so large and so—so gross, if I may use an imprecise word, they are much less susceptible to electromagnetic pulse than unshielded integrated circuits would be."

"Thank you, Technician-Second," Atvar said, reading the male's body paint for his rank. "Your data are valuable. Service to the Emperor." Hearing himself dismissed, the technician cast down his eyes in salute to the sovereign, then took back the radio set and pushed himself away from the fleetlord's presence.

"You see, Exalted Fleetlord, the Tosevites' communications system retained its utility only because it is so primitive," Kirel said.

"Their radios are primitive, and that ends up being useful to them. They don't yet know how to make decent missiles, so they fling outsized artillery shells instead, and that ends up being useful. Now they *are* trying to build missiles. Where will it end, Shiplord?"

"In our victory," Kirel said stoutly.

Atvar gave him a grateful look. Maybe the only reason Kirel was acting so loyally was that he did not want command of what looked like an effort that promised more in the way of trouble than glory. At the moment, Atvar didn't care. Just having someone to whom he could complain worked wonders.

And complain he did: "When the Tosevites aren't primitive, they hurt us, too. By the memories of all the ancient Emperors, who would have been mad enough to imagine making boats big enough to put airplanes on them? Who but the Big Uglies, I mean?"

Home, Rabotev 2, and Halless 1 all had free water, yes, but in the form of rivers and ponds and lakes (Rabotev 2 even had a couple of smallish seas). None of them was troubled by the vast, world-bestriding oceans of Tosev 3, and neither the Race, the Rabotevs, nor the Hallessi used their waters to anything like the extent the Big Uglies did. Having planes appear out of nowhere, as when they raided the base on the Chinese Coast, was a rude surprise. So were the ships with big guns that pounded bases anywhere near water.

Kirel waggled his fingers in a shrug. "Now that we know they fight from the sea, we can sink their big boats, and faster than they can hope to build them. The boats aren't exactly inconspicuous, either. That problem will go away, and soon."

"May it be so." But once Atvar got to worrying out loud, he wasn't about to let himself be mollified so easily. "These missiles they're trying to build—how are we supposed to shoot them all down? We came here intending to fight savages whose only missiles came from bows. And do you know what the latest is?"

"Tell me, Exalted Fleetlord," Kirel said, in the tones of a male who understands he'd better listen sympathetically if he knows what's good for him.

"In the past few days, for the first time, jet planes rose against our aircraft from both Deutschland and Britain. They're still badly inferior to ours—especially the Britainish ones—but not nearly so much so as the primitive crates with revolving airfoils we've been facing."

"I—hadn't heard that, Exalted Fleetlord." Now Atvar really had Kirel's attention again. After that moment of surprise, the shiplord continued,

"Wait a bit. Deutschland and Britain were enemies to each other before we landed, am I right?"

"Yes, yes. Britain and the U.S.A. and the SSSR and China against Deutschland and Italia; Britain and the U.S.A. and China against Nippon; but not, for some eggless reason, Nippon against the SSSR. If the Tosevites didn't keep coming up with new things to throw at us, I'd swear on the Emperor's name they were all mad."

"Wait a bit," Kirel repeated. "If Deutschland and Britain were foes until we landed, it's not likely they'd share jet plane technology, is it?"

"*I* wouldn't think so, but who can tell for certain *what* the Big Uglies would do? Maybe it's having so many different empires on so little land that makes them the way they are." The scrambled, convoluted way the Tosevites played the game of politics made even the maneuvers of the imperial court tame by comparison. Dealing with any one Tosevite official made Atvar feel out of his league. As for playing them off against one another, as the manuals suggested, he counted himself lucky that they weren't exploiting him.

But Kirel was still worrying over the jets: "Exalted Fleetlord, if they don't share technology, that means they can only have each developed it independently. They are like a bad virus, Fleetlord; they mutate—not physically, but technically, which is worse—too fast, maybe faster than we can handle. Perhaps we should sterilize the planet of them."

The fleetlord turned both eye sockets to bear on his subordinate. This, from the male who had urged giving the Big Uglies a chance to surrender before the Race choked off their communications?—or rather, failed to choke off their communications? "You think they represent so great a danger to us, Shiplord?"

"I do, Exalted Fleetlord. We are at a high level, and have been steady there for ages. They are lower, but rising quickly. We must smash them down while we still can."

"If only the filthy creatures hadn't hit the *56th Emperor Jossano*," Atvar said mournfully. *If only we hadn't kept so many of our bombs aboard one ship*, he added mentally. But no, he was not to blame for that; ancient doctrine ordained entrusting large stores of nuclear weapons only to the most reliable shiplords. As an officer of the Race should, he'd followed that ancient doctrine. No one could possibly think less of him for that—except that in so doing, he'd suffered a disaster. The way ancient doctrine corroded whenever it touched matters Tosevite worried him even more than the fighting down on the surface of Tosev 3.

"We still have some of the devices left," Kirel persisted. "Maybe the Big Uglies will be more willing to submit if they see what we can do to their cities."

Atvar threw back his head in disagreement. "We do not destroy the world toward which a settler fleet is already traveling." That was what ancient doctrine said, doctrine based on the conquests of Rabotevs and Hallessi.

"Exalted Fleetlord, Tosev 3 appears to me to be dissimilar to our previous campaigns," Kirel said, pressing his superior up to the edge of politeness. "The Tosevites have a greater capacity to resist than did the other subject races, and so seem to require harsher measures. The Deutsche in particular, Exalted Fleetlord—the cannon that wrecked the *56th Emperor Jossano* was theirs, even if it was on the land of the SSSR, and the missile the Big Uglies tried to launch, and now, you tell me, they fly jet planes as well."

"No," Atvar said. Ancient doctrine declared that new planets were not to be spoiled by radioactivity, which was apt to linger long after the war of subjugation ended. After all, the Race would be living here in perpetuity, integrating Tosev into the fabric of the Empire . . . and Tosev 3 didn't have that much land to begin with.

But it did have hideously troublesome natives. Just moments before, the fleetlord had thought how poorly ancient doctrine worked when dealing with the Big Uglies. Moving away from it frightened him as he'd never been frightened before, as if he were cut off from the Emperor's favor, adrift and alone. Yet would he deserve the Emperor's favor if he led the Race to more disasters?

"Wait, Shiplord—I have changed my mind," he told Kirel, who had begun to turn away. "Go ahead and use one on—what is the name of the place?"

"Berlin, Exalted Fleetlord," Kirel answered. "It shall be done."

"Paris," George Bagnall said wearily. "I was here on holiday a couple of years before the war started. It's not the same."

"Nothing's the same as it was before the war started," Ken Embry said. "Hell, nothing's the same as it was before the Lizards came, and that was bare weeks ago."

"A good thing, too, else we'd all be kriegies by now, sitting behind barbed wire and waiting for our next Red Cross packages," Alf Whyte said. The navigator lifted a leg and shook his tired foot, then laughed wryly. "If we were kriegies with Red Cross packages, we'd likely see better grub than we've had on the way up here."

"Right on both counts," Bagnall said. The German occupiers of northern and central France could have swept up the English fliers a dozen times over on their hike to Paris, but hadn't bothered. Some, in fact, cheered the men they might have shot under other circumstances. French peasants shared what they had with the Englishmen, but what they had was mostly potatoes and greens. Their rations made the ones back home sybaritic by comparison, a true testimonial to how meager they were.

Ken Embry said, "Talk about the Lizards, who'd've dreamt he'd be sorry to hear Berlin was smashed to flinders?"

The French papers, still German-dominated, had screamed of nothing else the past few days, shrieked about the fireball that consumed the city, wailed over unbelievable devastation, wept at the hundreds of thousands reported dead. Bagnall understood most of what the sheets proclaimed; his French was better than he'd giddily claimed in the moment of relief after the Lanc got down safe. Now he said, "I'd not have shed a tear if they'd managed to toast Hitler along with everyone else."

"Nor I," Embry agreed. "I'd not have minded carrying one of those bloody big bombs when we flew over Cologne, either. So long as it was us or the Nazis—but the Lizards complicate everything."

"Too right they do." Bagnall cast a wary eye to the sky, as if to watch for a Lizard plane. Not that seeing one would do any good, if it had on

100

board a superbomb like the one that hit Berlin. If the papers were to be believed—always a risky business in France, and all the more so after 1940—one single bomb had leveled an area miles across. You couldn't even run from a bomb like that, let alone hide. What point in watching the skies, then?

As Bagnall brought his gaze back to earth, it settled on a faded, tattered propaganda poster from the Vichy government; though it had never held sway in the German-occupied parts of France, this was not the first such poster he'd seen. In big, tricolor letters, it proclaimed, LABOURAGE ET PÂTURAGE SONT LES DEUX MAMELLES DE LA FRANCE. Underneath, someone had neatly chalked a comment: *Merde.*

The flight engineer ignored the editorial remark. He stared in wonder and fascination at the slogan, marveling that anyone could have written it in the first place, let alone committed it to print and spread it broadcast. But there it was, in letters four inches high, all tricked out and made to look patriotic. Quite unable to help himself, he broke out in great, braying guffaws.

"What's so bleeding funny?" asked Joe Simpkin, the Lanc's rear gunner.

Bagnall still could not speak. He simply pointed at the Vichy poster. Their attention drawn to it, Embry and Alf Whyte started laughing, too.

Simpkin didn't. He really had no French, though he'd picked up a few words, not all of them printable, since the bomber had to land. The edifying sentiment of the poster still remained beyond him, however. He scowled and asked, "What's it say?"

"Something like, 'Work and farming are France's two tits,'" Bagnall answered between wheezes. Translating it into English set him off again, and everyone else with him. A thin Frenchman in a ragged jacket and a black beret frowned at the spectacle of seven obvious foreigners falling to pieces in the middle of the street. Because there were seven of them, he didn't do anything more than frown.

"Tits, is it?" Simpkin said. He was from Gloucester, and spoke with a western accent. "France has better tits'n those, and legs, too."

As if to prove him right, a pretty girl rode by on a rattling bicycle that was probably older than she was. Her skirt showed a lot of tanned leg. Bagnall could hear every click of the bicycle chain as it traveled over the sprocket. He could hear other bicycles, around the corner and out of sight. He could hear horses' hooves, and the rattle of iron tyres on cobblestones as a horse-drawn wagon made its slow way along the street. He could hear someone working a hand-powered sewing machine, and an old woman calling her cat, whose name was Claude and who was, she said, a very naughty fellow. He felt as though he could hear the whole city.

"Paris isn't Paris without a horde of motorcars, all trying to run you down at once," he said.

"No, but it's cleaner than it used to be because the cars are gone," Embry said. "Smell how fresh the air is. We might as well still be out in the country. Last time I was here, the petrol fumes were bad as London."

"No petrol fumes to worry about now," Bagnall agreed. "No petrol to worry about, either—the Jerries have taken it all for their planes and tanks."

Footsteps from around the corner told of someone approaching. The footsteps rang, as if even the fellow's shoes were imbued with a sense of his importance. When he appeared a few seconds later, he proved better fed and much better dressed than most of the Frenchmen Bagnall had seen. Something gleamed silver on his lapel. As he drew near, Bagnall saw what it was: a little pin in the shape of a double-headed ax—the *francisque*, symbol of Vichy and collaboration.

The man started to walk on by, but the sight of men in unfamiliar uniforms, even ones as dirty and ragged as those of the Lanc's crew had become, roused his curiosity. *"Pardonnez-moi, messieurs, mais—êtes-vous allemands?"* he asked, then switched languages: *"Sind Sie deutsche?"*

"Non, monsieur, nous sommes anglais," Bagnall answered.

The Frenchman's eyes opened wide. Of itself, his left hand twitched toward that lapel pin, as if to hide the *francisque*. Bagnall wondered what was going through his head, how he felt, having accommodated himself to the German yoke, on meeting men from a country which refused to wear it.

He spoke English, too. "All the world today is a part of humanity." With a nod, he edged past the Englishmen and hurried away, looking back once over his shoulder.

"Slimy beggar," Alf Whyte muttered. "All the world, my left one. I'd like to give him my boot up his backside."

"So would I," Bagnall said. "But the devil of it is, he's right, or how long d'you think we'd last here traipsing about in RAF blue? It'd be a *Stalag* for us faster than you can say, 'Hands up!' "

"Maybe so, but I don't much care to count blighters like that as part of humanity," Whyte said. "If it was Lizards in Paris, he'd be sucking up to them instead of the Germans."

The navigator didn't bother keeping his voice down. The Frenchman jerked as if stung by a bee and walked even faster. Now his footfalls sounded like those of a mere mortal, not of one who was lord of all he surveyed.

Ken Embry clicked his tongue between his teeth. "We should count our blessings. We haven't had to live under Jerry's thumb the last two years. I daresay if Hitler had invaded and won, he'd have found his share of English collaborators, and plenty more who'd do what they had to to stay alive."

"I don't mind the second sort," Bagnall said. "You have to live, and that means you have to get on about your job and all. But I'm damned if I can see any of us sporting a silver jackboot or whatever the Mosley maniacs use. There's a difference between getting along and sucking up. Nobody *makes* you wear the *francisque;* you do it because you want to."

The rest of the aircrew nodded. They walked deeper into Paris. The nearly empty streets were not all that made it feel strange to Bagnall. When he'd been here before, the Depression still held sway; one of the things he'd never forgotten was the spectacle of men, many of them well dressed, suddenly stooping to pluck a cigarette butt out of the gutter. But well-dressed men in London were doing the same thing then. Somehow the Frenchmen managed to invest even scrounging with panache.

"That's what's gone," Bagnall exclaimed, as pleased at his discovery as if he were a physicist playing with radium. His comrades turned to look at him. He went on, "What did we always used to think of when we thought of Paris?"

"The Folies-Bergère," Embry answered at once. "What's her name, the Negro wench—Josephine Baker—prancing about wearing a few bananas and damn all else. All the girls behind her wearing even less. The orchestra sawing away down in the pit and no one paying it any mind."

"Sounds good to me," Joe Simpkin said. "How do we get there from here?"

Not without effort, Bagnall ignored the gunner's interruption. "Not quite what I meant, Ken, but close enough. Paris stood for good times—Gay Paree and all that. You always had the feeling everybody who lived here knew how to enjoy himself better than you did. Lord knows whether it was really true, but you always thought so. You don't, now."

"Hard to be gay when you're hungry and occupied," Alf Whyte said.

"Occupied, yes," Ken Embry said softly. "Straighten up, lads, here comes Jerry himself. Let's look like soldiers for him, shall we?"

The German infantry of propaganda photographs looked more machined than born of man and woman: all lines and angles; all motions completely identical; hard, expressionless faces under coalscuttle helmets that added a final intimidating touch. The squad ambling up the street toward the aircrew fell a good ways short of Herr Göbbels' ideal. A couple of them were fat; one wore a mustache that had more gray than brown in it. Several had the top buttons of their tunics undone, something a Göbbels soldier would sooner have been shot than imagine. Some were missing buttons altogether; most had boots that wanted polishing.

Third-line troops, Bagnall realized, *maybe fourth-.* The real German army, the past year, was locked in battle with the Russians or grinding now forward, now back across the Sahara. Beaten France got the dregs of German manpower. Bagnall wondered how happy these Occupation warriors were at the prospect of holding back the Lizards, a worse enemy than the Red Army ever dreamed of being.

He also wondered, rather more to the point, if the tacit Anglo-German truce held on the ground as well as in the air. The Germans up ahead might be overage and overweight, but they all carried Mauser rifles, which made the aircrew's pistols seem like toys by comparison.

The *Feldwebel* in charge of the German squad owned a belly that made him look as if he were in a family way. He held up a hand to rein in his men, then approached the British fliers alone. He had three chins and his eyes were pouchy, but they were also very shrewd; Bagnall would not have wanted to sit down at a card table with him.

"Sprechen Sie deutsch?" the sergeant asked.

The Englishmen looked at one another. They all shook their heads. Ken Embry asked, "Do any of your men speak English? Or *parlez-vous français?"*

The *Feldwebel* shook his head; his flabby flesh wobbled. But, as Bagnall had suspected, he was a resourceful fellow. He went back to his squad, growled at his men. They hurried into shops on the boulevard. In less than a minute, one of the soldiers emerged with a thin, frightened-looking Frenchman whose enormous ears looked ready to sail him away on the slightest breeze.

That, however, was not why the soldier had grabbed him. He proved to speak not only French but also fluent German. The *Feldwebel* spoke through him: "There is a *Soldatenheim*, a military canteen, at the Café Wepler, Place Clichy. That is where English fliers are being dealt with. You will please come with us."

"Are we prisoners?" Bagnall asked.

The Frenchman relayed the question to the German sergeant. He was more at ease now that he saw he was to serve as interpreter rather than, say, hostage. The sergeant answered, "No, you are not prisoners. You are guests. But this is not your country, and you will come with us."

It did not sound like a request. In English, Embry said, "Shall I point out it's not his bloody country, either?" With the rest of the aircrew, Bagnall considered that. The Germans had his comrades outnumbered and outgunned. No one said anything. The pilot sighed and returned to French: "Tell the sergeant we will go with him."

"Gut, gut," the *Feldwebel* said expansively, cradling that vast belly of his as if it were indeed a child. He also ordered the Frenchman to come along so he could keep on interpreting. The fellow cast a longing glance back at his little luggage store, but had no choice save to obey.

It was a long walk; the *Soldatenheim* lay on the right bank of the Seine, north and east of the Arc de Triomphe. The Germans and the English had both respected the monuments of Paris. The Lizards knew no such compunctions; a chunk had been torn out of the Arc, like a cavity in a rotting tooth. The Eiffel Tower still stood, but Bagnall wondered how many days more it would dominate the Paris skyline.

In the end, though, what lay longest in the flight engineer's memory about the journey to the canteen was a small thing: an old man with a bushy white mustache walking slowly along the street. At first glance, he looked like Marshal Pétain, or anyone's favorite grandfather. He carried a stick, and wore a homburg and an elegant, double-breasted pinstripe suit with knife-sharp creases. On the left breast pocket of that suit was sewn a yellow six-pointed star with one word: *Juif.*

Bagnall looked from the old Jew with his badge of shame to the fat *Feldwebel* to the French interpreter. He opened his mouth, then closed it again. What could he possibly say that would not make matters worse both for himself and, all too likely, for the Jew as well? He found nothing, but silence was bitter as wormwood to him.

German military signs, white wooden arrows with angular black letters, had sprouted like mushrooms on every Paris streetcorner. The British aircrew probably could have found the military canteen through them without an escort, but Bagnall supposed he could not blame the sergeant for taking charge of them. If not exactly enemies, they were not exactly friends, either.

The canteen had a big sign, again white on black, that announced what it was: *Soldatenheim Kommandantur Cross-Paris.* On another panel of the sign was a black cross in a circle. Men in field gray came in and out below. Those who recognized the fliers' RAF uniforms stopped to stare. No one did anything more than stare, for which Bagnall was duly grateful.

The *Feldwebel* turned the interpreter loose just outside the doorway without even a tip. The fellow hadn't translated more than half a dozen sentences, most of them banal, in the hour and a half it had taken to get here. Now he faced an equally long walk back. But he left without a backward glance or a word of complaint, as if escaping without trouble was payment enough. For a man in his shoes, perhaps it was.

Not far inside the entrance, a table with a sign lettered in both German and English had been set up. The English section read, FOR BRITISH MILITARY SEEKING REPATRIATION FROM FRANCE. Behind the table sat an officer with steel-rimmed spectacles; the single gold pip on his embroidered shoulder straps proclaimed him a lieutenant colonel.

The German sergeant saluted, spoke for a couple of minutes in his own language. The officer nodded, asked a few questions, nodded again, dismissed the *Feldwebel* with a few offhand words. Then he turned to the Englishmen. "Tell me how you came to Paris, gentlemen." His English was precise and almost accent-free. "I am Lieutenant-Colonel Maximilian Höcker, if knowing my name puts you more at ease."

As pilot, Ken Embry spoke for the aircrew. He told the tale of the attack on the Lizard installation in considerable detail, though Bagnall noted that he did not name the base from which the Lancaster had set out. If Höcker also noted that—and he probably did; he looked sharp as all get-out—he let it pass.

His gray eyes widened slightly when Embry described the forced landing on the French road. "You were very fortunate, Flight Lieutenant, and no doubt very skillful as well."

"Thank you, sir." Embry took up the tale again, omitting the names of the Frenchmen who had helped the aircrew along the way. They'd learned only a couple of those, and then just Christian names. Even so, Embry did not mention them. Again, Höcker declined to press him. The pilot finished, "Then your sergeant found us, sir, and brought us here. By the sign in front of you, you don't intend to hold us prisoner, so I hope you'll not take it amiss if I ask you how we go about getting home."

"By no means." The German officer's smile did not quite reach his eyes—or maybe it was a trick of the light reflecting off his spectacle lenses. He sounded affable enough as he continued: "We can put you on a train for Calais this evening. God and the Lizards permitting, you will be on British soil tomorrow."

"It can't be as simple as that," Bagnall blurted. After going on three years of war with the Nazis—and after seeing the old Jew wearing the yellow star—he was not inclined to take anything German on trust.

"Very nearly." Höcker plucked seven copies of a form off the table in front of him, gave them to Embry to pass out to his crew. "You have but to sign this and we shall send you on your way."

The form, hastily printed on the cheapest of paper, was headed PAROLE. It had parallel columns of text, one German, the other English. The English version was florid legalese made worse by some remaining Germanic word order, but what it boiled down to was a promise not to fight Germany so long as either London or—no, not Berlin, but the country of which it had been the capital—remained at war with the Lizards.

"What happens if we don't sign it?" Bagnall asked.

If the smile had got to Lieutenant-Colonel Höcker's eyes, it vanished from them now. "Then you will also go on a train this evening, but not one bound for Calais."

Embry said, "What happens if we do sign and then end up flying against you anyhow?"

"Under those circumstances, you would be well-advised to avoid capture." Höcker's face was too round and mild to make him fit the film cliché of a German officer; he seemed more Bavarian peasant than Prussian aristocrat. But he packed enough menace into his voice for any three cinematic Huns.

"Have you received any communication from the RAF or His Majesty's government permitting us to sign such a document?" Embry asked.

"I have not," Höcker said. "Formally, we are still at war. I give you my word of honor, however, that I have learned of no punishment given to any who have so signed."

"Please be so good as to put that assurance in writing, for us to present to our superiors. If it should prove false, we shall consider ourselves at liberty to deem our paroles null and void, nor should sanctions be applied against us in the event we are captured in arms against your country."

"Jolly good, Ken," Bagnall whispered admiringly.

Höcker inked a pen, wrote rapidly on the back of another parole form. He handed it to the pilot. "I trust this meets with your approval, Flight Lieutenant?" He pronounced it *leftenant*, as a native Englishman would have.

Embry read what he had written. Before he replied, he passed it to Bagnall. Höcker's script, unlike his speech, was distinctly Germanic; the flight engineer had to puzzle it out word by word. But it seemed to set forth what Embry had demanded. Bagnall gave it to Alf Whyte.

The German lieutenant-colonel waited patiently until the whole Lancaster crew had read it. "Well, gentlemen?" he asked when Embry had it back.

The pilot glanced from one flier to the next. No one said anything. Embry sighed, turned back to Höcker. "Give me the bloody pen." He signed his parole with a few slashing strokes. "Here."

Höcker raised an eyebrow. "You are not pleased with this arrangement?"

"No, I'm not pleased," Embry said. "If it weren't for the Lizards, we'd be fighting each other. But they're here, so what can I do?"

"Believe me, Flight Lieutenant, my feelings are the same in every particular," the German answered. "I had a sister in Berlin, however, and two nieces. So I shall adjourn my quarrel with you for the time being. Perhaps we shall take it up again at a more auspicious moment."

"Coventry," Embry said.

The lieutenant-colonel answered, "Beside Berlin, *Engländer*, Coventry is as a toddler's scraped knee." Höcker and Embry locked eyes with each other for most of a minute.

Bagnall took the pen, wrote his name on his parole form. "One enemy at a time," he said. The rest of the aircrew also signed theirs. But even as Höcker called for an escort to take the Englishmen to the train station, Bagnall wondered how many nieces the old Jew with the yellow star had, and how they were faring.

A squadron of devils tramped down the main street of the prison camp. Like everyone else who saw them, Liu Han bowed low. No one knew what would happen if the little scaled devils were denied all the out-ward trappings of respect their captives could give. No one, least of all Liu Han, wanted to find out.

When the devils were gone, a man came up to Liu Han and said some-thing. She shook her head. "I am sorry, but I do not understand your dia-lect," she said. He must not have been able to follow hers, either, for he grinned, spread his hands, and walked away.

She sighed. Hardly anyone here spoke her dialect, save the few villag-ers taken with her. The scaly devils threw people from all over China to-gether in their camps; they either did not know or did not care about the differences among them. For the educated few, those who could read and write, the lack of a common dialect mattered little. They spoke together with brush and paper, since they all used the same characters.

Such was the ignorance of the demons that they had even put Japa-nese in the camp. No Japanese were left any more. Some had slain them-selves in despair at being captured. Those whose despair was less deep died anyhow, one by one. Liu Han did not know just how they'd met their ends. So long as they were dead, and the little devils none the wiser, she was satisfied.

Two streets over from the one the devils most regularly patrolled, a market had sprung up. People landed in camp with no more than what they had on their backs, but they soon started trading that—no reason for a man with a gold ring or a woman whose purse had been full of coins to do without. Inside days, too, chickens and even piglets had made their ap-pearance, to supplement the rice the devils doled out.

A bald man with a wispy mustache sat on the ground, his straw hat upside down in front of him. In it nestled three fine eggs. Seeing Liu Han looking at them, he nodded and spoke to her. When he saw she did not fol-low him, he tried another dialect, then another. Finally he reached one she could also grasp: "What you give for these?"

Sometimes even understanding did not help. "I am sorry," she said. "I have nothing to give."

Back in her own village, it would have been the start of a haggle with which to while away most of a morning. Here, she thought, it was nothing but truth. Her husband, her child, dead at the hands of the Japanese. Her village, devastated first by the eastern barbarians and then by the devils in their dragonfly planes—and now gone forever.

The man with the eggs cocked his head to one side, smiled a bland merchant's smile up at her. He said, "Pretty woman never have *nothing* to give. You want eggs, maybe you let me see your body for them?"

"No," Liu Han said shortly, and walked away. The bald man laughed as she turned her back. He was not the first in the market who had asked her for that kind of payment.

She went back to the tent she shared with Yi Min. The apothecary was becoming an important man in the prison camp. Little scaly devils often visited him, to learn written Chinese and the dialects he spoke. Sometimes he made suggestions to them about the proper way to do things. They very often listened—that was what made him important. If he wanted eggs, he had influence to trade for them.

All the same, Liu Han sometimes wished she had moved in with the other prisoners from her village, or with people she'd never seen before. But she and he had come here in the belly of the same dragon plane, he had been a speck of the familiar in a vast strange ocean—and so she had agreed. He'd been diffident when he asked her. He wasn't diffident anymore.

She lifted the tent flap. A startled hiss greeted her. She bowed almost double. "I am very sorry, lord devil, sir. I did not mean to disturb you," she said rapidly.

Too rapidly. The demon turned back to Yi Min, from whose words she had distracted it. "She say—what?" it asked in abominably accented Chinese.

"She apologizes—says she is sorry—for bothering you." Yi Min had to repeat it a couple of times before the little devil understood. Then he made a noise like a boiling pot. "Is that how to say the same thing in your language?" he asked, switching back to Chinese once more.

The scaly devil hissed back at him. The language lesson went on for some time, with both Yi Min and the devil ignoring Liu Han as completely as if she'd been the sleeping mat on which they squatted. Finally the little demon bubbled out what must have been a farewell, for it got to its clawed feet and scurried out of the tent. Even in going, it brushed past Liu Han without a word in either Chinese or devil talk.

Yi Min patted the mat. With some reluctance, Liu Han sat down beside him in the place the little scaled demon had just occupied. The mat was still warm, almost hot; devils, fittingly enough, were more fiery creatures than human beings.

Yi Min was in an expansive mood. "I shall be rich," he chortled. "The Race—"

"The what?" Liu Han asked.

"The Race. It is what the devils call themselves. They will need men to serve them, to be their viceroys, men who can teach them the way real people talk and also learn their ugly language. It is difficult, but Ssofeg—the devil who was just here—says I pick it up more quickly than anyone else in this whole camp. I will learn, and help the devils, and become a great man. You were wise to stick by me, Liu Han, truly wise."

He turned to her and kissed her. She did not respond, but he hardly noticed; his tongue pushed its way into her mouth. She tried to fend him off. His greater weight overbore her, pressed her down to the mat. Already he was tugging at her tunic. She sighed and submitted, staring up at the gray fabric of the tent ceiling and hoping he would finish soon.

He thought he was a good lover. He did everything a good lover should, caressing her, putting his face between her legs. But Liu Han did not want either him or his attentions, and so they failed to stir her. Again, Yi Min was so full of himself that her response, or rather lack of it, did not even reach him. Had she not been there at a convenient moment, she was sure he would simply have taken himself in hand. But she was there, so he took her instead.

"Let us try the hovering butterflies today," he said, by which he meant that he wanted her on top. She sighed again. He would not even give her the chance just to lie there limply. Once more she wished the scaly devils had herded someone else into the dragonfly plane with her. She did not know why she'd yielded the first time he forced himself on her, save that he was the last link she had to the vanished life she was used to. Having yielded once, saying no became more nearly impossible every time afterward.

Looking in every direction but at his flushed, rather greasy face, she straddled him, lowered herself. He filled her, but that was all she felt: none of the delight she had known from her husband. She moved vigorously just the same—that was the way to make it over soonest.

He was thrashing beneath her like a gaffed carp when the tent flap opened. She gasped and grabbed for her cotton trousers at the same moment that Yi Min, oblivious as usual to everything not himself, groaned with his final pleasure.

Liu Han wanted to die. How could she show her face anywhere in camp now that her body had been seen in truth? She felt like killing Yi Min for piling such humiliation on her shoulders. Maybe tonight, after he fell asleep—

The hiss from the entranceway brought her out of her dark fantasy and back to the present. That wasn't a person there seeing her shame, it was a little scaly devil. As she rolled off Yi Min and away, as she scrambled into trousers and tunic, she wondered if that was better or worse. Better, she supposed—a person would surely gossip about her, while a scaly devil might not.

The devil hissed and sputtered in his own devils' language, then tried to speak Chinese: "What you do?"

"We were enjoying the moment of Clouds and Rain, mighty lord devil Ssofeg," Yi Min answered, as coolly as if he'd said, *We were having a cup of green tea.* "I did not expect you back so soon." Much more slowly than Liu Han had, he began to put his clothes back on.

"Clouds and Rain? Not understand," the little devil named Ssofeg said. Liu Han could scarcely understand it.

"As well expect to trap the moon in a mirror as poetry from a little devil, it would seem," Yi Min said in a low, rapid aside to Liu Han. He turned back to Ssofeg. "I am very sorry, mighty lord devil. I shall speak plain words for you: we were making love, doing what makes a baby, mating, balling, screwing, fucking. Do any of those make sense to you?"

Wanting as she did to find all things about Yi Min odious, Liu Han had to notice he was good at using simple words, and at using a whole cluster of them in the hope that the devil might grasp at least one.

Ssofeg did, too. "Make baby?" he echoed.

"Yes, that's right," Yi Min said enthusiastically. He smiled a broad, artificial smile and made extravagant gestures to show how pleased he was.

The little scaly devil tried to speak more Chinese, but words failed it. It switched to its own language. Now Yi Min was the one who had to grope for meanings. Ssofeg had patience, too, speaking slowly and simply as the apothecary had before. At one point, it aimed a clawed finger at Liu Han. She flinched back in alarm, but the scaly devil seemed just to be asking a question.

After a while, Yi Min asked a question or two in return. Ssofeg answered with a couple of short words. Without warning, Yi Min brayed laughter. "Do you know what this stupid turtle thinks?" he managed to wheeze out between guffaws. "Can you guess? You would never guess, not in a thousand years."

"Tell me, then," Liu Han said, afraid the joke would turn on her.

But it did not. Yi Min said, "The little scaly devil wanted to know if it was your breeding season, if you came into heat at a certain time of the year like a vixen or a ewe. If I understand him rightly, that is how his kind's females are made, and when they are not in season, he can feel no desire himself." The apothecary laughed again, harder than ever. "Poor, poor devil!"

"That is strange," Liu Han admitted. She had never given any thought to the little scaly devils' love lives; they were so ugly, she hadn't thought of their having any. Now, almost against her will, she found herself smiling. "Poor devils."

Yi Min gave his attention back to Ssofeg. He mixed Chinese and the devils' language to get across the idea that women could be receptive at any time. Ssofeg hissed and squeaked. So did Yi Min. Then, in Chinese, he said, "I give you oath, master devil, that I tell you the truth here."

Ssofeg squeaked again before it—no, *he*, Liu Han thought—tried Chinese again, too: "True all woman? Not just"—he pointed at Liu Han—"woman here?"

"True for all women," Yi Min agreed solemnly, though Liu Han saw the glint of laughter still in his eye. To make sure his own sex was not demeaned, he added, "It is also true that men—human men—have no fixed mating season, but can mate with women at any time of the year."

That started Ssofeg making cooking noises again. Instead of asking more foolish questions, the little scaly devil whirled and scampered out of the tent. Liu Han heard his clawed feet pattering away at a dead run. She said, "I'm glad he's gone."

"So am I," Yi Min said. "It lets me think—how can I best turn to my advantage this strange and sorrowful weakness of the scaly devils? If they were proper men, I could sell them proper medicine to strengthen their peerless pillars. But if I correctly follow Ssofeg, without devil females he and his brethren might as well be so many eunuchs—though even eunuchs have desires, they say. Hmm . . ."

Not five minutes after his *yang* essence had mingled with Liu Han's *yin*, he might as well have forgotten she remained in the tent. To Yi Min, Yi Min was all that truly mattered, with everyone and everything else to be rearranged at his whim for his convenience. Now he sat cross-legged on the mat, his eyes almost closed, feverishly planning how to turn the devils' debility into money or influence for him.

All at once, he let out a cry nearly as intense as the one he'd made when he spent himself inside her. "I have it!" he exclaimed. "I will—"

Liu Han never found out what Yi Min's latest scheme was. Before he could announce it, Ssofeg burst back into the tent. Three more little scaly devils were right behind him, all of them carrying guns. Liu Han's bowels turned to water. Now Yi Min bleated like a sheep facing the butcher's cleaver. "Mercy, kind devil!" he wailed.

Ssofeg pointed outside, then to Yi Min. "You come," he said in Chinese. Yi Min was so frightened, he had trouble getting to his feet. He stumbled out of the tent on stiff, numb legs. Two of the armed devils flanked him as he went.

Liu Han gaped at Ssofeg. At a stroke, the little devil had given her what she wanted most—freedom from Yi Min. And if he was gone, then she'd have this fine tent to herself. She felt like kissing Ssofeg. If he hadn't had a mouthful of sharp teeth and one armed retainer still standing by him, she might have done it.

Then the devil pointed at her. "Too come you," he said.

"Me?" Her sudden hopes crashed down. "Oh, no, kind devil, you don't want me, you don't need me, I am just a poor woman who knows not a thing in all the world." She knew she was talking too fast for the ignorant little devil to understand, but the words poured out of her like the sweat that all at once began to pour from her armpits.

Ssofeg paid no more attention to what she wanted than Yi Min had when he undressed her and satisfied his own urges. "Too come you, woman," he said. The scaly devil behind him moved his gun so it bore on her. The devils were not in the habit of taking no for an answer. Moaning, she followed Yi Min out into the street.

People stared and pointed and exclaimed as the little devils marched her along behind the apothecary. She understood a couple of their remarks:

"Ee, that doesn't look good!" "I wonder what they did?" Liu Han wondered what she'd done, too, aside from being foolish enough to let Yi Min take advantage of her. And why should the scaly devils care about that?

No one did anything more than stare and exclaim. The devils were little, but they were powerful. The three with guns could kill many Chinese by themselves, and even if they were somehow overwhelmed, the rest of the scaly devils would flay the prison camp with fire from their dragonfly planes. Liu Han had seen what such fire did to the Japanese in her village, and they had had arms to fight back. The people in the camp were utterly defenseless against assault from the air.

Yi Min yelled, "Help me, someone! I haven't done a thing. Save me from the terrible devils!" Liu Han snorted angrily and glowered at his back. He didn't care what happened to anyone else, so long as he saved his own worthless skin. She snorted again. It wasn't as if she didn't already know that.

Despite his bawling like a pig with a cut hock, no one did anything foolish, for which Liu Han was heartily glad. But she felt very lonely as the armed escort of devils led her out of the prison camp, away from her own people, and toward a dragonfly plane. "In!" Ssofeg said. Having no choice, first Yi Min and then Liu Han obeyed.

A few minutes later, the dragonfly plane scrambled noisily into the air. Even though her stomach lurched every time the plane changed direction, she wasn't as completely petrified as she had been the first time the little scaly devils forced her aboard one of their flying machines. After all, several of them were in here, too, and no matter how little they cared about her, she'd seen that they valued their own painted hides.

"This is all your fault!" Yi Min shouted at her. "If you weren't flaunting yourself there in my tent, I never would have gotten into this predicament."

The unfairness of that took her breath away. Before she could answer, one of the devils let out an ominous hiss. It punctured the apothecary's bluster like a pin popping an inflated sow's bladder. He shut up, though he didn't stop glaring at her. She glared right back.

After about half an hour's flight, the dragonfly plane set down not far from some much bigger machines of the scaly devils. The devils with guns urged her and Yi Min out, marched them along to one of those big machines, and up a ladder into its belly. Unlike the ones on the dragonfly plane, the seats in there were padded, though still not big enough even for her.

These seats had straps, too. A little devil waiting for them fastened those straps so Liu Han could not reach the buckles no matter how she squirmed. Her fear came back. Yi Min writhed even more violently than he had under her. Here, though, his thrashing won no release.

The door to the outside world slammed shut. The devil twisted a handle to make sure it stayed that way. Then he scrambled up an interior ladder into a higher room, leaving the two people alone and helpless.

"Your fault," Yi Min insisted. He went on in that vein for some time. Liu Han stopped listening to him. Nothing, obviously, had ever been his fault in all his born days, and if you didn't believe it, you had but to ask him.

Without warning, the machine shuddered beneath them. "Earthquake," Liu Han squalled. "We'll be crushed, we'll be killed—" She'd never heard anything like the roar that went with the terrible, unending shaking.

Without warning, she felt as if two or three people—or maybe a brick wall, knocked down by the earthquake—had fallen on top of her. She tried to scream, but produced no more than a gurgle; the dreadful, unending weight made it hard to breathe at all, let alone drag in enough air for a shriek. After a little while, much of the racket went away, though a more muted rumble and several medium-loud mechanical noises persisted.

"What's happening to us, Yi Min?" Liu Han gasped out. However much she disliked him, he was the only other human being caught in this devilish trap. Besides, with his education, he might even have known the answer.

"I have ridden on the railroad," he replied, his voice also coming forth in effortful grunts. "When a train starts to move, it presses you back into your seat. But—never like this."

"No, never like this. This is no train," Liu Han said scornfully. His words satisfied her no better than his body had.

The rumble from beneath them abruptly cut off. At the same instant, the crushing pressure on Liu Han's chest also went away. Her own weight somehow seemed to disappear, too. Were it not for the prisoning straps that grasped her, she felt as if she could have floated away from her seat, perhaps even flown like a magpie. Exhilaration she'd never known flooded through her. "It's wonderful," she exclaimed.

The only answer Yi Min gave was a sick, gulping noise that reminded her of a fish trying to breathe after it was hauled out of its pond. She twisted her neck so she could look over at him. His face was pale as whey. "I will not vomit," he whispered fiercely, as if trying to make himself believe it. "I will not vomit."

Big drops of sweat grew on his cheeks and forehead. He shuddered, still fighting to control his rebellious stomach. Liu Han watched, fascinated, as one of the drops broke free. It didn't fall. It just hung almost motionless in midair, as if hooked to the ceiling with an invisible line of spider silk. But no, no silk here.

Yi Min let out another gulp, this one louder than the last. All at once, Liu Han hoped he would not be sick. If his vomit hung as the drop of sweat had, it was liable to smother him—and if it drifted through the air, it was liable to smother her.

Then the apothecary quavered, "L-look at the devil, Liu Han."

Liu Han turned back toward the ladder up which the little scaly devil had climbed. He was there in the hatchway again, peering down at the two humans with his unnerving, independently mobile eyes. But those eyes, at the moment, were the least unnerving thing about him. He floated head-down, a couple of yards above Liu Han, with neither hands nor feet holding onto anything. He did not fall, any more than the drop of Yi Min's sweat had.

When he saw that the people could not escape, he twisted in midair so his legs were toward them. The practiced maneuver might have been part of a dance in three dimensions; for the first time, Liu Han found a devil graceful. He reached out, grabbed a rung of the ladder, pushed. Sure enough, just as Liu Han had imagined, he flew upward into his own cabin.

"Isn't that the most amazing thing you ever saw?" she said.

"It's impossible," Yi Min declared.

"Who knows what's impossible for devils?" Liu Han asked. Through his sickness, Yi Min stared at her. She needed a moment to read the expression on his face. Then she realized that without thinking about it, she had spoken to him as to an equal. That was not proper, but it was the truth; here, caught by the devils' cords, they were equals, equal nothings. And of the two of them, she was having the better time of coping with this strange (*she* would not say impossible) place.

If Yi Min had reprimanded her, shoved her back down into the subservient role she'd taken all her life, likely she would have accepted it without a murmur. But he didn't; he was too filled with his own nausea, too filled with his own fear. Because of that, some things—not everything, but some things—changed forever between them in the next few silent minutes.

She didn't know how long they traveled with their weight left behind. She enjoyed every second of it, and wished only that she were free to float about and try the twisting move the little scaly devil had used. Yi Min lay huddled on his seat. Every so often, he made another sick gulping noise. Liu Han did her best not to laugh at him.

The plane in which they were flying made noises of its own. The pops and hisses meant nothing to Liu Han, so she hardly noticed them. But the metallic bangs and the grating sound that came from the front end after a while were impossible to ignore. She said, "Are we going to crash?"

"How should I know?" Yi Min answered peevishly, diminishing himself in her sight yet again.

They did not crash. More strange noises came from the front end of the plane, then the harsh sounds of the little scaly devils' speech. Three devils came floating back into the compartment where Liu Han was strapped down, though she had not known the plane held more than one. Her fear came back with them, for two of the devils bore long knives that were almost swords. She'd imagined Yi Min's vomit drifting through the air like stinking fog. Now in her mind's eye she saw a red mist of her own blood filling the room. She shuddered and tried to make herself as small as she could.

The devil with a sword-knife glided down to the seat on which she lay, reached out. She shuddered again. A thousand times better Yi Min's caresses than the touch of the scaly devil. But all he did was unfasten the straps that held her in place, then those confining the apothecary. When they were both free, the devil pointed upward, in the direction from which he and his companions had come.

All at once, in an almost blinding flash of enlightenment, Liu Han saw that the armed devils were there to protect the other one from her and from Yi Min. Just as it hadn't occurred to her that she could talk back to Yi Min, so she hadn't imagined mere humans might be dangerous to devils. Again something changed for good in the way she looked at the world.

Yi Min spoke hesitantly in the devils' language. The one who had released him answered. "What does he say?" Liu Han asked; her tone said she had a right to know.

"He's telling us to go that way," Yi Min replied, pointing in the same direction the little devil had. "He says they will not hurt us if we do as they say."

Liu Han pushed against the arms of her seat. She floated up, lighter than a feather. The scaly devil did grab her, but only to straighten her course. Yi Min followed, still making queasy noises in the back of his throat.

The room from which the devils had come was smaller than the one in which they'd confined the humans. One wall was nothing but dials and buttons and screens. A scaly devil with a short sword floated in front of it. He hissed at Liu Han, as if warning her to come no closer. She wanted to laugh at him—she had no intention of doing that.

The devil's small, skinny body did not cover all the screens. One showed cloud-covered blue and brown slowly moving past, as if seen from far above. The pretty colors had a sharp, curved edge; above was only black. "Look, Yi Min," Liu Han said. "They can make pretty pictures. I wonder what it is."

Yi Min looked at the screen, pointed to it, tried out his small command of the devils' tongue on the one guarding it. That one answered at some length, Yi Min interrupting a couple of times with new questions. The apothecary said, "That's our world going round many miles below us, Liu Han, our whole world. The Western devils with whom I studied were right, it seems—the world really is round like a ball."

Liu Han kept her own opinion of that to herself. The world had always looked flat to her. But it certainly did seem to have a round edge now. Now was not the time to worry about it, not with so many more urgent concerns closer to hand.

The scaly devil hissed and pointed with his blade, urging her forward. She grabbed what had to be a handhold and went through another opening. Two more armed devils waited in the much bigger space out there. They pointed to an open circular doorway in the curved wall of that space. Liu Han obediently propelled herself toward it. It had handholds all around, for those whose aim was poor.

Hers wasn't. She almost collided with the devil waiting inside that tunnel. Yi Min missed the doorway and had to scrabble in with the handholds. He was nursing a sprained wrist and cursing under his breath when he appeared. The two floating devils followed him.

The trip along that corridor was the strangest journey Liu Han had ever known, even surpassing the weightless flight in the roaring plane. With every foot she traveled away from the doorway, she grew heavier. From floating, she went to bounding, then to walking with long strides, then to ordinary steps with what felt like about her proper weight.

"How do they do that?" she asked Yi Min; he was, after all, the only other person available, and could also talk with the devils, which she could not although, now that she thought about it, what held her back from learning their words for herself?

He spoke, listened, spoke, listened, finally gave up. "I do not understand. It has something to do with spinning round and round, but how could that make us heavier or lighter?" He wiped his sweaty forehead with a sleeve. "It's too hot in here, too."

"It certainly is," Liu Han said. It was as bad as any midsummer day, though less humid than usual in her village in summer. That helped, but not enough. The devils seemed perfectly happy in the heat. She remembered how warm the mat on which the devil was sitting had felt, just a few hours before. And the Christian priest, she recalled, had said devils lived in a hot place. She hadn't taken him seriously, but he must have known what he was talking about. Maybe, being a Western devil himself, he'd had more intimate acquaintance with other sorts of devils than was possible for a Chinese.

The armed devils took the two humans out of the corridor and into another one. Other devils bustled past on errands of their own. Some of them turned one turreted eye toward Liu Han and Yi Min. Most just ignored the two people.

The escort led Liu Han and Yi Min into a large room. Already inside were several devils with fancier body paint than any Liu Han had yet seen and a mat covered not with cotton cloth but with some smooth shiny stuff, obviously of devilish manufacture. One of the waiting devils surprised Liu Han by speaking Chinese. What he said surprised her even more: "You two go screw now."

She gaped at him, wondering if she'd heard correctly (his accent was dreadful) and whether he knew what he was saying. She knew a certain amount of relief to see that Yi Min looked as befuddled and as dismayed as she felt. To have endured both terror and wonder to get here, only to receive a blunt order to fornicate . . . She wondered about the little scaly devils in ways that had never occurred to her before.

"You go screw now," the devil repeated.

"No," she said, the word out of her mouth before she had time to wonder about its consequences.

And, "No," Yi Min echoed, which surprised her very little. It was soon after he had taken her before, and he'd been through quite a lot since. Few men wanted to try when they weren't likely to succeed.

"Not go screw, not leave," the scaly devil said.

Liu Han and Yi Min stared at each other, appalled. No matter how interesting the journey hither had been, Liu Han did not want to spend the rest of her days in the company of devils and Yi Min. But she had no desire to exhibit herself to the devils, either. "You are perverts if you think we will perform for you," she burst out. "Go away and leave us alone; then we will see."

"You can't talk to them that way," Yi Min said fearfully. But the devil who spoke Chinese hissed at the others. They filed out of the chamber, one by one. The last one closed the door. What sounded like a lock clicked. The devils might have left (and even that surprised her), but they hadn't changed their minds.

Liu Han looked around. Without the scaly devils, the chamber was dreadfully bare: no food, no water, not even a pot for night soil. Just that cursed shiny mat. She looked from it to Yi Min, back again. She wished she could persuade herself otherwise, but she was convinced that door wouldn't open again until she and the apothecary did what the devils wanted.

Resignedly, she started taking off her clothes. "What are you doing?" Yi Min said.

"What do you think I'm doing? I'm getting this over with," she retorted. "If the choice is between having you and staying locked up here among the devils, I'd sooner have you. But once we're back in camp, Yi Min, you'll never touch me again."

That warning was nothing but a bluff, and she knew it; she had no family in the camp to protect her from the apothecary, and he was bigger and stronger than she. But he did not argue. Muttering "Whatever you say," he undid the waistband of his trousers, let them fall to the metal floor of the chamber.

He did not have an easy time of it. She had to help him with her hand

and then her mouth before he would rise at all. He moved slowly and carefully within her, shepherding his strength, and went on almost endlessly
before at last he managed to spend.

Maybe that long, slow passage was what helped Liu Han startle herself by also ascending to the Clouds and Rain. More probably, though, she
decided later, she'd let herself go because for the first time the coupling
was of her choosing, not forced upon her. True, the choice—Yi Min or the
devils—had not been a good one, but it was her own. That made a lot of
difference.

The apothecary was still puffing as he rolled off her. "I wonder what
the little blinking orange light over there in the corner of the ceiling was,"
he said, pointing.

"I didn't notice it," she confessed. That annoyed her; every time till
now, she'd been more interested in where she was than in what Yi Min
was doing to her. Now when they were finally in new and fascinating surroundings, her foolish body kept her from seeing everything there was to
see. She glanced toward the ceiling. "It's not there now."

"It was," Yi Min said.

Liu Han dressed, then walked over to the door and knocked on it,
again and again. "We kept our part of the bargain," she said. "Now you
devils keep yours."

Whether thanks to the racket she was making or not, the door slid
open a couple of minutes later. The devil who opened it was the one who
spoke Chinese. "You come," he said, pointing to her and Yi Min.

She followed without fuss; every other choice looked worse. Yi Min
walked right behind her. She gave a long, slow nod when she noticed that.
She'd taken the lead here, as in their just-completed joining, simply by acting as if she had the right to do so. She wondered if it was always that simple.

Certainly it was not while facing the little scaly devils, especially here
in their lair. Here she was only too aware she was in their power. She
ducked to get through the entrance of the chamber to which the devil led
her. So did Yi Min; being taller, he had to bend farther. If they had to stay
in this strange place any length of time, she was sure they would both end
up smashing their foreheads in doorways every so often.

The devils who had been in the original chamber (or at least the same
number of devils; Liu Han was still shaky about telling them apart) now
gathered around what looked like a tall pedestal with no statue on top of
it. Their heads turned when the two people came in. Their mouths
dropped open, almost in unison.

Liu Han did not like the look of all those pointed teeth. The scaly
devil who spoke Chinese said, "You watch you go screw."

That made no sense to Liu Han. She turned to Yi Min. "What is the
little devil trying to say? Try and find out, since you speak his language."

Yi Min made hissing and bubbling noises. Liu Han listened, bemused. Getting him to do what she wanted had been easy—all she needed to do was tell him in a firm way. In this weird place, his man's arrogance had dried up and blown away: he was no master here, and he knew it.

"The devil says we're going to watch ourselves couple," Yi Min reported after a couple of minutes' back-and-forth. "It's the same in his speech as it is in Chinese. He seems very sure. He—"

The apothecary shut up. One of the other little scaly devils, impatient with all the chatter, had stuck a clawed finger into a recess near the top of the pedestal. An image sprang into being above it—an image of the two people making love on the shiny mat in the other chamber.

Liu Han stared and stared. She had spent coppers to see moving pictures two or three times, but this was no ordinary moving picture. For one thing, it was not in shades of gray, but perfectly reproduced the tans and golds and pinks of flesh. For another, the image looked solid, not flat, and, as she discovered when she took a step, her view of it shifted whenever she moved. She walked all the way around the pedestal and saw herself and Yi Min from every side.

The devils watched her, not the image. Their mouths fell open again. All at once, she was sure they were laughing at her. And no wonder—there she lay in miniature, doing publicly what she'd thought private. Watching herself made a third difference from seeing an ordinary moving picture, and made her hate the little devils for tricking her so.

"You people, you screw any time, no season?" the Chinese-speaking devil demanded. "This true for all peoples?"

"Of course it is," Liu Han snapped. Yi Min didn't say anything. He was watching his rather beefy buttocks move up and down, twisting his head to get the best possible view of things. As far as he was concerned, being in a moving picture was just fine.

The devil said, "Any man screw any woman any time?"

"Yes, yes, yes." Liu Han felt like screaming at the nasty little creature. Had it no decency? But then, who could say what was decent for a devil?

The devils talked back and forth among themselves. Every so often, one or another of them would point at the two people, which made Liu Han nervous. The devils' voices rose. Yi Min said, "They're arguing. Some of them don't believe it."

"What could it matter to them, anyhow?" Liu Han said.

The apothecary shook his head; he had no idea, either. But the Chinese-speaking scaly devil answered the question a little later: "Maybe this screw so what do you Big Uglies so different than Race. Maybe screw any man, woman all time make you so—" He needed a brief colloquy with Yi Min before he found the word he wanted: "So progressive. Yes. Progressive."

The words, the sentences, made sense to Liu Han, but she did not really take hold of the concepts behind them. *Progressive*, to her, was a word from Communist propaganda that meant "our way." As far as she could see, people and the little scaly devils had no way in common. In fact, they seemed to use *progressive* to mean "The opposite of our way."

She could not ask them to explain, either, for they were arguing among themselves again. Then the one who spoke Chinese said, "We find out if you speak true. We make test. Make—" He went word hunting with Yi Min again. "Make *experiment*. Bring for man many womans here, for woman many mans. See if screw all time like you say."

When he heard that, when he understood it through bad grammar and twisted syntax, Yi Min smiled beatifically. Liu Han stared in disbelieving horror at the little devil, who seemed pleased at his own cleverness. She'd wondered what could be worse than coming to this strange, unpleasant place. Now she knew.

Bobby Fiore picked up a rock, chucked it at a crumpled piece of paper forty or fifty feet away. He didn't miss by more than a couple of inches. His chuckle was sour. Chucking rocks was as close as he'd come to taking infield since the Lizards grabbed him. He didn't even dare do that near the perimeter of the camp. The last time anybody'd thrown a stone at a Lizard, five people were shot immediately afterward. That stopped that.

One of the Lizards' whirligig planes racketed in from the northwest. It landed at their encampment, right outside the fence that cut off the peninsula on which sat Cairo, Illinois. Fiore found another rock, chucked it too, let out a new chuckle more sour than the old. He'd never expected to come back to—to come down to— Cairo again. He'd played there in the Class D Kitty League in—was it 1931 or 1932? He didn't remember any more. He did remember it had been a funny kind of town. It still was.

A levee surrounded the place to protect it from floods on the Mississippi and the Ohio, at whose confluence Cairo sat. Over the top of the eastern barrier, Fiore could see magnolias and gingkos. They gave the town a Southern atmosphere that seemed out of place for Illinois. Also Southern was the feel of good times now long gone. Cairo had thought it would end up as the steamboat capital of the Mississippi. That didn't happen. Now it was just a Lizard prison camp.

He supposed it made a good one. Because it had water on three sides, the Lizards had just wrecked the Mississippi highway bridge and run up their fast fences across the neck of Cairo Point. They didn't have gunboats in the river, but they did have soldiers with machine guns and rockets on the levee and on the far shores. A couple of boats were supposed to have snuck across at night, but a lot more than a couple got sunk.

Fiore mooched along till he came to the Lizards' fence. It wasn't exactly barbed wire; it was more like long strips of narrow, double-edged razor blade. It did the same job as barbed wire, though, and did it just as well.

On the far side—on the free side—of the fence, the Lizards had run up guard towers. They looked the same way, say, Nazi prison-camp guard towers would have looked. A soldier in the nearest one swung the muzzle of his machine gun toward Fiore. "Go, go, go!" he said. It might have been the only word of English he knew. As long as he had that machine gun, it was certainly the only one he needed.

Bobby went, went, went. You didn't disobey a prison guard, not more than once. Fiore's shoulders sagged as he walked slowly down Highway 51, back toward town. The United States had been going to kick Japan's and Germany's asses. Everybody knew it. Everybody felt good about it. And then, suddenly, without the least warning in the world or out of it, a prison camp—probably a lot of prison camps—right in the middle of the U.S.A.

It wasn't so much that it didn't seem right. It was more as if it didn't seem possible. From the top of the world to sitting in a prison camp like a Pole or an Italian or a Russian or a poor damned Filipino. Americans weren't supposed to have to go through this kind of nonsense. His parents had left the old country to make sure they never went through this kind of nonsense. And here it came to them.

He tramped down the middle of the highway, wondering how his parents were; he hadn't heard word one about Pittsburgh since the Lizards came. When he got into Cairo, Highway 51 changed its name to Sycamore Street. Fiore kept walking on the white dashes of the center line. No cars were running, though a couple of burned-out shells remained of ones that had tried. Only a handful of men in their nineties remembered the last time war visited the United States at home. It was here again, all uninvited.

A colored man came up Sycamore toward Fiore. The fellow was pushing a cart that looked as if it had started life as a baby buggy. An old cowbell held on with a bent coat hanger clanked to announce his presence. As if that wasn't enough, he sang out every few steps: "Tamales! Git yo' hot tamales!"

"What are you charging today?" Fiore asked as the hot-tamale man drew near.

The Negro pursed his lips. "Reckon a dollar apiece'll do."

"Jesus. You're a goddamn thief, you know that?" Fiore said.

The hot-tamale man gave him a look that in other times he never would have taken from a Negro. His voice was cool and distant as he answered, "You don't want none, friend, there's plenty what does."

"Shit." Fiore unbuttoned the flap on his hip pocket, dug out his wallet. "Give me two."

"Okay, boss," the colored man said, but not until the dollar bills were in his hand. He flipped open the cart's steel lid, used a pair of tongs to dig out the greasy tamales. He blew on them to cool them off before he gave them to Fiore, something for which, in other times, the Board of Health would have come down on him like a ton of bricks.

Bobby didn't much care for a Negro's breath on his hot tamales, either, but kept his mouth shut. He was glad enough to have the money to buy them. When the Lizards pushed him off their whirligig flying machine, he'd had $2.27 in his pockets, and that was counting his lucky quarter. But it was enough to get him into a poker game, and endless hours on endless train and bus rides from one minor league town to the next had honed his skills sharper than those of the local boys he sat down with. More than two bills rubbed against each other in his wallet now.

He bit through corn husks into spicy tomato sauce, onions, and meat. He chewed slowly, trying to identify it a little closer than that. It wasn't beef and it wasn't chicken; the last tamales he'd bought, a couple of days before, had had chicken in them. These tasted different, stronger somehow, almost like kidney but not that either.

Something his father used to say, a phrase he hadn't thought of in years, floated through his mind: *times so tough, we had to eat roof rabbit.* In an instant, suspicion hardened to certainty: "You son of a bitch!" he shouted, half choking because he couldn't decide whether to swallow or spit. "That's cat meat in there!"

The hot-tamale man didn't waste time denying it. "What if it is?" he said. "It's the onliest meat I got. Case you didn't notice, mister, ain't nobody bringin' no food into Cairo these days."

"I oughta beat the crap outta you, givin' a white man cat meat," Fiore snarled. If he hadn't still held a tamale in each hand, he might have done it.

The threat alone should have made the Negro cringe. Cairo not only looked like a Southern town, it acted like one. Jim Crow was alive and well here. Colored children went to their own school. Their mothers were domestics, their fathers mostly longshoremen or factory hands or sharecroppers. They knew better than to disturb the powers that be.

But the hot-tamale man just stared steadily back at Bobby Fiore. "Mister, I can't sell you what I don' got. An' if you beat on me, maybe I won't hit back, though you ain't such a real big man as that. What I do, mister, I tell the Lizards. Y'all may be white, but them Lizards, they treats all kinds o' folks like they was niggers. White, black, don't make no never mind to them. We ain't free no more, but we is equal."

Fiore gaped at him. He looked back, steady still. Then he nodded, as peaceably as if they'd been talking about the weather, and started pushing his cart up Sycamore Street. The cowbell clanked. "Hot tamales! Git yo' hot tamales!"

Fiore looked down at the two he'd bought. His father had known hard times. He thought he had, too, but till now he'd been wrong. Hard times were when you ate cat and were happy you had it to eat. He ate both tamales, then deliberately licked his fingers clean.

He walked farther into town. Then he heard behind him the click of Lizards' nails on asphalt. He turned around to look. That was a mistake. The Lizards all pointed their guns at him. One made an unmistakable gesture—*come here*. Gulping, he came. The Lizards surrounded him. None of them came up past his shoulder, but with their weapons, that didn't matter.

They marched him back toward their razor-blade fence. When he passed the slow-moving tamale man, the fellow just grinned. "I'll get you if it's the last thing I do!" Fiore shouted. The hot-tamale man laughed out loud.

6

Warsaw knew naked war again, the crack of rifles, the harsh, abrupt roar of howitzers, the screech and whine of incoming shells, the crash when they struck and the slow rumbling crumple of collapsing masonry afterward. Almost, Moishe Russie longed for the days of the sealed-off ghetto, when dying came slow rather than of a sudden. Almost.

Ironic that Jews could come and go in the whole city now, just when the whole city became a battlefield. As the Poles had fought to the last in Warsaw against vastly superior Nazi forces, so now the Germans, embattled in turn, were making Warsaw a fortress against the overwhelming might of the Lizards.

A Lizard plane screamed overhead, almost low enough to touch but too fast for antiaircraft guns to hit. Bombs fell, one after another. The explosions that followed were bigger than those the usual run of Lizard bombs produced unaided (like everyone else in Warsaw, German, Pole, or Jew, Russie had become a connoisseur of explosions); the Lizards must have set off some German ammunition.

"What shall we do, *Reb* Moishe?" wailed a man in the shelter (actually, it was only a room in the ground floor of a reasonably stout building, but calling it safety might make it so—names, as any kabbalist knew, had power).

"Pray," Russie answered. He'd begun to grow used to the title with which the Jews of Warsaw insisted on adorning him.

More explosions. Through them, the man cried, "Pray for whom? For the Germans who would kill us in particular or for the Lizards who would kill everyone who stands in their way, which is to say, all of mankind?"

"Such a question, Yitzkhak," another man chided. "How is the *reb* to answer a question like that?"

With the Jewish love of disputation even in the face of death, Yitzkhak retorted, "What is a *reb* for, but to answer questions like that?"

It was indeed the question of the moment. Russie knew that, only too well. Finding an answer that satisfied was hard, hard. Through the different-toned roars and crashes of aircraft, shells, bullets, and bombs, the people huddled against one another and passed the terrifying time by arguing. "Why should we do anything for the *ferkakte* Nazis? They murder us for no better reason than that we're Jews."

"This makes them better than the Lizards, who would murder us for no better reason than that we're people? Remember Berlin. In an instant, as much suffering as the Germans took three years to give us."

"They deserve it. God made the Germans as a scourge for us, and God made the Lizards as a scourge for the Germans." A near miss from a bomb sent chunks of plaster raining down from the ceiling onto the heads and shoulders of the people in the shelter. If the Lizards were God's scourge on the Germans, they also chastised the Jews, Russie thought. But then, scourges were not brooms, and did not sweep clean.

Someone twisted the argument in a new direction: "God made the Lizards? I can't believe that."

"If God didn't, Who did?" someone else countered.

Russie knew the answer the Poles outside the ghetto's shattered walls gave to that. But no matter what the *goyim* thought, Jews put no great stock in the Devil. God was God; how could He have a rival?

But fitting the Lizards into God's scheme of things wasn't easy, either, even as scourges. The Germans had plastered Warsaw with posters of a *Wehrmacht* soldier superimposed over a photograph of naked burnt corpses in the ruins of Berlin. In German, Polish, and even Yiddish, the legend below read, HE STANDS BETWEEN YOU—AND THIS.

It was a good, effective poster. Russie would have reckoned it more effective still had he not seen so many naked Jewish corpses in Warsaw, corpses dead on account of the Germans. Still, he said, "I will pray for the Germans, as I would pray for any men who sin greatly."

Hisses and jeers met his words. Someone—he thought it was Yitzkhak—shouted, "I'll pray for the Germans, too—to catch the cholera." Cries of agreement rang loud and often profane—*no way to speak of prayer*, Russie thought disapprovingly.

"Let me finish," he said, and won a measure, if not of quiet, then of lowered voices: the advantage of being thought a *reb*, someone whose words were reckoned worth hearing. He went on, "I will pray for the Germans, but I shall not aid them. They want to wipe us from the face of the earth. However badly these Lizards treat all mankind, they will treat us no worse than any other part of it. Thus I see in them God's judgment, which may be harsh but is never unjust."

The Jews in the shelter listened to Russie, but not all followed his way of thinking. Punctuated by blasts outside, the dispute went on. Someone tapped Russie on the arm: a clean-shaven young man (Russie was almost sure the fellow had fewer years than his own twenty-six, though his beardless cheeks also accented his youth) in a cloth cap and shabby tweed jacket. He said, "Will you do more than simply stand aside while Lizards and Germans fight, *Reb* Moishe?" From under the stained brim of the cap, his eyes bored into Russie while he awaited his reply.

"What more can I do?" Russie asked cautiously. He wanted to shift his feet. He'd not been under such intense scrutiny since his last oral examination before the war, and maybe not then; this young, secular-looking Jew had eyes sharp and piercing as slivers of glass. "And who are you?"

"I'm Mordechai Anielewicz," the smooth-faced young man answered, his offhand tone making his name seem small and unimportant. "As for what you can do . . ." He put his head close to Moishe's—not, Russie thought, that there was much danger of anyone overhearing them in the noisy chaos of the makeshift shelter. "As for what you can do—you can help us when we hit the Germans."

"When you what?" Russie stared at him.

"When we hit the Germans," Anielewicz repeated. "We have grenades, pistols, a few rifles, even one machine gun. The *Armja Krajowa*"— the Home Army, the Polish resistance forces—"has many more. If we rise, the Nazis won't be able to fight us and the Lizards both, and Warsaw will fall. And we will have our vengeance." His whole face, thin and pale like everyone else's, blazed with anticipation.

"I—I don't know," Russie stammered. "What makes you think the Lizards will make better masters than the Germans?"

"How could they be worse?" Every line of Anielewicz's body was a shout of contempt.

"This I do not know, but after we have seen so much suffering, who knows what may be possible?" Russie said. "And the Poles—will they really rise with you, or sit on their hands and let the Nazis slaughter you? For every *Armja Krajowa* man, there's another in the dark blue police." The German-led Order Police wore uniforms of a shade nearly navy. Russie added, "Sometimes the *Armja Krajowa* man *is* in the dark blue police. There are traitors everywhere."

Anielewicz shrugged, as if hearing nothing he didn't already know. "Most of them hate Germans worse than Jews. As for those who don't, well, we'll have more guns after the rising than we do now. If we fight Germans, we can fight Poles, too. Come on, *Reb* Moishe—you've said all along the Lizards were God's means of delivering us from the Nazis. Say it again when we rise, to hearten us and bring new fighters to our cause."

"But the Lizards are not even human beings," Russie said.

Anielewicz impaled him on another stare. "Are the Nazis?"

"Yes," he answered at once. "Evil human beings, but human beings all the same. I don't know what to tell you. I—" Russie stopped, shaking his head in bewilderment. Ever since God granted him a sign—ever since the Lizards came to Earth—he'd been treated as someone important, as someone whose opinion mattered. *Reb* Moishe: even Anielewicz called him that. Now he discovered that with importance came responsibility; hundreds, more like thousands, of lives would turn on what he decided. All at once, he wished he were simply a starving onetime medical student once more.

But that was not the sort of wish God was in the habit of granting. Russie temporized: "By when must I decide?"

"We strike tomorrow night," Anielewicz answered. Then, with a couple of quick wriggles, he slid away from Russie and lost himself in the packed shelter.

After a while, Lizard bombs stopped raining down. No sirens wailed to announce the all clear, but that proved nothing. Power was erratic in Warsaw these days. For that matter, power had always been erratic in the ghetto. People took advantage of the lull to make their escape, to try to rejoin their loved ones.

As he made his way to the door with the rest, Russie looked for Mordechai Anielewicz. He did not find him; one shabby Jew looked all too much like another, especially from behind. Russie came out onto Gliniana Street, a couple of blocks east of the overflowingly full Jewish cemetery.

He glanced toward the graveyard. The Germans had positioned a couple of 8.8-centimeter antiaircraft guns in it; their long barrels stuck up from among the tumbled headstones like monster elephant trunks. Russie could see the gun crews moving around now that the bombardment had eased up.

The sun sparked dully off the matte finish of their helmets. *Nazis,* Russie thought, *the source of endless misery and death and ruin.* A plume of cigarette smoke floated up from one of them. They were Nazis, but they were also human beings. Would life be better under things called Lizards?

"Send me a sign, God," he begged silently, as he had on the night when the Lizards came. One of the gunners assumed a spraddle-legged stance Russie recognized: the fellow was urinating. Hoarse German laugher floated to Russie's ears. It filled him with rage—how like the Nazis to piss on dead Jews and then laugh about it.

All at once, he realized he had his sign.

An intelligence officer set a new stack of documents in front of Atvar. As was his habit, he skimmed through the summaries till he found one that engaged his full attention. It didn't take long this time. He read every word of the second report in the stack, then turned one eye toward the intelligence male. "This report is confirmed as accurate?"

"Which one do you have there, Exalted Fleetlord?" The officer peered down to see where Atvar had paused. "Oh, that one. Yes, Exalted Fleetlord, no possible mistake there. The Big Uglies in the town in the empire of Deutschland are fighting amongst themselves—quite ferociously, too."

"And the radio intercepts? Those are reliable as well?"

The intelligence male nervously twitched his tailstump. "There we are less certain, Exalted Fleetlord. One of the languages seems close to Deutsch, the other rather farther from Russki—these cursed Tosevites have altogether too many languages. But if we correctly understand the import of these signals, one faction in the city appears to be seeking our aid against the other."

"It's not the Deutsche themselves calling for our assistance, surely?"

"By the Emperor, no, Exalted Fleetlord," the intelligence officer said. "It's the others, the ones fighting against them. Our estimates are that the empire of Deutschland as it now stands is a jerry-built structure, most of its territory having been added in the course of the inter-Tosevite war in progress when our fleet arrived. Some of the inhabitants of that empire remain restive under Deutsch control."

"I see," Atvar said, though he didn't, not altogether. Product of an empire—of *the* Empire—which had been itself for tens of millennia, he felt himself failing to grasp what it was like to try to build one in a couple of years (without even the symbol of an emperor to bind it together, in most cases), or, for that matter, to pass suddenly out of the control of one empire and into that of another.

The intelligence officer said, "The groups involved in the fighting against the Deutsche appear to be prominently represented in the camp our forces overran east of the town now involved in strife."

"Which camp do you mean?" Atvar asked; a fleetlord's life is full of minutiae. Then he let out a hiss. "Yes, I remember. *That* camp. What was its name?"

The intelligence officer had to check the computer before he answered. "It is called Treblinka, Exalted Fleetlord." Even spoken by a male of the Race, the Tosevite word sounded harsh and ugly. "Do you wish me to call up the images our combat teams recorded when they captured the place?"

"By the Emperor, no," Atvar said quickly. "Once was sufficient."

Once, as a matter of fact, had been excessive. Atvar thought he'd hardened himself to the horrors of war. Even such hardening as he'd gained had not come easy; his own forces were taking far more casualties than the grimmest estimates had predicted before the fleet left Home. But then, no one had expected the Tosevites to be able to fight an industrialized war.

What the Race's advancing armor discovered at Treblinka wasn't industrialized war, though. It wasn't even industrialized exploitation of criminals and captives. The Race had camps of that sort on all its planets, and had overrun more on Tosev 3; the SSSR, especially, seemed full of them, all far more brutal than anything the Emperor, in his mercy, would have permitted.

But Treblinka . . . the fleetlord did not need the computer screen to replay images of Treblinka. Once reminded of the place, his mind called up the pictures, and he could not turn his eyes away from what his mind saw. Treblinka wasn't industrialized war or industrialized exploitation. Treblinka was industrialized murder—mass graves full of Tosevites shot in the head, trucks designed so the waste products of their inefficient, dirty engines were vented into a sealed compartment to kill those inside, and, just installed before the Race seized Treblinka, chambers to slaughter large numbers of Big Uglies at once with poisonous gas. It was as if the Deutsche had kept working to find the most effective way to get rid of as many other Big Uglies at a batch as they could.

Even if Treblinka represented no more than one set of barbarians tormenting another, it was plenty to sicken Atvar. It also set him thinking. "You say the groups now opposing the Deutsche in this town are the same ones the Deutsche have been massacring?"

"Linguistic evidence and preliminary interrogations suggest this is so, yes, Exalted Fleetlord," the intelligence officer answered.

"We shall promise them help, then, and deliver it," Atvar said.

"As the exalted fleetlord wishes." The intelligence officer deserved higher rank, Atvar thought. He kept any trace of what he thought about the fleetlord's order from his voice. Whether he agreed with it or thought it demented, he would obey it, as males of the Race were trained to obey from their hatchling days.

Atvar said, "We have here at last an opportunity to use some Big Uglies as gloves, with our hands inside. Despite their losses, the leading empires refuse to yield to us. Italia is wavering, but—"

"But Italia has too many Deutsch soldiers in it to be fully a free agent. Yes," the male said.

He was not only submissive but keen, Atvar thought happily, forgiving him the interruption because he had been right. "Exactly so. Perhaps we shall presently help them as we shall go to the aid of the, the—"

"The Polska and the Yehudim," the male supplied.

"Thank you, those are the kinds of Big Uglies I had in mind, yes," Atvar said. "And our assistance to them should not be grudging, either. If they give us a secure zone from which we may with impunity assail both Deutschland and the SSSR, we shall derive great benefits therefrom. We can promise them whatever they want. Once Tosev 3 is fully under our control . . . well, it's not as if they belong to the Race."

"Or even the Rabotevs or Hallessi," the intelligence officer said.

"Quite so. They remain wild, and thus we have no obligations toward them save those which we choose to assume." Atvar studied the male. "You are perceptive. Remind me of your name, that I may record your diligence."

"I am Drefsab, Exalted Fleetlord," the officer said.

"Drefsab. I shall not forget."

■

Georg Schultz raised up on his elbows to peer at the ripening fields of wheat and oats and barley, made a sour face. "The crop at this *kolkhoz* is going to be shitty this year," he said with the certainty of a man who had grown up on a farm.

"That, at the moment, is the least of our worries," Heinrich Jäger answered. He hefted the Schmeisser that had belonged to Dieter Schmidt. Schmidt himself had lain under the black soil of the Ukraine for the past two days. Jäger hoped he and Schultz had heaped on enough to keep the wild dogs from tearing up the body, but he wasn't sure. He and his gunner had been in a hurry.

Schultz's chuckle had a bitter edge to it. "*Ja*, we're a pair out of a jumble sale, aren't we?"

"You can say that again," Jäger answered. Both men wore scavenged infantry helmets and infantry tunics of field gray rather than tanker's black; Schultz carried an infantry rifle as well. Jäger's new, bristly beard itched all the time. Schultz complained about his, too. It was coming in carroty red, though his hair was light brown. Any inspector who saw them would have locked them in the guardhouse and thrown away the key.

Tankmen are usually neat to the point of fussiness. A tank without things stowed just so, and with working parts dirty and poorly maintained, is a tank waiting for breakdown or blowup. But Jäger had jettisoned spit and polish when he bailed out of his killed Panzer III. His Schmeisser was clean. So was his pistol. Past that, he'd stopped worrying. He was alive, and for a German on the south Russian steppe, that remained no small achievement.

As if to remind him he was still alive, his stomach growled. The last time he'd been full was the night he got a bellyful of kasha, the night before the Lizards came. He knew what he had in the way of rations: nothing. He knew what Schultz had: the same.

"We have to get something from that collective farm," he said. "Take it by force, sneak up in the night, or go up and beg—I don't much care which any more. But we have to eat."

"I'm damned if I want to be a chicken thief," Schultz said. Then, more pragmatically, he added, "Shouldn't be too hard, just going on in. Most of the men, they'll be off at the front."

"That's true," Jäger said; almost all the figures he saw working in the field wore babushkas. "But this is Russia, remember. Even the women carry rifles. I'd sooner get something peaceably than by robbery. With the Lizards all around, we may need help from the Ivans."

"You're the officer," Schultz said, shrugging.

Jäger knew what he meant: *you're the one who gets paid to think*. Trouble was, he didn't know what to think. The Lizards were at war with Russia no less than with the Reich, which meant he and these *kolkhozniks* shared a common foe. On the other hand, he hadn't heard anything to let him know Germany and the Soviet Union weren't still fighting each other (for that matter, he hadn't heard anything at all since his panzer died).

He got to his feet. The south Russian steppe had seemed overpoweringly vast when he traversed it in a tank. Now that he was on foot, he felt he could tramp the gently rolling country forever without coming to its end.

Georg Schultz stood up beside him, though the gunner muttered, "Might as well be a bug walking across a plate." That was the other side of Russia's immensity: if one could see a long way, one could be seen just as far.

The peasants spotted the two Germans almost instantly; Jäger saw their movements turn jerky even before they swung his way. He kept his submachine gun lowered as he strode toward the cluster of thatch-roofed wooden buildings that formed the heart of the *kolkhoz*. "Let's keep this peaceful, if we can."

"Yes, sir," Schultz said. "If we can't, no matter what we take from the Ivans now, they're liable to stalk us through the grass and kill us."

"Just what I'm thinking," Jäger agreed.

The workers in the fields converged on the Germans. None of them put down their hoes and spades and other tools. Several, young women and old men, carried firearms—pistols stuck in belts, a couple of rifles slung over shoulders. Some of the men would have seen action in the previous war. Jäger thought he and Schultz could have taken the lot of them even so, but he didn't want to find out the hard way.

He turned to the gunner. "Do you speak any Russian?"

"*Ruki verkh!*—hands up! That's about it. How about you, sir?"

"A little more. Not much."

A short swag-bellied fellow marched importantly up to Jäger. It really was a march, with head thrown back, arms pumping, legs snapping forward one after the other. The *kolkhoz* chairman, Jäger realized. He rattled off a couple of sentences that might have been in Tibetan for all the good they did the major.

Jäger did know one word that might come in handy here. He used it: "*Khleb*—bread." He rubbed his belly with the hand that wasn't holding the Schmeisser.

All the *kolkhozniks* started talking at once. The word "Fritz" came up in the gabble, again and again; it was almost the only word Jäger understood. It made him smile—the exact Russian equivalent of the German slang "Ivan."

"*Khleb, da,*" the chairman said, a broad grin of relief on his wide, sweaty face. He spoke another word of Russian, one Jäger didn't know. The German shrugged, kept his features blank. The chairman tried again, this time in halting German: "Milk?"

"*Spasebo,*" Jäger said. "Thank you. *Da.*"

"Milk?" Schultz made a face. "Me, I'd rather drink vodka—there, that's another Russian word I know."

"Vodka?" The *kolkhoz* chief grinned and pointed back toward one of the buildings behind him. He said something too rapid and complicated for Jäger to follow, but his gestures left no doubt that if the Germans wanted vodka, the collective farm could supply it.

Jäger shook his head. "*Nyet, nyet,*" he said. "Milk." To his gunner, he added, "I don't want us getting drunk here, not even a little bit. They're liable to wait until we go to sleep and then cut our throats."

"Likely you're right, sir," Schultz said. "But still—milk? I'll feel like I'm six years old again."

"Stick to water, then. We've been drinking it for a while now, and we haven't come down with a flux yet." Jäger was thankful for that. He'd been cut off from the medical service ever since the battle—skirmish, he supposed, was really a better word for it—that cost his company its last panzers. If he and Schultz hadn't stayed healthy, their only chance was to lie down and hope they got better.

Another old woman—a *babushka* in the grandmotherly sense of the word—hobbled toward the Germans. In her apron she carried several rings of dark, chewy-looking bread. Jäger's stomach growled the second he saw it.

He took two rings. Schultz took three. It was food fit for peasants, he knew; back in Münster, before the war, he would have turned up his nose at black bread. But compared to some of the things he'd eaten in Russia—and especially compared to nothing at all, of which he'd had far too much lately—it was manna from heaven.

Georg Schultz somehow managed to cram a whole ring of bread into his mouth at once. His cheeks bulged until he looked like a snake trying to swallow a fat toad. The *kolkhozniks* giggled and nudged one another. The gunner, his face beatific, ignored them. His jaws worked and worked. Every so often, he swallowed. His enormous cud of bread began to shrink.

"That's not the best way to do it, Sergeant," Jäger said. "See, I've almost managed to finish both of mine while you were eating that one."

"I was too hungry to wait," Schultz answered blurrily—his mouth was still pretty full.

The *babushka* went away, came back with a couple of carved wooden mugs of milk. It was so fresh, it warmed Jäger's cup. Its creamy richness went well with the earthy, mouth-filling taste of the bread. Peasants' food, yes, but a peasant who ate it every day was likely to be a contented man.

For politeness' sake, Jäger declined more, though he could have eaten another two dozen rings—or so he thought—without filling himself up. He drained the mug of milk, wiped his mouth on his sleeve, asked the *kol-*

khoz chief the most important question he could think of: *"Eidechsen?"* He necessarily used the German word for Lizards; he did not know how to say it in Russian. He waved his hand along the horizon to show he wanted to find out where the aliens were.

The *kolkhozniks* didn't get it. Jäger pantomimed short creatures, imitated the unmistakable screech of their airplanes as best he could. The *kolkhoz* chief's eyes lit up. "Ah—*yasheritsi*," he said. The peasants clustered round him exclaimed. Jäger memorized the word; he had the feeling he would need it again.

The chief pointed south. Jäger knew there were Lizards in that direction; that was the way he'd come. Then the chief pointed east, but made pushing motions with his hands, as if to say the Lizards over there weren't close. Jäger nodded to show he understood. And then the *kolkhoz* chief pointed west. He didn't do any dumb show to indicate the Lizards thereabouts were far away, either.

Jäger looked at Georg Schultz. Schultz was looking at him, too. He suspected he looked as unhappy as the gunner did. If there were Lizards between them and the bulk of the *Wehrmacht* . . . Jäger didn't care to follow that thought to its logical conclusion. For that matter, if there were Lizards over that way, the *Wehrmacht* might not have much left in the way of bulk.

The *kolkhoz* chief gave him another piece of bad news: "Berlin *kaput*, Germanski. *Yasheritsi.*" He used those expressive hands of his to show the city going up in a single huge explosion.

Schultz grunted as if he'd been kicked in the belly. Jäger felt hollow and empty inside, himself. He couldn't imagine Berlin gone, or Germany with Berlin gone. He tried not to believe it. "Maybe they're lying," Schultz said hoarsely. "Maybe it's just the God-damned Russian radio."

"Maybe." But the more Jäger studied the *kolkhozniks*, the less he believed that. If they'd gloated at his reaction to the news, he would have doubted them more, have thought they were trying to fool him. But while a few looked pleased at his discomfiture (as was only natural, when his country and theirs had spent a year locked in a huge, vicious embrace), most looked at him and his companion with sympathetic eyes and somber faces. That convinced him he needed to worry.

He found a useful Russian word: *"Nichevo."* He knew he pronounced it badly; German had to use the clumsy letter-group *tsch* even to approximate the sound that lay at its heart.

But the *kolkhozniks* understood. *"Tovarisch, nichevo,"* one of them said: Comrade, it can't be helped, there's nothing to be done about it. It was a very Russian word indeed: the Russians were—and needed to be—long on resignation.

He hadn't quite meant it that way. He explained what he had meant:

"Berlin *da, yasheritsi*—" He ground the heel of his boot into the dirt. "Berlin *nyet, yasheritsi*—" He ground his heel into the dirt again.

Some of the Russians clapped their hands, admiring his determination. Some looked at him as if he was crazy. *Maybe I am*, Jäger thought. He hadn't imagined anyone could hurt Germany as the Lizards had hurt it. Poland, France, and the Low Countries had gone down like ninepins. England fought on, but was walled away from Europe. And though the Soviet Union remained on its feet, Jäger was sure the Germans would have finished it by the end of 1942. The fighting south of Kharkov showed the Ivans hadn't learned much, no matter how many of them there were.

But the Lizards—the Lizards were an imponderable. They weren't the soldiers they might have been, but their gear was so good it didn't always matter. He'd found that out for himself, the hard way.

A faint buzz in the sky, far off to northward. Jäger's head whipped around. Any sky noise was alarming these days, doubly so when it might come from an almost invulnerable Lizard aircraft. This, though, was no Lizard plane. "Just one of the Ivans' flying sewing machines, Major—not worth jumping out of your skin for."

"Anything that's up there without a swastika on it makes me nervous."

"Can't blame you for that, I guess. But if we aren't safe from the Red Air Force here in the middle of a *kolkhoz*, we aren't safe anywhere." The tank gunner ran a hand along his gingery whiskers. "Of course, these days we really *aren't* safe anywhere."

The Soviet biplane didn't go into a strafing run, although Jäger saw it carried machine guns. It skimmed over the collective farm, a couple of hundred meters off the ground. Its little engine did indeed make a noise like a sewing machine running flat out.

The plane banked, turned in what looked like an impossibly tight circle, came back over the knot of people gathered around the two Germans. This time it flew lower. Several *kolkhozniks* waved up at the pilot, who was clearly visible in the open cockpit, goggles, leather flying helmet, and all.

The biplane banked once more, now north of the collective farm again. When it turned once more, it was plainly on a landing run. Dust spurted up as its wheels touched the ground. It bounced along, slowed to a stop.

"Don't know as how I like this, sir," Schultz said. "Dealing with the Russians here is one thing, but that plane, that's part of the Red Air Force. We shouldn't have anything to do with something connected to the Bolshevik government like that."

"I know we shouldn't, Sergeant, but everything's gone to hell since the Lizards got here," Jäger answered. "Besides, what choice have we?" Too many *kolkhozniks* carried guns to let him think about hijacking the toy plane with the red star on its flank, even assuming he knew how to fly it—which he didn't.

The pilot was climbing out of the plane, putting his booted foot in the stirrup on the side of the dusty fuselage below his seat. *His* boot, *his* seat? No, Jäger saw: a blond braid stuck out under the back of the flying helmet, and the cheeks under those goggles (now shoved up onto the top of the flying helmet) had never known—or needed—a razor. Even baggy flying clothes could not long conceal a distinctly unmasculine shape.

Schultz saw the same thing at the same time. His long jaw worked as if he were about to spit, but he had sense enough to remember where he was and think better of it. Disgust showed in his voice instead: "One of their damned girl fliers, sir."

"So she is." The pilot was coming their way. Jäger made the best of a situation worse than he really cared for: "Rather a pretty one, too."

Ludmila Gorbunova skimmed over the steppe, looking for Lizards or anything else interesting. No matter what she found, she wouldn't be able to report back to her base unless the emergency was great enough to make passing along her knowledge more important than coming home. Planes that used radios in flight all too often stopped flying immediately thereafter.

She was far enough south to start getting alert—and worried—when she spotted a crowd around a collective farm's core buildings at a time when most of the *kolkhozniks* should have been in the fields. That in itself wasn't so unusual, but then she caught a glint of light reflecting up from a couple of helmets. As the angle at which she viewed them shifted, she saw they were blackish gray, not the dun color she had expected.

Germans. Her lip twisted. What the Soviet government had to say about Germans had flip-flopped several times over the past few years. They'd gone from being bloodthirsty fascist beasts to peace-loving partners in the struggle against imperialism and then, on June 22, 1941, back to being beasts again, this time with a vengeance.

Ludmila heard the endless droning propaganda, noted when it changed, and changed her thinking accordingly. People who couldn't do that had a way of disappearing. Of course, for the past year the Germans themselves had been worse than any propaganda about them.

She wished that meant no one in the Soviet Union had anything good to think about the Nazis. The measure of Hitler's damnation was that imperialist England and the United States joined the Soviets in the struggle against him. The measure of the Soviet Union's damnation (though Ludmila did not think of it in those terms) was that so many Soviet citizens—Ukrainians, Baltic peoples, Byelorussians, Tatars, Cossacks, even Great Russians—collaborated with Hitler against Moscow.

Were these *kolkhozniks* collaborators, then? If they were, a quick pass with her machine guns would rid the world of a fair number of them. But the line from Radio Moscow on Germany had changed yet again since the Lizards came. They were not forgiven their crimes (no one who had fled from them would ever forgive their crimes), but they were at least human. If they cooperated with Soviet forces against the invaders from beyond the moon, they were not to be harmed.

So Ludmila's forefinger came off the firing button. She swung the *Kukuruznik* back toward the collective farm for a closer look. Sure enough, those were Germans down there. She decided to land and try to find out what they were up to.

Only when the U-2 was bumping along the ground to a stop did it occur to her that, if the *kolkhozniks* were collaborators, they would not want a report going back toward Moscow for eventual vengeance. She almost took off again, but chose to stay and see what she could.

The farmers and the Germans came toward her peacefully enough. She saw several weapons in the little crowd, but none pointed at her. The Germans kept their rifle and submachine guns slung.

"Who is the chief here?" she asked.

"I am, Comrade Pilot," said a fat little fellow who stood with his back very straight, as if to emphasize how important he was. "Kliment Yegorevich Pavlyuchenko, at your service."

She gave her own name and patronymic, watching this Pavlyuchenko with a wary eye. He'd spoken her fair and called her "comrade," but that did not mean he was to be trusted, not with two Germans at his elbow. She pointed at them. "How did they come to your collective farm, comrade? Do they speak any Russian?"

"The older one does, a word here and there, anyhow. The one with the red whiskers knows only how to eat. They must have been straggling a good while—they hadn't even heard about Berlin."

Both Germans looked at Pavlyuchenko when they heard the name of their capital. Ludmila studied them as if they really were a couple of dangerous beasts; she'd never before been close enough to see Hitlerites as individuals.

Rather to her surprise, they looked like neither the inhuman-seeming killing machines that had swept the Soviet armies east across a thousand kilometers of Russia and the Ukraine nor like Winter Fritz of recent propaganda, with a woman's shawl round his shoulders and an icicle dangling from his nose. They were just men, a little taller, a little skinnier, a little longer-faced than Russian norms, but just men all the same. She wrinkled her nose. They smelled like men, too, men who hadn't bathed any time lately.

The younger one, the bigger one, had a peasant look to him despite his foreign cast of feature. She could easily imagine him on a stool milking a cow or on his knees plucking weeds from a vegetable plot. The unabashed way he leered at her was peasantlike, too.

The other German was harder to fathom. He looked tired and clever at the same time, with pinched features that did not match the lined and sun-darkened skin of an outdoorsman. Like the red-whiskered one, he wore a helmet and an infantryman's blouse over the black trousers of panzer troops. The blouse had a private's plain shoulder straps, but she did not think it was part of the gear he'd started out with. He was too old and too sharp to make a proper private.

In secondary school, a million years before, she'd had a little German. This past year, she'd done her best to forget it, and hoped her transcript had perished when Kiev was lost: knowing the enemy's language could easily make one an object of suspicion. If these soldiers had little or no Russian, though, it would prove useful. She dredged a phrase out of her memory: *"Wie heissen Sie?"*

The Germans' worn, filthy faces lit up. Till now, they'd been nearly mute, tongue-tied among the Russians (which was also the root meaning of *Nemtsi*, the old Russian word for Germans—those who could make no intelligible sounds). The ginger-whiskered one grinned and said, *"Ich heisse* Feldwebel *Georg Schultz, Fräulein,"* and rattled off his pay number too fast for her to follow.

The older one said, *"Ich heisse Heinrich Jäger, Major,"* and also gave his number. She ignored it; it wasn't something she needed to know right now. The *kolkhozniks* murmured among themselves, either impressed she could speak to the *Wehrmacht* men in their own tongue or mistrustful of her for the same reason.

She wished she recalled more. She had to ask their unit by clumsy circumlocution: "From which group of men do you come?"

The sergeant started to answer; the major (his name meant "hunter," Ludmila thought; he certainly had a hunter's eyes) cleared his throat, which sufficed to make the younger man shut up. Jäger said, "Are we prisoners of war, Russian pilot? You may ask only certain things of prisoners of war." He spoke slowly, clearly, and simply; perhaps he recognized Ludmila's hesitancy with his language.

"Nyet," she answered, and then, *"Nein,"* in case he hadn't understood the Russian. He was nodding as she spoke, so evidently he had. She went on, "You are not prisoners of war. We fight the"—she perforce had to say *yasheritsi*, not knowing the German word for "Lizards"—"first. We fight Germans now only if Germans fight us. Not forget war against Germany, but put it to one side for now."

"Ah," the major said. "Yes, that is good. We fight the Lizards first also." (*Eidechsen* was what the German said. Ludmila made a mental note of it.) Jäger went on, "Since we have this common foe, I will tell you that we are from Sixteenth Panzer. I will also tell you that Schultz and I have together killed a Lizard panzer."

She stared at him. "This is true?" Radio Moscow made all sorts of claims of Lizard armor destroyed, but she had flown over too many battle-fields to take them seriously any more. She'd seen what was left of German panzer units that tried to take on the Lizards, too: not much. Were these tankmen lying to impress her with how masterful the Germans remained?

No, she decided after a moment of watching and listening to them. They described the action in too much vivid detail for her to doubt them: if they hadn't been through what they were talking about, they belonged on the stage, not in the middle of a collective farm. Most convincing of all was Jäger's mournful summary at the end: "We hurt them, but they wrecked us. All my company's tanks are gone."

"What are they saying, Comrade Pilot?" Pavlyuchenko demanded.

She quickly translated. The *kolkhozniks* gaped at the Germans as if they were indeed the superior beings they claimed to be. Their wide eyes made Ludmila want to kick them. Russians always looked on Germans with a peculiar mixture of envy and fear. Ever since the days of the Vi-kings, the Russian people had learned from more sophisticated Germanic folk to the west. And ever since the days of the Vikings, the Germanic peoples had looked to seize what they could from their Slavic neighbors. Teutonic Knights, Swedes, Prussians, Germans—the labels changed, but the Germanic push to the east seemed to go on forever. Though latest and worst, Hitler was but one of many.

Still, these particular Germans could be useful. They hadn't beaten the Lizards, far from it, but they'd evidently made them sit up and take notice. Soviet authorities needed to learn what they knew. Ludmila returned to their language: "I will take you with me when I fly back to my base, and send you on from there. I promise nothing bad will happen to you."

"What if we don't care to go?" asked the major—*Jäger*, she reminded herself.

She did her best to put authority in her gaze. "If you do not go, you will at best wander on foot and alone. Maybe you will find Lizards. Maybe you will find Russians who think you are worse than Lizards. Maybe these *kolkhozniks* are only waiting for you to fall asleep . . ."

The panzer major was a cool customer. He did not turn to give Kliment Pavlyuchenko a once-over, which meant he'd already formed his judgment of the chief. He did say, "Why should I trust your promises? I've seen the bodies of Germans you Russians caught. They ended up with their noses and ears cut off, or worse. How do I know Sergeant Schultz and I won't wind up the same way?"

The injustice of that almost choked Ludmila. "If you Nazi swine hadn't invaded our country, we never would have harmed a one of you.

I've seen with my own eyes what you do to the part of the Soviet Union you took. You should have everything you get."

She glared at Jäger. He glared back. Then Georg Schultz surprised her—and, by his expression, the major as well—by saying, *"Krieg ist Scheisse*—war is shit." He surprised her again when he came up with two Russian words, *"Voina—gavno,"* which meant the same thing.

"Da!" the *kolkhozniks* roared as one. They crowded round the sergeant, slapping his back, pressing cigarettes and coarse *makhorka* tobacco into his hands and tunic pockets. All at once, he was not an enemy to them, but a human being.

Turning back to Jäger, Ludmila pointed at the *kolkhozniks* and the gunner. "This is why we have stopped fighting Germans who do not fight us, and why I can say no harm will come to you. Germany and Soviet Union are enemies, *da*. People and Lizards are worse enemies."

"You speak well, and, as you say, we have little choice." Jäger pointed to her faithful *Kukuruznik*. "Will that ugly little thing carry three?"

"Not with comfort, but yes," she answered, stifling her anger at the adjective he'd chosen.

One corner of his mouth tugged upward in an expression she had trouble interpreting: a smile, she supposed, but not like any she'd seen on a Russian face, more like a dry white wine than a simple vodka. He said, "How do you know that, once we get into the air, we will not make you fly us toward German lines?"

"I do not have the petrol to reach the nearest I know of," she said. "Also, the most you can make me do is fly into the ground and kill us. I will not fly west."

He studied her for perhaps half a minute, that curious, ironic smile still on his face. Slowly, he nodded. "You are a soldier."

"Yes," she said, and found she had to return the compliment. "And you. So you must understand why we need to learn how you killed a Lizard panzer."

"Wasn't hard," Schultz put in. "They have wonderful panzers to ride around in, *ja*, but they're even worse tankmen than you Ivans."

Had he said that in Russian, he would have forfeited the goodwill he'd won from the *kolkhoz's* farmers. As it was, Ludmila gave him a dirty look. So did Kliment Pavlyuchenko, who seemed to have a smattering of German.

"He is right," Jäger said, which distressed Ludmila more, for she was convinced the major's judgment needed to be taken seriously. "You cannot deny our panzer troops have more skills than yours, Pilot"—he gave the word a feminine ending—"or we could never have advanced in our Panzer IIIs against your KVs and T-34s. The Lizards have even less skill than you Russians, but their tanks are so good, they do not need much. If we had comparable equipment, we would slaughter them."

So here is German arrogance at first hand, Ludmila thought. Having admitted the Lizards had smashed his unit to bits, all the panzer major cared to talk about was the foe's shortcomings. Ludmila said, "Since our equipment is unfortunately not a match for theirs, how do we go about fighting them?"

"*Das ist die Frage,*" Sergeant Schultz said solemnly, for all the world like a Nazi Hamlet.

Jäger's mouth quirked up once more. This time, he raised an eyebrow, too. Ludmila found herself smiling back, if only to show that she'd noticed the allusion and was no uncultured peasant. The German turned serious: "We must find places and situations where they cannot use to best advantage all they have."

"As the partisans fight behind your lines?" Ludmila asked, hoping to flick him on a raw spot.

But he only nodded. "Exactly so. We are all partisans now, when set against the forces we aim to oppose."

Somehow, his refusal to take offense irritated her. Brusquely, she pointed back toward her airplane. "The two of you will have to go into the front cabin side by side. Keep your machine pistols if you like; I do not try to take your arms away. But, Sergeant, I hope you will leave your rifle behind here. It will not"—she had to pantomime the word "fit"—"in a small space, and may help the *kolkhozniks* against the Lizards."

Schultz glanced to Jäger. Ludmila eased fractionally when she saw the major give an almost invisible nod. Schultz presented the Mauser to Kliment Pavlyuchenko with a flourish. Startled at first, the collective farm chief folded him into a bear hug. When the sergeant broke free, he went through his pockets for every round of rifle ammunition he could find. Then he set a foot in the stirrup and climbed up into the U-2.

Jäger followed him a moment later. The space into which they were crammed was so tight that they ended up sitting half facing each other, each with an arm around the other's back. "Would you care to kiss me, sir?" Schultz asked. Jäger snorted.

Ludmila had the back cabin, the one with working controls, to herself. At her shouted direction, a *kolkhoznik* spun the little biplane's prop. The sturdy radial engine buzzed to life. The two Germans set their jaws against the noise but otherwise ignored it. She remembered they had their own intimate acquaintance with engine noise.

When she saw all the peasants were clear of her takeoff path, she released the brakes, eased the stick forward. The *Kukuruznik* needed a longer run than she'd expected before it labored into the air. A sedate performer under the best of conditions, it was positively sluggish—or, better, sluglike—with more than three times the usual crew weight aboard. But it flew. The collective farm receded behind it as it made its slow way north.

■

"Be alert for Big Uglies, both of you," Krentel warned from the cupola of the landcruiser.

"It shall be done, commander," Ussmak agreed. The driver wished the male newly in charge of the landcruiser would shut up and let the crew do their jobs.

"It shall be done," Telerep echoed. Ussmak envied the way the gunner could keep the faintest hint of scorn from his voice. What Telerep had to say privately about Krentel would addle an egg, but he was all respect when the landcruiser commander was around.

Males of the Race learned to show respect from their smallest days, but Telerep was unusually smooth even by that high standard. Maybe, Ussmak thought, his low-voiced gibes about Krentel were a reaction to the need for public deference. Or maybe not. Telerep had never talked that way about Votal when the previous commander was alive.

Thinking about Votal made Ussmak think about the Big Uglies who had killed him, and did more to make him alert than all of Krentel's warnings. The natives of Tosev 3 had learned in a hurry that they could not oppose the Race landcruiser against landcruiser, aircraft against aircraft. That lesson should have marked the end of conquest and the beginning of consolidation. So officers had promised the males of the invasion force when battle commenced.

The promises had not come true. The Big Uglies stopped throwing hordes of males and landcruisers and planes into the grinder to be minced up, but they hadn't stopped fighting. Thus this landcruiser squadron kept rolling over the broad, cool steppeland of the SSSR, seeking to flush out a band of Tosevite raiders and bushwhackers who had shown up on a reconnaissance photo the day before.

A wail from the sky— "Rockets!" Telerep shrieked. Ussmak had already slammed the hatch shut over his head. A moment later, a metallic clang in the button taped to his hearing diaphragm announced that Krentel had done the same. Ussmak twiddled his fingers in approval: previous appearances to the contrary notwithstanding, the new commander wasn't a complete idiot.

The salvo of rockets slammed down all around the landcruisers. Their warheads kicked up great gouts of earth, blinding one of Ussmak's vision slits. Closed in as he suddenly was, he couldn't hear very much, but he knew he would have heard a landcruiser going up. When he didn't, he took it for a good sign.

Krentel, meanwhile, had been on the command circuit with base. "The range of the launcher is 2,200, bearing 42," he reported. "Gunner, send the Big Uglies back there two rounds of high explosive. That will make them think twice about harassing the Race again."

"Two rounds of high explosive. It shall be done," Telerep said tonelessly. The turret spun in its ring until it faced more nearly south than west. The big gun barked twice. Two or three of the other landcruisers in the squadron also fired, though none more than once.

Ussmak thought all those commanders fools, and Krentel a double fool. He doubted the Big Uglies who had fired the salvo were anywhere near their launcher any more; if they had any sense, they'd have touched it off with a long electric wire. That's what he would have done in their place, certainly. And they made better guerrillas than stand-up soldiers.

Krentel told him, "Shift to bearing 42, driver. I want to finish off that clutch of bandits. They shall not flourish within the bounds of territory controlled by the Race."

"Bearing 42. It shall be done," Ussmak said. He swung the landcruiser almost in a half circle, drove back in a direction close to the one from which the squadron had advanced. This time, he admitted to himself, Krentel had a point.

"Watch the ground carefully," the commander added. "We must not risk driving over a mine. Our landcruiser, like every other, is precious to the Race and its expansion. Exert unusual caution."

"It shall be done," Ussmak repeated. He wished Krentel would stop jumping around like a female waiting for her first pair of eggs. How was he supposed to get a good look at the ground while driving buttoned up? He didn't want to open his hatch, not yet. The Big Uglies had a habit of lobbing a second rocket salvo just about when males were taking a deep breath after the first one.

Even if his head was out in the open, he didn't think he'd spot a buried mine. The Tosevites were extraordinarily good at concealing them under leaves or stones or chunks of the rubble that littered the area from previous battles. He took comfort in remembering the Tosevite mines were designed to disable the weak and clumsy landcruisers the Big Uglies built. Even if one exploded right under his own machine, it might not wreck it. Looking at it with the other eye turret, though, it might.

Sure enough, more rockets rained down on the squadron. Krentel must have reopened the hatch at the top of his cupola, for Ussmak heard him slam it again in a hurry. The driver opened his jaws in amusement. No, the new commander wasn't as smart as he thought he was. With luck, he'd learn.

A clump of low Tosevite trees, their colors duller than the ones of Home, stood by the landcruisers' path about halfway to the place from which the natives had touched off their rockets. Ussmak thought about warning Telerep to fix his machine gun on those trees, but decided not to. Telerep knew his business perfectly well. And besides—

"Watch those trees, gunner." Before Ussmak could finish thinking Krentel would give the unnecessary order, Krentel gave it.

"It shall be done, commander." Again Telerep's subordination was perfect.

Ussmak watched the trees, too. Just because the order was unnecessary didn't make it stupid. If he were a Big Ugly bandit, he'd post males in those trees to see what he could do about the Race's landcruisers. In fact . . .

If Krentel had been reading his mind before, now Telerep was. The gunner fired a burst into the little stretch of wood. With luck, he'd kill a Big Ugly or two and flush out some more. Ussmak wouldn't have wanted to crouch in hiding while bullets snarled through the trees searching for him.

And sure enough, he spied motion at the edge of the trees. So did Telerep. Tracers walked the machine gun toward it. Then Ussmak shouted, "Hold fire!" The stream of bullets had already stopped: Telerep did know his business.

Krentel didn't. "Why are you holding?" he demanded angrily.

"It's not a Big Ugly, commander, just one of the animals they keep for pets," the gunner answered in soothing tones. "Be a waste of ammunition to kill it. Besides, for a creature covered with fuzz, it's not even that homely."

"Yes it is," Krentel said. Ussmak sided with Telerep. He'd seen several of these animals now, and thought them far more handsome than their masters. They were lean and graceful, obviously descended from hunting beasts. They were also friendly; he'd heard that a couple of males from another squadron had used raw meat to tame one and get a pet of their own.

"I still think we ought to kill it," Krentel said.

"Oh, please, no, commander," Ussmak and Telerep said in the same breath. The gunner added, "See how nice a creature it is? It's coming straight toward us, even though we're in a big noisy landcruiser."

"That doesn't make it nice," Krentel said. "That makes it stupid, if you ask me." But he did not order Telerep to kill the Tosevite animal.

Taking the commander's silence as consent, Ussmak slowed the landcruiser to let the animal approach. That seemed to please it; it opened its mouth, almost as if it were a male of the Race, laughing. Ussmak knew it was making sharp yelping noises, even if he couldn't hear them through the landcruiser's armor. The animal ran right for the machine.

That gave Ussmak pause; maybe it really was stupid, as Krentel had said. Then the driver noticed it had a square package strapped onto its back, a package with a cylindrical rod sticking straight up from it. He'd never seen one of these beasts so accoutered before, and didn't trust it. "Telerep!" he said sharply, "I think you'd better shoot it after all."

"What? Why?" the gunner said. "It—" He must have spotted the package the Tosevite animal was carrying, for the machine gun started to chatter in the middle of his sentence.

Too late. By then the animal was very close to the landcruiser. With a sudden burst of speed, it ran under the right track, even though Ussmak tried to swerve away at the last instant. The strapped-on mine exploded even as the animal was crushed to red pulp.

Ussmak felt as if he'd been kicked in the base of the tail by a Big Ugly wearing solid-iron foot coverings. The landcruiser's right corner lifted up, then slammed back to the ground. Hot fragments of metal flew all around the driver; one buried itself in his arm. He screeched, then started to choke as fire-fighting foam gushed into the compartment.

He opened and closed his hand. That hurt, but he could still use it. He tried the landcruiser's controls. The tiller jerked; a horrible grinding noise came from the right side of the machine. He snapped his jaws in fury, swore as foully as he knew how. Then he realized Krentel and Telerep were both screaming into his audio button: "What happened? Are you all right? Is the landcruiser all right?"

"We had a track blown off, may the spirits of the Emperors of blessed memory curse the Tosevites forevermore," Ussmak answered. He sucked in another breath that stank of foam, then spoke more formally: "Commander, this landcruiser is disabled. I suggest that we have no choice but to abandon it." He flipped up the hatch over his head.

"Let it be done," Krentel agreed. His voice turned vicious. "I told you to slaughter that Tosevite beast." That he'd been right made the rebuke sting worse. As far as Ussmak was concerned, it didn't make him a better landcruiser commander.

The driver pulled himself up and out of the compartment. It wasn't easy; his bleeding right arm didn't want to bear its share of his weight. He scrambled down behind the left side of the landcruiser. He would have liked to find out just what the mine had done to the other track and sprocket, but not enough to go around to the side exposed to the trees. That animal hadn't been a wandering stray, not with a mine strapped to its back. Somewhere in the copse lay Big Uglies with guns. He was as sure of it as he was of his own name, or the Emperor's.

Sure enough, bullets began snapping by, pinging off the armor of the landcruiser. Krentel let out a hiss of pain. "Are you all right, Commander?" Ussmak said. He still didn't think Krentel was fit to carry Votal's equipment bag, but the new landcruiser commander remained a male of the Race.

"No, I'm not all right," Krentel snapped. "How can I be all right with a hole in my arm and two crewmales who are mental defectives?"

"I regret your arm is wounded," Ussmak said. He wished the commander had been hit in the head instead. Those of lower rank gave unswerving deference to their superiors; that was the way of the Race. But the way of the Race defined obligations that ran in the other direction, too. Superiors gave underlings respect in exchange for their loyalty. Those who didn't often brought misfortune on themselves.

Along with Ussmak and Krentel, Telerep also huddled behind the protective flank of the landcruiser. He waggled his left eye, the one that faced Ussmak, back and forth to show he was thinking along with the driver. Krentel remained oblivious to the dismay he caused his crew.

A couple of the other landcruisers in the squadron slowed down, poured suppressive fire into the trees. The hail of bullets and high-explosive shells was so intense that the wood caught fire. But when Ussmak dashed away to scramble into the landcruiser that had pulled up behind his own wounded machine, Tosevite bullets flew all around him.

He heard one of those bullets strike home with a dull, horribly final-sounding smack. He couldn't look back; he was scrambling through the front hull hatch, almost falling down on top of the other landcruiser's driver. That male swore. "One of your crewmales just got hit. He won't get up, either."

"Was it—?" But it wasn't, Ussmak knew, for there was Krentel, nattering away over nothing in particular up in the turret. *Telerep*, the driver thought with a surge of pain. They'd been together all through training; they'd awakened from cold sleep side by side, within moments of each other; with Votal they'd fought their landcruiser across this seemingly endless plain. Now Votal was dead, and the landcruiser, and Telerep. And there was Krentel, nattering.

"The Big Uglies are getting too stinking good at this ambush business," the driver of the other landcruiser said.

Ussmak didn't answer. He'd never felt so completely alone. Among the Race, one always knew one's place in the mosaic, and the places of those all around one. Now all those around Ussmak were gone like fallen tesserae, and he felt himself rattling around in the middle of a void.

The landcruiser grunted into motion once more, and sensibly so. No point to staying still an instant longer than needed; the Tosevites didn't need more than a moment to work the most appalling mischief. As the armored fighting vehicle built up speed, Ussmak began to rattle around literally as well as in the bitter corners of his mind.

Here, though, he was not in the middle of a void. The driver's compartment barely had room to hold an extra male. Worse, everything from foam spray nozzle to the bracket that held the driver's personal weapon on the wall was hard and had sharp edges. He'd never noticed that while he was in the driver's chair. The chair, of course, had padding and safety belts to hold him where he belonged. Now he was just jetsam, tossed in here at random.

"Too bad about your other crewmale," the other driver said as he shoved the landcruiser up into the next higher gear. "How did your machine get hit?"

So Ussmak had to tell him about the Tosevite animal with the mine on its back, and how a moment's kindness had cost so much. He felt half-strangled as he spoke; he couldn't begin to say what he thought about either Krentel or Telerep, not even to a male who was a squadronmate. He hissed helplessly. That void around him again . . .

The driver hissed, too. "Yes, I know the beasts you mean. We haven't bothered them, either. Now I suppose we'll have to shoot them on sight, if the eggless Big Uglies have taken to strapping mines on their backs. Too bad."

"Yes," Ussmak said, and fell silent again. Rattle, rattle, rattle . . .

A little later, the driver of the other landcruiser made a sharp, disgusted noise. "They're gone," he said.

Recalled to himself, Ussmak asked, "Who's gone?" He had no vision slits, not in his present awkward perch, and no way of seeing outside.

"The Big Uglies. All that's here is a couple of wrecked launcher boxes for their stinking rockets. Not even any dead ones lying around. They must have touched them off at long range, then run away." The driver clicked off the intercom switch that connected him to the turret before he added one quiet sentence more: "This whole trip back here was for nothing."

For nothing. The words reverberated inside Ussmak's head. For nothing Krentel had ordered them to turn around. For nothing his landcruiser had been wrecked. For nothing Telerep had caught a bullet. For nothing Ussmak huddled here on a steel and ceramic floor, about as useful to the Race as the sack of dried meat he felt like. For nothing.

The other driver, still secure in his web of duties rather than all alone and falling, let out a sigh of both annoyance and—infuriating to Ussmak—resignation. "So it goes," he said.

Two or three times, in his travels through the bush leagues, Sam Yeager had had to dig in at the plate against every hitter's nightmare: a fireballing kid who couldn't find the plate if you lit it up like Times Square. Whenever he did it, he faced a deadly weapon. At the time, he hadn't thought about it in quite those terms, but it was true. The worst sound in baseball was the mushy *splat* of a ball getting somebody in the head. He'd seen friends lose careers in an instant of inattention and bad lights. He knew it was only luck he hadn't lost his the same way.

All that helped now, against weapons more overtly deadly. When bombs and bullets flew, a tin hat seemed small protection. For that matter, a tin hat *was* small protection. Yeager had seen more than one man gruesomely dead, helmet holed or smashed in or simply blown right off. But he wore his gladly, as better than nothing. Come to that, he wouldn't have minded wearing it, or even something that covered rather more, whenever he went to bat against a hard-throwing righthander.

He peeked up from behind the blackened pile of bricks which until recently had been the back wall of a dry-cleaning establishment; its sign lay fallen in the middle of Main Street. He ducked down again in a hurry. A Lizard autogiro was growling through the air toward him. The Invaders from Space (he thought of them that way, with the capital letters) were trying to push the ragtag American force of which he was a part out of Amboy and trap them against the Green River, where there'd be easy prey.

When he said that out loud, Mutt Daniels grunted and answered, "Reckon you're right, boy, but we're gonna have the devil's own time stoppin' 'em."

A roar in the sky—Yeager automatically threw himself flat. He'd learned that even before he took the soldier's oath, and had it reinforced when a fellow a few feet from him got smashed to a red smear for being a split second too slow to hit the dirt.

But the roar came from two piston-engined fighters that streaked west toward the autogiro. The machine guns of the P-40 Warhawks hammered.

Yeager stuck his head up again. The autogiro was firing back, and turning in midair to try to flee. The Lizards' jets far outclassed anything humanity could make, but their flying troop carriers were vulnerable.

The Warhawks whizzed past the autogiro, one to the right, the other to the left. They banked into tight turns for another firing pass, but no need. The Lizard machine, spurting smoke from just below the rotor, settled to the ground in what was half landing, half crash. The fighters darted away before anything more dangerous appeared over the horizon.

Yeager scowled to see live Lizards scuttling out of the autogiro. "They left too soon," he growled. "It wasn't a clean kill."

Mutt Daniels worked the bolt on his Springfield to chamber a new round. "Means it's up to us, don't it?" Moving with a grace that belied his fleshy form, he scuttled forward.

Yeager followed. He also had a rifle now, taken from a man who would never need one again. Back on the farm where he'd grown up, he'd shot at tin cans and gophers and the occasional crow with his father's .22. The military weapon he carried now was heavier and kicked harder, but that wasn't the main difference from those vanished days. When he shot at tin cans or gophers or crows, they didn't shoot back.

A heavy machine gun began to bark, up near the intersection of Main Street and Highway 52. Pieces flew off the Lizards' autogiro and sparkled in the sunlight as they twirled through the air. As for the Lizards themselves, they took cover with the speed and alacrity of their small reptilian namesakes. One by one, they opened fire. Their weapons chewed out short bursts, not the endless racket of a belt-fed machine gun, but not single shots, either.

Was that a flicker of motion, over there behind the ornamental hedge? Yeager didn't care to find out the hard way. He threw his rifle to his shoulder and fired. He scurried away to a new position before he looked toward the hedge again. Nothing moved there now.

Another rumble in the air, this one from the southwest . . . Yeager fired at the incoming autogiro, but it stayed out of rifle range. Flame shot from under its stubby wings. With a cry of fear, Yeager buried his face in grass and mud.

The rockets burst all around him, lances of fire that lashed the American position. The heavy machine gun fell silent. Through stunned ears, Yeager heard the Lizards on the ground moving forward.

Then another roar announced that the Warhawks had returned. Their guns tore at the new autogiro. This time they did the job right. The aircraft slammed the ground sideways and became a fireball. Smoke rose into the blue sky. It was less smoke than would have come from a human-built plane; the Lizards used cleaner fuel. But fuel wasn't all that burned in there. Seats, paint, ammunition, the bodies of the crew . . . they all went up.

Cheering, the Americans moved forward against the Lizards. "Careful there, you God-damned fools!" Sergeant Schneider bellowed, trying to shout over battlefield din. "You want to stay low." As if to underscore the advice, someone who hadn't stayed low enough suddenly pitched forward onto his face.

The Warhawks came back to strafe the Lizards on the ground. Something rose on a pillar of fire from behind a boulder in the middle of a Main Street lawn that marked a spot where Lincoln had spoken. The P-40 fled, twisting with all the skill the pilot had. It was not enough. The rocket tumbled it from the sky.

"Damn if it didn't look like a Fourth of July skyrocket, right down to the big boom at the end," Daniels said.

"It flew like it had eyes," Yeager said, thinking of the turning path the rocket had scrawled across the sky. "I wonder how they make it do that."

"Right now I got more important things to wonder about, like if I'm gonna be alive this time tomorrow," Mutt said.

Yeager nodded, but his bump of curiosity still itched. Writers in *Astounding* and the other pulps had talked about detection devices for as long as he'd been reading them, and likely longer than that. He'd discovered on the night the Invaders from Space descended on the world that living through science fiction was a lot stranger—and a lot more deadly—than just reading it.

A hiss in the sky, a whistle, a noise like a train pulling into a station—an artillery shell burst among the embattled Lizards, then another and another. Dirt fountained skyward. The enemy's fire slackened. Yeager didn't know whether the Lizards were killed or hurt or just playing possum, but he used the lull to slide closer to them . . . and also closer to where the shells were landing. He wished he hadn't thought of that, but kept crawling ahead.

A Lizard plane shot past, heading east. Yeager cringed, but the pilot wasted no time on a target as trivial as infantry. No doubt he wanted that battery of field guns. The shells kept coming for about another minute, maybe two, then abruptly stopped.

By that time, though, Yeager and the other Americans were on top of the Lizard position. "Surrender!" Sergeant Schneider shouted. Yeager was sure he was wasting his breath; where would the Lizards have learned English? And even if they had, would they quit? They seemed more like Japs than any other people Yeager knew of—at least, they were small and liked sneak attacks. Japs didn't surrender for hell, so would the Lizards?

One of them had got some English, God knew where. "No—ssrenda," came the reply, a dry hiss that made the hair stand up on Yeager's arms. A burst of machine-rifle fire added an exclamation point.

The burst was close, close. Yeager grabbed a grenade, pulled the pin, lobbed it as if he were aiming for a cutoff man. It flew toward the concrete block fence behind which he thought the Lizard who didn't want to surrender was hiding. He didn't see it go over. By the time it did, he was behind his own cover once more. He hadn't needed more than one or two bullets snapping past his head to learn that lesson forever.

The grenade went off with a crash. Before the echoes died, Yeager sprinted up to the gray fence. He fired over it, once, twice, blindly. If the Lizard wasn't badly hurt, he wanted to rattle it as much as he could. Then, gulping, he vaulted over the fence into the alleyway on the other side.

The Lizard was down and thrashing and horribly wounded; its red, red blood stained the gravel of the alley. Yeager's stomach did a slow, lazy loop. He'd never expected the agony of a creature from another world to reach him, but it did. The Lizard yammered something in its own incomprehensible language. Yeager had no idea whether it was defiance or a plea for mercy. All he wanted to do was put the alien out of its misery and make it be quiet. He raised his rifle, shot it through the head.

It twitched once or twice, then lay still. Yeager let out a whistling sigh of relief; he'd thought too late that it didn't necessarily have to store its brains in its head. He wondered if that would have occurred to any of the men fighting around him. Probably not; science-fiction readers were thin on the ground. As things worked out, it hadn't mattered anyway.

He bent over the scaly corpse, scooped up the machine rifle the Lizard had carried. He was amazed at how light it was. Somebody, he thought, would have to take it apart and figure out how it worked.

Sergeant Schneider yelled again: "Surrender, you Lizards! Throw down your guns! Give up and we won't hurt you."

Yeager thought he was wasting his breath, but the bursts of enemy fire quickly ceased. Schneider came out in the open with something white—it was a by-God pillowcase, Yeager saw—tied to his rifle. He waved toward the houses and stores in which the last few Lizards were holed up, then made a peremptory gesture no human could have misunderstood: *come out.*

From behind Yeager, Mutt Daniels said, "He oughta get the Medal of Honor for that." Yeager nodded, trying not to show how shaken he was; he hadn't heard his manager—no, his ex-manager now, he supposed—come up at all.

Sergeant Schneider simply stood and waited, his big feet splayed apart, his belly hanging over his belt. He looked as though he would have made three of the dead Lizard sprawled by Yeager; he looked hard and tough and quintessentially human. Seeing him defy the Lizards' machine rifles, Yeager felt tears sting under the lids of his eyes. He was proud to belong to a people that could produce such a man.

After the hammering racket of battle, silence seemed strange, wrong, almost frightening. The eerie pause hung in the balance for almost half a minute. Then a door opened in one of the houses from which the Lizards had been fighting. Without conscious thought on Yeager's part, his rifle snapped toward it. Schneider held up a hand, ordering the Americans not to shoot.

A Lizard came slowly through the doorway. He hadn't dropped his weapon, but held it reversed, by the barrel. Like Sergeant Schneider, he'd fastened something white to the other end. The shape was familiar to Yeager, but he needed a moment to place it. All at once, he bent double in a guffaw.

"What is it?" Mutt Daniels asked.

Between chuckles, Yeager wheezed, "First time I ever saw anybody make a flag of truce out of a pair of women's panties."

"Huh?" Mutt stared, then started laughing, too.

If the improvised white flag amused Sergeant Schneider, he didn't let on. He gestured again: *come here*. The Lizard came, moving with careful deliberation rather than his kind's usual quick skitter. When he got within about twenty feet of Schneider, the sergeant pointed to his machine rifle, then to the ground. He did it two or three times before the Lizard, even more hesitantly than before, set the weapon down.

Schneider made another *come here* gesture. The Lizard came. It flinched when he put an arm around it, but it did not flee. It came up to only the middle of his chest. Schneider turned to where the rest of the Lizards were holed up. "You see? No harm will come to you. Surrender!"

"Jesus, they're really doing it," Yeager whispered.

"Looks that way, don't it?" Mutt Daniels whispered back.

The Lizards emerged from their hiding places. There were only five more of them, Yeager saw, and two of those were wounded, leaning on their fellows. The Lizard who had surrendered first called something to them all. The three with machine rifles set them down.

"What are we going to do with hurt Lizards?" Yeager asked. "If they're proper prisoners of war, we have to try and take care of them, but do we yell for a medic or a vet? Hell, I don't even know if they can eat our food."

"I don't know either, and frankly, I don't give a damn." Round and pudgy and filthy, Mutt made a most unlikely Rhett Butler. He shifted the plug in his cheek, spat, and went on, "It's right nice, though, havin' prisoners of their'n, not so much on account of what they can tell us but to keep 'em honest with all of our people they got."

"Something to that." Yeager wondered what had happened to the rest of the Decatur Commodores. Nothing good, he feared, remembering how the Lizards had strafed their train. The invaders could do whatever they pleased throughout big stretches of the United States. If holding prisoners—hostages—would help restrain them, Yeager was all for it.

Along with the rest of the Americans, he hurried forward at Sergeant Schneider's waved command to take charge of the alien POWs. Having surrendered, the Lizards seemed abjectly submissive, hurrying to obey the soldiers' gestures as best they could. Even to Invaders from Space, *come along* and *this way* were easy enough to put across.

Schneider seemed convinced the band he led—with everything from officers to weapons to organization in short supply, slapping a more formally military name than that on it was optimistic—had done something important. "We want to get these scaly sons of bitches out of here and back up to Ashton just as fast as we can, before more of 'em come along." He told off half a dozen men: "You, you, you, you, you, and you." Yeager was the fourth "you," Mutt Daniels the fifth. "Get back to the bus that brought us here and take 'em away on it. The rest of us'll dig in and hope we see more men before the Lizards decide to push harder. Good Lord willing, you can drop 'em off and head down this way again inside a couple of hours. Now get your butts in gear."

Flanked by men with loaded, bayonet-tipped rifles, the Lizards picked their way through and over debris toward the yellow school bus that had been pressed into service as a troop hauler. Yeager would have preferred the dignity of a proper khaki Army truck, but up at Ashton, a school bus was what they had.

The key was still in the bus ignition. Otto Chase looked at it with a certain amount of apprehension. "Anybody here able to drive this big honking thing?" the onetime cement-plant worker asked.

"I reckon Sam and I just might be able to handle it," Mutt Daniels said with a sidelong glance at Yeager. The ballplayer puffed up his cheeks like a chipmunk to hold in his laughter. After half a lifetime bouncing around in buses, helping to repair them by the side of the road, pushing them when they broke down, there wasn't a whole lot about them he didn't know.

Mutt, moreover, had been bouncing around in buses essentially ever since there were buses. If there was anything about them he didn't know, Yeager had no idea what it was. Daniels waited for the rest of the men to herd the Lizards to the wide rear seat, then started the engine, turned the bus around in a street most people would have thought too narrow for turning around a bus, and headed back to Ashton.

He stayed off Highway 52 and Highway 30, preferring the backcountry roads less likely to draw attention from the air. Raising his voice to be heard over the noise of the motor, he said, "Reminds me of the country just back of the front line in France in 1918, right where the Boches got farthest. Parts of it are all tore up, but you go fifty yards on and you'd swear nobody ever heard o' war."

The description was apt, Yeager thought. Most of the farms that sprawled among belts of forest between Amboy and Ashton were untouched. Men wearing wide-brimmed hats and overalls worked in several fields; cows grazed here and there, black and white splotches vivid against the cheerful green of grass and growing crops. By the calm way life went on, the nearest Lizard might have been ten billion light-years off.

But every so often, the bus would rattle past a bomb or shell crater, an ugly brown scar on the land's smooth green skin. There were cattle by those craters, too, cattle on their sides bloating under the warm summer sun. And a couple of the neat frame farm buildings were neither neat nor buildings any longer, but more like a giant's game of pick-up-sticks. Fat crows, startled by the bus' racket, flapped into the air, cawing resentment at having their feasting interrupted.

Still, as Mutt had said, the eye could mostly forget the war whose border the bus had just left behind. The nose had a harder time. Yeager wondered if the faint reek of smoke and corruption simply clung to him, the other Americans, and the Lizards; if it came in through the open windows of the bus from the lightly damaged countryside through which they were driving; or if the breeze, which was out of the west, swept it along the front line.

The four unwounded Lizards did what they could for the two who were hurt. It wasn't much; the humans had stripped them of the belts that along with their helmets were all they wore—no telling what deadly marvels they might have concealed inside.

Yeager had never thought about how Invaders from Space might feel if they were wounded and captured by humans who were as alien to them as they were to people. They didn't look all-powerful or supremely evil. They just looked worried. In their shoes (if they'd worn shoes), he would have been worried, too.

He picked up one of the belts, started opening pouches. Before long, he found what looked like a bandage, wrapped in some clear stuff smoother and more pliable than cellophane. If it concealed a deadly marvel, he decided, he'd eat his helmet. He pushed past the rest of the Americans—who still had their rifles leveled at the Lizards—and held out the bandage pack.

"What the hell you doing?" Otto Chase growled. "Who cares whether them damn things live or die?"

"If they're prisoners of war, we're supposed to treat 'em decent," Yeager answered. "Besides, they hold a lot more of our kind than we do of theirs. Tormenting 'em might not be what you call smart."

Chase grunted and subsided. The Lizards' eyes swiveled from Yeager's face to the bandage and back again. They reminded him of the chameleon he'd seen at the zoo in—was it Salt Lake? Maybe Spokane. Whichever, it was a long time ago now.

One of the Lizards took the bandage pack in its small hand. As it used its claws to tear open the wrapping, it hissed something at Yeager. It and all its companions, even the two injured ones, lowered their turreted eyes to the floor of the bus for a second or two. Then it deftly began to bandage a gash in a wounded Lizard's flank.

"Paw through those belts," Yeager said over his shoulder. "See if you can find some more bandages." He was afraid the others would argue more, but they didn't. He heard their feet shift. Somebody—he didn't look back to see who—handed him another pack and then another. He passed them on to the Lizards.

By the time the bus pulled up in front of the Mills and Petrie Memorial Center in Ashton, the injured Lizards were swathed in enough gauze to make them look like something halfway between real wounded soldiers and Boris Karloff as the Mummy. Men in Army khaki, civilian denim and plaid flannel, and every possible combination thereof milled around in front of the stone and yellow brick building.

Through the open driver's window, Mutt Daniels yelled, "We got Lizard prisoners in here. What the devil we supposed to do with 'em?"

That drew all the attention he wanted and then some. People converged on the school bus at a dead run. Some pushing and elbowing followed, as men of higher rank made those below them give way. The first officer who actually got into the bus was a full colonel, the highest-ranking fellow Yeager had seen in Ashton (when he'd joined up a couple of weeks before, Sergeant Schneider had been the highest-ranking soldier in Ashton).

"Tell me how you took them, soldier," he said in a drawl almost as thick as Mutt's. "They're some of the very first Lizard captives we've managed to get our hands on."

"Yes, sir, Colonel Collins," Daniels answered, reading the name badge on the officer's right breast pocket. He ended up telling only part of the story, though, for the rest of the men, Yeager among them, kept interrupting with details of their own. Sam knew that wasn't showing proper military discipline, but he didn't care. If this Colonel Collins, whoever he was, didn't want to listen to Americans speaking their minds, to hell with him.

Collins listened without complaint. When the story was done, he said, "You boys had the luck of the devil—I hope you know that. Hadn't been for those Warhawks takin' out the enemy helicopters" (*So that's the right name for them*, Yeager thought), "you could've had a mighty thin time of it."

The colonel strode down the center aisle of the bus to get a closer look at the Lizards; like almost everyone else in the still free part of the United States, he hadn't yet really seen any of them. He brushed past Yeager, studied the prisoners for a couple of minutes, then turned back to their captors. "Don't look like so much, do they?"

"No, sir," Yeager said, in chorus with the other Americans. Collins, he thought, looked like quite a lot. The colonel was about Mutt's age, but with that and their accents the resemblance between them ceased. Collins was tall, still slim, handsome, with a full head of silver hair. He didn't keep a chaw in his cheek. Without the uniform, Yeager would have guessed him a politician, say, the mayor of a medium-sized and prosperous city.

He said, "You boys did somethin' special here; I'll see you're all promoted for it."

All the men grinned. Mutt said, "Sergeant Schneider, back there in Amboy, he deserves a big part o' the credit, sir." Yeager nodded vigorously.

"I'll see that he gets it, then," Collins promised. "Any time privates speak well of a sergeant when he's not around to hear it, I reckon he's some sort of special man." As the soldiers chuckled, Collins went on, "Now the thing we have to do is get these Lizards someplace where they can be studied by people who have a chance of figuring out what they're all about and what they're up to."

Yeager spoke up. "I'll help get 'em there, sir."

Colonel Collins fixed him with a cold gray stare. "You so eager to get out of the front line, eh, soldier?"

"No, sir, that doesn't have a thing to do with it," Yeager said, first flustered and then angry. He wondered if Collins had ever been *in* the front line. Maybe during the First World War, he admitted to himself. He didn't know how to read the fruit salad of service ribbons on the colonel's left breast.

"Why should I pick you in particular, then?" Collins demanded.

"Best reason I can think of, sir, is that I've been reading science fiction for a long time. I've been thinking about men from Mars and invaders from space a lot longer and harder than anybody else you're likely to find, sir."

Collins was still staring at him, but not in the same way. "Damned if I know what kind of answer I expected, but that's not it. You're saying you're more likely to be mentally flexible around these—things—than someone chosen at random, are you?"

"Yes, sir." Yeager hadn't been in the Army long, but he'd learned in a hurry not to promise too much, so he hedged: "I hope so, sir, anyhow."

Like managers, officers earn their pay by making up their minds in a hurry and then following through. After what couldn't have been more than a ten-second pause, Collins said, "Okay, soldier, you want it so bad, you've got it. Your name is—?"

"Samuel Yeager, sir," Yeager said, saluting. He could hardly keep the grin off his face as he spelled Yeager.

The colonel pulled out a little notebook and a gold-plated mechanical pencil. He was, Yeager saw, a southpaw. He put the notebook away as soon as he'd jotted down Sam's name. "All right, Private Yeager—"

Mutt Daniels spoke up: "Ought to be Co'poral Yeager, sir, or at least PFC." When Collins turned to frown at him, he went on blandly, "You did say you were promotin' us."

Yeager wished Mutt had kept his mouth shut, and waited for Colonel

Collins to get angry. Instead, the colonel burst out laughing. "I know an old soldier when I hear one. Tell me you weren't in France and I'll call you a liar."

"Can't do it, sir," Mutt said with a wide, ingratiating smile that kept a lot of umpires from throwing him out of the game no matter how outrageously he carried on.

"You better not try." Collins gave his attention back to Sam. "All right, *PFC* Yeager, you will serve as liaison to these Lizard prisoners until they are delivered to competent authorities in Chicago." He took out his notebook again, wrote rapidly. As he tore out a couple of sheets, he added, "These orders give discretion to your superiors in Chicago. They may send you back here, or they may let you stay on with the Lizards if you show you're more valuable in that role."

"Thank you, sir," Yeager exclaimed, pocketing the orders Collins gave him. They reminded him of Bobby Fiore's brief tryout with Albany—if he didn't perform right away, they'd ship him out and never give him another chance to show he could do the job. But he wouldn't even get as long as Bobby'd had; they'd likely be in Chicago tonight, though God only knew who competent authorities were or how long it would take to find them. Still, he had to get on the Lizards' good side in a hurry. One way to do that seemed obvious: "Sir, if there's a doctor or medic out there, to see to the wounds on these two . . ."

Collins nodded crisply. He strode back to the door of the bus. As if that were a signal, all the lower-ranking officers waiting outside swarmed toward it. Collins' upraised hand did what King Canute only dreamed of: it held back the tide. The colonel stuck his head out of the bus and shouted, "Finkelstein!"

"Sir!" A skinny fellow with glasses and a thick head of uncombed curly black hair pushed his way through the crowd.

"He's a Jew," Collins remarked, "but he's a damned fine doctor."

Yeager would not have cared—much—if Finkelstein were a Negro. It didn't matter one way or the other to the Lizards, that was for sure. Black bag in hand, the doctor scrambled up into the bus. "Who's hurt?" he asked in a thick New York accent. Then his eyes went wide. "Oh."

"Come on," Yeager said; if he was going to be Lizard liaison, he had to get on with the job. He led Finkelstein back to the Lizards, who had sat quietly through the colloquy with Collins. He hoped the creatures from another planet recognized him as the man who had let them have the bandages to bind up their wounds. Maybe they did; they showed no agitation when he brought the doctor right up to them.

But when Finkelstein made as if to tug at one of those bandages, the unhurt Lizards let out a volley of evil-sounding hisses. One of them stood up from his seat, clawed hands outstretched. "How can you let them know I'm not going to do anything bad to them?"

Sam thought, *How the devil do I know?* But if he couldn't invent an answer, somebody else would end up trying. He hoped for inspiration, and for once it came. He handed his rifle to Otto Chase, rolled up a sleeve. "Make like you're putting a bandage on my arm, then take it off again. Maybe they'll get the idea that that's what you're supposed to do."

"Yeah, that might work," Finkelstein said enthusiastically. He opened his medical bag, took out a paper-wrapped bandage. "Hate to waste anything sterile," he muttered as he opened it. He wrapped it around Yeager's arm. His hands were deft and quick and gentle. The Lizards watched him intently.

Yeager sighed and did his best to pantomime relief. He had no idea whether he got the idea across to the Lizards. Finkelstein undid the bandage. Then he tried moving toward one of the wounded prisoners again. This time, their uninjured companions, though they hissed among themselves, made no move to stop him.

The edge of a bandage came up easily. "It's not tape," the doctor said, as much to himself as to Yeager. "I wonder how it stays on." He peeled it back further, looked at the wound in the Lizard's side. He let out a hiss of his own. "Shell fragment, I'd guess. Give me my bag, soldier." He grabbed a probe. "Warn him this may hurt."

Who, me? But this was what Yeager had asked for. He got the Lizards' attention, pinched himself, did his best to imitate the noises the wounded captives had made. Then he pointed to Finkelstein, the probe, and the injury. He looked at that as briefly as he could; he found torn flesh to be torn flesh, whether it belonged to man or Lizard.

Finkelstein slowly inserted the probe. The wounded Lizard sat very still, then hissed and quivered at the same moment as the doctor exclaimed, "Found it! Not too big and not too deep." He withdrew the probe, took out a pair of long, thin grasping tongs. "Almost there, almost there . . . got it!" His hands drew back; the tongs came out of the wound clenched on a half-inch sliver of metal. A drop of the Lizard's blood fell from it to the floor of the bus.

All the alien prisoners, even the wounded one, spoke excitedly in their own language. The one who had threatened the doctor with claws lowered his weird eyes toward the ground and stood very still. Yeager had seen the captives do that before. It had to be a kind of salute, he thought.

The doctor started to replace the bandage, then paused and glanced toward Yeager. "Think I ought to dust the wound with sulfa? Can Earth germs live on a thing from God knows where? Or would I be running a bigger risk of poisoning the Lizard?"

Again, Yeager's first thought was, *How should I know?* Why was a doctor asking medical questions of a minor league outfielder without a high school diploma? Then he realized that when it came to Lizards, he might not know a whole lot less than Finkelstein. After a few seconds' thought, he answered, "Seems to me they must come from a planet that isn't too different than ours, or they wouldn't want Earth in the first place. So maybe our germs would like them."

"Yeah, that makes sense. Okay, I'll do it." The doctor poured the yellow powder into the wound, patted the bandage down. It clung as well as it had before.

Colonel Collins walked to the back of the bus. "How are you doing, Doctor?"

"Well enough, sir, thank you." Finkelstein nodded at Yeager. "This is one sharp man you have here."

"Is he? Good." Collins headed up to the bus door again.

"I'm sorry, soldier," the doctor said. "I don't even know your name."

"I'm Sam Yeager. Pleased to meet you, sir."

"There's a kick in the head for you—I'm Sam Finkelstein. Well, Sam, shall we see what we can do for this other Lizard here?"

"Okay by me, Sam," Yeager said.

Of all the places Jens Larssen had ever expected to end up when he set out from Chicago to warn the government how important the Metallurgical Laboratory's work was, White Sulphur Springs, West Virginia, might have been the last. Staying at the same hotel as the German chargé d'affaires hadn't been high on his list of things to anticipate, either.

But here he was at the Greenbrier Hotel by the famous springs, and here—again—was Hans Thomsen. The German had been interned here, along with diplomats from Italy, Hungary, Romania, and Japan, when the United States entered the war. Thomsen had sailed back to Germany on a Swedish ship, lit up to keep it safe from U-boats, in exchange for Americans interned in Germany.

Now Thomsen was back again. In fact, he had a room right across the hall from Larssen's. Down in the hotel dining room, he'd boomed, in excellent English, "I was worried going home, yes. But coming back here once more, on a dreadful little scow too small and ugly, God be thanked, for the Lizards to notice, then I was not worried. I was far too seasick to think for a moment of being worried."

Everyone who heard him laughed uproariously, Jens included. Having Thomsen back in the United States was a forcible reminder that humanity had more important things to do than slaughtering itself. It still made Larssen nervous. As far as he was concerned, Germany remained an enemy even if it happened to be forced into the same camp as the United States. It was the same feeling he'd had about allying with the Russians against Hitler, but even stronger here.

Not everybody in White Sulphur Springs agreed with him, not by a long shot. A lot of important people were here, fled from Washington when the government dispersed in the face of Lizard air raids. Larssen had heard that Roosevelt was here. He didn't know whether it was true. Every new rumor put the President somewhere else: back in Washington, in New York, in Philadelphia (W. C. Fields would not have approved), even in San Francisco (though how he was supposed to travel cross-country with the Lizards running loose was beyond Jens).

Larssen sighed, walked over to the sink in his room to see if he'd get any hot water. He waited and waited, but the stream stayed cold. Sighing, he scraped whiskers off his face with that cold water, lather from a hotel-sized bar of Lifebuoy soap, and a razor blade that had definitely seen better days. The resulting nicks tempted him to cultivate a beard.

His suits were wrinkled. Even his ties were wrinkled. He'd spent a long time getting here, and service at the hotel ranged from lousy on down. At that, he knew damned well he was lucky. No one in Washington or White Sulphur Springs had heard from Gerald Sebring, who'd headed east from Chicago by train instead of by car.

Larssen stooped to tie his shoelaces. One of them broke when he pulled at it. Swearing under his breath, he got down on one knee and tied the lace back together, then made his bow. It was ugly, but he'd already found out how badly picked over the Greenbrier's little sundries store was: it had been plundered first by Axis diplomats and then by invading American bureaucrats. He knew the place didn't have shoelaces. Maybe somebody in town did.

His nose wrinkled when he went out into the hall. Along with the brimstone odor of the springs, it still smelled of the dogs and cats the interned diplomats had brought with them from Washington. *Really gives me an appetite for breakfast,* he thought as he headed downstairs to the dining room.

Breakfast didn't rate much of an appetite. His choice was between stale toast with jam and corn flakes floating in reconstituted powdered milk. Either one cost $3.75. Jens suspected he might have to declare bankruptcy before he got out of White Sulphur Springs. He'd been making good money by wartime standards—great money by the lean standards of the 1930s—but inflation headed straight for the roof when the Lizards landed. Demand stayed high, and they played merry hell with supply.

He ended up eating toast; one taste of the powdered milk had been enough to last him a lifetime. He left a niggardly tip, and begrudged even that. Escaping quickly, before the waiter could see how he'd been stiffed, Larssen got his car and drove five miles into town, to the Methodist church to which he'd been directed to report.

White Sulphur Springs was a beautiful little town. It had probably been even more beautiful before herds of olive-drab trucks fouled the air with their exhaust and honked at each other like bellowing bulls disputing the right of way. The antiaircraft guns which blossomed on every streetcorner also did little for the decor.

But even so, the rolling, green-clad slopes of the Alleghenies, the clear water of nearby Sherwood Lake, and the fuming springs that gave the place its name made it easy for Jens to understand why White Sulphur Springs had been a presidential resort in the days before the Civil War, when it was part of Virginia and no one had ever imagined West Virginia would become a separate state.

On the outside, the white-painted church with its tall steeple maintained the serenity the town sought to project. One step through the door told Larssen he had entered another world. The pastor retained half his office, but that was all. From everywhere else came the clatter of typewriters, the raucous chatter of people with too much to do and not enough time to do it, and the purposeful clomp of government-issue footgear on a hardwood floor.

A harassed corporal looked up from whatever he was typing. Seeing a veritable civilian before him, he dispensed with even military politeness: "Watcha want, mac? Make it snappy."

"I have a nine o'clock appointment to see Colonel Groves." Larssen looked down at his watch. He was five minutes early.

"Oh." The corporal visibly shifted gears as he reassessed this civilian's likely importance. A good piece of his big-city tough-guy accent disappeared when he spoke again: "You want to come along with me, sir?"

"Thank you." Larssen followed the noncom through the pews on which more enlisted men were awkwardly working rather than praying, crabwise down a hallway pinched by mountains of file boxes that clung like clots to either wall, and into what had been the pastor's sanctum. New plywood partitions restricted that worthy to a fraction of his former domain—the fraction thereof that lacked a telephone.

Colonel Leslie Groves sat behind a desk that held said telephone. He employed the instrument with vim and gusto: "What the hell do you mean, you can't ship those tracks up to Detroit? . . . So the bridge is out and the road has a hole in it? So what? Get 'em on a barge. The Lizards aren't blasting half the shipping they might, the stupid bastards. We have to get those tanks made, or we can kiss everything good-bye . . . I'll call you tonight, so I can keep up with what you're doing. Get it done, Fred, I don't care how."

He hung up with no more of a good-bye than that, fixed Larssen with an intense blue stare. "You're from that Chicago project." It was not a question. A flick of the colonel's left hand dismissed the corporal.

"That's right." Larssen wondered how much Groves knew about it, and how much he ought to tell him. More than he wanted to; he was already sure of that. "After Berlin, sir, you have to know how important that project is. And the Lizards are advancing on Chicago."

"Son, we all got troubles," Groves rumbled. He was a big man with auburn hair cut short, a thin mustache, and blunt, competent features. He filled the pastor's chair to overflowing and sat well back from the desk; a hefty belly kept him from getting any closer.

"I know it," Jens said. "I mean, I drove here from Chicago, after all."

"Sit down; tell me about that," Groves urged. "I've been holed up here almost since the Lizards came. I ought to know more about the world outside than what I can find out over a phone line." As if on cue, the telephone jangled. "Excuse me."

While the colonel barked instructions to someone on the other end of the line, Larssen perched on the uncomfortable chair in front of the desk and tried to marshal his thoughts. Groves gave him the impression of a man who worked hard every waking moment, so he was ready when the handset went back into its cradle: "It's not a trip I'm looking forward to reversing. Lizard planes are everywhere, and I had to take the side roads up into upstate New York to get around the Lizard pocket east of Pittsburgh."

"They're in Pittsburgh now," Groves said.

Jens grunted. The news didn't surprise him, but it was like a kick in the belly just the same. He made himself go on: "Gas is hard as the devil to get. I drove a few miles on a half gallon of grain alcohol I bought from a little old man I think was a moonshiner. My engine hasn't been the same since, either."

"You kept going, which is what counts," Groves said. "The alcohol was a good dodge. One of the things we're looking at is adapting engines to burn it, in case the Lizards hurt our refining capacity even worse than they have already. If the revenuers haven't been able to put a stop to stills, damned if I see the Lizards doing it."

"I suppose not," Larssen agreed. But the colonel's words brought home to him how bad things were. Somehow all the terror and trouble that had befallen him on the way from Chicago, all the horrors he'd edited out of his brief account to Groves, seemed to have happened to him in isolation; he could imagine other parts of the United States going on about their usual business while hell didn't seem half a mile off for him. He could imagine it, yes, but Groves was warning him it wasn't true. He said, "As bad as that?"

"Some places worse," Colonel Groves said somberly. "The Lizards are like a cancer on the country. They don't just hurt the places where they are—they hurt other places, too, because supplies can't go through the territory they hold." The phone rang again. Groves delivered a crisp series of orders, then returned to his conversation with Jens without missing a beat: "They cut off our circulation, you might say, so we die inch by inch."

"That's why the Metallurgical Laboratory is so important," Larssen said. "It's our best chance at a weapon that will let us fight them on something like equal terms." He decided to push a little. "Washington could go the same way as Berlin, you know."

Groves started to say something, but was interrupted by the phone once more. When he hung up, he did say it: "You really think your people will be able to make an atomic bomb in time for us to get some use out of it?"

"We're close to starting up a sustained reaction," Larssen said. Then he shut up; even saying that much trampled on the security he'd lived with ever since he became a part of the project. The times, though, were not what they had been before the Lizards proved atomic weapons didn't belong just on the pages of pulp magazines. He added, "Speaking of Berlin, nobody here knows how far along the Germans are on their own special project." No matter how things had changed, he couldn't bring himself to say *uranium* to someone not in the know.

"The Germans." Groves scowled. "I hadn't thought of that. Nothing's ever simple, is it? After Berlin, they have some kind of incentive to push ahead, too. Heisenberg wasn't in the city when the bomb hit, I hear."

"If you know about Heisenberg, you know quite a bit about this," Larssen said, surprised and impressed. He'd taken Groves for just another man in a uniform, if one more overstuffed than most.

The colonel's gruff laugh said he understood what Larssen was thinking. "I do try to remind myself I'm living in the twentieth century," he noted dryly. "I spent a couple of years at MIT before I got my West Point ring, and took an engineering doctorate afterward. All of which and a nickel will buy me a cup of coffee—or would have, before the Lizards came. Costs more now. So you really think this gang of yours is on to something, do you?"

"Yes, I do, Colonel. We're too far along to make it easy for us to move, too. The Lizards are advancing on Chicago from the west, and after my adventures coming east, moving that way looks just about as risky. If we're going to go on doing our research, the United States has to hold on to Chicago."

Groves rubbed his chin. "What we have to do and what we can do too often aren't nearly the same thing these days, worse luck. Anyway"—he tapped the eagle that perched on one shoulder—"I don't have the authority to order us to hold Chicago no matter what and forget about the other nine million emergencies all over the country."

"I know that." Jens' heart sank. "But you're the best contact I've made. I was hoping you would—"

"Oh, I will, son, I will." Groves heaved his bulk out of the chair. The phone rang again. Swearing, Groves flopped down again, so hard Larssen half expected the seat to break under him. It held, and Groves, as he had several times already, crisply and authoritatively dealt with a new string of problems. Then he got up once more, and went on talking as if he'd never been interrupted: "I'll run interference for you, best I can. But you're the one who's carrying the ball." He stuck a fore-and-aft cap on his head. "Let's go."

Larssen had played football in high school. If he'd run the ball behind a lineman as huge as Groves, he'd have put so many touchdowns on the board that people would have thought him the second coming of Red Grange. The image made him smile. "Where are we going?" he asked as Groves pushed past him.

"To see General Marshall," the colonel said over his shoulder. "He has the power to bind and to loose. I'll get you in to talk to him—today, I hope. After that, it's up to you."

"Thank you, sir," Larssen said. George Marshall was Army Chief of Staff. If anyone could order Chicago defended at all cost, he was the man (although, against the Lizards, ordering something and having it come to pass were not the same thing). Hope rose in Jens. As he followed Groves out into the street, he drew in a lungful of air ripe not only with exhaust but also with the sulfurous reek of the springs.

Groves took a deep breath, too. A grin made him look years younger. "That smell always reminds me of walking into a freshman chemistry lab."

"It does, by God!" Jens hadn't made the connection, but the colonel was absolutely right. The very next breath brought with it memories of Bunsen burners and reagent bottles with frosted glass stoppers.

Colonel Groves literally ran interference for Larssen on the streets of White Sulphur Springs, using his blocky body to bull ahead where a thinner or less confident man might have hesitated. He had a good deal of muscle beneath the fat, and also a driving energy that made him walk with a forward lean, as if into a headwind.

Getting in to see the Chief of Staff wasn't as simple as Groves had made it sound back in his office. The lawn of the house in which Marshall stayed was clogged with officers. Jens had never seen so many sparkling silver stars in his life. To generals, a colonel like Groves might as well have been invisible.

He did not stay invisible long. Sheer physical bulk got him near enough to the doorway to catch the eye of a harried-looking major inside. In a ringing voice that cut through the hubbub, Groves announced his name and declared, "Tell the general I have a fellow here from the Metallurgical Laboratory in Chicago. It's urgent."

"What isn't?" the major answered, but he ducked back inside. Groves peacefully yielded up his place to a major general.

"Now what?" Larssen asked. He could feel the sun pounding his head and his arms—he wore a short-sleeved shirt. He was so fair he didn't tan worth a damn; he just burned layer by layer.

"Now we wait." Groves folded his own arms across his broad, khaki-clad chest.

"But you said it was urgent—"

The colonel's booming laugh made heads swing toward him. "If it weren't urgent, I wouldn't be here at all. Same with everybody else, son.

As that major said, everything is urgent nowadays. But if he delivers that message, well, I expect we're urgent *enough*, if you know what I mean."

As seconds crawled by on hands and knees, Jens began to wonder. He also wondered where in White Sulphur Springs he'd be able to find calamine lotion to slather on his poor toasting arms and nose. As inconspicuously as he could, he moved into Groves' massive shadow. He felt a stab of jealousy when the major returned to call out the name of a brigadier general. Groves only shrugged.

The major came out again. "Colonel, uh, Graves?"

"That's me," Groves declared; since no Colonel Graves rose up in righteous anger to dispute his claim, Larssen supposed he was right. More officers' heads turned toward him as he surged forward with Jens in his wake. Envy and anger were the main expressions Jens saw—who was this mere colonel to take precedence over men with stars on their shoulders?

"This way, sir," the major said. This way led to a closed door, in front of which Groves and Larssen spent the next several minutes cooling their heels. Larssen didn't care; the hall was hot and airless, but at least he'd got out of the sun.

The door opened. The brigadier general came out, looking grimly satisfied. He returned Groves' salute, gave Larssen a brusque nod, and strode away.

"Come in, Colonel Groves, and bring your companion," General Marshall called from behind his desk. Jens noticed that he got the name straight.

"Thank you, sir," Groves said, obeying. "Sir, let me present Dr. Jens Larssen; as I told your adjutant, he's reached us from the project at the University of Chicago."

"Sir." As a civilian, Larssen reached across the desk to shake hands with the Army Chief of Staff. The general's grip was firm and precise. Jens' first impression was that despite the uniform, despite the three rows of campaign ribbons, Marshall looked more like a senior research scientist than a soldier. He was in his early sixties, spare and trim, with hair going from iron gray toward white. Under a wide forehead, his face was rather narrow. He looked as though he seldom smiled. His eyes were arresting; they said he'd seen a lot and thought hard about every bit of it.

If not warm, he was gracious enough, waving Larssen and Groves to chairs and listening closely to Jens' brief retelling of his trip across the eastern half of the United States. Then he put his elbows on the desk and leaned forward. "Tell me the status of the Metallurgical Laboratory as you know it, Dr. Larssen. You may speak freely; I am cleared for this information."

"If you'd like me to step outside, sir—" Groves started to get up again.

Marshall raised a hand to stop him. "That will not be necessary, Colonel. Security requirements have changed considerably since the end of

May. The Lizards already know the secrets we are trying to extract from nature."

"Do the Germans?" Larssen asked. Being a civilian had advantages; he could question the Army Chief of Staff where military discipline held Groves silent. "Do we want the Germans to learn them from us? I'd better know the answer to that, sir, not least because Hans Thomsen has the room across the hall from mine at the Greenbrier."

"The Germans have an atomic research program of their own," Marshall said. "It is in our interest to keep them fighting the Lizards, not least because, to speak frankly, they are doing a better job of it than anyone else at the moment. They have their army and their economy already geared to war on a large scale, while we were still readying our resources when the Lizards came."

Larssen nodded before he realized General Marshall hadn't really answered his question. Being able to talk like a politician, he supposed, was one of the job qualifications for Army Chief of Staff.

As if thinking along with him, Marshall said, "Before I tell you what you may say to the German chargé, Dr. Larssen—and you may say nothing without direct authorization from me or someone at a higher level—I do need to know where the Metallurgical Laboratory presently stands in its researches."

"Of course, sir." But Larssen remained bemused as he mustered his thoughts. Who was at a higher level than General Marshall? Only two men he could think of—the secretary of war and President Roosevelt. Was Marshall implying he might meet them? Jens shook his head. It didn't matter now. He said, "When I left Chicago, sir, we were assembling an atomic pile which, we hoped, would have a k-factor greater than one."

"You'll have to explain a bit further than that, I'm afraid," Marshall said. "While I have studied your group's reports with great attention, I do not pretend to be a nuclear physicist."

"It means arranging the uranium so that, as atomic nuclei are split—*fission*, the term is—the neutrons they release will split more atoms, and so on. Think of it as a positive feedback cycle, sir. In a bomb like the ones the Lizards have, it happens in a split second and releases enormous energy."

"What you are working toward is not a bomb in and of itself, then," Marshall said.

"That's right." Larssen eyed the older man with respect. As Marshall had said, he was no nuclear physicist, but he had no trouble drawing implications from data. Jens continued, "It is an essential first step, though. We'll control the nuclear reaction with cadmium rods that capture excess neutrons before they strike uranium atoms. That will keep it from getting out of hand. We have to walk before we can run, sir, and we need to understand how to produce a controlled chain reaction before we can think about making a bomb."

"And Chicago is the place where this research is going on?" Marshall said musingly.

"In the United States, yes," Larssen said.

He'd hoped Marshall might tell him what, if anything, was happening elsewhere. The Chief of Staff, however, had taken security for granted longer than Jens had been alive. He did not even change expression to acknowledge he'd noticed the hint. He said, "We intended to fight for Chicago for other reasons. This gives us one more. Thank you for your courage in coming here to report on the Metallurgical Laboratory's progress."

"Yes, sir." Larssen wanted to ask more questions, but General Marshall did not strike him as a man given to loose talk even in private circumstances, which these emphatically were not. Nevertheless, he blurted what was uppermost in his mind: "General, *can* we beat the damned Lizards?"

Colonel Groves shifted weight in his chair, making it squeak; Jens abruptly realized that wasn't the way you were supposed to talk to the Army Chief of Staff. He felt himself flushing. He was so fair, he knew the flush would show. That only embarrassed him more.

But Marshall did not seem angry. Maybe the perfectly unmilitary question touched a responsive chord in him, for he said, "Dr. Larssen, if you find anybody who *knows* the answer to that one, he wins the prize. We're doing everything we can, and we'll go on doing everything we can. The alternative is to surrender and live in slavery. Americans won't accept that—maybe your grandfather was one who helped prove it."

"Sir, if you mean the Civil War, my grandfather was still back in Oslo then, trying to make a living as a cobbler. He came to the United States in the 1880s."

"Looking for something better than he had over there, no doubt," Marshall said, nodding. "That's a very human thing to do. I'll be frank with you, Dr. Larssen: in purely military terms, the Lizards have us outclassed. Up to now, no one—not us, not the Germans, not the Russians, not the Japs—has been able to stop them. But no one has stopped trying, and we've put most of our own conflicts on the back shelf for the time being, as witness Mr. Thomsen's presence here—across the hall from you, didn't you say?"

"That's right." Cooperating with the Third Reich still left a bad taste in Larssen's mouth. "Didn't I hear that Warsaw fell when the people there rose against the Nazis and for the Lizards?"

"Yes, that's true," Marshall said soberly. "From the intelligence we have of what those people were suffering, I can see how the Lizards might have seemed the better bargain to them." His voice went flat, emotionless. The very blankness of his face convinced Jens he wasn't telling all he knew there. After a moment, that blankness lifted. "On a global scale, however, it is a small matter, as are the Chinese uprisings against the Japs and in favor of the Lizards. But the Lizards have weaknesses of their own."

Colonel Groves leaned forward. His chair squeaked again. "May I ask what some of those weaknesses are, sir? Knowing them may help me assign priorities in allocating matériel."

"The chief one, Colonel, is their rigid adherence to doctrine. They are methodical to a fault, and slow to adapt tactics to fit circumstances. Some of our nearest approaches to success have come from creating situations where we used their patterns to lure units into untenable situations and then exploited the advantages we gained in so doing. And now, if you will excuse me . . ."

The dismissal was polite, but a dismissal nonetheless. Groves rose and saluted. Jens got up, too. He decided not to shake hands again; General Marshall's attention had already returned to the papers that clogged his desk. The general's aide took charge of them as they came out of the office, led them back to the door by which they'd entered.

"I think you did pretty well there, Dr. Larssen," Groves said, making slow headway against the tide of officers that flowed toward the entrance.

"Call me Jens," Larssen said.

"Then I'm Leslie." The heavyset colonel made an extravagant gesture. "Where now? The world lies at your feet."

Larssen laughed. Till now, he hadn't known any senior military men. They were different from what he'd thought they'd be—Marshall scholarly and precise, plainly a first-class mind (a judgment Jens did not make lightly, not after working with several Nobel laureates); Groves without the Chief of Staff's unbounded mental horizons, but full of bulldog competence and just enough whimsy to leaven the mix. Neither was the singleminded fighting man evoked by the label "general" or "colonel."

After a little thought, Larssen decided that made sense. The group at the Met Lab weren't the effete eggheads layfolk thought of when they imagined what nuclear physicists were like, either. People were more complicated than any subatomic particles.

He wondered what the Lizards made of people. If the invaders were as compulsively orderly as Marshall had said, mankind's aggressive randomness likely confused them no end. He hoped so—every weakness of theirs, no matter how tiny, was a corresponding strength for humanity.

He also wondered what it would be like in one of their spaceships, cruising along far above the surface of the Earth, flying between planets, perhaps even between stars. They were the ones who could literally have the world under their feet. Cold, clear envy pierced him.

Despite his musings, he was only a beat slow in answering Groves: "Unless you've got FDR up your sleeve there, Leslie, I think you've done as much as any man could. Thanks more than I can say for all your help."

"My pleasure." Groves stuck out a hand. He had a grip like a hydraulic press. "You convinced me you and your group are on to something important, and my superiors need to understand that, too, so they can factor it into their calculations. As for Roosevelt, hmm . . ." He actually did look up his sleeve. "Sorry, no. He seems to have stepped out."

"Too bad. If you do happen to see him" —Larssen had no idea how probable that was, but believed in covering his bets—"mention the project if you get the chance."

"I'll do that, Jens." Groves glanced at his wrist again, this time just to check his watch. "I'd best get back to it. I've been away too long already. God only knows what's stacking up on my desk. No rest for the weary, as they say." With a last nod, he turned and headed back toward the Methodist church. Larssen hadn't been able to park any closer than several blocks away. Watching Groves' broad back recede, he concluded the colonel got results from those around him by working twice as hard as any of them. In that, he would have fit in well at the Metallurgical Lab.

The physicist looked at his own watch. Nearly noon—no wonder his stomach was sounding reveille. He wondered what epicurean delight the Greenbrier was offering for lunch. Yesterday it had been canned pork and beans, canned corn, and canned fruit cocktail. Wryly shaking his head, he wondered about the consequences of excessive tin in the diet.

Today's menu, he discovered when he got to the hotel restaurant, was extravagant by current standards: Spam and canned peas. The peas were more nearly olive drab than green, but he ate them all the same, hoping they retained at least some of their vitamins. He also put down an extra buck and a half for a nickel bottle of Coke—that, nobody could snafu. The bottle, he noted, was closer to the color peas ought to be than the peas themselves were.

As he was chasing the last sad, soft, overcooked peas with his fork, there was a stir at the entrance to the dining room. A couple of people started to clap. Larssen looked up, saw a short, pale, bullet-headed man wearing a homburg, steel-rimmed spectacles, and a suit of European cut. That face had looked out at him from countless newsreels, but he'd never thought to encounter Vyacheslav Molotov in the flesh.

Something else occurred to him. His gaze flicked from table to table. Sure enough, there sat Hans Thomsen, also with a plate of Spam. The German chargé d'affaires was affable, genial, a fluent English-speaker who'd worked hard to put the best face on the activities of the Nazi government until Hitler declared war on the United States. Larssen wondered how he felt to be in the presence of the Soviet foreign minister after Germany's unprovoked invasion of Russia. He also wondered how Molotov would react to finding a Nazi representative here in the heart of the American government in refuge.

Nor was his the only such curiosity. The dining room grew silent for a few seconds as people stopped talking and suspended forks in midair to see what would happen next. Thomsen, Jens thought, recognized Molotov before the latter saw him. Maybe Molotov would not have noticed him at all but for the Nazi party badge he wore on his left lapel.

The Russian had a face as impassive as any Larssen had ever seen. He did not change expression now, but he did hesitate before proceeding into the dining room. Then he turned to the man beside him, a squarely built fellow whose suit was similar in cut to his own but much more poorly fitted. He spoke a single sentence of Russian.

From the explosive coughs that went up, a few people understood what he had to say in the original. The squarely built man's function was then revealed; he translated Molotov's words into elegant, Oxford-accented English: "The foreign commissar of the USSR observes that, having already entered into diplomatic discussions with the Lizards, he has no objection to speaking to serpents as well."

More coughs rose, Larssen's among them. His eyes swung back to Hans Thomsen. He doubted he could have been as politely insulting as Molotov, given what the Nazis had done to the Soviet Union. On the other hand, all of humanity was supposed to be joining together to resist the invaders from another planet. If everyone kept remembering what was going on before the Lizards came, the united front would come crashing down. And if it did, that literally handed the Lizards the world.

Thomsen was a trained diplomat. If he noticed Molotov had given him the glove, he never let on. He was smiling as he replied, "There is in English an old saying about the enemy of one's enemy."

The interpreter murmured to Molotov. Now the Communist official looked straight back at the German. "It was on this basis, no doubt, that the imperialist powers of Great Britain and the United States allied with the peace-loving people of the USSR against the Hitlerite regime."

Watch out for this guy, Jens thought. *He's dangerous*. Thomsen kept his smile, but it looked held in place by force of will. Still, he had a counterthrust ready: "No doubt it was also on this basis that Finland allied with Germany after being invaded by the peace-loving people of the USSR."

As if at a tennis match, Larssen turned his head to look at Molotov. The match here, though, he thought, used a live hand grenade for a ball. Molotov's lips might have drawn back from his teeth a millimeter or two. Through his interpreter, the Soviet foreign minister replied, "As we have both noted, the principle admits of broad application. Thus I am willing to discuss our own differences at another time."

The sigh of relief that filled the dining room was quite audible. Larssen didn't consciously notice; he was too busy adding to it.

The hologram of Tosev 3 hung in space above its projector, just as it had before the Race began to add a fourth world to the Empire. Today, though, Atvar did not urge Kircl to project the image of the ferocious Tosevite warrior with his sword and chain mail that the Race's probes had brought Home. Like everyone else in the fleet, Atvar had found out more about Tosevite warriors than he'd ever wanted to learn.

The fleetlord turned to the assembled shiplords. "We are met here to day, valiant males, to evaluate the results of the first half-year's fighting"—he used the Race's chronology, of course; sluggish Tosev 3 had completed only a fourth of its orbit—"and to discuss our plans for the combat yet to come."

The shiplords accepted the introduction better than he'd dared hope. When the schedule for the conquest of Tosev 3 was drawn up back on Home, the half-year meeting was the last one included. After half a year, everyone was certain, Tosev 3 would be firmly attached to the Empire. The Race lived by schedules and plans drawn up long before they were carried out. That Atvar's chief underlings recognized the need for much more work was a measure of how much the Tosevites had shaken them.

"We make progress," Atvar insisted. "Large parts of Tosev 3 are under our virtually complete control." On the hologram, portions of the planet's land area changed color from their natural greens and browns to a bright golden hue: the southern half of the smaller continental mass, much of the southwestern part of the main continental mass. "The natives in these areas, while not as primitive as previously available data led us to believe, have been unable to offer resistance much above the nuisance level."

"May it please the exalted fleetlord," Shiplord Straha of the *206th Emperor Yower* said, "but much of this territory strikes me as being that on Tosev 3 least worth the having. True, it's warm enough to suit our kind, but much of it is so beastly wet that our fighting males break out in molds and rots."

"Molds and rots are a small price to pay for victory," Atvar answered.

More of the hologram turned gold, so that Tosev 3 itself looked blotched and diseased. "Here are our holdings in the regions where the Big Uglies are most technologically advanced. As you can see for yourselves, valiant males, these have expanded considerably since last we gathered together." The hologram rotated to give the shiplords a view of the entire planet.

Brash as usual, Straha said, "Certainly we have made great gains. How could it be otherwise, when we are the Race? The question that arises, however, Exalted Fleetlord, is why our gains have not been greater still, why Tosevite forces yet remain in arms against us."

"May I speak, Exalted Fleetlord?" Kirel asked. At Atvar's assent, the shiplord of the *127th Emperor Hetto* went on, "The principal reason for our delays, Shiplord Straha, strikes me as obvious to a hatchling still wet from the egg: the Big Uglies' capabilities are far greater than we imagined while readying the expeditionary force."

"Oh, indeed, as we have discovered to our sorrow," Straha said sarcastically, eager to score points off his rival. "But why is this so? How did our probes fail us so badly? How did the Tosevites become a technological species while the Race turned its eye turrets in the other direction?"

Kirel turned to Atvar in protest. "Exalted Fleetlord, the blame for that must surely rest with the Big Uglies themselves, not on the Race. We merely applied procedures which had proved themselves eminently successful on our two previous conquests. We could not know in advance that they would be less effective here."

"That is so." Atvar glanced down to check some data on a computer screen. Before Kirel could look too smug at having his commander's support, the fleetlord added, "Nevertheless, Straha poses a legitimate question, even if impolitely: why *are* the Tosevites so different from us and our two previous subject races?"

Now Straha brightened up. Atvar needed to keep his rivalry with Kirel active; that way both powerful shiplords, and the lesser leaders who inclined to one of them or the other, would continue to labor zealously to seek the fleetlord's support.

After reviewing his electronic notes once more, Atvar said, "Our savants have isolated several factors which, they feel, cause the Tosevites to be as they are." A muffled hiss ran through the shiplords as they gave their commander full attention. Some of these speculations had already gone out in bulletins and announcements, but bulletins and announcements flowed from the fleetlord's ship in such an unending stream that no one, no matter how diligent, could pay attention to them all. Words straight from the fleetlord's jaws, though, were something else again.

He said, "One element contributing to the Tosevites' anomalous nature is surely the anomalous nature of Tosev 3." Now all at once the planet's immense, innumerable oceans and seas and lakes and rivers glowed bright blue. "The excessive amount of free water serves, along with mountains and deserts, to wall off groups of Big Uglies from one another and allow them to go their own separate ways. This is obvious from one eye's glance at the globe, and is not too different from our own most ancient days back on Home."

"But, Exalted Fleetlord—" Kirel began. Not only had he read all the bulletins and announcements, he'd discussed them with Atvar—the advantage of being shiplord to the bannership of the fleet.

"But indeed." Atvar wanted to lay out this exposition himself, without interruptions. "What follows is more subtle. Because land dominates water on the worlds of the Empire, we have little experience with boats and other aquatic conveyances. That is not the case among the Tosevites, who lavish endless ingenuity upon them. When some Big Uglies stumbled upon technology, they were quickly able to spread its influence—and theirs—by sea to most of the planet."

"Then why do we not face one unified Tosevite empire, Exalted Fleetlord?" asked Feneress, a shiplord of Straha's faction.

"Because the Tosevites in the area where the breakthrough took place were already divided among several competing groups," Atvar answered. "Travel by sea let them all expand their influence outward without consolidating into a single empire."

The assembled shiplords hissed again, more quietly this time, as implications began to sink in. Back on Home, the ancestral Empire had grown step by small step. That was the only way it could grow, on a normal world where there were no great oceans to let its influence suddenly metastasize in a hundred directions at once. Atvar hissed himself as that word crossed his mind; it seemed the perfect metaphor for the Tosevites' malignantly rapid technological growth.

"You must also bear in mind the constantly competitive nature of the Big Uglies themselves," he went on. "As we have recently discovered, they are sexually competitive throughout the year, and remain in a state permitting sexual excitement even in the long-term absence of any breeding partner."

Atvar knew he sounded faintly disgusted. Without pheromones from females in heat, his own sexual urge remained latent. He didn't miss it. On a mission like this, it would have been a distraction. The Rabotevs and Hallessi were like the Race in that regard, which had led its savants to believe all intelligent species followed the same pattern. There as elsewhere, Tosev 3 was proving a theorist's crematorium.

Straha said, "Exalted Fleetlord, I recently received a shiplord's-eyes-only report noting that the Tosevite empires opposing us are in fact not empires at all. I find this a contradiction. Granted that the scale of area ruled may vary, but how can there be government without empire?"

"Before I came here, Shiplord, I assure you I found that concept as unimaginable as you do now," Atvar answered. "Tosev 3, unfortunately, has taught us all a variety of unpleasant new ideas. Of the lot, government without empire may be the most repugnant, but it does exist and must be dealt with."

The shiplords stirred uncomfortably. Talking about government without empire was worse than talking about sexual interest in the absence of females in heat. For the Race, the latter was just an intellectual exercise, a study in abstraction. Government without empire, though, tore at the underpinnings of a thousand millennia of civilized life.

Feneress said, "Without emperors, Exalted Fleetlord, how can the Big Uglies administer their affairs? I too saw the report to which the senior shiplord Straha refers, but I confess I dismissed it as just another flight of fancy from savants drawing broad conclusions without enough data. You are saying this is not the case?"

"It is not, Shiplord. For my own peace of mind, I wish it were, but the data are irrefutable," Atvar replied. "Moreover, revolting as it surely seems to us, the Big Uglies in many cases seem proud of their success at ruling themselves without emperors." The Big Ugly named Molotov had seemed proud of belonging to a band that had slaughtered his empire's emperor. The very idea still gave Atvar the horrors.

"But how do they administer their affairs?" Feneress persisted. Several other shiplords, males from both Straha's faction and Kirel's, made gestures of agreement. Here the whole Race united in finding the Tosevites baffling.

Atvar found them baffling, too, but he had been working hard to understand. He said, "I will summarize as best I can. In some Tosevite, uh, non-empires—the two most powerful examples are Deutschland and the SSSR—the ruler has full imperial power but draws on no hereditary loyalty and affection from his subjects. This may be one reason these two Tosevite areas are ruled with more brutality than most: obedience out of affection being unavailable to them, they force obedience out of fear."

That made a certain amount of logical sense, anyway, no matter how much it appalled the fleetlord. Since logical sense was hard enough to come by on Tosev 3, he cherished it when he found it. Deutschland and the SSSR were models of comprehensibility when set beside some of the other—maybe *lands* was a good word for them, Atvar thought—on Tosev 3.

He went on, "Italia, Nippon, and Britain *are* empires in our sense of the word. Or so they claim, at any rate; nothing the Big Uglies do can be trusted to be what it appears. In the first two empires I mentioned, the emperor serves as a false front for other Tosevites who hold the actual power in their regimes."

"This phenomenon was also known among the Rabotevs before we integrated them into the Empire," Kirel noted. "In fact, some of our own ancient records may be interpreted to imply that it occurred among the Race as well, in the long-ago days when the Empire was limited, not merely to one planet, but to a portion of that planet."

The shiplords muttered among themselves. Atvar did not blame them. Anything that cast doubt on the sovereignty of the Emperor had to be intensely disturbing. The Emperor was the rock to which their souls were tethered, the central focus of all their lives. Without him, they could only wander through existence alone and afraid, no better than the Big Uglies or any other beasts of the field.

Yet this briefing held more that would disquiet them. As the mutters died away, Atvar spoke again: "The case of Britain is more obscure. Again, though it is an empire, its emperor holds no real power. Some of you will have noticed the name of the male, uh, Churchill, as appearing repeatedly among those who urge the Tosevites to continue their futile and foredoomed resistance to the Race. This Churchill, it seems (admittedly from the limited data we have and our own imperfect—the Emperor be praised!—understanding of Tosevite customs), is but the leader of the Britainish faction which currently musters more support than any other. If the factions shift, their leaders meeting together may at any time choose for themselves a different chief."

Straha's jaws gaped in amusement. "And when they do, Exalted Fleetlord, how will this war leader, this—Churchill, did you say?— respond? By abandoning the power he has seized? Isn't he more likely to set soldiers on them to cure their presumption? Isn't that what you or I or any sane male would do?"

"We have reason to believe he would abandon power," Atvar answered, and had the satisfaction of seeing Straha's mouth close with a snap. "Intercepted radio signals indicated such—how best to put it?— resignation to factional shifts is a commonplace of government (or lack of government) among the Britainish."

"Madness," Straha said.

"What else would you expect from the Big Uglies?" Atvar said. "And if you think the Britainish mad, how do you account for the Tosevite land called the United States?"

Straha did not answer. Atvar had not expected him to answer. The rest of the shiplords also fell silent. Without a doubt the most prosperous land on Tosev 3, the United States was by any rational standard an anarchy. It had no emperor; as far as any of the Race's savants could tell, it had never had an emperor. But it also had few of the trappings of a land ruled by force like the SSSR or Deutschland.

Atvar summed up the Race's view of the United States in one scornful word: "Snoutcounters! How do they have the hubris to imagine they can build a land that amounts to anything by counting one another's snouts?"

"And yet they have," Kirel said, as usual soberly sticking to observable truth. "Analysis suggests they acquired the snoutcounting habit from the Britainish, with whom they share a language, and then extended it further than even the Britainish countenance."

"They even count snouts in the prison camps we have established on their soil," Atvar said. "When we needed Big Ugly representatives through whom to deal with their kind, that's how they chose them—instead of picking ones known to be wise or brave, they let several vie for the jobs and counted snouts to see which had the most in favor."

"How are these representatives working out?" asked Hassov, who was rather a cautious male and thus inclined to Kirel's faction. "How much worse are they than those selected by some rational means?"

"Our officers have noted no great differences between them and similar representatives elsewhere on Tosev 3," Atvar said. "Some are better and more obedient than others, but that is the case all around the planet."

The admission bothered him. It was as if he were confessing that the manifest anarchy of the United States worked as well as a system that made sense. As a matter of fact, it did seem to work well, by Tosevite standards anyhow. And the American Big Uglies (he did not understand how they derived *American* from *United States*, but he did not pretend to be a linguist, either) fought as hard for the sake of their anarchy as other Big Uglies battled for their emperors or non-imperial rulers.

Straha said, "Very well, Exalted Fleetlord, the Tosevites rule themselves in ways we find incomprehensible or revolting or both. How does this affect our campaign against them?"

"A relevant question," Atvar said approvingly. He did not trust Straha; the male had enough ambition to be—why, he had almost enough ambition to be one of those freewheeling American Big Uglies himself, Atvar thought with the new perspective he'd gained from half a year on Tosev 3. But no denying his ability.

The fleetlord resumed: "The Tosevites, with these ramshackle, temporary governments of theirs, have shown themselves to be more versatile, more flexible, than we are. No doubt those back on Home would be shocked at the improvisations we have been forced to make in the course of our conquest here."

No doubt a good many of you are, too, Atvar added silently to himself. From lack of practice or need, the Race did not improvise well. When change came in the Empire (which was seldom), it came in slow, carefully planned steps, with likely results and plans to meet them mapped out beforehand. The Emperor and his servants thought in terms of millennia. That was good for the Race as a whole, but did not promote quick reflexes. Here on Tosev 3, situations had a way of changing even as you looked at them; yesterday's perfect plan, if applied day after tomorrow, was as apt to yield fiasco as triumph.

"Improvising, though, seems a way of life for the Big Uglies," Atvar said. "Witness the antilandcruiser mines they mounted on animals' backs.

Would any of us have imagined such a ploy? Bizarre as it is, though, it has hurt us more than once. And the supply of munitions available to us, as compared to that which the Tosevites continue to produce, remains a source of some concern."

"By the Emperor, we rule the skies on this world," Straha said angrily. "How is it that we've failed to smash the factories down below?" Just too late, he added, "Exalted Fleetlord." Several shiplords stirred uneasily at the implied criticism of Atvar.

The fleetlord did not let his own anger show. "The answer to your question, Shiplord Straha, has two parts. First, Tosev 3 has a great many factories, scattered through several areas of the planet's surface. Destroying them all, or even most of them, is no easy task. Besides which, the Tosevites are adept at quickly repairing damage. This, I suppose, is another result of their having been at war among themselves when we arrived. They cannot match our technology, but are extremely effective within the limits of their own."

"We should have had more resources before we undertook the conquest of an industrialized planet," Feneress complained.

Now Atvar did project the image of the mail-clad Tosevite warrior captured by the earlier probe from Home. "Shiplord, let me remind you that this is the opposition we expected to face. Do you think our forces adequate to defeat such foes?" Feneress sensibly stood silent—what reply could he hope to make? Against sword-swinging primitives, the fight would have been over in days, probably without the loss of a single male of the Race.

Atvar touched the controls again. New images replaced the familiar one of the Tosevite fighting male: a gun-camera hologram of a swept-wing fighter with two jet engines and the hooked-cross emblem of Deutschland; a landcruiser from the SSSR, underpowered and undergunned by the standards of the Race, certainly, but needing only scaling up to become a truly formidable weapon; a bombed-out factory complex in the United States that had been turning out several bombing planes every day; and, finally, the satellite picture of the unsuccessful Deutsch missile launch.

Into the shiplords' sudden silence, Atvar said, "Considering the unexpectedly strong struggle the Big Uglies have been able to maintain, we can be proud of our successes thus far. As we gradually continue to cripple their industrial base, we may find future victories coming more easily."

"Simply because we did not have the walkover we expected, we need not twitch our tailstumps and yield to despair or pessimism," Kirel added. "Instead, we should give thanks that the Emperor in his wisdom sent us forth with force overwhelming for our anticipated task, thus allowing us to accomplish the far more difficult one that awaited us here."

The fleetlord sent him a grateful look. He could not imagine a more encouraging note on which to close the gathering. But before he had the chance to dismiss the shiplords, Straha asked, "Exalted Fleetlord, in view of the technological base the Tosevites do have, could they be working toward nuclear weapons of their own and, if so, how can we prevent this development short of sterilizing the planet's surface?"

Some of the lesser shiplords, and those less given to paying attention to their briefings, twitched in alarm. In a way, Atvar did not blame them; he had trouble thinking of anything more horrid than Tosevites armed with fission bombs. But they also annoyed him, for they should have been able to envision the potential problem for themselves, without Straha's prodding. The more Atvar had to deal with Tosevites, the more he thought his own people lacked imagination.

"We have no evidence that they are," he said. "How much this extrapolation from a negative means, however, is uncertain. If one of their warring empires were involved in such research, I doubt it would trumpet the fact over the radio, lest it encourage its enemies to do the same."

"You have spoken truth, Exalted Fleetlord," Straha agreed. "Let me ask the question another way: do the Big Uglies know enough about the inner workings of the atom to envision nuclear weapons?"

"After our initial bombardment to disrupt their communications, and especially after we smashed the capital of Deutschland, they need not envision nuclear weapons," Kirel said. "They have seen them."

"They have seen them, yes." Straha would not let his rival distract him from the point he was trying to make. "But can they understand what they have seen?"

Atvar hadn't thought of the question in quite those terms. Finding out just what the Tosevites knew wasn't easy. Even if they were reticent on the radio, their books surely revealed a great deal. But in only half a year (half of half a year, by Tosevite reckoning), who among the Race had had the chance to find and translate the relevant texts? The fleetlord knew the answer perfectly well: no one. The war of conquest left no leisure for such fripperies as translation.

Except that now it was not a frippery. Straha had a point: finding out exactly what the Big Uglies knew about the inner workings of the atom could prove as important as anything else in this campaign. With hope, but without too much, Atvar put a hushmike to his mouth and asked the bannership's computer what it knew.

He'd expected it to report back that it had no information. Instead, though, it gave him a translated radio intercept of a news item from the United States. "X-rays reveal the Cincinnati Reds outfielder Mike McCormick suffered a fractured leg in yesterday's contest. He is expected to be out for the season."

Like a lot of translated intercepts, this one didn't tell Atvar everything he might have wanted to know. He wondered what sort of contest an outfielder (whatever an outfielder was) took part in, and for what season he was lost. Spring? Summer? Harvest? The fleetlord also wondered whether Cincinnati (whose name he did recognize) had Greens and Blues and Yellows to go with its Reds.

But all that was by the bye. The important thing about the intercept was that it showed this Mike McCormick's leg fracture had been diagnosed by X-rays. Atvar presumed that meant X-rays were in common use down on Tosev 3: if they weren't, then the Big Uglies wouldn't have freely talked about them on the radio during wartime. And if X-rays were in common use . . .

"They know something about the inner workings of the atom," he said, and explained his reasoning. Dismay spread through the ranks of the shiplords.

Straha spelled out the reason for that dismay: "Then they may indeed be covertly seeking a means of producing nuclear weapons."

"So they may," Atvar admitted. Oddly, the notion appalled him less than he would have guessed. He'd been appalled so many times already by the Tosevites and the unexpected things they did that he was getting hard to shock. He just let out a long, hissing sigh and said, "One more thing to worry about."

The White Horse Inn smelled of beer and sweat and the tobacco smoke that made the air nearly as thick as a London pea-soup fog. The bar maid named Daphne set pints of what was misleadingly called best bitter in front of David Goldfarb and Jerome Jones. She scooped up the shillings they'd laid on the bar, slapped Jones' wrist when he tried to slip an arm around her waist, and spun away, laughing. Her skirt swirled high on her shapely legs.

Sighing, Jones followed her with his eyes. "It's no use, old man," Goldfarb said. "I told you that weeks ago—she only goes with fliers."

"Can't shoot a man for trying," Jones answered. He tried every time they came to the White Horse Inn, and as consistently crashed in flames. He took a moody pull at his beer. "I do wish she wouldn't giggle that way, though. Under other circumstances, it might discourage me."

Goldfarb drank, too, then made a face. "This beer discourages me. Bloody war." Thin and sour, the yellow liquid in his glass bore only the faintest resemblance to what he fondly recalled from the days before rationing. He sipped again. "Pah! I wonder if it's saltpeter they're putting in it, the way they do in schools to keep the boys from getting randy."

"No, I know that taste, by God."

"That's right, you went to a public school."

"So what? Back before the Lizards smashed our radar, you were better with it than I ever was."

To cover his thoughts, Goldfarb drained his glass, raised a finger for another. Eventually, even bad beer numbed the tongue. Jerome could say

So what? sincerely enough, but after the war was done—if it ever ended—he'd go back to Cambridge and end up a barrister or a professor or a business executive. Goldfarb would go back, too, back to repairing wireless sets behind the counter of a dingy little store on a dingy little street. To him, his friend's egalitarianism rang hollow.

Blithely oblivious, Jones went on, "Besides, if there is saltpeter in this bitter, it's not working worth a damn. I'd really fancy a go right now—but it's the sods with wings on their shirtfronts who'll get one. Look at that, will you?" He pointed. "Disgraceful, I call it."

Now you know what it's like, down in the lower classes, Goldfarb thought. But Jerome didn't, not really. Just seeing Daphne perched on a flight engineer's knee over by the electric fire wasn't enough to take away his ingrained advantages in society. All it did was make him jealous.

It made Goldfarb jealous, too, especially when Sylvia, the other barmaid, also went over to the table full of aircrew. She quickly ended up in the bomb-aimer's lap. It wasn't fair. Goldfarb tried to remember the pithy phrase he'd heard in an American film not long before. *Them as has, gits,* that was it. No grammar there, but a lot of truth.

As for himself, he didn't even seem able to git his pint refilled. That struck him as excessive. He got up, started over to the table where the fliers were monopolizing the barmaids. Jerome Jones put a hand on his arm. "Are you bloody daft, David? There's seven of them there; they'll wipe the floor with you."

"What?" Goldfarb stared, then realized what Jones was talking about. "Oh. I don't want a fight, I just want a fresh pint. Maybe they'll stop feeling up the girls long enough to let one of them draw me another."

"Maybe they won't, too," Jerome said. But Goldfarb ignored him and walked across the pub to the aircrew and the barmaids.

Nobody there took any notice of him for a few seconds. The fellow who had Daphne on his knee was saying, ". . . worst thing I saw there, or at least the nastiest, was that old fellow walking down the street with a yellow Star of David on his chest." He looked up from his comrades, saw Goldfarb standing there. "You want something, friend?" His tone was neither hostile nor the reverse; he waited to hear what Goldfarb had to say.

"I came over to see if I could borrow Daphne just for a moment." Goldfarb held up his empty pint glass. "But what you were just talking about—I hope I'm not prying, but you're newly back from France?"

"That's right. Who wants to know?" The flight engineer was a pint or two ahead of Goldfarb, but still alert enough. One of his eyebrows rose. "I hope I'm not prying in turn, radarman, but are you by any chance of the Jewish faith?"

"Yes, I am." Goldfarb knew he didn't look quite English; his hair was too wavy, and the wrong color brown, while no Anglo-Saxon—or even Celt—wore a nose like his. "I have relatives in Warsaw, you see, and I thought I'd ask someone who'd seen with his own eyes how Jews are faring under the Germans. If I'm interrupting your party, I do apologize. Perhaps if I gave you my name, you could look me up at the station when it's convenient for you."

"No, that's all right. Pull up a chair," the flight engineer said after a quick eyecheck of the rest of the aircrew. He straightened his leg, so Daphne started to slide down it. She squeaked indignantly as she sprang to her feet. The flight engineer said, "Hush, love. Bring this lad his new pint, will you?"

Pert nose in the air, Daphne snatched Goldfarb's glass out of his hand and marched behind the bar. "That's very kind of you," Goldfarb said. He pointed back at Jerome Jones. "May my friend join you as well?" On receiving a nod, he waved Jones over.

"I suppose *he'll* want another pint, too," Daphne said darkly as she returned with the filled glass. "The one he has is empty now, that's bloody sure." Without waiting for an answer, she carried Jones' dead soldier away to be revivified.

The newly enlarged group exchanged names. The pilot of the aircrew, Ken Embry, said, "You have to remember two things, Goldfarb: Warsaw isn't likely to be just like Paris by any means, and it isn't under the Germans any more."

"I understand all that," Goldfarb said. "But anything I can find out will be of value to me."

"Fair enough," said the flight engineer, whose name was George Bagnall. "Aside from the six-pointed stars, I saw shops and even telephone booths with signs saying things like 'No Jews allowed' and 'Patronage by Jews prohibited.' Other shops had special late-afternoon hours for Jews, so they could only pick over what other people had left."

"Bastards," Goldfarb muttered.

"Who, the Jerries? Too right they are," Embry said. "We didn't see anything, though, like the photos the Lizards have released from Warsaw, or like what the people who live there talk about on the Lizards' wireless programs. If even a tenth part of that's true, by God, I'm damned if I blame those poor devils for rising up against the Nazis, not a bit of it."

The rest of the aircrew spoke up in agreement, all save Douglas Bell; the bomb-aimer and Sylvia were so wrapped up in each other that Goldfarb half expected them to consummate their friendship on the table or the floor. If Bell aimed his bombs as well as he did his hands, he'd done some useful work.

Embry said, "Even with pictures, I have trouble believing the Jerries built a slaughterhouse for people at whatever the name of that place was."

"Treblinka," Goldfarb said. He had trouble believing it, too, but less trouble, he guessed, than Embry. To a young Englishman whose accent said he came from the comfortable classes, organized murder like that

might really be unthinkable. To Goldfarb, whose father had fled less organized but no less sincere persecution, the notion of a place like Treblinka
was merely dreadful. Where Embry couldn't imagine it, Goldfarb could,
and had to hope he was wrong.

"How has it been back here, day by day?" Bagnall asked. "Until Jerry
shipped us home from Calais, we've been in the air so much all we did on
the ground was sleep and eat."

Goldfarb and Jones looked at each other. "It's not been the push-
button war we had during the Blitz," Goldfarb said at last. "The Lizards
are smarter than Jerry; they took out our radar straightaway and send more
rockets after it whenever we try to light it up again. So we've been reduced
to field glasses and telephones, like in the old days."

Daphne came back with Jerome Jones' new pint. He leered at her.
"David's been using his field glasses to peer in your window."

"Really?" she said coolly, setting the pint down. "And all the time I
thought it was you."

Jones' fair English skin made his flush visible even by the light of the
fireplace. Goldfarb and the aircrew howled laughter. Even Douglas Bell untangled himself from Sylvia long enough to say, "There's a fair hit, by
God!" Jones buried his nose in the pint.

"Do you know what I hear has worked well, though?" Goldfarb valiant-
ly tried to get back to George Bagnall's question. "Barrage balloons have cost
the Lizards some of their aircraft. They fly so low and so fast they haven't
a prayer of evading if the balloon's wire happens to lie in their path."

"Nice to know something does a bit of good," Bagnall said. "But that
wasn't quite what I meant—not the war, I mean. Just—life."

"Radarmen don't have lives," Jones said. "It's against His Majesty's articles of war, or something like that." He shoved his reemptied pint toward Daphne. "Try not to put so much arsenic in this one, my darling."

"Why? You'd likely thrive on it." But the barmaid went to fill the pint
again.

"She's sweet, Daphne is. I can tell that already," Bagnall said.

"Ah, but you got her on your knee," Goldfarb said morosely. "Do you
know how many months Jerome and I have been trying to do that?"

"Quite a few, by your long face. Aren't there any other women in Dover?"

"I expect there may be. Have we looked, Jerome?"

"Under every flat stone we could find," Jones answered. He was
watching Douglas Bell and Sylvia. If he'd had a pad in front of him, he'd
have taken notes, too.

"I'm going to pour this over your head, dearie," Daphne told him.

"They say it makes a good hair-set," he said, adding, "Not that I'd
know," just in time to keep the barmaid from making good on her threat.

Goldfarb finished his second pint, but wasn't quite in his friend's hurry to get another one. Everything the Lancaster aircrew had told him about life for the Jews in France made him worry more about what had been happening to them in Warsaw, where traditions of persecution ran back centuries and where the Nazis had no one within hundreds of miles to keep an eye on what they did. German radio could scream all it liked about "traitors to mankind"; he feared the Jews in Warsaw had been so desperate that even alien invaders looked better to them than the benign and humane rule of Hans Frank.

He wondered how his uncles and aunts and cousins were doing in Poland. Thinking about the broadcasts in Yiddish and German over the Warsaw shortwave station the Lizards had set up, he wondered how many—or how few—of his uncles and aunts and cousins were still alive.

He stared down at his empty pint. Would another help him forget his fears or bring them more strongly to the surface? The latter, he suspected. He held out the glass to Daphne anyhow. "Since you're still on your feet, dear, would you bring me one more?" Enough bitter and he'd stop caring about anything at all—if not this pint, then the next one or the one after that.

Then Jerome asked the aircrew, "And what happens to you lads next?"

Ken Embry said, "I expect we'll be going up again in another day or two. By all they've said, experienced aircrew are getting rather thin on the ground, if you'll forgive something of a mixed metaphor."

"How can you be so bloody calm about it?" Jones burst out. "Flying against the Jerries was one thing, but against the Lizards . . ."

Embry shrugged. "It's what we do. It's what we have to do. What else is there for anyone to do, but do what he has to do the best he can for as long as he can do it?"

Goldfarb studied the pilot and the rest of the aircrew. While he worried about his relatives—and from all he'd heard, with reason—they carried on in the face of their own nearly certain deaths. He looked at Sylvia, who might have been trying to squeeze Douglas Bell to death, and suddenly understood, on a level deeper than words, why she and Daphne would sleep with fliers but not with men who stayed on the ground. He remained rueful about that, but his jealousy disappeared.

When Daphne came back with his bitter, he stood up, dug in his pocket, came out with a handful of silver. "Fetch these lads a round, would you?"

Jerome Jones stared at him. "Such largess! Did your rich grandfather just cork off, or have you forgotten you're a Jew?"

He would have gone for anyone else's throat, especially with a couple of pints in him. Bagnall and a couple of the other members of the aircrew shifted in their seats to get ready to grab him if he tried. Instead, he started to laugh. "Bloody hell, Daphne, I'll buy one for this big-mouthed sod, too."

The aircrew relaxed. Jones' eyes got even bigger than they had been. "If I'd known calling you names was the way to pry beer out of you, I'd've tried it long ago."

"*Geh kak afen yam,*" Goldfarb said, and then disgusted everybody by refusing to translate.

Moishe Russie felt his heart pound in his chest. Meeting the Lizard governor whose forces had driven the Nazis out of Warsaw always frightened him, though Zolraag had treated him well enough—certainly better than he would have fared had he fallen under the eye of Hans Frank. He did not know whether Frank was dead or fled. Hoping him dead was sinful. Russie knew that. He was willing to make the wish even so.

Tadeusz Bor-Komorowski, the leader of the Home Army, came out of Zolraag's office. He did not look happy. He looked even less happy on seeing Russie. "What are you going to pry out of him now, Jew?" he growled. "They will give you anything you like, it seems."

"That is not so," Russie said. Bor-Komorowski frightened him, too. He hated Germans, yes, but he also hated Jews. The Germans were gone now. That left him only one target.

Scowling still, Bor-Komorowski stamped out, his boot heels ringing on the marble floor. Russie hurried into Zolraag's office; keeping his people's protector waiting would not do.

"Your Excellency," he said in German. He could speak to a Lizard easily enough now. A couple of weeks before, when the Nazis fled, beset from within and attacked from without at the same time, the first of the little, scampering creatures had seemed like demons to him. Though they were allies, they were weird almost beyond his power to take in. There the German propaganda had not lied.

But dealing with Zolraag day by day had begun to make strangeness familiar—and also brought the suspicion that the Lizard found him in particular and humanity in general at least as peculiar as he thought the governor.

"Herr Russie." Zolraag spoke slowly and with an accent that almost swallowed *r*'s and turned the middle sound in Russie's name into a long hiss. "You are well, I hope?"

"Yes, Your Excellency, thank you." Russie hissed himself, and made a gargling sound: he'd learned how to say "thank you" in Zolraag's language. He was doing his best to pick up words of the Lizards' speech; as he was already fluent in Yiddish, Hebrew, German, and Polish, acquiring a new tongue held no terror for him. He got the idea that Zolraag found the idea of there being many languages as alien as anything else about the Earth.

The Lizard was working hard with German, though. While his accent remained (Russie thought part of it due to the shape of his mouth), he'd picked up new words every time he spoke with the Jew, and his grammar, if less than good, was better than it had been. Now he said, "The German prisoners, Herr Russie, what do you think we do with them?"

"They are prisoners, Your Excellency; they ought to be treated like any other prisoners of war." Russie had walked out to the camp in the ruins of the Rakowiec district, just to see Germans behind the razor strips the Lizards used in place of barbed wire. He wished he hadn't. Looking at the crowds of dirty, battered, hungry men milling around reminded him overpoweringly of looking down any street when the ghetto was packed tight.

"Not all your people so think, Herr Russie. Who is your emperor here?"

"Our ruler, you mean?"

"Your emperor—he who decides for you," Zolraag said. He seemed to think it was very simple. Maybe it was, among the Lizards. Russie gathered that their supreme commander—the fleetlord, Zolraag called him— had chosen Zolraag governor of Warsaw, and that was that.

Things in human Warsaw, and especially inside the Jewish quarter, were less simple. The old German-backed ghetto administration still functioned after a fashion, doling out rations from the Lizards now rather than from the Nazis. Russie himself held moral authority because of the night the Lizards came. How that translated varied from day to day, sometimes from minute to minute.

And there was Mordechai Anielewicz. He'd taken a bullet through the left hand during the attack on the Germans, but it hadn't slowed him down. If anything, the fat white bandage seemed to mark him as a hero. His men swaggered through the streets of the Jewish quarter with captured German rifles on their shoulders. They walked boldly when they went into the rest of Warsaw, too: they were men whose comrades could avenge slights, and they knew it. For Jews, the feeling was rich and heady, like a fine new brandy.

The *Armja Krajowa* hated them. Many of the Mausers they bore had come to them from the Lizards: more arms than the new conquerors gave the Polish Home Army. Of course, the Poles had had far more guns at the start of the Warsaw rebellion than the Jews. Maybe the Lizards were working to balance the two groups in the newly conquered territory.

Maybe too, Russie admitted to himself, Zolraag and the rest of the Lizards were using the Jews and their plight under the Nazi regime as a tool against the rest of mankind. He listened to shortwave radio, just as he'd spoken on it from a studio for the Lizards. Though he'd told no more than the truth—and much less than all the truth—human broadcasters dismissed his reports as obvious propaganda. Even the dreadful pictures that came out of the ghetto brought little belief.

Because of that, Russie said, "Your Excellency, you will hurt yourself if you treat these captured Germans different from any other prisoners of war. People will only say you are cruel and ruthless."

"This you say, Herr Russie?" Unnervingly, Zolraag looked at Moishe with one eye and down at the papers on his desk with the other. "You, a Jew, a—how do you say it?—a sufferer, no, a victim of these Germans? Not treat them as killers? Why? Killers they are."

"You asked what I wanted done, Your Excellency," Russie answered. "Now I've told you. Revenge is a meal better eaten hot than cold." He spent the next few minutes explaining that, and reminded himself not to use figurative language with the Lizard governor again any time soon.

Zolraag turned both eyes on him. That was almost as unnerving as being examined with just one, for his stare was steadier than any man's could be. "You are emperor for your people when you so say? You— decide?"

"This is what I say for myself," Russie answered. He knew that if he lied, Zolraag's backing of his policy would transmute the lie to truth. But if he started lying, where would he stop? He didn't want to find out; he'd discovered too many horrors, in both himself and the world around him, over the past few years. After a moment, he added, "I am fairly sure I can bring my people with me." That wasn't a lie: more in the way of an exaggeration.

The governor studied him a while longer, then looked away in two directions at once. "Maybe you do this, Herr Russie; maybe you bring people with you. Maybe this end up by being good. Maybe we say, look at Jews, see how Germans do to them, see how Jews not want—what was word you use?—revenge, yes, revenge. Kind Jews, gentle Jews, better than Germans, yes?"

"Yes," Russie said in a hollow voice. More clearly than ever, he saw that Zolraag cared nothing for the Jews as Jews, and little for them as victims of the Nazis. He himself remained as much a *thing* to the Lizards as he had been to Hans Frank. The only difference was, to Zolraag he was a useful rather than an abhorrent thing. That marked an improvement, surely; a little while longer under the German *Generalgouvernement* and he would have been a dead thing. All the same, the realization tasted bitter as the bitter herbs of the Seder.

Zolraag said, "Maybe we make picture, Jew give German prisoner food. Maybe we do that, Herr Russie, yes? Make picture make men think."

"Any Jew who let himself be used for that sort of picture would find himself hated by other Jews," Russie answered. Despair tinged his thoughts: *propaganda, that's all they want us for. They rescued us for their own purposes, not out of any special kindness.*

A moment later, the Lizard echoed his worries. "We help you then,

Herr Russie. You help us now. You owe us—what is word?—debt, yes. You owe us."

"I know, but after what we went through, this is a hard way to repay the debt."

"What else you Jews good for, Herr Russie, now to us?"

Russie flinched, as from a blow. Never before had Zolraag been so brutally frank with him. *Change the subject a little, before you get in deeper,* he thought. The ploy had served him well in medical school, letting him use his strengths and minimize weakness. He said, "Your Excellency, how can Jews think of giving Germans food when we still haven't enough for ourselves?"

"Have as much as anyone else now," Zolraag said.

"Yes, but we were starving before. Even what we have now is none too good." The Poles resented having their rations cut to help feed the Jews, and the Jews were angry at the Poles for not understanding—or for approving of—their plight under the Nazis. Fair rations meant everyone ate too little. Russie said, "With all your power, Your Excellency, can't you bring in more food for everyone in Warsaw? Then we would worry less about sharing it with the Germans."

"Where we get food, Herr Russie? No food here, not by Warsaw, no. This place where fight happen, not farming. Fight ruin farming. You tell me where food is, I get. Otherwise . . ." Zolraag spread clawed hands in a very human seeming gesture of frustration.

"But—" Russie stared at the Lizard in dismay. He knew only God was omnipotent, but the Lizards, aside from seeming like manifestations of His will when they drove the Germans out of Warsaw and saved the Jews from certain destruction, were able to do so many other things with so little effort that Moishe had assumed their abilities were for all practical purposes unlimited. Discovering that was not so rocked him. He faltered. "Could you not, uh, bring food in from other parts of the world where you are not fighting hard?"

Zolraag let his mouth hang open. Russie glowered at rows of little, sharp-pointed teeth and the unnerving snakelike tongue; he knew the governor was laughing at him. Zolraag said, "Can do that, when you people give up stupid fight, join Empire. Now, no. Need all we have in fight. Tosev 3—this world—big place. Need all we have."

"I see," Russie said slowly. Here was news he would have to pass on to Anielewicz. Maybe the combat leader would have a better feel for what it meant than he did. What it sounded like was that the Lizards were stretched thinner than they wanted to be.

A world was indeed a big place. Till the war started, Russie hadn't really worried about anything outside Poland. The Germans' crushing triumph taught him the folly of that. Afterward, his hope against the

Germans rested first on England and then on the even more distant United States.

But when Zolraag spoke of this world, he implied the presence of others. That should have been obvious; the Lizards plainly were from nowhere on Earth. Till now, though, what all that meant hadn't got through to Russie. He wondered how many worlds the aliens knew, and if any besides Earth and their own home held thinking beings.

Having gained a secular education—indispensable in medicine—Russie believed in Darwin alongside of Genesis. They coexisted uneasily in his mind, one dominant when he thought, the other when he felt. In the ghetto, God gained the upper hand, for prayer seemed likelier to do some good than anything merely rational. And when the Lizards came, prayer was answered.

But Russie suddenly wondered what part God had had in creating the Lizards and whatever other thinking races there might be. If He had shaped them all, what was man that He should notice him especially? If Lizards and any others were not His creatures, what was His place in the universe? Had He any place in the universe? Posing the question in those terms was even more frightening than coming to meet with Zolraag.

The governor said, "We have more food, we give you more. Maybe soon." Russie nodded. That meant he wasn't supposed to hold his breath. Zolraag went on, "You find out who is emperor of Jews about German prisoners, Herr Russie, tell what you think to do. Not wait—must know."

"Your Excellency, it shall be done." Russie repeated the phrase in the Lizards' language. To them, it was one to conjure with, one almost as important as the *Sh'ma Yisroayl* for an observant Jew. They built their lives around elaborate patterns of obedience, in the same way people did around families. *It shall be done* was the most potent promise they had.

When Zolraag seemed to have nothing further to say, Russie got to his feet, bowed to the Lizard governor, and started to leave. Then the Lizard said, "A moment, please." Moishe obediently turned back. Zolraag continued, "Is always so . . . not cold—how do you say, a little cold?—in Warsaw?"

"Cool?" Russie asked.

"Cool, yes, that is word, thank you. Is always so cool in Warsaw?"

"It will be cooler yet later in the year, Your Excellency," Russie answered, puzzled. It was still summer in Warsaw, not a hot summer, but summer nonetheless. He remembered the winter before, when heat of any sort—electricity, coal, even wood—had been next to impossible to come by. He remembered huddling with his whole family under all the bedclothes they had, and his teeth chattering like castanets even so. He remembered the endless sound of coughing that had filled the ghetto, and picking out by ear the soft tubercular coughs from those brought on by pneumonia or influenza. He remembered scrawny corpses lying in the snow, and his relief that they might not start to stink until they were picked up.

If Zolraag thought this August day cool, how could he explain to the Lizard what winter really meant? He saw no way: as well explain the Talmud to a five-year-old, and a *goyishe* five-year-old at that. What he'd already said would have to do.

Zolraag hissed something in his own language. Russie caught a word or two: "—inside a refrigerator." Then the governor switched back to German. "Thank you, Herr Russie, for saying beforehand what may be bad about what comes, for, ah . . ."

"For warning you?" Russie said.

"Warning, yes, that is word. Thank you. Good day, Herr Russie."

"Good day, Your Excellency." Russie bowed again; this time Zolraag did not detain him with more questions. In the waiting room outside the governor's office sat a handsome, strikingly masculine-looking young Catholic priest. His pale eyes went icy for a moment when they met the Jew's, but he managed a civil nod.

Russie nodded back; civility was not to be despised. Asking Poles to love Jews was asking for a miracle. Having asked for one miracle and received it, Moishe did not aim to push his luck with God. But asking for civility—that was within the realm of the possible.

Zolraag's headquarters lay in a block of two- and three-story office buildings on Crójccka Street in southwestern Warsaw. A couple of the buildings had taken shell hits, but most were intact save for such details as bullet holes and broken-out windows. That made the block close to unique in the city, Russie thought as he scrunched through shards of glass.

Nazi artillery and unending, unchallenged streams of *Luftwaffe* bombers had torn gaping holes in Warsaw when the city stood siege after the Germans invaded Poland. Most of that rubble still remained: the Germans did not seem to care what sort of Warsaw they ruled, so long as it was theirs. The buildings smashed in 1939 now had a weathered look to them, as if they'd always been part of the landscape.

More ruins, though, were fresh, sharp-edged. The Germans had fought like men possessed to hold the Lizards out of Warsaw. Russie walked by the burnt shell of a Nazi panzer. It still exhaled the dead-meat stench of man's final corruption. Shaking his head, Russie marveled that so many Germans, here as elsewhere, had expended so much courage for so bad a cause. God had given mankind that particular lesson at least since the days of the Assyrians, but its meaning remained obscure.

A Lizard fighting vehicle purred past the wrecked German tank. When the Nazis entered Warsaw, their roaming, smoke-belching panzers, all hard lines and angles as if the faces of SS men were somehow turned to armor plate, seemed dropped into 1939 straight from a malign future. The Lizards' smoother, faster, nearly silent machines showed that the Germans were not quite the masters of creation they fancied themselves to be.

It was a couple of kilometers back to the edge of the Jewish quarter. Russie wore his long black coat unbuttoned, but he'd started to sweat by the time he drew near the ruined walls that marked off the former (God be praised!) ghetto. *If Zolraag thinks this is cool weather, let him wait until January*, he thought.

"*Reb* Moishe!" A peddler pushing a cart full of turnips paused to doff his cloth cap.

"*Reb* Moishe!" A very pretty girl, no more than thirteen or fourteen, smiled. She was gaunt, but not visibly starving.

"*Reb* Moishe!" One of Anielewicz's fighters came to a fair approximation of attention. He wore an old Polish helmet, a peasant blouse, and baggy trousers tucked into German army boots. Twin bandoliers full of gleaming brass cartridges crisscrossed his chest.

The salutes pleased Russie, and reminded him he'd become an important man here. He gravely gave back each in turn. But as he did so, he wondered whether any of the people he'd greeted would still have been alive had the Lizards not come and, if so, how much longer they would have survived. He wondered how much longer he would have survived himself.

And so I decided to help the Lizards, in the hope that they would then help my people, he thought. *And they did, and we were saved. And what have I gained from this? Only to be branded a liar and a traitor and a renegade by those who will not believe their fellow men capable of what the Germans did here.*

He tried to tell himself he did not care, that the recognition of those inside Warsaw, those who knew the truth, counted for more than anything anyone else could say. That was true and not true at the same time. Given a choice, he would sooner have worked with any human beings—save only the Germans—against the invaders from another world.

But what choice had he had? When the Lizards came, the Russians were far away and themselves reeling under German attack. The British were beleaguered, the Americans so distant they might as well have been on the dark side of the moon. Set beside the Nazis, the Lizards looked like a good bargain. No, they *were* a good bargain.

All the same, he sometimes wished he'd not had to make it.

Such thoughts flew away when he turned a corner and saw Mordechai Anielewicz coming toward him. The young leader of the Jewish fighters was surrounded by several of his men, all of them heavily armed, all in the ragged mishmash of military gear and ordinary clothes Russie had seen on the other warrior.

Anielewicz himself carried no weapons. Though he dressed as shabbily as his followers, his firm stride and the space the others kept clear around him proclaimed him to be cock o' the walk here.

He nodded, cautiously, to Russie. Allies and rivals at the same time, they drew their power from different sources: Anielewicz straight from the barrels of his fighters' guns, Russie from the confidence the Jews of Warsaw placed in him. Because of that, neither was as confident with the other as he would have been with one of his own kind.

Anielewicz spoke first: "Good day to you, *Reb* Moishe. How did your meeting with the Lizard governor go?"

"Well enough," Russie answered. "He complained the weather was too cool to suit him, though."

"Did he?" Anielewicz said. A couple of the Jewish fighters laughed. Anielewicz's smile was broad, but never quite reached his eyes. "He'll complain more in a few months, and that's a fact. What else did he have to say?"

"It doesn't sound as though there's much hope for more rations any time soon." Russie explained Zolraag's supply problems. They were something the Jews' military leader needed to know.

"Too bad." Anielewicz scowled. "We really need more than the Poles, because we had so much less for so long. But if he can't, he can't. I don't want to start a war with the *Armja Krajowa* over this; they outnumber us too badly."

"Bor-Komorowski was in to see Zolraag just before me. He isn't too happy about how much we're getting now."

"Too bad," Anielewicz said again. "Still, it's worth finding out, and it's not what you'd call a surprise." His gaze sharpened; he peered at Russie as if over a gunsight. "And what did His Lizardy Excellency have to say about the Nazi bastards and SS swine who couldn't run fast enough when they got thrown out of here? Has he figured out what he's going to do with them yet?"

"He asked me what I thought, as a matter of fact," Russie said.

"And what was your answer?" Anielewicz asked softly.

Russie took a deep breath before he answered: "I told him that, if it were up to me, I would treat them as prisoners of war." Almost all the fighters growled at that. Ignoring them, Moishe went on: "Doing so would pull the teeth from the propaganda the Germans are putting out against us. And besides, if we treat them as they treated us, how are we any better than they?"

"They did it to us for sport. When we do it to them, it's for vengeance," Anielewicz said, with the same exaggerated patience he would have used in explaining to a child of four. "Do you *want* to be the perfect ghetto Jew, *Reb* Moishe, the one who never hits back no matter what the *goyim* do to you? We've come too far for that." He slapped one of his men on the shoulder. The fellow's slung Mauser bounced up and down.

Standing up to armed ruffians, Russie discovered, was hardly easier when they were Jews than it had been when they were Germans. He said, "You know what I am. Was I not with you when we rose? But if murder in cold blood was wrong for the Germans, I tell you again that it does not magically become right for us."

"What did Zolraag think when you said this to him?"

"If I understand him rightly, he thought I was out of my mind," Russie admitted, which jerked a few startled laughs from the fighters around Anielewicz.

"He may well have a point." The smile Anielewicz gave Russie was far from pleasant; it reminded him of a wolf curling back its lip to show its teeth. He studied the young Jewish fighting leader. Anielewicz was different from the Germans who had until lately been his models in matters military. Most of them were professionals, going about their business no matter how horrific that business might be. Anielewicz, by contrast, gave the impression that he loved what he was doing.

Did that make him better or worse? Russie couldn't decide. He said, "As may be. He wants some sort of consensus from us before he acts— you'll have noticed that the Lizards think we must have someone who can make binding decisions for our whole community."

Now Mordechai Anielewicz let out a snort of genuine amusement. "Has he ever watched anyone trying to get three Jews to agree about anything?"

"I would say not. But I would also say something else: we used the Lizards to save our own lives, because nothing they did to us could be worse than what the Nazis were already doing. Well and good thus far, Mordechai. No one who knows the truth of what we suffered could blame us for that—a drowning man grabs any plank in the sea."

One of the fighters growled, "What about the ones who won't believe the truth even when it's shoved in their fat faces?"

"If you'd believed the Nazis would do all they said they'd do, would you have stayed in Poland?" Russie asked. Like a lot of Polish Jews, Russie had relatives in England and more distant ones in the United States. His parents had got letters after Hitler came to power, urging them to get out while they could. They hadn't listened—and they were dead now.

The fighter grunted. He was in his late thirties; maybe he'd made the choice to stay himself instead of having his parents do it for him.

Anielewicz put the conversation back on track. "Were you coming to some sort of point about the Lizards, *Reb* Moishe? I do hope so, for you've said nothing to convince me thus far."

"Think about this, then: we did what we had to do with the Lizards, I grant you that. But are we wise to do any more than we have to do? Telling them to shoot their German prisoners for us plays into their hands, and into the hands of the rest of the Germans as well. If you do not think well of mercy for mercy's sake, look at that before you urge a slaughter."

"Are you sure you intended to be a doctor? You argue like a *reb*, that's certain." But Anielewicz really did think about what Russie'd said; Russie could see it in his face. Slowly, the fighting leader said, "You're telling me you don't want us to be the Lizards' cat's-paws."

"That's it exactly." Maybe Russie had found the key to reaching the fighting leader after all. "We have to be, to some extent, because we're so much weaker than they are. But when we let them put our name on their wickedness, it becomes ours as well in the eyes of the world."

The fighter who'd spoken before said, "He may have something there, boss." He sounded reluctant to admit it; Moishe admired him the more for speaking.

"Yes, he just may." The glance Anielewicz shot Russie was no more friendly for that. "By God, *Reb* Moishe, I want vengeance on those Nazi bastards. When the Lizards bombed Berlin, I cheered, do you know that? I cheered."

"I would be lying if I said I was as sorry as I should have been," Russie said.

"Well, there you are," Anielewicz said, as if he'd proven something. Maybe he had.

If so, Russie did not care to concede it. "Cheering, though, was wrong, don't you see? Most of those Germans had done nothing more to the Lizards than we'd done to the Germans. They just happened to be in Berlin when the Lizards dropped their bomb. The Lizards didn't care that they weren't soldiers; they went ahead and killed them anyhow. They aren't angels, Mordechai."

"This I know," Anielewicz answered. "But better our devils than the devils on the other side."

"No, that's not the lesson." Moishe stubbornly shook his head. "The lesson is, better that we not become devils ourselves."

Anielewicz's scowl was fearsome. Russie felt the fear. If the leader of the Jewish fighting forces chose to ignore him, what could he do about it? But before Anielewicz replied, he glanced at the fighters who accompanied him. A couple of them were nodding at Russie's words. That seemed only to make Anielewicz angrier.

"All right!" He spat on the filthy cobblestones. "We'll keep the stinking Germans alive, then, if you love them so well."

"Love them? You must be out of your mind. But I hope I still know what justice is. And," Russie added, "I hope I still know that what mankind thinks of me is more important than any Lizard's good opinion—and that includes Zolraag's." His own vehemence surprised him, the more so because he got on well with the aliens' governor.

Anielewicz also surprised him. "There for once we agree, *Reb* Moishe. There, in fact, we might even find common ground with General Bor-Komorowski, should the need ever arise."

"Really?" Russie was not sure he wanted to find common ground with Bor-Komorowski on anything save the desirability of getting rid of the Germans. Bor-Komorowski was a good Polish patriot, which made him only a little less fascist—or perhaps just less efficiently fascist—than Heinrich Himmler. Still . . . "That may be useful, one of these days."

Moscow! The winter before, German troops had seen the spires of the Kremlin from the Russian capital's suburbs. None came any closer than that, and then they'd been thrown back in bitter fighting. Yet now Heinrich Jäger walked freely through the streets the *Wehrmacht* had been unable to reach.

Beside him, Georg Schultz looked this way and that, as he did every day going to and from the Kremlin. Schultz said, "I still have trouble believing how much of Moscow is still in one piece. We bombed it, the Lizards bombed it—and here it is still."

"It's a big city," Jäger answered. "It can take a lot of punishment and not show much. Big cities are hard to destroy, unless . . ." His voice trailed away. He'd seen pictures of Berlin now, and wished he hadn't.

He and Schultz both wore ill-fitting civilian suits of cheap fabric and outdated cut. He would have been ashamed to put his on back in Germany. Here, though, it helped him fit in, for which he was just as glad. He would not have been safe in his tankman's uniform. In the Ukraine, the panzer troops had sometimes been welcomed as liberators. Germans remained enemies in Moscow, even after the coming of the Lizards.

Schultz pointed to a poster on a brick wall. "Can you read what that says, sir?"

Jäger's Russian was better than it had been, but still far from good. Letter by unfamiliar Cyrillic letter, he sounded out the poster's message. "*Smert* means 'death,' " he said. "I don't know what the second word is. Something to do with us."

"Something nasty," Schultz agreed. The poster showed a pigtailed little girl lying dead on the floor, a doll beside her. A footprint in blood led the eye to a departing soldier's marching boot, on the heel of which was a German swastika.

Before he got to Moscow, Jäger had been certain down to the very core of him that the *Wehrmacht* would have beaten the Red Army for good this year had the Lizards not intervened. Now he wondered, though he'd never said so out loud. It wasn't just that Russia was so much bigger than Germany; he had known that all along. But despite the stubbornness of Soviet resistance, he hadn't believed the Russian people were as firmly behind Stalin as the Germans were behind Hitler. Now he did, and it was a disturbing thought.

His shoes scuffed on the paving of Red Square. The Germans had planned a victory parade there, timed for the anniversary of the Bolshevik Revolution. It hadn't happened. Russian sentries still paced back and forth in front of the Kremlin wall in their own stiff version of the goose step.

Jäger and Schultz came up to the gateway by which they entered the Kremlin compound. Jäger nodded to the guards there, a group of men he saw every third day. None of the Russians nodded back. They never did. Their leader, who wore a sergeant's three red triangles on his collar patches, held out his hand. "Papers," he said in Russian.

As usual, he carefully examined the documents the Germans produced, compared photographs to faces. Jäger was certain that if he ever forgot his papers, the sergeant would not pass him through even though he recognized him. Breaking routine was not something the Russians did well.

Today, though, he and Schultz had everything in order. The sergeant started to stand aside to pass them through when someone else came trotting across Red Square toward the checkpoint. Jäger turned to see who was in such a tearing hurry. As he did, his mouth fell open. "I'll be Goddamned," Schultz said, which about summed things up.

Unlike the tankmen, the fellow approaching wore a German uniform—an SS uniform at that—and wore it with panache. His every aggressive stride seemed to warn that anyone who gave him trouble would have a thin time of it. He was tall and broad-shouldered and would have been handsome had a scar not seamed his left cheek. Actually, he was handsome anyhow, in a piratical sort of way.

Instead of bristling at him as Jäger had expected, the Russian guards grinned and nudged each other. The sergeant said, "Papers?"

The SS man drew himself up to his full impressive height. "Stuff your papers, and stuff you, too!" he said in a deep, booming voice. His German held an Austrian accent. The sentries practically hugged themselves with glee. The sergeant came to an attention stiffer than he might have granted Marshal Zhukov, waved the big bruiser into the Kremlin.

"Why didn't we ever try that?" Schultz said admiringly.

"I don't have the balls for it," Jäger admitted.

The SS man spun toward them. For all his size, he was light on his feet. "So you are Germans after all," he said. "I thought you might be, but what with those rag-pickers' getups, I couldn't be sure till you opened your mouths. Who the devil are you, anyway?"

"Major Heinrich Jäger, Sixteenth Panzer," Jäger answered crisply.

"Here is my tank gunner, Sergeant Georg Schultz. And now, *Herr Hauptsturmführer*, I might ask you the same question." The SS rank was the equivalent of captain; however much brass this fellow had, Jäger was his superior.

The SS man's brace was almost as rigid—and as full of parody—as the Soviet sergeant's had been. Clicking his heels, he declared in falsetto, "SS *Hauptsturmführer* Otto Skorzeny begs leave to report his presence, sir!"

Jäger snorted. The scar on Skorzeny's cheek partly froze the left corner of his mouth and turned his smile into something twisted. Jäger asked him, "What are you doing here, especially in that suit? You're lucky the Ivans haven't decided to take your nose and ears."

"Nonsense," Skorzeny said. If he ever had doubts about anything, he didn't show them in public. "Russians only know how to be one of two things: masters or slaves. If you convince them you're the master, what does that leave them?"

"If," Georg Schultz murmured, too softly for the SS man to hear.

"You still haven't said why you're here," Jäger persisted.

"I am acting under orders from—" Skorzeny hesitated; Jäger guessed he'd been about to say *from Berlin*. He resumed: "from my superiors. Can you say the same?" He gave Jäger's Russian suit a fishy stare.

Beside Jäger, Schultz stirred angrily. Jäger wondered if this arrogant *Hauptsturmführer* had ever seen action that required him to get those polished boots dirty. But that question answered itself: Skorzeny wore the ribbon for a wound badge between the first and second buttons of his tunic. All right, he had some idea of what was real, then. And his counterquestion made Jäger think—what *would* the authorities have to say about how he was working with the Red Army?

He briefly summarized how he had come to be in Moscow. Maybe Skorzeny had done some fighting, but could he say he'd taken out a Lizard panzer? Not many had, and not many of those who had still lived.

When he was through, the SS man nodded. Now he blustered less. "You might say we're both in Moscow for the same reason, then, Major, whether with official approval or without. We have a common interest in showing the Ivans how to make themselves more effective foes for the Lizards."

"Ah," Jäger said. Just as the Soviets no longer treated Germans caught on Russian soil as prisoners of war (or worse), the surviving pieces of the government of the *Reich* must have decided to do their best to keep the Russians in the fight now and worry about their being Bolshevik Slavic *Untermenschen* later.

The three Germans walked together toward the Kremlin. The heart of Soviet Russia still wore the camouflage it had donned after the Russo-German war began. Its bulging onion domes, an architecture alien and oriental to Jäger's eyes, had their gilding covered over with battleship gray paint. Walls were mottled with patches of black and orange, yellow and brown, rather like the hide of a leprous giraffe, to confuse attackers from the air.

Such tricks had not entirely spared it from damage. Stolid, wide-shouldered women in shawls and drab dresses carried bricks and chunks of wood away from a recent bomb hit. The sick-sweet stink of day before yesterday's battlefield hung over the place. That smell always made Jäger's heart beat faster in remembered fear.

Skorzeny grunted and put a hand over the right side of his belly. Jäger thought the SS man's reaction similar to his own until he realized Skorzeny's face held real pain. "What's wrong?" he asked.

"My fucking gall bladder," the *Hauptsturmführer* answered. "It had me in the hospital for a while earlier this year. But the doctors say it isn't going to kill me, and lying around on my backside is a bloody bore, so here I am up and doing again. A good thing, too."

"You were here on the Eastern Front before, sir?" Georg Schultz asked.

"Yes, with *Das Reich*," Skorzeny said.

Schultz nodded and said nothing more. Jäger could guess what he was thinking. A lot of people who saw action on the Eastern Front would fall down on their knees and thank God for an illness that got them sent back to Germany and safety. Skorzeny, by the way he talked, would sooner have stayed and fought. He didn't sound as though he were bluffing, either. Jäger's respect for him went up a notch.

In spite of the Lizards' air raids, the Kremlin still swarmed with life. Occasional holes merely showed Jäger the soldiers and bureaucrats bustling about within, in the same way as he could have seen the humming life inside an anthill with its top kicked off.

He was not surprised to find Skorzeny heading for the same doorway as he and Jäger used: naturally, the SS man would also be meeting with officers from the Defense Commissariat. The doorway into the Kremlin itself, like the one into the compound around it, was guarded. The lieutenant who headed this detachment put out his hand without a word. Without a word, Jäger and Schultz gave him their documents. Without a word, he studied and returned them.

Then he turned to Skorzeny, his hand still outstretched. An impish grin lit the big man's face. He seized the Russian lieutenant's hand, vigorously pumped it up and down. The guards stared in disbelief. The lieutenant managed to return a sickly smile. A couple of his men had raised their submachine guns. When he smiled, they lowered them again.

"Talk about balls, one of these days he's going to get his blown off, playing games like that," Schultz said out of the side of his mouth.

"Maybe, maybe not," Jäger answered. He'd known a few people who simply bulled their way through life, charging at the world with such headlong aggression that it gave way before them. Skorzeny seemed to be of that stripe. On a larger scale, so did Adolf Hitler . . . and Stalin.

It was easier to think of the Soviet leader than of Hitler as Jäger let the immensity of the Kremlin swallow him and Schultz. Skorzeny followed. Just inside the doorway stood a pair of Russian lieutenant-colonels: no Germans would go wandering unescorted through the Red Army's holy of holies.

One of the Russian officers wore a tankman's black collar patches. "Good morning, Major Jäger, Sergeant Schultz," he said in excellent German.

"Lieutenant-Colonel Kraminov," Jäger said, nodding back politely. Viktor Kraminov had been assigned to Schultz and him since they came to Moscow. They might have traded shots with each other the year before, for Kraminov had been part of Marshal Budenny's southern Soviet army before being transferred to staff duty in Moscow. He had an old man's wise eyes set in a face of childlike innocence, and knew more about handling panzers than Jäger would have expected from the Russians' battle performance.

The other lieutenant-colonel, a fellow Jäger had not seen before, wore green collar patches. Georg Schultz frowned. "What's green stand for?" he whispered.

Jäger needed a minute to think. Russian infantry patches were maroon; tanks, artillery, and engineers black; cavalry dark blue; air force light blue. But what Soviet service wore green as its *Waffenfarbe*? Jäger stiffened. "He's NKVD," he whispered back.

Schultz flinched. Jäger didn't blame him. Just as no Russian soldier would want to run across the *Gestapo*, so the Germans naturally grew nervous at the sight of an officer of the People's Commissariat for the Interior. If he'd come across the NKVD man a year ago, he would have shot him at once; German orders were to take no secret policemen or political commissars alive, regardless of the laws of war.

After one brief glance, the NKVD lieutenant-colonel ignored the two Germans in civilian clothes; he'd been waiting for Otto Skorzeny. "A very good day to you, *Herr Hauptsturmführer*," he said. His German was even better than Kraminov's. He sounded fussily precise, like about half of Jäger's old *Gymnasium* teachers.

"Hello, Boris, you skinny old prune-faced bastard," Skorzeny boomed back. Jäger waited for the heavens to fall. The NKVD man, who really was a skinny old prune-faced bastard, just gave a tight little nod, from which Jäger inferred he'd been working with Skorzeny for a while and had decided he'd better make allowances.

The NKVD man—Boris—turned toward Lieutenant-Colonel Kraminov. "Perhaps all five of us will work together today," he said. "In chatting before you gentlemen arrived, Viktor Danielovich and I discovered that we all may be able to contribute to an operation which will benefit both our nations."

"It is as Lieutenant-Colonel Lidov says," Kraminov agreed. "Cooperation here will aid both the Soviet Union and the *Reich* against the Lizards."

"You mean you want German help for something you don't think you can do on your own," Skorzeny said. "Why do you need us for an operation which I presume will be on Soviet soil?" His gaze came to a sudden, sharp focus. "Wait! It's on territory we took from you last year, isn't it?"

"That may be," Lidov said. The noncommittal reply convinced Jäger that Skorzeny was right. He made a mental note: the SS man might bluster, but he was anything but stupid. Lieutenant-Colonel Kraminov evidently saw dissimulation was useless, too. He sighed, perhaps regretting it. "Come, all of you."

The Germans followed the two Russian officers down the long, high-ceilinged halls of the Kremlin. Other Russian soldiers sometimes paused in their own duties to stare at Skorzeny's SS uniform, but no one said anything: they seemed to accept that the world had grown stranger these past few months.

The office Jäger and Schultz entered was not the one Kraminov used. Like Kraminov's, though, it was surprisingly light and airy, with a large window that gave a view of the grounds of the Kremlin compound. Jäger had looked for nothing but dank gloom at the heart of Soviet Russia, but a moment's reflection after finding the opposite told him that was silly. Even Communists needed light by which to work. And the Kremlin was far older than either Communism or electricity; when it was raised, the only light worth having came from the sun. So, large windows.

Lieutenant-Colonel Lidov pointed to a samovar. "Tea, *tovarishchii*?" he asked. Jäger frowned; Kraminov didn't call Schultz and him "comrades," as if they were Reds themselves. But then, Kraminov was a tank-man, a warrior, not NKVD. At home, Jäger drank coffee thick with cream. But he hadn't been at home for a long time. He nodded.

Lidov poured for all of them. At home, Jäger didn't drink tea from a glass, either. He had done that before, though, with captured samovar sets in steppe towns and collective farms overrun by the *Wehrmacht*. Lidov brewed better tea than he'd had there.

The NKVD man set down his glass. "To business," he said. Jäger leaned forward and looked attentive. Georg Schultz just sat where he was. Skorzeny slouched down in his chair and looked bored. If that disconcerted Lidov, he didn't let it show.

"To business," he repeated. "As the *Hauptsturmführer* has suggested, the proposed action will take place in an area where the fascist invaders had established themselves prior to the arrival of the alien imperialist aggressors commonly known as Lizards."

Jäger wondered if Lidov talked that way all the time. Skorzeny yawned. "By fascist invaders, I presume you mean us Germans." He sounded as bored as he looked.

"You and your lackeys and running dogs, yes." Maybe Lidov did talk that way all the time. However he talked, he didn't retreat a centimeter, though Skorzeny could have broken him over his knee like a stick. "To resume, then: along with bands of gallant Soviet partisans, German remnant groups remain in the area under discussion. Thus the apparent expedience of a joint Soviet-German operation."

"Where *is* the area in question?" Jäger asked.

"Ah," Lidov said. "Attend the map here, if you please." He stood up, pointed to one of the charts tacked onto the wall. The lettering, of course, was Cyrillic, but Jäger recognized the Ukraine anyhow. Red pins showed Soviet positions, blue ones surviving German units, and yellow the Lizards. The map had more yellow measles than Jäger liked.

Lidov went on, "We are particularly concerned with this area north and west of Kiev, near the town of Komarin. There, early in the struggle against the Lizards, you Germans succeeded in wrecking with heavy artillery two major ships of the common enemy."

That made Georg Schultz sit up straighter. So did Jäger—it was news to him, too. Skorzeny said, "And so? This is no doubt excellent, but how does it concern us here?"

"In and around the wreckage of one of these ships, the Lizards appear to be making no more than an ordinary effort at salvage. This is emphatically not the case at the other."

"Tell us about the second one, then," Jäger urged.

"Yes, that is what I was getting to, Major," the NKVD man said. "We have reports from witnesses that the Lizards are operating as if in an area of poison gas, although no gas seems to be present. Not only do they wear masks, in fact, but also bulky full-body protective suits. You see the significance of this, I trust?"

"*Ja,*" Jäger said absently. Except for helmets and sometimes body armor, Lizards didn't wear clothes. If they felt they needed to be protected from something, whatever it was had to be pretty fierce. As for gas—he shivered a little as he remembered his own days in the trenches back in the first war. A gas mask was torment, made worth wearing only because it warded against worse.

"It is not gas, you say?" Skorzeny put in.

"No, definitely not," Lidov answered. "There has been no problem due to wind or anything of that sort. The Lizards appear to be engaged in recovering certain chunks of metal strewn about over a wide area when their ship exploded. These are loaded into lorries which seem to be very heavy for their size, judging by the tracks they leave in dirt."

"Armor-plated?" Jäger asked.

"Possibly," Lidov said. "Or possibly lead."

Jäger thought about that. Lead was good for plumbing, but for shielding? The only time he'd ever seen anyone use lead for shielding was when the fellow who'd X-rayed him after he was wounded put on a lead waistcoat before he took his pictures. He made a sudden connection—he'd heard inside these very Kremlin walls that the weapon which destroyed Berlin had had some sort of effect (not being a physicist, he didn't know quite what) related to X-rays.

He said, "Is this salvage related to these dreadful bombs the Lizards have?"

Skorzeny's dark eyes widened. Lidov's rather narrow ones, already constricted by a Tatar fold at their inner corners, now thinned further. In a voice silky with danger, he said, "Were you one of ours, Major Jäger, I doubt you would long survive. You speak your thoughts too openly."

Georg Schultz surged halfway out of his chair. "You watch your mouth, you damned Red!"

Jäger set a hand on the gunner's shoulder, pushed him back into the seat. "Do remember where we are, Sergeant," he said dryly.

"That is an excellent suggestion, Sergeant Schultz," the NKVD man agreed. "Your loyalty does you credit, but it is foolish here." He turned back to Jäger. "You, Major, may be too clever for your own good."

"Not necessarily." Otto Skorzeny spoke up for the panzer officer. "That we are here, Lieutenant-Colonel Lidov, that you have said even so much on this sensitive matter, argues that you need German assistance for whatever you have in mind. You shall not get it unless Major Jäger here remains unharmed. You do need us, do you not?" In other circumstances, his smile would have been sweet. Now it mocked.

Lidov glared at him. Lieutenant-Colonel Kraminov, who had let the other man do the talking till now, said, "You are right, worse luck, *Herr Hauptsturmführer*. This area has only Russian partisans, no regular Red Army forces, as you Germans drove these out last fall. While brave enough, the partisans lack the heavy armament required to attack a Lizard lorry convoy. There are, however, also fragmentary *Wehrmacht* units in the area—"

"In regard to the Lizards, these are hardly more than partisan forces themselves," Lidov interrupted. "But they do retain more arms than our own glorious and heroic partisans, that is true." By his expression, the truth tasted bad in his mouth.

"Thus we suggest a joint undertaking," Kraminov said. "You three will serve as our liaison with whatever German units remain north of Kiev. In the event we succeed in despoiling the convoy, our two governments will share equally in what we capture. Is it agreed?"

"How do we know you won't keep everything for yourselves?" Schultz asked.

"You fascist aggressors were the ones who brutally violated the non-aggression pact the great Stalin generously granted to Hitler," Lidov snapped. "We are the ones who tremble at the thought of trusting you."

"You would've jumped us if we hadn't," Schultz said angrily.

"Comrades," Lieutenant-Colonel Kraminov said—in German, which gave the word a different feel from the harsh Russian Lidov had used. "Please, comrades. If we are to be comrades, we shall need to work together. If we go at each other's throats, only the Lizards will benefit."

"He's right, Georg," Jäger said. "If we start arguing, we'll never get anything done." He hadn't forgotten his own dislike and contempt for nearly everything he'd seen in the Soviet Union, but could not deny the Russians fought hard—nor that they were masters of partisan warfare. "For now, let ideology wait."

"Can you get me a telegraph line to Germany?" Otto Skorzeny asked. "I must have authorization before proceeding with this scheme."

"Provided the latest Lizard advances have not cut it, yes," Lidov said. "I can also let you transmit on the frequency arranged with your government. You must talk around what you truly wish to say there, however, to keep the Lizards from following if they intercept the signal, as they very likely will."

"The telegraph first, then," Skorzeny said. "That failing, the radio. The mission strikes me as worth accomplishing. Other concerns can wait." He studied the NKVD lieutenant-colonel as if through the eyepiece of a panzer cannon sight. Lidov scowled right back at him. Without words, both men said that, while other concerns could wait, they were not forgotten.

Liu Han sat naked on the shiny mat in her room in the giant airplane that somehow never fell down from the sky. She made herself into the smallest bundle she could, legs drawn up tight, hands clasped on her shins, head pressed down till it touched her knees. With her eyes closed, she could imagine the entire universe around her had disappeared.

Her world view did not include the concept *experimental animal*, but that was what she had become. The little scaly devils who held her here wanted to discover certain things about the way people functioned, and were using her to help them learn. They cared not at all what she thought of the process.

The door to the chamber slid open. Before she could will herself to stillness, she looked up. Two Lizards marched in, with a man—a foreign devil, not even decently Chinese—between them. The man wore no more clothes than she did. "Another one here," one of the scaly devils said in his hissing Chinese.

She lowered her head again, refused to answer. *Another one,* she thought. When would they be satisfied that she could indeed fit the prongs of however many men they brought her? This was—the fifth? The sixth? She couldn't remember. Maybe, after a while, it ceased to matter. How could her defilement grow any greater?

She tried to recapture the feeling of power, the feeling of being her own person, she'd known for that little while when Yi Min was helpless and afraid. Then her own will had mattered, if only for a short time. Before then, she'd been held in her place by the customs of her village and her people, afterward by the terrifying might of the Lizards. Just for a moment, though, she'd almost been free.

"You two show what you do, you eat. You not, no food for you," the devil said. Liu Han knew he meant it. After the first couple of men in this grim series, she'd tried to starve herself to death, but her body refused to obey her. Her belly cried louder than her spirit. Eventually, she did what she had to do to eat.

The other Lizard spoke to the foreign devil in a language that was neither Chinese nor the Lizards' own speech—Liu Han still tried to pick up words of that whenever she could. Then the scaly devils went out of the chamber. They were probably (no, certainly) taking pictures, but that was not the same as having them in the room. She still drew the line there.

Reluctantly, she looked up at the foreign devil. He was very hairy, and had grown a short thick beard that reached to within a couple of fingers' breadth of his eyes. His nose seemed nearer a hawk's beak than what a proper person should grow. His skin was not too different in color from hers.

At least he did not simply ravage her, as one man had the second the door closed behind him. He stood quietly, watching her, letting her look him over. Sighing, she stretched herself out flat on the mat. "Come ahead; let's get it over with," she said in Chinese, her weary voice full of infinite bitterness.

He stooped beside her. She tried not to cringe. He said something in his own language. She shook her head. He tried what sounded like a different tongue, but she understood no better. She expected him to get on top of her then, but instead he let out hisses and grunts which, she realized after a moment, were words in the Lizards' speech: "Name—is." He ended with the cough that showed the sentence was a question.

Her eyes filled with tears. None of the others had even bothered to ask. "Name is Liu Han," she answered, sitting up. She had to repeat herself; the accents she and he gave the Lizards' words were so different that they had trouble following each other. Once she'd given her name, she saw she ought to treat him as a human being, too. "You—name—is?"

He pointed to his furry chest. "Bobby Fiore." He turned toward the doorway by which the little scaly devils had departed, spoke their name for themselves. "Race—" Then he delivered an extraordinary series of gestures, most of which she'd never seen before but all obviously a long way from compliments. Either he didn't know his picture was being taken or he didn't care. Some of his antics were so spirited, almost like those of a traveling actor in a skit, that she found herself smiling for the first time in a long while.

"Race bad," she said when he was done, and gave the different cough that put extra stress on what she said.

Instead of answering with words, he just repeated the emphatic cough. She'd never heard a little scaly devil do that, but she followed him well enough.

No matter how they despised their captors, though, they remained captive. If they were going to eat, they had to do what the scaly devils wanted. Liu Han still didn't understand why the Lizards thought it important to prove that men and women didn't go into heat and could lie with each other any time, but they did. She lay back again. Maybe it wouldn't be so bad this time.

As far as skill went, Yi Min was three times the lover the foreign devil with the unpronounceable second name proved to be. But if he was rather clumsy, he treated her as though it were their wedding night, not as if she was a handy convenience. She hadn't imagined foreign devils had so much kindness in them; few enough Chinese did. She hadn't known any kindness since her husband died in the Japanese attack on her village.

To thank him, she did her best to respond to his caresses. She'd been through too much, though; her body would not answer. Still, when he closed his eyes and groaned atop her, she was moved to reach up and stroke his cheek. The beard there was almost as rough as a bristle brush. She wondered if it itched.

He slid out of her, sat back on his knees. She drew up one leg to hide her secret place—foolish, when he'd just been inside her. He pantomimed smoking a cigarette with such nimble gestures that she started to laugh before she could catch herself. He raised a bushy eyebrow, took another drag on the imaginary smoke, then made as if to crush it out on his chest.

He'd so convinced her the nothing between his two fingers was real, she exclaimed in Chinese: "Don't get burned!" That set her laughing again. She groped for words in the Lizards' tongue, the only one they had in common: "You—not bad."

"You, Liu Han"—he said her name so strangely, she needed a moment to recognize it—"you—not bad also."

She looked away from him. She didn't know she was crying till the first scalding tears ran down her cheeks. Once she started, she discovered she could not stop. She wailed and keened for all she'd lost and suffered and endured, for her husband and her village, for her very world and her own violation. She'd never imagined she had so many tears inside her.

After a little while, she felt Bobby Fiore's hand on her shoulder. "Hey," he said. "Hey." She didn't know what it meant in his language. She didn't know if it meant anything or was just a sound. She did know his voice held sympathy, and that he was the only human being who'd shown her any since her nightmare began. She twisted around and clung to him till she'd cried herself out.

He didn't do much but let her hold him. He ran a hand through her hair once or twice and quietly said "Hey" a few more times. She hardly noticed, so consumed was she by her own grief.

As her sobs at last slowed to gasps and hiccups, she felt his erection pressed against her belly, hot as the tears she'd shed. She wondered how long he'd had it. It didn't surprise her; she would have been surprised if a naked man in the arms of a naked woman failed to rise. What surprised her was that he'd been content to ignore it. What could she possibly have done to stop him if he'd decided to take her again?

His restraint made her want to cry again. She realized how desperate she'd grown when simply not being raped became a kindness worth tears.

He asked her something in his own language. She shook her head. He shook his, too, maybe angry at himself for forgetting she couldn't understand. His eyebrows came together as he looked thoughtfully past her shoulder toward the blank metal wall of the chamber. He tried the scaly devils' speech: "You, Liu Han, not bad now?"

"Not *so* bad, Bobby Fiore." When she tried to say his name, she botched it at least as badly as he had hers.

"Okay," he said. She did understand that; a city person in one of the films she'd seen had said it. People in the city picked up foreign devils' slang along with their machines and funny clothes.

He let go of her. She looked down at herself. She'd held him so tight, the smooth skin of her chest had the marks of his hair pressed into it. His erection started to droop now that she no longer lay against him. She reached out and closed her hand around him. The Lizards had taken everything she'd ever had, leaving her with only her body with which to thank him.

That eyebrow of his went up again. So did what she was holding. Somehow, the heat of it against the palm of her hand brought comfort. If it was good this time, if she lost herself in her body, sheer sensation might let her forget for a little while the metal room in which she was trapped and the scaly devils who kept her here to satisfy their own perverse curiosity.

She moaned softly as she lay back on the mat once more. She wanted it to be good, hoped it would be. Bobby Fiore moved beside her. His lips came down on hers; his hand roamed her body. A bit sooner than she would have liked, his fingers found their way between her legs. They didn't go quite to the right place. After a few seconds of frustration, she reached down and moved them to where they belonged.

He frowned for a moment. She hoped she hadn't angered him. Who could say what might anger a foreign devil? He didn't put his hand back where it had been, though. And now it was better, now her eyes closed and her buttocks clenched and her back began to arch. As if from far away, she heard him laugh, deep in his throat.

She was at the edge of the Clouds and Rain when he took his hand away. Her eyes opened. It was her turn to start to frown. But his weight pressed her against the slick surface of the mat. His tongue teased her left nipple as he guided himself into her. Her legs rose, clenched around him. With her inner muscles, she squeezed him as hard as she could. "Ah," he said, in surprise or delight or both at once. Then she stopped listening to anything but what her body told her.

Afterward, they were both sweaty and breathing hard. The only thing wrong with making love, Liu Han thought as the afterglow faded, was that it didn't really help. All the troubles pleasure had let her ignore were still here. None had got any better. Ignoring troubles was not meeting them. She knew that, but what else, here, could she do?

She wondered if foreign devils had the wit to be disturbed by such worries. She glanced over at Bobby Fiore. His hairy face had turned serious, his own gaze distant and inward. Surely thoughts much like her own were passing through his head.

But when he noticed her looking at him, he smiled and sat up in one smooth motion. He might have been imperfectly skilled in matters of the mattress, but he had a well-muscled body which he handled well otherwise. He also had a sense of foolishness—this time he pretended to smoke two cigarettes at once, one in each hand.

Liu Han laughed. A few seconds later, she rolled over and gave the foreign devil with the funny name a long, grateful hug. Whatever private fears or worries he'd been brooding about, he'd set them aside to make her feel better. That was something else that hadn't happened since the scaly devils came (and not often before then; she was, after all, only a woman).

As if thinking of the little devils was enough to make them appear, the door to the hallway outside her chamber slid open. The devils who had brought Bobby Fiore in now returned to take him away again. That was how it went: they forced a man on her, then took him away so she never saw him again. Up till now, that had been only a relief. Now it wasn't, or not so much. But the devils didn't care one way or the other.

Or so she thought, until the scaly devil who spoke Chinese after a fashion said, "You do mating two times. Why two times? Never two times before." Absurdly, he sounded suspicious, as if he'd caught her enjoying herself at what was supposed to be hard work. Well, in a way, he had.

She'd learned honest answers worked best with the little devils. "We did it twice because I liked him much more than I liked any of the others. I just wanted to be rid of them. But he is not a bad man; if he were Chinese, he might be a very good man."

The other devil was talking with Bobby Fiore. He answered in his own language. It wasn't Chinese, so Liu Han could make nothing out of it. Because it had no tones, it sounded to her more like animals grunting than speech. She wondered how—and if—foreign devils managed to understand one another. But compared to the hisses and coughs the scaly devils used, Bobby Fiore's foreign devil language was as lovely as a beautiful song.

The little scaly devil who had been talking with her turned and spoke to the one who'd been talking with Bobby Fiore. They made their snaky noises back and forth. Liu Han tried to follow what they were saying, but couldn't: they talked too fast. She worried. The last time she'd had a moment of feeling partway safe and secure, the scaly devils had turned her into a whore. What new horror were they plotting now?

The one who spoke Bobby Fiore's language said something to him. He nodded as he answered. That seemed to mean the same thing to him as it did to her, so he'd probably just said yes. But yes to what?

The Lizard who knew a little Chinese turned both his eyes back to her. "You want come back again this man?"

The question took her by surprise. Again she gave an honest answer. "What I really want is to go back to the camp you took me from. If you will not do that, I wish you would just leave me alone here and not make me give my body for food."

"This one choice not for you," the scaly devil said. "This other choice not for you, either."

"What choices do you give me?" Liu Han asked bleakly. Then she realized this was the first time the little scaly devils had offered her any choices at all. Up till now, they'd simply done with her as they pleased. Maybe she had reason to hope.

"Come back again this man one choice," the little devil said. "Other choice come in here new man. You pick choice now."

Liu Han felt like screaming at him. He would not free her; he just let her choose between two kinds of degradation. But any choice was better than none. Bobby Fiore had not hit her; though he'd gone into her, he hadn't forced her; he'd let her clutch at him when she cried; he'd even made her laugh with his silly imaginary cigarettes. And he hated the little scaly devils, maybe nearly as much as she did.

"I would rather have this man come back again," she said as fast as she could, not wanting to give the little devil a chance to change his mind.

He turned to the other devil. They talked back and forth once more. The one who spoke Chinese said, "Big Ugly male say he want come again, too. We do that, see what happen, you him. We learn plenty, maybe."

She couldn't have cared less what the scaly devils learned, except insofar as she hoped they learned nothing whatever. But she smiled her thanks to Bobby Fiore. If he hadn't been willing to come back to her, then whatever she wanted probably wouldn't have mattered. He smiled back. "Liu Han—not bad," he said, and gave the emphatic cough.

The two scaly devils both made noises like kettles bubbling over. The one who spoke Chinese asked, "Why use our tongue, talk you, him?"

"We don't know each other's languages," Liu Han answered, shrugging. The scaly devils could do all sorts of things she'd never imagined possible, but sometimes they were genuinely stupid.

"Ah," this one said. "We learn again." He and his companion led Bobby Fiore out of the chamber. Just before the door slid shut and hid him, he raised yet another pretended cigarette to his lips.

Liu Han stood for a while, staring at the closed door panel. Then she noticed, or rather paid heed to, being messy and dripping. The cubicle had a faucet that released a few seconds' worth of water when she pushed a button by it. She went over and cleaned herself as best she could. When she was done, she didn't feel the need to wash again and again and again, as she had several times before. Once was enough. That, to her, meant progress.

Flight Leader Teerts felt like a longball. Back on Home, two males would toss a ball back and forth, starting out at arm's length from each other. Every time one of them caught it, he'd take a step backwards. Good longball players could keep the game going until they were a city block apart. Championship players could go almost twice that far.

The shiplords of the invasion fleet had them all beat. They'd thrown Teerts and his flight of killerplanes back and forth across the whole length of Tosev 3's main continental mass. He'd begun the campaign by swatting Britainish bombardment aircraft out of the sky. Now he was attacking Nipponese ground positions almost halfway around this cold, wet world.

"There they are." Gefron's voice came through the flight leader's headphones. "I have them on my terrain mapper."

Teerts checked the display. Yes, those were the Race's landcruisers and other fighting vehicles up ahead, their IFF transponders all glowing cheerily orange. Ahead of them lay the Nipponese trench lines in front of—what was the name of the town? Harbin, that was it—which the killerplanes were supposed to soften up.

"That is affirmative, Gefron," Teerts said. "I say again, affirmative. Pilot Rolvar, have you also acquired the target?"

"I have, Flight Leader," Rolvar answered formally. Then his voice changed: "Now let's go smash it!"

Teerts would not have wanted to be one of the Big Ugly soldiers down there. The peaceful night was about to turn hideous for them. At the precise programmed instant, rockets leapt away from his killercraft to slice into the gashed earth in which the Nipponese huddled. The flames from their motors reminded him of knives of fire.

Since he was flight leader, he had a display Rolvar and Gefron lacked, one that showed they'd also launched their rocket packs. A moment later, ground explosions confirmed that: there were far more of them than his own munitions load could have accounted for by itself.

"Let's see how they like that!" Gefron shouted jubilantly. "We should have given it to them a long time ago, by the Emperor."

Pilots got special training so their eyes did not leave their instruments when they heard the Emperor's sacred name. Teerts kept on paying attention to his cabin displays. He felt the same excitement Gefron had shown; it was as close to arousal as a male could know in the absence of females.

He also wished his flight had been able to attack the Nipponese sooner. But there were only so many killerplanes, and *so many* Tosevite positions to smash. This one had had to wait its turn. It would have waited longer still had the shiplords not thrown his flight east against it.

His aircraft roared low over the shattered trench line. Little dots of flame sprang into being on the ground as the surviving Big Uglies fired blindly at him. The Nipponese were not the only Tosevite army to do that. Teerts had listened to the briefings. He supposed shooting back made the Big Ugly soldiers feel less like the helpless victims they really were. Its probability of doing anything more than that was very small.

Teerts didn't gamble. Gambling was a vice of support for males who had time to kill, which was not one of his problems. He'd been in action from the start. But if he'd sat down with the little plastic dodecahedrons a few times, he would have understood with his gut rather than just with his brain the difference between a small probability and zero probability.

The left engine made a horrible noise, then died. His killercraft lurched in midair. A small town's worth of warning lights came on all over his instrument panel. At the same time, he keyed his radio: "Flight Leader Teerts, aborting mission and attempting to return to base. I must have sucked a bullet or something right into one turbofan."

"May the spirits of departed Emperors take you safely home," Rolvar and Gefron said in the same breath. Rolvar added, "We will finish the attack run on the Tosevites, Flight Leader."

"I'm sure you will," Teerts said. Rolvar was a good, reliable male. So was Gefron, in a different, more primitive way. Between the two of them, they'd make the Nipponese wish they'd never been hatched. Teerts swung his killercraft westward, back toward the base from which he'd set out. He could fly on one engine, though he wouldn't be very fast or maneuverable. Get repairs made and he'd be good as new tomorrow—

The right engine made a horrible noise, then died.

All at once, Teerts' instrument panel was nothing *but* warning lights. *This isn't fair*, the flight leader thought. His hard-won altitude began to slip as the aircraft became nothing more than an aerodynamic stone in the sky.

"Ejecting! I say again, ejecting!" he yelled. His thumbclaw hit a button he'd never expected to have to use. Something about the size of the invasion fleet's bannership booted him in the base of the tail as hard as it could. His eyes stayed open, but he briefly saw only gray mist.

Pain soon brought him back to his senses. One of the three bones in his left wrist had surely broken. At the moment, though, that was the least of his worries. Still strapped into his seat, he floated above the Nipponese lines like the biggest, most tempting target in the whole Empire.

The Big Uglies blazed away at him for all they were worth. He watched in fearful fascination as holes appeared in the ripstop fabric of his parachute. Too many holes, or three or four too close together, and ripstopping wouldn't matter much. Then a bullet smacked the armored bottom of the seat. He hissed in fright and tried to draw up his legs.

Not fair, he thought again. The whole killercraft was armored, not just the bottom of the seat. Bullets that hit were nearly harmless. But turbofan blades, immensely strong though they were, couldn't chew up lead. If you were colossally unlucky enough to lose both engines that way . . .

If you were that unlucky, you had to hope the Big Uglies wouldn't catch you and do the frightful things rumor said they did to prisoners. You had to hope you landed a little ways away from them, so you could unstrap (one-handed, it wouldn't be easy or fast) and try to evade until the rescue helicopter got there to pick you up.

But if you were that unlucky, who cared what you hoped? Teerts had spilled wind from his canopy, trying to float as far back toward the Race's lines as he could. That would have made rescuing him a lot easier . . . if he hadn't come down right in the middle of a Nipponese trench.

He was sure he was dead. The Big Uglies swarmed around him, shouting at one another and brandishing rifles with knives stuck onto the ends of their barrels. He waited for them to shoot him or stick him. A little more pain, he told himself, and everything would be over. His spirit would join those of the Emperors now departed, to serve them in death as he had served the Race in life.

One of the Nipponese outshouted the rest. By the way they cleared a path for him, he must have been an officer. He stood in front of Teerts, hands on hips, staring at him with the small, immobile eyes that characterized the Big Uglies. Instead of a rifle, he carried a sword not too different from the one borne by the Tosevite warrior in the picture the Race's probe had sent Home.

Teerts wondered why he didn't draw it and use it. Why else had the others drawn back, but to give their commander the privilege of the kill? But the officer did not strike. Instead, he gestured for Teerts to free himself from the straps that held him in his seat.

The flight leader obeyed, awkwardly because his left hand wouldn't work. As soon as he'd moved a couple of paces away from the seat, the Nipponese did take his sword from its sheath. He slashed two-handed at the lines that held Teerts' parachute to the ejection seat. The sword must have had good metal in it, for the tough lines parted almost at once. The parachute canopy blew away.

The officer said something to his males. Several of them raised their rifles and fired repeatedly into the seat. The blasts almost deafened Teerts. They also dismayed him right down to the claws on his toes. Those bullets were certain to smash the homing beacon buried in the padding.

Baring his small, flat teeth, the Nipponese pointed east with his sword. He barked out a phrase that probably meant something like *get moving*. Teerts got moving. The officer and several of his males followed, to make sure the flight leader didn't try to run.

Teerts had no intention of running. Since he hadn't been killed out of hand, he expected to be treated fairly well. The Race held far more Tosevite captives than the other way round, and mistreatment of prisoners could be avenged ten-thousandfold. Not only that, the Big Uglies, barbarous though they were, fought among themselves so often that they'd developed protocols for dealing with captured enemies. Teerts couldn't remember offhand whether Nippon adhered to those protocols, but most Tosevite empires did.

Jets screamed overhead, back where the ejection seat had landed. That would be Gefron and Rolvar, trying to keep him from being captured. Too late, unfortunately; not only had he landed among the Big Uglies, but this officer was alert enough to have wrecked the beacon and got him away from it in a hurry.

Still, he didn't think things would be too bad. The officer first took him to a medical station. A Nipponese doctor with corrective lenses held in front of his eyes by a weird contraption of bent wires bandaged his wrist and poured a stinging disinfectant over the cuts and scrapes he'd got in his ejection and landing. By the time the doctor was done, Teerts felt halfway decent.

Then the Nipponese officer started hustling him away from the front line again. The jets' wail vanished; the other two pilots in the flight must have expended their munitions and had to head home. Artillery shells whistled overhead every so often. Most came from the west and landed on Tosevite positions. The Big Uglies kept firing back, though. They seemed too stubborn to know when to give up.

Teerts walked toward the dawn that was breaking in the east. As light grew, Nipponese artillery fire also picked up. Lacking night-vision gear, the Tosevites were limited to targets they could actually see. Each salvo of theirs drew quick counterbattery fire from the gunners of the Race.

Back at the rear edge of the Nipponese trench system, a new party of

Big Uglies took charge of Teerts. By the way the officer who had captured him acted toward the one who now received him, the latter was far more prominent. They bowed to each other one last time before the junior officer and the males who had accompanied him headed back to their position.

Teerts' new keeper surprised him by speaking the language of the Race. "You come this way," he said. His accent was mushy and he barked out his words, but the flight leader followed him well enough.

"Where are you taking me?" Teerts asked, glad for the chance to communicate with something more expressive than gestures.

The Nipponese officer whirled and struck him. He staggered and almost fell; the blow had been cleverly aimed. "Not talk unless I say you can talk!" the Big Ugly shouted. "You prisoner now, not master. You obey!"

Obedience had been drilled into Teerts his whole life long. His captor might be a savage, but he spoke as one who had the right to command. Almost instinctively, the flight leader responded to his tone. "May I speak?" he asked, as humbly as if he were addressing a shiplord.

"*Hai*," the Nipponese said, a word Teerts did not understand. As if realizing that, the Tosevite abandoned his own jargon. "Speak, speak."

"Thank you, exalted male." With no notion of the officer's rank, Teerts laid the honorifics on with a trowel. "Without asking where, exalted male, do you have places in which you keep your captives from the Race?"

The Nipponese showed his teeth. Among the Big Uglies, Teerts knew, that was a gesture of amiability, not amusement. The officer, however, looked not the least bit amiable. He said, "You prisoner now. No one care what happen to you."

"Forgive me, exalted male, but I do not understand. You Tosevites"— Teerts carefully did not say *Big Uglies*—"take prisoners in your own wars and mostly treat them well. Is it just to use us so differently from your own?"

"Not do so," the Nipponese officer answered. "Be prisoner go against *bushido*." The word was in Nipponese. The officer explained it: "Against way of fighting male. Proper fighting male die before become prisoner. Become prisoner, not deserve to live. Become—how you say?—sport for those who catch."

"That's—" Teerts caught himself before he blurted out *insane*. "That's not the way most other Tosevites act."

"They fools, idiots. We Nipponese, we—how you say?—people of the emperor. Our way right, proper. Same family rule us two thousand five hundred year." He drew himself up as if that paltry figure were a matter for pride. Teerts didn't think it wise to point out that *the* Emperors' family had ruled the Race for fifty thousand years, which was twenty-five thousand revolutions of Tosev 3. A small pride, he reasoned, might be more easily hurt by a large truth.

He said, "What will you do with me, then?"

"What we want," the officer answered. "You *ours* now."

"If you mistreat me, the Race will avenge itself on your people," Teerts warned.

The Nipponese officer made a peculiar barking noise. After a bit, Teerts realized it had to be what the Big Uglies used for laughter. The officer said, "Your Race already hurt Nippon so bad, how you do worse on account of prisoners, eh? You try make me afraid? I show you. I not afraid to do this—"

He kicked Teerts, hard. The flight leader hissed in surprise and pain. When the Big Ugly kicked him again, he whirled round and tried to fight back—even if he was smaller than a Tosevite, he had teeth and claws. They did him no good. The officer did not even bother reaching for the sword or the small firearm he carried on his belt. He'd somehow learned to use his legs and arms as deadly weapons. Teerts couldn't so much as tear his tunic.

The beating and stomping went on for some time. Finally the Nipponese officer kicked the flight leader's broken wrist. Teerts' vision blurred and threatened to go out, just as it had when the ejection seat hurled him away from his killercraft. As if from very far away, he heard someone screaming, "Enough! Enough!" He needed a while before he recognized the voice as his own.

"You talk stupid again?" the Big Ugly asked. He stood balanced on one leg, ready to kick Teerts some more. If the flight leader said no, the Tosevite might stop; if he said yes, he was sure he'd get kicked to death. He got the feeling the officer didn't much care one way or the other what he answered. In a way, that indifference was even more frightening than the beating itself.

"No, I won't talk stupidly again, or I'll try not to, anyway," Teerts gasped. The tiny qualification held all the defiance left in him.

"You get up, then."

Teerts didn't think he could. But if he failed, the Big Ugly would have another excuse to hurt him. He struggled to his feet, did his best to wipe the mud off his scales one-handed.

"What you learn from this?" the Nipponese officer asked.

The flight leader could hear the danger in that question. It wasn't just rhetoric; he'd better answer it in a way that satisfied the Tosevite. Slowly, he said, "I learned that I am your prisoner, that I am in your power, that you can do whatever you want with me."

The Big Ugly moved his head up and down. "You keep this in your mind, eh?"

"Yes." Teerts didn't think he was likely to forget.

The Nipponese officer gave him a light shove. "You come on, then."

Moving hurt, but Teerts managed. He didn't dare fail; maybe the Big Ugly really had taught him a lesson after all. Dawn was breaking when they came to a transport center. The Race had worked it over at least once: truck carcasses lay here and there, some flipped over, others burnt out, still others both.

But the center still functioned. Nipponese soldiers, chanting as they worked, unloaded cloth sacks from a few intact motor vehicles and from a great many animal-drawn wagons. The officer shouted to the males there. A couple of them came rushing over. They exchanged bows with the flight leader's captor, spoke rapidly back and forth.

The officer shoved Teerts again, pointed toward a wagon. "You go on that one."

Teerts awkwardly climbed into the wagon. The Nipponese officer gestured for him to sit in one corner. He obeyed. The wooden bottom and sides scratched against his sore hide. The officer and a Big Ugly soldier got into the wagon with him. Now the officer took out his small firearm. The soldier kept his rifle aimed at Teerts, too. The flight leader's mouth wanted to fall open. The Tosevites had to be crazy if they thought he was in any shape to try something.

Crazy they might have been, but they weren't stupid. The officer spoke again in his own language. The males around the wagon obeyed with an alacrity that would not have shamed members of the Race. They snatched up a heavy, dirty tarpaulin and draped it over Teerts and his guards.

"No one see you now," the officer said, and laughed his noisy, barking laugh once more.

Teerts was afraid he was right. From the air, the wagon would look like any other, hardly worth shooting up and certainly not worth investigating. Oh, in an infrared scan the wagon bed might show up warmer than it would have were it just carrying supplies, but no one was likely to bother scanning it.

Somebody with heavy, booted feet got up onto the front of the wagon, the part the tarpaulin didn't cover. The wagon shifted under his weight. The newcomer said something, though not to Teerts or the Big Uglies. The only answer he got was a soft snort from one of the two animals tethered to the front end of the wagon.

The animals started to walk. In that instant, Teerts discovered the wagon had no springs. He also discovered the road over which it traveled did not deserve the name. The first two jounces made him bite his tongue. After that, with the iron taste of blood in his mouth, he deliberately clamped his jaws shut and endured the rattling as best he could. He was jolted worse here at a walking pace than he'd ever been inside his killercraft.

After a while, daylight began to seep through the space between the tarpaulin and the top of the wagon. The two Tosevites did not seem to have so much as twitched since they sat down. Their weapons remained pointed straight at Teerts. He wished he were as dangerous as they thought he was.

"May I speak?" he asked. The Nipponese officer's head moved up and down. Hoping that meant yes, the flight leader said, "May I please have some water?"

"*Hai,*" the officer said. He turned to the other male, spoke briefly. The soldier shifted his weight—he could move after all. He carried a water bottle slung on his right hip. He undid it with one hand (the other kept his rifle aimed at Teerts), passed it to his commander. The officer in turn gave it to Teerts, making sure all the while that the flight leader could not grab his small firearm.

Teerts found the water bottle hard to use. The Toscvites could wrap their flexible lips around its opening to keep from spilling it. His own mouthparts were less mobile. He had to hold the bottle above his head, pour the water down into his mouth. Even so, some of it dribbled out the corners of his jaws and made a couple of small puddles on the floor of the wagon.

Refreshed, he dared ask, "May I also have some food?" Saying the word told him how empty his belly was.

"You eat food like us?" The officer paused, tried to make himself clearer: "You eat food from this world?"

"Of course I do," Teerts answered, surprised the Big Ugly could doubt it. "Why would we conquer this world if we could not support ourselves upon it afterwards?"

The officer grunted, then spoke to the other soldier again. This time, the junior male moved slowly, grudgingly. He had to put down his rifle to reach into the pack on his back. From it he took out a cloth wrapped around a couple of flat, whitish grainy cakes. He handed one of them to Teerts, carefully refolded the cloth, and put the other cake back into the pack. Then he picked up the rifle again. By the way he held it, he wouldn't have been sorry to shoot the flight leader.

Teerts stared down at the cake he held in his good hand. It didn't look particularly appetizing—why was the male so unhappy to give it up? The flight leader took a while to realize the two cakes might have been the only food the soldier had. *They're barbarians, after all,* he reminded himself. *They still have things like hunger—and we've been hitting their supply lines as hard as we can.*

He knew about hunger himself now. He bit into the cake. It tasted bland and starchy—given a better choice, it wasn't anything he would have eaten. Of itself, though, his tongue flicked out to clean the last couple of crumbs off his claw. He wished he had another cake just like it—or maybe another three.

Maybe, he thought too late, he shouldn't have shown just how hungry he was. He didn't like the way the Nipponese officer stretched out his lips and showed his teeth.

Vyacheslav Molotov glanced around the room. Here was a sight that would have been impossible to imagine a few months before: diplomats from Allies and Axis, imperialists and progressives, fascists and Communists and capitalists, all gathered together to seek a common strategy against a common foe.

Had Molotov been a different man, he might have smiled. As it was, his expression never wavered. He had been in a place more unimaginable than this when he floated feather-light in the Lizard leader's bake-oven of a chamber hundreds of kilometers above the Earth. But this London room was remarkable enough.

The room might have been anywhere in the world. It was in London because Great Britain lay relatively close to all the powers here save only Japan, the Lizards hadn't invaded the islands, and their attacks on shipping were haphazard enough to have given everyone a reasonable chance of arriving safely. And, indeed, everyone *had* arrived safely, though the conference was starting late because the Japanese foreign minister had been delayed zigzagging around the Lizard-held areas of North America.

The only disadvantage Molotov could see to meeting in London was that it gave Winston Churchill the right to preside. Molotov had nothing personal against Churchill—though imperialist, he was a staunch antifascist, and without him Britain might well have folded up and come to terms with the Hitlerites in 1940. That would have left the Soviet Union in a bad way when the Nazis turned east the next year.

No, it wasn't personal animosity. But Churchill did have a habit of going on and on. He was by all accounts a master orator in English. Molotov, unfortunately, spoke no English; even masterful oratory, when understood only through the murmurs of an interpreter, soon palled.

That didn't bother Churchill. Round and plump and ruddy-faced, waving a long cigar, he looked the very picture of a capitalist oppressor. But his words were defiant: "We cannot yield another inch of ground to these creatures. It would mean slavery for the human race forevermore."

"If we didn't all agree in this, we would not be here today," Cordell Hull said. The U.S. secretary of state raised a wry eyebrow. "Count Ciano isn't, for instance."

Molotov appreciated the dig at the Italians, who had given up even pretending to fight the Lizards a couple of weeks before. The Italians had named fascism, and now they showed its bankruptcy by yielding essentially at the first blow. The Germans at least had the courage of their convictions; Mussolini seemed to lack both.

Translators murmured to their principals. Joachim von Ribbentrop spoke fluent English, so the five leaders got along with three languages and thus only two interpreters per man. That made the talks cumbersome, but not unmanageably so.

Shigenori Togo said, "I feel our primary goal here is not so much to affirm the fight against the Lizards, with which we all agree, but to ensure that we do not allow the hostilities previously existing among ourselves adversely to affect our struggle."

"That is a good point," Molotov said. The Soviet Union and Japan had been neutral, which allowed each of them to devote its full energies to foes it reckoned more important (though Japan's foes were the USSR's allies in its battle against Germany, Japan's Axis partner—diplomacy could be a strange business).

"Yes, it is," Cordell Hull said. "We have come a long way in that direction, Mr. Togo—a short while ago, you'd not have been welcome in London, and even less welcome traveling across the United States to get here." Togo bowed in his seat, politely acknowledging the American's reply.

Churchill said, "Another point we must address is the trouble we have rendering aid to one another. As matters now stand, we must sneak about on our own world like so many mice fearing the cat. It is intolerable; it shall not stand."

"Bravely spoken as usual, Comrade Prime Minister," Molotov said. "You set forth an important and inspiring principle, but unfortunately offer no means of putting it into effect."

"To find such a means is the reason we have agreed to meet in spite of past differences," Ribbentrop said.

Molotov did not dignify that with a reply. If Churchill's gift was for inspiration, the Nazi foreign minister's was for stating the obvious. Molotov wondered why the pompous, posturing fool couldn't have been in Berlin when it disappeared from the face of the earth. Hitler might have had to replace him with a capable diplomat.

Air-raid sirens began to wail. Lizard jets shrieked by on low-level attack runs. Antiaircraft guns pounded—not as many as warded Moscow, Molotov thought, but a goodly number. None of the diplomats at the table moved. Everyone looked at everyone else for signs of fear and tried not to give any of his own. They had all come under air attack before.

"Times like these make me wish I were back in the wine business," Ribbentrop said lightly. He had animal courage, if nothing else; he'd been decorated for bravery during the First World War.

"I want those God-damned planes shot down," Churchill said, as if giving someone unseen an order. *If only it were that easy,* Molotov thought. *If Stalin could have done it by giving an order, the Lizards would long since have ceased to trouble us—as would the Hitlerites.* Some things, unfortunately, yielded to no man's orders. Maybe that was why foolish people imagined gods into being: to have someone whose orders were sure to be obeyed.

A stick of bombs crashed down not far from the Foreign Office building. The noise was cataclysmic. Windows rattled. One broke and fell in tinkling shards to the floor. The interpreters were less obliged to show sangfroid than the men they served. Several of them muttered; one of Ribbentrop's aides crossed himself and began fingering a rosary.

More bombs fell. Another window broke, or rather blew inward. A fragment of glass flew past Molotov's head and shattered against the wall. The translator who'd been praying cried out and clapped a hand to his cheek. Blood leaked between his fingers. *So much for your imaginary God,* Molotov thought. As usual, though, his face revealed nothing of what went on in his mind.

"If you like, gentlemen, we can adjourn to the shelter in the basement," Churchill said.

Interpreters looked hopefully at foreign ministers. Molotov checked his confreres. None of them said anything, in spite of the suggestion's obvious good sense. Molotov took the bull by the horns. "Yes, let us do that, Comrade Prime Minister. In all candor, our lives are valuable to the nations we serve. Foolish displays of bravado gain us nothing. If we can keep safe, we should do so."

Almost as one, the diplomats and interpreters rose from their seats and moved toward the door. No one thanked Molotov for cutting through the façade of bourgeois manners, but he'd expected no thanks from class enemies. As the Soviet foreign minister set foot on the stairs leading down, another irony struck him. For all their advanced technology, the Lizards appeared in Marxist-Leninist terms still to be in the ancient economic organizational system, using slave labor and plunder from captive races to maintain their imperial superstructure. Next to them, even Churchill—even Ribbentrop!—was progressive. The thought amused and appalled Molotov at the same time.

Another stick of bombs shook the Foreign Office as the diplomats descended to the cellar. Cordell Hull slipped and almost fell, catching himself at the last instant by grabbing the shoulder of the Japanese interpreter in front of him.

"Jesus Christ!" the secretary of state exclaimed. Molotov understood that without translation, though the American pronounced *Christ* as if it were *Chwist*. Hull followed it with several more sharp-sounding remarks.

"What is he saying?" Molotov asked his English-speaking translator.

"Oaths," the man answered. "Forgive me, Comrade Foreign Commissar, but I do not follow them easily. The American's accent is different from Churchill's, with which I am more familiar. When he speaks deliberately, I have no trouble understanding him, but the twang he gives his words when he is excited makes them difficult for me."

"Do your utmost," Molotov said. He hadn't thought about there being more than one dialect of English; to him it was all equally incomprehensible. Stalin and Mikoyan spoke Russian with an accent, of course, but that was because the one came from Georgia and the other from Armenia. The interpreter seemed to imply something else, more like the differences between the Russian of a *kolkhoznik* near the Polish border (*the former Polish border*, Molotov thought) and that of a Moscow factory worker.

The shelter proved low-roofed, crowded, and smelly. Molotov looked around scornfully: was this the best the British could protect their essential personnel? Corresponding quarters in Moscow were farther underground, surely better armored, and much more spacious.

Clerks and officials gave the diplomats as much room as they could, which was not a great deal. Churchill said, "Shall we continue, gentlemen?"

Molotov wondered if he had lost his mind. Resume, in front of all these people? Then he reflected that what happened here was not likely to be reported back to the Lizards; unlike the powers negotiating today, the invaders had no long-established spy network to pick up their rivals' every word.

But then he realized that might not matter. He said, "I make no secret"—which meant Stalin had told him to make no secret—"of the fact that I have met the enemy's commanding officer in his ship above the Earth. As I expected, those negotiations proved fruitless, the Lizards demanding nothing less than the unconditional surrender we all find unacceptable. In the course of the meeting, however, I also learned the German foreign minister had held talks with this Atvar creature. I desire to know now whether this also holds true for Great Britain, the United States, and Japan. If so, I desire to know the status of their conversations with the Lizards. In short, are we in danger of betrayal from within?"

Joachim von Ribbentrop spluttered something indignant in German, then switched to English. The translator murmured into Molotov's ear: "Yes, I discussed certain matters with the Lizards. After the fire that fell on Berlin, this is surely understandable, not so? I betrayed nothing, however, and resent the imputation. As proof I offer the *Reich*'s continuing struggle against the invading forces."

"No imputation was intended," Molotov said, though he remembered

Atvar had implied Ribbentrop was more pliable than the German painted himself. Of course, it was as likely the Lizard lied for his own advantage as that Ribbentrop did so. More likely still, they both lied. Molotov resumed: "What of the rest of you?"

Cordell Hull said, "I haven't done any of this Buck Rogers stuff." ("By which he means he has not traveled into space," the interpreter glossed.) "No one from the government of the United States has. We have held lower-level talks with the Lizards on our soil regarding such matters as transportation of food and other noncombat supplies to areas they control, and we are also attempting to arrange exchanges of prisoners of war."

Soft, Molotov thought. The handful of prisoners the Soviets had taken from the invaders were interrogated until no longer useful and then disposed of, just as if they were Germans or *kulaks* with important information. As for supplying food to Lizard-held areas, Moscow had enough trouble feeding the people it still ruled. Those the Lizards had overrun made useful partisans and spies, but that was all.

Shigenori Togo spoke in German; Molotov remembered he had a German wife. The Soviet foreign minister's English-speaking interpreter also knew German. He translated for Molotov: "He says there is no excuse for treating with this enemy."

Ribbentrop scowled at the Japanese representative. Ignoring the glare, Togo switched to his own language and went on for some time. Molotov's other translator took over: "The Emperor Hirohito's government has consistently refused to deal with the Lizards except on the battlefield. We see no reason to discontinue this policy. We shall continue to fight until events prove favorable for us. We understand this fight will be difficult; that is why I am here today. But Japan will fight on regardless of the course any other nation may take."

"The same holds true for Britain," Churchill declared. "We may talk with the foe, consistent with the usages of war, but we shall not surrender to him. Resistance is our sacred duty to our children."

"You say this now," Ribbentrop said. "But what will you say when the Lizards strike London or Washington or Tokyo or Moscow with the same dreadful weapon that destroyed Berlin?"

Silence reigned for the next several seconds. It was a better question than Molotov had expected from the plump, prosperous, foolish Ribbentrop. He did notice the Nazi foreign minister had put the Soviet capital last on his list. Annoyed by that, he said, "Comrade Stalin has pledged a fight to the finish, and the Soviet workers and people shall hold to the pledge, come what may. In any case, if I may use a bourgeois analogy, having continued to resist despite wholesale murder at the hands of Germany, we shall not quail at the prospect of retail murder from the Lizards."

Ribbentrop's protuberant blue eyes glared balefully. Shigenori Togo, whose nation had been at war with neither the Soviet Union nor Germany when the Lizards came, was in the best position to address both their representatives: "Such talk as this, gentlemen, aids no one but the invaders. Of course we remember our own quarrels, but to use them to interfere with the struggle against the Lizards is shortsighted."

He could not have picked a better word to gain Molotov's attention. The ineluctable nature of the historical dialectic made Marxist-Leninists long-term planners almost by instinct. The Five-Year Plans that had made the Soviet Union an industrial match for Germany were a case in point.

Molotov said, "I merely used the analogy to demonstrate that we shall not be intimidated by brute force. In fact, the Soviet Union and Germany are even now cooperating in areas where our two states can effectively bring combined resources to bear against the common enemy." He stopped there. Another word would have been too much.

Ribbentrop nodded. "We will do what we must do to secure final victory."

Glee danced behind Molotov's unchanging visage. He would have bet a prewar Crimean *dacha* against a trip to the *gulag* that Ribbentrop had no idea what sort of cooperation he'd meant. He knew perfectly well that he would never have told the pompous ass anything important.

"Instead of bemoaning the dreadful weapons the Lizards have, one of the things we should be doing is discovering how to make them for ourselves," Cordell Hull said. "I am authorized by President Roosevelt to tell you all that the United States has such a program in progress, and that we will share resources with our allies in the struggle."

"The United States and Britain are already operating under such an arrangement," Churchill said, adding with a touch of smugness, "nor is the sharing to which Secretary Hull referred by any means a one-way street."

Now Molotov's stony façade trapped amazement. Had he been as indiscreet as Hull, he'd have earned—and deserved—a bullet in the back of the head. Yet the American secretary of state spoke at his president's orders. Astonishing! Molotov more easily understood the Lizards than the United States. Combining the technical expertise implicit in Hull's words with such unbelievable naïveté . . . Incredible—and dangerous.

Ribbentrop said, "We are prepared to cooperate with any nation against the Lizards."

"As are we," Togo said.

Everyone looked at Molotov. Seeing silence would not serve here, he said, "I have already stated that the Soviet Union is currently working with Germany on projects of benefit to both nations. We have no objection in principle to pursuing similar collaborative efforts with other states actively resisting the Lizards."

He glanced round the tight circle of diplomats. Ribbentrop actually smiled at him. Churchill, Hull, and Togo remained expressionless, save that one of Churchill's eyebrows rose a little. Unlike the Nazi buffoon, they'd noticed he hadn't really promised anything. A wide gap lay between "no objection in principle" and genuine cooperation. Well, too bad. If they wanted to keep fighting the Lizards, they were in no position to call him on it.

Cordell Hull said, "Another area of concern for all of us is dealing with nations which have, for whatever reasons, made devil's bargains with the Lizards." He ran a hand through the strands of gray hair he'd combed over the top of a mostly bald skull. The Americas had a lot of nations like that.

"Many of them will have done so only under compulsion, and may well remain willing to carry on the fight and to work with us even while nominally under the invaders' yoke," Churchill said.

"That may be true in some cases," Molotov agreed. His own judgment was that Churchill kept the cockeyed optimism which he'd demonstrated in defying Hitler after British forces were booted out of Europe in 1940. That kind of optimism often led to disaster, but sometimes it saved nations. Bourgeois military "experts" hadn't given the Red Army six weeks of life against the *Wehrmacht*—but the Soviets were still fighting almost a year later when the Lizards came to complicate the situation yet again.

Molotov went on, "Partisan movements against both the invaders and the governments collaborating with them should also be organized and armed as expeditiously as possible. Leaders who favor submission must be removed by whatever means prove necessary." He said the last with a hard look at Joachim von Ribbentrop.

The German foreign minister was dense, but not too dense to miss that message. "The *Führer* still feels a personal fondness for Mussolini," he said, sounding more than a little embarrassed.

"No accounting for taste," Churchill rumbled. "Still, Minister Molotov is correct: we are past the stage where personal likes and dislikes ought to influence policy. The sooner Mussolini is dead and buried, the better for all of us. Some German forces remain in Italy. They might well be the ones to give him the boot, or rather take him from it for good."

The interpreter stumbled over the idioms in the last sentence, but Molotov got the gist. He added, "Having the Pope join Mussolini in the grave would also be a progressive development. Since the Lizards do not interfere with his bleating preachments, he fawns on them like a cur."

"But would a successor prove any better?" Shigenori Togo asked. "Along with this, we must also ask ourselves whether making the Pope into a martyr would in the long run prove harmful by generating hatred for our cause among Catholics all over the world."

"This may perhaps need to be considered," Molotov admitted at last. His own instinct was to strike at organized religion wherever and however he could. But the Japanese foreign minister had a point—the political repercussions might be severe. The Pope had no divisions, but many more followed him than had backed Leon Trotsky, now dead with an ice ax in his brain. Not one to yield ground lightly, Molotov added, "Perhaps the Pope could be eliminated in a way which makes the Lizards appear responsible."

Cordell Hull screwed up his face. "This talk of assassination is repugnant to me."

Soft, Molotov thought again. The United States, large, rich, powerful, and shielded by broad oceans east and west, had long enjoyed the historical luxury of softness. Not even two world wars had made Americans feel in their guts how dangerous a place the world was. But if they could not awake to reality with the Lizards in their own back yard, they would never have another chance.

"In war, one does what one must," Churchill said, as if gently reproving the secretary of state. The British prime minister could see past his button of a nose.

The all-clear sirens began to wail. Molotov listened to the long sigh of relief that came from the Foreign Office workers all around. They'd got through to the far side of another raid. None of them thought that only meant they'd have the dubious privilege of facing another soon.

The office staff formed a neat queue to leave the shelter and get back to work. Molotov had seen endless queues in the Soviet Union, but this one seemed somehow different. He needed a few seconds to put his finger on why. Soviet citizens queued up with a mixture of anger and resignation, because they had no other way to get what they needed (and because they suspected even queuing up often did no good). The English were more polite about it, as if they'd silently decided it was the one proper thing to do.

Their revolution is coming, too, Molotov thought, *to sweep away such bourgeois affectations.* Meanwhile, affected bourgeois though they were, they seemed likely to stay in the fight against the Lizards. So did the other three powers, though Molotov still had his doubts about Germany: any nation that let a nonentity like Ribbentrop become foreign minister had something inherently wrong with it. But the chief capitalist states were not giving up yet, even if Italy had stabbed them in the back. That was what he'd needed to learn, and that was the word he would take back to Stalin.

Sam Yeager shepherded two Lizards down the corridor of the Zoology Building of the Hull Biological Laboratories. He still carried his rifle and wore a tin hat, but that was more because he'd grown used to them than because he thought he'd need them. The Lizards made docile prisoners—more docile than he'd have been if they'd caught him, he thought.

He stopped in front of room 227A. The Lizards stopped, too. "In here, Samyeager?" one of them asked in hissing English. All the Lizard POWs pronounced his own name as if it were one word; what their mouths did to *Sam Finkelstein* was purely a caution.

Yeager got the idea his command of their tongue was as villainous as their English. He was doing his best with it, though, and answered, "Yes, in here, Ullhass, Ristin, brave males." He opened the door with the frosted-glass window, gestured with the barrel of the rifle for them to precede him.

In the outer office, a girl was clattering away on a noisy old Underwood. She stopped when the door opened. Her smile of greeting froze when she saw the two Lizards. "It's all right, ma'm," Yeager said quickly. "They're here to see Dr. Burkett. You must be new, or else you'd know about them."

"Yes, it's my first day on the job," answered the girl—actually, Yeager saw with a second look, she was probably in her late twenties, maybe even early thirties. His eyes flicked automatically to the third finger of her left hand. It had a ring. Too bad.

Dr. Burkett came out of his sanctum. He greeted Ullhass and Ristin in their own language; he was more fluent than Yeager, though he hadn't been learning for nearly as long. *That's why he's a fancy-pants professor and I'm a bush-league outfielder,* Yeager thought without much resentment. Besides, the Lizards liked him better than they did Burkett; they said so every time they went back to their own quarters.

Now, though, Burkett waved them into his office, shut the door behind them. "Isn't that dangerous?" the girl asked nervously.

"Shouldn't be," Yeager answered. "The Lizards aren't troublemakers. Besides, Burkett's window is barred, so they can't get away. And besides one more time"—he pulled out a chair—"I sit here until they come out, and I go in and get 'em if they don't come out inside of a couple of hours." He reached into his shirt pocket, drew out a pack of Chesterfields (not his brand, but you took what you could get these days) and a Zippo. "Would you like a cigarette, uh—?"

"I'm sorry. I'm Barbara Larssen. Yes, I'd love one, thanks." She tapped it against the desk, put it in her mouth, leaned forward to let him light it. Her cheeks hollowed as she sucked in smoke. She held it, then blew a long plume at the ceiling. "Oh, that's nice. I haven't had one in a couple of days." She took another long drag.

Yeager introduced himself before he lit his own smoke. "Don't let me get in your way if you're busy," he said. "Just pretend I'm part of the furniture."

"I've been typing nonstop since half past seven this morning, so I could use a break," Barbara said, smiling again.

"Okay," Yeager said agreeably. He leaned back in his chair, watched her. She was worth watching: not a movie-star beauty or anything like that, but pretty all the same, with a round, smiling face, green eyes, and dark blond hair that was growing out straight though its ends still showed permanent waves. To make conversation, he said, "Your husband off fighting?"

"No." That should have been good news, but her smile faded anyhow. She went on: "He was working here at the university—at the Metallurgical Laboratory, as a matter of fact. But he drove to Washington a few weeks ago. He should have been back long since, but—" She finished the cigarette with three quick savage puffs, ground it out in a square glass ashtray that sat by her typewriter.

"I hope he's all right." Yeager meant it. If the fellow needed to travel bad enough to do it with the Lizards on the loose, he was up to something important. For that matter, Yeager wasn't the sort to wish bad luck on anybody.

"So do I." Barbara Larssen did a game best to hold fear out of her voice, but he heard it all the same. She pointed to the pack of Chesterfields. "I hope you won't think I'm just scrounging off you, but could I have another one of those?"

"Sure."

"Thanks." She nodded to herself as she started to smoke the second cigarette. "That *is* good." She tapped ash into the ashtray. When she saw Yeager's eyes follow the motion of her hand, she let out a rueful laugh. "Typing is hell on my nails; I've already broken one and chipped the polish on three others. But after a while I got to the point where I couldn't stand just sitting around cooped up in my apartment any more, so I thought I'd try to do something useful instead."

"Makes sense to me." Yeager got up, stubbed out his own smoke. He didn't light another for himself; he wasn't sure where his next pack was coming from. He said, "I suppose keeping busy helps take your mind off things, too."

"It does, some, but not as much as I hoped it would." Barbara pointed to the door behind which Dr. Burkett was studying the Lizards. "How did you end up standing guard over those—things?"

"I was part of the unit that captured them, out west of here," he answered.

"Good for you. But how did you get picked to stay with them, I mean? Did you draw the short straw, or what?"

Yeager chuckled. "Nope. Matter of fact, I broke an old Army rule—I volunteered."

"You did?" Her eyebrows shot upward. "Why, for heaven's sake?"

Rather sheepishly, he explained about his fondness for science fiction. Her eyebrows moved again; this time, their inner ends came together in a tight little knot above her nose. He'd seen that expression before, more times than he could easily count. "You don't care for the stuff," he said.

"No, not really," Barbara said. "I was doing graduate work in medieval English literature before Jens had to move here from Berkeley, so it's not my cup of tea." But then she paused and looked thoughtful. "Still, I suppose it's done a better job of preparing you for what's happening here than Chaucer has for me."

"Mmm—maybe so." Sam had been ready with his usual hot defense of what he read for pleasure; finding out he didn't need it left him feeling like a portable phonograph that had been wound up and forgotten without a record on its turntable.

Barbara said, "As for me, if I couldn't type, I'd still be stuck in that Bronzeville flat."

"Bronzeville?" Now Yeager's eyebrows went up. "I don't know a lot about Chicago—*If I'd ever played here, I would* (the thought was there and gone fast as a Lizard jet)—"but I do know that's not the real good part of town."

"Nobody's ever bothered me," Barbara said. "With the Lizards here, the differences between whites and Negroes look pretty small all of a sudden, don't they?"

"I suppose so," Yeager said, though he didn't sound convinced even to himself. "But whatever color they are, you'll find more than its share of crooks in Bronzeville. Hmm—tell you what. What time do you get off here?"

"Whenever Dr. Burkett feels like turning me loose, it sounds like," she answered. "I already told you, I'm new on the job. Why?"

"I'd walk you home, if you like . . . Hey, what's so darn funny?"

Laughing still, Barbara Larssen threw back her head and made a noise that might have been a wolf's howl. Yeager's cheeks turned hot. Barbara said, "I think my husband might approve of that idea in the abstract, but not walking along the concrete, if you know what I mean."

"That's not what I had in mind at all," Yeager protested. Not until the words were out of his mouth did he realize he wasn't telling the whole truth. The front of his mind had made the offer innocently enough, but some deeper part knew he might have kept quiet if he hadn't found her attractive. He was embarrassed that she'd seen through him faster than he saw through himself.

"No harm in your asking, and I'm sure it was kindly meant," she said, giving him the benefit of the doubt. "Men only turn really annoying when they can't hear 'no thank you' or don't believe it, and I see you're not like that."

"Okay," he said, as noncommittal a noise as he could come up with.

Barbara put out her second cigarette, looked at her wristwatch (the electric clock on the wall wasn't running), and said, "I'd better get back to work." She bent over the typewriter. Her fingers flew; the keys made machine-gun bursts of noise. Yeager had known a few reporters who could crank more words a minute than Barbara was putting out now, but not many.

He leaned back in his chair. He couldn't imagine an easier duty: unless something went wrong inside Dr. Burkett's office, or unless Burkett needed to ask him something (not likely, since the scientist seemed convinced he already knew everything himself), he had nothing to do but sit around and wait.

A lot of people would have got bored in a hurry. Being a veteran of long hours on trains and buses, Yeager was made of tougher stuff than that. He thought about baseball, about the science fiction he read to kill time between one town and the next, about the Lizards, about his small taste of combat (plenty to last him a lifetime if he got his way, which he probably wouldn't).

And he thought about Barbara Larssen. There she sat in front of him, after all. She wasn't ignoring him, either; every so often, she'd look up from her work and smile. Some of his thoughts were the pleasant but meaningless ones with which any man will while away the time in the presence of a pretty girl. Others had a bitter edge to them: he wished his former wife had cared about him while he was traveling the way Barbara obviously cared about her husband. What was his name? Jens, that was it. Whether he knew it or not, Jens Larssen was one lucky fellow.

After a while, the door to Dr. Burkett's office opened. Out came Burkett, looking plump and pleased with himself. Out came Ristin and Ullhass. Yeager wasn't so good at figuring out what their expressions meant, but they weren't in any obvious distress. Burkett said, "I'll want to see them again same time tomorrow, soldier."

"I'm sorry, sir," said Yeager, who was not sorry at all, "but they're scheduled to spend all day tomorrow with a Doctor, uh, Fermi. You'll have to try another time."

"I know Dr. Fermi!" Barbara Larssen exclaimed. "Jens works with him."

"This is most inconvenient," Dr. Burkett said. "I shall complain to the appropriate military authorities. How is one to conduct a proper experimental program when one's subjects are snatched away at inconvenient and arbitrary times?"

What that meant, Sam thought, was that Burkett hadn't bothered to check the schedule before he made his list of experiments. Too bad for him. Aloud, Yeager said, "I'm sorry, sir, but since we have a lot more experts than we do Lizards, we have to spread the Lizards around as best we can."

"Bah!" Burkett said. "Fermi is just a physicist. What can they possibly have to teach him?"

He plainly meant it as a rhetorical question, but Yeager answered it anyhow: "Don't you think he might be a little interested in how they came to Earth in the first place, sir?" Burkett stared at him; maybe he'd assumed joining the Army precluded a man from having a mind of his own.

Barbara said, "Shall I schedule you for another session with the Lizards as soon as they're available, Dr. Burkett?"

"Yes, do that," he answered, as if she were part of the furniture. He stamped back into his private chamber, slamming the door behind him. Barbara Larssen and Yeager looked at each other. He grinned; she started to giggle.

"I hope your husband comes home safe, Barbara," he said quietly.

Her laughter stopped as abruptly as if cut by a knife. "So do I," she answered. "I'm worried. He's been gone longer than he said he would." Her gaze settled on the two Lizards, who stood waiting for Yeager to tell them what to do next. He nodded. Everyone's life would have been simpler without the Lizards.

"Anybody gives you a bad time because he's not around, you let me know," he said. He'd never had a reputation for being a hard case while he was playing ball, but he hadn't carried around a bayonet-tipped rifle then, either.

"Thanks, Sam; I may do that," she said. Her tone was just cool enough to let him know again that he shouldn't be the one who gave her a bad time. He answered with a sober expression that let her know he got the message.

He turned to the Lizards, gestured with his gun. "Come on, you lugs." He stood aside to let them precede him out of the office. Barbara Larssen picked up the telephone on her desk, made a face, put it down. No dial tone, Yeager guessed—everything was erratic these days. Burkett's next go-round with the Lizards would have to wait a while.

The Plymouth's engine made a sudden, dreadful racket, as if it had just been hit by machine-gun fire. Jens Larssen knew a mechanical death rattle when he heard one. On the dashboard panel in front of him, the battery and temperature lights both glowed red. He wasn't overheated and he knew he still had juice. What he didn't have any more was a car. It rolled forward another couple of hundred yards, until he pulled off onto the shoulder to keep from blocking Highway 250 for anyone else.

"Shit," he said as he sat and stared at the dashboard lights. If he hadn't had to use garbage for fuel so much of the time, if he hadn't had to try to make his way over bombed-out roads or sometimes over no roads at all, if the damned Lizards had never come . . . he wouldn't have been stuck here somewhere in eastern Ohio, two whole states away from where he was supposed to be.

He raised his eyes and looked out through the dusty, bug-splashed windshield. Up ahead, the buildings of a small town dented the skyline. Small-town mechanics had helped keep the car going more than once before. Maybe they could do it again. He had his doubts—the Plymouth had never made a noise like this one before—but it was something he had to try.

He left the key in the ignition when he got out—good luck to anybody who tried to drive the car away. Slamming the driver's-side door relieved his anger a little. He took off his jacket, slung it over his shoulder, and started up the road toward the town.

There wasn't much traffic. In fact, there wasn't any traffic. He tramped past a couple of cars that looked as if they'd been sitting on the shoulder a lot longer than his, and past a burnt-out wreck that must have been strafed from the air and then shoved over to the roadside, but no cars passed him. All he could hear was his own footfalls on asphalt.

Just outside the outskirts of town, he came to a signboard: WELCOME TO STRASBURG, HOME OF GARVER BROTHERS—WORLD'S BIGGEST LITTLE STORE. Below that, in smaller letters, it said POPULATION (1930), 1,305.

Jens blew air out between his lips to make a snuffling noise. Here was Smalltown U.S.A., all right: even though the "new" census was already two years old, the mayor or whoever hadn't got around to fixing the numbers yet. Why bother, when they probably hadn't changed by more than a couple of dozen?

He walked on. The first gas station he came to was closed and locked. A big fat spider was sitting in a web spun between two of the gas pumps, so it had likely been closed for a while. That didn't look encouraging.

The drugstore half a block farther on had its door open. He decided to go in and see what they had at their soda fountain. At the moment, he wouldn't have turned down anything cold and wet, or even warm and wet. He still had some money in his pocket; Colonel Groves had been generous down in White Sulphur Springs. Being treated as a national resource was something he'd have no trouble getting used to.

Gloom filled the inside of the drugstore; the electricity was out. "Anybody in here?" Larssen called, peering down the aisles.

"Back here," a woman answered. But that wasn't the only answer he got. From much closer came startled hisses. Two Lizards walked around a display of Wildroot Creme Oil that was taller than they were. One carried a gun; the other had his arms full of flashlights and batteries.

Larssen's first impulse was to turn around and run like hell. He hadn't known he'd blundered into enemy-held territory. He felt as if he were carrying a sign that said DANGEROUS HUMAN—NUCLEAR PHYSICIST in letters three feet high. Fortunately, he didn't give in to the impulse. As he realized after a moment, to the Lizards he was just another person: for all they knew, he might have lived in Strasburg.

The Lizards skittered out of the drugstore with their loot. "They didn't pay for it!" Jens exclaimed. It was, on reflection, the stupidest thing he'd ever said in his life.

The woman back near the pharmacy had too much sense even to notice idiocy. "They didn't shoot me, either, so I guess it's square," she said. "Now what can I do for *you*?"

Confronted by such unshakable matter-of-factness, Larssen responded in kind: "My car broke down outside of town. I'm looking for somebody to fix it. And if you have a Coca-Cola or something like that, I'll buy it from you."

"I have Pepsi-Cola," the woman said. "Five dollars."

That was robbery worse than back at White Sulphur Springs, but Larssen paid without a whimper. The Pepsi-Cola, unrefrigerated and fizzy, went down like nectar of the gods. It tried to come up again, too; Jens wondered if you could explode from containing carbonation. When his eyes stopped watering, he said, "Now, about my car . . ."

"Charlie Tompkins runs a garage up on North Wooster, just past Garver Brothers." The woman pointed to show him where North Wooster was. "If anybody can help you, he's probably the one. Thank you for shopping at Walgreen's, sir."

He wondered if she'd have said that to the Lizards had he not come in and interrupted her. Very likely, he thought; nothing seemed to faze her. When he handed her the empty soda bottle, she rang up NO SALE on the cash register, reached in, and took out a penny, which she handed to him. "Your deposit, sir."

Bemused, he pocketed the coin. Deposits hadn't gone up with prices. *Of course not*, he thought—*shopkeepers have to pay out deposits*.

Strasburg wasn't big enough to get lost in; he found North Wooster without difficulty. An enormous sign proclaimed the presence of the Garver Brothers store. The signboard outside of town, unlike a lot of small-town signboards, hadn't exaggerated: the store sprawled over a couple of acres. The parking lot off to one side had room for hundreds of cars. At the moment, it held none.

That did not mean it was empty. Trucks ignored the white lines painted on concrete. They were not trucks of a sort Jens had seen before: they were bigger, somehow smoother of outline, quieter. When one of them rolled away, it didn't rattle or rumble or roar. No smoke belched from its exhaust.

The Lizards were plundering Garver Brothers.

A couple of them stood in front of the store, guns at the ready, in case the small crowd of people across the street got boisterous. In the face of that firepower, and of everything the Lizards had behind it, nobody seemed inclined toward boisterousness.

Jens joined the crowd. Two or three people gave him sidelong looks: he was a Stranger, with a capital *S*. He'd grown up in a small town before he went off to college; he knew he could live here for twenty years and still be thought a stranger, though perhaps by then a lower-case one.

"Damn shame," somebody said. Somebody else nodded. Larssen didn't. As someone from out of town, his opinion was automatically less than worthless. He just stood and watched.

The Lizards knew the kinds of goods they wanted. They came out of Garver Brothers with coils of copper wire slung over their scaly shoulders, with hand tools of all sorts, with an electric generator trundled along on a wheeled cart, with a lathe on another cart.

Jens tried to find a pattern to their depredations. At first he saw none. Then he realized most of what the Lizards were taking was tools that would help them make things of their own rather than already finished products of Earthly manufacture.

He scratched his head, not quite knowing what to make of that. It might have been a sign the invaders were settling in for a long stay. On the other hand, it might also have meant their own resources were short and they were having to eke them out with whatever they could steal. If that was so, it was encouraging.

"They're just a bunch of damn chicken thieves, that's what they are," someone in the crowd said as another truck rolled away. Most of the rest of the people murmured agreement. This time, Larssen did let himself nod. Whatever their reasons for cleaning out Garver Brothers, the Lizards were doing a good, workmanlike job of it.

A vehicle came up Wooster Street toward the store. It was about as far removed as possible from the smooth, silent trucks the Lizards ran: it was a horse-drawn buggy, driven by a bearded man with a broad-brimmed black hat. He pulled into the parking lot as casually as if it had been filled with Fords and De Sotos, put a feed bag on his horse's nose, and strode toward the guarded front door.

"The Amish have been coming to Garver Brothers for years," someone observed.

"I wish I had me a buggy like that," somebody else said. "A horse'll run on grass, but my car sure as hell won't."

The Lizards with guns blocked the Amish farmer's path into the store. He spoke to them; since he didn't raise his voice and his back was turned, Larssen couldn't make out what he said. He braced himself for trouble all the same.

Another Lizard came bounding up to the doorway. Maybe he spoke English, because the farmer started talking to him instead of to the guards. And then, to Jens' surprise, the aliens stood aside and let him go in. He emerged a few minutes later with a shovel, a pickax, and a bolt of black cloth. Nodding politely to the Lizards as he passed them, he returned to his wagon, climbed in, and rolled away.

He didn't want anything the Lizards needed, so they let him have his stuff, Jens thought. That was smart of them. As for the farmer, he might not have seen them as being that different from anyone else who failed to share his own rigorous faith. The idea of living in a simple, orderly world with strict laws held no small appeal for Larssen: as a physicist, he thought well of order and law and predictability. But the tools he used to seek them were necessarily more complex than pick and shovel, horse and buggy.

That reminded him why he'd come this way in the first place. "Does anybody know if Charlie Tompkins' garage is open?" he asked.

"Not right now it isn't," said the fellow who'd called the Lizards chicken thieves, "on account of I'm Charlie Tompkins. What can I do for you, stranger?"

"My car broke down about a mile outside of town," Larssen answered. "Any chance you can take a look at it?"

The mechanic laughed. "Don't see why not. I'm not what you'd call real busy these days—I expect you can tell that by lookin'. What's your machine doin', anyhow?" When Jens described the symptoms, Tompkins looked grave. "That doesn't sound so good. Well, we'll go see. Come on up to my shop so as I can get some tools."

As the woman at the drugstore had said, the garage lay just a little past the Garver Brothers store. Tompkins picked up his tool kit. It didn't look light, so Larssen said, "I'll carry it for you, if you like. We've got a ways to walk."

"Don't worry about it. Here, come on with me." The mechanic led Larssen over to a bicycle which had a bracket welded to the head tube. The handle of the tool kit fit neatly over the bracket. Tompkins climbed onto the saddle, gestured to Larssen. "You ride behind me. I don't use any gas this way, a bike's got fewer parts than a car, and they're easier for somebody like me to fix if they do break."

All that made perfect sense, but Jens hadn't ridden on one of those little flat racks since about the third grade. "Will it carry both of us?" he asked.

Tompkins laughed. "I've put bigger men than you back there, my friend. Sure, you're tall, but you're built like a pencil. We won't have any trouble, I promise."

They didn't have much. What there was came because Larssen hadn't been on any bicycle at all for a good many years, and needed a little while before his body remembered how to balance. Charlie Tompkins compensated for his lurches without saying a word. In a way, that only made them more embarrassing: weren't you never supposed to forget how to stay on a bicycle? Jens sighed as he did his best not to maim himself while exploding the cliché.

"Whereabouts you from, mister?" Tompkins asked as they rolled past the sign welcoming people to Strasburg.

"Chicago," Larssen answered.

The mechanic twisted his head. That struck Larssen as foolhardy, but he kept his mouth shut. After a moment, Tompkins turned back to watch where he was going. He spoke over his shoulder: "And you were heading back there, were you, from wherever you were coming from?"

"That's right. What about it?"

"Nothing, really." Tompkins pedaled along for a few more seconds, then went on in a sad tone, "Thing is, though, you might not want to say that to just anybody around here who asks. Chicago's still free, right? Sure it is. I'm not asking whether you would or you wouldn't, mind, but I can see where you might not want the Lizards to get wind of whatever reasons you've got for going that way."

"How would the Lizards . . ." Larssen's voice trailed away. "You don't mean people would tell them?" He knew the Lizards had human collaborators: the Warsaw Jews, Chinese, Italians, Brazilians. Up till this second, though, he'd never imagined there could be such a thing as an American collaborator. He supposed that was naive of him.

Evidently it was. Tompkins said, "Some people, they'll do anything to get in good with the boss, no matter who the boss is. Some other people have gotten hurt on account of it." He didn't seem to care for the subject, either. Instead of giving details, he took one hand off the handlebars and pointed. "That your car up ahead there, that Plymouth?"

"Yes, that's it."

"Okay, let's see what we've got." Tompkins stopped the bike with the soles of his shoes against the asphalt. He and Jens both got off. The mechanic unhooked the tool box, walked over to the deceased automobile, reached through the grill, and popped the hood latch. Once the long piece of sheet metal was up and out of the way, he bent over and peered into the engine compartment.

A low, mournful whistle floated up. "Mister, I hate to tell you, but you got yourself a cracked block." Another whistle, not much later. "Your valves are shot to shit, too, pardon my French. What the hell you been burnin' in this machine, anyhow?"

"Whatever I could get my hands on that would burn," Larssen answered honestly.

"Well, I know how that goes, what with the way things are, but Jesus, even if times were good I couldn't fix this poor bastard by my lonesome. What with the way things are, I don't think I can fix her at all. Hate to have to tell you that, but I'm not gonna lie to you, either."

"How am I supposed to get back to Chicago, then?" Larssen wasn't really asking Tompkins; it was more a cry to the unhearing gods. When he'd come east through Ohio, the Lizards hadn't been anywhere near this far north. When he'd come east through Ohio, his car had been in reasonably good shape, too.

"Wouldn't take you forever to walk there," Tompkins said. "What is it, maybe three, four hundred miles? Could be done."

Jens stared at the mechanic in dismay. At least two weeks on shank's mare, more likely a month? Dodging in and out of the Lizards' territory? Dodging bandits, too, likely enough (one more thing he'd never expected in America, at least outside the vanished Wild West)? Winter was on the way, too; already the sky had lost the perfect, transparent blue of summer. Barbara would think he was dead by the time he got back—if he got back.

His eye fell on Tompkins' bicycle. He pointed. "Tell you what—I'll trade you my set of wheels for yours. You can use the parts that are still good to keep other cars running." Before the Lizards came, swapping a two-year-old Plymouth for an elderly bicycle would have been insane. Before the Lizards came, of course, his car could have been fixed if it broke down. Before the Lizards came, his car wouldn't have broken down because he wouldn't have had to abuse it so.

Now— Now Charlie Tompkins looked from the bike to the Plymouth, slowly shook his head. "What's the point to that, mister? You take off for Chicago, you gonna carry your car on your back? I'll get to scavenge it whether I give you my bike or not."

"Why, you—" Larssen wanted to murder the mechanic. The force of the feeling frightened him, left him almost sick. He wondered how many killings had sprung from the chaos the Lizards spread across the United States, across the world. Times grew ever more desperate, the risk of getting caught shrank . . . so why not kill, if you needed to?

To fight the temptation, he jammed his hands deep into his trouser pockets. Amidst keys and small change, the fingers of his right hand closed round his cigarette lighter. The Zippo, unlike the Plymouth, would work forever, or at least as long as he could keep coming up with flints. It would also burn moonshine a lot better than the car had.

He yanked out the buffed steel case, flipped open the top. His thumb went to the lighter's wheel. "You don't trade me your bike, Charlie, I'll *burn* the goddamn car. Let's see how you like that."

The mechanic started to grab for a wrench from his tool kit. Larssen's mouth went dry—maybe he hadn't been the only one thinking of murder. Then Tompkins' hand stopped suddenly. His high-pitched laugh sounded unnatural, but it was a laugh. "Godawful times," he said, to which Jens could only nod. "All right, Larssen, take the bike. I expect I'll be able to come up with another one from somewheres."

Larssen relaxed, but not very far. His Zippo might torch the Plymouth, but it didn't stack up very well against a monkey wrench. He walked over to the rear end of the car, opened the trunk. He took out the smaller of the two suitcases there and a ball of twine, slammed the trunk shut. He did the best job he could of tying the suitcase to the rack on which he'd ridden, then pulled the trunk key off the ring and tossed it to Charlie Tompkins.

He swung his right leg over the bicycle saddle, as if he were mounting a horse. If he'd wobbled as a passenger, he was even more unsteady up there by himself. But he managed to stay upright and keep the bike rolling forward. After a couple of hundred yards, he took a chance and looked back over his shoulder. Tompkins was already going through the suitcase he'd had to leave behind. He scowled and kept pedaling.

The U-2 buzzed through the night, so low that an instant's inattention or simply a hillock she'd forgotten would have cost Ludmila Gorbunova her life. The *Kukuruznik* was proving the Soviet Union's ace in the hole in the war against the Lizards. Newer Red Air Force planes with greater speed and better guns, but also with more metal in their airframes and higher minimum ceilings, had all but vanished from the skies. The obsolescent little biplane trainer, too small, too slow, and too low to be noticed, soldiered on.

The slipstream blew chilly over Ludmila's goggled face. Fall was in the air. The rains would start any day now. Her lips curled upwards in a mirthless smile. The *rasputitsa*, the time of mud, had hurt the fascists badly last year. She wondered how the Lizards' armored vehicles would enjoy trying to push forward through slimy porridge.

She also wondered, just for a moment, what her superiors had done with the two Germans she'd delivered to them from the Ukrainian collective farm. Having deadly foes suddenly turn into allies was disconcerting, as was the realization the Nazis were human beings like her own side. Better when they'd seemed only small field-gray shapes scurrying like lice before the bullets from her machine guns.

She glanced down at the map book balanced on her knees. The lights from her instrument panel let her trace her assigned flight path. She flew over a river. A quick peek at her watch told her how long she'd been in the air. Yes, it ought to be the Slovechna, which meant she needed to swing farther south . . . now.

Her breath came short and fast when she spotted lights on the horizon ahead. Some of the Lizards still kept the stupid habit of lighting up their campsites at night. Maybe they thought it made them safer from ground attack. Given the range and power of their weapons, maybe it even did; Ludmila was no Marshal of the Soviet Union, to know everything there was to know about ground tactics. She did know being able to see what she was shooting at made her own job easier.

She couldn't gain altitude and then glide silently to the attack, as she had against the Nazis. Aircraft that attacked the Lizards from anything much above ground height came down in pieces, a lesson learned from bitter experience. Stay low and you had a chance.

It wasn't always a good chance. Her air regiment was chewed to bits. She knew of only three or four other pilots from it still flying. The regiment was long since broken up, of course—large concentrations of aircraft on the ground drew the Lizards' wrath like nothing else. These days, the *Kukuruzniks* flew by ones and twos, not in formation.

The lighted area swelled ahead of her. Her finger went to the firing button for the machine guns. She spied what looked at first like bumpy ground but proved as she drew nearer to be some sort of vehicles under camouflage netting. Trucks, she thought—Lizard tanks, being almost impervious to human weapons, were seldom concealed so carefully.

She started her firing run. The machine guns hammered under her wings. The little U-2 shook like a leaf in an autumn wind. The flying sparks of tracer bullets helped guide her aim.

Almost in the same instant, the Lizards began shooting back. They owned more firepower than the Germans had been able to bring to bear; by the muzzle flashes on the ground, Ludmila thought ten thousand automatic weapons had opened up on her all at once. The fabric skin of the *Kukuruznik*'s wings made cheerful popping noises as bullets pierced it.

Then one of the trucks blew up in a blue-white ball of hydrogen fire, so different from the orange flames of blazing petrol. The blast of heat seared Ludmila's cheeks as she flew past; it tried to fling her aircraft tumbling out of control. She wrestled with stick and pedals, held it steady in the air.

Touched off by the first, more trucks exploded behind her. She gave the U-2 all the meager power it had, banked away toward the friendly darkness. A few Lizards kept shooting at her, but only a few; more ran to fight the fires she'd touched off. As night drew its cloak around her, she took one hand off the stick for a moment, pounded fist against thigh. She'd hurt them this time.

Now to find her way home. Even without flying a combat mission, navigating at night was anything but easy. She straightened onto compass course 047. That would bring her somewhere close to the airstrip from which she'd been operating. She checked her watch and her airspeed indicator, the other vital tools of night flying. After about—hmm—fifty minutes, she'd begin to circle and look for landing lights.

Just surviving a mission was enough to make her proud—and to make her remember all her friends who would never fly again. That thought quickly leached joy from her, leaving behind only weariness and the jittery residue of terror.

Either she was a better navigator than she'd thought or much luckier than usual, for she spotted the dim landing lanterns after only a couple of circles. They were hooded so as not to be visible from high overhead. The Red Air Force had learned the dangers of that from the *Luftwaffe*; the lesson was all the more vital against the Lizards.

Her approach in the dark was tentative, the makeshift airstrip anything but smooth. The landing she made would have earned only scorn from her *Osoaviakhim* instructor (she wondered if the man was still alive). She didn't care. She was down and among her own people and safe—until her next mission. She didn't even have to think about that, not yet.

As soon as she got out of the U-2, groundcrew started dragging it to cover. A woman mechanic pointed to the bullet holes. Ludmila shrugged. "Patch them as you get the chance, comrade. I'm all right and so is the aircraft."

"Good," the mechanic said. "Oh—you have a letter down in the bunker."

"A letter?" The Soviet post, erratic since the start of the war, had grown frankly chaotic once the Lizards added their ravages to those of the Nazis. Eagerly, Ludmila asked, "From whom?"

"I don't know. It's in an envelope, and it doesn't say on the outside," the mechanic answered.

"An envelope? Really?" The very occasional letters Ludmila had had from her brothers and her father and mother were all written on folded single sheets of paper, with her name and unit scrawled on the reverse. She'd had only one note since the Lizards came, three hasty lines, from her younger brother Igor, letting her know he was alive. She trotted for the shelter bunker, saying, "I'll have to see who's gotten rich."

Curtains and doglegs in the entry passage kept candlelight from leaking out. Yevdokia Kashcrina looked up from the tunic she was darning. "How did it go?" she asked with a fellow pilot's concern. It was a long way from the formal debriefings of earlier missions, but the Soviet Air Force was too dispersed and battered to have much room for formalities these days.

"Well enough," Ludmila said. "I shot up some trucks that weren't hidden well enough, and I got back here alive. Now what's this I hear about a letter?"

"It's over there on your blankets," Yevdokia said, pointing. "You don't think anyone would dare do anything with it, do you?"

"Better not," Ludmila said fiercely. Both women laughed. Ludmila hurried over to where she slept. The clean, white envelope gleamed against the dark blue wool of the blankets. She snatched it up, carried it over to a candle.

She'd expected to recognize the script on the envelope at a glance, and thus know who had written to her before she started the letter itself. Hearing from any of her family would be so good . . . But, to her surprise and disappointment, the handwriting was unfamiliar to her. Indeed, handwriting was too good a word for it; her name and unit were printed in large copybook letters of the sort a bright eight-year-old might make.

"Who's it from?" Yevdokia asked.

"I don't know yet," Ludmila said.

The other pilot laughed. "A secret admirer, Ludmila Vadimovna?"

"Hush." Ludmila tore open the envelope, pulled out the piece of paper inside. The words on that were also printed rather than written. For a moment, they seemed utterly meaningless to her. Then she realized she had to switch languages and even alphabets: the letter was in German.

Her first reaction was fright. Before the Lizards came, a letter in German would have been delivered by a harsh-faced NKVD man certain she was guilty of treason. But censors must have seen this note and decided to let it go through. Reading it probably would not endanger her.

To the brave flier who plucked me from the kolkhoz, it began. *Flier* had a feminine ending tacked on, and *kolkhoz* was spelled out in those copybook Cyrillic letters. *I hope you are well and safe and hitting back against the Lizards. I write this as simply as I can, as I know your German is slow, though much better than my Russian. I am now in Moscow, where I work with your government to hurt the Lizards in new ways. These will—*

A few words were neatly clipped out of the letter. A censor *had* been at it, then. Some of Ludmila's fear returned: somewhere in Moscow, her name appeared in a dossier for getting mail from a German. As long as Germany and the Soviet Union kept on working together against the Lizards, that dossier would not matter. If they had a falling out . . .

Ludmila read on: *I hope one day we may see each other again. This may be so, because—* The censor had excised another section. The letter finished, *Your country and mine have been enemies, allies, enemies, and now allies again. Life is strange, not so? I hope we shall not be enemies ourselves, you and I.* The signature was a scrawl that looked to her eyes nothing like *Heinrich Jäger*, but that was surely what it said. Underneath, in the clear printing that marked the rest of the note, he had appended *Major, 16th Panzer*, as if she were unlikely to remember him without being reminded.

She stared at the piece of paper for a long time, trying to sort out her own feelings. He was polite, he was well-spoken, he was not the ugliest man she had ever seen . . . he was a Nazi. If she answered his letter, another note would go down in the dossier. She was as certain of that as of tomorrow's sunrise.

"Well?" Yevgenia said when she did not comment.

"You were right, Yevgenia Gavrilovna—it *is* from a secret admirer."

The other pilot made a rude noise. "The Devil's nephew, no doubt."

"How did you guess?"

A shell screamed down and landed in the middle of the grove of
larches south of Shabbona, Illinois. Mutt Daniels threw himself flat. Splinters of wood and more deadly splinters of metal whined past overhead. "I
am getting too old for this shit," Daniels muttered to no one in particular.

A flock of black-crowned night herons—"quawks," the locals called
them, after the noise they made—leapt into the air in panic. They were
handsome birds, two feet tall or more, with long yellow legs, black or
sometimes dark green heads and backs, and pearl-gray wings. Quawking
for all they were worth, they flew south as fast as they could go.

Mutt listened to their receding cries, but hardly looked up to watch
them go. He was too busy deepening the foxhole he'd already started in
the muddy ground under the larches. In the generation that had passed
since he'd got back from France, he'd forgotten how fast you could dig
while you were lying on your belly.

Another shell burst, this one just east of the grove. The few quawks
that hadn't taken fright at the first explosion did at this one. From a hole
a few feet away from Daniels', Sergeant Schneider said, "They likely won't
be back this year."

"Huh?"

"The herons," Schneider explained. "They usually head south for the
winter earlier in the year than this, anyhow. They come in in April and fly
out when fall starts."

"Just like ballplayers," Daniels said. He flipped up more dirt with his
entrenching tool. "I got a bad feeling this grove ain't gonna be the same
when they come north after spring training next year. Us and the Lizards,
we're kind of rearranging the landscape, you might say."

He didn't find out whether Sergeant Schneider would say that or not.
A whole salvo of shells crashed down around them. Both men huddled in
their holes, heads down so they tasted mud. Then, from east of the
larches, American artillery opened up, pounding back at the Lizard positions along the line of Highway 51. As he had in France, Mutt wished the

big guns on both sides would shoot at one another and leave the poor damned infantry alone.

Tanks rumbled past the grove under cover of the American barrage, trying to push back the Lizard vanguard still moving on Chicago. Daniels raised his head for a moment. Some of the tanks were Lees, with a small turret and a heavy gun mounted in a sponson on the front corner of the hull. More, though, were the new Shermans; with their big main armament up in the turret, they looked like the Lizard tanks from which Daniels had been retreating since the Lizards came down from beyond the sky.

"The closer they get to Chicago, the more stuff we're throwin' at 'em," he called to Schneider.

"Yeah, and a fat lot of good it's doing us, too," the other veteran answered. "If they weren't spread thin trying to conquer the whole world at once, we'd be dead meat by now. Or maybe they don't really care whether they get into Chicago or not, and that's why they've moved slower than they might have."

"What do you mean, maybe they don't care? Why wouldn't they?" Mutt asked. When he thought about strategy, he thought about the hit-and-run play, when to bunt, and the right time for a pitchout. Since he got home after the Armistice, he'd done his best to forget the military meaning of the word.

Schneider, though, was a career soldier. Though only a noncom, he had a feel for the way armies functioned. He said, "What good is Chicago to us? It's a transportation hub, right, the place where all the roads and all the railroads and all the lake and river traffic come together. Just by being this close, and by their air power, the Lizards have smashed that network to smithereens."

Daniels pointed to the advancing American tanks. "Where'd those come from, then? They must've got into Chicago some kind of way, or they wouldn't be here."

"Probably by ship," Sergeant Schneider said. "Things I've heard, they don't quite understand what ships are all about and how much you can carry on one. That probably says something about wherever they come from, wouldn't you think?"

"Damned if I know." Mutt looked at Sergeant Schneider with some surprise. He might have expected that remark from Sam Yeager, who'd enjoyed reading about bug-eyed monsters before people knew there were any such things. The sergeant, though, seemed to have a one-track military mind. What was he doing wondering about other planets or whatever you called them?

As if to answer the question Mutt hadn't asked, Schneider said, "The more we know about the Lizards, the better we can fight back, right?"

"I guess so," said Daniels, who hadn't thought of it in quite those terms.

"And speaking of fighting back, we ought to be moving up to give those tanks some support." Schneider scrambled out of his foxhole, shouted and waved one arm so the rest of the troops in the grove would know what he meant, and dashed out into the open.

Along with the others, Daniels followed the sergeant. He felt naked and vulnerable away from his hastily dug shelter. He'd seen more than enough shelling, both in 1918 and during the past weeks, to know a foxhole often gave only the illusion of safety, but illusions have their place, too. Without them, most likely, men would never go to war at all.

Westbound American shells tore through the air. Their note grew fainter and deeper as they flew away from Mutt. When he heard a rising scream, he threw himself into a ditch several seconds before he consciously reasoned that it had to spring from an incoming Lizard round. His body was smarter than his head. He'd seen that in baseball often enough—when you had to stop and think about what you were doing, you got yourself in trouble.

The shell burst a few hundred yards ahead of him, among the advancing Lees and Shermans. It had an odd sound. Again, Daniels didn't stop to think, for more rounds followed the first. Cursing himself and Schneider both for breaking cover, he tried once more to dig in while flat on his belly. The barrage walked toward him. He wished he were a mole or a gopher—any sort of creature that could burrow far underground and never have to worry about coming up for air.

His breath sobbed in his ears. His heart thudded inside his chest, so hard he wondered if it would burst. "I *am* too old for this shit," he wheezed. The Lizard barrage ignored him. He remembered that the Boche artillery hadn't paid any attention when he cursed it, either.

The shells rained down for a while, then stopped. The one blessing about going through Lizard barrages was that they didn't last for days on end, the way German pounding sometimes had in 1918. Maybe the invaders didn't have the tubes or the ammunition dumps to raise that kind of hell.

Or maybe they just didn't need to do it. Their fire was more accurate and deadly than the Boches had ever dreamed of being. When Daniels ever so cautiously raised his head, he saw that the field he'd been crossing was churned into a nearly lunar landscape. Up ahead, two or three tanks were burning. As he watched, smoke and flame burst from under another one. A tread thrown, it ground itself into the mud.

"How'd they do that?" Mutt asked the air. No new shell had struck the Lee; he was sure of that. It was almost as if the Lizards had a way to pack antitank mines inside their artillery rounds. Before the invaders came down from Mars or wherever, he would have laughed at the idea. He wasn't laughing now; the Lizards were nothing to laugh about.

A couple of feet in front of his new foxhole, half hidden in yellowing grass, lay a shiny blue spheroid a little smaller than a baseball. Daniels was sure it hadn't been there before the shelling started. He reached out to pick it up and see what it was, then jerked back his hand as if the thing had snarled at him.

"Don't fool around with what you don't know nothin' about," he told himself, as if he were more likely to obey a real spoken order. Just because that little blue thing didn't look like a mine didn't mean it wasn't one. He was certain the Lizards hadn't shot it at him out of the goodness of their hearts, assuming they had any. "Let a sapper screw around with it. That's his job."

Mutt gave the spheroid a wide berth as he started moving forward again. He didn't go as fast as he wanted to; he kept looking down to see if any more of them had been scattered about. A flat *bang!* and a shriek off to his right told him his caution wasn't wasted.

Ahead and to his left, Sergeant Schneider trotted westward, steady as a machine. Daniels started to call out a warning to him, then noticed that even though the sergeant was making better time than he (not surprising, since Schneider was both taller and trimmer), he was also carefully noting where he planted his feet. Soldiers in wartime didn't necessarily live to grow old, but Schneider was not about to die from doing something stupid.

Farther up ahead, another tank rolled over a mine. This one, a Sherman, started to burn. The five-man crew bailed out seconds before the tank's ammunition began cooking off. The rest of the American armor, fearful of meeting a like fate, slowed almost to a crawl.

"Come on!" Sergeant Schneider shouted, perhaps to the suddenly lagging tanks, perhaps to the infantrymen whose advance had also slowed. "We've got to keep moving. If we bog down in the open, they'll slaughter us."

That held enough truth to keep Mutt slogging forward after the sergeant. But he soon began looking for a good place in which to dig in. Despite Schneider's indomitable will, the advance was running out of steam. Even the sergeant recognized that after another couple of hundred yards. When he stopped and took out his entrenching tool, the rest of the men followed his example. Trench lines began to spiderweb their way across the field.

Daniels worked for half an hour extending his hole toward the one nearest to him on the right before he realized the Lizards had halted the American counterattack without ever once showing themselves. That did not strike him as encouraging.

Atvar studied the situation map of the northern part of Tosev 3's secondary continental map. "This does not strike me as encouraging," he said. "I find it intolerable that the Big Uglies continue to thwart us in this way. We must do a more effective job of destroying their industrial base. I have repeatedly spoken of this concern, yet nothing seems to be accomplished. Why?"

"Exalted Fleetlord, the situation is not as black as you make it," Kirel said soothingly. "True, not all the enemy's factories are wrecked as completely as we might like, but we have damaged his road and rail networks to the point where both raw materials and finished goods move with difficulty if at all."

Atvar refused to be mollified. "We ourselves are moving with difficulty if at all," he said with heavy sarcasm as he stabbed a finger toward the representation of a lakeside city. "This place should have fallen some time ago."

Kirel leaned forward to read the name of the town. "Chicago? Possibly so, Exalted Fleetlord, yet again we have rendered it essentially useless to the Big Uglies as a transport center. The deteriorating weather has not helped our cause, either. And in spite of all obstacles, we do continue to advance on it."

"At a hatchling's crawl," Atvar sneered. "It should have fallen, I tell you, before the weather became a factor in any way."

"Possibly so, Exalted Fleetlord," Kirel repeated. "Yet the Big Uglies have defended it with unusual stubbornness, and now the weather *is* a factor. If I may . . ." He touched a button below the video screen in front of Atvar. The fleetlord watched as rain poured down from a soggy sky, turning the ground to thick brown porridge. The Big Uglies, evidently used to such deluges, were taking full advantage of this one. They'd destroyed a good many roads leading toward Chicago themselves, forcing the vehicles of the Race off into the muck. The vehicles didn't like muck very well. The mechanics who tried to keep them running in it liked it even less.

"The same thing is happening in the SSSR, and against the Nipponese in—what do they call it?—in Manchukuo, that's right," Atvar said. "It's even worse in those places than in the United States, because they don't need to wreck their roads to make us go into the mud. As soon as it rains for more than two days straight, the roads themselves turn into mud. Why didn't they pave them to begin with?"

The fleetlord knew Kirel could not possibly answer a question like that. Even if he could have answered it, responsibility still rested with Atvar. The Race's landcruisers and troopcarriers, of course, were tracked. They managed after a fashion, even churning through sticky mud. Most supply vehicles, though, merely had wheels. Back before Atvar went into cold sleep, that had seemed sufficient, even extravagant. Against spear-carrying warriors riding on animals, it would have been.

"If this cursed planet were anything like what the stinking probes claimed it to be, we would have conquered it long since," he growled.

"Without a doubt, Exalted Fleetlord," Kirel said. "Should you care to use it, we still have one major advantage of the Big Uglies. A nuclear weapon exploded above Chicago would end its resistance once and for all."

"I have considered this," Atvar said. That he had considered it was the measure of his frustration. But he went on, "I am also obligated, however, to consider our occupation of Tosev 3 as well as our conquest of it. Chicago is a natural center of commerce for the region, and will be again when peace returns under our administration. Creating another such nexus after destroying this one would prove troublesome and expensive for those who come after us."

"Let it be as you say, then, Exalted Fleetlord," Kirel replied; he knew when to set a topic aside. In any event, he had plenty of other titbits with which to worry Atvar: "I have a report that the Deutsche launched two medium-range missiles against our forces in France last night. One was intercepted in flight; the other impacted and exploded, fortunately without damage worse than a large hole in the ground. Their guidance systems leave much to be desired."

"What I would most desire is that they had no guidance systems," the fleetlord said heavily. "May I at least hope we destroyed the launchers from which these missiles came?"

Kirel's hesitation told him he could not so hope. The shiplord said, "Exalted Fleetlord, we scrambled killercraft and vectored them over the area from which the missiles were discharged. It is heavily forested terrain, and they failed to discover the launchers. Officers speculate the Deutsche used either launchers concealed in caves, portable launchers, or both. More information will become available upon subsequent firings."

"More damage will become available, too, unless we are more careful than we have been," Atvar said. "We have the capability to knock these things out of the sky; I expect us to live up to that capability."

"It shall be done," Kirel said.

Atvar relaxed, a little; when Kirel said something would be done, he meant it. "What other news of interest have you for me, Shiplord?"

"Some intriguing data have come in from the study we began when we learned the Tosevites were sexually active at all seasons of the year," Kirel replied.

"Tell me," Atvar said. "Anything that will help me understand the Big Uglies' behavior is an asset."

"As you say, Exalted Fleetlord. You may recall that we took a fair number of Tosevites of each gender and had them mate with one another to confirm they did indeed lack a breeding season. This they have done, as you know. Even more interesting, however, is that several more-or-less-permanently mated male-female pairs have emerged from the randomly chosen individuals. Not all subjects in the experimental study have formed such pairs; we are currently investigating the factors which cause some to do so and others to abstain."

"That is interesting," the fleetlord admitted. "I remain not entirely sure of its relevance to the campaign as a whole, however."

"Some may well exist," Kirel said. "We have had instances all over the planet of Tosevites, some military personnel but others nominally civilians, attacking males and installations of the Race without regard for their own lives or safety. In those cases where the assailants survived for interrogation, a reason frequently cited for their actions was the death of a mate at our hands. This male-female bonding appears to be part of the gluc which holds together Tosevite society."

"Interesting," Atvar said again. He felt faintly disgusted. When he smelled the pheromones of females in estrus, all he thought about was mating. At other seasons of the year—or indefinitely, if no females were around—not only was he not interested, he was smug about not being interested. Among the Race, the two words *arousal* and *foolishness* sprang from a common root. *Trust the Big Uglies to build their societies based on a facet of foolishness*, he thought. He asked, "Can we exploit this Tosevite aberration so it works to our advantage rather than against us?"

"Our experts are working toward this goal," Kirel said. "They will test strategies both among our shipboard experimental specimens and, more cautiously, with select members of the populations of Big Uglies under our control."

"Why more cautiously?" Atvar asked. Then he answered his own question: "Oh, I see. If the experiments down on Tosev 3 produce undesirable results, that might lead to situations where Big Uglies will seek to harm members of the Race in the manner you previously described."

"Exactly so, Exalted Fleetlord," Kirel answered. "We have learned from painful experience that suicidal attacks are most difficult to guard against. We can much more easily protect ourselves against dangers from rational beings than from fanatics who are willing, sometimes even eager, to die with us. Not even the threat of large-scale retaliation against the captive populace has proven a reliable deterrent."

Half of Atvar heartily wished he'd been passed over for this command; he'd be living in peaceful luxury back on Home. But he had a duty to the Race, and knew somber pride at having been chosen the male best suited to the task of fostering the Empire's growth. He said, "I hope our experts will soon be able to suggest ways in which we can use the Big Uglies' perpetual randiness against them. And speaking of using things Tosevite against the Tosevites, how fare we in turning the captured portion of their industrial capacity to our benefit?"

Kirel did not let the change of subject fluster him. "Not as well as we would have liked, Exalted Fleetlord," he replied, earning Atvar's respect for unflinching honesty. "Part of the problem rests with the Tosevite factory workers we must necessarily employ in large numbers: many are apathetic and perform poorly, while others, actively hostile, sabotage as much of what they produce as possible. Another issue involved is the general primitiveness of their manufacturing plants."

"By the Emperor, they're not too primitive to keep from turning out guns and landcruisers and aircraft to use against us," Atvar exclaimed. "Why can't we use some of that capacity for ourselves?"

"The only way to do so, Exalted Fleetlord, is to adapt ourselves—resign ourselves might be a better way to put it—to arms and munitions at the Big Uglies' current technological level. If we do so, we forfeit our chief advantage over them and the contest becomes one of numbers—wherein the advantage is theirs."

"Surely some of these facilities, at any rate, can be upgraded to our standards," Atvar said.

Kirel made an emphatic gesture of negation. "Not for years. The gap is simply too wide. Oh, there are exceptions. A bullet is a bullet. We may be able to adapt their factories to produce small arms to our patterns, though even that will not be easy, as hardly any of their individual infantry weapons are automatic. We have had some success reboring captured artillery tubes to fire our ammunition, and could perhaps manufacture more tubes to our own specifications."

"I have seen these reports," Atvar agreed. "From them I inferred greater progress would also be possible."

"I wish it were so, Exalted Fleetlord," Kirel said, repeating the gesture of negation. "You will notice the examples I cited were of unsophisticated weapons. As soon as electronics of any sort become involved, any hope of our using Tosevite facilities goes straight out the window."

"But they have electronics, some at least," Atvar said. "They have both radar and radio, for instance. Our task would be simpler if they didn't."

"True enough, they have electronics. But they have no computers whatever, and they know nothing of integrated circuits or even transistors. The vacuum-filled glass tubes they use in place of proper circuitry are so large and bulky and fragile and produce so much heat as to make them useless for our purposes."

"Can we not introduce what we need into their factories?"

"Simpler to build our own, by what the technical experts tell me," Kirel answered. "Besides which, we run the risk of Tosevite workers learning our techniques from us and transmitting them to their unsubdued brethren. This is a risk we take with every venture that involves the Big Uglies."

Atvar made an unhappy noise. None of the manuals from Home warned about that sort of risk. Neither the Rabotevs nor the Hallessi had been far enough along to be in a position to steal the Race's technology and turn it against its creators. Therefore the planners, drawing on precedent as they always did, failed to envision that any race could do so.

The fleetlord should have thought of the danger for himself. But Tosev 3 presented so many unexpected difficulties, and the Race was so little used to dealing with unexpected difficulties, that not all of them became obvious at once. Precedent, organization, and long-term planning were splendid things within the Empire, where change, when it occurred, did so in tiny, closely supervised increments over the course of centuries. They did not prepare the Race to handle Tosev 3.

"We and the Big Uglies are both metals," Atvar said to Kirel, "but we are steel and they are quicksilver."

"An excellent comparison, Exalted Fleetlord, right down to the poisonous vapors they exude," his subordinate answered. "May I make a suggestion?"

"Speak."

"You are gracious, Exalted Fleetlord. I can understand the reasons for your reluctance to employ nuclear weapons against Chicago. But the natives of the United States continue to resist, if not with the skill of the Deutsche, then with equal or greater stubbornness and with far greater industrial capacity, even if their weapons are generally less sophisticated. They need to have the potential price of such resistance brought home to them. Their capital— Washington, I believe they call it—is merely an administrative center, with limited commercial or manufacturing significance. It is, moreover, not far from the eastern coast of the continent; prevailing winds would blow most nuclear waste products harmlessly out to sea."

One of Atvar's eyes swung across the map from Chicago to Washington. The situation was as Kirel described. Still . . . "Results in the case of Berlin were not altogether as we anticipated," he said, a damning indictment among the Race.

But Kirel said, "It had unexpected benefits as well as shortcomings. We gained the allegiance of Warsaw and its environs shortly after employing that first device."

"Truth," Atvar admitted. It was an important truth, too; the Race too often saw only hazard in the unexpected, even if opportunity could also hatch from it.

"Not only that," Kirel continued, "but it will also create uncertainty and fear on the part of the Big Uglies who do continue to resist. Destroying a single imperial capital might be an isolated act on our part. But if we destroy a second one, that shows them we can repeat the action anywhere on their planet at any time we choose."

"Truth," Atvar said again. Like any normal male of the Race, he distrusted uncertainty; the idea of using it as a weapon was unsettling to him. But when he thought of it as inflicting uncertainty on the foe, in the same way that his forces might inflict hunger or death, the concept became clearer—and more attractive. Moreover, Kirel was usually a cautious male; if he thought such a step necessary, he was likely to be right.

"What is your command, Exalted Fleetlord?" Kirel asked.

"Let the order be prepared for my review. I shall turn both eyes upon it the instant it appears before me. Barring unforeseen developments, I shall approve it."

"Exalted Fleetlord, it shall be done." Tailstump quivering with excitement, Kirel hurried away.

"This is Radio Deutschland." *Not Radio Berlin*, Moishe Russie thought as he moved his head closer to the speaker of the shortwave set. *Not any more.* Nor was the signal, though on the same frequency as Berlin had always used, anywhere near as strong as it had been. Instead of shouting, it was as if the Germans were whispering now, in hope of not being overheard.

"An important bulletin," the news reader went on. "The government of the *Reich* is grieved to report that Washington, D.C., capital of the United States of America, appears to have been the victim of a bomb of the type which recently made a martyr of Berlin. All radio transmissions from Washington ceased abruptly and without warning approximately twenty-five minutes ago; confused reports from Baltimore, Philadelphia, and Richmond speak of a pillar of fire mounting into the night sky. Our *Führer*, Adolf Hitler, has expressed his condolences for the American people, victims like the Germans of the insane aggression of these savage alien invaders. The *Führer*'s words—"

Russie clicked off the set. He did not care what Adolf Hitler had to say; he wished with all his heart that Hitler had been in Berlin when the Lizards dropped their bomb on it. The regime there had deserved to go up in a pillar of fire.

But Washington! If Berlin represented everything dark and bestial in the human spirit, Washington stood for just the opposite: freedom, justice, equality . . . yet the Lizards destroyed them both alike.

"Yisgadal v'yiskadash shmay rabo—" Russie murmured the memorial prayer for the dead. So many would be dead, across the ocean; he remembered the posters the Germans had plastered all over Warsaw before the city fell to the Lizards . . . before the Jews and the Polish Home Army rose up and helped the Lizards drive the Germans out of Warsaw.

No doubt that had been justified; without the Lizards, Russie knew he and most if not all his people would have died. That reasoning had let him support them after they entered Warsaw. Gratitude was a reasonable emotion, especially when as fully deserved as here. That the outside world thought him a traitor to mankind hurt deeply, but the outside world did not know—and refused to see—what the Nazis had done here. Better the Lizards than the SS; so he still believed.

But now— Booted feet pounded down the corridor toward his office, breaking in on his thoughts. The door flew open. The moment he saw

Mordechai Anielewicz's face, he knew the fighting leader had heard. "Washington—" they both said in the same breath.

Russie was the first to find more words. "We cannot go on comfortably working with them after this, not unless we want to deserve the hatred the rest of mankind would give us for such a deed."

"*Reb* Moishe, you're right," Anielewicz said, the first time in a long while he'd given Russie such unqualified agreement. But where Russie thought in terms of right and wrong, the Jewish soldier almost automatically began considering ways and means. "We cannot simply rise up against them, either, not unless we want the bloodbath back again."

"Heaven forbid!" Russie said. Then he remembered something he would sooner have forgotten: "I'm supposed to go on the radio this afternoon. What shall I say. God help me, what can I say?"

"Nothing," Anielewicz answered at once. "Just the sound of your voice would make you the Lizards' whore." He thought for a moment, then gave two words of blunt, practical advice: "Get sick."

"Zolraag won't like that. He'll think I'm faking, and he'll be right." But Russie had been a medical student; even as he spoke, his mind searched for ways to make false sickness seem real. He thought of some quickly enough; the punishment they'd inflict on him would also scourge him for letting the Lizards make him into their willing tool. "A purgative, a good strong one," he said. "A purgative and a stiff dose of ipecac."

"What's ipecac?" Anielewicz asked. Russie made ghastly retching noises. The fighter's eyes went big and round. He nodded and grinned. "That should do the job, all right. I'm glad they have you in front of the microphone instead of me."

"Ha." It wasn't a laugh, only one syllable of resignation. But Russie thought such florid symptoms would convince Zolraag something truly was wrong with him. The epidemics in the ghetto, the endemic diseases from which all humanity suffered, seemed to horrify the Lizards, who gave no signs of being similarly afflicted. Russie would have liked to study at one of their medical schools; no doubt he would have learned more there than any Earthly physician could teach him.

"If we want this to work, we're going to have to do something else, you know," Anielewicz said. At Russie's raised eyebrow, he elaborated. "We're going to have to talk with General Bor-Komorowski. The Poles have to be in on this with us. Otherwise the Lizards will turn them loose on us and stand back and smile while we beat each other to death."

"Yes," Russie said, though he both distrusted and feared the commander of the *Armja Krajowa*. But he had other, more immediate concerns. "Even if I manage not to broadcast today, I'll still have to go back to the studio next week. The week after that at the latest, if I take to my bed and swallow more ipecac in a few days." His stomach lurched unhappily at the prospect.

"Don't worry past this afternoon." Anielewicz's eyes were cold and calculating. "Yes, I can piece together enough uniforms, and I can find enough blond fighters or fellows with light brown hair."

"Why do you need fighters with—?" Russie stopped and stared. "You're going to attack the transmitter, and you want the Nazis to get the blame for it."

"Right both times," Anielewicz said. "You should have been a soldier. I just wish I had some men who weren't circumcised. Humans would know the difference. The Lizards might not, but I hate to take the chance. Some Poles think the only thing the Germans did wrong was to leave some of us alive. They might rat on us if they get the chance."

Russie sighed. "Unfortunately, you're right. Send one of your fighters out for the ipecac and another for the purgative. I don't want to be remembered for getting either one, in case the Lizards ask questions later." He sighed. "I have the feeling I won't want to remember the next few hours anyway."

"I believe that, *Reb* Moishe." Anielewicz eyed him with amusement and no small respect. "You know, I think I'd rather be wounded in combat. At least then it comes as a surprise. But to deliberately do something like this to yourself . . ." He shook his head. "Better you than me."

"Better nobody." Russie glanced at his watch (the former property of a German who no longer needed it). "But you'd better arrange for it quickly. The Lizards will be coming in less than three hours, and I ought to be good and sick by then." He started going through the papers on his desk. "I want to move the ones that truly matter—"

"So you can puke all over the rest," Anielewicz finished for him. "That's good. If you pay attention to the small details in a plan, that helps the big pieces go well." He touched one finger to the brim of his gray cloth cap. "I'll take care of it."

He was as good as his word. By the time the Lizard guards came to escort Russie to the studio, he wished Anielewicz had been less efficient. The Lizards hissed and drew back in dismay from his door. He could hardly blame them; the office would need an airing out before anyone wanted to work there again. A pair of good trousers weren't going to be the same any more, either.

One of the Lizards ever so cautiously poked his head back into the office. He stared at Russie, who sprawled, limp as wet blotting paper, over his chair and befouled desk. "What—wrong?" the Lizard asked in halting German.

"Must be something I ate," Russie groaned feebly. The small part of him that did not actively wish he were dead noted he was even telling the truth, perhaps the most effective way to lie ever invented. Most of him, though, felt as if he'd been stretched too far, tied in knots, and then kneaded by a giant's fingers.

A couple of more Lizards looked in at him from the hallway. So did some people. If anything, they seemed more horrified than the Lizards, who did not have to fear catching whatever horrible disease he'd come down with and simply found him most unaesthetic.

One of the Lizards spoke into a small hand-held radio. An answer came back, crisp and crackling. Regretfully, the Lizard advanced into the office. He spoke into the radio again, then held it out to Russie. Zolraag's voice came from the speaker: "You are ill, *Reb* Moishe?" the governor asked. By now his German was fairly good. "You are too ill to broadcast for us today?"

"I'm afraid I am," Russie croaked, most sincerely. He added his first untruth of the afternoon: "I'm sorry."

"I also am sorry, *Reb* Moishe," Zolraag answered. "I wanted your comments on the bombing of Washington, D.C., about which we would have given you full information. I know you would say this shows the need for your kind to give up their foolish fight against our stronger weapons."

Russie groaned again, partly from weakness, partly because he'd expected Zolraag to tell him something like that. He said, "Excellency, I cannot speak now. When I am well, I will decide what I can truthfully say about what your people have done."

"I am sure we will agree on what you would say," Zolraag told him. The governor was trying to be subtle, but hadn't really found the knack. He went on, "But for now, you must get over your sickness. I hope your doctors can cure you of it."

He sounded unconvinced of the skills of human physicians. Russie wondered again what wonders Lizard medical experts could work. He said, "Thank you, Excellency. I hope to be better in a few days. This sort of illness is not one which is usually fatal."

"As you say." Again, Zolraag seemed dubious. Russie supposed he had reason. When the Lizards broke into Warsaw, thousands of starving Jews in the ghetto had suffered from one form of intestinal disease or another, and a great many had died. The governor continued, "If you want, my males will take you from your office to your home."

"Thank you, Excellency, but no," Russie said. "I would like to preserve as much as possible the illusion of free agency." He regretted the words as soon as they were out of his mouth. Better if the Lizards kept on thinking of him as a willing cat's-paw. He hoped Zolraag wouldn't understand what he'd said.

But the Lizard did. Worse, he approved. "Yes, this illusion is worth holding to, *Reb* Moishe," he answered, confirming that, as far as he was concerned, Russie's freedom of action *was* an illusion. Even in his battered, nauseated state, he felt anger stir.

The governor spoke in his own hissing language. The Lizard who held the radiotelephone answered, then skittered out of Russie's office with every evidence of relief. He and the rest of the aliens left the Jewish headquarters; Russie listened to their claws clicking on linoleum.

A few minutes later, Mordechai Anielewicz came back in. He wrinkled his nose. "It stinks like a burst sewer pipe in here, *Reb* Moishe," he said. "Let's clean you up a little and get you home."

Russie surrendered himself to the fighting leader's blunt, practical ministrations. He let Anielewicz manhandle him down the stairs. Waiting on the street was a bicycle with a sidecar. Anielewicz poured him into it, then climbed onto the little saddle and started pedaling.

"Such personal concern," Russie said. The wind blowing in his face did a little to revive him. "I'm honored."

"If I'd brought a car for you, then you'd have some business being honored," Anielewicz said, laughing. Russie managed a wan chuckle himself. These days, gasoline was more precious than rubies in Warsaw: rubies, after all, remained rubies, but gasoline, once burned, was gone forever. Even diesel fuel for fire engines was in desperately short supply.

A few dry leaves whirled through the streets on the chilly fall breeze, but only a few; a lot of trees had been cut down for fuel. More would fall this winter, Russie thought, and buildings wrecked in two rounds of fighting would be cannibalized for wood. Warsaw would be an uglier city when the fighting ended—if it ever did.

Rain began falling from the lead-gray sky. Mordechai Anielewicz reached up, yanked down the brim of his cap so it did a better job of covering his eyes. He said, "It's set. We'll have a go at the transmitter tomorrow night. Stay sick till then."

"What happens if you don't take it out?" Russie asked.

Anielewicz's laugh had a grim edge to it. "If we don't take it out, *Reb* Moishe, two things happen. One is that some of my fighters will be dead. And the other is that you'll have to go on taking your medicines, so that by this time next week you'll likely end up envying them."

Maybe the fighting leader meant it for a joke, but Russie didn't find it funny. He felt as if the *Gestapo* had been kicking him in the belly. His mouth tasted like—on second thought, he didn't want to try to figure out what his mouth tasted like.

Many of the Jews the Nazis forced into the Warsaw ghetto had left it since the Lizards came (many more, of course, were dead). Even so, the streets remained crowded. Adroit as a footballer dodging through defensemen toward the goal, Anielewicz steered his bicycle past pushcarts, rickshaws, hordes of other bicycles, and swarms of men and women afoot. No one seemed willing to yield a centimeter of space to anyone else, but somehow no one ran into anyone else, either.

Then, suddenly, there was space. Anielewicz stopped hard. A squad of Lizards tramped past on patrol. They looked cold and miserable. One turned his strange eyes resentfully up toward the weeping sky. Another wore a child's coat. He hadn't figured out buttons, but held the coat closed with one hand while the other clutched his weapon.

As soon as the Lizards moved on, the crowds closed in again. Anielewicz said, "If those poor creatures think it's cold now, what will they do come January?"

Freeze, was the answer that immediately sprang into Russie's mind. But he knew he was probably wrong. The Lizards knew more than mankind about so many things; no doubt they had some simple way to keep themselves warm out in the open. That patrol certainly had *looked* chilly, though.

Anielewicz pulled up in front of the apartment block where Russie lived. "Can you make it up to your flat?" he asked.

"Let's see." Russie unfolded himself from the sidecar. He wobbled when he took a couple of tentative steps, but stayed on his feet. "Yes, I'll manage."

"Good. If I had to walk you up, I'd worry about the bicycle being here when I got back. Now I can worry about other things instead." Anielewicz nodded to Russie and rode off.

Had Moishe felt more nearly alive, he might have laughed at the way people in the courtyard started to come up to greet him, then took a better look and retreated faster than they'd advanced. He didn't blame them; he would have sheered off from himself, too. If he didn't look horribly contagious, it wasn't from lack of effort.

He turned the key, walked into his flat; one perquisite of his position was that his family had it all to themselves. His wife whirled round in surprise. "Moishe! What are you doing here so early?" Rivka said, starting to smile. Then she got a good look at him—and maybe a good whiff of him as well—and asked a better question: "Moishe! What happened to you?"

He sighed. "The Lizards happened to me."

She stared at him, her eyes wide in a face that, while not skeletal as it had been a few months before, was still too thin. "The Lizards did—that—to you?"

"Not directly," he answered. "What the Lizards did was to treat Washington, D.C., exactly as they had Berlin, and to expect me to be exactly as happy about it."

Rivka did not much concern herself with politics; the struggle for survival had taken all her energy. But she was no fool. "They wanted you to praise them for destroying Washington? They must be *meshuggeh*."

"That's what I thought, so I got sick." Moishe explained how he'd manufactured his illness on short notice.

"Oh, thank God. When I saw you, I was afraid you'd come down with something dreadful."

"I feel pretty dreadful," Russie said. Though drugs rather than bacteria induced his illness, his insides had still gone through a wringer. The only difference was that he would not stay sick unless it proved expedient.

His little son, Reuven, wandered out of the bedroom. The boy wrinkled his nose. "Why does Father smell funny?"

"Never mind." Rivka Russie turned briskly practical. "We're going to get him cleaned up right now." She hurried into the kitchen. The water had been reliable since the Lizards took the town. She came back with a bucket and a rag. "Go into the bedroom, Moishe; hand me out your filthy clothes, clean yourself off, and put on something fresh. You'll be better for it."

"All right," he said meekly. Shedding the soiled garments was nothing but relief. He discovered he'd managed to get vomit on the brim of his hat. In a horrid sort of way, that was an accomplishment. The rag and bucket seemed hardly enough for the job for which they were intended; he wondered if the Vistula would have been enough. Thoughts of the Augean stables ran through his mind as he scrubbed filth from himself. He hadn't discovered Greek mythology until his university days. Sometimes the images it evoked were as telling as any in the Bible.

In clean clothes he felt a new, if hollow, man. He didn't want to touch what he had been wearing, but finally bundled the befouled outfit so the filthiest parts were toward the middle. He brought everything out to Rivka.

She nodded. "I'll take care of them soon." Living in the ghetto had made stenches just part of life, not something that had to be swept away on the instant. At the moment, questions were more urgent: "What will you do if the Lizards insist that you speak for them after you're better?"

"I'll get sick again," he answered, though his guts twisted at the prospect. "With luck, though, I won't have to." He told her what Anielewicz had planned for the transmitter.

"Even if that works, it only puts off the evil day," Rivka said. "Sooner or later, Moishe, either you will have to do what the Lizards want or else you will have to tell them no."

"I know." Moishe grimaced. "Maybe we never should have thrown our lot in with them in the first place. Maybe even the Nazis were a better bargain than this."

Rivka vigorously shook her head. "You know better. When you are dead, you can't bargain. And even if we have to disobey the Lizards, I think they will kill only the ones who disobey, and only because they disobey, rather than making a sport of it or killing us simply because we are Jews."

"I think you are right." The admission failed to reassure Russie. He, after all, would be one of those who disobeyed, and he wanted to live. But to praise the Lizards for using one of their great bombs on Washington . . . better to die with self-respect intact.

"Let me make you some soup." Rivka eyed him as if gauging his strength. "Will you be able to hold it down?"

"I think so," he said after making his own internal assessments. He let out a dry chuckle. "I ought to try, anyhow, so I have something in my stomach in case I, ah, have to start throwing up again. What I just went through was bad enough, but the dry heaves are worse."

The soup was thick with cabbage and potatoes, not the watery stuff of the days when the Germans starved the ghetto Jews and every morsel had to be stretched to the utmost. Though no one who had not known those dreadful days would have thought much of it, its warmth helped ease the knots in Russie's midsection.

He had just finished the last spoonful when somebody came pounding down the hall at a dead run. A fist slammed against his front door. The somebody shouted, "*Reb* Moishe, *Reb* Moishe, come quick, *Reb* Moishe!"

Russie started to get up. His wife took him by the shoulders and forced him back into his chair. "You're sick, remember?" she hissed. She went to the door herself, opened it. "What's wrong? My husband is ill. He cannot go anywhere."

"But he has to!" the man in the hallway exclaimed, as if he were a two-year-old convinced his word was law.

"He cannot," Rivka repeated. She stepped aside to let the fellow get a look at Moishe, adding, "See for yourself if you don't believe me," which told Russie he had to look as bad as he felt.

"I'm sorry, *Reb* Moishe," the man said, "but we really do need you. Some of our fighters are facing off with some *Armja Krajowa* louts up on Mickiewicza Street, and it's getting ugly. They're liable to start shooting at each other any minute now."

Russie groaned. Of all the times for hotheaded Jews and prejudiced Poles to start butting heads, this was the worst. Rivka was too far away to make him keep sitting down. He rose, ignoring her look of consternation. But before he could do anything more, the man in the hallway said, "The Lizards are already bringing heavy equipment up there. They'll slaughter everyone if a fight breaks out."

With another groan, Russie clutched his belly and sank back down. Rivka's alarmed expression turned to real concern. But she rallied quickly. "Please go now," she told the man. "My husband would come if he possibly could; you know that. But he really is ill."

"Yes, I see he is. I'm sorry. God grant you health soon, *Reb* Moishe." The fellow departed at the same breakneck pace at which he'd arrived.

Rivka shut the door, then turned on Russie. "*Are* you all right?" she demanded, hands on hips. "You were going out there, I know you were. Then all of a sudden—"

He knew a moment's pride that his acting had been good enough to give her doubts. He said, "If the Lizards are already there, I can't let them see me, or they'll know I'm not as sick as I let on."

Her eyes widened. "Yes, that makes sense. You—"

"I'm not done," he interrupted. "The other thing is, I don't think our men are tangling with the *Armja Krajowa* Poles by accident. Think where the quarrel is—at the opposite end of Warsaw from the Lizard headquarters. I think they're trying to draw troops—and maybe Zolraag's attention, too—away from the studio and the transmitter. Mordechai said tomorrow night, but he works fast. Unless I miss my guess, this is a put-up fight."

"I hope you're right." For most of the next minute, Rivka looked as intensely thoughtful as a yeshiva student following a rabbi's exegesis of a difficult Talmudic text. A smile broke through like sunrise. "Yes, I think you are."

"Good," Russie said. He did feel better with the warm soup inside him. He hoped he wouldn't have to spew it up again, but carried another vial of ipecac in a coat pocket.

He got up and walked over to the battered sofa. Springs poked through here and there and the fabric was filthy, but just owning a sofa was a mark of status among Warsaw Jews these days. The Nazis hadn't stolen it in one of their ghetto sweeps, and the family hadn't had to break it up and burn it to keep from freezing the winter before. As he lay down on it, Russie was conscious of how lucky that made him.

Rivka draped a threadbare blanket over him. "How can you look sick if you're not covered up?" she asked.

"I seem to have managed," he said, but she ignored him. He let the blanket stay.

About the time he came close to dozing off, Reuven started banging on a pot with a spoon. Rivka quickly hushed the boy, but the damage was done. A few minutes later, a new, more ominous racket filled the flat: the distant rattle of guns. "Where is it coming from?" Russie asked, turning his head this way and that. If it was from the north, the Jews and Poles might really have opened up on each other; if from the south, Anielewicz's fighters in German uniform were hitting the radio transmitter.

"I can't tell, either," Rivka said. "The sound is funny inside a block of flats."

"That's true." Russie settled himself to wait. The shooting and explosions lasted only a couple of minutes. He'd nearly forgotten the echoing silence that followed gunfire, though he'd heard it almost daily before the Lizards seized Warsaw from the Germans.

Half an hour later, another knock came at the apartment door. Rivka opened it. Without ceremony, a Lizard walked in. He fixed both eyes on Russie. In hissing German, he said, "I am Ssfeer, from the governor Zolraag's staff. You know me now?"

"Yes, I recognized your body paint," Moishe answered. "How can I help you? I fear I cannot do much at the moment; I was taken ill this morning."

"So the prominent Zolraag learned," Ssfeer said. "He—how say you?—he gives permissions to you to get well more slow. Bandits from Deutschland just now they—how say you?—shoot up radio, maybe to keep you quiet, not let you speak. We need maybe ten days to fix."

"Oh, what a pity," Russie said.

The Lancaster rumbled down the runway, engines roaring. The plane bounced and shuddered as it gained speed; Lizard bomblets had cratered the runway the week before, and repairs were crude. George Bagnall knew nothing but relief that they weren't trying to take off with a full bomb load. Bombs were delicate things; once in a while, a bump would set one off . . . after which, the groundcrew would have another crater, a big one, to fill in.

The bomber fairly sprang into the air. In the pilot's seat next to Bagnall's, Ken Embry grinned. "Amazing what lightening the aircraft will do," Embry said. "I feel like I'm flying a Spitfire."

"I think it's all in our head," Bagnall replied. "The radar unit back there can't be a great deal lighter than the ordnance we usually carry." The flight engineer flicked an intercom switch. "How is it doing, Radarman Goldfarb?"

"Seems all right," he heard in his earphones. "I can see a long way."

"That's the idea," Bagnall said. A radar set in an aircraft several miles above the Earth could peer farther around its curve, pick up Lizard planes as they approached, and give England's defenses a few precious extra minutes to prepare. Bagnall shivered inside his flight suit and furs as the Lanc gained altitude. He switched on his oxygen, tasted the rubber of the hose as he breathed the enriched air.

Goldfarb spoke enthusiastically. "If we can keep just a few planes in the air, they'll do as much for us as all our ground stations put together. Of course," he added, "we also have a good deal farther to fall."

Bagnall tried not to think about that. The Lizards had pounded British ground radar in the opening days of their invasion, forcing the RAF and ground defenses to fight blind ever since. Now they were trying to see again. The Lizards were not likely to want to let them see.

"Coming up on angels twenty," Ken Embry announced. "Taking station at the altitude. Radioman, how is our communication with the fighter pack?"

"Reading them five by five," Ted Lane replied. "They report receiving us five by five as well. They are eager to begin the exercise, sir."

"Bloody maniacs," Embry said. "As far as I'm concerned, the ideal mission is one devoid of all contact with the enemy whatsoever."

Bagnall could not have agreed more. Despite machine gun turrets all over the aircraft, the Lancaster had always been at a dreadful disadvantage against enemy fighters; evasion beat the blazes out of combat. The knowledge made bomber aircrew cautious, and made them view swaggering, aggressive fighter pilots as not quite right in the head.

From back in the bomb bay, David Goldfarb said, "I ought to be able to communicate directly with the fighter aircraft rather than relaying through the radioman."

"That's a good notion, Goldfarb," Bagnall said. "Jot it down; maybe they'll be able to use it on the Mark 2." *And maybe, if we keep on being luckier than we deserve, we'll live to try out the Mark 2*, he added to himself. He didn't need to say it aloud; Goldfarb had known what the odds were when he volunteered for this mission.

Bagnall wiped the inside of the curved Perspex window in front of him with a piece of chamois cloth. Nothing much to see out there, not even the exhaust flames from other bombers ahead, above, below, and to either side—reassuring reminders one was not going into danger all alone. Now there was only night, night and the endless throb of the four Merlins. Consciously reminded of the engines, the flight engineer flicked his eyes over the gauges in front of him. Mechanically, all was well.

"I have enemy aircraft," Goldfarb exclaimed. Back in the bomb bay, he couldn't see even the night, just the tracks of electrons across a phosphor-coated screen. But his machine vision reached farther than Bagnall's eyes. "I say again, I have enemy aircraft. Heading 177, distance thirty-five miles and closing, speed 505."

Ted Lane passed that word on to the Mosquitoes that lurked far above the radar-carrying Lancaster. The twin-engine planes not only had the highest operational ceiling of any British fighters, they were also, with their wooden skins and skeletons, harder for radar to acquire.

"Rockets away from the Lizard aircraft," Goldfarb yelped. "Bearing—straight for us. Speed—too bloody fast for my machine here."

"Shut it down," Embry ordered. He threw the Lanc into a violent, corkscrewing dive that made Bagnall glad for the straps that held him in his seat. His stomach felt a couple of thousand feet behind the aircraft. He gulped, wishing he hadn't had greasy fish and chips less than an hour before the mission started.

An excited yell from Joe Simpkin in the tail gunner's turret echoed in his headset. The gunner added, "One of those rockets flew through where we used to be."

"Well, by God," Ken Embry said softly. The pilot, who made a point of never letting anything impress him, added, "Who would have thought the boffins could actually get one right?"

"I'm rather glad they did," Bagnall said, stressing his broad "a"s to show he also took such miracles for granted. The engineers down on the ground had been confident the Lizards would attack a radar-carrying aircraft with the same radar-homing rockets they'd used to wreck the British ground stations. Turn off the radar and what would they have to home on? Nothing. Down on the ground, it all seemed as inexorably logical as a geometric proof. The boffins, however, didn't have to test their theories in person. That was what aircrews were for.

"Shall I start it up again?" Goldfarb asked over the intercom.

"No, better not, not quite yet," Embry said after a moment's thought.

"It does us no good if it isn't running," the radarman said plaintively.

It does us no bloody good if it gets us shot down, either, Bagnall thought. But that wasn't fair, and he knew it. For someone whose only time in the air had been practicing for this mission, Goldfarb was doing fine. And not only was it natural for him to want to play with his toy, he had a point. A radar set that had to shut down as soon as action started to keep from being destroyed was better than no radar set at all, but not much. Along with letting Goldfarb talk directly with the fighters his radar directed, the boffins would have to come up with a way to let him keep the set operating without getting it and its aircraft blown out of the sky.

Ted Lane let out an ear-piercing Red Indian whoop. "A Mosquito just took out one of their planes. Bounced him from above, almost head-on—couldn't very well come up on him from behind, could he, what with the Lizards' being the faster aircraft. Says he saw the enemy break up in midair, and then he was diving for the deck for all he was worth."

Everyone in the Lancaster cheered. Then Ken Embry said, "What about the rest of the Mosquitoes?"

After a moment, the radioman answered, "Er—several of them do not respond to my signal, sir." That dashed the moment of exultation. The RAF was slowly, painfully learning how to hurt the Lizards. The Lizards already knew only too well how to hurt the RAF. Bagnall hoped the fighter pilots had managed to bail out. Trained men were harder to replace than airplanes.

From his station in front of the now-dark radar screen, Goldfarb said, "The chaps on the ground have been listening to us, too. With a bit of luck, they'll also have hurt the Lizards: at least, they'll have had the advantage of knowing a bit sooner from which direction they're coming."

"Fat bloody lot of good it'll do them," Embry said. Like any pilot, he pretended to disbelieve flak crews could possibly hit anything with their guns. If that attitude made flying seem safer for him, Bagnall was not about to complain. A calm pilot was a smooth pilot, and a smooth pilot was likeliest to bring his aircrew home again.

Goldfarb repeated, "May I turn the set on again, sir?"

Embry took his right hand off the stick, pounded a closed fist up and down on his thigh. Bagnall didn't think he knew he was doing it. At last the pilot said, "Yes, go ahead; you may as well. As you've noted, that is the purpose of our being up here on this lovely fall evening."

"Really?" Bagnall said. "And all the time I thought it was to see how fast the Lizards could shoot us down. The groundcrew have formed a pool on it, I understand. Did you toss in your shilling, Ken?"

"I'm afraid not," Embry answered, imperturbable. "When they told me someone had already chosen twenty seconds after takeoff, I decided my chances for winning were about nil, so I held onto my money out of consideration for my heirs. What about you, old fellow?"

"Sorry to have spoiled your wager, but I'm afraid I'm the chap who took the twenty seconds after we left the ground." Bagnall was not about to let the pilot outdo him in offhandedness, not this time. "I admit I did wonder how I'd go about collecting if I happened to win."

The radar set, like any human-built piece of electronic apparatus, needed a little while to warm up after it went on. Bagnall had heard rumors that Lizard gear taken from shot-down planes went on instantly. He wondered if they were true; from what he knew, valves (tubes, the Americans called them) by their very nature required warm-up time. Maybe the Lizards didn't use valves, though he had no idea what might take their place.

"Another flight incoming, same bearing as before," Goldfarb announced. "Range . . . twenty-three miles and closing too bloody fast. Shall I shut it down now?"

"No, wait until they launch their rockets at us," Embry said. Bagnall wondered if the pilot had lost his mind, and even wondered if there really was a groundcrew pool and if Embry was trying to win it. But Embry proved to have method in his madness: "We've already seen we can evade the rockets that track us by our own radar. If we shut down before they fire those, they may get closer and shoot rockets of a different sort at us, ones we can't evade."

"Their tactics do tend to be stereotyped, don't they?" Bagnall agreed after a little thought. "Given a choice, they'll do the same thing over and over, regardless of whether it's the right thing. And if it's wrong, why give them the excuse to change?"

"Just what was in my—" Embry began.

Goldfarb interrupted him: "Rockets away! Shutting down—*now.*"

Again the Lancaster spun through the air; again Bagnall wondered if the fish and chips would stay down. And again, the Lizards' rockets failed to bring down the British aircraft. "Maybe this isn't a suicide mission after all," Bagnall said happily. He'd had his doubts as the Lanc rolled down the runway.

Ted Lane listened to the surviving Mosquitoes as they made their runs at the attackers. "Another hit!" he said. This time, though, no one in the Lancaster shouted for joy. The aircrew had realized the price the fighter pilots were paying for every kill.

Then the radioman told Embry, "We are ordered to break off operations and return to base. The air vice marshal remarks that, having been lucky twice, he's not inclined to tempt fate by pushing for a third bit of good fortune."

"The air vice marshal is a little old woman," the pilot retorted. He added hastily, "You need not inform him of my opinion, however. We shall of course obey his instructions like the good little children we are. Navigator, if you would be so kind as to suggest a course—"

"Suggest is the proper word, all right," Alf Whyte said from his little curtained-off space behind the pilot's and flight engineer's seats. "What with some of the twists you put the aircraft through, I thought the compass was jitterbugging to a hot swing band. If we are where I think we are, a course of 078 will bring us to the general neighborhood of Dover in ten or twelve minutes."

"Oh-seven-eight it is," Embry said. "Turning to that course now." He swung the bomber through the sky as if it were an extension of himself.

George Bagnall watched the neatly ordered phalanx of gauges in front of him as intently as if they monitored his own heartbeat and breathing. In a very real way, they did: if the Lancaster's engines or hydraulic system failed, his heart would not go on beating for very long.

"I have contact with the airfield," the radioman announced. "They read us five by five and report no damage from the Lizards this evening."

"That's good to hear," Embry said. Bagnall nodded. The landing would be rough enough as it was, what with the hasty repairs to earlier repairs from the sky. The Lanc wouldn't be coming in with combat damage or unexpended bombs, as it might have from a mission over Germany or France, but its fuel tanks were much fuller than they would have been on the return flight from such a mission. The petrol the plane burned made a more-than-satisfactory explosive when things went wrong.

Bagnall stared out through the Perspex. He tapped Embry on the arm. "Isn't that the ocean approaching?"

Embry looked, too. "Sod me if it's not. Alf, we're coming up on the bloody North Sea. Are we north or south of where we want to be? I feel like a blind man tapping down the path with his stick, all the more so with that radar set back in the bomb bay. It ought to be able to find our way home for us all by its lonesome."

"I dare say it will do precisely that one of these days," the navigator answered. "I suggest you bear in mind, though, that the Lizards doubtless monitor every sort of signal we produce. Do you really care to guide them to the runway as you set down?"

"Now that you mention it, no. Ha!" Embry pointed down into the darkness. Bagnall's eyes followed his finger. He too spied the red torch winking on and off. He flicked on the Lancaster's wing lights, just for a moment, to acknowledge the signal.

Other torches, these white along one side of the runway and green

along the other, sprang to life. Embry pointed. "Looks like a bloody aircraft carrier flight deck down there. I thought this was the RAF, not the
Fleet Air Arm."

"Could be worse," Bagnall remarked. "At least the runway's not
pitching in a heavy sea."

"There's a cheerful thought." Embry lined up the Lancaster on the
two rows of torches, went into the final landing descent. The hasty touch-
down was less than smooth, but also less than disastrous: about par for a
landing under war conditions, Bagnall thought. Along with the rest of the
aircrew, he got out of the Lanc in a hurry and sprinted across the tarmac—
now blacked out again—for the Nissen hut whose corrugated metal walls
were surrounded by sandbags to protect against blast.

A tent of blackout curtains in front of the hut's doorway let people go
in and out without leaking light for all the world—and for unfriendly visitors from another world—to see. The glare of the bare bulbs strung from
the Nissen hut's ceiling smote Bagnall's dark-accustomed eyes like a pho-
tographer's flash.

The aircrew hurled themselves onto chairs and couches. Some,
drained by the mission, fell asleep at once in spite of the glare. Others,
Bagnall among them, dug out pipes and cigarettes.

"May I have one of those?" David Goldfarb asked, pointing to the
flight engineer's packet of Players. "I'm afraid I'm all out."

Bagnall passed him a cigarette, leaned close to give him a light off the
one he already had going. As the radarman inhaled, Bagnall said, "I expect
you'll be off to the White Horse Inn after the boffins get done grilling you
over how things went tonight."

"What's the point?" Goldfarb said, more in resignation than bitterness. "Oh, I expect I'll drink there, but the girls—as I say, what's the
point?"

Bagnall also knew about the barmaids' preferences. Now he stuck his
tongue far into his cheek. "I think staring into the radar screen must have
a deleterious effect on the brain. Did it never occur to you that you've just
returned from flying a combat mission?"

The end of Goldfarb's cigarette suddenly glowed a fierce red. His eyes
glowed, too. "I knew it only too bleeding well when those Lizard rockets
homed on us. I confess I hadn't thought of it in other terms, though.
Thank you, sir."

Bagnall waved a hand in a parody of aristocratic elegance. "Delighted
to be of service." Service it had been, too—in an instant, he'd made the radarman forget all about the fear he'd just endured. He wished he could perform the same service for himself.

Ussmak cursed the day the Race had first discovered Tosev 3. He cursed the day the probe the Race had sent to this miserable world returned safely. He cursed the day he'd been hatched, the day he'd gone into cold sleep, the day he'd awakened. He cursed Krentel, something he'd been doing every day since the blundering idiot replaced Votal. He cursed the Big Uglies for killing Votal and then Telerep and leaving Krentel alive.

Most of all, he cursed the mud.

The landcruiser he drove was built to handle difficult terrain. On the whole, it did well. But Tosev 3, being a wetter place than any of the three worlds already in the Empire, had mixtures of water and dirt more thorough and more spectacularly gloppy than any of the Race's engineers had imagined.

Ussmak was in the middle of one of those mixtures. As far as he could tell, it was most of a continent wide and most of a continent long. The Russkis only made matters worse by not paving any of their stinking roads. Once the rain soaked into what was allegedly a roadbed, the mud there was most of a continent deep, too.

He pressed his foot down on the accelerator. The landcruiser lurched forward. So long as he moved every little while, he was all right. If he stayed too long in one place, the machine started to sink. Its tracks were more than wide enough to support it on any reasonable surface. This gluey, slimy stuff was a long way from reasonable.

Ussmak accelerated again. The landcruiser plowed through the bog. Its tracks flung muck in all directions. Some of the muck—dead Emperors only knew how—splashed down onto Ussmak's vision slit. He pressed a button. Detergent solution sprayed the armorglass clean. That was a relief. At least he wouldn't have to unbutton and stick his head into the refrigerator outside.

Krentel had his cupola in the turret dogged down tight, too. A landcruiser commander was supposed to look out over the top of that cupola as much as he could, but Ussmak, though he blamed Krentel for a lot of things, couldn't blame him for not wanting to freeze his snout off.

At that, the driver thought, gunning the landcruiser forward once more, things could have been worse. He could have been driving a truck instead. The wheeled vehicles the landcruiser was supposed to be protecting had a much rougher time in this accursed bog than he did. He'd already used his towing chain to pull two or three of them out of places where they'd sunk worse than axle-deep. That the trucks had to be shielded just made them heavier and the sticking problem worse.

For that matter, Ussmak could have been one of the poor wretches in radiation suits who guddled around in the freezing Tosevite slime for the bits of radioactive material their detectors found. The radiation suits weren't heated—no one had foreseen the need (no one had foreseen that the Big Uglies would be able to blow the *67th Emperor Sohrheb* all over the landscape, either). The males in those suits had to labor in shifts, one group going back to a warming station while the other emerged to work.

Krentel's voice rang in the intercom button taped to Ussmak's hearing diaphragm. "Maintain heightened alertness, driver. I have just received a report that Tosevite bandit groups may be operating in the area. Primary defense responsibilities fall on our glorious landcruiser forces."

"As you say, Commander," Ussmak answered. "It shall be done." How he was supposed to be especially alert for bandits when he could see only straight ahead with the landcruiser buttoned was beyond him. Maybe Krentel ought to open up the cupola and look around after all.

He thought about saying as much to the landcruiser commander, but decided not to bother. The Race did not encourage lower ranks to reprove their superiors; that way lay anarchy. In any case, Ussmak doubted that Krentel would have listened; he seemed to think the Emperor had personally granted him all the answers. And finally, Ussmak's own sense of isolation from everything going on around him had only grown worse since his two original landcruiser crewmales died. A good replacement for Votal would have taken pains to reforge the team. Krentel just treated him like a piece of machinery. Machines don't care.

Machinelike, Ussmak kept the landcruiser out of as much trouble as he could. He'd found some better ground, where the grass, now yellow and dying rather than green and shiny with life, was still thick enough under his tracks to keep the landcruiser from sinking as fast as it had on barer terrain.

Ahead lay a stand of low, scrubby trees. Their bare branches groped for the sky like thin, beseeching arms. They'd dropped their leaves when the rains started. Ussmak wondered why; it seemed wasteful to him. Certainly none of the trees back on Home behaved in such profligate fashion.

He missed Home. Although the idea of turning Tosev 3 into another version of his own world had seemed good and noble when he got into the cold-sleep capsule, everything he'd seen since he came out of it screamed that it wasn't going to be as easy as everybody had thought. Given the Big Uglies' intractability, he wondered how the Race had succeeded so well on Rabotev 2 and Halless 1.

He also wondered why no one else seemed to have any doubts about what the Race was doing here. The males had just formed their own rather compressed version of society back Home and gone on about their business, changing original plans only because the Tosevites had more technology than anyone expected. No one worried about the rightness of what they were doing.

Even Ussmak had no real idea of what the Race's forces ought to be doing now that they'd come to Tosev 3. He supposed the doubts he did have sprang from his own feeling of apartness from everyone around him, from having been wrenched out of his comfortable niche in the original landcruiser crew and thrust into the unwanted company not merely of strangers, but of pompous, inept strangers.

Behind him, the turret traversed with a whir of smooth machinery The coaxial machine gun began to chatter. "We shall rout out any Big Uglies lurking among the trees," Krentel declared with his usual grandiloquence.

For once, though, the commander's tone failed to grate on Ussmak. Krentel was actually doing something sensible. Ussmak cherished that when it happened. Had it happened more often, he might have been content even on this miserable, cold, wet ball of mud.

Machine-gun bullets whined less than a meter above Heinrich Jäger's head. Had any leaves remained on the birch trees, the bullets would have shaken the last of them down. As it was, he used the fallen leaves to help conceal himself from the Lizard panzer firing from the open country ahead.

The wet ground and wet leaves soaked Jäger's shabby clothes. Rain beat on his back and trickled down his neck. He suppressed a sneeze by main force. A round ricocheting from a tree trunk kicked mud up into his face.

Beside him, Georg Schultz let out a ghostly chuckle. "Well, Major, aren't you glad we never had to mess with this infantry shit before?"

"Now that you mention it, yes." It wasn't just the manifold discomforts of crawling around bare to the elements, either. Jäger felt naked and vulnerable without armor plate all around him. In his Panzer III, machine-gun bullets had been something to laugh at. Now they could pierce his precious, tender flesh as easily as anything else they happened to strike.

He raised his head a couple of centimeters, just enough to let him peer out at the Lizard panzer. It seemed sublimely indifferent to anything a mere foot soldier could hope to do to it. All at once, Jäger understood the despair his own tank must have induced in French and Russian infantry who'd tried and failed to stop it. The shoe was on the other foot now, sure enough.

One of the partisans who huddled with Jäger might have been reading his mind. The fellow said, "Well, there it is, Comrade Major. What the fuck do we do about it?"

"For the time being, we wait," Jäger answered. "Unless you're really keen on dying right now, that is."

"After what I've been through the last year and a half from your fucking Nazi bastards, dying is the least of my worries," the partisan answered.

Jäger twisted his head to glare at the ally who would have been anything but a few months before. The partisan, a skinny man with a gray-streaked beard and a big nose, glared back. Jäger said, "I find this as ironic as you do, believe me."

"Ironic?" The partisan raised bushy eyebrows. Jäger had trouble understanding him. He wasn't really speaking German at all, but Yiddish, and about every fourth word made the major stop and think. The Jew went on, "Fuck ironic. I asked God how things could be worse than they were with you Germans around, and He had to go and show me. Let it be a lesson to you, Comrade Nazi Major: never pray for something you don't really want, because you may get it anyhow."

"Right, Max," Jäger said, smiling a little in spite of himself. He hadn't fought side by side with any Jews since the first World War; he had no great use for them. But the Russian partisan band sprawled in the dripping woods with him was more than half Jewish. He wondered whether the Ivans back in Moscow had set it up that way on purpose, to make sure the partisans didn't think about betraying Stalin. That made a certain amount of sense, but it was also likely to make a fighting unit less efficient than it would have been without mutual suspicion and, on the Jews' side, outright hatred.

The Lizard panzer's machine gun stopped spitting flame. It swung away from the woods; Jäger envied the turret's quick power traverse. If he'd had himself a machine like that, now, he could have accomplished something worthwhile. It was wasted on the Lizards, who had hardly a clue about how to exploit it.

The tank wallowed forward through the mud. Jäger had made the acquaintance of Russian mud the previous fall and spring. It had done its best to glue his Panzer III in one place for good; he was not altogether disappointed to watch it give the Lizards trouble, too.

His attention shifted from the tank to the trucks and soldiers it was guarding. The trucks, like any wheeled vehicles, were having a lot of trouble in the mud. The NKVD man back in Moscow had been right; they were unusually heavy. Every so often a Lizard soldier, looking even more alien than usual in a shiny gray suit that covered him from toe claws to crown, would go over and put something—at this distance, Jäger couldn't tell what—into the back of a truck.

I hope we don't have to hijack a vehicle, he thought. Given the state of what the Russians, for lack of a suitably malodorous word, called roads, he wasn't sure the band *could* hijack a Lizard truck.

From a position carefully camouflaged by tall dead grass, a German machine gun began to bark. A couple of Lizards fell. Others started to run, while still others, wiser or more experienced, flattened out on the ground as human soldiers would have done. The glass blew out of a truck's windshield when a round or two struck home; Jäger couldn't see what happened to the driver.

The commander of the Lizard panzer needed longer to notice the machine gun had opened up than he should have. The *Dummkopf* had his cupola buttoned up, too; Jäger would have demoted a man (to say nothing of blistering his ears and maybe his backside) for a piece of stupidity—or was it cowardice?—like that.

When the Lizard finally deigned to pay some attention to the machine gun nest, he did just what Jäger had hoped he would: instead of standing off and annihilating it with a round or two from his cannon, he charged toward it, his own machine gun chattering.

The German weapon fell silent. That worried Jäger; if the Lizard got lucky with his own machine gun, the partisan band might have to back off and come up with a new plan. But then the concealed machine gun started up again, now firing straight at the oncoming tank.

Save as a goad, that was useless; Jäger watched 7.92mm bullets spark off the Lizard panzer's invincible front armor and fly away uselessly. The popgun onslaught, though, was intended only as a goad, to make sure the enemy tank commander took the machine-gun nest too seriously to worry about anything else.

Georg Schultz let out a gleeful grunt. "God damn me to hell if he isn't taking the bait, sir."

"*Ja,*" Jäger answered absently. He watched the panzer slog through the mud until it was just past the edge of the woods. Then its main armament did speak, a bellow that made Jäger's ears ring. Mud fountained up from just behind the German machine-gun nest, but the weapon kept returning fire.

Jäger turned his head to glance over at Max. "Brave men there," he remarked.

The muzzle of the cannon lowered a centimeter or so, fired again. This time, the machine gun was put out of action—a singularly bloodless term, Jäger thought, for having a couple of men suddenly made into mangled chunks of raw meat.

But Otto Skorzeny was already dashing forward from the birch trees toward the Lizard panzer. The enemy tank commander must have been looking straight through his forward cupola periscope, for he never saw the big SS man pounding toward him from the flank and rear. Muck flying from his boots as he ran, Skorzeny covered the couple of hundred meters out to the panzer in time an Olympic sprinter might have envied.

The big machine started to move just as he came up on it. He scrambled onto the rear deck, chucked a satchel charge under the overhang of the turret, and dove off headfirst. The charge exploded. The turret jerked as if kicked by a mule. Blue flames spurted from the engine compartment. An escape hatch in the front of the panzer popped open. A Lizard sprang out.

Jäger took no notice of the alien enemy. He was watching Skorzeny leg it back toward the shelter of the woods. Then his gaze slid to Max again. "Fuck you, Nazi," the Jewish partisan repeated. But even he saw that would not do, not by itself. Grudgingly, he added, "That SS bastard isn't just brave, he's fucking crazy."

Since Jäger had thought the same thing since he met Skorzeny in Moscow, he declined to argue. Along with everyone else in the band, he grabbed his rifle, got to his feet, and ran toward the Lizards of the salvage crew, shouting at the top of his lungs.

The heavy protective suits made the Lizards slow and awkward. They fell like ninepins. Jäger wondered how safe it was for him to be tramping about with no more protection than his helmet, but only for a moment. Getting shot was a much more pressing concern.

"Come on, come on, come on!" he shouted, pointing toward the truck the German machine gun had shot up. It hadn't moved since. When he got up to it, he found out why: one of the rounds that shattered the windshield had also blown out the back of the driver's head. The blood and brains splashed over the inside of the cab looked no different from those of a human being similarly killed.

Having made sure the truck driver was in fact dead, Jäger hurried around to the rear of the vehicle. The latch there was very much like the one on an earthly truck. The partisans already had it open. Jäger peered into the cargo compartment, which was lit by fluorescent tubes that ran from front to back across the ceiling.

The mud-covered little misshapen chunks of metal that lay on the floor of the compartment seemed hardly worth the trouble to which the Lizards had gone to recover them. But they were what the raiders had come to steal: if the Lizards wanted them so badly, they ought to be worth having.

Along with his rifle, Max carried an entrenching tool. He scooped up several of those innocuous-looking muddy lumps, dumped them into a lead-lined wooden box a couple of the other partisans hauled between them. The instant he finished, they slammed on the lid. Three men spoke together. "Let's get out of here."

The advice was, to say the least, timely. The Lizards had another panzer off in the distance, maybe a kilometer and a half away. It started churning toward them. In the same instant, muzzle flashes sprang from the machine gun on its turret. Bullets cracked past the running men. One of them fell with a groan. Long-range machine-gun fire wasn't much good for taking out any particular individual, but it could decimate troops caught in the open. Jäger had fought on the Somme in 1916. German machine guns then had done a lot worse than decimating the oncoming British.

Unlike those brave but foolish Englishmen a generation before, the partisans were not advancing into barbed-wire entanglements but running for the cover of the woods. They were almost there when one of the men carrying the lead-lined chest threw up his hands and pitched forward onto his face. Jäger was only a few meters away. He grabbed the handle the partisan had dropped. The box was astonishingly heavy for its size, but not too heavy to lift. Jäger and the Jew on the other side ran on.

The sound of dead leaves scrunching wetly under his feet was one of the loveliest things he'd ever heard: it meant he'd made it into the woods. He and his fellow bearer dodged around tree trunks, trying to take advantage of as much cover as they could.

Behind them, the Lizard panzer kept firing, but it didn't sound as if it was getting any closer. Jäger turned to the partisan beside him. "I think the bastard bogged down." The Jew nodded. The two men grinned at each other as they hurried away from the tank.

Jäger felt surprising confidence build in him. He'd thought of this mission as suicidal ever since the NKVD man proposed it back in Moscow. That hadn't kept him from taking part; suicidal missions were part of war and, if they served the cause, were often worth attempting. But now he began to think he might actually get away with this one. Then—well, he'd worry about *then* later. He began to think he'd have a *later* in which to worry about *then*.

A whirring thutter in the air brought all his fears flooding back. Knowing it was foolish, knowing it was dangerous, he glanced over his shoulder. The helicopter swelled in the split second he watched it. Its guns started to chatter. Mud wouldn't slow it down. Left alone, it could hover over the bare-branched woods and lash the raiders with fire until they had to give up their mission.

Wham, wham, wham! From among the trees, a 2-centimeter antiaircraft cannon opened up on the helicopter. With its light mount, designed for mountain warfare, it had made up twenty-seven man-portable loads; Jäger had hauled one of them himself. It was a German weapon, served by a German crew: part of the reason the Soviets had been willing to include *Wehrmacht* men along with their own partisans in this band.

The Lizard helicopter just hung in midair for a moment, as if disbelieving the guerrillas could seriously attack it. It was proof against rifle bullets, but not against the antiaircraft gun's shells. Jäger watched them chew it to pieces, watched chunks of metal fly from it at every hit.

Too late, the helicopter swung toward its tormentor. The 2-centimeter *Flak 38* kept pounding away. Like a sinking ship, the helicopter heeled over onto one side and crashed.

The raiders' cheers filled the woods. Max pumped his fist in the air and screamed, "Take that, you—" Jäger couldn't follow the rest of the Yiddish he called it, but it sounded explosive. The panzer major yelled himself, then blinked. Fighting alongside a Jew was one thing; tactics dictated that. Finding you agreed with him, finding you might even like him as a man, was something else again. If he lived long enough, Jäger would have to think about that.

Otto Skorzeny came dodging through the trees. Even filthy, even in dappled SS camouflage gear, he managed to look dapper. He shouted, "Move, you stupid fools! If we don't get away now, we never will. You think the Lizards are going to sit there with their thumbs up their arses forever? It's your funeral if you do."

As usual, Skorzeny galvanized everyone around him. The Red partisans undoubtedly hated him still, but who could argue with a man who'd just singlehandedly wrecked a Lizard panzer? The raiders hurried deeper into the woods.

None too soon—again Jäger heard the thuttering roar of helicopters in the air. He glanced back and saw a pair of them now. The Germans manning the antiaircraft cannon opened up at long range this time, hoping to knock down one in a hurry so they could fight the other on more even terms—and also hoping to draw both machines' fire onto themselves and away from their fleeing comrades.

The helicopters separated, swung around to engage the antiaircraft cannon from opposite sides. Jäger wished the gun were a big 88; it could have swatted the copters like flies. But an 88 was anything but a man-portable weapon—it had a barrel almost seven meters long and weighed more than eight tonnes. The stubby mountain antiaircraft gun would have to do.

One of the helicopters blew up in midair, showering flaming debris over the woods. The other bored in for a firing run. Jäger watched tracers from the cannon on the ground swivel through a wild arc, then stab up at the second helicopter while tracers from its machine guns stabbed down.

The 2-centimeter *Flak 38* suddenly fell silent. But the helicopter did not go on to pursue the partisans. A rending crash moments later told him why. The gunners had done their duty as well as they were able—better than anyone dared hope when the mission was planned.

The partisan carrying the lead-lined box with Jäger was at the end of his tether, stumbling and staggering and gasping like a man breathing his last. Jäger scowled at him. "Get away from there and put somebody else on that handle before you ruin the mission and get us both killed." Only after he'd spoken did he notice the order in which he'd put those two elements. He grunted. In case he hadn't noticed, that would have told him he was a thoroughly trained soldier.

The raider nodded his thanks and reeled away. Georg Schultz hurried up. "Here, I'll take some of that, sir," he said, nodding to the burden Jäger now held alone.

"No, let me." It was Max, the foul-mouthed Jewish partisan.

He wasn't as big, probably wasn't as strong as Schultz, but he'd shown himself to be wiry and tough. All other things being equal, Jäger would have preferred his tank gunner beside him, but all other things were not equal. The mission might depend on cooperation between surviving Germans and Russians. Having two Germans carrying the precious whatever-it-was inside that chest might make the Reds think harder about selling them out.

All that ran through Jäger's head in a couple of seconds. He couldn't afford to think very long; hanging onto the chest solo was hard work. He said, "Let the Jew do it, Georg." Schultz looked unhappy but fell back a couple of paces. Max took one of the handles from Jäger. Together, they started moving again.

Even as he trotted beside Jäger, Max glared at him. "How would you like it if I said, 'Let the fucking Nazi do it,' eh, Mister fucking Nazi?"

"That's Major fucking Nazi to you, Mister Jew," Jäger retorted. "And the next time you want to go swearing at me, kindly remember those flak men back there who stayed at their gun and got shot up to help you make your getaway."

"They did their jobs," Max snapped. But after he spat into a clump of brown leaves, he added, "Yeah, all right, I'll remember them in the *kaddish*."

"I don't know that word," Jäger said.

"Prayer for the dead," Max said shortly. He glanced toward Jäger again. Now his gaze was measuring instead of hostile, but somehow no easier to bear. "You don't know fucking much, do you? You don't know Babi Yar for instance, eh?"

"No," Jäger admitted. "What's that?"

"Place a little outside of Kiev, not far from here, as a matter of fact. You find a big hole in the ground, then line Jews up at the edge of it. Men, women, children—doesn't matter. You line 'em up, you shoot 'em in the back of the neck. They fall right into their own graves. You Germans are fucking efficient, you know? Then you line up another row and shoot them, too. You keep doing it till your big hole is full. Then you find yourself another fucking hole."

"Propaganda—" Jäger said.

Without a word, Max used his free hand to pull down the collar of his peasant's blouse and bare his neck. Jäger knew a gunshot scar when he saw one. The Jew said, "I must have jerked just as the gun went off behind me. I fell down. They had bastards down in the hole with more guns, making sure everybody really was dead. They must have missed me. I hope they don't get a fucking reprimand, you know? More people fell on me, but not too many—it was getting late. When it was dark, I managed to crawl out and get away. I've been killing fucking Germans ever since."

Jäger didn't answer. He hadn't gone out of his way to notice what happened to Jews in Russian territory taken by the Germans. Nobody in the *Wehrmacht* went out of his way to notice that. It wasn't safe for your career; it might not be safe for you personally. He'd heard things. Everybody heard things. He hadn't worried much about it. After all, the *Führer* had declared Jews the enemies of the *Reich*.

But there were ways soldiers treated enemies. Lining them up at the edge of a pit and shooting them from behind wasn't supposed to be one of those ways. Jäger tried to imagine himself doing that. It wasn't easy. But if the *Reich* was at war and his superior gave him the order . . . He shook his head. He just didn't know.

From across the chest, less than a meter away, his Jewish yokemate watched him flounder. Watching Max watch him only made Jäger flounder harder. If Jews could flip-flop from enemies of the *Reich* to comrades-in-arms, that just made massacring them all the harder to stomach.

Max's voice was sly. "You maybe have a fucking conscience?"

"Of course I have a conscience," Jäger said indignantly. Then he shut up again. If he had a conscience, as he'd automatically claimed, how was he supposed to ignore what Germany might well have been doing? (Even in his own mind, he didn't want to phrase it any more definitely than that.)

To his relief, the woods started thinning out ahead. That meant the most dangerous part of the mission—crossing open country with what they'd stolen from the Lizards—lay ahead. Beside the abyss whose edge he'd been treading with Max, physical danger suddenly seemed a welcome diversion. As long as he was putting his own life on the line, he'd be too busy to look down into the abyss and see the people piled there with neat holes in the backs of their necks.

The survivors of the raiding party gathered near the edge of the trees. Skorzeny took charge of them. From under the thick layer of dead leaves, he pulled out several chests which looked the same as the one Jäger and

Max carried but were not lead-lined. "Two men to each one," he ordered, pausing to let the Russian partisans who understood German translate for those who didn't. "We scatter now, two by two, to make it as hard as we can for the Lizards to figure out who has the real one."

One of the partisans said, "How do we know the real one will go where it's supposed to?"

All the worn, dirty men, Russians and Germans alike, nodded at that. They still had no great trust in one another; they'd fought too hard for that. Skorzeny said, "We have one from each side holding the prize. The *panje* wagon that's waiting for them has one from each side, too. If they don't try to murder each other, we'll be all right, *ja*?"

The SS man laughed to show he'd made a joke. Jäger looked over to Max. The Jew was not laughing. He wore the expression Jäger had often seen on junior officers who faced a tough tactical problem: he was weighing his options. That meant Jäger had to weigh his, too.

Skorzeny said, "We'll go out one pair at a time. The team with the real chest will go third."

"Who told you you were God?" a partisan asked.

The SS man's scarred cheek crinkled as he gave an impudent grin. "Who told you I wasn't?" He waited a moment to see if he got any more argument. When he didn't, he swatted a man from the pair closest to him on the shoulder and shouted "Go! Go! Go!" as if they were paratroopers diving out of a Ju-52 transport plane.

The second pair followed a moment later. Then Skorzeny yelled "Go! Go! Go!" again and Jäger and Max burst out of the woods and started off toward the promised *panje* wagon. It waited several kilometers north and west, outside the Lizards' tightest security zone. Jäger wanted to sprint the whole way. Slogging through mud carrying a heavy chest, that wasn't practical.

"I'm fucking sick of rain," Max said, though he knew as well as Jäger that the snow which would follow was even harder to endure.

Jäger said, "Right now I don't mind rain at all. The Lizards will have a harder time chasing us through it than they would on dry ground. The low clouds will make us harder to spot through the air, too. If you want to get right down to it, I wouldn't mind fog, either."

"I would," Max said. "We'd get lost."

"I have a compass."

"Very efficient," Max said dryly. Jäger took it for a compliment until he remembered it was the word the Jew had used to describe the assembly-line murder at—what was the name of the place?—at Babi Yar, that was it.

Anger surged in the panzer major. The trouble was, he had trouble deciding whether to turn it on his own people for dishonoring the uniforms they wore or the Jew for telling him about it and making him notice it. He glanced over at Max. As usual, Max was watching him. *He* had no trouble finding a focus for his fury.

Jäger twisted his head, looked behind him. The driving rain had already obscured the woods. He could see one of the decoy pairs, but only one. He wouldn't have wanted to track anyone in weather like this, and wished just as much trouble on the Lizards. They wouldn't pursue in panzers, anyhow; from what he'd seen, their armor had at least as much trouble coping with Russian mud as the *Wehrmacht* did.

He must have been thinking aloud. Max grinned an unsympathetic grin and said, "You poor bogged-down bastards."

"Fuck you, too, Max." In the wrong tone of voice, that would have started the fight Skorzeny had not-quite-joked about. As it was, the Jewish partisan's expression changed shape as if he, like Jäger, had to change some of his thinking.

Then both men's faces congealed to fear. The Lizards had more helicopters in the air, and this time no *flak* cannon would stop them. Rifle shots rang out from back in the woods, but using a rifle against one of these machines was as magnificently futile as the Polish lancers' charges against German panzers back when the war—the human war—was new.

But these rifle bullets did have some effect. The whistling roar of the copter rotors grew no louder. The deadly machines hovered over the trees. Their guns snarled. When they paused, more rifle fire announced that they hadn't finished off all the raiders. The yammering resumed.

The sound from the helicopters changed. Jäger looked back, but could see nothing through the curtains of rain. He tried to be optimistic anyhow: "Maybe they're settling down so they can comb through the woods—if they are, they'll be looking in the wrong place."

Max was less sanguine: "Don't count on them to be so fucking stupid."

"They aren't what you'd call good soldiers, not in the tactical sense," Jäger answered seriously. "They're brave enough, and of course they have all that wonderful equipment, but ask them to do anything they haven't planned out in advance and they start floundering around." *They're even worse than Russians that way*, he thought, but he kept quiet about that.

The strafing from the helicopters hadn't slaughtered all the raiders. Rifles barked again; a Soviet submachine gun added its note to the din. Then, harsher and flatter, Lizard automatic small arms answered.

"They *have* landed troops!" Jäger exclaimed. "The longer they waste time back there, the better the chance the mission has of succeeding."

"And the likelier they'll kill off my friends," Max said. "Yours too, I suppose. Does a fucking Nazi have friends? After a tough day shooting Jews in the back of the neck, do you go out and drink some beer with your *Kameraden*?"

"I'm a soldier, not a butcher," Jäger said. He wondered whether Georg Schultz had got one of the dummy chests. If so, he was tramping through the mud, too. If not . . . He also wondered about Otto Skorzeny. The SS captain seemed to have a gift for creating impossible situations and then escaping from them. He'd need all that gift now. But thinking of the SS made Jäger think of Babi Yar. That would have been their doing; *Wehrmacht* men couldn't have stomached it. He added, "You Russians have butchers, too."

"So?" Max said. "Does that make you right?" Jäger found no good answer. The Jewish partisan went on, "I wish they'd sent me to the *gulag* in Siberia years before you fucking Germans ever got to Kiev. Then I wouldn't have had to see what I saw."

Further argument cut off abruptly when Jäger fell headlong into the muck. Max helped him haul himself to his feet. They pushed on. Jäger felt as if he were a hundred years old. A kilometer through this clinging goo was worse than a day's march on hard, dry ground. He wistfully wondered whether the Soviet Union contained so much as a square centimeter of hard, dry ground at the moment.

He also wondered for what the soft, wet ground over which he was fleeing had been used. In Germany, land had a clearly defined purpose: meadow, crops, forest, park, town. This stretch met no such criteria. It was just land—raw terrain. Of that the Soviet Union had unending inefficient abundance.

Jäger abruptly cut off his disparaging thoughts about Soviet inefficiency. His head went up like a hunted animal's. The tiny, atrophied muscles in his ears tried to make them prick like a cat's. Lizard helicopters were in the air again. "We have to move faster," he said to Max.

The partisan pointed to his own trousers, which were covered in mud up to the knees. He dismissed Jäger's suggestion with three sardonic words: "Good fucking luck."

Rationally, Jäger knew Max was right. Still, as the whirring drone from the sky grew louder, he wanted to drop the heavy chest and run. He looked over his shoulder. The driving rain veiled the helicopter from sight. He could only hope it helped hide him from the Lizards.

Off to the south, from the middle of this big open field, shots cracked; Jäger recognized the deep bark of a *Gewehr*-98K, the standard German infantry rifle (no way to tell now, of course, whether it was borne by a standard German infantryman or a very definitely nonstandard Russian partisan). The helicopter that had been closest to him droned off to meet the fleabite challenge.

"I think some of the decoys just drew them away from us," Jäger said.

"It might be a Jew saving your neck, Nazi. How does that make you feel?" Max said. After a moment, though, he added in wondering tones, "Or it might be a fucking Nazi saving mine. How does that make *me* feel? You know the word *verkakte*, Nazi? This is a *verkakte* mess, and no mistake."

A village—maybe even a small town—loomed out of the rain ahead.

In instant unspoken agreement, both men swerved wide around it. "What's the name of that place?" Jäger asked.

"Chernobyl, I think," Max said. "The Lizards drove the people out after their ship blew up, but they might keep a little garrison there."

"Let's hope they don't," Jäger said. The Jewish partisan nodded.

If the village held a garrison, it didn't come forth to search for the raiders . . . or maybe it did, and simply missed Jäger and Max in the downpour. Once past the clump of ugly wooden buildings and even uglier concrete ones, Jäger glanced down at his compass to get back onto the proper course.

Max watched him put it back in his pocket. "How are we going to find the fucking *panje* wagon?"

"We keep on this heading until—"

"—we walk past them in the rain," the Jew put in.

"If you have a better idea, I'd love to hear it," Jäger said icily.

"I don't. I was hoping you did."

They pushed on, skirting another small patch of woods and then returning to the course the compass dictated. Jäger had a piece of black bread and some sausage in his pack. Getting them out one-handed was awkward, but he managed. He broke the bread, bit the sausage in half, and passed Max his share. The Jew hesitated but ate. After a while, he pulled a little tin flask from his hip pocket. He yanked out the cork, gave the flask to Jäger for the first swig. Vodka ran down his throat like fire.

"Thanks," he said. "That's good." He put his thumb over the opening so the rain couldn't get in, passed the flask back to Max.

Off to one side, somebody spoke up in Russian. Jäger started, then dropped the chest that had become like an unwelcome part of him and grabbed for the rifle slung on his back. Then a German voice added, "*Ja, we could use something good about now.*"

"You found them," Max said to Jäger as the *panje* wagon came up through the muck. "That's fucking amazing." Instead of hatred, he looked at Jäger with something like respect. Jäger, who was at least as surprised as the Jewish partisan, did his best not to show it.

The horse that pulled the *panje* wagon had seen better days. The light wooden wagon itself rode on large wheels; it was low, wide, and flat-bottomed, so it could float almost boatlike across the surface of even the deepest mud. It looked as if its design hadn't changed for centuries, which was probably true; no vehicle was better adapted to coping with Russia's twice-yearly *rasputitsa*.

The driver and the fellow beside him both wore Red Army greatcoats, but instead of a *shlem*, a Russian cloth helmet rather like a balaclava, the man who wasn't holding the reins had on the long-brimmed cap of a German tropical-weight uniform. The weather was anything but tropical, but the cap kept the rain out of his eyes.

He said, "You have the cabbages?"

"Yes, by God, we do," Jäger said. Max nodded. Together, they lifted the lead-lined chest into the wagon. Jäger had grown so used to the burden that his shoulder ached when he was relieved of it. Max handed the flask of vodka to the driver, then clambered up over the side of the wagon. Jäger followed him. Between them, they almost filled the wagon bed.

The fellow with the *shlem* spoke in Russian. Max turned it into Yiddish for Jäger. "He says we won't bother with roads. We'll head straight across country. The Lizards aren't likely to find us that way."

"And if they do?" Jäger asked.

"*Nichevo,*" the Russian answered when Max put the question to him: "It can't be helped." Since that was manifestly true, Jäger just nodded. The driver twitched the reins, clucked to the horse. The *panje* wagon began to roll.

"It's true," Yi Min declared. "I floated through the air light as a dandelion seed in the little scaly devils' airplane, and it flew so high that I looked down on the whole world." The apothecary conveniently forgot to mention—in fact, he'd just about made himself forget altogether—how sick he'd been while he floated light as a dandelion seed.

"And what did the world look like when you looked down on it?" one of his listeners asked.

"The foreign devils are right, believe it or not—the world is round, like a ball," Yi Min answered. "I have seen it with my own eyes, so I know it is so."

"Ahh," some of the men said who sat crosslegged in front of him, either impressed at his eyewitness account or astonished Europeans could be right about anything. Others shook their heads, disbelieving every word he said. *Foolish turtles,* he thought. He'd had a lot of lies taken for granted in his time; now that he was telling nothing but the truth, half the people in the scaly devils' prisoner compound made him out to be a liar.

In any case, his audience hadn't gathered to hear him talk about the shape of the world. A man in a blue cotton tunic said, "Tell us more about the women the little scaly devils gave to you." Everyone, believers and skeptics alike, spoke up in favor of that; even if Yi Min were to lie about it, he'd still be amusing.

The best part was, he didn't need to lie. "I had a woman whose skin was black as charcoal all over, save only the palms of her hands and the soles of her feet. And I had another who was pale as milk, even her nipples only pink, with eyes of fine jade and hair and bush the color of a fox's fur."

"Ahh," the men said again, imagining it. One of them asked, "Did their strangeness make them better on the mat?"

"Neither of those two was particularly skilled," Yi Min said, and his audience sighed with disappointment. He quickly added, "Still, their being so different to look at was piquant, like pickle after sweet. If you ask me, the gods first made the black folk, but left them in the oven too long. Then they tried again, but took the white folk—the foreign devils most of us had seen—out too soon. Finally they made us Chinese, and cooked us to perfection."

The men who listened to him laughed; some of them clapped their hands. Then the fellow in the blue tunic said, "From what oven did the gods take the little scaly devils?"

Nervous silence fell. Yi Min said, "To know that for certain, you would have to ask the little devils themselves. If you want to know what I think, my guess is that a whole different set of gods made them. Why, do you know they have a mating season like cattle or songbirds, and are impotent all the rest of the year?"

"Poor devils," several men chorused, the first sympathy Yi Min had heard for the Lizards.

"It's true," he insisted. "That's why they took me up into their airplane that never lands in the first place: to see for themselves that real human beings could mate at any season of the year." His smile was very nearly a leer. "I proved it to their satisfaction—and to mine."

He smiled again, this time happily, at the grins and laughter his words won. Being back among people with whom he could speak, back among people who appreciated his undoubted cleverness, was the greatest joy in returning to the ground after so long aloft.

Then a bald old fellow who sold eggs said, "Didn't the little devils also kidnap that pretty girl who was living in your tent? Why didn't she come back with you?"

"They wanted to keep her up there," Yi Min answered, shrugging. "Why, I don't know; they would not tell me. What does it matter? She's only a woman."

He was just as glad Liu Han remained with the scaly devils. She'd been a pleasant convenience to him, certainly, but no more than that. And she'd seen him sick and vulnerable while he floated without weight, a weakness he was doing his best to pretend had never happened. Now, with the prestige of his journey and the connections he retained with the little scaly devils, women both prettier and more willing than Liu Han were happy to share his mat. He sometimes wondered what the little devils were doing to her, but his curiosity remained abstract.

Bowing as he sat, he said, "I do hope I've held your interest, my friends, and that you'll reward me for helping you pass an idle hour."

The gifts the audience gave were about what he'd expected: a little cash, a pair of old sandals that wouldn't fit him but which he could trade for something he wanted, some radishes, a smoked duck breast wrapped in paper and tied with string, a couple of tiny pots filled with ground spices.

He lifted their lids, sniffed, smiled appreciatively. Yes, he'd been paid well for entertaining.

He gathered up his loot and walked back toward the hut in which he was living. Nothing was left of the tent he'd shared with Liu Han. He could not honestly say he missed it, either; with winter nearly at hand, he was glad to have wooden walls around him. Of course, the people in the camp had also stolen everything he'd accumulated before the scaly devils took him up into the sky, but so what? He was already well on his way to getting more and better. Getting more and better of everything, as far as he could see, was what the world was all about.

From the changes in the camp while he'd been flying, he had to conclude just about everyone agreed with him. Instead of several square *li* of flapping canvas, it now boasted houses of wood and stone and sheet metal, some of them quite substantial. None of the construction materials had been here when the scaly devils' prisoners were herded into the wire-enclosed compound, but they were here now. One way or another, people managed. Sharp wire wasn't enough to keep them from managing.

As he came up to his own shelter, Yi Min readied the key that he carried on a bit of string around his neck. Key and lock both had cost only a couple of pig's feet; the smith who made them out of scrap metal was too skinny to have bargained hard. Yi Min knew they weren't very good, but what did that matter? The lock on his door publicly proclaimed him a man of property, which was what he had in mind. It wasn't supposed to keep thieves away. His close connections with the little devils took care of that.

On about the fourth try, the key clicked, the lock opened, and Yi Min went inside. He started a fire in the little charcoal brazier by his sleeping mat. The feeble warmth the brazier gave made him long for his old home, where he slept on top of the low clay hearth and stayed snug even in the worst weather. He shrugged. The gods dealt the tiles in the game of life; a man's job was to arrange them into the best hand he could.

Sudden silence clamped down on chattering friends, shouting husbands, screeching wives, even squalling children. Yi Min instinctively understood what that meant: little scaly devils close by. He was already turning toward the door when the knock came.

He raised the inner bar (regardless of connections, no sense taking chances), pulled the door open. He bowed low. "Ah, honored Ssofeg, you do me great favor by honoring my humble dwelling with your presence," he said in Chinese, then went on in the devil's speech: "What is your will, superior of mine? Speak, and it shall be done."

"You are dutiful," Ssofeg said in his own language. It was polite formula and praise at the same time; the scaly devils were even more punctilious than Chinese about respect for superiors and elders. Then Ssofeg switched to Chinese, which he used with Yi Min as the apothecary used the little devils' language with him. "You have more of what I seek?"

"I have more, superior of mine," Yi Min said in the Lizards' speech. One of the little spicepots he'd received for his talk of women and other marvels was full of powdered ginger. He took out a tiny pinch, put it in the palm of his other hand, and held it out for Ssofeg.

The little devil flicked out his tongue, for all the world like a kitten lapping from a bowl—although the tongue itself so much reminded Yi Min of a serpent's that he had to steel himself to keep from jerking away. Two quick licks and the ginger was gone.

For a couple of seconds, Ssofeg simply stood where he was. Then he quivered all over and let out a long, slow hiss. It was the nearest approach to a man's ecstatic grunt at the moment of Clouds and Rain that Yi Min had ever heard from a little scaly devil. As if he'd forgotten Chinese, Ssofeg spoke in his own language: "You can have no idea how fine that makes me feel."

"No doubt you are right, superior of mine," Yi Min said. He liked to get drunk; he enjoyed a pipe of opium every so often, too, though there he was very moderate for fear of permanently blunting his drive and ambition. As an apothecary, he'd come across and sampled a lot of other substances alleged to produce pleasure: everything from hemp leaves to powdered rhinoceros horn. Most, so far as he could tell, had no effect whatever. That didn't keep him from selling them, but it did keep him from trying them twice.

But ginger? As far as he was concerned, ginger was just a condiment. Some people claimed it had aphrodisiac powers because ginger roots sometimes looked like gnarled little men, but it had never done anything to harden Yi Min's lance. But when Ssofeg tasted it, he might have died and gone to the heaven Christian missionaries always talked about in glowing words.

The little scaly devil said, "Give me more. Every time I taste the pleasure, I crave it again." His bifurcated tongue went out, then in.

"I will give you more, superior of mine, but what will you give me in return? Ginger is rare and expensive; I have had to pay much to get even this little amount for you." Yi Min was lying in his teeth, but Ssofeg didn't know that. Nor did the people from whom he got ginger know he was selling it to the scaly devils. They would eventually figure it out, of course, at which point competition would cut into his profits. But for now—

For now, Ssofeg let out another hiss, this one redolent of distress. "Already I have given you much, very much." His tailstump lashed in agitation. "But I must know this—this delight once more. Here." He took from around his neck something that most closely resembled the field glasses Yi Min had once seen a Japanese officer using. "These see in darkness as well as light. I will report them missing. Quick, give me another taste."

"I hope I will be able to get any kind of price for them," Yi Min said peevishly. In fact, he wondered whether the Nationalists, the Communists, or the Japanese would pay most for the new trinket. He had contacts with all three; the little scaly devils were naive if they thought mere wire cut a prison camp off from the world around it.

Such decisions could wait. By the way Ssofeg stood swaying slightly, he couldn't. Yi Min gave him another pinch of ginger. He licked it off the apothecary's palm. When his pleasure-filled shiver finally stopped, he said, "If I report much more gear as missing, I shall surely be called to account. Yet I must have ginger. What shall I do?"

Yi Min had been hoping for just that question. As casually as he could, keeping any trace of a chortle from his voice, he said, "I could sell you a lot of ginger now." He showed Ssofeg the spicepot full of it.

The scaly devil's tailstump lashed again. "I must have it! But how?"

"You buy it from me now," Yi Min repeated. "Then you keep some—enough for yourself—and sell the rest to other males of the Race. They will make up your cost and more."

Ssofeg turned both eyes full upon the apothecary, staring as if he were the Buddha reincarnated. "I could do that, couldn't I? Then I could pass on to you what they convey to me, my own difficulties with inventory control would disappear, and you would gain the wherewithal to acquire still more of this marvelous herb which I desire more with each passing day. Truly you are a Big Ugly of genius, Yi Min!"

"The superior of mine is gracious to this humble inferior," Yi Min said. He did not smile; Ssofeg was a clever little devil, and might notice and start asking questions better left unraised.

No, on second thought, Ssofeg was unlikely to notice anything. He was caught in the gloom that always seemed to seize him when ginger's exhilaration wore off. Now he shook as if from an ague rather than with delight. He moaned, "But how can I in good conscience expose other males of the Race to this constant craving I feel myself? That would not be right."

He stared hungrily at the spicepot full of ginger. Fear bubbled through Yi Min. Some opium addicts would kill to keep from being separated from their drug, and ginger seemed to hit Ssofeg far harder than opium did its human users. The apothecary said, "If you take this from me now, superior of mine, where will you get more when you have used it all?"

The little devil made a noise like a boiling kettle. "Plan for tomorrow, plan for next year, plan for the generations yet to come," he said, sounding as if he were repeating a lesson learned long ago in school. He resumed, "You are right, of course. Thievery would in the long run prove futile. What then is your price for the pot of precious herb you hold here?"

Yi Min had an answer ready: "I want one of the picture-taking machines the Race has made, the ones that take pictures you can look at from all around. I want also a supply of whatever it is the machine takes the pictures on." He remembered how—interesting—the pictures the devils had taken of Liu Han and him were. Many men in the camp would pay well to watch such pictures ... while he could give the young men and girls who would perform in them next to nothing.

But Ssofeg said, "I myself cannot get you one of these machines. Give me the ginger now, and I will use it to find a male who has access to them and can abstract it so it will not be missed."

Yi Min laughed scornfully. "You called me wise before. Do you all at once think me a fool?" Hard bargaining followed. In the end, the apothecary surrendered a quarter of the ginger to Ssofeg, the rest to remain with him until payment was forthcoming. The little scaly devil reverently enclosed the ground spice in a transparent envelope, put that envelope into one of the pouches he wore on the belt round his waist, and hurried out of Yi Min's hut. The devils' gait always struck Yi Min as skittery, but Ssofeg's movements seemed downright furtive.

Well they might, the apothecary thought. The Japanese had strict laws against selling equipment to the Chinese; since the little devils' gear was so much better than that of the Japanese, it only stood to reason that their regulations would be harsher. If Ssofeg got caught by his people's inspectors, he would probably be in even bigger trouble than he thought.

Well, that was his lookout. Yi Min had been certain almost from the day the scaly devils landed that they would make his fortune. At first he'd thought it would be as an interpreter. Now, though, ginger and—with luck—interesting films looked likely to prove even more profitable. He wasn't fussy about how he got rich, as long as he did.

I'm on my way, he thought.

Sweat trickled through Bobby Fiore's beard, dripped down onto the smooth, shiny surface of the mat on which he sat. When he got up to walk over to the faucet, his buttocks made rude squelching noises as they pulled free from the mat. The water that came when he pushed a button was warmer than luke- and had a faint chemical tang. He made himself drink anyhow. In heat like this, you had to drink.

He wished he had some salt tablets. He'd spent a couple of seasons playing ball in west Texas and New Mexico; the weather there hadn't been a lot cooler than the Lizards kept their spaceship. Every team in that part of the country kept a bowl of salt tablets by the bat rack. He thought they did some good: without them, how were you supposed to replace what you sweated away?

The door to his cubicle silently slid open. A Lizard brought in some rations for him, and a magazine as well. "Thank you, superior of mine," Fiore hissed politely. The Lizard did not deign to reply. It got out of the cubicle in a hurry. The door closed behind it.

The rations, as usual, were Earthly canned goods: this time, a can of pork and beans and one of stewed tomatoes. Fiore sighed. The Lizards seemed to pull cans off the shelf at random. The meal before had been fruit salad and condensed milk, the one before that chicken noodle soup (cold, undiluted, and still in the can) and chocolate syrup. After weeks on such fare, he would have killed for a green salad, fresh meat, or a scrambled egg.

The magazine, however, was a treat, even if it did date from 1941. When he wasn't with Liu Han, he was here by himself and had to make his own amusement. Something new to look at would keep him interested for several meals. The title—*Signal*—even let him hope it would be in English.

He found out it wasn't as soon as he opened it. Just what the language was, he couldn't tell, his formal education having stopped in the tenth grade. Something Scandinavian, he guessed: he'd seen *o*'s with lines through them like these on Minnesota shopfronts in towns where everybody seemed to be blond and blue-eyed.

He didn't need to be able to read the *Signal* to figure out what it was—a Nazi propaganda magazine. Here was Göbbels smiling from behind his desk, here were Russians surrendering to men in coalscuttle helmets, here were a rather beefy cabaret dancer and her soldier boyfriend. Here was the world that had been before the Lizards came. He clenched his teeth; tears stung his eyes. Being reminded of that world also reminded him how much things had changed.

One thing fifteen years of playing minor-league ball had taught him was how to roll with the punches. That meant eating pork and beans and stewed tomatoes when the Lizards gave them to him, lest his next meal be worse or fail to come at all. It meant looking at the pictures in the *Signal* when he couldn't read the words. And it meant hoping he could see Liu Han some time soon, but not letting himself get downhearted when he had to stay in his cubicle alone.

He was washing molasses and tomato juice off his fingers and trying to rinse his beard clean when the door opened again. The Lizard that had brought in the cans now carried them away. Fiore looked at the *Signal* a while longer, then lay down on the mat and went to sleep.

The lights in the cubicle never dimmed, but that didn't bother him. The heat gave him a harder time. Still, he managed. Anyone who could sleep on a bus rattling between Clovis and Lubbock in the middle of July could sleep damn near anywhere. He'd never realized how rough life was in the bush leagues until he found all the rugged things for which it had prepared him.

As usual, he woke slick with sweat. He splashed water over himself to get some of the greasy feel off his skin. For a little while, as it evaporated, he felt almost cool. Then he started sweating again. At least it was dry heat, he told himself. Had it been humid, he would have cooked long since.

He was glancing through the *Signal* again, trying to figure out what some of the Norwegian (or were they Danish?) words meant, when the door opened. He wondered what the Lizards wanted. He wasn't hungry yet; the pork and beans still felt like a medicine ball in his stomach. But instead of a Lizard with canned goods, in walked Liu Han.

"Your mate," said one of the Lizards escorting her. His mouth fell open. Fiore thought that meant he was laughing. That was all right. He laughed at the Lizard, too, for not being able to mate.

He gave Liu Han a hug. Neither of them wore anything; they stuck to each other wherever they touched. "How are you?" he said, letting her go. "It's good to see you." It was good to see anyone human, but he didn't say that aloud.

"Good also to see you," Liu Han said, adding the Lizards' emphatic cough to end the sentence. They spoke to each other in a jargon they invented and expanded each time they were together, one no other two people could have followed: English, Chinese, and the Lizards' language pasted together to yield ever-growing meaning.

She said, "I am glad the scaly devils do not force us to mate"—she used the Lizards' word for that—"each time we see each other now."

"You're glad?" He laughed. "I can only do so much." He flicked his tongue against the inside of his upper lip as he blew air out through his mouth, making a noise like a window shade rolling up—and him with it.

He'd done that often enough for her to understand it. She smiled at his foolishness. "Not that I don't like what you do when we mate"—again she used the Lizards' emotionless word, which let her avoid choosing a human term with more flavor to it—"but I do not like having to do it at their order."

"Yeah, I know," he said. Being a specimen didn't appeal to him, either. Then he wondered what they ought to do instead. Besides their bodies, the only thing they had in common was that the Lizards had shanghaied both of them.

Since Liu Han plainly didn't feel like screwing to pass the time, he went through the *Signal* with her. He'd decided a while ago that she was anything but stupid, but he found how little she knew of the world outside the village from which she'd come. He couldn't read the text of the magazine, but he recognized faces and places in the pictures: Göbbels, Marshal Pétain, Paris, North Africa. To Liu Han, they were all strange. He wondered if she'd even heard of Germany.

"Germany and Japan are friends," he told her, only to discover that Japan wasn't *Japan* in Chinese. He tried again: "Japan fights"—that in pantomime—"America and fights China, too."

"Oh, the eastern devils," she exclaimed. "Eastern devils kill my man, my child, just before little scaly devils come. This Germany friends with eastern devils? Must be bad."

"Probably," he said. He'd been sure the Germans were the bad guys when they declared war on the United States. Since then, though, he'd heard they had done a better job of fighting the Lizards than most. Did that all of a sudden turn them back into good guys? He had trouble figuring out where loyalty to his own country stopped and loyalty to—to his planet, would it be?—started. He wished Sam Yeager were around. Yeager was more used to thinking in terms like those.

He also noticed, not for the first time but more strongly than ever before, that anything not Chinese was somehow devilish to Liu Han. The Lizards were scaly devils; he himself, when he wasn't *Bobbyfiore* pronounced all as one word, was a foreign devil; and now the Japs were eastern devils. Given what they'd done to her family, he couldn't blame her for thinking of them like that, but he was pretty sure she would have hung the same label on them no matter what.

He asked her about it, using multilingual circumlocutions. When she finally understood, she nodded, surprised he needed to put the question to her. "If you are not Chinese, of course you are a devil," she said, as if stating a law of nature.

"That's not how it is," Fiore told her; but she didn't look convinced. Then he remembered that, till he'd started playing ball and meeting all sorts of people instead of just the ones from his neighborhood, he'd been sure everybody who wasn't Catholic would burn in hell forever. Maybe this devil business was something like that.

They went back to looking at the *Signal.* The high-kicking nightclub dancer in her skimpy satin outfit made Liu Han laugh. "How can she show herself, wearing so little?" she asked, forgetting for the moment that she herself wore nothing. Fiore laughed in turn. Except when he stuck to the mat, he often forgot he was naked, too. Amazing what you got used to.

Liu Han pointed to an advertisement for an Olympia typewriter. "What?" she said in English, adding the Lizard interrogative cough.

Fiore had more trouble explaining it than he'd expected. After a while, he figured out that she couldn't read or write. He'd known a few ballplayers, mostly from the South, who had the same trouble, but it wasn't something that automatically occurred to him.

Now he wished more than ever that the *Signal* was in English; he would have started teaching her on the spot. He thought about showing her the alphabet—despite crossed *o*'s and *a*'s with little circles above them, the ABCs didn't change much. But if he didn't understand what he was reading, how was she supposed to? He gave it up as a bad job and turned to the next page.

It showed a flight of German bombers over some Russian city. In spite of the sweltering heat, she shivered and pressed herself against him. She might not know what a typewriter was for, but she recognized bombers when she saw them. Fiore clicked his tongue between his teeth. Wasn't that a hell of a thing?

They came to the article about Marshal Pétain. Fiore thought he was going to have trouble putting across what Vichy France was all about, the more so as he didn't understand all the details himself. But as soon as he managed to convey to her that it was a German puppet state, she nodded and exclaimed, "Manchukuo!"

"That's right, the Japs have puppets, too, don't they?" he said.

"Puppets?" She had the concept, but the word eluded her. He resorted to pantomime again until she got the idea. He hammed up his dumb show as much as he could; she always enjoyed that. She did smile now, but only for a moment. Then she said, "The scaly devils have made puppets of us all."

He blinked; that was as serious an idea as she'd ever gotten across. She was also dead right. If it weren't for the Lizards, he'd be . . . doing what? The answer he arrived at brought him up short. If it weren't for the Lizards, all he'd be doing was trying to keep a floundering minor-league career alive, getting an off-season job, and waiting for Uncle Sam to send him a draft notice. When you stepped back and looked at it, none of that was worth writing home about.

"Maybe we were already puppets before the Lizards came," he said harshly. His voice grew softer as he added, "If they hadn't come, I never would have known you, so I guess I'm glad they did."

Liu Han did not answer right away. Her face was unreadable as she studied Fiore. He flinched from that quiet scrutiny, wondering how badly he'd just stuck his foot in his mouth. He knew she'd been through hard times, and it was a lot rougher for a woman to have to lie down with a strange man than the other way around. He suddenly wondered exactly what she thought of him. Was he something good, or simply something better than she'd known in captivity before?

How much the answer mattered surprised him. Till now, he hadn't asked himself what Liu Han meant to him, either. Sure, getting laid was fine, and he'd found out more about that from her than he'd thought he needed to learn until the Lizards brought him up here. But there was more to it. In spite of all the dreadful things that had happened to her, she remained good people. He wanted to take care of her. But did she want him for anything more than an insurance policy?

She never did answer, not in words. She put her head on his chest, smoothing away the hairs with her hand so they wouldn't tickle her nose. His arms closed around her back. He could have rolled over on top of her, but it didn't cross his mind, not now. They held each other for a while.

He wondered what his mother would say if he told her he was falling in love with a Chinese girl. He hoped he'd have the chance to find out.

Then he wondered how he'd say "I love you" to Liu Han. He didn't know the Chinese for it, she didn't know the English, and it was one place where the Lizards' language helped not at all. He patted her bare shoulder. One way or another, he'd get the idea across.

The latest storm had finally blown out of Chicago, leaving a fine dusting of snow on the ground. The Lizards stared at it in swivel-eyed wonder as Sam Yeager marched them along toward the Metallurgical Laboratory. He was comfortable enough in a wool sweater, but they shivered in too-large peacoats scrounged from the Great Lakes Naval Base. Their breath, hotter than his, made puffs of steam in the crisp air.

In spite of intermittent Lizard air raids, a couple of students were playing catch on the dying grass by the walk. *Doing their best to pretend everything's normal,* Yeager thought. He envied them their determination.

As athletes, they weren't much. One of them flat-out missed the ball when it came to him. It skidded through the slush and stopped almost at Yeager's feet. He set down the rifle he was still required to carry, scooped up the baseball, and fired it back to the student who'd thrown it. If the kid hadn't caught it, it would have hit him right in the middle of the chest. He stared at Yeager, as if to say *Who is this old guy?* Yeager just grinned, picked up his piece, and started shepherding the Lizards down the walk again.

Ristin said, "You"—he followed it with a Lizard word Yeager didn't know—"very well."

As best he could, Yeager echoed the croaked word. "Not understanding," he added in the Lizards' language. Ristin obligingly gestured while repeating the word. A light went on in Yeager's head. He dropped back into English: "Oh, you mean *throw.*" He made as if to throw again, this time without a baseball. "Throw."

"Ssrow," Ristin agreed. He tried English himself: "You—ssrow—good."

"Thanks," Yeager said, and let it go at that. How was he supposed to explain to an alien that he'd made a living (not much of a living, sometimes, but he'd never gone hungry) because he could throw and hit a baseball? If he didn't have a better arm than a couple of half-assed college kids, he'd better leave town.

It wasn't much warmer inside Eckhart Hall than it had been outside. Heat was as hard to come by as electricity these days. Army engineers did a marvelous job of repairing bomb damage, but the Lizards could wreck things faster than they could fix them. Since the elevator wasn't running, Yeager took Ristin and Ullhass up the stairs to Enrico Fermi's office. He didn't know about them, but the exercise made him warmer.

Fermi bounced up out of his chair when Yeager walked the Lizards through his open door. "So good to see you and your friends here," he said effusively. Yeager nodded, hiding a smile at the physicist's heavy accent. He would have bet Bobby Fiore's father sounded the same way.

Fermi had a glass coffeepot set up above a tin of canned heat. Heavy china mugs, cafeteria-style, stood beside the Sterno. The physicist gestured for Yeager to take one. "Thank you, sir," Yeager said. He hadn't noticed little things like cigarettes and coffee until he couldn't get them whenever he wanted. Scarcity made them precious—and besides, the coffee was hot.

He glanced at Ullhass and Ristin. They'd tried coffee, too, but found it too bitter to stand. That was their tough luck, he thought; it cut them off from something that could heat them up from the inside out. He took another sip from his cup, felt his eyes opening wider. Coffee hit harder when you couldn't have it every day. So did tobacco; he remembered how Barbara Larssen had reacted to her first smoke in a while.

At Fermi's gesture, the Lizards perched themselves on a couple of chairs in front of the desk. Their feet barely touched the ground; human furniture was too big for them. Yeager sat down too, off to one side, his Springfield resting in his lap. He was still on guard duty, though that wasn't his chief reason for being here. Enrico Fermi had more important things to do than learning the Lizards' language, so Yeager interpreted whenever Ristin and Ullhass ran out of English.

Till the past few weeks, everything he knew about nuclear physics had come from the pages of *Astounding*. If stories like "Blowups Happen" and "Nerves" hadn't had good science in them as well as good fiction, he would have been no use to Fermi—not because he couldn't understand the Lizards, but because he wouldn't have been able to understand the physicist.

Fermi asked the Lizards, "How long have your people known how to control and release the energy contained within the atomic nucleus?"

Yeager translated. He knew he didn't do perfectly for *nucleus*; the word he used actually meant something closer to *center*. But the Lizards understood him well enough. They chattered back and forth between themselves for a few seconds before Ullhass said, "Somewhere between seventy and eighty thousand years, we think."

Ristin added, "That's our years, of course. Yours are about twice as long."

Yeager did the arithmetic in his head. Even after dividing by two, it was still an ungodly long time. If Ristin and Ullhass were telling the truth, the Lizards had known about atomic power since humanity's newest superweapon was fire against cave bears. If— He turned to Fermi. "Do you believe them, Professor?"

"Let me say that I know of no reason for them to lie," Fermi answered. He looked like the fellow you'd find behind the counter of a delicatessen in half the medium-sized towns in the United States. He sounded like him, too, until you listened to what he had to say. Now he went on, "I think if we had had this power for so long, we would have accomplished more with it than they have."

What the Lizards *had* done looked like plenty to Yeager. They'd crossed space to land on Earth, they'd kicked the tar out of every army they'd come up against, and they'd blown Berlin and Washington clean off the map. What did Fermi want, egg in his beer?

The physicist gave his attention back to the aliens. "How do you proceed in separating the useful U-235 from the much more abundant U-238?" In one form or another, he'd been asking that same question since he first set eyes on the Lizards.

As usual, they left him frustrated. Ullhass spread his clawed hands in a very human-seeming gesture of frustration. "You keep pestering us about this. We have told you before—we are soldiers. We do not know all the fine details of our technology."

This time, Fermi turned to Yeager. "Can you credit what they say?"

Not for the first time, Yeager wondered why the devil the experts were asking him questions. All at once, though, he realized he too was an expert of sorts: an expert on the Lizards. That made him chuckle; the only thing on which he'd been an expert before was hitting the cutoff man. He certainly hadn't been an expert at hitting a curve ball, or he'd have played at fields a lot fancier than the ones in the Three-I League.

He still didn't believe he had much expertise, but he did know more about the Lizards than most people. Mixing what he did know with his common sense (which, except for keeping him at a baseball career, had always been pretty good), he answered, "Professor, I think maybe I do believe them. You yank a couple of privates out of the American army and they might not be able to tell you everything you want to know about how an electrical generator works."

Fermi's sigh was melodramatic. "*Sì,* this may be so. And yet I have learned a great deal from what they do know: they take for granted so many things which are for us on the cutting edge of physics—or beyond it. Just by examining what they know 'of course' to be true, we have tremendously refined our own lines of investigation. This will help us a great deal when we relocate our program."

"I'm glad you've—" Yeager broke off. "When you what?"

"When we move away from here," Fermi said. Sadness filled his liquid brown eyes. "It will be very hard, this I know. But how are we to do physics in a city where we have not even electricity most of the day? How are we to proceed when the Lizards may bomb us at any time, may even capture Chicago before long? The line, I hear, is nearly to Aurora now. Under these circumstances, what is there to do but go?"

"Where will you go to?" Yeager asked.

"It is not yet decided. We will leave the city by ship, surely—much the safest way to go, as your little friends"—Fermi nodded toward Ullhass and Ristin—"do not seem to have grasped the importance of travel by water on this world. But where we shall try to set down new roots, that is still a matter for debate."

Yeager looked at the Lizards, too. "Are you going to want to take them with you?" he asked. If the answer was yes, he'd have to figure out whether he should try to finagle a way to come, too. He supposed he should; he couldn't think of any way in which he'd be more useful to the war effort.

But he seemed to have taken Fermi by surprise. The physicist rubbed his chin. Like most men's in Chicago, it was poorly shaven and had a couple of nicks; no new razor blades had made it into town for a long time. Yeager felt smug for using a straight razor, which required only stropping to keep its edge. That also endeared him to his sergeant, who was an old-time graduate of the cleanliness-is-one-step-ahead-of-godliness school.

After a moment, Fermi said, "It may well be that we shall." He glanced at Yeager. In a lot of science fiction, scientists were supposed to be so involved in research that they took no notice of the world around them. Yeager's little while at the University of Chicago had shown him it didn't usually work that way in real life. Now Fermi confirmed that yet again, saying, "This affects you, no?"

"This affects me, yes," Yeager said.

"We do not leave tomorrow, or even the day after," Fermi said. "You will have time to make whatever arrangements you must. Ah! Would you like me to send a request for your services to your commanding officer? This will help you with your military formalities, not so?"

"Professor, if you'd do that, it would save me from a lot of red tape," Yeager said.

"I will see to it." To make sure he did see to it, Fermi jotted a note to himself. His head might have been in the clouds much of the time, but his feet were firmly on the ground. He also shifted gears as smoothly as a chauffeur. "At our last session, Ullhass was telling what he knew of the cooling systems employed by the Lizards' atomic power plants. Perhaps he will elaborate a little more on these." His poised his pencil above a fresh sheet of paper. Questions flew, one after another.

Finally Yeager had to call time. "I'm sorry, Professor, but I've got to take our friends here on to their next appointment."

"*Sì, sì*," Fermi said. "I understand. You do what you must do, Mr. Yeager. You have been helpful to us here. I want you to know that, and know you will be very welcome to come with us as we depart to—who knows where we are to depart to?"

"Thank you, sir. That means a lot to me." A proud smile stretched itself across Yeager's face. He gave Ullhass and Ristin a grateful look—if it hadn't been for them, he'd have been reading about scientists for the rest of his life without ever meeting one, let alone being useful to one. He got up, gestured with the rifle that had lain half-forgotten across his lap. "Come on, you two. Let's go. Time for us to be on our way."

One nice thing about the Lizards was that, unlike most people he knew, they didn't give him any back talk. Ullhass said, "It shall be done, superior sir," and that was that. They preceded him out the door. He'd long since been convinced that his standing orders never to let them get behind him were foolish, but he obeyed anyhow. Army orders were like baseball fundamentals: you couldn't go far wrong with them and you couldn't do anything right without them.

He almost bumped into Andy Reilly, the custodian, when he came out the door, and he and his charges hadn't taken more than a couple of steps down the hall when someone else called, "Hi, Sam!"

He couldn't just turn around; that would have put the Lizards at his back. So he went around behind them before he answered, "Hi, Barbara. What are you doing up here?"

She smiled as she came up; she wasn't skittish about Ullhass and Ristin any more. "I'm here a lot. My husband works for the Met Lab, remember?"

"Yeah, you did tell me. I forgot." Yeager wondered if Barbara Larssen knew how big a misnomer "Metallurgical Laboratory" was. Maybe, maybe not. Secrecy about atomic energy research wasn't as tight as it had been before the Lizards proved it worked, but he'd been warned in no uncertain terms about what would happen to him if he talked too much. He didn't want a cigarette bad enough to get a blindfold with it. He didn't even want to think about that. He asked, "Any word?"

"Of Jens? No, none." Barbara kept up a brave front, but it was getting tattered. Worry—no, fear—showed in her voice as she went on, "He should have been back weeks ago—you know he was long overdue the first time you brought these little fellows into Dr. Burkett's office. And if he doesn't get back soon—"

From the way she stopped short, he thought he scented the great god Security. He said, "Professor Fermi told me the project is going to pull out of Chicago."

"I wasn't sure if you knew, and I didn't want to say too much if you didn't," Barbara answered: security, sure enough. "Wouldn't it be awful if he did make it here, only to find out there isn't any Met Lab to come back to?"

"There may not be any Chicago to come back to," Yeager answered. "From what Fermi said, the line's just outside Aurora now."

"I hadn't heard that." Her lips thinned; a small vertical worry line appeared between her eyes. "They're—getting close."

"What will you do?" he asked. "Will you go with the Met Lab people when they pull out?"

"I just don't know," Barbara said. "That's what I came up here to talk about, as a matter of fact. They're holding a slot for me, but I don't know if I should use it. If I were sure Jens was coming back, I'd stay no matter what. But he's been gone so long, I have trouble believing that any more. I try, but—" She broke off again. This time, security had nothing to do with it. She groped in her purse for a hanky.

Yeager wanted to put an arm around her. With the two Lizards standing between them, that wasn't practical. Even without them, it probably would have been stupid. She'd just think he was coming on to her, and she'd be at least half right. He didn't even tell her Fermi had asked him to evacuate with the Metallurgical Lab staff. Feeling awkward and useless, he said, "I hope he makes it back soon, Barbara."

"Oh, God, so do I." Her hands shaped themselves into claws; her red nail polish made them look like bloody claws. Her face twisted. "God *damn* the Lizards for coming down here and wrecking everything people have tried to do for as long as there've been people. Even the bad things— they're *our* bad things, nobody else's."

Ullhass and Ristin had picked up almost as much English as Yeager had learned of their language. They flinched away from Barbara's fury. "It's all right," Yeager told them. "Nothing's going to happen to you two." He understood how Barbara felt; he knew much of that same rage himself. But constantly being around the Lizard POWs had made him start thinking of them as people, too—sometimes almost as friends. He hated the Lizards collectively but not individually. It got confusing.

Barbara seemed to share some of that confusion. She'd gotten to the point where she could tell one of the captive Lizards apart from another. "Don't worry," she said to Yeager's two charges. "I know it's not your fault in particular."

"Yes, you know this," Ullhass said in his hissing voice. "But what can we do if you not know this? No thing. We are—how you say it?—in your grisp?"

"Grip, maybe," Yeager answered. "Or do you mean grasp?"

"I do not know what I mean," Ullhass declared. "It is your speech. You teach, we learn."

"They're like that," Yeager said to Barbara, trying to find less emotionally charged things to talk about. "Now that they're our prisoners, it's like we've become their superior officers and anything we say goes."

"Dr. Burkett has talked about the same thing," she said, nodding. She turned back to the Lizards. "Your people are trying to take our whole world into their grasp. Do you wonder that we don't like you?"

"But we are the Race," Ristin said. "It is our right."

Yeager had got pretty good at reading tone in the Lizards' voices. Ristin sounded surprised Barbara would question that "right." Yeager clicked his tongue between his teeth. Both Lizard POWs swung their eyes toward him; it was something he did when he wanted to get their attention. He said, "You'll find not everybody on this planet agrees with you about that."

Teerts wished his ejection seat had malfunctioned. Better to have crashed with his aircraft than to fall into the hands of the Nipponese. Those hands lacked the Race's claws, but were no less cruel for that.

He'd found out about the Nipponese in a hurry. Even before they'd got him to Harbin, his illusion that they treated prisoners decently had been shattered. From what he'd seen of the way they treated their own kind, that shouldn't have come as a surprise to him.

The rest of the Tosevite empires were barbarous, yes, but their leaders had the sense to recognize that war was a risky business in which things could go wrong, and that both sides were liable to lose prisoners when things did go wrong. Nipponese soldiers, however, were supposed to commit suicide before they let themselves be captured. That was bad enough. Worse, they expected their foes to play by the same set of rules, and scorned captives as cowards who deserved whatever happened to them.

Teerts looked down at himself. From his neck all the way down to his groin, every rib was clearly visible. The food they gave him was vile, and they didn't give him very much of it. He had the feeling that if they hadn't been interrogating him, they might not have bothered to feed him at all.

The door to the little room where they kept him swung noisily open on rusty hinges. A couple of armed guards came in. Teerts jumped to his feet and bowed to them. They'd beaten him once for forgetting. After that, he didn't forget.

The officer who had brought him to Harbin followed the guards into the smelly little cell. Teerts bowed again, deeper this time; the Nipponese made a point of being insanely punctilious about such things. Teerts said, "Good day, Major Okamoto. I hope you are well?"

"I am well." Okamoto did not ask how Teerts was; a prisoner's health was beneath his notice. He shifted from Nipponese to the tongue of the Race. Despite a heavy accent, he was growing fluent: "You shall come with me at once."

"It shall be done," Teerts said.

Okamoto turned his back and walked out of the chamber. Short for a Tosevite, he still towered over Teerts. So did the Nipponese guards; the knives mounted on the ends of their rifles looked very long and cold and sharp. They gestured with the guns for Teerts to precede them. He was already in motion. By now, captivity had become a routine like any other.

Cold smote him when he left the building where he was imprisoned. He was always chilly, even inside; what the Tosevites called heat was arctic to the Race. Outside, the weather really was arctic, with frozen water falling from the sky in feathery flakes. It clung to the ground, to trees, to buildings, coating everything with a layer of white that helped mask its inherent ugliness.

Teerts began to shiver violently. Okamoto paused, snapped an order to the guards. One of them set down his rifle for a moment, pulled a blanket out of his pack, and draped it over Teerts. The captured pilot pulled it as tight around himself as he could. Slowly, the shivers subsided.

Okamoto said, "You lucky you important prisoner. Otherwise, we let you freeze."

Teerts would willingly have forgone such luck. A truer measure of his importance was the vehicle that waited outside his prison to take him to his next interrogation session. It was noisy and smelly and had a ride like a killercraft out of control and about to crash, but at least it boasted an engine rather than a Big Ugly pedaling hard enough to grow warm even in this frigid weather. Better yet, it also had an enclosed cabin.

One of the guards drove. The other sat beside him in the front seat. Major Okamoto sat behind the driver, Teerts behind the other guard. Okamoto did not have a rifle with a long knife on the end, but he did carry both a sword and a pistol. And even if Teerts could somehow have overcome him, what was the point? How could he flee out of this teeming den of Big Uglies without getting caught and meeting a fate even worse than the one he was now suffering?

Den was the right word for Harbin, he thought as the military vehicle made its slow way through the narrow, twisting streets of Harbin. It was a city in size, but not, to his mind, in design. Indeed, it didn't seem to have a design. Streets ran every which way. Big, important buildings sprawled next to appalling hovels. Here and there, piles of rubble testified to the effectiveness of the Race's bombardment. Half-naked Big Uglies labored at the piles, clearing them away a brick at a time.

Teerts thought longingly of Rosspan, the city back on Home where he'd grown up. Sunshine, warmth, cleanliness, streets wide enough for traffic, sidewalks wide enough for pedestrians—he'd taken all those things for granted till he came to Tosev 3. Now, by dreadful counterexample, he knew how lucky he'd been to enjoy them.

The truck rumbling along in front of Teerts' vehicle ran over one of the scavenger beasts that roamed the streets of Harbin. The animal's yelp of agony pierced the deep engine rattle that was the main traffic noise in Harbin. The truck never slowed as the animal passed under its wheels. It had somewhere important to go; what did one animal matter? Teerts got the idea it wouldn't have paused after running over a Big Ugly, either.

It could have, easily enough. If Harbin owned any traffic rules, Teerts hadn't discovered them. Vehicles with engines pushed their way as best they could through swarms of animal-drawn wagons and carts and even thicker swarms of Tosevites—Tosevites on foot, Tosevites carrying burdens on poles balanced on their shoulders, Tosevites riding two-wheeled contraptions that looked as if they ought to fall over but never did, Tosevites pedaling other Tosevites about in bigger contraptions or pulling them in carts as if they were beasts of burden themselves. Sometimes, at a particularly insane intersection, a Nipponese with white gloves and a swagger stick would try to bring a little order into the chaos. The next Big Ugly Teerts saw obeying any of them would be the first.

He got the idea Harbin was a peculiar kind of place even by Tosevite standards, which was saying a good deal. Nipponese troops were the most aggressively visible piece of the blend; in a town near a fighting front, that was not surprising. What was surprising was the way they knocked around Big Uglies not in uniform, natives who, to Teerts' inexperienced eyes, looked no different from themselves save in clothing.

The farther east Teerts' vehicle went, the more he saw of another variety of Big Ugly: pink-skinned, with light-colored—brown or even yellow—tufts of fluff or fur or whatever it was on top of their heads. They seemed less voluble than the darker natives who made up most of the local population, and went about their business with a stolid determination that impressed Teerts.

He turned to Major Okamoto. "These pale Tosevites"—he'd learned, by painful experience, never to say *Big Ugly* to a Big Ugly's face—"may I ask where they come from?"

"No," Okamoto answered at once. "Prisoners may not spy. No questions from you, do you hear me? Obey!"

"It shall be done," Teerts said, anxious not to anger his captor. The small part of him that was not hungry and afraid insisted the Big Ugly was being foolish: he would never escape to tell what he knew. But Okamoto tolerated no argument, so Teerts gave him none.

The vehicle pulled up in front of a building from which flew Nipponese flags, red ball on white ground. Several antiaircraft guns poked their noses into the sky from sandbagged installations around it. When Teerts was flying killercraft, he'd laughed at such puny opposition. He'd stopped laughing when the Big Uglies shot him down. He hadn't laughed since.

The guards got out of the vehicle. One unlocked Teerts' door and pulled it open, then jumped back so the other could level his rifle at the pilot. "Out!" they yelled together in Nipponese. Out Teerts came, marveling as usual that the Big Uglies could find his unarmed and miserable self so dangerous. He only wished they were right.

Since they were unfortunately mistaken, he let them lead him into the building. The stairs did not fit his size or his gait. He climbed them anyhow; the interrogation chamber was on the third floor. He walked in with trepidation. Some very unpleasant things had happened to him in there.

Today, though, the three Big Uglies behind the desk all wore pilot's wings. That relieved Teerts, a little. If these questioners were pilots, they'd presumably ask him about his killercraft. At least he would know the answers to their questions. Other interrogators had grilled him about the Race's landcruisers, ground tactics, automatic weapons, even its diplomatic dealings with other Tosevite empires. He'd pleaded ignorance, and they'd punished him for it even though he told the truth.

As he'd learned, he bowed low to the interrogation team and then to Major Okamoto, who interpreted for them. They didn't bow back; he gathered a prisoner forfeited the right to any gesture of respect.

The Big Ugly in the middle turned loose a torrent of barking Nipponese. Okamoto translated: "Colonel Doi is interested in the tactics you use with your killercraft against our planes."

Teerts bowed to the Tosevite who had asked the question. "Tactics are simple: you approach the enemy as closely as you can, preferably from behind and above so you are not detected, then you destroy him with missiles or cannon shells."

Doi said, "True, this is the basis of any successful fighter run. But how do you achieve it? Where precisely do you deploy your wing man? What is his role in the attack?"

"We commonly fly in groups of three," Teerts answered: "a leader and two trailers. But once in combat, we fly independent missions."

"What? That is nonsense," Doi exclaimed.

Teerts turned and bowed nervously to Okamoto, hoping to appease him. "Please tell the colonel that, while it would be nonsense for his aircraft, ours are superior enough to those you Tosevites fly to make my words the truth."

He didn't like the grunt that came from the colonel. Of itself, one of his eye turrets swiveled to the collection of nasty tools hung on the wall behind him. When the Race needed to interrogate one of its own, or a Rabotev, or a Hallessi, they pumped the suspected offender full of drugs and then pumped him dry. No doubt physicians were hard at work developing drugs that would let them do the same for the Big Uglies.

The Nipponese were more primitive and more brutal. Techniques to gain information by inflicting pain were lost in the mists of the Race's ancient history. The Nipponese, however, had proved intimately familiar with such techniques. Teerts suspected they could have hurt him much worse had he been one of their own kind. Since he was strange and valuable, they'd gone easy for fear of killing him before they'd wrung out everything they wanted to know. What they had done was quite ingenious enough.

He felt like cheering when the Big Ugly named Doi changed the subject: "How do these missiles of yours continue to follow aircraft even through the most violent evasive actions?"

"Two ways," Teerts answered. "Some of them home on the heat from the target aircraft's engine, while others use radar."

The Nipponese translation of that took a good deal longer to say than Teerts' words had. Colonel Doi's answer was also lengthy, and Major Okamoto fumbled a good deal in putting it into the language of the Race. What he did say sounded like a paraphrase: "The colonel instructs you to give us more information on this radar."

"Do you mean he doesn't know what it is?" Teerts asked.

"Do not be insolent, or you shall be punished," Okamoto snapped. "He instructs you to give us more information on radar. Do so."

"The Deutsche, the Americans, and the British use it," Teerts said, as innocently as he could. When that got translated, all three of his interrogators let out excited exclamations. He just stood quietly, waiting for the hubbub to die down. He thought—he hoped—he'd managed to imply the Nipponese were barbarous even by Tosevite standards.

Eventually, Doi said, "Go on, prisoner. Speak of this device as *you* use it."

"It shall be done." Teerts bowed, granting the Big Ugly reluctant respect for not conceding Nipponese ignorance. "We shoot out a beam of rays like light but of longer wavelength, then detect those that reflect back from the objects they strike. From these we learn distance, speed, altitude, and bearing of targets."

The Nipponese chattered among themselves again before the one on the left directly addressed Teerts. Okamoto translated: "Lieutenant Colonel Kobayashi says you are to help our technicians build one of these radar machines."

"I can't do that!" Teerts blurted, staring appalled at Kobayashi. Did the Big Ugly have any idea what he was asking for? Teerts couldn't have built, or even serviced, a radar set with the Race's tools, parts, and instruments. To expect him to do it with the garbage that passed for electronics among the Tosevites was insane.

Kobayashi spoke a few ominous-sounding words. They sounded even more ominous when Okamoto turned them into the language of the Race: "You refuse?"

Again, Teerts' eyes involuntarily swung back to the instruments of pain on the wall behind him. "No, I don't refuse, I am not able," he said, so quickly that Okamoto had to force him to repeat himself. "I have not the knowledge either of radar itself or of your forms of apparatus. I am a pilot, not a radar technician."

"*Hontō?*" Kobayashi asked Okamoto. That was one Nipponese word Teerts had learned; it meant *Is it true?* He waited fearfully for the interpreter's reply. If Okamoto thought he was lying, he would likely renew his acquaintance with some of those instruments.

"*Hontō, hai,*" Okamoto said: "Yes, it is true." Teerts did his best not to show his relief, as he had tried not to reveal fear before.

Kobayashi said, "What good is this Lizard if he can only babble of marvels without being able to share them?" Teerts took the return ride from relief to fear. The Nipponese kept him alive mainly because they were interested in what he could teach them. If they decided they weren't learning, they wouldn't hesitate to dispose of him.

Colonel Doi spoke at some length. Teerts had no idea what he said; instead of interpreting, Okamoto joined the discussion that came when the senior officer stopped talking. It grew loud. Several times, stubby Tosevite fingers stabbed out at Teerts. He did his best not to flinch. Any one of those gestures could have meant his death.

All at once, the antiaircraft cannon outside the tower where he was being interrogated began to roar. The scream of killercraft overhead was incredibly loud and incredibly terrifying. The jolting thud of bombs going off made the floor shiver as if in an earthquake. If the Race had targeted this hall for destruction, it could kill Teerts along with the Nipponese. How dreadful, to die from the weapons of one's friends!

He had to admit the Big Ugly officers showed courage. They sat unmoving while the building shook around them. Colonel Doi looked at Teerts and said something in his own language. Major Okamoto translated: "The colonel says that if he joins his ancestors in the next little while, he will have the happy—no, the pleasure—that you go with him."

Maybe Doi's words were intended to make Teerts afraid. Instead, they gave him one of the very few moments of pleasure he'd had since his aircraft swallowed those indigestible Nipponese bullets. He bowed first to Doi, then to Okamoto. "Tell the colonel I feel exactly the same way, with roles reversed." Too late to regret the defiant words; they were already spoken.

Okamoto turned them into Nipponese. Instead of getting angry, Colonel Doi leaned forward in his chair, a sign of interest. Ignoring the dreadful racket all around, he said, "Is that so? What do you believe happens to you when you die?"

Had Teerts' face been flexible like a Tosevite's, he would have grinned enormously. At last, a question he could answer without fear of getting himself into deeper trouble! He said, "When we are through here, our spirits join those of the Emperors who guided the Race in the past so that we may go on serving them." He didn't just believe that, he was as sure of it as he was that this part of Tosev 3 would turn away from its star tonight. Billions of individuals of three species on three worlds shared that certainty.

When his remarks had been translated, Colonel Doi made that mouth-motion of amiability, the first time Teerts had seen it from an interrogator. The officer said, "We have much the same belief. I shall be honored to serve my emperor in death as I have in life. I wonder if the spirits of our dead war against those of your kind."

The notion made Teerts queasy; material Tosevites were quite troublesome enough, and he didn't care to think of Emperors past being compelled to struggle against their spiritual counterparts. Then he brightened. Up until a handful of years before, the Big Uglies had enjoyed no industrial technology. If their barbarous spirits dared assail those of the Race, surely they would be smashed.

He did not say that to Colonel Doi. "It may be so," seemed a much safer answer. Then he swung his eyes toward Okamoto. "Please ask the colonel if I may ask him a question that has nothing to do with spying."

"*Hai,*" Doi said.

Teerts asked, "Do all Tosevites hold the same idea about what will happen after you die?"

Even in the midst of chaos, that sent the Nipponese officers into gales of their barking laughter. Through Major Okamoto, Doi said, "We have as many beliefs as we have different empires, maybe more. That of us Nipponese is the correct one, however."

Teerts bowed politely. He did not presume to contradict his captors, but Doi's answer left him unsurprised. Of course the Big Uglies were divided in opinion about the world to come. The Big Uglies, as far as he could see, were divided about everything. Their little makeshift empires had all been fighting one another when the Race came; no doubt their little makeshift beliefs fought one another, too.

Then his scorn faded. In an odd way, the Big Uglies' innumerable different beliefs and languages and empires might have proved a source of strength for them. They competed so savagely among themselves that less effective methods fell by the wayside. Maybe that was why the sword-swinging savages the Race had expected to meet no longer inhabited Tosev 3.

Like any right-thinking member of the Race, Teerts automatically assumed unity and stability desirable in and of themselves. Until he came to Tosev 3, he'd never had any reason to assume otherwise. Now, as if a cold breeze blew through his thoughts, he wondered what price his species, and the Hallessi and Rabotevs with them, paid for their secure, comfortable lives.

Until the Race came to Tosev 3, it hadn't mattered. Now it did. Even if the exalted fleetlord Atvar were to pull every starship off this chilly mudball tomorrow (which of course the exalted fleetlord would not do), the Race would not be finished with the Tosevites. One fine day—surely sooner than anyone back on Home would expect—starships full of fierce, savage Big Uglies would follow where Atvar had gone.

What did that leave? The only thing that occurred to Teerts was conquering the Tosevites and so thoroughly integrating them into the Empire that their competitiveness would be stifled for good. Failing that . . . he didn't want to think about *failing that*. The next best choice he came up with was sterilizing the planet altogether. That would keep the Empire safe, no matter how hard it was on the Big Uglies. All other choices looked worse.

Bombs stopped falling; the turbofans of the Race's killercraft faded into the distance. In the streets of Harbin, a few Nipponese still fired rifles into the air at imaginary targets. "It is over," Lieutenant-Colonel Kobayashi said. "Until the next time they come back."

"Let us resume the questioning, then," Colonel Doi said. He turned his face toward Teerts once more; his poor immobile eyes could not do the job by themselves. Whatever friendliness and recognition of Teerts as a fellow intelligent being he had shown while discussing the nature of the world to come now vanished as abruptly as it had appeared. "We were speaking of radar machines. I find your answer evasive and unsatisfactory. If you do not prove more forthcoming, you will be punished. Major Okamoto . . ."

Teerts braced for what he knew was coming. Okamoto bowed to Doi, then stepped forward and slapped Teerts across the muzzle, just in front of his left eye turret. He staggered. When he regained his balance, he bowed to Okamoto, though he would sooner have killed him. "Please tell the colonel I will do my best to answer his question, but I am ignorant of the knowledge he seeks."

Okamoto translated that. Doi said, "Ha! More likely you are a liar. Major . . ." Okamoto slapped Teerts again. While he desperately tried to think of something that might satisfy Doi, Okamoto drew back his hand for yet another blow. Teerts began to think that being killed by bombs from the Race might not have been so dreadful after all.

Atvar said, "We can now take it as certain that the Big Uglies know enough to covet nuclear weapons of their own." His voice had the dreadful finality of a physician's when telling a patient only a little time was left.

The assembled shiplords stirred restlessly. Atvar tried to think of worse news he might have given them. Maybe that the Big Uglies had exploded a nuclear weapon under one of the Race's landed ships. Of course, they would have found out about that without his telling them.

Straha said, "Exalted Fleetlord, how did our security procedures fail so abominably as to permit the Tosevites to raid a nuclear recovery team?"

Atvar wondered how his own security procedures had failed so abominably as to permit Straha to find out just what the Big Uglies had done. He said, "Investigations are continuing, Shiplord." He was also investigating how Straha had learned what had happened, but forbore to mention it.

The shiplord said, "Forgive me, Exalted Fleetlord, but I would be grateful for somewhat more detail than you have furnished."

"Forgive me, Shiplord, but I have difficulty in providing them." Before Straha could come back with more sarcasm, Atvar went on, "One of the unfortunate things we have observed about the Big Uglies is that, while we have better technology, they are better soldiers than we in tactical terms. We have practiced and studied war; they have lived it. To our cost, we are discovering what a difference that makes."

"Let me give an example of this," Kirel said, supporting the fleetlord. "In and around several of our positions, we installed sensors that detected Tosevites by sniffing out the uric acid that is one of the wastes they excrete. The concentration of it in the air lets us gauge the number of Big Uglies in the vicinity."

"This is adapted from standard techniques we use back on Home," Straha said in challenging tones. "Why do you mention it now? What relevance has it to our failure?"

"Its relevance is that the Tosevites do not think in our standard terms," Kirel answered. "They must somehow have become aware of our sensors—possibly by stumbling over one of them—and learned how they functioned."

"So?" Straha said. "I assume this story has a point."

"It does," Kirel assured him. "The Tosevites began discharging their liquid wastes directly onto the sensors."

"Disgusting," Straha said. There if nowhere else, Atvar agreed with him. Having evolved on a hotter, drier planet than Tosev 3, the Race did not casually cast off water, but passed all its excreta in neat, solid form. Big Ugly prisoners had strained the fleet's plumbing systems.

"Disgusting, true, but also informative," Kirel said. "Some of our technicians suddenly began screaming in panic that four billion Tosevites were heading straight for their position. By our best estimates, that is about double the total population of Tosev 3, but it is also what the drenched, befouled, and overloaded sensors were reporting. And while we reacted to these frightening data, the Big Uglies worked mischief elsewhere. Is this a ploy that would have occurred to any of us?"

Straha did not answer. None of the other shiplords said anything, either, though a few let their mouths fall open in amusement. Atvar thought the story was funny, too, in a scatological way, but it also had a point. He drove that point home: "The Big Uglies are ignorant, but they are far from stupid. Within their limits, they can be very dangerous. They have learned

better than to stand up to us in large-scale combat, but at these little pinprick raids they excel."

"*This* raid was more than a pinprick," Straha insisted.

"Strategically, yes, but not tactically," Atvar said. "The Big Uglies
also use this world's revolting weather to good advantage. They are accustomed to wet and cold, even to the various forms of frozen water which
occur on Tosev 3. We have to learn to deal with these case by case, and
they are making our education expensive."

Straha said, "In my opinion, this world may not be worth our settling.
The weather is not its only revolting feature: the Big Uglies themselves
certainly merit that description."

"As may be," Atvar said. "The Emperor has ordained that we bring
Tosev 3 into the Empire, and so it shall be done." That statement of unconditional obedience to the Emperor's will brought up short the shiplords
who before had plainly agreed with Straha. Atvar went on, "Many parts of
this world will suit us well, and its resources, which the Big Uglies exploit
only inefficiently, will be most valuable to us."

"If this be so, let us use its resources as if they were on a lifeless
planet of one of our own solar systems," Straha said. "Kill all the Big Uglies and we solve most of our problems with Tosev 3."

Atvar did not like the number of shiplords who looked as though they
agreed with Straha. He said, "You forget one thing: the colonizing fleet is
already on its way behind us. It will be here in less than forty years—
twenty turns for this planet—and its commander will not thank us for presenting him with a dead world."

"Given a choice between presenting him with a dead world and a lost
war wherein the Big Uglies learn of nuclear weapons, Exalted Fleetlord,
which would you prefer?" Straha demanded. Even the shiplords of his aggressive faction stirred restlessly at that; such acid sarcasm was rare
among the Race.

The best way to defuse it, Atvar thought, was to pretend not to recognize it. He said, "Shiplord, I do not believe those are the only choices left
to us. I intend to present the commander of the colonizing fleet a planet
ready for his settlers."

If the war went well, that still remained possible. Even Atvar, though,
was beginning to doubt whether Tosev 3 would be as ready for the colonists as the plans back Home called for. Conditions on the planet were too
different from what the Race had expected: too many Big Uglies here with
too many of their own factories.

And Straha, curse him, would not shut up. He said, "Exalted Fleetlord,
how can we claim to be winning this war, conquering this world, when even
the little gimcrack Tosevite empires which have allegedly surrendered to us
continue to maintain armed resistance to our occupying forces?"

"If the sagacious shiplord has a solution to this difficulty, hearing it would gladden my spirit," Atvar replied. "We continue to defend ourselves, of course, and to strike back against raiders as we may. What else would you have us do?"

Straha was never short on opinions. He said, "Retaliate massively for every act of banditry and sabotage. Slay ten Big Uglies for every truck damaged, a hundred for every soldier of the Race harmed. Force them to respect us and eventually they will."

"Exalted Fleetlord, may I speak to this issue?" Kirel asked.

"Speak," Atvar said.

"I thank you, Exalted Fleetlord. Straha, I want you to know I formerly held a view similar to yours; as you may or may not have heard, I strongly advocated the destruction of the Big Ugly city called Washington to terrify the Tosevites of the United States into ceasing their resistance to us. The strategy likely would have succeeded against the Hallessi or Rabotevs, or even against the Race. Against the Tosevites, it has failed."

Straha started to interrupt; Kirel stuck out his tongue to stop him. "Let me finish, if you please. I do not claim we have failed to cow many of the Big Uglies by massive shows of force. But there also exists among the Tosevites a strong minority impelled to ever greater resistance by such acts on our part. Your policy plays into the hands of these fanatics."

"Why should the Big Uglies be different from any civilized species?" Straha said.

"Our scholars will be debating that for thousands of years to come, as they review the records of this campaign," Kirel said. Mouths lolled open here and there among the assembled shiplords; the Race's scholars were notoriously more sure but slow than slow but sure. Kirel went on, "I, however, lack the luxury of leisure, as is true of everyone here on Tosev 3. Were I to speculate, I would say the Big Uglies' differences go back to their peculiar—I might say unique—mating patterns."

Straha made a disgusted noise. "Always we come back to mating. Do the miserable Big Uglies think of nothing else?"

"The answer to this may be no," Atvar said. "The intense emotional bonds they form with sexual partners and with offspring make them willing to take risks any member of the Race would reckon insane, and also provoke them to take vengeance should partners or offspring be harmed."

"There may even be more to it than that," Kirel added. "Some of our scholars speculate that the Big Uglies, because of the familial attachments they are accustomed to forming, also are predisposed toward forming equally strong attachments to the causes of their little empires and their implausible religious systems. We are in effect dealing with a species full of fanatics—and fanatics, by definition, are not to be constrained by threats of force which would deter more rational individuals."

"Let me see if I understand you, Honored Shiplord," Straha said. "You are advancing the hypothesis that Tosev 3 may never be as fully pacified as Halless 1 and Rabotev 2 are, and that the Big Uglies may continue suicidal resistance to us even after overall military victory is achieved."

"You extrapolate further than I have been willing to go, but the answer is basically yes," Kirel said unhappily.

Atvar said, "Let us eat the worms ahead of the soup, Shiplords. Before we can discuss ways to reduce harassment of our forces after we conquer, we must first complete our conquest. The truly atrocious winter weather prevailing over much of the northern hemisphere of Tosev 3 makes matters no easier for us."

"Our males should have been better trained to withstand such conditions," Straha said.

The fleetlord wished one of the fearsome Tosevite snipers would draw a bead right in the middle of Straha's snout. All he did was complain and intrigue; he didn't care for solving the problems he pointed out. Atvar said, "I might remind the shiplord that no territory within the Empire closely simulates the climate of the Tosevite lands wherein, to our misfortune, our most formidable opponents dwell."

Several males even of Straha's faction showed their agreement with that. It relieved Atvar a little. He was coming to dread these assemblages. Too often he had bad news to report, and news bad in ways he never would have imagined before the fleet left Home. He'd expected his principal concern on this campaign to be how many soldiers carelessly got hurt in traffic accidents, not whether the Big Uglies would soon be fighting him with nuclear weapons of their own.

He'd also expected much better data from the Race's probes. He'd already resigned himself to their missing the weird technological jump the Tosevites had taken after they departed: that was the Big Uglies' fault, not theirs. But they should have done a better job of reporting on Tosevite social and sexual habits, so Kirel's research crews wouldn't have had to start learning about them from scratch.

What really worried him was the thought that maybe the probes had sent accurate data back to home, only to have those data ignored, misinterpreted, or downright disbelieved by scholars who analyzed them from a Race-centered perspective. If similar mistakes had been made before the conquests of the Rabotevs and Hallessi, the Race not only got by with them but didn't even notice them—the subject species really weren't very different from their overlords. But the Big Uglies were . . . and finding out how much so was proving more costly than anyone could have imagined.

"Exalted Fleetlord, how shall we minimize the mischief the Tosevites may cause with nuclear material in their possession?" Kirel asked.

"I shall summarize for the shiplords new orders which will soon reach them in written form," Atvar answered. "In essence, we will increase our bombardment of major urban centers in which important scientific research is likeliest to take place. Let us see how well they do at such research if, for instance, their facilities lack electrical power."

Horrep, one of the males of Straha's faction, waggled his tailstump to ask to be recognized. When Atvar turned both eyes in his direction, he said, "I would respectfully remind the exalted fleetlord that our own stockpiles of munitions are not so high as they might be. We have used far more than we anticipated when we set out from Home, and our replenishment facilities have not been established here at the pace originally planned, due to both commitment of our resources to the actual fighting and unexpectedly heavy damage from Tosevite resistance."

Several other males spoke up to support Horrep. Again Atvar had that unsettling mental image of expending his last round of ammunition, only to see one more Big Ugly landcruiser crawl out from behind a pile of rubble. "Do you say you cannot obey the forthcoming order?" he demanded.

"No, Exalted Fleetlord—it shall be done," Horrep answered. "But I must warn you that such a program cannot be sustained indefinitely. I very much hope the results it achieves will be in proportion to the munitions it expends."

So do I, Atvar thought. He thanked the forethoughtful spirits of Emperors past that the Race had brought far more weapons of war to Tosev 3 than would have been necessary to conquer the semisavages they'd expected to find here. If his people had done things hastily, they might have walked headlong into ignominious defeat.

On the other hand, if the Race had been hasty and come to Tosev 3 a few hundred years sooner, the Big Uglies would have been much easier prey, because they wouldn't have had the time to develop their own technology. Did that mean haste would have been advisable here? The harder one looked at a complicated question, the more complicated it generally became.

The fleetlord reluctantly decided to scrap for the time being another part of the order he'd intended to issue: he'd wanted to command increased efforts against the boats on which the Big Uglies lavished so much effort and ingenuity. Because Tosev 3 had so much water, the locals made much more use of it than any species within the Empire. Atvar had the feeling they used water transport enough to make suppressing it worthwhile for the Race . . . but with munitions in shorter supply than he would have liked, he'd have to preserve as much as he could for targets of the highest priority.

He sighed. Back on Home, the aptitude tests had said he might make a successful architect as well as a soldier. The choice had been his. He'd always been an idealist, eager to serve the Emperor and the Race as fully as possible. Only when confronted with the unending morass of the conquest of Tosev 3 had he seriously started wondering whether he wouldn't have been happier putting up buildings after all.

He sighed again. That choice was dead for him now. He had to do the best he could with the one he'd made. He said, "Shiplords, I know this meeting has been imperfectly satisfying. The Big Uglies have shown a re-volting knack for making everything we do appear unsatisfactory. Before I dismiss you back to your commands, has any of you anything further to note?"

More often than not, the formal question went unanswered. This time, however, a male named Relek signaled for recognition. When Atvar acknowledged him, he said, "Exalted Fleetlord, my vessel, the *16th Emperor Osjess*, is grounded in the eastern part of Tosev 3's main continental mass, in the Big Ugly empire called China. Lately a fair number of males have made themselves unfit for duty due to excessive consumption of some local herb which apparently has a stimulant and addictive effect on them."

"My ship is based in the center of that continental mass, and I've had the same experience with a handful of my troopers," said another shiplord, this one called Tetter. "I thought I was the only shiplord so affected."

"You are not," said Mozzten, a shiplord whose vessel was based in the U.S.A. portion of the smaller continental mass—Atvar took notice of that. Mozzten went on, "The Big Ugly name—*a* Big Ugly name, I should say—for the herb is 'ginger.' Its effects on the males in my command have been deleterious."

"I shall issue a general order condemning this herb in no uncertain terms," Atvar declared. "To add to its effectiveness, I would have each shiplord—especially you three who have indicated a problem—issue his own order forbidding the individuals under his jurisdiction from having anything to do with this—ginger, was that the name I heard?"

"It shall be done," the shiplords chorused.

"Excellent," Atvar said. "There's one problem settled, at least."

The mechanic spread his thick-fingered, greasy hands, shook his head helplessly. "I am very sorry, Comrade Pilot," he said, "but I cannot find the cause of the trouble. As best I can tell, the devil's grandmother has set up shop in your engine."

"Move out of the way, then, and I will see for myself," Ludmila Gorbunova snapped. She wanted to kick some sense into the stupid *muzhik*, but both his head and his arse were probably hard enough to break her foot. She wished she still had her old mechanic; unlike this oaf, Katya Kuznetsova had actually understood engines and gone after problems instead of babbling about the devil and his stupid relatives.

It wasn't as if the little five-cylinder Shvetsov radial was the most complicated piece of machinery ever built, either. It was about as simple as an engine could be and still work, and as reliable as anything that didn't walk on all fours.

As soon as she got a good look at the engine, she became certain this idiot mechanic walked on all fours. She reached up, asked, "Do you think this loose spark-plug wire might have something to do with the aircraft's poor performance of late?" As she spoke, she connected the wire firmly.

The mechanic's head bobbed up and down, as if on a string. "*Da*, Comrade Pilot, very likely it could."

She wheeled on him. "Why didn't you see it, then?" she shouted shrilly. She wished she were a man; she wanted to bellow like a bull.

"I'm sorry, Comrade Pilot." The mechanic's voice was humble, as if she were a priest who had caught him at some sordid little sin. "I am trying. I do the best I can."

With that, Ludmila's rage evaporated. She knew the fellow was telling the truth. The trouble was, his best just wasn't good enough. The Soviet Union's pool of skilled manpower had never been big enough to meet the country's needs. The purges of the 1930s hadn't helped, either; sometimes simply knowing something was enough to make one an object of suspicion. Then the Germans came, and after them the Lizards ... Ludmila supposed it was a miracle any reliable technicians were left alive. *If* any were—she knew she hadn't seen one lately.

She said, "We have here manuals for the *Kukuruznik* and its engine. Study them carefully, so we won't have this kind of problem any more."

"*Da*, Comrade Pilot." The mechanic's head bobbed up and down again. Ludmila was dully certain they wouldn't have this kind of problem any less, either. She wondered if the mechanic could read the manuals. Before the war, he'd probably been a tinker or a blacksmith at a *kolkhoz*, good enough at patching a pot or hammering out a new blade for a shovel. Whatever he'd been, he was hopelessly out of his depth when it came to engines.

"Do the best you can," she told him, and left the shelter of the U-2's enclosure. It had been cold in there. Away from the heaped banks of earth that shielded from blast, away from the roof of camouflage netting covered over with dead grass, the wind bit with full force, driving sleet into her face. She was glad for her flying clothes of fur and leather and thick cotton padding, for the oversized felt *valenki* that kept her feet from freezing. Now that winter was here, she seldom took anything off.

The *valenki* acted almost like snowshoes, spreading her weight as she squelched along the muddy edge of the equally muddy landing strip. Only the slush-filled ruts from her plane and others distinguished the runway from any other part of the steppe. Even more than most Soviet aircraft, the *Kukuruznik* was made to operate from landing fields that were fields in truth.

Her head came up; her right hand went to the pistol she wore on her hip. Someone not part of the battered Red Air Force detachment was trudging across the airstrip, very likely without realizing it was one. A Red Army man, maybe—he had a rifle slung across his back.

No, not a Red Army man: he wasn't dressed warmly enough, and the cut of his clothes was wrong. Ludmila needed only a moment to recognize the nature of the wrongness; she'd seen it enough. *"Germanski!"* she yelled, half to call to the fellow, half to warn the rest of the Russians on the little base.

The German spun, grabbed for his rifle, flopped down on his belly in the mud. *A combat veteran,* Ludmila thought, unsurprised: most of the German soldiers still alive in the Soviet Union were the ones with reactions honed by battle. This one was also smart enough not to start blazing away before he knew what he'd walked into, even if his thick red whiskers gave him the look of a bandit.

Ludmila frowned. She'd seen whiskers like those before. *On the* kolkhoz, *that's right,* she thought. What had the fellow's name been. "Schultz," she murmured to herself. Then she shouted it, going on in German, "Is that you?"

"*Ja.* Who are you?" the red-bearded man yelled back: like her, he needed a few seconds to make the connection. When he did, he exclaimed, "You're the pilot, right?" As it had back at the collective farm, the word sounded exotic with a feminine ending tacked onto it.

She waved for him to approach. He got to his feet; though he didn't resling his rifle, he didn't point it at her, either. He was grimy and ragged and looked cold: if not quite the pathetic Winter Fritz of Soviet propaganda, still a long way from the deadly-dangerous figure he'd seemed back in the summer. She'd forgotten how tall he was. He was skinnier than he had been, too, which further exaggerated his height.

He asked, "What are you doing here, out in the middle of nowhere?"

"This isn't nowhere. This is an airfield," she answered.

He looked around. There wasn't much to see. He grinned impudently. "You Ivans really know how to camouflage things."

She let that pass; she wasn't sure whether it was a compliment or he was saying there wasn't anything here worth hiding. She said, "I didn't expect to see you again. I thought you and your major were on your way to Moscow." As she spoke, she saw out of the corner of her eye that several pilots and mechanics had come out of their shelters and were watching her talk with the German. They all carried guns. No one who had fought the Nazis was inclined to trust them, not even now when the Soviet Union and Germany both faced the same foe.

"We were there," Schultz agreed. He saw the Russians, too. His eyes were never still, not even for a second; he scanned everything around him, all the time. He unobtrusively shifted his feet so Ludmila stood between him and most of her countrymen. With a wry smile, he went on, "Your people decided they'd rather have us go out and work for a living than sit around eating their kasha and borscht. So we did—and here I am."

"Here you are," she said, nodding. "Where is the major?"

"He was alive last I saw him," Schultz answered. "We got separated; it was part of the operation. I hope he's all right."

"Yes," Ludmila said. She still kept the letter Jäger had sent her. She'd thought about answering, but hadn't done it. Not only did she have no idea how to address a reply, but writing to a German would make another suspicious mark go down in her dossier. She'd never seen that dossier—she never would, unless charges were brought against her—but it felt as real as the sheepskin collar of her flying jacket.

Schultz said, "Anything to eat here? After what I've been stealing lately, even kasha and borscht would seem mighty fine."

"We haven't much for ourselves," Ludmila answered. She didn't mind feeding Schultz once or twice, but she didn't want to turn him into a parasite, either. Then she had a new thought. "How good a mechanic are you?"

"Pretty good," he said, not arrogant but confident enough. "I had to help keep my panzer running, after all."

"Do you think you could work on an aircraft engine?"

He pursed his lips. "I don't know. I never tried. Do you have the manuals for it?"

"Yes. They're in Russian, though." Ludmila switched to her own language: "You didn't know any back at the *kolkhoz*. Do you understand it better now?"

"*Da*, a little," Schultz answered in Russian, his accent not too scurrilous. But he dropped back into German with every sign of relief: "I still can't read it worth a damn, though. But numbers don't change, and I can make sense out of pictures. Let me see what you have."

"All right." Ludmila led him back toward the U-2 she'd just left. Members of the ground crew watched with hard, mistrustful stares as she approached. Some of that mistrust was aimed at Ludmila, for having anything to do with a German. She thought about her dossier again. But she said, "I think he can help us. He knows engines."

"Ah," everyone said, almost in unison. Ludmila didn't care for that much more than she liked the mistrustful stares. Along with hating and fearing Germans, too many Russians were in the habit of attributing nearly magical abilities to them just because they came from the west. She hoped she knew better. They were good soldiers, yes, but they weren't supermen.

When Georg Schultz saw the *Kukuruznik*, he rocked back on his heels and started to laugh. "You're still flying these little bastards, are you?"

"What about it?" Ludmila said hotly. He'd have done better to insult her family than her beloved U-2.

But the panzer man answered, "We hated these stupid things. Every time I had to go out and take a dump, I figured one of 'em would fly by and shoot my ass off. I swear they could stand on tiptoe and peek in through a window, and I bet the Lizards don't like 'em one bit better'n we did."

Ludmila translated that into Russian. As if by magic, the ground crew's hostility melted. Hands fell away from weapons. Somebody dug out a pouch of *makhorka* and passed it to Schultz. He had some old newspaper in an inside pocket that hadn't got wet. When he'd rolled himself a cigarette, a Russian gave him a light.

He shielded it with one hand from the drips that splattered down off the camouflage netting, walked around so he could get a good look at the engine and two-bladed wooden prop on the nose of the Wheatcutter. When he turned around, he wore a disbelieving grin. "It really flies?"

"It really flies," Ludmila agreed gravely, hiding her own smile. She said it again in her own language. A couple of the mechanics laughed out loud. She returned to German: "Do you think you can help keep it flying?"

"Why not?" he said. "It doesn't look near as bad as keeping a panzer going. And if that engine were any simpler, you'd run it off a rubber band like a kid's toy."

"Hmm," Ludmila said, not sure she cared for the comparison. The little Shvetsov was made to be rugged as a mule, but surely that was something to be proud of, not to scorn. She pointed to Schultz. "Turn your back."

"*Jawohl!*" He clicked his heels as if she were a field marshal in red-striped trousers, and performed a smart about-turn.

She gestured for a couple of Russians to stand behind him so he couldn't see what she was doing, then loosened the spark-plug wire she'd noticed and her alleged mechanic hadn't. "You can turn back now. Find out what's wrong with the machine."

Schultz walked over to the U-2, inspected the engine for perhaps fifteen seconds, and fixed the wire Ludmila had tampered with. His smile seemed to say, *Why don't you ask me a hard one next time?* The mechanic who had failed to find the same defect glared at the German as if suspecting the devil's grandmother had somehow migrated from the Shvetsov to him.

"This man will be useful on this base," Ludmila said. Her eyes dared the ground crew to argue with her. None of the men said anything, though several looked ready to burst with what they weren't saying.

The German panzer sergeant seemed at least as bemused as his Soviet counterparts. "First I fight alongside a bunch of Jewish partisans, and now I'm joining the Red Air Force," he said, maybe more to himself than to Ludmila. "I hope to God none of this ever shows up in my file."

So the Nazis worried about dossiers, too. The thought gave Ludmila something in common with Schultz, though it wasn't one she'd be able to share with him. Somehow that didn't matter, either. They both knew what was safe to talk about and what wasn't.

Schultz also knew what the hostile looks he was getting meant. He undid his canteen, tossed it to the mechanic who was glaring hardest. *"Vodka, russki vodka,"* he said in his pidgin Russian. He smacked his lips. *"Ochen khorosho."*

The startled groundcrew man undid the stopper, sniffed, then grinned and enfolded Schultz in a bear hug. "That was clever," Ludmila said as the ground crew passed the flask from one eager hand to the next. A moment later, she added, "Your Major Jäger would have approved."

"Do you think so?" She'd found the right praise with which to reach him—his long, bony face glowed as if he were a small boy who'd just been told he'd written his school's prize essay for the year. He went on, "The major, miss, I think he's one hell of a man."

"Yes," Ludmila said, and realized she and Schultz might have something else in common after all.

Bicycling across Ohio, Indiana, and Illinois to Chicago had seemed a good idea when Jens Larssen set about it. In summer, in a country that had never known invasion, it might even have been a good idea. In winter, pedaling through territory largely occupied by the Lizards, it looked stupider with every passing moment.

He'd seen newsreel footage of half-frozen German soldiers captured by the Russians in front of Moscow. The Russians, in their white snow suits, many of them on skis, had looked capable of going anywhere any time. That was how Jens had thought he would do, if he'd really thought about it at all. Instead, he feared he much more closely resembled one of those Nazi ice cubes with legs.

He didn't have the clothes he needed for staying out in the open when the temperature dropped below freezing and stayed there. He'd done his best to remedy that by piling on several layers at a time, but his best still left him shivering.

The other thing he hadn't thought about was that nobody was plowing or even salting the roads this winter. In a car, he would have done all right. A car was heavy, a car was fast—best of all, his Plymouth had had a heater. But drifted snow brought a bicycle to a halt. As for ice . . . he'd fallen more times than he could count. Only dumb luck had kept him from breaking an arm or an ankle. Or maybe God really did have a soft spot in his heart for drunks, children, and damn fools.

Jens looked at a map he'd filched from an abandoned gas station. If he was where he thought he was, he'd soon be approaching the grand metropolis of Fiat, by God, Indiana. He managed a smile when he saw that, and declaimed, "And God said, *Fiat, Indiana*, and there was Indiana."

His breath puffed out around him in a cloud of half-frozen fog. A couple of times, on really frigid days, he'd had it freeze in the mustache and beard he was growing. He hadn't seen himself in a mirror any time lately, so he didn't know what he looked like. He didn't care, either. He'd decided scrounging for razor blades was a waste of time, and shaving without either mirror or hot water hurt too much to be worthwhile. Besides, the new growth helped keep cheeks and chin warm. He wished he could sprout fur all over.

As he had on most of his journey, he owned the road. Cars and trucks just weren't moving, especially not in this Lizard-occupied stretch of country. Trains weren't moving much, either, and the few he'd seen had Lizards aboard. He'd wished for a white snow suit of his own, to keep from drawing their notice. But the aliens hadn't paid any attention to him as they chugged by.

He supposed that was one advantage to having been invaded by creatures from another planet as opposed to, say, Nazis or Japs. The Lizards didn't have a feel for what was normal on Earth. A *Gestapo* man, spotting a lone figure pedaling down a road, might well have wondered what he was up to and radioed an order to pick him up for questions. To the Lizards, he was just part of the landscape.

He rolled past a burned-out farmhouse and the twisted wreckage of a couple of cars. Snow covered but did not erase the scars of bomb craters in the fields. There had been fighting here, not so long ago. Jens wondered how far west into Indiana the Lizards' control reached, and how hard crossing back into American-held territory would be.

(Down deep, he wondered if Chicago was still free; if Barbara was still alive; if this whole frozen trek wasn't for nothing. He seldom let those thoughts rise to the surface of his mind. Whenever he did, the urge to keep going faltered.)

He peered ahead, shielding his eyes against snow glare with the palm of his hand. Yes, those were houses up there—either Fiat or, if he'd botched his navigation, some other equally unimpressive little hamlet.

Off to one side of the road, he saw little dark figures moving against the white-splashed background. *Hunters*, he thought. In hard times, anything you could add to your larder was all to the good. A deer might mean the difference between starving and getting through the winter.

He was not a great outdoorsman (though he'd learned a lot lately), but one good glance at how the dark figures moved warned him his first hasty thought was wrong. Hunters, at least of the human variety, did not walk like that. It was some sort of Lizard patrol.

And, worse luck, they'd seen him, too. They broke off whatever they were doing and came toward the road. He thought about diving off his bike and running away from them, but no surer way to get himself shot came to mind. Better to assume the air of an innocent traveler out and about.

One of the Lizards waved to him. He waved back, then stopped his bicycle and waited for them to come up. The closer they got, the more motley and miserable they looked. That struck him as somehow wrong; bug-eyed monsters weren't supposed to have troubles of their own. At least, they never did in the Buck Rogers and Flash Gordon serials.

But a couple of the Lizards were tricked out in their own kind's shiny cold-weather gear, while the rest had draped themselves with a rummage sale's worth of stolen human coats, mufflers, hats, snow pants, and boots. They looked like sad little tramps, and they also looked frozen in spite of everything they had on. They were, in fact, so many Winter Fritzes in the scaly flesh.

The one who had waved led the squad out onto the roadway, which was hardly less snow-covered than the surrounding fields. "Who you?" he asked Larssen in English. His exhaled breath steamed around him.

"My name is Pete Smith," Jens answered. He'd been questioned by Lizard patrols before, and never gave his real name on the off chance that they'd somehow compiled a list of nuclear physicists. He didn't give the same alias twice, either.

"What you do, Pete Ssmith? Why you out?" The Lizard turned the first sound in Larssen's assumed surname into a long hiss and pronounced the *th* at the end as a Cockney's *ff*.

"I'm going to visit my cousins. They live a little past Montpelier," Jens said, naming the small town just west of Fiat on his map.

"You not cold?" the Lizard said. "Not cold on that—that thing?" He'd evidently forgotten the word *bicycle*.

"Of course I'm cold," Larssen answered; he had the feeling the Lizard would have shot him if he'd dared deny it. Hoping he sounded properly indignant, he went on, "Have to go by bike if I want to go, though. Don't have any gas for my car." That was true for everybody these days. He didn't mention that his dead car was back in eastern Ohio.

The Lizards sounded like steam engines as they talked among themselves. The one who'd been questioning Larssen said, "You come with us. We ask you more things." He gestured with his gun to make sure Jens got the point.

"I don't want to do that!" Larssen exclaimed, which was true for both his Pete Smith persona and his very own self. If the Lizards did any serious questioning, they'd find out he didn't know much about his alleged cousins west of Montpelier. They might even find out he didn't *have* any cousins west of Montpelier. And if they found that out, they'd likely start doing some serious digging about who he really was and why he was biking across eastern Indiana.

"Not care what you want," the Lizard said. "You come with us. Or you stay." He brought the rifle up to point straight at the middle of Larssen's chest. The message was clear: if he stayed here, he'd stay forever. The Lizard spoke in his own language, maybe translating for his friends what he'd told Jens. Their mouths fell open. Larssen had seen that before, often enough to figure out what it meant. They were laughing at him.

"I'll come," he said, as he had to. The Lizards formed up on either side of his bicycle and escorted him into Fiat.

The town wasn't even a wide spot on Highway 18, just a few houses, a general store, an Esso station (its pumps now snow-covered mounds), and a church along the side of the road. The store was probably the main reason the town existed. A couple of children ran shouting across the empty pavement of the highway, pelting each other with snowballs. They didn't even look up when the Lizards went past; by now they were used to them. *Kids adapt fast*, Larssen thought. He wished he did.

The Lizards had turned the general store into their headquarters. A razor-wire fence ringed the building to keep anyone from getting too close. A portable pillbox sat in front of the store. Larssen wouldn't have envied a human on duty in there. It had to seem even chillier for one of the invaders.

A blast of heat hit him in the face when the Lizards opened the store's front door. He went from too cold to too hot in the space of a few seconds. Sweat glands he'd thought dormant till summer suddenly returned to life. In his wool hat, overcoat, and sweater, he felt like a main dish in a covered kettle that had just been moved from the icebox to the oven.

"Ahh!" The Lizards all said it together. As one, they stripped off their layers of insulation and drank in the heat they loved so well. They did not object when Larssen shed his own coat and hat and, a moment later, his sweater. Even in shirt and trousers, he was too warm. But while the Lizards took nudity in stride, the last time he'd been naked in public was at a swimming hole when he was thirteen years old. He left the rest of his clothes on.

The Lizard who spoke English led him to a chair, then sat down across a table from him. The alien reached forward and poked a knob on a small Lizardy gadget that lay on the table. Behind a small, transparent window, something inside the machine began to spin. Jens wondered what it was for.

"Who you?" the Lizard asked, as if seeing him for the first time. He repeated his Pete Smith alias. "What you do?" the alien said, and he gave back his story about the mythical cousins west of Montpelier.

The Lizard picked up another contraption and spoke into it. Larssen jumped when the contraption hissed back. The Lizard spoke again. He and the machine talked back and forth for a couple of minutes, in fact. Larssen thought at first that it was some kind of funny-looking radio or telephone, but the more the Lizard used it, the more he got the feeling the device itself was doing the talking. He wondered what it was saying, especially when it spoke his name.

The Lizard turned one of its turreted eyes toward him. "We have of you no record, Pete Smith." It might have been pronouncing sentence. "How you explain this?"

"Well, uh, sir, uh—what is your name?"

"I am Gnik," the Lizard said. "You call me superior sir."

"Well, superior sir, Gnik, I guess the reason you don't have any record of me is that till now I've just stayed on my own little farm and not bothered anybody. If I'd known I'd run into you, I'd have stayed there longer, too." That was the best excuse Larssen could come up with on the spur of the moment. He wiped his forehead with a sleeve.

"It could be," Gnik said neutrally. "These cousins of you—who, what they are?"

"They're my father's brother's son and his wife. His name is Olaf Smith, hers is Barbara. They have two children, Martin and Josephine." By naming the imaginary cousins (*what's the square root of minus one cousin?* flashed across his mind) after his father, wife, brother, and sister, he hoped he'd be able to remember who they were.

Gnik talked to his gadget again, listened while it talked back. "No record of these Big Uglies," he said, and Larssen thought he was doomed. Then the Lizard went on, "Not have all records yet," and he breathed again. "One day soon, put in machine here." Gnik tapped the talking box with a clawed forefinger.

"What is that thing, anyway?" Larssen asked, hoping to get the Lizard to stop asking him questions about relatives he didn't have.

But Gnik, though too short for basketball and too little for football, was too smart to go for a fake. "You not ask questions at I. I ask questions at you." Lizards didn't have much in the way of facial expressions, but what Gnik had, Larssen didn't like. "You ask questions at me to spy out secrets of Race, yes?"

Yes, Jens thought, though he didn't think coming out and admitting it would be the smartest thing he'd ever done. He didn't have to fake a stammer as he answered, "I don't know anything about your secrets and I don't want to know anything about them. I just never saw a box that talked back to somebody before, that's all."

"Yes. You Big Uglies are pri-mi-tive." Gnik pronounced the three-syllable English word with obvious relish; Larssen guessed he'd learned it so he could score points off uppity humans. He was still suspicious, too. "Maybe you find this things out, pass on to other sneaky Big Uglies, eh?"

"I don't know anything about sneaky Big Uglies—I mean, people," Larssen said, noticing that the Lizards had as unflattering a nickname for human beings as humans did for their kind. "I just want to go see my cousins, that's all." Now he wanted Gnik to ask questions about Olaf and his nonexistent family. That suddenly seemed safer than being grilled about spies who might very well be real.

Gnik said, "We see more about this, Pete Smith. You not leave town called Fiat now. We keep your travel thing here"—he still couldn't remember how to say *bicycle*—"ask more questions to you later."

Larssen started to exclaim, "You can't do that!" He opened his mouth, but shut it again in a hurry. Gnik damn well *could* do that, and if he didn't care for the cut of Jens' jib, he could reslice it—and Jens—into a shape that better pleased his fancy. Losing a bicycle was the least of his worries.

No, that wasn't so. Along with the bike, he was also losing precious time. How long would he take to hike across Indiana in the dead of winter? How long before another Lizard patrol picked him up and started asking unanswerable questions? Not long, he feared. He wanted to ask Gnik where the Lizard-human frontier through Indiana ran, but didn't think it wise. For all he knew, the invaders had conquered the whole state by now. And even if they hadn't, Gnik almost certainly wouldn't answer and almost certainly would get even more suspicious.

He couldn't fail to make some kind of protest, though, not if he wanted to keep his self-respect, so he said, "I don't think you ought to take my bicycle when I haven't done anything to you."

"You say this. I not know this," Gnik retorted. "You put on now your warm things. We take you to other Big Uglies we keep here."

Putting on sweater, overcoat, and hat in the sweltering general store and then going outside reminded Jens of the runs from steam room to snow he'd shared with his grandfather when he was a kid. The only thing missing was his father standing out there to whack him with birch twigs. The Lizards didn't seem invigorated when they left the store. They just seemed cold.

They took him over to the church. Lizard guards stood outside it. When they opened the closed door, he found it was heated to a more humanly tolerable level. He also found Gnik was using it as a holding pen for people who came through or near Fiat.

People sat up on the pews; turned around to look him over; and started talking, both at him and among themselves. "Look, another poor sucker." "What did they get him for?" "What *did* they get you for, stranger?"

"Sstay—here," one of the Lizards said to Jens, his words accented almost past comprehension. Then he left the church. As the door swung shut, Larssen saw him and his companion racing back toward the general store and what they thought of as a decent temperature.

"What *did* they get you for, stranger?" repeated the woman who'd asked the question before. She was a brassy blonde not far from Jens' age; she might have been pretty if her hair (which showed dark roots) hadn't been a snaky mess and if she didn't look as if she'd been wearing the same clothes for quite a while.

Everybody in the church had that same grubby look. The faces that turned toward Larssen were mostly clean, but a strong, almost barnyard odor in the air said no one had bathed lately. He was sure he contributed to that odor; he hadn't seen a bar of Lifebuoy for a while himself. Without hot water, baths in winter were more likely to be next to pneumonia than to godliness.

He said, "Hello, folks. I don't know just what they got me for. I don't think they know, either. One of their patrols spotted me on my bicycle and pulled me in so they could ask me questions. Now they don't want to let me go."

"Sounds like the little bastards," the woman said. She wore no lipstick (maybe she'd run out) but, as if to make up for it, had rouged her cheeks almost bloodred.

Her words touched off a torrent of abuse from the other involuntary churchgoers. "I'd like to squeeze their skinny necks till those horrible eyes of theirs pop," said a man with a scraggly reddish beard.

"Put 'em in a cage and feed 'em flies," suggested a skinny, swarthy gray-haired woman.

"I wouldn't mind if they bombed us off the face of the Earth here, so long as the Lizards went with us," added a stout, red-faced fellow. "The scaly sons of bitches won't even let us go out to scrounge around for cigarettes." Larssen missed his nicotine fix, too, but Redface sounded as though he'd forgive the Lizards anything, up to and including bombing Washington, if they'd only let him have a smoke. That struck Jens as excessive.

He gave his Pete Smith alias, and was bombarded with the others' names. He wasn't especially good at matching faces and monickers, and needed a while to remember that the gray-haired woman was Marie and the bleached blonde Sal, that the fellow with the red beard was Gordon and the man with the red face Rodney. Then there were also Fred and Louella and Mort and Ron and Aloysius and Henrietta to keep straight.

"Hey, we still have pews to spare," Rodney said. "Make yourself at home, Pete." Looking around, Larssen saw people had made nests of whatever clothes they weren't wearing. Sleeping wrapped in an overcoat on a hard pew did not strike him as making himself at home, but what choice had he?

He asked, "Where's the men's room?"

Everyone laughed. Sal said, "Ain't no such thing, or powder room neither. No running water, see? We've got—what do you call 'em?"

"Slop buckets," Aloysius said. He wore a farmer's denim overalls; by the matter-of-fact way he spoke, he was more than familiar with such appurtenances of rural life.

The buckets were set in a hall behind a door which stayed sensibly closed. Larssen did what he had to do and got out of there as fast as he could. "My father grew up with a two-seater," he said. "I never thought I'd have to go back to one."

"Wish it *was* a two-seater," Aloysius said. "Dang sight easier on my backside than squattin' over one o' them buckets."

"What do you folks—what do *we*, I mean—do to pass the time here?" Jens asked.

"Cuss the Lizards," Sal answered promptly, which brought a chorus of loud, profane agreement. "Tell lies." She batted her eyes at him. "I can make like I was in Hollywood so good I almost believe it myself." He found that more pathetic than alluring, and wondered how long she'd been cooped up here.

Gordon said, "I've got a deck of cards, but poker's no damn good without real money. I've won a million dollars three or four times and thrown it away again on nothing better than a pair of sevens."

"Do we have four for bridge?" Larssen was an avid contract player. "You don't need to have money to enjoy bridge."

"I know how to play," Gordon admitted. "I think poker's a better game, though." A couple of other people also said they played. At first, Jens was as close to ecstatic as a prisoner could be; study and work had never left him as much time for cards as he would have liked. Now he could play to his heart's content without feeling guilty. But the men and women who didn't know bridge looked so glum that his enthusiasm faded. Was it really fair for some people to enjoy themselves when others couldn't?

The church door opened. A tall, thin woman with her hair pulled back in a tight bun and her face set in disapproving lines put down a box of canned goods. "Here's your supper," she said, each word clipped as precisely as if by scissors. Without waiting for an answer, she turned and walked out, slamming the door behind her.

"What's eating her?" Larssen said.

"Eating's the word." Sal tossed her head in fine contempt. "She says we're eating the people who live in this miserable little town out of house and home. As if we asked to get stuck here!"

"You notice we're eating out of tin cans," Rodney added, his features darkening even more with anger. "Nothing but farms around here, but they save all the good fresh food for themselves. We haven't seen any of it, anyhow, that's for sure."

There weren't enough spoons to go around; the town woman either hadn't noticed or hadn't cared that the church held a new arrival. Jens ate with somebody else's, washed in cold water and dried on a trouser leg. Even though he'd given up on hygiene since leaving White Sulphur Springs, that was a new low.

As he chewed on tasteless beef stew, he worried what—if anything—Chicago was eating these days. Rather more to the point, he worried about Barbara. Fiat had at the outside a couple of hundred people for the surrounding countryside to feed. Chicago had three million, and was under Lizard attack, not safely under the Lizards' thumb.

He wished he'd never left for Washington. He'd thought he was going into the worse danger himself, not leaving his wife behind to face it. Like most Americans under the age of ninety, he'd thought of war as something that happened only to unfortunate people in far-off lands. He hadn't thought through all the implications of its coming home to roost.

Something strange happened as he was getting to the bottom of the can of stew. A Lizard skittered into the church, peered down into the box of food the grim-faced woman had brought. The alien looked up in obvious disappointment, hissed something that could equally well have been English or its own language. Whatever it was, Larssen didn't understand it.

The people who'd been stuck in church longer did. "Sorry," Marie said. "No crabapples in this batch." The Lizard let out a desolate hiss and slunk away.

"Crabapples?" Larssen asked. "What does a Lizard want with crabapples?"

"To eat 'em," Sal said. "You know the spiced ones in jars, the ones that go so nice with a big ham at Christmas time? The Lizards are crazy about 'em. They'd give you the shirt off their backs for a crabapple, except they mostly don't wear shirts. But you know what I mean."

"I guess so," Larssen said. "Crabapples. Isn't that a hell of a thing?"

"Gingersnaps, too," Gordon put in. "I saw a couple of 'em damn near get into a fight one time over a box of gingersnaps."

Marie said, "They look a little like gingerbread men, don't they? They're not all that far from the right color, and the paint they wear could do for icing, don't you think?"

It was, without a doubt, the first time a Baptist church had ever resounded to the strains of "Run, run, as fast as you can! You can't catch me—I'm the gingerbread man!" Laughing and cheering one another on, the prisoners made up verses of their own. Some were funny, some were obscene, some—the best ones—were both.

Jens flogged his muse, sang, "I've blown up your cities, and I've shot up your roads, and I can take your crabapples, too, I can!" He knew it wasn't very good, but the chorus roared out: "Run, run, as fast as you can! You can't catch me—I'm the gingerbread man!"

When at last they ran out of verses, Sal said, "I hope that sour old prune who brings us our food is listening. 'Course, she probably thinks having a good time is sinful, especially in church."

"If she had her way, the Lizards would shoot us for having a good time in here," Mort said.

Sal chuckled. "One thing is, the Lizards don't pay no more attention to what she wants than we do. Other thing is, she don't know what all goes on in here, neither."

"Got to make our own fun," Aloysius agreed. "Ain't nobody gonna do it for us. Never thought how much I liked my radio till I didn't have it no more."

"That's true, that's a fact," several people said together, as if they were echoing a preacher's amens.

The short winter day wore on. Darkness poured through the windows and seemed to puddle in the church. Rodney walked over to the box the local woman had brought. "God damn her," he said loudly. "She was supposd to bring us more candles."

"Have to do without," Marie said. "No use complaining about it. We'll get by as long as we don't run out of coal for the furnace."

"And if we do," Aloysius said, "we'll be frozen hard enough that we won't start to stink till they got around to buryin' us."

That cheerful thought pretty well halted conversation. Sitting huddled in his overcoat in the darkness, Larssen thought how important the discovery of fire had been, not just because it heated Neanderthal man's caves but because it lit them as well. A man with a torch could go out at midnight unafraid, knowing it would show him any lurking danger. And electricity had all but banished night altogether. Now the age-old fears proved not dead but merely sleeping, ready to rouse whenever precious light was lost.

He shook his head. The best way he could think of to fight the night terrors was to sleep through them. Sleep was what day-loving animals did in the dark—stay cozy and quiet so nothing dangerous could find them. He stretched out on the hard pew. It wouldn't be easy.

After a long spell of tossing and turning and twisting—and once almost rolling onto the floor—he managed at last to fall asleep. When he woke, he almost fell off the pew again before he remembered where he was. He looked at his wrist. The luminous dial on his watch said it was half past one.

The inside of the church was absolutely dark. It was not, however, absolutely quiet. He needed a few seconds to identify the noises floating up from a few rows behind him. When he did, he was surprised his ears didn't glow brighter than his watch. People had no business doing that in church!

He started to sit up and see who was screwing on the pews, but paused before he'd even leaned onto one elbow. For one thing, it was too dark for him to tell anyway. And was it any of his business? His first shock had sprung straight from the heart of his upper Midwestern Lutheran upbringing. But when he thought about it a little, he wondered how long most of these people had been cooped up together and where else they were supposed to go if they wanted to make love. He lay back down.

But sleep would not return. The whispered gasps and moans and endearments, the small creaking of the pew itself, shouldn't have been enough to keep him awake. They weren't, not really, not by themselves. Listening to them, though, smote him with the realization of how long it had been since he'd slept with Barbara.

He hadn't even looked at another woman in his erratic journey back and forth across the eastern half of the United States. Pedaling a bicycle a good many hours a day, he thought wryly, was liable to take the edge off other physical urges. Besides, it was *cold*. But if just then Sal or one of the other women in here had murmured a suggestion to him, he knew he would have pulled his pants down (if not off) without a moment's hesitation.

Then he wondered what Barbara was doing about such matters. He'd been gone a long time, a lot longer than he'd thought when he set out in the late, lamented Plymouth. She might think he was dead. (For that matter, she might be dead herself, but his mind refused to dwell on that.)

He'd never imagined he needed to worry about whether she'd stay faithful. But then, he'd never thought he needed to worry about whether he would, either. The middle of the night on a cold, hard pew was hardly the time or place for such thoughts. That didn't keep him from having them.

It did keep him from going back to sleep for a long, long time.

"So," Zolraag said. Moishe Russie knew the Lizard's accent was the main thing that stretched the word into a hiss, but the knowledge didn't make it sound any less menacing. The governor went on, "So, *Herr* Russie, you will no longer for us speak on the radio? This is your measure of— what is the Deutsch word—gratitude, is that it?"

"Gratitude is the word, yes, Excellency," Russie said, sighing. He'd known this day was coming. Now it had arrived. "Excellency, not a Jew in Warsaw is ungrateful that the Race delivered us from the Germans. Had you not come when you did, there might be no Jews left in Warsaw. So I have said on the radio for your benefit. So much I would say again."

The Lizards had shown him the extermination camp at Treblinka. They'd shown him the much bigger one at Oświecim —the Germans called it Auschwitz—which had just been starting up when they came. Both places were worse than anything he'd imagined in his worst nightmares. Pogroms, malignant neglect: those were standard tools in the anti-Semite's kit. But murder factories . . . his stomach twisted whenever he thought of them.

Zolraag said, "If you are gratitudeful, we expect you to show this in ways of usefulness to us."

"I thought I was your friend, not your slave," Russie answered. "If all you want of me is to repeat the words you say, better you should find a parrot. There must be one or two left in Warsaw."

His defiance would have been more impressive, even to himself, if he hadn't had to go back and explain to Zolraag what a parrot was. The Lizard governor took a while to get the whole idea. "One of these animals, then, would speak our message in your words? This could be done?" He sounded astonished; maybe Home didn't have any animals that could learn to talk. He also sounded excited. "You Tosevites would listen to such an animal?"

Russie was tempted to say yes: let the Lizards make laughingstocks of themselvcs. Reluctantly, he decided he had to tell the truth instead; that much he owed to the beings who had saved his people. "Excellency, human beings would listen to a parrot, but only to be amused, never to take it seriously."

"Ah." Zolraag's voice was mournful. So was the Lizard's whole demeanor. His office was heated past what Russie found comfortable, yet he still draped himself in warm clothing. He said, "You know our studio has been repaired after the damage the Deutsch raiders caused."

"Yes." Russie also knew the raiders had been Jews, not Nazis. He was glad the Lizards had never figured that out.

Zolraag went on, "You know you are now in good health."

"Yes," Moishe repeated. Suddenly the governor reminded him of a rabbi laying out a case for his interpretation of a Talmudic passage: this was so, and that was so, and therefore . . . He didn't like the *therefore* he saw ahead. He said, "I will not go on the radio and thank the Race for destroying Washington."

The irrevocable words, the ones he'd tried so long to evade, were spoken at last. A large lump of ice seemed to grow in his belly in spite of the overheated room. He had always been at the Lizards' mercy, just as before he and all the Warsaw Jews were at the mercy of the Germans. A quick gesture from the governor and Rivka would be a widow.

Zolraag did not make the gesture—not yet, anyhow. He said, "I do not understand your trouble. Surely you did not object to the identical bombing of Berlin, which helped us take this city from the Deutsche. How does the one differ from the other?"

It was so obvious—but not to the Lizards. Looked at dispassionately, the distinction wasn't easy to draw. How many Germans incinerated in Berlin had been women, children, old men, people who hated everything for which the regime centered there stood? Thousands upon thousands, surely. Their undeserved deaths were as appalling as anything Washington had suffered.

But that regime itself was so monstrous that no one—least of all Moishe Russie—could look at it dispassionately. He said, "You know the kinds of things the Germans did. They wanted to enslave or kill all their neighbors." *Rather like you Lizards*, he thought. Saying that out loud, however, seemed less than expedient. He went on, "The United States, though, has always been a country where people could be freer than they are anywhere else."

"What is this freedom?" Zolraag asked. "Why do you esteem it so?"

A quotation from a scripture not his own ran through Russie's mind: *Pilate saith unto him, What is truth?* Unlike the Roman, Zolraag seemed to want a serious answer. That only made Russie the sadder for him; he suspected he would be explaining music to a deaf man.

Nonetheless, he had to try. "When we are free, we may think as we like, believe as we like, and do as we like so long as what we do does not harm any of our neighbors."

"All this you would enjoy under the beneficent rule of the Race." No, Zolraag heard no music.

"But we did not—do not—choose to come under the rule of the Race, beneficent or not," Russie said. "Another side of freedom is being able to choose our own leaders, our own rulers, rather than having them forced upon us."

"If you enjoy the other freedom, how could this one possibly matter?" Zolraag sounded all at sea. Though he and Moishe both used a hodgepodge of Lizard and German words, they did not speak the same language.

"If we cannot choose our own leaders, we keep the other freedoms only on sufferance, not because they are truly ours," Russie replied. "We Jews, we know all about having freedom taken away from us at a ruler's whim."

"You still have not answered my very first question," the Lizard governor insisted. "How can you condone our bombing of Berlin while you condemn the bombing of Washington?"

"Because, Excellency, of all the countries on this world, Germany had the least freedom of either kind and, when you came, was busy trying to take away whatever freedom its neighbors possessed. That's why most of the countries—empires, you would say, though most of them aren't—had banded together to try to defeat it. The United States, now, the United States gives its citizens more freedom than any other country. In hurting Berlin, you were helping freedom; in hurting Washington, you were taking it away." Russie spread his hands. "Do you understand what I am trying to say, Excellency?"

Zolraag made a noise like a leaky samovar coming to a boil. "Since you Tosevites cannot come close to agreeing among yourselves in matters political, I hardly see how I am to be expected to grasp your incomprehensible feuds. But have I not heard that the Deutsche chose their—what is his name?—their Hitler for themselves in the senseless manner you extol so highly? How do you square this with your talk of freedom?"

"Excellency, I cannot." Russie looked down at the floor. He wished the Lizard had not known about how the Nazis came to power. "I do not claim any system of government will always work well, only that more folk are likely to be made content and fewer harmed with freedom than under any other arrangement."

"Not so," Zolraag said. "Under the Empire, the Race and its subject species have prospered for thousands upon thousands of years without ever worrying about choosing their own rulers and the other nonsense of which you babble."

"To this I say two things," Moishe answered: "first, that you have not been trying to govern human beings—"

"To which I say, on short experience, that I am heartily glad," Zolraag broke in.

"Humanity would be glad if you still weren't," Russie said. He did not stress that, though; as he'd already admitted, he and his people would have been exterminated had the Lizards not come. He tried another tack: "How would these subject races of yours feel about what you say?"

"They would agree with me, I believe," Zolraag said, "They can scarcely deny their lives are better under our rule than they were in their barbarous days of what you, I suppose, would call freedom."

"If they like you so well, why haven't you brought any of them with you to Earth?" Russie was trying to make the governor out to be a liar. The Germans had had no trouble recruiting security forces from among the peoples they'd conquered. If the Lizards had done the same, why weren't they using their subjects to help conquer or at least police this world?

But Zolraag answered, "The Empire's soldiers and administrators come only from the ranks of the Race. This is partly tradition, dating from the epoch when the Race was the only species in the Empire . . . but then, you Tosevites care nothing for tradition."

Russie wanted to bristle at that, belonging as he did to a tradition that stretched back more than three thousand years. But he'd gotten the idea that, to Zolraag, three thousand years was about the equivalent of summer before last—hardly worth mentioning if you wanted to talk about a long time ago.

The Lizard governor went on, "That the security of the Race's rule is another consideration, I will not deny. You should be honored that you are allowed to aid us in our efforts to pacify Tosev 3. Such a privilege would not be afforded to a Hallessi or a Rabotev, I assure you, though the members of subject races may freely pursue careers in areas not affecting the government and safety of the Empire."

"We do not use the word *freely* in the same way," Russie said. "If I weren't useful to you, I'm sure you wouldn't grant me this privilege." He packed all the irony he could into that last word. Zolraag had as much as said that if the Lizards brought Earth into their Empire, humans would be reduced to hewers of wood and drawers of water, with no voice in their own fate forevermore.

Zolraag answered, "You are undoubtedly correct, *Herr* Russie. I suggest you bear that in mind, make the most of the opportunity you are presented, and cease your foolish complaints against our dominion." Using irony against him was about as futile as German antitank guns firing on Lizard panzers.

Russie said, "I cannot do as you ask of me, not only for the sake of my own self-respect but also because no human who heard me praise you for destroying Washington could ever take my words seriously again."

"You have been useful to us up until this time, so I have given you many chances to change your mind: more than I should have, very likely. But after this you will have no more chances. Do you understand what I say to you?"

"Yes. Do what you want to me. I cannot speak as you wish." Russie licked dry lips. As he had when the Nazis ruled the ghetto, he hoped he could endure whatever the Lizards inflicted on him.

Zolraag said, "We will not do anything to you, *Herr* Russie. Direct intimidation has shown itself to be less valuable on this world than we might have wished." Russie stared at him, hardly believing his own ears. But the governor was not finished: "Research has suggested another tactic which may prove more effective. As I said, you will not suffer personally for this refusal. But we shall exact reprisals upon the female with whom you are mated and upon your hatchling. I hope this may suggest a possible change in your view."

Moishe stared at him, not so much in disbelief as in dreadful disappointment. "And here I thought I'd helped drive the Nazis out of Warsaw," he said at last.

"The Deutsche are indeed well and truly driven from this city, and with your help," Zolraag said, missing the point completely. "We seek your continued assistance in persuading your fellow Tosevites of the justice of our cause."

The governor spoke without apparent irony. Russie concluded he'd noticed none. But even a Nazi might have hesitated to threaten a woman and child in one breath and proclaim the justice of his cause in the next. *Alien*, Russie thought. Not till now had he had his nose rubbed in the meaning of the word.

He wanted to point out to Zolraag the errors in his reasoning, as if he were a rabbi correcting a young *yeshiva-bucher*. In the first days after the Lizards came, he could have done just that. Since then, little by little, he'd had to learn discretion—and now his temper could endanger not just himself but also Rivka and Reuven. Softly, then.

"You understand you offer me no easy choice," he said.

"Your lack of cooperation has forced me to this step," Zolraag answered.

"You ask me to betray so much of what I believe in," Russie said. That was nothing but truth. He tried to put a whine in his voice: "Please give me a couple of days in which to think on what I must do." Getting sick wouldn't be enough this time. He was already sure of that.

"I ask you only to go on working with us and for our cause as you have in the past." Just as Russie was getting more cautious in what he said to Zolraag, so Zolraag was getting more suspicious about what he heard from Russie. "Why do you need time in which to contemplate this?" The governor spoke in his own language to the machine on the desk in front of him. It was no telephone, but it answered anyway; sometimes Moishe thought it did Zolraag's thinking for him. The Lizard resumed: "Our research demonstrates that a threat against a Tosevite's family is like to be the most effect way to ensure his obedience."

Something in the way he phrased that made Russie notice it. "Is the same not true among the Race?" he asked, hoping to distract Zolraag from wondering why he needed extra time to think.

The ploy worked, at least for a little while. The governor emitted a most human-sounding snort; his mouth fell open in amusement. "Hardly, *Herr* Russie. Among our kind, matings are but for a season, driven by the scent females exude then. Females brood and raise our young—that is their role in life—but we do not have these permanent families you Tosevites know. How could we, when parentage is less certain among us?"

The Lizards were all bastards, then, in the most literal sense of the word. Moishe liked that notion, especially with what Zolraag was putting him through now. He asked, "This is so even with your Emperor?"

Zolraag cast down his eyes at the mention of his ruler's title. "Of course not, foolish Tosevite," he said. "The Emperor has females reserved for him alone, so his line may be sure to continue. So it has been for a thousand generations and more; so shall it ever be."

A harem, Russie thought. That should have made him all the more scornful of the Lizards, but somehow it did not. Zolraag spoke of his Emperor with the reverence a Jew would have given to his God. *A thousand generations.* With a past of that depth upon which to draw, no wonder Zolraag saw the future as merely a continuation of what had already been.

The governor returned to the question he'd asked before: "With your family as security for your obedience, why do you still hesitate? This appears contrary to the results of our research on your kind."

What sort of research? Russie wondered. He didn't really want to know; the bloodless word too likely concealed more suffering than he could think about with equanimity. In doing as they pleased to people without worrying about the consequences of their actions, the Lizards weren't too different from the Nazis after all. But all of mankind was for them as Jews were for the Germans.

I should have seen that sooner, Russie thought. Yet he could not blame himself for what he'd done before. His own people were dying then, and he'd helped save them. As so often happened, though, the short-term solution was proving part of a long-term problem.

"Please answer me, *Herr* Russie," Zolraag said sharply.

"How can I answer now?" Russie pleaded. "You put me between impossible choices. I must have time to think."

"I will give you one day," the governor said with the air of one making a great concession. "Past that time, I shall have no more patience with these delaying tactics."

"Yes, Your Excellency; thank you, Your Excellency." Russie scurried out of Zolraag's office before the Lizard got the bright idea of attaching a couple of guards to him. Whatever invidious comparisons he'd drawn, he had to recognize that the invaders were less efficient occupiers than the Nazis had been.

What do I do now? he wondered as he went back out into the cold. *If I praise the Lizards for bombing Washington, I deserve an assassin's bullet. If I don't . . .*

He thought of killing himself to escape Zolraag's demands. That would save his wife and son. But he did not want to die; he'd survived too much to throw away his life. If any other way was open, he would seize it.

He was not surprised to find his feet taking him toward Mordechai Anielewicz's headquarters. If anyone could help him, the Jewish fighting leader was the man. Trouble was, he didn't know if anyone could help him.

The armed guards outside the headquarters came, if not to attention, then at least to respectful alertness as he approached. He had no trouble getting in to see Anielewicz. The fighter took one look at his face and said, "What's the Lizard said he's going to do to you?"

"Not to me, to my family." Russie told the story in a few words.

Anielewicz swore. "Let's go for a walk, *Reb* Moishe. I have the feeling they can listen to whatever we say in here."

"All right." Russie went out into the street again. Warsaw this winter, even outside the former ghetto, was depressingly drab. Smoke from soft-coal and wood fires hung over the city, tinting both clouds and scattered snow a dingy brown. Trees that would be green and lovely in summer now reached toward the sky bare branches that reminded Russie of skeletons' arms and fingers. Piles of rubble were everywhere, swarmed over by antlike Poles and Jews out to take away what they could.

"So," Anielewicz said abruptly. "What did you have in mind to do?"

"I don't know, I don't know. We expected this would happen, and now it has. But I thought they would strike only at me, not at Rivka and Reuven." Russie rocked back and forth on his heels, as if mourning lost chances.

Anielewicz's eyes were hooded. "They're learning. They aren't stupid by any means, just naive. All right, here's what it comes down to: do you want to disappear, do you want your family to disappear, or should you all vanish at the same time? I've set up plans for each case, but I need to know which to run."

"What I would like," Russie said, "is for the Lizards to disappear."

"Ha." Anielewicz gave that exactly as much laughter as it deserved. "A wolf was devouring us, so we called in a tiger. The tiger isn't eating us right now, but we are still made of meat, so he's not a good neighbor to have, either."

"Neighbor? Landlord, you mean," Russie said. "And he will eat my family if I don't throw myself into his mouth."

"I asked you once already how you want to keep from doing that."

"I can't afford to disappear," Russie said reluctantly; he would have liked nothing better. "Zolraag would just pick someone else from among us to mouth his words. He may decide to do that anyhow. But if I'm here, I serve as a reproach to whoever might want to take such a course—and to Zolraag himself, not that he cares much about reproaches from human beings. But if you can get Rivka and Reuven away . . ."

"I think I can. I have something in mind, anyhow." Anielewicz frowned, thinking through whatever his scheme was. In what seemed a *non sequitur*, he asked, "Your wife reads, doesn't she?"

"Yes, of course."

"Good. Write a note to tell her whatever you need to say about escaping: I'd bet the Lizards can hear what goes on at your flat, too. I'd be able to do that, if I were wearing their shoes."

Russie looked at the Jewish fighting leader in sharp surprise. Sometimes Anielewicz was amazingly matter-of-fact about his own deviousness. Maybe only accident of birth separated him from a *Gestapo* man. The thought was depressing. Even more depressing that in times like these the Jews desperately needed such men.

Anielewicz had barely paused. Now he went on, "Out loud, you talk to her about the three of you going out shopping to the marketplace on Gesia Street. Then go, but in a couple of hours. Have her wear a hat that stands out."

"What will happen then?"

The fighting leader let out an exasperated snort. "*Reb* Moishe, the more you know, the more somebody can squeeze out of you. Even after you see what we do, you won't know all of it—which is for the best, believe me."

"All right, Mordechai." Russie glanced over at his companion. "I hope you're not putting yourself in too much danger on account of me."

"Life is a gamble—we've learned about that these past few years, haven't we?" Anielewicz shrugged. "Sooner or later you lose, but there are times when you have to bet anyhow. Go on, do what I told you. I'm glad you don't want to go into hiding yourself. We need you; you're our conscience."

Moishe felt like a conscience, a guilty one, all the way back to his block of flats. He paused along the way to scribble a note to his wife along the lines Anielewicz had suggested. As he stuck it back into his pocket, he wondered if he'd really have to use it. When he turned the last corner, he saw Lizard guards standing at the entrance to the apartment building. They hadn't been there the day before. Guilt evaporated. To save his family, he would do what he must.

The Lizards scrutinized him as he approached. "You—Russie?" one of them asked in hesitant German.

"Yes," he snapped, and pushed past. Two steps later, he wondered if he should have lied. The Lizards seemed to have as much trouble telling people from one another as he did telling them apart. He stamped angrily on the stairs as he climbed up to his own flat. Maybe he'd wasted a chance.

"What's the matter?" Rivka asked, blinking, when he slammed the door behind him.

"Nothing." He answered as lightly as he could, mindful Zolraag's minions might be listening. "Why don't we go shopping with Reuven this afternoon? We'll see what they're selling over on Gesia Street."

His wife looked at him as if he'd suddenly taken leave of his senses. Not only was he anything but an enthusiastic shopper; his cheery manner did not match the way he'd stormed into the apartment. Before she could say anything, he pulled out the note and handed it to her.

"What is—?" she began, but fell silent at his urgent shushing motions. Her eyes widened as she read what he'd written. She rose to the occasion like a trouper. "All right, we'll go out," she said happily, though all the while her glance darted this way and that in search of the microphones he'd warned her about.

If we could spot them so easily, they wouldn't be a menace, he thought. He said, "When we go, why don't you put on that new gray fur hat you bought? It goes so nicely with your eyes." At the same time, he nodded vigorously to show her he wanted to be certain she did just that.

"I will. In fact, I'll fetch it now so I don't forget," she said, adding over her shoulder, "You should tell me things like that more often." She sounded more mischievous than reproachful, but he felt a twinge of guilt just the same.

The hat, a sturdy one with earflaps, had once belonged to a Red Army soldier. It wasn't feminine, but it was warm, which counted for more in a city full of scarcity and too near empty of fuel. And it *did* set off her eyes well.

They made small talk to kill the time Anielewicz had asked them to kill. Then Rivka buttoned her coat, put a couple of extra layers of outer clothes on Reuven—who squealed with excitement at the prospect of going out—and left the apartment with Moishe. As soon as they were outside, she said, "Now what exactly is this all about? Why are we—?"

While they walked to the stairs and then down them, he explained more than he'd been able to put in his note. He finished, "So they'll spirit the two of you away somehow, to keep the Lizards from using you to get a hold on me."

"What will they do with us?" she demanded. "Where will we go?"

"I don't know," he said. "Mordechai wouldn't tell me. He may not know himself, but leave the choice to people the Lizards won't automatically question. Though any rabbi would have a fit to hear me say it, sometimes ignorance is the best defense."

"I don't want to leave you," she said. "Running from danger while you stay in it isn't right. I—"

Before she could say *won't*, he broke in, "This is the best thing you can do to keep me safe, too." He wanted to say more, but by then they were at the entrance to the flats, and he couldn't be sure how much Yiddish or Polish the Lizard guards there knew.

Somehow he wasn't surprised when those guards, instead of staying at their post, started following him and his family. They didn't come right alongside as if they were jailers, but they never let the Russies get more than ten or twelve meters ahead. If he or Rivka had tried to break and run, the Lizards would have had no trouble capturing or shooting them. Besides, if they broke and ran, they'd wreck whatever plan Anielewicz had made.

So they kept walking, outwardly as calm as if nothing unusual were happening. By the time they got to the market, four Lizards trailed them and two more walked ahead; with their swiveling eyes, the aliens could keep watch without constantly turning their heads back over their shoulders.

Gesia Street, as usual, boiled with life. Hawkers loudly peddled tea, coffee, and hot water laced with saccharine from samovars, turnips from pushcarts. A man with a pistol stood guard over a crate of coal. Another sat behind a table on which he had set out spare parts for bicycles. A woman displayed bream from the Vistula. The weather was cold enough to keep the fish fresh till spring.

Several stands sold captured German and Russian military clothing. More German gear was available, but the Red Army equipment brought higher prices—the Russians knew how to fight cold. Rivka had bought her hat at one of these stands. Now, Moishe saw, even Lizards crowded around them. That made him abruptly move away.

"Where are we going?" Rivka asked when he swerved.

"I don't exactly know," he said. "We'll just wander about and see what there is to see." *Wander about and let Anielewicz's men see us*, he thought.

As if from a distant dream, he remembered the days before the war, when he could walk into any tailor's or grocer's or butcher's in Warsaw, find what he wanted, and be sure he had the zlotys to buy it. Compared to those days, the market on Gesia Street was privation personified. Compared to what the ghetto market had been like when the Nazis ruled Warsaw, it seemed cigar-smoking Wall Street capitalist affluence.

People surged this way and that, buying and bartering, trading bread for books, marks for meat, vodka for vegetables. The Lizards who were watching Russie and his family had to get closer to make sure their quarry did not somehow vanish in the crowds. Even then, they had no easy time because they couldn't even see over or through the taller humans who kept stepping between them and the Russies.

Moishe suddenly found himself in the middle of a large knot of large men. By main force of will, he made himself keep his face straight—a lot of them came from the ranks of Mordechai Anielewicz's fighters. Whatever happened would happen now.

One of Anielewicz's men bent down, muttered something in Rivka's ear. She nodded, squeezed Moishe's hand hard, then let go. He heard her say, "Come on, Reuven." A couple of burly fighters shouldered themselves between him and his wife and son. He looked away, biting the inside of his lip and fighting back tears.

A few seconds later, a hand joined his again. He spun round, half afraid something was wrong, half delighted he wouldn't have to be separated from Rivka and Reuven after all. But the young woman whose fingers interlaced with his, though a fair-skinned, gray-eyed brunette who wore Rivka's hat, was not his wife. Nor was the boy beside her his son.

"We'll wander around the marketplace a few more minutes, then go back to your flat," she said quietly.

Russie nodded. This impostor's coat was much like his wife's, the hat was hers. He didn't think the ploy would have fooled, say, SS men, but to the Lizards, one human looked much like another. They might well have recognized Rivka by her hat rather than her features—that obviously was Anielewicz's gamble, at any rate.

Russie's first urge was to crane his neck to see where the fighters were taking his family. He fought it down. Then he really realized he was holding the hand of a woman not his wife. He jerked away as if she'd suddenly become red-hot. He would have been even more mortified if she'd laughed at him. To his relief, she just nodded in sympathetic understanding.

But his relief did not last long. "Could we leave now?" he asked. "It's not only the Lizards, and it's not that I'm not grateful, but people will see us together and wonder what on earth we're doing. Or rather, they won't wonder—they'll decide they know."

"Yes, that is one of the things that can go wrong," the woman agreed, as coolly as if she were one of Anielewicz's rifle-toting fighters herself. "But this was the best way we could come up with to make the switch on short notice."

We! Russie thought. *She is a fighter, then, regardless of whether she carries a gun. So is the boy.* He said, "What's your name? How can I thank you properly if I don't know who you are?"

She smiled. "I'm Leah. And this is David."

"Hello, David," Russie said. David nodded back, as soberly as any adult might have. Moishe felt a stab of guilt at using a child to protect himself.

A short woman with curly gray hair pushed her way between the fighters around him. "*Reb* Moishe, I need to ask you—" she began. Her words trailed away as she noticed Leah was not Rivka. She backed off, her eyes as wide and staring as if Russie had sprouted a second head.

"That's torn it," Leah muttered. "You're right, *Reb* Moishe; we'd better go. I'm sorry for the damage I'm doing to your reputation."

"If I have to choose between my reputation and my family, I know which is more important," Russie said firmly, adding, "Besides, the way we gossip here, before long everyone will know why I'm playing this game." He spoke for Leah's benefit, but also eased his own mind because he realized he was probably right.

For the moment, though, what would spread was scandal. Before people started gathering around and pointing fingers, he and Leah and David left the market and strolled, not too fast and not too slow, back toward his home. The Lizard guards moving along in front and behind them were in a way a blessing, because they kept most folk from coming too close and puncturing the masquerade.

Russie's conscience twinged again when he closed the door to his flat behind him. Bringing a woman—a young, attractive woman—here . . . *shameful* was the mildest word he thought of. But Leah remained utterly prosaic. She took off the fur hat, handed it back to him, smiled without saying anything: she must have been warned the Lizards might be listening. She pointed to the hat, then to herself, and shrugged as if to ask how anyone, even a Lizard, could imagine she was Rivka if she didn't have it on her head. Then she walked out the door and was gone.

The simplicity of the escape took Moishe's breath away. The Lizards hadn't posted guards right outside the flat, only at the entrance to the building. Maybe they didn't want to act as if they were intimidating him, even though they were. Or maybe, as Anielewicz had said, they were just naive about how tricky human beings could be. Whichever was true, Leah, now that she was no longer disguised as Rivka, plainly intended to stroll right past them and off to freedom.

The boy David sat on the floor and played with Reuven's toys for a little while. Then he got up and stood by the door. Moishe opened it for him. He nodded again with that surprising gravity, then went out into the hall. Russie closed the door.

The flat seemed achingly huge and achingly empty now that he was here alone. He walked into the bedroom, shook his head, came out again in a hurry. Then he went into the kitchen and shook his head for a different reason—he was no cook, and now he'd have to feed himself for a while. He found some black bread and a slab of cheese on the counter. He picked a knife from the dairy service, made himself a sandwich. If he wanted anything fancier than that, he'd need to get someone else to fix it for him.

Of course, the Lizards might fix things so he wouldn't have to worry about food any more. He tried not to dwell on that. He went back into the main room, pulled out an old medical text on diseases of the large intestine. His eyes went back and forth, he turned pages, but he remembered nothing of what he read.

He slept badly that night. Rivka's bed next to his, Reuven's little cot, painfully reminded him his loved ones were not here. He was used to soft breathing and occasional snores in the bedroom with him. The silence their absence imposed on him somehow was more disturbing than a dreadful racket; he felt smothered in thick wool batting.

He ate more bread and cheese the next morning. He was still puttering around afterward, trying to figure out what to do next, when something clicked against the front door. Lizard claws tapping the wood in the quick little drum-rattle the aliens used in place of a knock.

Russie's mouth went dry. He'd hoped he'd have a full day in which to pretend to be making up his mind. But no. He opened the door. To his surprise, Zolraag himself stood in the hall, along with a large contingent of guards. "Excellency," Russie stammered. "I am honored. W-won't you come in?"

"There is no need," Zolraag answered. "I ask you one question, *Herr* Russie: will you speak over the radio as we desire and require of you?"

"No, Excellency, I shall not." Moishe waited for the sky to fall.

The Lizard governor remained businesslike. "Then we shall persuade you." His eyes swiveled toward one of the guards. "Your males shall now seize the Tosevite female and hatchling." He spoke, of course, in his own language, but Russie followed him well enough.

"It shall be done." The guard—officer?—hissed orders to the Lizards with him. One of them pointed his rifle at Russie, who stood very still.

"You will not interfere, *Herr* Russie," Zolraag said.

"I will not interfere," Moishe agreed.

Some guards went into the kitchen, others into the bedroom. All returned in short order. "The other Big Uglies are not here, superior sir, Provincelord," one of them reported. Had he been a man, Russie would have said he sounded worried.

"What?" the guard leader and Zolraag said together. The Lizard governor's eyes drilled into Russie. "Where are they?"

"Excellency, I do not know." Russie wished he could be as brave as Anielewicz's fighters, who seemed to go into combat without a trace of worry. If Zolraag had been angry at him before, he'd be furious now—but at least he could no longer vent that fury on the innocent. Russie went on, "As your male said, they are not here."

"Where did they go?" Zolraag demanded.

"I don't know that, either."

"You cannot deceive me as easily as you would hope," Zolraag said.

"The female and hatchling were observed to return to this dwelling with you yesterday. They were not seen to leave. Therefore they must be in the building somewhere." He turned to the guard officer with whom he'd spoken before. "Summon more males. We shall peel this hovel as if it were a *klegg*fruit."

"Provincelord, it shall be done." The guard spoke into one of the incredibly small, incredibly light radiotelephones the Lizards carried.

Watching him, Russie tried not to show the jubilation he felt. Whatever happened to him, Rivka and Reuven were out of Zolraag's clawed, scaly hands. The Lizards were welcome to search the block of flats from now until the Messiah came. They wouldn't find what wasn't there.

They made a good game try of it, though. Moishe didn't hear their lorries pull up, as he had too many times when the Nazis rumbled into the ghetto on a sweep. But the noises that came through his open doorway after the Lizards swarmed into the building were all too familiar—rifle butts hammering on doors, frightened Jews wailing as they were herded into hallways, overturned furniture crashing to the ground.

"Excellency, out of all the people in the world, we hailed you as rescuers when you came to Warsaw, and fought on your side against other men," Russie said. "Now you are doing your best to turn us into foes."

"You turn yourselves into foes by failing to obey," Zolraag answered.

"We were happy to be your allies. I told you before that being your slaves, obeying because we have to rather than because we think you are in the right, is something else again."

Zolraag made his unhappy-samovar noise. "Your effrontery is intolerable."

Time dragged on. Every so often, a Lizard would come in and report to the governor. Not surprisingly, the searchers had no luck. Zolraag kept right on sounding like a teakettle with something wrong with it. Russie wondered if he could have hidden his wife and son in plain sight. Maybe so. The Lizards had already shown they weren't any good at telling one human from another. What they were probably doing now was looking for anyone in hiding.

They did bring one little old man with a white beard up in front of Zolraag, but the governor knew enough to dismiss him as a likely spouse for Moishe. By late afternoon, the Lizards confessed failure. Zolraag glared at Russie. "You think you have won a victory, do you, Big Ugly?" He hardly ever hurled the Lizards' offensive nickname for humanity into Moishe's face. That he did so now was a measure of his wrath. "Let me tell you, you shall not prove the happier for it."

"Do what you like with me, Excellency," Russie said. "From your point of view, I suppose you have that right. But I think no one has any business taking hostages and enforcing his will through fear."

"When I seek your opinions, be assured I shall request them of you," the governor replied. "Until that time, keep them to yourself."

Russie tried to figure out what he would do in Zolraag's position. Probably stick a gun to the recalcitrant human's head, hand him a script, and tell him to read it or else. And what would he do himself in the face of a threat like that? He hoped for defiance, but was far from sure he could come up with it. Few men had within them the stuff of martyrs.

Zolraag was not quite so peremptory as he'd feared. The Lizard said, "I shall consult with my superiors, *Herr* Russie, over the proper steps to take in response to this unprecedented act of defiance on your part." He strode away, his retinue trailing after him.

Limp as a wet blotter, Russie sank down onto the sofa. *Unprecedented*, he decided, was the word that had saved him. The Lizards were not good at thinking on their feet, at knowing what to do when something failed to go according to plan. That didn't mean he was out of danger, though, only that it was deferred for the moment. Somewhere higher in the Lizards' hierarchy was a male who could tell Zolraag what to do. And Zolraag, Russie knew, would do it, whatever it was.

He went into the kitchen, ate more bread and cheese. Then he opened the door—the bathroom was down at the end of the hall. Two armed Lizard guards stood outside; they'd been so quiet, he'd had no clue they were there.

They marched to the toilet with him. Despite his indignant protest, one went inside and kept watch on him while he made water. Then they marched him back to the apartment. He wondered if they'd come in with him, but they didn't.

Still, they made sure he wasn't going anywhere they didn't want him to go. As Mordechai had said, they weren't stupid. He looked around the flat. He was trapped, awaiting sentence.

An hour outside Chicago. Crouched behind an overturned drill press in a shattered factory building in Aurora, Illinois, Mutt Daniels reflected that this was about as close to the Windy City as he'd come since he fell out of the big leagues thirty years before.

The noise he made was half laugh, half cough. Steam swirled from his mouth, thick as cigarette smoke. Even in a sheepskin coat, he shivered. Snow drifted down on him through holes in the roof. He kept his hands jammed in his pockets. If he happened to brush them against the frozen bare metal of the drill press, he knew it would strip off his skin like a scaling knife getting a bluegill ready for the frying pan.

Clanking outside in the rubble-strewn street. A few feet away, sprawled in back of a lathe, lay Sergeant Schneider. "That there's a Lizard tank," Daniels whispered, hoping Schneider would tell him he was wrong. But the veteran noncom just nodded. Daniels swore. "We didn't have to worry about these goddamn things when we were Over There in the last war."

"Too goddamn right we didn't," Schneider said. "And all the time then I thought things couldn't get any worse." He spat on the floor. "Shows what I know, don't it?"

"Yeah." Daniels' shiver had only a little to do with the cold that snuck into his very bones. He'd read about tanks since the new war began, seen them in newsreels. But until the Lizards turned the whole world upside down, he hadn't really understood what they did to fighting. It wasn't just that they picked up big guns and put them on tracks. Worse still, behind their thick armor, the crews that served those guns were almost invulnerable to infantry.

Almost. Mutt scuttled forward on hands and knees. If that tank—if any Lizard tank—forced its way to the eastern bank of the Fox River, the job of defending Chicago would take another step on the road to impossibility.

The tank's machine gun chattered, firing at one of the Americans defending Aurora or else at random to make humans keep their heads down. Combat here was house-to-house, concentrated; in fact, it reminded Daniels of the trench warfare he'd known in France. Aurora marked the western edge of the factory belt that spread out across the prairie from Chicago.

Fighting all the way into the big city would be like this—if anyone lived to retreat all the way into the big city. Mutt had his doubts about that. He'd had his doubts in 1918, too, but then he'd been on the side with more men and bigger guns. Now he was getting a taste of how the poor damned Boches must have felt as everything rained down on them.

The Germans had kept fighting like bastards right up till the Armistice. Mutt felt a similar obligation to keep going as long as he could. The front wall of the factory had been bombed not long before he holed up in it; its bricks were part of the rubble through which the Lizard tank was forcing its way. He crawled toward what had been a window opening and was now just a hole a little squarer than most. Knife-sharp shards of glass tore his pants and his knees.

Ever so cautiously, he peered out. The tank was about thirty yards east of him. It had slowed to shove aside some burned-out trucks the Americans were using as a roadblock. The commander had nerve. In spite of rattling small-arms fire, he stood head and shoulders out of his cupola so he could see what was going on around him.

His back was to Daniels. Mutt had grown up hunting squirrels and possums for the pot. He swung the rifle up to his shoulder, exhaled, saw the front of the Lizard's head explode in a red mist a split second before he threw himself away from his firing position.

"*Nailed* the son of a bitch!" he shouted through the din of gunfire and explosions. The other Americans sheltering in the ruined factory raised a cheer. Such a clear-cut cry of victory came their way too seldom. Had the Lizards had the numbers to match the might of their marvelous machines, Daniels knew the fight would have been long since lost.

Nor did he get more than a moment to exult in his successful piece of sniping. Bullets from the tank's machine gun lashed the factory building. He huddled in back of another broken power tool, grateful for the heavy chunk of iron and steel that shielded him from flying death.

"Good job, Mutt," Sergeant Schneider bawled. "You diverted him from the advance he was making. Taking us out doesn't mean a thing strategically."

Daniels wondered whether he'd be any less dead if he got killed in an action strategically meaningless. He didn't think so. "Damn shame," he muttered. He also marveled that Schneider could still think and talk like a professional soldier while being hosed down by machine-gun slugs.

Then there was a sudden hot yellow glare outside, as if the sun had come on in the middle of the street. The roar that accompanied it was loud, the *wham-crash!* of the shell from the tank's big gun even louder.

Chunks of brick rained down on Daniels; a timber that would have smashed him like a bug was instead smashed itself against the machine behind which he cowered.

The tank gave the factory two more rounds: *flash, boom crash; flash, boom, crash.* Mutt screamed for all he was worth, but couldn't hear himself or anyone else. He wondered if he'd ever hear anything again. At the moment, it was the least of his worries. He realized he'd wet his pants, but he didn't care about that, either.

When he tried to scramble away, his arms and legs shook so much he could hardly move. "Shell shock," he said, feeling the words on his lips but not hearing them at all. He'd seen men like this in the trenches after a good German barrage. Other soldiers would jeer at them, but not too hard—it wasn't as if the poor bastards could help themselves. He marveled at being alive.

"Hey, Schneider," he called, "you think them Lizards are fucking diverted enough for now?"

He didn't hear Schneider answer, but that was all right—he hadn't heard himself ask the question. He glanced over to where the sergeant had been hiding. Any further jokes stuck in his throat. The veteran was nothing but splashed blood and raw meat ground not too fine.

Daniels gulped. "Jesus," he whispered. Schneider was the best soldier he'd ever known—by a wide margin in this crazy war and, he thought, also better than any of the top sergeants he'd served under in France. One way you told good soldiers from bad was that the good ones lived to learn new things while the bad ones bought their farms in a hurry. Seeing a good soldier dead reminded you that you could end up the same way yourself. Mutt didn't want reminders like that.

He smelled smoke, sharp and fresh. It was a reminder, too, a reminder there were nastier ways to die than getting chewed to pieces by a storm of shell splinters. Schneider, at least, never knew what hit him. If you roasted, you'd have plenty of time to regret it. All at once, Daniels' shaky limbs worked, if not perfectly, then well enough.

He looked around the gloomy inside of the factory building—considerably less gloomy now that the Lizards had done some fresh ventilation work on the front—for the rest of the Americans who'd been in here with him. A couple of them weren't going anywhere: they lay dead as gruesomely as Schneider. Three or four others, as lucky as he'd been himself, were getting away from the fire as fast as they could. And a couple of wounded men flopped on the floor like fresh-landed fish in the bottom of a boat.

Both Mutt's grandfathers had fought in the War Between the States, and both, as old men will, told stories to the wide-eyed boy he'd been. He remembered Pappy Daniels, long white beard stained with tobacco juice, talking about the Battle of the Wilderness and how wounded men there had shot themselves before any of the little blazes all the musketry had started could wash over them.

That memory—one he hadn't called to mind in years—told him what he had to do. He hurried forward, grabbed one of the injured soldiers, and dragged him away from the spreading flames over to a tumbledown wall that might shelter him for a little while.

"Thanks," the fellow gasped.

"It's okay." Daniels quickly bandaged the worst of the man's wounds, then went back to pick up his comrade. He had to sling his rifle; the other fellow had passed out, and was a two-hand carry. He'd just taken him onto his shoulders when a Lizard infantryman skittered into the factory.

He was sure he was dead. After what seemed an age but had to have been only a heartbeat, the Lizard pointed the muzzle of its rifle to the floor, gestured with its free hand: *get your wounded buddy out of here.*

Sometimes—far from always—the Germans had extended that courtesy in France; sometimes—just as far from always—the Americans returned it. Daniels never expected to encounter it from a thing that looked like one of the monsters in the serials his ballplayers liked to watch.

"Obliged," he told the Lizard, though he knew it couldn't understand. Then he raised his voice to the men hiding somewhere in the ruins: "Don't shoot this one, fellas! He's all right."

Staggering under the weight of the soldier he'd lifted, he carried him back to the wall behind which he'd laid the other wounded man. At the same time, the Lizard slowly backed out of the factory building. Nobody fired at it.

The tiny truce held for perhaps half a minute. Mutt rolled the second injured soldier off his shoulder, discovered he wasn't breathing. He grabbed the fellow's wrist; his finger found the spot just on the thumb side of the tendons. No pulse. The soldier's arm flopped limply when he let it fall. "Aah, shit," he said dully. The strange moment of comradeship had gone for nothing, lost in the waste that was war.

More Lizards dashed into the building. They fired their automatic weapons from the hip, not aiming at anything in particular but making the Americans keep their heads down. Only a couple of rifle rounds answered them. *The fellow who shoots first has the edge,* Daniels thought. He'd learned that in the trenches, and it still seemed true.

All at once, he realized that with Schneider dead, he was the senior noncom present. He'd been in charge of more men than these as a manager, but the stakes hadn't been so high—nobody shot you for hanging a curve ball, no matter how much people talked about it.

The first wounded man he'd dragged to cover was still very much alive. "Fall back!" Mutt yelled. He started crawling away, dragging the hurt soldier after him. Stand up now and you'd stop one of those sprayed bullets just as sure as sunrise.

A beam crashed down behind him. Flames crackled, then roared at his back. He tried to crawl faster. "Over here!" somebody shouted.

He changed direction. Hands reached out to help pull the wounded man behind a file cabinet that, between its metal and the reams of paper spilling from it, probably could have stopped a Lizard tank round. Mutt got in back of it himself and lay there, panting like a dog on a Mississippi summer day.

"Smitty still alive up there?" asked the soldier already under cover.

Daniels shook his head. "For all I know, he could've been dead when I picked him up. Goddamn shame." He didn't say anything about the Lizard who'd refrained from shooting him. He had the strange feeling that mentioning it would take the magic away, as if it were the seventh inning of a building no-hitter.

The other soldier—his name was Buck Risberg—pointed and said, "The fire's holding the Lizards back."

"Good to know somethin' can." Daniels made a sour face. He was turning cynical fast in this fight. *I'm gettin' old*, he thought, and then, *Gettin'? Hell, I am old*. But he was also in command. He dragged his mind back to what needed doing right now. "Get Hank here out of this mess," he told Risberg. "There ought to be a medic a couple blocks north o'here, less'n the Lizards drove him out by now. But you gotta try."

"Okay, Mutt." Half dragging, half carrying the now-unconscious Hank, Risberg made his way out of the firing line. The burning beam helped light his way through the gloom, and also provided a barrier the Lizards hesitated to cross.

Shells screamed down on the factory and the street outside: not from Lizard tank cannon, these, but out of the west from American batteries still in place on Stolp's Island in the middle of the Fox River. The gunners were bringing the fire right down onto the heads of their own men in the hope of hitting the enemy, too. Daniels admired their aggressiveness, and wished he weren't on the receiving end of it.

The incoming artillery made the Lizards who were poking their snouts into the factory building stop shooting and hunker down. At least, that was what Mutt assumed they were doing—it was certainly what he was doing himself. But all too soon, even in the midst of the barrage, they started up again with nasty three- and four-bullet bursts that would chew a man to rags. Mutt felt as inadequate with the Springfield jammed against his shoulder as Pappy Daniels must have if he'd ever tried to fight Yankees toting Henry repeaters with his single-shot, muzzle-loading rifle musket.

Then from in back of him came a long, ripping burst of fire that made him wonder for a dreadful instant how the Lizards had got round to his rear. But not only did the Lizards usually have better fire discipline than that, the weapon did not sound like one of theirs. When Daniels recognized it, he yelled, "You with the tommy gun! Get your ass up here!"

A minute later, a soldier flopped down beside him. "Where they at, Corporal?" he asked.

Mutt pointed. "Right over that way; leastways, that's where they shot from last."

The tommy gun chattered. The fellow with it—not a man from Daniels' unit—went through a fifty-round drum as if he were going to have to pay for all the rounds he didn't fire off. Another submachine gun opened up behind Daniels and to his left. Grinning at Mutt's surprised expression, the soldier said, "Our whole platoon carries 'em, Corporal. We got enough firepower to make these scaly sons of bitches think twice about messin' with us."

Daniels started to say, "That's crazy," but maybe it wasn't. Out in open country it would have been; a tommy gun fired a .45-caliber pistol cartridge, and was accurate out to only a couple of hundred yards. But in street fighting or building-to-building combat like this, volume of fire counted for a lot more than accuracy. Since the U.S.A. couldn't match the Lizards' automatic rifles, submachine guns were probably the next best thing.

So instead of cussing the high command for a worthless brainstorm, Mutt said, "Yeah, some of the German assault troops in France carried those damn things, too. I didn't much care to go up against 'em, either."

The tommy-gunner turned his head. "You were Over There, were you? I reckon this is worse."

Daniels thought about it. "Yeah, probably. Not that that was any fun, mind you, but it's always easier bein' on the long end of the stick. And this here fightin' in factories—I didn't used to think they made anything worse'n trenches, but I'm comin' round to believe I was wrong."

An airplane roared by, just above rooftop height. "Ours," the tommy-gunner said in glad surprise. Daniels shared it; American planes were all too few these days. The aircraft pounded the advancing Lizards for a few seconds, machine guns bellowing. Then came another bellow, an almost solid wall of noise, from the ground. The airplane's engine stopped screaming; the machine guns cut off at the same time. The plane crashed with a boom that would have broken windows had Aurora had any windows left to break.

"Damn!" the tommy-gunner and Daniels said together. Mutt added, "I hope he came down on top of a whole pile of the bastards."

"Yeah," said the soldier with the Thompson gun. "I just wish he could have got away so he'd be able to hit 'em again tomorrow." Daniels nodded; he sometimes thought no American ever lived to fly more than one mission against the Lizards. Using up pilots as fast as planes was a losing way to do business.

The tommy-gunner squeezed off a burst in the direction of the Lizards. He said, "Corporal, I'll cover you if you want to slide away from here. You ain't much good in this fight with just your old Springfield."

Had he left off the second sentence, Daniels might have taken him up on the offer. But he discovered he had pride left to flick. He could think of himself as old and he'd already thought of his rifle as antiquated, but he wasn't about to let this punk kid tell him he couldn't cut it. "I'll stick," he said shortly.

"However you want it," the tommy-gunner said, shrugging. Mutt got the idea that only his stripes kept the kid from tacking *Pop* onto the end of the sentence.

The Lizards skittered forward, firing as they came. The flames that leapt from the burning beam lit them up but also helped screen their movements. Daniels snapped off a shot. A skitter turned into a tumble. He raised a Rebel yell his grandpappy would have been proud of. "No good in a fight, am I?"

The soldier beside him looked innocent. "Did I say something?"

The kid got up on one knee to fire, then went over backwards with almost the grace of a circus acrobat. Something hot and wet splashed Daniels. The flickering firelight showed red-streaked gray on the back of his hand. He violently wiped it against his trouser leg. "Brains," he said, shuddering. When he glanced over at the tommy-gunner, the top of the youngster's head was clipped off, as if by a hatchet. A spreading pool of blood reached toward him.

He didn't have time to be as sick as he would have liked. As far as he could tell, he was the forwardmost American still fighting. He fired at one Lizard—a miss, he thought, but he made the little monster duck—then whirled through a quarter-circle to shoot at another.

He had no idea what, if anything, that second round did. He did know that if he had to keep using a bolt-action rifle against what were in essence machine guns, he was going to get his ass killed—and the rest of him with it. He snatched up the tommy gun. The kid lying dead beside him was carrying another couple of drums of ammo, so he could use it for a while.

It bucked against his shoulder like an ornery horse when he opened up. He sprayed bullets hose-fashion out in front of him. The prolonged muzzle flash nearly blinded him before he dropped back behind cover. Hell of a way to fight, he thought—lay down a lot of lead and hope the bad guys walk into it.

It was, he realized, a hell of a place to fight, too: gloom-filled ruins lit only by fires and muzzle flashes, echoing with gunshots and screams, the air thick with smoke and the smells of sweat and blood and fear.

He nodded. If this wasn't hell, what the hell was it?

The hospital ship *13th Emperor Poropss—the Merciful* should have been a taste of Home for Ussmak. And so, in a way, it was: it was heated to a decent temperature; the light seemed right, not the slightly too blue glare that lit Tosev's third world; and, best of all, no Big Uglies were trying to kill him at the moment. Even the food was better than the processed slop he ate in the field. He should have been happy.

Had he felt more like himself, he might have been.

But when the Big Uglies blew the turret off his landcruiser, he'd bailed out of the driver's escape hatch into a particularly radioactive patch of mud. The detectors had chattered maniacally when males in protective suits got near him. And so here he was, being repaired so he could return to action and let the Tosevites figure out still more ways to turn him into overcooked chopped meat.

Radiation sickness had left him too nauseated to enjoy the good hospital food at first. By the time that subsided, his treatment was making him sick. He'd had a whole-blood-system transfusion and a cell transplant to replace his damaged blood-producing glands. The immunity-suppressing drugs and the others that resuppressed triggered oncogenes made him sicker than the radiation had. He'd spent a good many days being a very unhappy male indeed.

Now his body was beginning to feel as if it might actually be part of the Race again. His spirit, however, still struggled against the most insidious hospital ailment of all: boredom. He'd done all the reading, played all the computer simulations he could stand. He wanted to go back to the real world again, even if it was Tosev 3 full of large ugly aliens with large ugly cannon and mines and other unpleasant tools.

Yet at the same time he dreaded going back. They'd just make him part of another patched-together landcruiser crew, another piece of a puzzle forced into a place where he did not quite fit. He'd already had two crews killed around him. Could he withstand that a third time and stay sane? Or would he die with this next group? That would solve his problems, but not in a way he cared for.

An orderly shuffled by, pushing a broom. Like a lot of the males who did such lowly work, he had green rings painted on his arms to show he was being punished for a breach of discipline. Ussmak idly wondered what he'd done. These days, idle wondering was about the only sort in which Ussmak indulged.

The orderly paused in his endless round of sweeping, turned one eye toward Ussmak. "I've seen males who looked happier, friend," he remarked.

"So?" Ussmak said. "Last I heard, the fleetlord hadn't ordered everybody to be happy all the time."

"You're a funny one, friend, you are." The orderly's mouth fell open. The two males were alone in Ussmak's chamber. All the same, the orderly swiveled his eyes in all directions before he spoke again: "You *want* to be happy for a while, friend?"

Ussmak snorted. "How can you make me be happy?" *Except by leaving,* he added to himself. If this petty deviationist kept bothering him, he'd say it out loud.

The orderly's eyes swiveled again. His voice fell to a dramatic half-whisper: "Got what you need right here, friend, you bet I do."

"What?" Ussmak said scornfully. "Cold sleep and a starship ride back Home? And it's right there in a beltpouch, is it? Tell me another one." He nodded slightly while opening his own mouth: a sarcastic laugh.

But he did not faze the other male. "What I've got, friend, is better than a trip Home, and I'll give it to you if you want it."

"Nothing is better than a trip Home," Ussmak said with conviction. Still, the fast-talking orderly stirred his curiosity. That didn't take much; in the middle of stultifyingly dull hospital routine, anything different sufficed to stir his curiosity. So he asked, "What do you have in there, anyhow?"

The orderly looked all around again; Ussmak wondered if he expected a corrector to leap out of the wall and bring new charges against him. After that latest survey, he took a small plastic vial out of one of the pouches he wore, brought it over to Ussmak. It was filled with finely ground yellow-brown powder. "Some of this is what you need."

"Some of what?" Ussmak had guessed the male was somehow absconding with medications, but he'd never seen a medication that resembled this stuff.

"You'll find out, friend. This stuff makes you forgive the Big Uglies for a whole lot of things, yes it does."

Nothing, Ussmak thought, could make him forgive the Big Uglies either for the miserable world they inhabited or for killing his friends and landcruiser teammates. But he watched as the orderly undid the top of the vial, poured a little powder into the palm of his other hand. He held that hand up to Ussmak's snout. "Go ahead, friend. Taste it—quick, before somebody sees."

Ussmak wondered again why the orderly was sporting green stripes—had he poisoned someone with the stuff? All at once, he didn't care. The doctors had been doing their level best to poison him, after all. He sniffed at the powder. The smell startled him—sweet, spicy . . . *tempting* was the word that sprang to mind. Of itself, his tongue flicked out and licked the fine grains off the scales of the orderly's hand.

The taste was like nothing he'd known before. The powder bit at his tongue, as if it had sharp little teeth of its own. Then the flavor filled his whole mouth; after a moment, it seemed to fill his whole brain as well. He felt warm and brilliant and powerful, as if he were the fleetlord and at the same time in the bosom of the Race's deceased Emperors. He wanted to go out, hop into a landcruiser—by himself, for he felt capable of driving, gunning, and commanding all at the same time—and blast Big Uglies off their planet so the Race could settle here as it should. Getting rid of the Tosevites seemed as easy as saying, "It shall be done."

"You like that, friend?" the orderly asked, his voice sly. He put the vial of powder back into the pouch.

Ussmak's eyes followed it all the way. "I *like* that!" he said.

The orderly laughed again—he really was a funny fellow, Ussmak thought. He said, "Figured you would. Glad you found out it doesn't have to be a mope in here." He made a few haphazard swipes with his broom, then went out into the hallway to clean the next healing cubicle.

Ussmak reveled in the strength and might the Tosevite—herb, he supposed it was—had given him. He desperately wanted to be out and doing, not cooped up here as if he were being fattened for the stewpot. He craved action, danger, complication . . . for a while.

Then the feeling of invincibility started to fade. The harder he clung to it, the more it slipped between his fingers. Finally, too soon, it was gone, leaving behind the melancholy awareness that Ussmak was only himself (all the more melancholy because he so vividly remembered how he'd felt before) and a craving to know that strength and certainty once more.

Dull hospital routine was all the duller when set against that brief, bright memory. The day advanced on leaden feet. Even meals, till now the high points on Ussmak's schedule, seemed hardly worth bothering over. The orderly who took away Ussmak's tray—not the same male who'd given him his moments of delight—made disapproving noises when he found half the food uneaten.

Ussmak slept poorly that night. He woke up before the daytime bright lights in the ceiling went on. He lay tossing in the gloom, imagining time falling off a clock until at last the moment for the broom-pushing orderly to return arrived.

When that moment came, however, he was not in his cubicle. The doctors had trundled him into a lab for another in a series of metabolic and circulatory tests. Before he tasted the Tosevite powder, he hadn't minded being poked, prodded, and visualized by ultrasound and X-rays. None of it hurt very much, and it was more interesting than sitting around all day like a long-unexamined document in a computer storage file.

Today, though, he furiously resented the tests. He tried to get the technicians to hurry through them, snapped when they sometimes couldn't, and had them snapping back at him. "I'm sorry, landcruiser driver Ussmak," one of the males said. "I didn't realize you had an appointment with the fleetlord this forenoon."

"No, it must be an audience with the Emperor," another technician suggested.

Fuming, Ussmak subsided. He was so upset, he almost forgot to cast down his eyes at the mention of his sovereign. As if to punish him, the males at the lab worked slower instead of faster. By the time they finally let him go back to his cubicle, the orderly with the green rings on his arms was gone.

Another desolate day passed. Ussmak kept trying to recapture the sensation the powder had given him. He could remember it, and clearly, but that wasn't the same as—or as good as—feeling it again.

When the orderly did show up at last, Ussmak all but tackled him. "Let me have some more of that wonderful stuff you gave me the other day!" he exclaimed.

The orderly put up both hands in the fending-off gesture the Race used to show refusal. "Can't do it." He sounded regretful and sly at the same time, a combination that should have made Ussmak see warning lights.

But Ussmak wasn't picking up subtleties, not at that moment. "What do you mean, you can't do it?" He stared in blank dismay. "Did you use it all up? Don't tell me you used it all up!"

"As a matter of fact, I didn't." The orderly nervously turned his eyes this way and that. "Keep your voice down, will you, friend? Listen— there's something I didn't tell you about that stuff the other day, and you better hear it."

"What?" Ussmak wanted to grab the cutpurse or malingerer or whatever he was and shake the truth—or at least some more powder—out of him.

"Here, come on, settle down, friend." The orderly saw—would have needed to be blind to miss—his agitation. "Well, what you need to know is, this stuff—the Big Uglies call it ginger, so you know that, too—anyhow, this stuff is under ban by order of the fleetlord."

"What?" Ussmak stared again. "Why?"

The orderly spread clawed hands. "Am I the fleetlord?"

"But you had this—ginger, did you say?—before," Ussmak said. Suddenly, breaking regulations seemed a lot less heinous than it had.

"The ban was in force then, too." The orderly sounded smug. Of course, he had the green arm stripes to show what he thought of regulations he found inconvenient in one way or another.

Up until the moment his tongue touched ginger, Ussmak had been a law-abiding male, as most males of the Race were. Looking back on things, he wondered why. What had obeying laws and following orders ever gained him? Only a dose of radiation poisoning and the anguish of watching friends die around him. But breaking a lifetime of conditioning did not come easy. Hesitantly, he asked, "Could you get me some even if—even if it is banned?"

The orderly studied him. "I might—just might, you understand—be able to do that, friend—"

"Oh, I hope you can," Ussmak broke in.

"—but if I do, it's gonna cost you," the orderly finished, unperturbed.

Ussmak was confused. "What do you mean, cost me?"

"Just what I said." The orderly spoke as if he were a hatchling still wet with the liquids from his egg. "You want more ginger, friend, you're gonna have to pay me for it. I'll take commissary scrip, voluntary electronic transfer from your account to one I have set up, Big Ugly souvenirs that I can resell, all kinds of things. I'm a flexible male; you'll find that out."

"But you gave me the first bit of ginger for nothing," Ussmak said, confused more than ever and hurt now, too. "I thought you were just being kind, helping me get through one of those endless days."

The orderly's mouth dropped open. "Why shouldn't the first taste be free? It shows you what I've got. And you want what I've got, don't you, friend?"

Ussmak hated to be laughed at. The orderly's arrogant assumption of superiority also angered him. "Suppose I report you to the discipline-masters? We'll see how you laugh then, by the Emperor."

But the orderly retorted, "Suppose you do? Yeah, I'll draw some more punishment, and likely worse than this, but you, friend, you'll never taste ginger again, not from me, not from anybody else, either. If that's how you want it, you go ahead and make that call."

Never taste ginger again? The idea appalled Ussmak so much, he never wondered if the orderly was telling the truth. What did he know about ethics, or lack of ethics, among ginger sellers? Quickly, he said, "How much do you want?"

"Thought you'd be sensible." The orderly ticked off rates on his claws. "If it's just another taste you want, that'll cost you half a day's pay. But if you want a vial like the one you saw the other day, with enough ginger in it for maybe thirty tastes, that's a tenday's worth of pay. Cheap at the price, eh?"

"Yes." With little to spend his money on, Ussmak had most of it banked in the fleet's payroll accounting system. "Let me have a vial. What's your account code, so I can make the transfer?"

"Transfer it to this code." The orderly gave him the number, written down on a scrap of paper. "I'll be able to use it, but the computer won't pick up that it's mine."

"How did you manage that?" Ussmak asked, genuinely curious. Males could be bought, perhaps, but how did you go about bribing a computer?

The orderly let his mouth fall open again, but only a little: he wanted Ussmak to share the joke. "Let's say there's somebody who works in pay-rolls and likes ginger just as much as you do. I'm not gonna tell you any more than that, but I don't need to tell you any more than that, do I? You're a clever male, friend; I don't have to draw you a circuit diagram."

Well, well, Ussmak thought. He wondered how long this clandestine trade in ginger had been going on, how widely its corruption had spread among the Race, and whether anyone in authority had the slightest notion it was there.

Those were all interesting questions. None, though, was as urgent to Ussmak as getting his tongue on some of the precious powdered herb. Like any compartment in a starship, his cubicle had a computer terminal. He used his own account code to access his payroll records, transferred a tenday's salary to the code the orderly had given him. "There," he said. "Now, when do I get my ginger?"

"Eager, aren't you?" the orderly said. "Let's see what I can do."

Naive though he was, Ussmak belatedly realized the orderly might keep his money and give him nothing in return. If that happened, he resolved to tell the authorities about the ginger trade and take the cheater down into punishment with him. But the orderly, with the air of a stage magician producing a bracelet from someone's snout, handed him a vial full of what he craved.

He wanted to pop it open and start tasting it right then. Somehow, though, he didn't feel easy about doing it in front of the orderly: he didn't want the fast-talking male to see what a hold he had on him. He knew that was probably foolish; how could the orderly not have a good notion of how much he desired ginger? He held back even so.

He wondered about something else. "Suppose I start running out of pay but still want more ginger? What do I do then?"

"You could do without." The cold, callous ring in the orderly's voice chilled Ussmak. Then the fellow said, "Or you can find friends of your own to sell it to, and use what you make to buy more for yourself."

"I—see." Ussmak wondered about that. It might work for a while, but before too long, it seemed to him, every male in the invasion fleet would be selling ginger to every other male. He started to ask the orderly about that—the fellow certainly acted as if he had all the answers—but the male, having made his profit, left the healing cubicle without so much as a farewell.

Ussmak opened the plastic vial, poured a little ginger onto his palm as he'd seen the orderly do. His tongue flicked the precious powder into his mouth. And again—for a while—he felt powerful, clever, capable. As the wonderful sensation faded, he realized he'd do whatever he had to do to keep on having it as often as he could. Against that stark need, the careful planning that had been a hallmark of the Race for millennia suddenly was of small import.

If getting more ginger for himself meant peddling it to his friends . . . he hesitated. After the disasters that had befallen his landcruisers, few friends were left alive. But if he had to, he'd make more friends and then sell ginger to them.

He nodded to himself, pleased. He could still plan after all. Deliberately or not, he turned both eyes away from the shape of his plan.

■

Liu Han looked down at her belly. It did not bulge, not yet, but it would. Her homage to the moon had failed. Her breasts would never be large, but they felt tight and full; a new tracery of veins showed just below the skin. Her appetite was off. She knew the signs. She was with child.

She didn't think Bobby Fiore had noticed the absence of her monthly courses. She wondered if telling him she was pregnant was a good idea. She had no doubt the baby was his—given the way she was caged here, how could she? But she remembered how even her true husband had lost interest in her while she was carrying their child. If a Chinese treated her so, how would a round-eyed foreign devil react? She was afraid to have to find out.

Not too long after she began to worry, the door to her bare cubicle hissed open. Little scaly devils with guns escorted Bobby Fiore into the room. After so many trips where nothing untoward happened, she thought human guards would have fallen under the spell of routine. The scaly devils still acted as if they expected him—or her—to pull a gun out of the air and start shooting. They carefully backed out of the room, weapons at the ready all the time.

Liu Han got up from her mat, walked up to embrace Bobby Fiore while the door was still sliding shut. She'd long since resigned herself to the little devils' watching, knowing everything she did. Besides, she was starved for even the simplest contact with another human being.

His arms closed round her back. He kissed her. One hand slid down to cup a buttock. His manhood stirred against her hipbone. She smiled a little. Knowing he still wanted her was always reassuring. His mouth might lie, or even his hand, but not that part of him.

The kiss went on. He pulled her tightly to him. When at last he had to breathe, he asked her, "Shall we now?"

"Yes, why not?" she answered. If she did decide to tell him, what better time than when he was lazy and happy after love? And besides, what else was there to do in here?

They lay down together. His hands and mouth roamed her body. He was, she thought as she closed her eyes and let herself enjoy what he was doing, a much better lover than he had been when the scaly devils first put the two of them in the same cubicle and made them couple. She'd found ways to show him some of what she wanted without hurting his pride, while some he'd picked up on his own. All at once, she gasped and quivered. Yes, he'd learned quite nicely . . . and the hair of his beard and mustache added a little to what his tongue could do, something she hadn't imagined when she'd known only smooth-faced men.

He sat back on his haunches. "Again?" he asked her.

"No, not right now," she said after considering for a few seconds.

"Well, then," he said with a smile. "My turn."

She didn't mind taking him in her mouth. He kept himself as clean as he could with only warm water for washing, and she could tell how much pleasure she gave him. A sudden thought flashed through her mind: he'd been teaching her while she was teaching him. She'd never noticed till now.

His breath caught as she pulled back his foreskin. He was hot in her hand. But almost as soon as her lips and tongue touched him, she started to gag and had to pull away.

"Are you all right?" he asked, surprised. "What's the matter?"

Liu Han knew what the matter was. Just another proof she was pregnant, she thought. She hadn't been able to please her husband that way, either, not until she gave birth. Maybe that was one reason he'd ignored her so much.

"What's the matter?" Bobby Fiore said again.

She didn't know how to answer. If she told him and he turned cold to her . . . she didn't think she could stand that. But he'd find out before too long, anyway. She remembered how good having the initiative with Yi Min had felt, even if only for a little while (she also wondered, for a very little while, what the scoundrel was up to—something to his own advantage, she had no doubt). That memory helped make up her mind.

She didn't know how to say "baby" in English or the little devils' speech; she knew Bobby Fiore wouldn't understand it in Chinese. She sat up, used her hand to sketch the shape her belly would take in a few months. He frowned—he didn't get it. She pantomimed cradling a newborn in her arms. If that didn't put the idea across, she didn't know what she'd do.

His eyes widened. "Baby?" he said in English, giving her the word. He pointed to her, to himself, made the cradling motion.

"Yes, ba-bee." Liu Han repeated the word so she'd remember it. "Baby." She'd need to use it a lot in the months—in the years—to come. "You, me, baby." Then she waited to see how he would react.

At first, he didn't seem sure what to do, what to say. He muttered something in English—"Goddamn, who woulda thought my first kid would be half Chink?"—she didn't completely follow, but she thought he was talking more to himself than to her. Then he reached out and laid the palm of his hand on her still-flat belly. "Really?"

"Really," she said. She had no doubts. If she'd had any before (and she hadn't, not in truth), choking on him blew them away.

"How about that?" he said, a phrase he used when he was thinking things over. His hand slid lower, down between her legs. "Will you still want to . . . ?" Instead of finishing the question with words, he rubbed gently.

She wondered if he cared for her only because she gave him her body, but the worry that raised was more than balanced by relief that he did still want her. The other she could think about later. For now, she let her thighs fall open. "Yes," she said, and did her best to prove it when he climbed on top of her.

They separated quickly after he'd spent himself; the little scaly devils kept the chamber too hot for them to lie entwined when they weren't actually joined. Bobby Fiore kept staring at her navel, as if trying to peer inside her. "A baby," he said. "How about that?"

She nodded. "Yes, a baby. Not surprising, when we do"—she twitched her hips—"so much."

"I suppose not, not when you think about it like that, but it sure surprised me." Behind the hair that half masked him, his face was thoughtful. She wondered what was going on in his mind to make his eyebrows lower and come together, the slight furrows on his forehead deepen. At last he said, "I wish I could do more—hell, I wish I could do anything—to take care of you and the kid."

When he'd gone through the usual backing and filling to make her understand, Liu Han looked down at the smooth gray mat on which she was sitting. She didn't want him to see the tears that stung her eyes. Her husband had been a good enough man, but she wondered if he would have said as much. For a foreign devil to think that way . . . She'd known next to nothing about foreign devils before she was snatched up into this airplane that never landed, and Bobby Fiore was making her see that most of what she'd thought she knew was wrong.

"What is it?" he asked her. "What's the matter now?"

She didn't know how to answer him. "We both have to find a way to take care of—" As he had done before, she set her hand in the space between her navel and the small patch of short black hair that covered her secret place.

"Yeah," he said. "Ain't that a hell of a thing? How are we gonna be able to do anything at all for Junior, cooped up here like we are?"

As if to underscore his words, the door to the cubicle opened. A little scaly devil set down opened cans of food, then backed away from Liu Han and Bobby Fiore. She wondered if he thought it unsafe to turn around in their presence. She found that ludicrous, the more so as she knew herself to be so completely in the little devils' power. But the presence of armed devils in the doorway covering their comrade argued that they feared her kind, too. She thought that foolish, but the little devils always did it.

The food, as usual, was not much to her taste: some sort of salty pork in a square, dark blue tin, flavorless green beans, the little yellow lumps Bobby Fiore called "corn," and canned fruit in a cloyingly sweet syrup. She missed rice, vegetables briefly steamed or stir-fried, all the flavorings she'd grown up with: soy sauce, ginger, different kinds of peppers. She missed tea even more.

Bobby Fiore ate methodically and without complaint. This meal, like most they'd received, came from supplies canned by his people. Liu Han wondered if the foreign devils ever ate anything fresh.

Then another, more urgent, concern suddenly replaced that idle curiosity: she wondered if the pork and the rest were going to stay down. She hadn't been sick during her first pregnancy, but village gossip said every one was different. Saliva flooded into her mouth. She gulped. The tremor subsided.

"You okay?" Bobby Fiore asked. "You looked a little green there for a minute." Liu Han puzzled at the idiom, but he explained it a moment later: "You coming down with—what do they call it?—morning sickness?"

"I don't know," Liu Han answered faintly. "Please don't talk about it." While discovering that foreign devil women suffered from the same infirmity as Chinese was interesting, she didn't want to think about morning sickness. Thinking about it might make her—

She got to the plumbing hole just in time.

Bobby Fiore rinsed out the can the fruit had come in, filled it with water, and gave it to her so she could rinse her mouth. He put an arm around her shoulders. "I've got two married sisters. This happened to both of 'em when they were expecting. I don't know if you want to hear that or not, but they say misery loves company."

Liu Han did not understand all of what he said, which was perhaps just as well. She did appreciate the water; after she'd rinsed and spat a couple of times to take away the horrid taste, she felt much better. It wasn't like throwing up when she was ill: now that her body had done what it needed to do, it seemed willing to let her alone for a while.

"I wish the Lizards had a priest up here," Bobby Fiore said. "I want the kid to get brought up Catholic. I know I'm not the best Christian there ever was, but I try to do what's right."

Liu Han hadn't thought much of the Christian missionaries she'd seen in China. How to raise the baby was, however, the least of her worries at the moment. She said, "I wonder what the little scaly devils will do to me when they find out I am with child."

She did not think her fear was idle. After all, the little devils had snatched her from her village, then from the prison camp. While she was up here in the airplane that did not land, they'd made her submit to several men (and how relieved she was not to be carrying a baby by any of them!). They could do as they pleased with her, do whatever interested them ... without caring in the least what she thought about what they wanted.

"Whatever they do, they'll have to do it to both of us," Bobby Fiore said stoutly. She reached out and set a hand on his arm, grateful he stood by her. She would have been more grateful had she thought his brave words bore any relation to reality. If the little devils decided to keep the two of them in separate cubicles, what could he possibly do about it?

He said, "You ought to try and eat some more. You've got company in there, after all."

"I suppose so." Dutifully—but also cautiously—Liu Han ate a little corn, some of the beans, and even the last mouthful of pork left in the tin. She waited for her stomach to give them back, but it stayed quiet: having emptied once, it now seemed willing to relent. She hoped it would keep on being so forbearing.

Then, too late, she realized the little scaly devils would not have to wait until her belly bulged to learn she was pregnant. She'd grown so resigned to the moving pictures they made of her—not just when she was coupling but almost all the time—that she'd almost forgotten about them. But if the scaly devils could sort through the mix of Chinese, English, and their own language that she and Bobby Fiore spoke with each other, they'd know at once. And what would they do then?

If they were human, they'd have known when my courses didn't come, she thought. But the devils hadn't noticed that. Bobby Fiore didn't think they were devils at all, but creatures from another world. Most of the time, Liu Han remained convinced that was nonsense, but now and then she wondered. Could real devils be so ignorant of matters Earthly as her captors sometimes acted?

In the end, what they were didn't much matter. They had her—and Bobby Fiore—in their power either way. Liu Han wondered if any of the other women they'd brought up to the airplane that never landed were also pregnant. If they'd been used as she was, some probably were. She hoped so. She didn't want to face the ordeal alone.

She glanced over at Bobby Fiore. He'd been watching her; when her eyes met his, he looked away. *Wondering if I'll throw up again,* Liu Han guessed. She smiled wryly. What did a man know about a woman who was with child? Not much, which was why she hoped some of the others up here shared her predicament.

Then all at once she clung to Bobby Fiore, man though he was, foreign devil though he was, as she had not clung to him since the first day when he astonished her with his kindness. He might not know much about expectant mothers, but he was a veritable Kung Fu-Tze when set alongside even the wisest of the little scaly devils.

Smoke and a blast of heat greeted David Goldfarb when he walked into the White Horse Inn. "Shut the bloody door!" three people yelled from three different parts of the pub. Goldfarb quickly obeyed, then pushed his way through the crowd to get as close to the fireplace as he could.

The crackling wood fire, the torches that blazed in place of electric lights dark for want of power, took the White Horse Inn a long step back toward its medieval origins. Shadows jumped and flickered like live things, and puddled in corners as if they might creep out and pounce at any moment. Goldfarb had never been afraid of the dark, but these days he better understood why his ancestors might have been.

The reek of unwashed bodies was another step away from what had been the civilized norm. Goldfarb knew he added to it, but what could he do? Hot water was impossible to come by, and bathing in cold invited pneumonia.

Besides, when everyone stank, no one in particular stank. After a few breaths, the nose accepted the smell as part of the background and forgot about it, just as a radar operator learned to ignore echoes from the countryside in which his set was placed.

Had been placed, Goldfarb corrected himself. Ground-based radars had saved Britain against the Germans, but not against the Lizards. His own nervous forays in the belly of Ted Embry's Lanc continued. He hadn't been shot down yet, which was about as much as he could say for the project. The boffins were still trying to figure out whether the aircraft-mounted radar, used as intermittently as it had to be, helped them shoot down more Lizard planes.

Sylvia snaked her way through the crush. Smiling at Goldfarb, she asked, "What'll it be, dearie?" In the firelight, her hair glowed like molten copper.

"A pint of whatever you have," he answered; the White Horse Inn had never yet run out of beer, but it never got in the same brew twice running any more.

As he spoke, Goldfarb slipped his arm around the barmaid's waist for a moment. She didn't pull away or slap his hand, as she would have before he started climbing up into the cold and frightening night. Instead, she leaned closer, tilted her head up to brush her lips against his, and then slid away to find out what more drinkers wanted.

Wanting her, Goldfarb thought, had been more exciting than having her was. Or maybe he'd just expected too much. Knowing she shared her favors with a lot of men hadn't bothered him when he was on the outside looking in. It was different now that he'd become one of those blokes himself. He hadn't thought of himself as the jealous type—he still didn't, not really—but he would have wanted more of her than she was willing to give.

Not, he admitted to himself, that thinking of her bare under the covers didn't warm him when he sucked in frigid, rubber-tasting oxygen at Angels Twenty.

Her white blouse reappeared from out of the dark forest of RAF blue and civilian tweeds and serges. She handed Goldfarb a pint mug. "Here y'go, love. Tell me what you make of this." She took a step back and cocked her head, awaiting his reaction.

He took a cautious pull. Some of the alleged bitters he'd drunk since the Lizards came made the earlier war beer seem ambrosial by comparison. But his eyebrows went up in surprise at the rich, nutty taste that filled his mouth. "That's bloody good!" he said, amazed. He sipped again, thoughtfully smacked his lips. "It's nothing I've drunk before, but it's bloody good. Where'd our sainted landlord come by it?"

Sylvia brushed red wisps of hair back from her eyes. "He brewed it his own self."

"Go on," Goldfarb said, in automatic disbelief.

"He did," Sylvia insisted indignantly. "Me and Daphne, we helped, too. It's dead easy when you know how. Maybe after the war— if there ever is an after the war—I'll start my own little brewery and put a pub in front. I'd invite you there, if I didn't think you'd drink up my profit."

Goldfarb emptied the mug with a practiced twist of the wrist. "If you do as well as this, I'd surely try. Bring me another, will you?"

He kept staring after her once she'd disappeared among the acres of dark cloth. She was the first person he'd heard speak of what might be after the war since the Lizards came. Thinking of what to do once Jerry was beaten was one thing, but as far as he could see, the fight against the Lizards would go on forever . . . unless it ended in defeat.

"Hullo, old man," said a blurry voice at his elbow. He turned his head. By the list Jerome Jones had developed, he'd taken on several pints of ale below the waterline and would likely start sinking at any moment. The other radarman went on, "D'you know what I had with my spuds tonight? Baked beans, that's what." His eyes glittered in sodden triumph.

"Anything with spuds is reason enough to shout," Goldfarb admitted. Britain was hungry these days, not only because the island could not grow enough to feed itself, but also because Lizard bombing of the railway net kept what food there was from moving around the country.

"So you needn't feel so bloody smug about moving in with your bloody aircrew. Baked beans." Jones smacked his lips, exhaled in Goldfarb's direction. He didn't smell like baked beans—he smelled like beer.

"I'm not smug, Jerome," Goldfarb said, sighing. "It's what I was ordered to do, so I did it." He knew the other radarman resented not being chosen to take a seat aloft in the Lancaster; not only did he crave the duty (no one could fault Jones' pluck) but, being stuck on the ground, he still had no luck with the White Horse Inn's barmaids.

At the moment, he was probably too drunk to do either of them justice even if she performed a striptease in front of him and then dragged him into the bushes. He blinked, stared at Goldfarb as if he had no idea who his friend (former friend? Goldfarb hoped not, hoped his jealousy didn't run so deep) was. Then his pale eyes focused again. He said, "We had electricity in the barracks yesterday."

"Did you?" Goldfarb said, wondering where—if anyplace—the seemingly random remark would lead and wishing Sylvia would fetch him another pint so he wouldn't have to worry about it. Power had been out at his own quarters for several days.

"Yes we did," Jones said. "Electricity in the barracks. We had it. Why did I want to tell you that?" *As if I knew,* Goldfarb felt like shouting. But Jones, though his own mental railway net had taken some bombing, got his train of thought through. "I was listening to the shortwave, that's it. Got Warsaw in clear as day, we did."

"*Did* you?" The words were the same as before, but informed with a whole new meaning. "Was Russie on the air?"

"Not a word from him. Not a word." Jones repeated himself with owlish solemnity. "That's what I wanted to tell you. He's some sort of cousin of yours, what?"

"Yes, I'm afraid so. His grandmother was my grandfather's sister." No one had been more astonished than Goldfarb when his cousin surfaced as the Lizards' human spokesman. Unlike his gentile comrades, he'd believed most of what Russie said about Nazi horrors in Warsaw, though he remained unconvinced life under the Lizards was as invigorating as Russie painted it. Then, a few weeks before, his cousin disappeared from the airwaves as abruptly as he'd arrived. The Lizards had blamed illness at first. Now they didn't bother saying anything, which struck Goldfarb as ominous.

"Bloody traitor. Maybe the sod sold them out, too, and they put paid to him for it," Jones mumbled.

Goldfarb drew back a fist to smash him in the face—no one, he told himself, former friend, friend, or not, talked about his relatives like that and got away with it. But Sylvia chose that moment to return. " 'Ere now, David, don't even think of it," she said sharply. "You start the fight, you're out of the pub for good—them's the rules. *And* I won't see you any more."

The first threat was trivial. The second . . . Goldfarb considered, opened and lowered his hand. Sylvia put a new pint mug in it. Jones just stood, swaying slightly, not knowing how close he'd come to getting his features rearranged.

"That's better," Sylvia said. Goldfarb wasn't sure it was, but finally decided smashing a helpless drunk didn't count toward upholding the family honor. He emptied the third pint with one long pull. Sylvia surveyed him with a critical eye. "That should be about right for you, unless you want to get as lost as he is."

"What else have I to do?" Goldfarb's laugh sounded thick even in his own ears as the potent brew swiftly did its work. But the question, despite its sardonic edge, was serious. Without electricity, radio and the cinema vanished as amusements and reading through long winter nights became next thing to impossible. That left getting out among one's fellow men. And going up into the sky again and again to be shot at brought a need for the release only alcohol or sex could give. Since Sylvia was working to-night . . .

She sighed; it was not, Goldfarb thought, as if he were the first lover she'd seen who also had a need to get drunk—probably not even the first tonight. Resentment flared in him, then died. If he was out for what he could get, how could he blame her for acting the same way?

Jerome Jones nudged him. "Is she good?" he asked, as if Sylvia weren't standing beside him. "Do you know what I mean?" His wink was probably meant to be that of a man of the world, but the beery slackness to his features made it fail of its intention.

"Well, I like that!" Sylvia said with an indignant squeak. She swung round on Goldfarb. "Are you going to let him talk about me that way?"

"Probably," Goldfarb answered, which made Sylvia squeak again, louder. He waved his hands in what he hoped was a placating gesture. "You stopped a fight a few minutes ago, and now you want to start one?"

By way of reply, Sylvia stamped on his foot and then stamped off. He didn't figure he'd see that next pint, let alone the inside of her bedroom, any time soon. *Try and figure women,* he thought. He was no knight in shining armor, and she was a long way from being a maiden whose virtue needed defending. But if he'd said that, he'd probably have got a knee in the family jewels, not a spike-heeled foot on the instep.

Jones nudged him again. "Fight? What fight?" he asked, sounding more interested than he had been in how Sylvia performed.

Suddenly the absurdity of it all was too much for Goldfarb. He forced his way out through the crowd that jammed the White Horse Inn, then stood on the sidewalk wondering where to go next. The first breath of frosty air in his lungs, the nip of night against his nose, loudly insisted leaving had been a mistake. But he couldn't make himself go back into the pub.

The night was clear. Stars burned in the dark sky, more stars than he ever remembered seeing in the days before the blackout. The Milky Way shone like sparkling sugar crystals spilled across a black tile floor. Before the Lizards came, the stars had been friendly, or at worst remote. Now they felt dangerous, as any enemy's homeland would.

To the south, the gray stone pile of Dover Castle concealed some of those stars from view. The Saxons had had a fort there. When Louis VIII failed to take the place in 1216, it likely staved off a French invasion of England. Henry VIII had added to it, and more brickwork had gone up against another feared French invader, Napoleon. Later in the nineteenth century, a turret with a sixteen-inch gun was added to ward the port from attack by sea.

But the turret designers never foresaw attack by air. Goldfarb's own radar masts had done more to defend Dover, to defend all of England, from Hitler's wrath than all the stone and brickwork put together. Against the

Lizards, even the wizardry of radar seemed, if not futile, then surely inadequate.

A little red dot, fainter than a summer glowworm, came floating down St. James Street toward him. His hand twitched; he hadn't had a cigarette in it for a long time. With imports even of food cut first by German submarines and then by Lizard aircraft, tobacco had all but disappeared.

During the Depression, people had scooped cigarette butts out of the gutter to smoke. Goldfarb was never reduced to that, though the scorn he'd felt the first time he saw it had dwindled first to pity and then to acceptance. But that scavenging sprang from a shortage of money, not a shortage of cigarettes.

Now Goldfarb called to whoever hid behind that seductively burning coal, "Here, friend, have you got another fag you can sell me?"

The smoker stopped. The lit end of the cigarette glowed brighter for a moment, then moved as its owner shifted it to the side of his mouth. "Sorry, chum, I'm down to my last three, and I won't sell 'em: I couldn't use the money on anything I'd sooner have. But you can take a drag off this one, if you like."

Goldfarb hesitated; in a way, that struck him as worse than nipping up fag-ends. But the unseen smoker sounded kindly. Even if he wouldn't give up what he had, he'd share a little. "Thanks," Goldfarb said, and stepped quickly forward.

He held the single lungful of smoke as long as he could, let it out with real regret. The owner of the cigarette puffed again. In the faint crimson glow, his face was rapt with pleasure. "Bloody war," he said on the exhale.

"Too right," Goldfarb said. He coughed; however much he liked it, his body was out of the habit of smoking. "I wonder what we'll run short of next. Tea, maybe."

"There's a horrible thought. You're likely right, though. Don't raise a lot of bloody tea in the fields of Kent, eh?"

"No," Goldfarb said morosely. He wondered what he'd do when his morning cuppa ran out. He'd do *without*, was what he'd do. "What did we do before there was tea?"

"Drank beer, I expect." The smoker carefully extinguished the cigarette. "That's what I'm about to do now. Don't want to go in there with this lit, though. I've heard of men knocked over the head for a pipe's 'orth of tobacco, and I don't fancy it happening to me."

"Clever," Goldfarb said, nodding. "There's enough smoke inside already that no one will smell it on you."

"My very thought." Now the other man was just a voice in the darkness. He went on, "I might want to try and get close to that redheaded barmaid they have here, too—what's her name?"

"Sylvia," Goldfarb said dully.

"Sylvia, that's right. Have you seen her?" Without waiting for an answer, the smoker added, "I'd spend a cigarette on *her*, I would." He found the door to the White Horse Inn by ear, slipped inside.

Goldfarb stood out in the cold a few seconds longer, then started the long hike back to his quarters. He didn't think Sylvia could be bought for a fag, but what did it matter? She wasn't his now, and she'd never really been his. Slaking your lust was all very well—was, when you got down to it, better than all very well—but you had to be sensible about it. If that was all you were doing with a woman, stopping oughtn't to be the end of the world.

Far away, like distant screams, he heard the shriek of Lizard aircraft engines. His shiver had nothing to do with the cold. He wondered who was up in the night sky with a balky radar, and whether the chap would make it back to the ground again.

Antiaircraft guns began their almost surely futile pounding. Goldfarb shivered again. Losing Sylvia was not the end of the world. Off in the distance, he could hear the sound the end of the world made.

Off in the distance, antiaircraft guns yammered. Heinrich Jäger listened enviously. If the *Wehrmacht* had had guns like those, Red Air Force planes would have had a thin time of it indeed. Going up against the Lizards, the Red Air Force still had a thin time of it.

But, as the stutter of AA fire proved, the Russians kept coming. Jäger had found out about that, too, in the eleven months before the Lizards' invasion shoved the war between National Socialism and Communism onto the back burner. Now the Lizards were learning about Soviet stubbornness. Jäger hoped they enjoyed their education as much as he'd liked his.

Maybe the Russians hadn't lied when they told him his horse had served as a cavalryman's mount. It only twitched its ears at the distant gunfire. Of course, how it would react if he had to shoot from its back was anyone's guess. With luck, he wouldn't have to find out.

"The sons of whores should have put me in a plane," he said aloud, as much to hear the sound of his own voice in this snowy wilderness as for any other reason. The horse snorted. It didn't understand German; they'd given him a list of Russian commands for it. But it seemed glad to be reminded it was carrying a human. If ever there was a country for wolves, this was it.

Jäger slapped his lead-lined saddlebags with a gloved hand. They held the *Reich*'s fair share of the metal the partisan raid had stolen from the Lizards outside Kiev. And here he was, alone on horseback, carrying it to Germany.

"They want me to fail," he said. The horse snorted again. He patted its neck. "They really do."

When he and foul-mouthed Max made contact with a Red Army unit still in the direct chain of command from Moscow, the Soviets had been effusive in their praise and scrupulously exact in sharing out the precious booty Germans and Russians had combined to seize. Only afterward did things get difficult.

No, he'd been told, unfortunately air transportation wasn't available.

Yes, the Red Army colonel understood his urgent need to return to Germany. But did *he* understand how likely he was to be shot down before he got there? No, the colonel could not in good conscience let him risk his life by flying.

Now Jäger snorted, louder than the horse had. "When a Russian colonel says he won't risk a life, you know something's screwy somewhere." Against the Germans in the last war and this one, the Russian way of putting out a fire was to throw bodies on it till it smothered.

With knees, reins, and voice, Jäger urged the horse forward. He hadn't done much riding since before World War I broke out, but he still remembered the basics. It was a very different business from traveling by panzer. Inside that heavy steel turret, you felt cut off from the world and immune to whatever it might do to you . . . unless it decided to hit you with a shell, of course.

But on horseback, you met the world face to face. At the moment, the world was snowing in Jäger's face. The Russians had given him a fur hat, a padded jacket, and felt boots, so he wasn't chilly. Now that he was inside some of it, he discovered for himself how good Russian cold-weather gear really was. No wonder the Ivans had given the *Wehrmacht* such grief the winter before.

He leaned down, spoke confidentially into the horse's ear. "If anyone ever asks the Kremlin about this, they'll be able to say they gave me all the help they thought they could, but I just didn't make it back to Germany with this stuff." He slapped a saddlebag again. "But do you know what, Russian horse? I'm going to fool them. I'm going to get there whether they want me to or not. And if they don't like it, they can go piss themselves for all I care."

The horse, of course, had no idea what he was talking about. Not only was it a dumb animal, it was a Russian dumb animal. Till recently, it had been either pulling a plow for the enemy or carrying a Red Army cavalryman into action. But for the time being, its fate and his were bound together.

The snow muffled the animal's hoofbeats. Its body heat warmed the insides of his thighs and his rear end. His Panzer III, he remembered fondly, had had a heater that would warm all of him. On the other hand, he liked the horse's grassy smell better than the oil, petrol, cordite reek of the panzer.

"Yes, that's how the Kremlin wants it, horse," he said. "They needed German help to get this metal, but do they want the *Reich* to have the benefit of it? Not on your life they don't. They want to be the only ones who can make bombs like this, yes they do. They will use one on the Lizards, and if they beat the Lizards, wouldn't it be nice for them if they could hold one over Germany's head, too? But I already told you, horse, I don't intend to let that happen."

He peered ahead through the spattering snow. Unfortunately, what he intended to let happen and what would in fact happen were not necessarily one and the same. He didn't think he was inside what had been Soviet territory before the war any more, but rather in what was formerly Polish-held Ruthernia. Much of that land, after getting overrun first by the Russians and then by the Germans, was now in the Lizards' hands.

And here, as perhaps nowhere else on earth, the Lizards had their willing puppets—their quislings, the British would have called them, Jäger thought with wry amusement. In Moscow, he'd listened to Moishe Russie on the shortwave a couple of times. He'd judged the man a hysteric, a liar, and a traitor to mankind.

Now . . . now he was not so sure. Every time he tried to laugh off what the Jew said as just another atrocity story, he kept remembering the scar on the side of Max's neck and the Jewish partisan's obscenely embellished tale of slaughter and horror at Babi Yar. Much as he wanted to, he didn't think Max lied. And if Max's horror was true, then Moishe Russie's might be, also.

Riding a horse alone through winter gave you a chance to think, maybe more of a chance than you really wanted. What *had* the *Reich* been doing behind the lines of the territory it held? Jäger was a field-grade officer, not a policymaker. But German officers were supposed to think for themselves, not blindly follow superiors' orders like their Soviet or Lizard counterparts. He could not for the life of him see how massacring Jews moved the war effort forward even a centimeter.

Massacring Jews might in fact push the war effort back. It had driven the Polish Jews who survived into the Lizards' arms. A lot of those Jews lay between Jäger and the *Reich*. If they spotted him and let their new masters know a German was loose on their territory . . . if they did that, the Russians' scheme would be realized in full.

"Stupid," he muttered. What did Jews do in battle against the *Reich* except get in the way like any other civilians?

He rode by a deserted farmhouse, shook his head. So much devastation. How long would people take to recover from it? Even more to the point, on what terms would they recover? Would they be their own masters, or slaves to the Lizards for untold centuries to come? Jäger found no sure answer. Humanity had discovered ways to hurt the Lizards, but not to beat them, not yet. Maybe—he hoped—he held a way to beat them in his saddlebags.

The road he was following (actually, it was more of a track) took him into a stand of pale-barked birches a few hundred meters past the farmhouse. He unslung his rifle, set it across his knees. Unpleasant things and even more unpleasant people could lurk among trees. He showed his teeth in a not-quite-humorless grin. A few weeks before, he'd been one of those unpleasant people, or so the Lizards would have said.

A man stepped out from behind a tree trunk. Like Jäger, he wore a mixture of Russian and German winter gear; also like Jäger, he carried a rifle. He didn't aim it at the German, but he looked ready to use it. He said something in Polish. Jäger didn't know any Polish. He weighed his chances as he reined in. If he could get in a quick, sure shot—no guarantee while on horseback—then set spurs to his mount, he had a chance at getting away from this . . . bandit?

The fellow might have been thinking along with him. "I wouldn't try that," he said, now in accented German—or was it Yiddish? "Look behind you." Jäger didn't look. The man standing in the track laughed, leaned his rifle against the nearest tree. "No trick. Go ahead and look."

This time, Jäger did. He could see two men, both with guns. He wondered how many he couldn't see. He turned back to the fellow in front of him. "All right, you have me," he said equably. "What happens now?"

He didn't know which nonplussed the fellow more, his calm or his clear German. The man grabbed his rifle, a Mauser just like Jäger's. "I thought you were one of those Nazi bastards," he growled. "You don't ride like a Pole or a Russian. I ought to shoot you now." He *was* speaking Yiddish. Jäger's heart sank.

"Hold on, Yossel," called one of the men in back of the German. "We're supposed to take him in to—"

"If you're going to take me to the Lizards, do me the favor of shooting me instead," Jäger broke in. Here was his worst nightmare coming to life around him. If the Lizards made him talk—and who knew what the Lizards could do along those lines?—he might imperil the Russians' efforts with the stolen metal, and Germany's would never be born.

"Why should we do any favors for a German?" Yossel said. Jäger heard snarls from behind him. Here indeed was pointless cruelty coming home to roost.

But Jäger had an answer. "Because I fought alongside Russian partisans, most of them Jews, to get what I'm carrying away from the Lizards and bring it back toward Germany." There. It was done. If these were truly the Lizards' creatures, he'd just done himself in. But he was done in anyhow, the instant the Lizards found what his saddlebags held. And if his captors were men . . .

Yossel spat. "You're a fast liar, I give you that much. Where was this, on the road to Treblinka?" Seeing that that meant nothing to Jäger, he spoke a word of pure German: *"Vernichtungslager."* Extermination camp.

"I don't know anything of extermination camps," Jäger insisted. The men behind him growled. He wondered if they would shoot him before he could go on. He spoke quickly: "I never heard of this Treblinka. But one of the Jews in the partisan band came back alive from a place called Babi Yar, outside Kiev. He and I worked together for this common good."

Something changed in Yossel's face. "So you know of Babi Yar, do you, Nazi? Tell me what you think of it."

"It sickens me," Jäger answered at once. "I went to war against the Red Army, not—not—" He shook his head. "I am a soldier, not a murderer."

"As if a Nazi could tell the difference," Yossel said scornfully. But he did not raise his rifle. He and the other—well, what were they? soldiers? partisans? merely bandits?—talked back and forth, partly in Yiddish, which Jäger could follow, and partly in Polish, which he couldn't. Had the Jew in front of him looked less alert, Jäger might have made a break. As it was, he waited for his captors to figure out what to do with him.

After a couple of minutes, one of the men behind him said, "All right, off the horse." Jäger dismounted. His back itched uncontrollably. He was ready to whirl and start shooting at the least untoward sound; they would not find a passive victim, if that was what they wanted. But then the fellow he could not see said, "You can sling that rifle, if you care to."

Jäger hesitated. The invitation could have been a ruse to relax him for easier disposal. But the Jews already had him at their mercy, and no fighting man with even a gram of sense left an enemy armed. Maybe they'd decided he wasn't altogether an enemy, then. He slid the sling strap over his shoulder, asked, "What do you intend to do with me?"

"We haven't decided yet," Yossel said. "For now, you'll come with us. We'll take you to someone who can help us figure it out." Jäger's face must have said something, for Yossel added, "No, not a Lizard, one of us."

"All right," Jäger said, "but bring the horse, too; what he has in these saddlebags is more important than I am, and your officer will need to know of it."

"Gold?" asked the fellow who'd told Jäger to get off the horse.

He didn't want the Jews to think he was just someone to be robbed. "No, not gold. If the NKVD doesn't miss its guess, I have there some of the same kind of stuff as the Lizards used to bomb Berlin and Washington."

That got a reaction, all right, "Wait a minute," Yossel said slowly. "The Russians are letting you take this—this stuff to Germany? How does that happen?"

Why don't they keep it all themselves? he meant. "If they could have kept it all, they would have, I'm sure," Jäger answered, smiling. "But as I said, it was a joint German-Soviet combat group that won this material, and however much reason the Russians have to dislike us Germans, they know also our scientists are not to be despised. And so . . ." He slapped a saddlebag.

Further colloquy, now almost entirely in Polish, among the Jews. Finally Yossel said, "All right, German; if nothing else, you've confused us. Come along, you and your horse and whatever he's carrying."

"You have to keep me out of the Lizards' sight," Jäger insisted.

Yossel laughed. "No, no, we just have to keep you from being noticed. It's not the same thing at all. Get moving, we've already wasted too much time here on jabber."

The Jew proved to know what he was talking about. Over the next few days, Jäger saw more Lizards at closer range than he ever had before. Not one even looked at him; they all assumed he was just another militia-man, and so to be tolerated.

Encounters with armed Poles were more alarming. Although he'd grown a gray-streaked beard, Jäger was ironically aware he looked not the least bit Jewish. "Don't worry about it," Yossel told him when he said as much. "They'll think you're just another traitor."

That stung. Jäger said, "You mean the way the rest of the world thinks of you Polish Jews?" He'd been with the band long enough now to speak his mind without fearing someone would shoot him for it.

"Yes, about like that," Yossel answered calmly; he was hard to rile. "Of course, what the rest of the world still doesn't believe is that we had good reason to like the Lizards better than you Nazis. If you know about Babi Yar, you know about that."

Since he did know about that, and didn't like what he knew, Jäger changed the subject. "Some of those Poles looked like they'd just as soon start shooting at us as not."

"They probably would. They don't like Jews, either." Yossel's voice was matter-of-fact. "But they don't dare, because the Lizards have given us enough in the way of weapons to hurt them bad if they play their old games with us."

Jäger chewed on that for a while. The Jew frankly admitted his kind depended on the Lizards. Yet he'd had endless chances to betray Jäger to them and hadn't done it. Jäger admitted to himself that he didn't understand what was going on. With luck, he'd find out.

That evening, they came to a town bigger than most of the others through which they'd passed. "What's the name of this place?" Jäger asked.

At first he thought Yossel sneezed. Then the Jew repeated himself: "Hrubieszów." The town boasted cobblestone streets, three-story buildings with cast-iron awnings, and a central boulevard that had a median strip planted with trees, perhaps to achieve a Parisian effect. Having seen the real Paris, Jäger found the imitation laughable, but kept that to himself.

Yossel went up to one of the three-story buildings, spoke in Yiddish to the man who answered his knock. He turned to Jäger. "You go in here. Take your saddlebags with you. We'll get your horse out of town—a strange animal that stays around is plenty to make people start asking questions."

Jäger went in. The gray-haired Jew who stood aside to let him pass said, "Hello, friend. I'm Lejb. What shall I call you while you're here?"

"Ich heisse Heinrich Jäger," Jäger answered. He'd grown resigned to the looks of horror he got for speaking German, but it was his only fluent language—and, for better or worse, he *was* a German. He could hardly deny it. Stiffly, he said, "I hope my presence will not disturb you too much, sir."

"A Nazi—in my house. They want to put a Nazi—in *my* house?" Lejb was not talking to Jäger. The German didn't think he was talking to himself, either. Whom did that leave? God, maybe.

As if wound into motion by a key, Lejb bustled over and shut the door. "Even a Nazi should not freeze—especially if I would freeze with him." With what seemed a large effort of will, he made himself look at Jäger. "Will you drink tea? And there's potato soup in the pot if you want it."

"Yes, please. Thank you very much." The tea was hot, the potato soup both hot and filling. Lejb insisted on giving Jäger seconds; the Jew apparently could not force himself to be a poor host. But he would not eat with Jäger; he waited until the German finished before feeding himself.

That pattern persisted over the next two days. Jäger noticed he got the same chipped bowl, the same cup, at every meal; he wondered if Lejb would throw them away once he'd left, along with his bedding and everything else he'd touched. He didn't ask, for fear the Jew would tell him yes.

Just when he started to wonder if Yossel and the rest of the Jewish fighters had forgotten about him, his first captor returned, again under cover of darkness. Yossel said, "Somebody here wants to see you, Nazi." From him, unlike from Lejb, the word had somehow lost most of its sting, as if it were a label and nothing more.

An unfamiliar Jew stepped into the living room of Lejb's house. He was fair and thin and younger than Jäger would have expected for someone obviously important enough to be sent for. He did not offer to shake hands. "So you're the German with the interesting package, are you?" he said, speaking German himself rather than Yiddish.

"Yes," Jäger said. "Who are you?"

The newcomer smiled thinly. "Call me Mordechai." By the way Yossel started in surprise, that might even have been his real name. *Bravado*, Jäger thought. The more the German studied Mordechai, the more impressed he grew. Young, yes, but an officer all the way: those light eyes were hooded and alert, alive with calculation. If he'd worn German field-gray, he'd have had a colonel's pips and his own regiment before he hit forty; Jäger recognized the type. The Jews had themselves a hotshot here.

The hotshot said, "I gather you're a panzer soldier and that you've stolen something important to the Lizards. What I've heard from Yossel here is interesting, but it's also secondhand. Tell it to me yourself, Jäger."

"Just a minute," Jäger said. Yossel bristled, but Mordechai only grunted, waiting for him to go on. He did: "You Jews cooperate with the Lizards, yet now you seem ready to betray them. Show me I can trust you not to hand me straight over to them."

"If we wanted to do that, we could have done it already," Mordechai pointed out. "As for how and why we work with the Lizards—hmm. Think of it like this. Back three winters ago, Russia swamped the Finns. When you Nazis invaded Russia, Finland was happy enough to ride on your coattails and take back its own. But do you think the Finns go around yelling 'Heil Hitler!' all day long?"

"Mmm—maybe not," Jäger admitted. "And so?"

"And so we helped the Lizards against you Nazis, but for our own reasons—survival, for instance—not theirs. We don't have to love them. Now I've told my story, and more than you deserve. You tell yours."

Jäger did. Mordechai interrupted every so often with sharp, probing questions. The German's respect for him grew at every one. He'd figured the Jew would know something of war and especially partisan operations—he had him pegged for a high military official. But he hadn't figured Mordechai would know so much about the loot he carried in his saddlebags; he soon realized the Jew, though he'd never seen the mud-encrusted chunks of metal, understood them better than he did himself.

When Jäger was through (he felt squeezed dry), Mordechai steepled his fingers and stared up at the ceiling. "You know, before this war started, I worried more about what Marx thought than about God," he remarked. His speech grew more guttural; his vowels shifted so Jäger had to think to follow him—he'd fallen out of German into Yiddish. He went on, "Ever since you Nazis shut me up in the ghetto and tried to starve me to death, I've had my doubts about the choice I made. Now I'm sure I was wrong."

"Why now in particular?" Jäger asked.

"Because I would need to be the wisest rabbi who ever lived to decide whether I ought to help you Germans fight the Lizards with their own filthy weapons."

Yossel nodded vehemently. "I was thinking the same thing," he said.

Mordechai waved him to silence. "I wish this choice fell on someone besides me. All I wanted to be before the war was an engineer." His gaze and Jäger's clashed, swordlike. "All I am now, thanks to you Germans, is a fighting man."

"That's all I've ever been," Jäger said. Once, before another war, he'd had hopes of studying biblical archaeology. But he'd learned in the trenches of France what he was good at—and how much the fatherland needed folk with talents like his. Set against that knowledge, biblical archaeology was small beer.

"And so on us the future turns," Mordechai mused. "I don't know about you, Jäger"—it was the first time he'd used the German's name—"but I wish my own shoulders were wider."

"Yes," Jäger said.

Mordechai eyed him again, this time with a soldier's calculation. "Simplest would be to shoot you and dump your body into the Vistula. So many have gone in that no one would notice one more. Toss your saddlebags in after you and I'd never have to wake up sweating in the night for fear of what you damned Nazis were going to do with this stuff you've stolen."

"No—instead you'd wake up sweating in the night that no one could do anything to fight the Lizards." Jäger tried to keep his voice and manner calm. He'd hazarded his life often enough on the battlefield, but never like this—it felt more like poker than war. He tossed another chip into the pot: "And no matter what you do to me, Stalin already has his share of the loot. Will you also sweat for what the Bolsheviks do with it?"

"As a matter of fact, yes." Mordechai sighed, a sound that seemed to flow out from his whole body, not just his chest. "Better this choice should have fallen to Solomon the Wise than a poor fool like me. Then we would have some hope of a decision rightly taken."

He started to sigh again, but the noise turned into a sudden, sharp inhalation halfway through. When he looked at Jäger now, his eyes blazed. *Yes*, the German thought, *an officer indeed, one men would follow into hell.*

"Maybe Solomon shows the way after all," Mordechai said softly.

"What do you mean?" But even if he hadn't thought of archaeology in years, Jäger knew his Bible well enough. Of themselves, his eyes went to the saddlebags leaning against the wall. "You want to cut the baby in half, do you?"

"That's just what I want to do, Jäger," Mordechai said. "Just exactly. All right, keep some of what you have. You Nazi bastards are smart, I give you that; maybe you'll figure out what to do with it. But someone besides you and the Russians ought to have a chance with it, too."

"Whom did you have in mind? You?" Jäger asked. The idea of Polish Jews with such horror weapons alarmed him as much as the prospect of the Germans with them appalled Mordechai. These Jews had too good a reason to want to use it on Germany.

But Mordechai shook his head. "No, not us. We haven't the men, we haven't the research facilities we'd need to figure out what we'd have to do, and there'd be too many Lizards underfoot for us to keep the work secret."

"Who, then?" Jäger said.

"I was thinking the Americans," Mordechai answered. "They've lost Washington, so they know in their bellies this thing is real. For all we know, they were working on it already. They have enough scientists there—plenty who fled to America away from you fascists, by all accounts. And it's big, like Russia; they'd have plenty of places to hide from the Lizards while they figured things out."

Jäger thought about that. He had an instinctive reluctance to hand over strategic material to the enemy—but compared to the Lizards, the Americans were allies. And even in terms of purely human politics, the more counterbalances to Moscow, the better. But one large question remained: "How do you propose to get this stuff across the Atlantic?"

He'd expected Mordechai to blanch, but the Jew was unperturbed. "That we can manage, easier than you'd think. The Lizards don't trust us as far as they used to, but we can still move pretty freely through the countryside—and we can get to the sea."

"Then what?" Jäger said. "Put your saddlebag on a freighter and sail for New York?"

"You say it as a joke, but I think we could do it," Mordechai answered. "There's a surprising lot of water traffic going on; the Lizards don't automatically attack it the way they do trains and lorries. But no, I hadn't intended to put it on a freighter. We have ways of getting a submarine here without the Lizards' noticing. We've done it a couple of times already, and it ought to be good for one more run."

"A submarine?" *American?* Jäger thought. *No, more likely British.* The Baltic had been a German lake; a few months earlier, a British U-boat captain would have been suicidal to poke his periscope into it. Now, though, Germany had more urgent worries than British subs. "A submarine." This time, Jäger made it a statement. "You know, that might be crazy enough to work."

"Oh, we're crazy, all right," Mordechai said. "If we weren't crazy before the war, you Nazis made us that way." His laugh was full of self-mockery. "And now I must be crazier than ever, dickering to help Nazis make something that might be the end of the world. Only some ends are worse than others, eh?"

"Yes." Jäger felt just as strange, dickering with Communists and now Jews. Now that he was close to Germany again, he suddenly wondered how his superiors—and the *Gestapo*—would view his dealings since the Lizards blew his Panzer III out from under him. But unless the world had turned completely insane, what was in the lead-lined saddlebag would redeem almost any amount of ideological contamination. Almost.

"We are agreed?" Mordechai asked.

"We are agreed," Jäger said. Afterward, he was never sure which of them first stuck out a hand. They both squeezed, hard.

Atvar was busy checking the latest reports on how the Race was coping with the insane winter weather of Tosev 3 when a musical note from his computer reminded him of an appointment. He spoke into the intercom mike: "Drefsab, are you there?"

"Exalted Fleetlord, I am," came the reply from an antechamber. Of course no one would presume to make the commander of the Race's force wait, but formality persisted nonetheless.

"Enter, Drefsab," Atvar declared, and pressed a button on his desk that made it possible for the operative to enter.

The fleetlord hissed in shocked dismay when Drefsab came into the office. The investigator had been one of his brightest males, infiltrating Straha's staff to try to learn how the shiplord was spying on him and also dueling with Big Ugly intelligence agents who lacked his tools but made up for that with deceit unmatched even around the Emperor's court. He'd always been dapper and crisp. Now his body paint was smeared, his scales dull, his pupils dilated.

"By the Emperor, what's happened to you?" Atvar exclaimed.

"By the Emperor, Exalted Fleetlord, I find I must report myself unfit for duty," Drefsab answered, casting down his eyes. Even his voice sounded as if he had rust in the works somewhere.

"I can see that," Atvar said. "But what's wrong? How have you become unfit?"

"I took it in my mind, Exalted Fleetlord, to investigate how traffic in the Tosevite herb called ginger was affecting our males. I realize I did so without orders, but I judged the problem to be of sufficient importance to justify the breach in conduct."

"Go on," Atvar said. Males who did things without orders were vanishingly rare in the Race, though that kind of initiative seemed all too common among the Big Uglies. If this was what happened when the Race tried to match the Tosevites for sheer energy, the fleetlord wished his starships had never left Home.

Drefsab said, "Exalted Fleetlord, to evaluate both the traffic in ginger and the reasons for its spreading use, I deemed it necessary to seek out and sample the herb for myself. I regret to have to inform the fleetlord that I myself have fallen victim to its addictive properties."

Males of the Race's primitive ancestors had been hunters, carnivores. Atvar bent his fingers into the position that gave his claws the best opportunity to rend and tear. He did not need more bad news, not now. Tosev 3, and especially winter on Tosev 3's northern hemisphere, were giving him plenty of bad news by themselves.

He had to say something. He didn't know what. At last he tried, "How could you do such a stupid thing, knowing your value to the Race?"

Drefsab hung his head in shame. "Exalted Fleetlord, in my arrogance I assumed I could investigate, could even sample the illicit herb, with no ill effects. I was, unfortunately, mistaken. Even now the craving burns in me."

"What is it like, to be under the influence of this ginger substance?" The fleetlord had read reports, but his confidence in reports was not what it had been back Home. The report on Tosev 3, for instance, had made it sound like an easy conquest.

"I feel—bigger than myself, better than myself, as if I am capable of undertaking anything," Drefsab said. "When I don't have that feeling, I long for it with every scale of my skin."

"Does this drug-induced feeling have any basis in reality?" Atvar asked. "That is, viewed objectively, do you in fact perform better while taking ginger than without it?" He had a moment of hope. If the noxious powder turned out to be a valuable pharmaceutical, some good might yet spring from Drefsab's initiative.

But the agent only let out a long, whistling sigh. "I fear not, Exalted Fleetlord. I have examined work I produced shortly after tasting ginger. It contains more errors than I would normally find acceptable. I made them, but simply failed to notice them because of the euphoria the drug induces. And when I have not tasted ginger in some time . . . Exalted Fleetlord, it is very bad then."

"Very bad," Atvar echoed in a hollow voice. "How do you respond to this craving, Drefsab? Do you indulge it at every opportunity, or do you resist as best you can?"

"The latter," Drefsab answered with a certain melancholy pride. "I go as long as I can between tastes, but that period seems to decrease as time passes. And I am also at less than maximum effectiveness in the black interval between tastes."

"Yes." Although with regret, Atvar's thoughts now turned purely pragmatic: how could he get the best use out of this irrevocably damaged male? Decision came quickly. "If you find yourself more valuable to the Race than without taking it, use it at whatever level you find necessary for your continued function. Ignore all else. I so order you, for the good of the Race."

"It shall be done, Exalted Fleetlord," Drefsab whispered.

Atvar went on, "I further order you to record in diary form all your reactions to this ginger. Physicians' views of the problem are necessarily external; your analysis from the ginger user's perspective will furnish them valuable data."

"It shall be done," Drefsab repeated, more heartily now.

"Further, continue your investigation into the trafficking in this drug. Bring down as many of those involved in the foul trade as you can."

"It shall be done, Exalted Fleetlord," Drefsab said for the third time. For a moment, he sounded like the keen young male, the hunting *solmek*, he had always been for Atvar. But then he wilted before the fleetlord's eyes, asking piteously, "Exalted Fleetlord, if I bring them all down, whence shall my further supply of ginger come?"

Atvar hid his disgust. "Seize all you need to ensure your own stock for as long as you wish to continue your habit," he said, reasoning that

Drefsab on ginger was likely to make a better agent than he would pining for the herb, and was also likely to remain a better agent than any male, no matter how sober, he appointed in his place. To salve his conscience, Atvar added, "Our physicians will continue to seek a cure for this Tosevite herb. Spirits of dead Emperors grant they find it soon."

"Aye, Exalted Fleetlord. Even now, I crave—" With a shudder, Drefsab broke off in the middle of the sentence. "Have I the Exalted Fleetlord's gracious leave to depart?"

"Yes, go on, Drefsab, and may Emperors past look kindly on you."

Drefsab's salute was ragged, but the male seemed to pull himself together as he left the fleetlord's office. If nothing else, Atvar had imbued him with fresh purpose. The fleetlord himself was depressed as he returned to his paperwork. *I hate this cursed world*, he thought. *One way or another, it is made only for driving the Race mad.*

His treatment of Drefsab left him no happier. Subordinate males owed their superiors obedience; superiors, in turn, were bound to grant those males under them support and consideration. Instead, he'd treated Drefsab exactly as he would have handled a useful but inexpensive tool: he'd seen the cracks, but he'd go on using it till it broke, then worry about acquiring another one.

Back Home, he'd not have used a male so. Back Home, he had luxuries long forgotten on Tosev 3, not least among them time to think. The Race made it a point never to do anything without due reflection. When you planned in terms of millennia, what was a day—or a year—more or less? But the Big Uglies did not work that way, and forced haste and change on him because they were so cursedly mutable themselves.

"They've corrupted me along with Drefsab," he said mournfully, and went back to work.

"What is this thing, anyway?" Sam Yeager asked as he lifted a piece of lab apparatus off a table and stuck it in a cardboard box.

"A centrifuge," Enrico Fermi answered, which left Yeager little wiser than he had been before. The Nobel laureate crumpled old newspaper—not much in the way of new newspaper around these days—and padded the box with it.

"Don't they have, uh, centrifuges where we're going?" Yeager said.

Fermi threw his hands in the air in a gesture that reminded Yeager of Bobby Fiore. "Who knows what they have? The more we are able to bring, the less we shall have to rely on that which is and remains uncertain."

"That's true, Professor, but the more we bring, the slower we're liable to move and the bigger the target we make for the Lizards."

"What you say is so, but it is also a chance we must take. If, having relocated, we cannot perform the work required of us, we might as well have stayed here in Chicago. We flee not just as individuals, but as an operating laboratory," Fermi said.

"You're the boss." Yeager closed the box, sealed it with masking tape, pulled a grease pencil out of his shirt pocket. "How do you spell 'centrifuge?' " When Fermi told him, he wrote it on the top and two sides of the box in big black letters.

He ran out of tape while sealing another centrifuge, so he went down the hall to see if he could snag another roll. The supply room had plenty; these days, the Metallurgical Laboratory got the best of whatever was left in Chicago. He was heading back to give Fermi more help when Barbara Larssen came out of a nearby room. The frosted glass window in the door from which she emerged was striped with tape to keep splinters from flying if a bomb hit nearby.

"Hi, Sam," Barbara said. "How's it going?"

"Not bad," he answered, pausing for a moment. "Tired. How about you?"

"About the same." She looked tired. From somewhere, she'd got hold of some face powder, but it couldn't hide the dark circles under her eyes. The slump in her shoulders had nothing to do with the stack of file folders she carried. It spoke more of not enough sleep, too much work, too much fear.

Yeager hesitated, then asked, "Any good news?"

"About Jens, you mean?" Barbara shook her head. "I've just about given up. Oh, I still go through the motions: I just now left a note with Andy Reilly—do you know Andy?—saying where we were going to give to Jens in case he ever does come back."

"The janitor, you mean? Sure, I know Andy. That's a good idea; he's reliable," Yeager said. "Where *are* we going? Nobody's bothered to tell me. Of course, I'm just a cook and bottle-washer around here, so it's not surprising."

"Denver," Barbara said. "If we can get there."

"Denver," Sam repeated. "Yeah, I played there. I was with Omaha, I think." That had been in the days before he broke his ankle, when the Class A Western League was a step up on a road he hoped would lead to the big leagues. Somehow he'd stayed even when he knew the road went nowhere. He shook his head, forcing his thoughts back to the here-and-now. "Why Denver? We'll have the devil's own time getting there from here."

"I think that's part of the idea," Barbara said. "The Lizards haven't bothered it much, especially since winter started. We'll be safer there, with a better chance to work . . . if, as I said, we can get there."

Yeager noticed that *as I said*. From his lips, it would have come out *like I said*. But then, he hadn't done graduate work in English. They probably ran you out of the university on a rail if you used bad grammar; it had to be a sin on the order of trying to go from second to third on a ball hit too short. He snorted. He still had baseball on the brain.

Barbara said, "Listen, I'd better take these downstairs." She hefted the folders.

"I've got to get back to it, too," Yeager said. "You take care of yourself, you hear? I'll see you on the convoy."

"Okay, Sam. Thanks." She walked down the corridor toward the stairway. Sam's eyes followed her. Too bad about her husband, he thought. Now even she'd started admitting to herself that he wasn't coming back. But even worn as she was, she remained too pretty, and too nice, to stay a widow forever. Yeager told himself he'd do something about that, if and when he got the chance.

Not now. Back to work. He taped up the second centrifuge box, then, grunting, piled both of them onto a dolly. He set the sole of his Army boot against the bar in the back, tilted the dolly into the carrying position. He'd learned the trick as a moving man one off-season. He'd learned how to get a loaded dolly downstairs, too: backwards was slower, but a lot safer. And from what Fermi said, every gadget here had to be treated as irreplaceable.

He was sweating from effort and concentration both by the time he got down to ground level. Camouflage netting covered a large expanse of lawn in front of Eckhart Hall. Under it, with luck concealed from Lizard fighter-bombers, huddled a motley collection of Army trucks, moving vans, stakebed pickups, buses, and private cars. Uniformed guards with loaded rifles and fixed bayonets surrounded them, not so much to keep them from being stolen as from having their gas tanks siphoned dry. They were all full up, and in war-ravaged Chicago gasoline was more precious than rubies.

He didn't begin to understand all the things people were stowing in them. One olive-drab Studebaker truck was full of nothing but blocks of black, smeary stuff, each with a number neatly stenciled onto the end. It was as if somebody had taken apart a three-dimensional jigsaw puzzle and planned on putting it back together once he got to Colorado. But what was the thing *for*?

He turned and asked one of the men who'd got stuck behind him in a stairway traffic jam. The fellow said, "It's graphite, to moderate the pile, slow down neutrons so uranium atoms have a better chance of capturing them."

"Oh." The answer left Yeager less than enlightened. He clicked his tongue against the roof of his mouth. Not for the first time, he found that reading science fiction, while it put him ahead of where he would have been without it, didn't magically turn him into a physicist. Too bad.

Barbara came outside with another load of file folders. Yeager went back and gave the graphite blocks another look so he could walk back upstairs with her. If she noticed what he was doing, she didn't complain, but let him fall into step beside her.

They'd just got to the doorway when antiaircraft guns began to pound off to the west. In moments, the noise spread through the city. Above it, through it, came the scream of Lizard planes' jet engines, and then the flat, hard *cruump!* of bombs going off. Barbara bit her lip. "Those are close," she said.

"Mile, maybe two, north," Yeager said. Like everyone else in Chicago, he'd become a connoisseur of explosions. He put a hand on Barbara's shoulder, happy for the excuse to touch her. "You get under a roof. Shrapnel'll start falling any minute, and you aren't wearing a tin hat." He rapped his own helmet with his knuckles.

Right on cue, pieces of antiaircraft shell casing pattered down like hail. Barbara scurried inside Eckhart Hall—you didn't want to be under one when it landed. She said, "Those were between here and Navy Pier. I hope they don't fubar the evacuation route."

"I hope they don't, too." Sam stopped and stared. "You," he said severely, "have been listening to too many soldiers."

"What? Oh." Barbara's eyes widened in a good simulation of innocence. "It means 'fouled up beyond all recognition,' doesn't it?"

"Fouled up. Yeah. Right. Among other things." The noise Yeager made was half cough, half chuckle. Barbara stuck out her tongue at him. Laughing, they climbed the stairs together.

More Lizard planes hit Chicago that afternoon, and more again after night fell. They hadn't pounded the city so hard in a while. Yeager wished for bad weather, which sometimes kept the enemy away. Faint in the distance, he heard the wailing siren of a fire engine that still had fuel. He wondered if the firemen would find any water pressure when they got where they were going.

By the next morning, the loading was done. Yeager was crammed into a bus along with a bunch of boxes that could have held anything, a couple of other soldiers—and with Ullhass and Ristin. The two Lizard POWs were coming along to Denver for whatever help they could give the Met Lab project. Though swaddled in Navy peacoats that hung like tents on their slight frames, they still shivered. The bus had several broken windows; it was as cold inside as out.

All over the lawn, men grumbled about the cut fingers and mashed toes they'd gotten loading the convoy. Then, one after another, engines started up. The roar and vibration sank deep into Yeager's bones. Soon he'd be on the road again. After God only knew how many trips between towns, getting rolling felt good, felt normal. Maybe he was a nomad by nature.

Diesel and gasoline fumes wafted into the bus. Yeager coughed. He didn't remember the stink being so bad. But then, lately he hadn't smelled it much. Not a lot was on the roads these days to make a stink.

Inside of two gear changes, Yeager was convinced he had more business behind the wheel than the clod driving the bus. *No*, he thought with a touch of pride, *any fool can drive*. Guarding the Lizards was more important to the war effort.

The convoy rumbled north up University to Fifty-first, then swung left one vehicle at a time. The streets were mostly clear of debris and not too bumpy; rammed earth and rubble filled bomb craters and the subsidence caused by ruptured water mains. The sidewalks were something else again—bulldozers and pick-and-shovel crews had shoved up onto them all the garbage that had clogged the streets. These trucks were going to get through no matter what.

To help make sure it got through, soldiers had nests in the rubble and stood menacingly at streetcorners. Here and there, colored faces, eyes huge and white within them, stared at the passing traffic from windows of houses and apartment buildings. Bronzeville, Chicago's black belt, began bare blocks from the university and indeed almost lapped around it. The government feared its Negro citizens only a little less than it feared the Lizards.

Before the aliens came, a quarter of a million people had been jammed into Bronzeville's six square miles. A lot fewer than that were there now, but the district still showed the signs of crowding and poverty: the storefront churches, the shops advertising mystic potions and charms, the little lunch counters whose windows (those that hadn't blown out) advertised chitlins and sweet potato pie, hot fish and mustard greens. Poor man's fare, yes, and poor black man's fare to boot, but the thought of fresh greens and hot fish was plenty to set Yeager's stomach rumbling. He'd been living out of cans too long. That was even worse than the greasy spoons he'd haunted as he bounced from one minor-league town to the next. Some of those diners— He hadn't thought anything could be worse.

"Why we leave this place where we so long stay?" Ristin said. "I like this place, as much as can like any place on this cold, cold world. Where we go now is warmer?" He and Ullhass both swiveled their eyes toward Yeager, waiting hopefully on his reply.

They squeaked in disappointment when he said, "No, I don't think it will be much warmer." He didn't have the heart to tell them it would be colder for a while: once on the Great Lakes, they'd almost certainly sail north and then west, because the Lizards held big stretches of Indiana and Ohio and controlled most of the Mississippi valley. The colder the country, the better, as far as evading them went.

Yeager continued, "As for why we're leaving, we're tired of having your people drop bombs on us, that's why."

"We tired of that, too," Ullhass said. He'd learned to nod like a human being to emphasize his words. So had Ristin. Their heads bobbed up and down together.

"I wasn't real fond of it myself," Yeager said, adding the Lizards' emphatic cough; he liked the way it served as a vocal exclamation point. His two charges let their mouths fall open. They thought his accent was funny. It probably was. He laughed a little, too. He and Ullhass and Ristin had rubbed off on one another more than he would have imagined possible back when he became their link to humankind.

The convoy chugged past the domed Byzantine bulk of Temple Isaiah Israel, then past Washington Park, bare-branched and brown and dappled with snow. It swung right onto Michigan Avenue, picking up speed as it went. There were advantages to being the only traffic on the road and not having to worry about stop lights.

Though it was winter, though the Lizards had cut off most rail and truck transport into Chicago, the stink of the stockyards lingered. Wrinkling his nose, Yeager tried to imagine what it had been like on a muggy summer afternoon. No wonder colored folk had taken over Bronzeville—they usually ended up settling in places no one else much wanted.

He also wondered that Jens and Barbara Larssen had chosen to get an apartment somewhere near here. Maybe they hadn't known Chicago well when they moved, maybe they wanted to be close to the university for the sake of his work, but Yeager still thought Barbara lucky to have had no trouble getting back and forth each day.

At the corner of Michigan and Forty-seventh, a sign proudly proclaimed, MICHIGAN BOULEVARD GARDEN APARTMENTS. The brick buildings looked as if they held more people than some of the towns Yeager had played for. One of them had taken a bomb hit and fallen in on itself. More bomb craters scarred the gardens and courts around the apartments. Skinny colored kids ran back and forth, running like banshees.

"What they do?" Ristin asked.

"Probably playing Lizards and Americans," Sam answered. "It could be cowboys and Indians, though." He spent the next few minutes trying to get the alien to understand what cowboys and Indians were, to say nothing of why they were part of a game. He didn't think he had much luck.

The convoy kept rolling north up Michigan Avenue. Before long, though, the bus Yeager was riding slowed, then stopped. "What the hell's goin' on?" the driver said. "This was supposed to be a straight shot."

"It's the Army," one of the other passengers explained. "The next time something goes just according to plan will be the first." The fellow wore a major's gold oak leaves, so no one presumed to argue with him. Besides, he was obviously right.

After a minute or so, the bus started rolling again, more slowly now. Yeager leaned out into the aisle to peer through the front windows. At the corner of Michigan and Eleventh, soldiers waved vehicle after vehicle onto the latter street.

The driver opened the front door with a hiss of compressed air. "What got screwed up now?" he called to one of the men on traffic-cop duty. "Why you movin' us offa Michigan?"

The soldier jerked a thumb back over his shoulder. "You can't get through no more on Michigan. The goddamn Lizards knocked down the Stevens Hotel this morning, and they're still clearin' the bricks and shit away."

"So what am I supposed to do now?"

"Go over a block, then up Wabash to Lake. You can get back onto Michigan there."

"Okay," the driver said, and swung through the turn. No sooner had he rolled past the Woman's Club Building than more soldiers waved him right onto Wabash, one block west. St. Mary's Church there had had its spire blown off; the cross that had topped it lay half on the sidewalk, half in the gutter.

Since Wabash hadn't been cleared to let the convoy get through, the going was slow and bumpy. Once the bus had to jounce up onto the sidewalk to get around a crater in the road. Two empty gas stations, one Shell, the other Sinclair, stood across the street from each other at Wabash and Balbo. A dusty sign in front of the Sinclair station advertised its regular gasoline, six gallons for ninety-eight cents, tax paid. A fifteen-foot-tall plywood cutout of a waving man in a parking attendant's uniform plugged the parking lot next to the gas station: twenty-five cents for one hour or less (SAT. NITE 50¢ AFTER 6 P.M.). But for parked cars and rubble, the lot was empty.

Yeager shook his head. Up until the Lizards came, life in the United States had been within shouting distance of normal, war or no war. Now . . . He'd seen newsreel film of wreckage in Europe and China, seen black-and-white images of stunned people trying to figure out how to go on with their lives after they'd lost everything—and often everybody—that mattered to them. He thought they'd sunk in. But the difference between seeing pictures of war and having war brought home to you was like the difference between seeing a picture of a pretty girl and going to bed with her.

The elevated train curled round the corner of Wabash and Lake. Lizard bombs had torn great gaps in the steel-and-wood superstructure. The trains in Chicago did not run on time, not any more.

Back onto Michigan Avenue. Half a block north of Lake, the forty-story Carbide and Carbon Building had been a Chicago landmark with its black marble base, dark green terra cotta walls, and gilded trim. Now scorch marks ran up its flanks. Piles of the wall—hell, pieces of the building—were chewed out by bomb hits, as if a dog the size of King Kong had tried it for taste. The glass from hundreds of windows had been swept out of Michigan Avenue, but still glittered on the sidewalk.

The bus driver was evidently a native Chicagoan. Just past the Carbide and Carbon Building, he pointed to the opposite side of the street and said, "This here used to be the 333 North Michigan Building. Now it ain't."

Now it ain't. A mournful pronouncement, but accurate enough. The pile of debris—marble facings, wood floors, endless cubic yards of reinforced concrete, twisted steel girders beginning to be mangy with rust now that they were open to the snow and rain—had been a building once. It wasn't any more.

Nor was the double-decked Michigan Avenue Bridge a bridge any more. Army engineers had run a temporary pontoon bridge across the Chicago River to get the convoy to the other side. It would come down again as soon as the last truck rattled over it. If it didn't, the Lizards would blast it in short order.

Armchair strategists said the Lizards didn't really understand what all human beings used boats for. Yeager hoped they were right. He'd been strafed in a train the night the aliens came crashing down on Earth. Getting strafed on board ship would be ten times worse—no place to run, no place to hide.

But if the Lizards didn't understand boats, they sure knew what bridges were all about. Looking west as he bounced over the steel plates of the makeshift span the engineers had thrown up, Yeager saw that bridges had leapt over the Chicago River at every block. They didn't overleap it now. Every one of them, like the Michigan Avenue Bridge, had been bombed into oblivion.

"Ain't it a bitch?" the driver said, as if reading his mind. "This here bridge was only about twenty, twenty-five years old—my old man was back from France to watch 'em open it up. Fuckin' waste, if you ask me."

On the north side of the river, the gleaming white Wrigley Building looked intact but for broken windows. Across the street, though, the Tribune Tower had been gutted. Yeager found a certain amount of poetic justice in that. Even when reduced to a skinny weekly by paper shortages, the *Chicago Tribune* hadn't stopped laying into Roosevelt for not Doing Something about the Lizards. Just what he was supposed to be Doing was never quite clear— but he obviously wasn't Doing it, so the paper piled scorn on him.

Yeager felt like thumbing his nose at the ruined building. About all anyone could do about the Lizards was fight them as hard as he could for as long as he could. The United States was doing as well as any other country on Earth, and better than most. But Sam wondered if that would be enough.

Along with the rest of the convoy, the bus turned right on Grand Avenue toward the Navy Pier. The morning sun gleamed off Lake Michigan, which seemed illimitable as the sea.

The pier stretched more than half a mile into the lake. The bus rattled past sheds once full of merchandise, now mostly bombed-out shells. At the east end of the pier were playgrounds, a dance hall, an auditorium, a promenade—all reminders of happier times. Waiting at what had been the excursion landing was a rusty old freighter that looked like the maritime equivalent of the beat-up buses Yeager had been riding all his adult life.

Also waiting were a couple of companies of troops. Antiaircraft guns poked their noses into the sky. If Lizard planes swooped down on the convoy, they'd get a warm reception. Even so, Yeager wished the guns were someplace else—from everything he'd seen, they were better at attracting the Lizards than shooting them down.

But he wasn't the one who gave the orders—except to his Lizardy charges. "Come on, boys," he told them, and let them precede him off the bus and onto the pier. At his urging, Ullhass and Ristin headed toward the freighter, on whose side was painted the name *Caledonia*.

The gathered soldiers swarmed onto the convoy vehicle like army ants—Yeager smiled as the comparison struck him. One truck after another was emptied and sped back down Navy Pier toward Chicago. Working transport of any sort was precious these days. Watching them head west, Yeager got an excellent view of the proud city skyline—and of the gaps the Lizards had torn in it.

Barbara Larssen came over and stood by him. "They just want us small fry out of the way," she said unhappily. "They put the physicists on board first, and now the equipment they need. Afterward, if there's any room and any time, they'll let people like us get on."

Given the military needs of the moment, those priorities made sense to Yeager. But Barbara wanted sympathy, not sense. He said, "You know what they say—there's the right way, the wrong way, and the Army way."

She laughed, maybe a little more than the tired joke deserved. A chilly gust of wind off the lake tried to flip up her pleated skirt. She defeated it with the quick two-hand clutch women seem to learn as a tribal gesture, but shivered just the same. "Brr! I wish I were wearing pants."

"Why don't you?" he said. "With all the heaters to hell and gone, I bet you'd be a lot more comfortable. I wouldn't want to freeze my—well, I wouldn't want to freeze myself in a skirt just on account of fashion."

If she'd noticed what he started to say, she didn't let on. "If I find some that fit me, I think I will," she said. "Long johns, too."

Yeager let himself indulge in the fantasy of peeling her out of a pair of long johns until somebody bawled, "Come on, get those goddamn Lizards on board. We ain't got all day."

He urged Ullhass and Ristin ahead of him, then had a happy afterthought. Grabbing Barbara's hand, he said, "Make like you're a Lizard-keeper, too?" She caught on fast and fell into step behind him. She didn't shake off his hand, either.

The two Lizard POWs hissed in alarm as the gangplank swayed under their weight. "It's all right," Barbara reassured them, playing her part to the hilt. "If humans carrying heavy equipment didn't break this, you won't." Yeager had come to know Ullhass and Ristin well enough to tell how unhappy they were, but they kept walking.

They hissed again when they got up onto the deck of the *Caledonia* and discovered the ship was still shifting slightly to and fro. "It will fall over and put us all at the bottom of the water," Ristin said angrily. He didn't know nautical English, but got his meaning across.

Yeager looked around at the faded paint, the rust that streaked down from rivets, the worn woodwork, the grease-stained dungarees and old wool sweaters the crew wore. "I don't think so," he told the Lizards. "This boat's done a lot more sailing in its day. I expect it's good for some more yet."

"I think you're right, Sam," Barbara said, perhaps as much to reassure herself as to console Ristin.

"Out of the way, there," an officer in Navy uniform yelled at Yeager. "And get those damned things into the cabin we've set up for them."

"Yes, sir," Yeager said, saluting. "Uh, sir, where is this cabin? Nobody told me before I got here."

The Navy man rolled his eyes. "Why doesn't that surprise me?" He grabbed a passing sailor by the arm. "Virgil, take this guy and his pet Lizards up to cabin nine. That one can be locked from the outside—here's the key." He turned to Barbara. "Who are you, ma'am?" When she gave him her name, he checked a list, then said, "You can go along if you like, since you don't seem to mind being around these things—they give me the creeps. Anyway, you're in cabin fourteen, just up the corridor. I hope that's all right."

"Sure—why not?" Barbara said. The Navy man looked at her, looked back to the Lizards, rolled his eyes again. He obviously didn't want to have anything more to do with them than duty required.

"Come on," Virgil said. He had an engaging hillbilly twang, and seemed more curious than repelled by the Lizards. Nodding to Ristin, he said, "You speak English?"

"Yess," Ristin answered, fixing him with a baleful stare. "You are sure this—thing—will not fall over into the water?"

"Yup." The sailor laughed. "Hasn't yet, anyhow." Just then, other sailors cast off lines at stern and bow. The ship's engine roared into life, making the deck vibrate. Ristin and Ullhass both glared at Virgil as if they'd just convicted him of perjury in their minds. Black smoke poured from the *Caledonia*'s twin stacks. She slowly pulled away from the Navy Pier.

Back on the pier, some of the soldiers who'd done stevedore duty waved farewells. More, though, were too worn to do anything but stand or sit at the end of the pier. Yeager wondered how many of them had any idea why the cargo they'd loaded onto the freighter was so important. A handful if any, he guessed.

He was looking back toward Chicago when he saw flames and dust and smoke spurt up from an explosion, and then from another and another. Oddly flat across a widening stretch of water, the blasts reached his ears at about the same time he heard the screaming jets of the Lizard fighter-bombers.

The antiaircraft gunners on the Navy Pier started firing for all they were worth. All that accomplished was to draw the Lizards' attention to them. One of the planes zoomed along the length of the pier, turned loose a couple of bombs. The AA fire cut off as sharply as a chicken's squawks when the cleaver comes down.

The Lizard plane shot over the *Caledonia*, so low Yeager could see the seams where pieces of its skin were joined together. He breathed a sigh of relief when it screamed out over the lake.

Along with his charges, Virgil had stopped to watch the enemy aircraft again. Now he said, "Let's get you movin' again." But he kept his head cocked, as Yeager did, listening to the sound of the jet engine. Worry crossed his face. "I don't much like that it's—"

Before he could say *comin' back*, a sharp bark rose above the scream. Yeager had been under fire often enough to make his reaction almost reflexive. "Hit the deck!" he yelled, and had the presence of mind to knock Barbara down beside him.

Cannon shells raked the *Caledonia* from starboard to port. Glass shattered. Metal screamed. A moment later, so did men. The Lizard pilot, happy with the strafing run, darted westward toward his base.

Something hot and wet splashed Yeager. When he touched it, his hand came away smeared with red. He looked up. There on the deck, a little in front of him, lay Virgil's still-twitching legs. A few feet away were the soldier's head and shoulders and arms. Nothing but that red smear was left of the parts in between.

Ullhass and Ristin stared at the ruin of what had been a man with as much horror as if they'd been men themselves. As Yeager did, Barbara Larssen looked up into carnage. She was as smeared with blood as he, from her wavy hair to her pleated skirt and beyond—a neat line between silk-covered pink and crimson on her calf showed just how far down the skirt had gone.

She saw what was left of Virgil, stared down at the slaughterhouse survivor she'd become. "Oh God," she said, "Oh God," and was noisily sick on the deck in the middle of the blood. She clung to Yeager and he to her, his hands digging like claws into the firm, marvelously unbroken flesh of her back, her breasts pressing against his chest as if they grew there. Her head was jammed down into the hollow of his shoulder. He didn't know if she could breathe and he didn't care. In spite of the stink of the blood and the puke, he wanted her more than he'd ever wanted a woman in all his life and from the way his hard-on rubbed her leg and she didn't pull away but moaned and just shoved herself to him harder than ever he knew she wanted him too and of course it was crazy and of course it was shock but he didn't care about that either, not one bit.

"Move," he growled to the Lizards in a voice not his own. They skittered round the pieces of poor dead Virgil. He followed, still clutching Barbara, hoping desperately he could find the cabins before the moment broke.

The numbers on the doors of the first corridor he ducked into showed him he'd been lucky. He opened cabin nine, marched Ullhass and Ristin in, slammed the door behind them, turned the key. Then, almost running, he and Barbara hurried up the echoing metal hallway to fourteen.

The cabin was tiny, the bunk even tinier. Neither of them cared. They fell on it together. She happened to land on top. It could have been the other way round just as easily.

His hand dove under her shirt. He stroked her smooth thigh above the top of her stocking, then yanked at the crotch of her panties. At the same time, she pulled his pants down just far enough. She was so wet, he went deep into her the moment she impaled herself on him.

He'd never known such heat. He exploded almost at once, and in the first instant of returning self-consciousness feared he'd been too quick to satisfy her. But her spine was arched, her head thrown back; she made little mewling noises deep in her throat as she quivered above him. Then her eyes opened. Like him, she seemed to be coming to herself after a hard bout of fever.

She scrambled off him. He hastily put his trousers to rights. They'd both left bloodstains on the blanket that covered the bunk. Barbara stared wildly around the cabin, as if really seeing it for the first time. Maybe she was. "Oh God," she moaned, "what have I gone and done to myself now?" But of that there could be no possible doubt.

Sam took a step toward her, made as if to take her in his arms. He said what countless men have said to women after lust takes them by surprise: "Darling, it'll be all right—"

"Don't you call me that," she hissed. "Don't you touch me, don't you come near me." She backed as far away from him as she could, which wasn't very far. "Get out of here this instant. I never want to see you again. Go back to your damned Lizards. I'll scream. I'll—"

Yeager didn't wait to find out what she'd do. He left the cabin in a hurry, closed the door behind him. By sheer dumb luck, the corridor was empty. Through the steel door, he heard Barbara start to cry. He wanted to go back in and comfort her, but she couldn't have made it any plainer that she wanted no comfort from him. Since they were quartered right down the corridor from each other, she'd have to see him again, and soon. He wondered what would happen then.

"It'll be all right," he said without much conviction. Then, shoulders slumped, he walked slowly along the corridor to see how Ristin and Ullhass were. They didn't have to worry about the whole business of male and female; out of sight was truly out of mind for them. He'd never thought he'd be jealous of that, but right now he was.

A Lizard threw open the door to the Baptist church in Fiat, Indiana. The people inside jerked their heads around in surprise and alarm; this was not a usual time for the aliens to bother them. They'd learned a basic lesson of war and captivity: anything out of the ordinary was frightening.

Jens Larssen started with the rest, though as he already faced the big double doors he didn't have to spin toward them. He'd been standing around kibitzing a game of hearts. Sal the waitress was going for it— trying to take the queen of spades and all the hearts and stick all three of her opponents with twenty-six points each. He didn't think she had the cards to make it, but you never could tell—she played like a barracuda.

He never found out what happened with the hand. The Lizard stalked into the church, automatic weapon at the ready. Two others covered it from the doorway. The creature hissed, "Piit Ssmiff?"

Larssen needed a second to recognize his alias in the alien's mouth. As the Lizard started to repeat it, he said, "That's me. What do you want?"

"Come," the Lizard said, which might have come close to exhausting its English. A jerk of the gun barrel, however, was hard to misconstrue.

"What do you want?" Larssen said again, but he was already moving. The Lizards were not long on patience with captives.

"Good luck, Pete," Sal called softly as he headed out toward the doorway.

"Thanks. You, too," he answered. He hadn't put a move on her, not yet; he still had hopes of making it home to Barbara. But day by day *not yet* was rising higher in his thoughts than *hadn't put a move on her.* And when he did (*if I do*, he halfheartedly reminded himself), he was pretty sure—no, he *was* sure—she'd come across. Once or twice, she'd put what might have been a move on him.

A couple of other people also wished him luck. The Lizard just waited for him to arrive, then fell in behind him. Outside the church, cold smote. His eyes filled with tears; he'd been inside the gloomy building so long that sun sparkling off snow was almost overpoweringly bright.

His guards marched him along to the store the Lizards used as their Fiat headquarters. As soon as he went inside, he started to sweat; the place was at the bake-oven heat the aliens enjoyed. The three who had brought him there hissed blissfully. He wondered how they escaped pneumonia from the drastic temperature shifts they endured whenever they went in or out. Maybe pneumonia bugs didn't bite Lizards. He hoped they wouldn't bite him.

The guards led him back to the table where Gnik had interrogated him before. The Lizard lieutenant or whatever he was waited there now. He was holding something Lizardy in his left hand. Without preamble, he said, "Open your mouth, Pete Smith."

"Huh?" Jens said, taken aback.

"Open your mouth, I say. You do not understand your own speech?"

"No, superior sir. Uh, I mean, yes, superior sir." Larssen gave that up as a bad job and opened his mouth; with guns all around him, he had no real choice.

Gnik started to reach up with the gadget in his left hand, then paused. "You Big Uglies are too tall," he said peevishly. Nimble as his Earthly reptilian namesake, he scrambled up onto a chair, put the muzzle of the gadget into Larssen's mouth, squeezed a trigger.

The Lizardy thing hissed like a snake. A jet of something stung Jens on the tongue. "Ow!" he exclaimed, and involuntarily pulled back. "What the devil did you just do to me?"

"Injected you," Gnik answered; at least he didn't seem angry about Jens' retreat. "Now we will find out the truth."

"Injected me? But . . ." When Larssen thought about injections, he thought about needles. Then he took a long look at Gnik's scaly hide. Would a hypodermic pierce it? He didn't know. The Lizards' only easily available soft tissue was inside their mouths. Some sort of compressed gas jet must have forced the drug into his system. But what was it? "Find out the truth?" he asked.

"New from our base." Gnik was one smug Lizard. "You will not lie to me. You cannot lie to me. The injection will not permit it."

Uh-oh, Jens thought. The sweat that sprang out on his forehead now had nothing to do with the hot, dry interior of the store. He felt woozy; he needed a distinct effort of will not to see double. "May I sit down?" he said. Gnik jumped off the chair he'd used. Larssen sank into it. His legs did not seem to want to support him. *Why not?* he thought vaguely. *I always supported them.*

Gnik stood and waited for a few minutes, presumably to let the drug take full effect. Larssen wondered if he'd throw up all the canned goods he'd been eating lately. His mind felt detached from his body; it was almost as if he were looking down on himself from the ceiling.

Gnik asked, "What is your name?"

What is *my name?* Jens wondered. *What a good question.* He wanted to giggle, but didn't have the energy. What had he been calling himself lately, anyhow? Remembering was a triumph. "Pete Smith," he said proudly.

Gnik hissed. He and the other Lizards talked among themselves for a couple of minutes. The officer swung his turreted eyes back toward Larssen. "Where you going when we catch you on that—thing?" He still couldn't remember the name for a bicycle.

"To, to visit my cousins west of, of, Montpelier." Sticking to his story wasn't easy for Jens, but he managed. Maybe he'd already told it so many times that it felt true for him. And maybe the Lizards' drug wasn't as good as they thought it was. In a pulp science-fiction story, it was easy enough to imagine something one day, create it the next, and use it the day after that. Reality was different, as he'd found out time and again at the Met Lab: nature usually proved less tractable than pulp writers made it out to be.

Gnik hissed again. Maybe he wasn't convinced the drug was everything it was supposed to be—or maybe he had been convinced Jens was lying through his teeth and had got a nasty shock when he didn't come out with something new under the drug. Not only was the Lizard stubborn, he was sneaky as well. "Tell me more of the male of this grouping of yours, this cousin Osscar." He put a hiss in the middle of the name, too.

"His name is, is Olaf," Larssen said, scenting the trap just in time. "He's my father's brother's son." He quickly rattled off the names of the fictitious Olaf's equally fictitious family. He hoped that would keep Gnik from trying to trip him up with them; it also helped fix them in his own mind.

The Lizards went back to talking to one another again. After a while, Gnik returned to English. "We still do not find this—these—cousins of yours anywhere about."

"I can't help that," Larssen said. "For all I know, maybe it's because you've killed them. But I hope not."

"More probably because their neighbors do not tell us who they are." Did Gnik sound conciliatory? Larssen hadn't heard conciliation in a Lizard's voice often enough to be sure. "Some of you Big Uglies do not care for the Race."

"Why do you suppose that is?" Jens asked.

"It is a puzzlement," Gnik said, so seriously that Larssen knew he really was puzzled. *Are they that stupid?* he wondered. But the Lizards weren't stupid, not even slightly, or they'd never have been able to come to Earth, never have been able to make and drop their atomic bombs. They were sure naive, though. Had they expected to be welcomed as liberators?

Even under the mildly euphoric buzz of the not-quite-truth drug, Larssen worried a little. Suppose the Lizards decided to let him go and then followed him while he tried to find his cousins' farm? That would be the best way to make him out a liar. Or would it? He could always point to a ruined one and claim Olaf *et* mythical *cetera* had lived there.

The Lizards were chattering back and forth one more time. Gnik cut off debate with a sharp motion of his hand. He swung his eyes toward Larssen. "What you say with the drug in you must be true. So my superiors have told me; thus, so it must be. And if it is true, you is—*are*—no danger to the Race. You may go. Take up the things that are yours and travel on, Pete Smith."

"Just like that?" Larssen blurted. An instant later, he bit his tongue, which made him yelp—it was sore. But did he want the Lizard to change its mind? Like hell he did! His next question was distinctly more practical: "Where's my bike?"

Gnik understood the word, even if he couldn't recall it. "It will go to where you are being kept. Go there now yourself to take up the things that are yours."

Along with the drug-induced euphoria, Jens now had his own genuine variety. He put his cold-weather gear back on, all but floated over the snow back to the Baptist church. Questions rang out: "What happened?" "What'd they want with you?"

"They're letting me go," he said simply. He was still absorbing the magnitude of his own luck. Back in White Sulphur Springs, Colonel Groves—or was it General Marshall?—had told him the Lizards were worse than Russians for depending on their higher-ups to tell them what to do. Gnik's higher-ups had told him he had a real live truth drug here, and as far as he was concerned, that made it Holy Writ. As long as the higher-ups were right, it was a good enough system. When they were wrong . . .

Half the people in the church came running forward to pound his back and shake his hand. Sal's kiss was so authoritative, his arms automatically tightened around her. She molded herself to him, ground her hips against his crotch. "Lucky bastard," she whispered when she finally pulled away.

"Yeah," he muttered, dazed. All at once, he wanted not to leave . . . at least for one night. But no. If he didn't get out while he could, the Lizards were liable to wonder why—and liable to change their minds. That did not bear thinking about.

He pushed through the friendly little crowd to get his belongings from the pew he'd come to call his own. As he slung his knapsack over his shoulders, he noticed for the first time the men and women who'd hung back from offering best wishes. Not to put too fine a point on it, they looked as if they hated him. Several—women and men both—turned away so he would not see them cry. He all but ran toward the doorway. No, even if the Lizards allowed it, he could not stay another night, not for Sal and all her blowsy charms. Even a few seconds of that envy and rage were more than he could stand.

The Lizards were efficient enough. By the time he got outside, one of them had his bicycle waiting. As he swung up onto it, he got a last glimpse of pale, hungry faces staring out from inside the church at the freedom they could not share. He'd expected to feel a lot of different things when he was set free, but never shame. He started to pedal. Snow kicked up from under his wheels. In bare seconds, the hamlet of Fiat vanished behind him.

After less than an hour, he stopped for a blow. He wasn't in the shape he'd enjoyed before the Lizards put him out of circulation for a while. "Gotta keep going or I'll stiffen up," he said aloud. Unlike his wind, the habit of talking to himself came back right away.

When he came upon the signs announcing Montpelier, he skirted the town on the best paths he could find, then returned to Highway 18. For the next few days, everything seemed to go right. He rode around Marion as he had Montpelier, sailed right on through Sweetser and Converse, Wawpekong and Galveston. Whenever he needed food, he found some. Whenever he was tired, a hayloft or an abandoned farmhouse seemed to beckon.

Once, in a bureau drawer, he even found a pack of Philip Morrises. He hadn't had a cigarette since he couldn't remember when; he smoked himself light-headed and half-sick in an orgy of making up for lost time. "Worth it," he declared as he coughed his way through the next day.

He saw few people as he rolled through central Indiana. That suited him fine. He saw even fewer Lizards, and that suited him better—how was he supposed to explain what he was doing a good many miles west of where he'd told Gnik he was going? Luck stayed with him; he didn't have to.

The war between humans and aliens seemed far away from that nearly deserted winter landscape (although, of course, it wouldn't have been deserted but for the war). A couple of times, though, off in the distance, he heard gunfire, the widely spaced barks of sporting or military rifles and the chatter of the Lizards' automatic weapons. And, once or twice, Lizard planes screamed high overhead, scrawling trails—*ice crystals*, the physicist part of him said—across the sky.

Somewhere between Young America and Delphi, a new noise entered the mix: intermittent explosions. The farther west he traveled, the louder they got. Maybe half an hour after he first noticed them, his head went up like a hunted animal's when it catches a scent.

"That's artillery, is what that is!" he exclaimed. Excitement coursed through him—artillery meant people still fighting the Lizards on a level higher than bushwhacking. It also meant danger, since it lay in the direction he was riding.

The duel, he noticed as he drew near, was anything but intense. A few shells would come in, a few more go out. He rode past a Lizard battery. Instead of being towed, the guns were mounted on what looked like tank chassis. The Lizards serving them paid no attention to him.

Shortly after he passed the Lizard position, he started going by wrecked combat vehicles, most of them now just big shapes covered over with snow. The road, which had been pretty good, suddenly developed not just potholes but craters. The fighting hereabouts wasn't intense now, but had been not too long before.

He got off his bike before he went headlong into a snow-filled hole. Frustration ate at him. After fairly flying through Lizard-held territory, was he going to get delayed by humans? He'd started believing he'd get home to Chicago again fairly soon. Getting hopes up and then having them dashed seemed cruel and unfair.

Then he came to the first belt of rusty barbed wire. It was like something out of a movie about World War I. "How am I supposed to get through that?" he demanded of an uncaring world. "How am I supposed to get my bike through that?"

A hiss, a whistle, a scream, a crash! Frozen earth flew through the air off to his left. So did fragments of steel. One tore through a couple of spokes of the bicycle's rear wheel. It could have torn through Jens' leg just as easily. All at once, the artillery duel turned real for him. It wasn't just abstract shells flying back and forth on trajectories dictated by Newtonian mechanics and air resistance. If one of those shells hit a little nearer (or no nearer, but with an unlucky spray of fragments), he wouldn't have to worry about getting to Chicago any more.

Another freight-train noise in the air. This time Larssen dove into the snow before the shell burst. It landed in the middle of the barbed-wire belt, and chunks of wire probably flew along with its own fragments. Getting hit by one sort of jagged metal would be about as bad as the other, Jens thought.

He cautiously raised his head, hoping the shell had cleared a way through the wire. A generation of young Englishmen who'd fought at the Somme—or, at any rate, the fraction of that generation which survived— could have told him he was wasting optimism. Tanks could crush wire, but shells couldn't smash it aside.

How to cross, then? With shells still falling in the neighborhood every so often, he didn't even want to get up and walk around to look for a path to the other side of the wire. He turned his head so he could see how far to the north and west the barrier ran. Farther than his ground-level Mark One eyeball carried, anyhow. Was it no-man's-land all the way from here to Chicago? With his luck, it might well be.

"Okay, pal, don't even blink, or you'll get yourself some .30 caliber ventilation." The voice came from the direction in which Larssen wasn't looking. He obediently froze. Lying in the snow, he already had a good start on freezing, anyhow. "Awright," the voice said. "Turn toward me, nice and slow. I better see your hands every second, too."

Jens turned, nice and slow. As if he'd sprouted there like a mushroom, a fellow in a khaki uniform and a tin hat sprawled not fifty feet away. His rifle pointed right about at Larssen's brisket. "Jesus, it's good to see a human being holding a gun again," Jens said.

"Shut up," the soldier told him. The Springfield never wavered. "Likeliest guess is, you're a God-damned Lizard spy."

"A what? Are you crazy?"

"We shot two last week," the soldier said flatly.

Ice grew inside Larssen, to go with the snow all around. The fellow meant every word of it. Jens tried again: "I'm no spy, and I can prove it, by God."

"Tell it to the Marines, Mac. I'm a harder sell than that."

"Goddammit, will you listen to me?" Jens shouted, furious now as well as frightened. "I'm on my way back from White Sulphur Springs, West Virginia. Jesus, I talked with General Marshall while I was there. He'll vouch for me, if he's still alive."

"Yeah, pal, an' I was in Rome last week, for lunch with the Pope." But the unwashed, unshaven soldier did move his rifle so it wasn't aimed at Larssen's midriff. "Awright, I'll take you in. You can peddle your papers to my lieutenant. If he buys what you're pushin', that's his business. C'mere . . . No, dummy, leave the bike."

Sans bicycle, Larssen came. He wondered how he was supposed to get through that impenetrable-looking mass of barbed wire. But a path was cut, with strands looking as if they were firmly attached to their support posts but in fact just hanging from them. He didn't have much trouble crawling along after his captor, though he never could have navigated by himself. Although he tried to be careful, he got punctured a couple of times. He tried to remember when his last tetanus shot had been.

More dirty faces peered out at him from the zigzagging trenches behind the wire. The lieutenant, instead of a British-style tin hat, wore a domed steel helmet that looked very modern and martial. He listened to Larssen's story, reached into a shirt pocket, then laughed at himself. "I still want a butt to help me think, but I haven't seen one in weeks. Hellfire, buddy, I don't know what to do with you. I'll bump you on up the line, see if somebody else can figure you out."

Escorted by the soldier who'd found him—the fellow's name turned out to be Eddie Wagner—Larssen made the acquaintance of a captain, a major, and a lieutenant colonel. By then, he expected to be kicked on to a bird colonel, but the lieutenant colonel short-circuited the process, saying, "I'm going to send you to General Patton's headquarters, bud. If you say you've met Marshall, he's the one to decide what to do with you."

General Patton's headquarters proved to be in Oxford, something like twenty miles west. The march there, starting at dawn the next day, ended near dark and left Larssen footsore, weary, and mourning his lost bike. Little by little, as he tramped along, he began to notice how many field guns were disguised as tree trunks with branches wired onto their upright barrels, how many tanks inhabited barns or crouched under haystacks, how many airplanes rested beneath nets that hid them from the sky.

"You guys have a lot of stuff built up here," he remarked some time in the afternoon. "How'd you manage to do it right under the Lizards' snouts?"

"Wasn't easy," Wagner answered, who'd apparently decided he might not be a spy after all. "We been movin' it in a little at a time, just about all of it at night. The Lizards, they've let us do it. We hope to Jesus that means they ain't really noticed what we're up to. They'll find out, they sure as hell will."

Larssen started to ask what the Lizards would find out, then thought better of it. He didn't want to stir up his guide's suspicions again. Not only that, he could make a good stab at figuring it out for himself. Some sort of big push had to be in the offing. He wondered in which direction it would go.

General Patton's headquarters was in a white frame house on the outskirts of Oxford (though the town, with fewer than a thousand people, was barely big enough to have outskirts). The sentries on the covered porch— like everything else military hereabouts, they were concealed from aerial observation—were well shaved and wore neater uniforms than any Jens had seen for a while.

One of them nodded politely to him. "We've been expecting you, sir: Lieutenant-Colonel Tobin telephoned to say you were on your way. The general will see you at once."

"Thanks," Larssen said, feeling more draggled than ever in the presence of such all-but-forgotten spit and polish.

That feeling intensified when he went into the house. Major General Patton—he wore two stars on each shoulder of a sheepskin-collared leather jacket—was not only clean-shaven and neat, he even had creases in his trousers. The buttery light of a kerosene lamp left black shadows at the corners of his mouth, in the lines that grooved their way up alongside his nose, and beneath his pale, intense eyes. He had to be getting close to sixty, but Jens would not have cared to take him on.

He ran a hand through his short brush of graying sandy hair, then stabbed a finger out at Larssen. "I risked a radio call on you, mister," he growled, his raspy voice lightly flavored by the South. "General Marshall told me to ask you what he said to you about the Lizards in Seattle."

Panic quickly swamped relief that Marshall lived. "Sir, I don't remember him saying anything about the Lizards in Seattle," he blurted.

Patton's fierce expression melted into a grin. "Good thing for you that you don't. If you did, I'd know you were just another lying son of a bitch. Sit down, son." As Larssen sank into a chair, the general went on, "Marshall says you're important, too, though he wouldn't say how, not even in code. I've known General Marshall a lot of years now. He doesn't use words like *important* just for show. So who and what the devil are you?"

"Sir, I'm a physicist attached to the Metallurgical Laboratory project at the University of Chicago." Jens saw that didn't mean anything to Patton. He amplified: "Even before the Lizards came, we were working to build a uranium weapon—an atomic bomb—for the United States."

"Lord," Patton said softly. "No, General Marshall wasn't kidding, was he?" His laugh could have sprung from the throat of a much younger man. "Well, Mr. Larssen—no, you'd be Dr. Larssen, wouldn't you?—if you want to get back to Chicago, you've come to the right place, by God."

"Sir?"

"We are going to grab the Lizards by the nose and kick 'em in the ass," Patton said with relish. "Come over here to the table and have a look at this map."

Larssen came and had a look. The thumbtack-impaled map had come from an old *National Geographic*. "We're here," Patton said, pointing. Larssen nodded. Patton went on, "I've got Second Armored here, other assets, infantry, air support. And up *here*"—his finger moved to an area west of Madison, Wisconsin—"is General Omar Bradley with even more than I've got. Now all we're doing is waiting for a good, nasty blizzard."

"Sir?" Jens said again.

"We've found the Lizards don't like fighting in winter conditions, not even a little bit." Patton snorted. "Like any pansies, they wilt when it's cold. The bad weather'll help keep their aircraft on the ground. When the snow flies, my forces move northwest while Bradley comes southeast. God willing, we join hands somewhere not far from Bloomington, Illinois, and put the spearhead of the Lizard forces attacking Chicago in a pocket—a *Kessel*, the Nazis were calling it in Russia."

He shaped the movements of the two American forces with his hands, made Larssen see them, too. A real chance to hit back at the invaders from outer space . . . that made Jens catch fire, too. But a lot of people, all over the world, had tried to hurt the Lizards. Not many had much luck. "Sir, I'm no soldier and I don't pretend to be one, but—can we really pull this off?"

"It's a gamble," Patton admitted. "But if we don't, the United States is washed up, because we won't get another chance to make troop concentrations like these. And I refuse to believe my country is washed up. We'll be confused and scared in the attack, I don't doubt it for a second, but the enemy'll be more confused and scared than we are, because we'll be taking the fight to him, not the other way round."

A gamble. A chance. Larssen slowly nodded. A real victory against the Lizards would lift morale around the world. A defeat . . . well, humanity had known a lot of defeats. Why should one more be noticed?

Patton said, "You'll have to stay here now, till the attack goes in. We can't let you head through Lizard-held territory, not knowing what you do."

"Why not? Their truth drug doesn't work," Larssen said.

"Dr. Larssen, you are a gentle soul and have led what is, I fear, a sheltered life," Patton answered. "There are methods far more basic than drugs for extracting truth from a man. I'm sorry, sir, but I cannot afford the risk. In any case, hard fighting will start soon. You'll be far safer with us than traveling on your own."

Jens wasn't sure about that, either. Trucks and tanks were far more likely to draw more fire than a lone man on a bicycle—or, now, afoot. But he was in no position to argue the point. Besides, just then an orderly brought in a tray with a roasted chicken and several baked potatoes and a bottle of wine along with it.

"You'll take supper with me?" Patton asked.

"Yes, thank you." Larssen had all he could do not to grab the savory, golden-brown chicken and tear at it like a starving wolf. After cans in the church and a fast but hungry trip across Indiana, it looked wonderful beyond belief.

A little later, sucking the last scrap of meat off a drumstick, he said, "All I want to do is get back to my work, get back to my wife. Lord, she probably thinks I'm dead by now." For that matter, he could only hope Barbara was still alive.

"Yes, I miss my Beatrice, too," Patton said with a heavy sigh. He lifted his wineglass. "To snow, Dr. Larssen."

"To snow," Jens said. The glasses clinked together.

Moishe Russie had gone into the Lizards' broadcasting studio a good many times before, but never at gunpoint. Zolraag stood beside the table with the microphone. "You may be doing this broadcast under duress, *Herr* Russie," the Lizard governor said, "but you *will* do it." He added the emphatic cough.

"You've brought me here, anyhow." Russie was amazed at how little fear he felt. Almost three years in the ghetto under German torment had been a sort of dress rehearsal for death. Now that the time had come . . . He murmured in Hebrew: *"Sh'ma yisroyl, adonai elohaynu, adonai ekhod."* He didn't want to die with the prayer unspoken.

Zolraag said, "You would not have even this last chance to make yourself useful in our eyes if you had not shown you truly knew nothing about the disappearance of your mate and hatchling."

"So you have told me, Excellency." Russie made his voice submissive.

Let the governor think he was cowed. Inside, he exulted. Though he didn't know everything of how Rivka and Reuven had vanished, he knew enough to endanger a lot of people. His tongue twitched at the memory of the Lizards' gas jet in action. But in spite of their drug, he'd been able to lie.

Mere human nostrums all too often did much less than what they claimed; as a onetime medical student, he had some feel for how complex the human organism was. He'd feared the Lizards had mastered it, though, especially when he went all dreamy after his dose. Somehow, though, he managed to withhold the truth. He wondered what went into the drug. Even if it didn't work as advertised, it had promise.

No time to worry about that now. Zolraag said, "Read the script to yourself, *Herr* Russie, then read it aloud for our broadcast. You know the penalty for failure to comply."

Russie sat down in the chair. It and the table in front of it were the only human-sized pieces of furniture in the room. One of the Lizard guards stepped up behind Russie, set the muzzle of his rifle against the back of the Jew's head. Zolraag wasn't playing games, not any more.

Moishe wondered who had typed—and probably written—the script. Some poor human, accommodating himself to the new masters as best he could. So many Poles, even so many Jews, had accommodated themselves to the Nazis as best they could . . . so why not to the Lizards as well?

The words were what he'd expected: sycophantic praise for the aliens and for everything they did, including the destruction of Washington. The Lizard studio engineer looked at a chronograph, spoke first in his own language and then in German: "Quiet, all—we begin. *Herr* Russie, you speak."

Russie whispered the *Sh'ma* to himself one last time, bent low over the microphone. He took a deep breath, made sure he spoke clearly: "This is Moishe Russie. Because of illness and other personal reasons, I have not broadcast in some time." That much was on the paper in front of him. What came next was not: "I doubt I shall broadcast ever again."

Zolraag spoke German well enough to realize he'd deviated from the script. He waited for the bullet to crash through his skull. He wouldn't hear it; he hoped he wouldn't feel it. It would disrupt the program, by God! But the Lizard governor gave no sign he noticed anything wrong. The bullet did not come.

Russie went on, "I have been told to sing the praises of the Race's destruction of Washington to point out to all mankind that the Americans had it coming because of their stubborn and foolish resistance, that they should have surrendered. All these things are lies."

Again he waited for some reaction from Zolraag, for the bullet that would blow his head all over the studio. Zolraag just stood there listening. Russie plowed ahead, squeezing as much as he could from the Lizard's strange forbearance: "I told the truth when I said what the Germans did in

Warsaw. I am far from sorry they are gone. To us, the Jews of Warsaw, the Race came as liberators. But they seek to enslave all men. What they did in Washington proves this, for any who still need proof. Fight hard, that we may be free. Better that than subjection forever. Good-bye and good luck."

The silence in the studio lasted more than a minute after he stopped. Then Zolraag said, "Thank you, *Herr* Russie. That will be all."

"But . . ." Having prepared himself for martyrdom, Moishe felt almost cheated at failing to attain it. "What I said, what I told the world . . ."

"I recorded, *Herr* Russie," the Lizard engineer said. "Go out tomorrow, your regular time."

"Oh," Moishe said in a hollow voice. Of course the broadcast would not go out tomorrow. Once the Lizards listened to it carefully, really understood it, they'd hear the sabotage he'd tried to commit. The shadow of death had not lifted from him. He would just have to wear it a little longer.

In a way, it might have been better had the Lizards shot him now. That would have been quick. Given time to reflect, they might come up with a more ingenious end for him. He shivered. He'd overcome fear once, to say what he'd said. He hoped he could nerve himself to do it again, but feared the second time would be harder.

"Take him away," Zolraag said in his own language. The Lizard guards led Moishe out to one of their vehicles parked outside the studio. As they always did, they hissed and complained about the few meters of frigid cold they had to traverse between the bake ovens they thought comfortable.

Back in his flat, Russie puttered around, read the Bible and the apocryphal tale of the Maccabees, cooked himself supper with bachelor inefficiency. He did his best to sleep and eventually succeeded. In the morning, he heated up some of the potatoes he hadn't finished the night before. It wasn't much of a last meal for a condemned man, but he lacked the energy to fix anything finer.

A few minutes in front of the appointed hour, he turned on the short-wave set. He'd never listened to himself before; all his previous broadcasts had gone out live. He wondered why the Lizards chose to alter the pattern this time.

Music—a martial fanfare. Then a recorded tag: "Here is free Radio Warsaw!" He'd liked that, back when the city was freshly out from under the Nazis' bootheels. Now it seemed sadly ironic.

"This is Moishe Russie. Because of illness and other personal reasons, I have not broadcast in some time." Was that voice really his? He supposed it was, but he didn't sound the way he did when he listened to himself from inside, so to speak.

He dropped that thought as he listened to himself go on: "I sing the praises of the Race's destruction of Washington. I point out to all mankind

that the Americans had it coming because of their stubborn and foolish resistance. They should have surrendered. For any who still need proof, better subjection forever than to fight hard, that we may be free. What the
Race did to Washington proves this. Good-bye and good luck."

Russie stared in blank dismay at the speaker of the shortwave radio.
In his mind's eye, he saw Zolraag's mouth falling open in a hearty Lizard
guffaw. Zolraag had tricked him. He'd been ready to give up his life, but
not to live on to be used to another's purpose. Suddenly he understood
why rape was called a fate worse than death. Had his words not been
raped, employed in a way he would have died to prevent?

Distantly, abstractly, he wondered how the Lizards had managed their
perversion of what he'd said. Whatever recording and editing technology
they'd used was far ahead of anything men could boast. And so they'd
threatened him with what seemed a sure and grisly end, let him make his
defiant cry for liberty, and then not only smothered that cry but held up
the surgically altered corpse to the world and pretended it had life. As far
as the rest of mankind could tell, he was a worse collaborator now than
ever before.

Rage ripped through him. He was not used to feeling anything so raw;
it left him giddy and light-headed, as if he'd drunk too much plum brandy
at Purim. The shortwave set brayed on—more propaganda, this time in
Polish. Had the fellow talking really said these words in this order? Who
could tell?

Moishe lifted the radio over his head. It fit in the palm of one hand
and weighed hardly anything—it was of Lizard make, a gift from Zolraag.
But even had it been a heavy, bulky human-made set, fury would have
fueled his strength and let him treat it the same way. He smashed it to the
floor as hard as he could.

The lies the Pole was squawking died in midsyllable. Bits of metal and
glass and stuff that looked like Bakelite but wasn't flew in every direction.
Russie trampled the carcass of the radio, ground it into the carpet, turned
it into a forlorn puddle of fragments that bore no resemblance to what it
had been a moment before.

"Not half what the *mamzrim* did to me," he muttered.

He threw on his long black coat, stormed out of his flat, slammed the
door behind him. Three people along the corridor poked their heads out
their doorways to see who'd just had a fight with his wife. "*Reb* Moishe!"
a woman exclaimed. He stomped past without even looking her way.

Lizard guards still stood at the entrance to the block of flats. Moishe
stomped past them, too, though he wanted to snatch one of their rifles and
drop them both bleeding to the sidewalk. He knew just what the muzzle
of a Lizard rifle felt like, jammed against the curly hair at the back of his
head. What would it be like to hold one in his arms, have it buck as he
squeezed the trigger? He didn't know, but he wanted to find out.

Halfway down the block he stopped in his tracks. *"Gevalt!"* he exclaimed, deeply shocked. "Am I turning into a soldier?"

The prospect was anything but appetizing. As a medical student, he knew too well how easy a human being was to damage, how hard to repair. In the German siege of Warsaw and since, he'd seen that proved too many times, too many horrible ways. And now he wanted to become a destroyer himself?

He did.

His feet figured it out before the rest of him knew. He found himself on the way to the headquarters of Mordechai Anielewicz before he consciously realized where he was going.

A light snowfall swirled through the air. Not many people were on the streets. Every so often, one of them would nod to him from beneath a black felt fedora like his own or a Russian-style fur cap. He braced himself for shouts of hatred, but none came. If only the rest of the world paid as little attention to his broadcast as the Jews of Warsaw!

Here came someone striding briskly toward him. Who? His spectacles didn't help enough to let him be sure. His eyes had grown weaker lately; what had suited them in 1939 wasn't good enough any more. He scowled. He'd been shortsighted a lot of different ways.

Whoever it was, the fellow waved vigorously at him. He recognized the motion if not the man. Fear flooded through him. While he'd gone looking for Mordechai Anielewicz, Anielewicz was looking for him, too. Which meant Anielewicz, if no one else hereabouts, had heard him on the radio. Which meant the fighting leader without a doubt had blood in his eye.

Which he did. *"Reb* Moishe, are you *meshuggeh?"* he yelled. "I thought you weren't going to turn into the Lizards' *tukhus-lekher."*

The Lizards' *tukhus-lekher.* That was what it had come to. Mortification almost gagged Moishe. "I haven't. As God is my witness, I haven't," he choked out.

"What do you mean, you haven't?" Anielewicz said, still loudly. "With my own ears I heard you." He looked to right and left, lowered his voice. "Was it for this we made your wife and little boy disappear? So you could say what the Lizards wanted you to say?"

"But I didn't!" Russie wailed. Anielewicz's face was full of flinty disbelief. Stammering, almost sobbing, Russie told how he had gone into the Lizards' broadcast studio expecting to die, how he'd hoped and intended to give one last *cri de coeur* before he did, and how Zolraag and the Lizards' engineers cheated him out of a death that had meaning. "Do you think I want to be alive, to have my friends call me filthy names on the street?" He took a clumsy, unpracticed swing at Anielewicz.

The Jewish fighting leader easily blocked the blow. He caught Russie's arm, twisted a little. Russie's shoulder creaked like a dead branch about to fall off a tree; fire shot through the joint. He bit back a gasp.

"Sorry." Anielewicz let go at once. "Didn't mean to jerk it quite so hard there. Force of habit. You all right?"

Russie gingerly tested the injured member. "For that, yes. Otherwise—"

"And I'm sorry about that, too," Anielewicz said quickly. "But I heard you with my own ears—how could I not trust my ears? Of course I believe you, *Reb* Moishe; don't even think you need to ask me. You couldn't have guessed the Lizards would do things to a recording. They outfoxed you; it happens. The next question is, how do we get our revenge?"

"Revenge." Moishe tasted the word. Yes, it was right. He hadn't found a name for it himself. "That's what I want."

"I'll tell you something." Mordechai Anielewicz laid a finger alongside his nose. "It may just be taken care of. You haven't played a direct part, but all us Jews owe you a lot of what freedom we have. And if we hadn't been free to move through Poland, none of what I'm talking about would have happened."

"What *are* you talking about?" Russie demanded. "You haven't really said anything."

"No, and I don't intend to, either," Anielewicz answered. "What you don't know, you can't tell, and the Lizards may find better—more painful—ways of asking questions than that *vorkakte* drug of theirs. But one fine day before too long, the Lizards may have cause to notice something for which you'll be partly responsible. And if they do, you'll have your revenge, I promise you."

That all sounded very good, and Anielewicz was not in the habit of talking about what he couldn't deliver. Nonetheless ... "I want more," Russie said. "I want to hurt the Lizards myself."

"*Reb* Moishe, a soldier you're not," Anielewicz said, not unkindly but very firmly.

"I could learn—"

"No." Now the Jewish fighting leader's voice turned hard. "If you want to fight them, there are ways you can be more valuable than with a gun in your hand. You'd be wasted as a common soldier."

"What, then?"

"You're serious about this." To Moishe's relief, it was not a question. Anielewicz studied him as if trying to figure out how to field-strip some new kind of rifle. "Well, what could you do?" The fighting leader rubbed his chin. "How's this? How would you like to tell the world how much of a liar the Lizards have made you out to be?"

"You could arrange for me a broadcast?" Russie asked eagerly.

"A broadcast, no. Too dangerous." Anielewicz shook his head. "A recording, though, just possibly. Then we might smuggle it out for others to broadcast. That would make the Lizards blush—if they knew how to blush, that is. Only one trouble—well, more than one, but this you have to think about especially hard: once you make this recording, if you make it, you have to disappear."

"Yes, I see that. Zolraag would not be pleased with me, would he? But I'd sooner have him angry than laughing as he surely is now." Russie let his mouth hang open in an imitation of a Lizard chuckle. Then, in a sudden, completely human gesture, he stabbed a finger out at Anielewicz. "Could you arrange for me to vanish into the same place where Rivka and Reuven have gone?"

"I don't even know where that place is," Anielewicz reminded him.

"But that's more of your not knowing so you can't talk in case you're interrogated. Don't tell me you can't arrange to have me sent there without ever learning directly about that place, because I won't believe you."

"Maybe you *should* disappear. You're getting too cynical and suspicious to make a proper *reb* any more." But amusement glinted in Anielewicz's pale eyes. "I won't say yes to that and I won't say no." He waggled his hand back and forth. "For that matter, I don't even know for certain if I can arrange for you to make this recording, but if you want me to, I'll try."

"Try," Russie said at once. He cocked his head, peered sidelong at the Jewish fighting leader. "I notice you don't say you're worried about smuggling the recording out of Warsaw once it's made."

"Oh, no." Anielewicz looked like a cat blowing canary feathers off its nose. "If we make the recording, we'll get it out. That we can manage. We've had practice."

Ludmila Gorbunova stared at her CO. "But, Comrade Colonel," she exclaimed, her voice rising to a startled squeak, "why *me?*"

"Because your aircraft is suited to the task, and you are suited to be its pilot," Colonel Feofan Karpov replied. "The Lizards hack all sorts of aircraft out of the sky in large numbers, but fewer *Kukuruzniks* than any other type. And you, Senior Lieutenant Gorbunova, have flown combat missions against the Lizards since they came, and against the Germans before that. Do you question your own ability?"

"No, Comrade Colonel, by no means," Ludmila answered. "But the mission you have outlined is not—or should not become, let me say—one involving combat."

"It should not become such, no," Karpov agreed. "It will be the easier on account of that, though, not the more difficult. And having a combat-proved pilot will increase its chances for success. So—you. Any further questions?"

"No, Comrade Colonel." *What am I supposed to say?* Ludmila thought.

"Good," Karpov said. "He is expected to arrive tonight. Make sure your plane is in the best possible operating condition. Lucky you have that German mechanic."

"Yes, he's quite skilled." Ludmila saluted. "I'll go check out the airplane with him now. Pity I can't take him with me."

Back at the revetments, she found Georg Schultz already tinkering with the *Kukuruznik*. "Wire to one of your foot pedals here wasn't as tight as it could have been," he said. "I'll have it fixed in a minute here."

"Thank you; that will help," she answered in German. Speaking it with him every day was improving her own command of the language, though she had the feeling several of the phrases she now used casually around him were unsuited for conversation with people who didn't have greasy hands. Feeling her way for words, she went on, "I want the machine to be as good as it can. I have an important flight tomorrow."

"When isn't a flight important? It's your neck, after all." Schultz checked the feel of the pedal with his foot. He was always checking, always making sure. Just as some men had a feel for horses, he had a feel for machines, and a gift for getting them to do what he wanted. "There. That ought to fix it."

"Good. This one, though, is important for more than just my neck. I'm to go on a courier mission." She knew she should have stopped there, but how important the mission was filled her to overflowing, and she overflowed: "I am ordered to fly the foreign commissar, Comrade Molotov, to Germany for talks with your leaders. I am so proud!"

Schultz's eyes went wide. "Well you might be." After a moment, he added, "I'd better go over this plane from top to bottom. Pretty soon you're going to have to trust it to Russian mechanics again."

The scorn in that should have stung. In fact, it did, but less than it would have before Ludmila saw the obsessive care the German put into maintenance. She just said, "We'll do it together." They checked everything from the bolt that held on the propeller to the screws that attached the tailskid to the fuselage. The brief Russian winter day died while they were in the middle of the job. They worked on by the light of a paraffin lantern. Ludmila trusted the netting overhead to keep the lantern from betraying them to the Lizards.

Bell above the center horse—the one in shafts—jangling, a *troika* reached the airstrip about the time they were finishing. Ludmila listened to the team approaching the revetment. The Lizards mostly ignored horse-drawn sledges, though they shot up cars and trucks when they could. Anger filled her. More even than the Nazis, the Lizards aimed to rob mankind of the twentieth century.

"Comrade Foreign Commissar!" she said when Molotov came in to have a look at the airplane that would fly him to Germany.

"Comrade Pilot," he answered with an abrupt nod. He was shorter and paler than she'd expected, but just as determined-looking. He didn't bat an eye at the sight of the beat-up old U-2. He gave Georg Schultz another of those die-cut jerks of his head. "Comrade Mechanic."

"Good evening, Comrade Foreign Commissar," Schultz said in his bad Russian.

Molotov gave no overt reaction, but hesitated a moment before turning back to Ludmila. "A German?"

"*Da*, Comrade Foreign Commissar," she said nervously: Russians and Germans might cooperate against the Lizards, but more out of desperation than friendship. She added, "He is skilled at what he does."

"So." The word hung ominously in the air. Behind his trademark glasses, Molotov's eyes were unreadable. But at last he said, "If I can talk with them after they invaded the *rodina*, no reason for those who are here not to be put to good use."

Ludmila sagged with relief. Schultz did not seem to have followed enough of the conversation to know he'd been in danger. But then, he'd been in danger since the moment he rolled across the Soviet border. Perhaps he'd grown used to it—though Ludmila never had.

"You have the flight plan, Comrade Pilot?" Molotov asked.

"Yes," Ludmila said, tapping a pocket in her leather flying suit. That made her think of something else. "Comrade Foreign Commissar, your clothing may be warm enough on the ground, but the *Kukuruznik*, as you see, is an airplane with open cockpits. The wind of our motion will be savage . . . and we will be flying north."

To get to Germany at all, the little U-2 would have to fly around three sides of a rectangle. The short way, across Poland, lay in the Lizards' hands. So it would be north past Leningrad, then west through Finland, Sweden, and Denmark, and finally south into Germany. Ludmila hoped the fuel dumps promised on paper would be there in fact. The *Kukuruznik*'s range was only a little better than five hundred kilometers; it would have to refuel a number of times on the journey. On the other hand, if travel arrangements for the foreign commissar of the Soviet Union went awry, the nation was probably doomed.

"Can I draw flying clothes like yours from the commandant of this base?" Molotov asked.

"I am certain Colonel Karpov will be honored to provide you with them, Comrade Foreign Commissar," Ludmila said. She was just as certain the colonel would not dare refuse, even if it meant sending one of his pilots out to freeze on the fellow's next mission.

Molotov left the revetment. Schultz started to laugh. Ludmila turned a questioning eye on him. He said, "A year ago this time, if I'd shot that little hardnosed pigdog, the *Führer* would have stuck the Knight's Cross, the Swords, and the Diamonds on me—likely kissed me on both cheeks, too. Now I'm helping him. Bloody strange world." To that Ludmila could only nod.

When the foreign commissar returned half an hour later, he looked as if he'd suddenly gained fifteen kilos. He was bundled into a leather and sheepskin flight suit, boots, and flying helmet, and carried a pair of goggles in his left hand. "Will these fit over my spectacles?" he asked.

"Comrade Foreign Commissar, I don't know." Ludmila had never heard of a Red Air Force flier who needed spectacles. "You can try them, though."

Molotov looked at his wristwatch. Just getting to it under the bulky flight suit was a struggle. "We are due to depart in less than two hours. I trust we shall be punctual."

"There should be no trouble," Ludmila said. A lot of the mission would be flown at night to minimize the chance of interception. The only problem with that was the U-2's aggressively basic navigational gear: compass and airspeed indicator were about it.

As things happened, there was a problem: the little Shvetsov engine didn't want to turn over when Georg Schultz spun the prop. In the seat in front of Ludmila's, Molotov clenched his jaw. He said nothing, but she knew he was making mental notes. That chilled her worse than the frigid night air.

But this problem had a solution, borrowed from the British: a Hicks starter, mounted on the front of a battered truck, revolved the propeller shaft fast enough to kick the engine into life. "God-damned sewing machine!" Schultz bawled up to Ludmila, just to see her glare. The acrid stink of the exhaust was perfume in her nostrils.

The U-2 taxied to the end of the airstrip, bumped along the couple of hundred meters of badly smoothed ground as it built up speed—and at the end of one bump, didn't come back to earth. Ludmila always relished the feeling of leaving the ground. The wind that blasted into her face over and around her little windscreen told her she was really flying.

And tonight she relished taking off for another reason as well. As long as the *Kukuruznik* stayed in the air, she was in charge, not Molotov. That was a heady feeling, like being on the way to drunk. If she did a tight snap roll and flew upside down for a few seconds, she could check how well he'd fastened his safety belt . . .

She shook her head. Foolishness, foolishness. If people had disappeared in the purges of the thirties—and they had, in great carload lots—the German invasion proved there were worse things. Some Soviet citizens had been willing (and *some* Soviet citizens had been eager) to collaborate with the Nazis, but the Germans showed themselves even more brutal than the NKVD.

But now Soviets and Nazis had a common cause, a foe that threatened to crush them both, regardless, even heedless, of ideology. Life, Ludmila thought with profound unoriginality, was very strange.

The biplane droned through the night. Snow-draped fields alternated with black pine forests below. Ludmila stayed as low as she dared: not as low as she would have during the day, for now a swell of ground could be upon her before she knew it was there. Her route swung wide around the Valdai Hills just to cut that risk.

The farther north she flew, the longer the night became, also. It was as if she drew darkness around the aircraft . . . though winter nights anywhere in the Soviet Union were quite long enough.

Her first assigned refueling stop was between Kalinin and Kashin, on the upper reaches of the Volga. She buzzed around the area where she thought the airstrip was until her fuel started getting dangerously low. She hoped she wouldn't have to try to put the U-2 down in a field, not with the passenger she was carrying.

Just when she thought she would have to do that—better with power than dead stick—she spied a lantern or electric torch, swung the *Kukuruznik* toward it. More torches came on, briefly, to mark the borders of a landing strip. She brought in the U-2 with gentleness that surprised even herself.

Whatever Molotov thought of the landing, he kept it to himself. He rose stiffly, for which Ludmila could hardly blame him—after four and a half hours in the air, she too had cramps and kinks aplenty.

Ignoring the officer in charge of the airstrip, the foreign commissar stumped off into the darkness. *Looking for a secluded place to piss*, Ludmila guessed: the most nearly human response she'd yet seen from Molotov.

The officer—the collar tabs of his greatcoat were Air Force sky-blue and bore a winged prop and a major's two scarlet rectangles—turned to Ludmila and said, "We are ordered to render you every assistance, Senior Lieutenant Gorbunov."

"Gorbunova, sir," Ludmila corrected, only a little put out: the heavy winter flight suit would have disguised any shape at all.

"Gorbunova—pardon me," the major said, eyebrows rising. "Did I read the despatch wrong, or was it written incorrectly? Well, no matter. If you have been chosen to fly the comrade foreign commissar, your competence cannot be questioned." His tone of voice said he did question it, but Ludmila let that go. The major went on, more briskly now, "What do you require, Senior Lieutenant?"

"Fuel for the aircraft, oil if necessary, and a mechanical check if you have a mechanic who can do a proper job." Ludmila put first things first (she also wished she could have lashed Georg Schultz to the U-2's fuselage and carried him along). Almost as an afterthought, she added, "Food and someplace warm for me to sleep through the day would be pleasant."

"Would be necessary," Molotov amended as he came back to the *Kukuruznik*. His face remained expressionless, but his voice betrayed more animation; Ludmila wondered how hard he'd been fighting to hold it in. Her own bladder was pretty full, too. Perhaps confirming her thought, the foreign commissar continued, "Tea would also be welcome now." *Not before*, ran through Ludmila's mind—*he would have exploded.* She knew that feeling.

The major said, "Comrades, if you will come with me . . ." He led Ludmila and Molotov toward his own dwelling. As they kicked their way through the snow, he bawled orders to his groundcrew. The men ran like wraiths in the predawn darkness, easier to follow by ear than by eye.

The major's quarters were half hut, half dug-out cave. A lantern on a board-and-trestle table cast a flickering light over the little chamber. A samovar stood nearby; so did a spirit stove. Atop the latter was a pot from which rose a heavenly odor.

With every sign of pride, the major ladled out bowls of borscht, thick with cabbage, beets, and meat that might have been veal or just as easily might have been rat. Ludmila didn't care; whatever it was, it was hot and filling. Molotov ate as if he were stoking a machine.

The major handed them glasses of tea. It was also hot, but had an odd taste—a couple of odd tastes, in fact. "Cut with dried herbs and barks, I'm afraid," the major said apologetically, "and sweetened with honey we found ourselves. Haven't seen any sugar for quite a while."

"Given the circumstances, it is adequate," Molotov said: not high praise, but understanding, at any rate.

"Comrade Pilot, you may rest there," the major said, pointing to a pile of blankets in one corner that evidently served him for a bed. "Comrade Foreign Commissar, for you the men are preparing a cot, which should be here momentarily."

"Not necessary," Molotov said. "A blanket or two will also do for me."

"What?" The major blinked. "Well, as you say, of course. Excuse me, comrades." He went back out into the cold, returned in a little while with more blankets. "Here you are, Comrade Foreign Commissar."

"Thank you. Be sure to awaken us at the scheduled time," Molotov said.

"Oh, yes," the major promised.

Yawning, Ludmila buried herself in the blankets. They smelled powerfully of their usual user. That didn't bother her; if anything, it was reassuring. She wondered how Molotov, who was used to sleeping softer than with blankets on dirt, would manage here. She fell asleep herself before she found out.

Some indefinite while later, she woke with a start. Was that horrible noise some new Lizard weapon? She stared wildly around the Air Force major's quarters, then started to laugh. Who would have imagined that illustrious Vyacheslav Mikhailovich Molotov, foreign commissar of the USSR and second in the Soviet Union only to the Great Stalin, snored like a buzzsaw? Ludmila pulled the blankets up over her head, which cut the din enough to let her get back to sleep herself.

After more borscht and vile, honey-sweetened tea, the flight resumed. The U-2 droned slowly through the night—an express train could have matched its speed—north and west. Snow-dappled evergreen forests slid by below. Ludmila hugged the ground as tightly as she dared.

Then, without warning, the trees disappeared, to be replaced by a long stretch of unbroken whiteness. "Lake Ladoga," Ludmila said aloud, pleased at the navigational check the lake gave her. She flew along the southern shore toward Leningrad.

Well before she got to the city, she skimmed low over the lunar landscape of the German and Soviet lines around it. The Lizards had pounded both impartially. Before they came, though, the heroism and dreadful privations of the defenders of Leningrad, home and heart of the October Revolution, had rung through the Soviet Union. How many thousands, how many hundreds of thousands, starved to death inside the German ring? No one would ever know.

And now she was flying Molotov to confer with the Germans who had subjected Leningrad to such a cruel siege. Intellectually, Ludmila understood the need for that. Emotionally, it remained hard to stomach.

Yet the *Kukuruznik* she flew had been efficiently maintained by a German, and, from what Georg Schultz had said, he and Major Jäger had fought alongside Russians to do something important: either he didn't understand exactly what or he was keeping his mouth shut about that or both. So it could be done. It would have to be done, in fact. But Ludmila did not like it.

As the shore of Lake Ladoga had before, now the Gulf of Finland gave her something to steer by. She began to peer ahead, looking for landing lights: the next field was supposed to be not far from Vyborg.

When Ludmila finally spotted the lights, she bounced the biplane in a good deal more roughly than she had at the last airstrip. The officer who greeted her spoke Russian with an odd accent. That was not unusual in the polyglot Soviet Union, but then she noticed that several of his men wore coalscuttle helmets. "Are you Germans?" she asked, first in Russian and then *auf Deutsch*.

"*Nein*," he answered, though his German sounded better than hers. "We are Finns. Welcome to Viipuri." His smile was not altogether pleasant; the town had passed from Finnish to Soviet hands in the Winter War of 1939–40, but the Finns took it back when they joined the Nazis against the USSR in 1941.

"Can one of your mechanics handle this type of aircraft?" she asked.

With an ironic glint in his eye, he scanned the *Kukuruznik* from one end to the other. "Meaning no disrespect, but I think any twelve-year-old who is handy with tools could work on one of these," he answered. Since he was probably right, Ludmila kept her annoyance to herself.

The Finnish base had better food than Ludmila had tasted in some time. It also seemed cleaner than the ones from which she'd been fighting. She wondered whether that was because the Finns hadn't seen as much action against the Lizards as the Soviets had.

"Partly," the officer who'd greeted her said when she asked. His greatcoat, she noticed once they were inside, was gray, not khaki; it had three narrow bars on the cuffs. She wondered what rank that made him. "And partly, again meaning no disrespect, you may see that other people are often just generally neater about things than you Russians. But never mind that. Would you care to use our *sauna*?" When he saw she didn't understand the Finnish word, he turned it into German: "Steam-bath."

"Oh, yes!" she exclaimed. Not only was it a chance to get clean, it was a chance to get *warm*. The Finns didn't even leer at her when she went in alone, as Russians would have done. She wondered how manly they were.

Flying over Finland and then over Sweden, she thought about what the Finnish officer had said. Just looking down at countryside that war had not ravaged was new and different; flying past towns that weren't burned-out ruins took her thoughts back to better days she'd almost forgotten in the midst of combat's urgency.

Even under snow, though, she could see the orderly patterns of fields and fences. Everything was on a smaller scale than in the Soviet Union, and almost toylike in its tiny perfection. She wondered if the Scandinavians were neater than Russians simply because they had so much less land and had to use it more efficiently.

That impression grew stronger in Denmark, where even forest had all but vanished and every square centimeter seemed put to some useful purpose. And then, past Denmark, she flew into Germany.

Germany, she saw at once, had been at war. Though her flight path took her a couple of hundred kilometers west of murdered Berlin, she saw devastation that matched anything she'd come across in the Soviet Union. In fact, first the British and then the Lizards had given Germany a more concentrated beating from the air than the Soviet Union as a whole had received. Town after town had factories, train stations, and residential blocks pounded to ruins.

For that matter, the Lizards were still pounding Germany. When Ludmila heard the roar of their jets, she flew doubly low and slow, as if her U-2 were a tiny gnat buzzing by the floor, too small to be worth noticing.

The Germans were still fighting back, too. Tracers spiderwebbed across the night sky like fireworks. Searchlights stabbed, trying to pin Lizard raiders with their beams. Once or twice, off in the distance, Ludmila heard piston engines racing. *So*, she thought, *the* Luftwaffe *still has fighters in the air, too.*

As she flew farther south, the land began to rise. Her landing strip the fourth night of her flight, outside a little town called Suilzbach, was in what looked to have been a potato field. A ground crew dragged her plane to cover while a *Luftwaffe* officer drove her and Molotov to town in a horse-drawn wagon. "The Lizards are too likely to shoot at automobiles," he explained apologetically.

She nodded. "It is so with us, too."

"Ah," said the *Luftwaffe* man.

Every so often, *Pravda* or *Izvestia* would describe the atmosphere in diplomatic talks as "correct." Ludmila hadn't quite understood what that meant. Now, seeing the way the Germans treated her and Molotov, she did. They were polite, they were attentive, but they couldn't hide that they wished they didn't have to deal with the Soviets at all. It was mutual, Ludmila thought, at least as far as she was concerned. As for Molotov, he was seldom more than civil to anyone, Russian or German.

Ludmila had to work hard to suppress a yelp of glee at the prospect of sleeping in a real bed for the first time in she couldn't remember how long. Suppress it she did, lest the Nazis take her for uncultured. She also studiously ignored the *Luftwaffe* officer's hints that he wouldn't mind sleeping in that same bed with her.

To her relief, he didn't get obnoxious about it. He did say, "You will, I hope, forgive me, but I would not recommend trying to fly to Berchtesgaden by night, *Fräulein* Gorbunova."

"My rank is senior lieutenant," Ludmila answered. "Why would you not recommend this?"

"Flying at night is difficult enough—"

"I have flown a good many night attack missions, both against the Lizards and against you Germans," she said: let him make of that what he would.

His eyes widened, but only momentarily. Then he said, "Maybe so, but those, I dare say, were out on the Russian steppe, not in the mountains." He waited for her response; she nodded, yielding the point. He went on, "The danger is worse in the mountains, not only because of the terrain but also from gusts of wind. Your margin of error would be unacceptably low for a mission of this importance, especially since you will want to stay as low to the ground as you can."

"What do you suggest, then? A flight by day? The Lizards are too likely to shoot me down."

The German said, "I admit this. To protect you as you fly by day, though, we will sortie several squadrons of fighters—not to escort you, for that would attract unwanted attention to your aircraft, but to distract the Lizards from the area through which you will be passing."

Ludmila considered that. Given the inequality between German planes and what the Lizards flew, some pilots would almost certainly be sacrificing their lives to make sure she and Molotov got through to this Berchtesgaden place. She also knew she had no experience in mountain flying. If the Nazis were willing to help her mission so, she decided she had to accept. "Thank you," she said.

"Heil Hitler!" the *Luftwaffe* man answered, which did nothing to make her happier about working with Germans.

When she and Molotov went clip-clopping out to the airstrip next morning, she discovered the German ground crew had daubed the U-2's wings and fuselage with splotches of whitewash. One of the fellows in overalls said, "Now you'll look more like snow and rocks."

Soviet winter camouflage was more thoroughly white, but snow drifted more evenly across the steppe than it did in mountains. She didn't know how much the whitewash would help, but supposed it couldn't hurt. The groundcrew man grinned as she thanked him in her accented German.

When she got a good look at the mountains toward which she was flying, she was glad she'd taken the *Luftwaffe* officer's advice and not tried to make the trip by night. The landing field to which she was ordered lay not far outside the village of Berchtesgaden. When she set the *Kukuruznik* down there, she assumed Hitler's residence lay within the village.

Instead, a long wagon ride up the side of the mountain—Obersalzberg, she learned it was called—followed. Molotov sat staring stonily straight ahead the whole way up. He said nothing much. Whatever went on behind the mask of his face, he kept it there. He glared right through the soldiers at two checkpoints, ignored the barbed wire that ringed the compound.

Hitler's *Berghof*, when the wagon finally reached it, reminded Ludmila of a pleasant little resort house (the view was magnificent) swallowed up by a residence that met the demands of a world leader. Molotov was whisked away into the *Berghof*; Ludmila thought she recognized his German counterpart, von Ribbentrop, from newsreels during the strange couple of years when the Soviet Union and Germany held to their friendship treaty.

She wasn't important enough to be lodged in the *Berghof*. The Germans escorted her over to a guesthouse not far away. As she stood in the splendid lobby, all she could think was how many workers and peasants had had their labor exploited to create it. She was primly certain no one in the classless Soviet Union cared to live in such unnecessary splendor.

Down the staircase came an officer in the natty black uniform and beret of the German panzer formations: a colonel, by the two pips on each braided shoulder strap. On his right breast he wore a large, garish eight-pointed gold star with a swastika in the center. He was lean and perfectly shaved and looked quite at home here close by his *Führer*; just watching his smooth stride made Ludmila feel short and dumpy and out of place. She swung the knapsack that held her few belongings over one shoulder.

The motion drew the natty colonel's eye. He stopped, stared, then hurried across the parquet floor to her. "Ludmila!" he exclaimed, and went on in fair Russian: "What the devil are you doing here?"

She recognized his voice even if she hadn't known his face. "Heinrich!" she said, trying hard not to pronounce it with an initial *g* as Russians often did. She was so glad to find someone she knew that, heedless equally of startled looks from her German escorts and of what Molotov would think when the news got back to him, she gave Jäger a hug he enthusiastically returned. "You've been promoted two grades," she observed. "That's wonderful."

His grin was self-deprecating. "They offered me a choice: lieutenant-colonel and the Knight's Cross or colonel and just Hitler's fried egg here." He patted the gaudy medal. "Excuse me, the German Cross in gold. They thought I'd take glory. I took rank. Rank lasts."

"Hitler's fried egg?" Ludmila echoed in delicious amazement. She noticed her escorts were ostentatiously pretending they hadn't noticed that. She shook her head. "My, we'll have a lot to talk about."

"Yes, we will." For a moment, Jäger's face assumed the watchful expression she'd first seen at the Ukrainian *kolkhoz*. Then the smile came back. "Yes, we will," he repeated. "Quite a lot."

Atvar stared out at the assembled shiplords. They silently stared back. He tried to gauge their mood before he called the meeting to order. Nothing short of mutiny—maybe not even that—would have surprised him. Well past one of the Race's years into a campaign even expected to be a walkover, no one had yet turned one eye turret, let alone two, toward victory.

The fleetlord decided to confront that head-on: "Assembled males, I know we face new problems almost every day on Tosev 3. Sometimes we are even forced to face old problems over again, as in the Tosevite empire called Italia."

The shiplord Straha stood, crouched, and waited to be recognized. When Atvar pointed to him, he asked, "How *did* the Deutsche manage to kidnap what's-his name—the Big Ugly in charge of Italia—"

"Mussolini," Atvar supplied.

"Thank you, Exalted Fleetlord. Yes, Mussolini. How did the Deutsche manage to steal him when we shut him up in that castle away from everything after he had surrendered his empire to us?"

"How they learned where he was, we do not know," Atvar admitted. "They are skilled at such irregular warfare, and I must concede the move has embarrassed us."

"Embarrassed us? I should say so." Straha added an emphatic cough. "His radio broadcasts from Deutschland negate much of the value we got from that Big Ugly from Warsaw, the one who spoke so convincingly against the Deutsche."

"Russie," Atvar said after a quick glance at a tickler file on the computer screen in front of him. The file also told him something else: "We'd reached the point of diminishing returns with that one in any case. His last statement had to be electronically altered to make it conform to our requirements."

"The Big Uglies have not yet adjusted themselves to the idea that the Race will rule over them," the shiplord Kirel said mournfully.

"And why should they?" Straha retorted, his voice dripping sarcasm. "As far as I can see, they have no reason to. This affair with Mussolini is but one more embarrassment in a long series. Now Italia seethes with sabotage, where before it was among the calmest of the empires under our control."

Feneress, a male of Straha's faction, chimed in, "Moreover, it lets the Deutsche make a folk hero of this"—he checked his own computer for the name he sought—"this Skorzeny who led the raid, and encourages other Tosevites to try to emulate his feat."

Kirel started to come to Atvar's defense, but the fleetlord held up a hand. "What you say is true, Feneress," he replied. "For his failure, the male in charge of the Big Ugly Mussolini's security would normally have found himself liable to severe disciplinary action. As, however, he perished in the Tosevite raid, this has become impracticable."

The assembled shiplords stirred and murmured among themselves. For the fleetlord to admit failure so frankly was strange and untoward. No wonder they murmured: they had to be trying to figure out what Atvar's concession meant. Did it signal a change in strategy? Did it mean Atvar would resign his post, perhaps in favor of Straha? If so, what did that imply for each shiplord?

Atvar raised his hand again. Slowly, the murmurs died away. The fleetlord said, "I did not summon you to the bannership to dwell on failure, assembled shiplords. On the contrary. I summoned you here to outline a course which, I believe, will give us victory."

The officers stirred and murmured all over again. Some of them, Atvar knew, had begun to despair of victory. Others still thought it could be attained, but the means they wanted to use would leave Tosev 3 a ruin unfit for settlement by the colonization fleet now traveling across interstellar space toward the planet. If he could prove them wrong and still make the Big Uglies submit, Atvar would be ahead indeed. And he thought he could.

He said, "We have been discomfited by the disturbingly advanced technology the Tosevites have demonstrated. Were it not for those advances—whose causes we are still investigating—the conquest of Tosev 3 would have been routine."

"And we all would have been a lot happier," Kirel put in. Atvar saw shiplords' mouths fall open. That they could still laugh was a good sign.

"We have been perhaps slower than we should in appreciating the implications of the Big Uglies' technology," the fleetlord said. "Compared to the Tosevites, the Race *is* slow. They have used that fact to their advantage against us. But we are also thorough. Compare our Empire, *the* Empire, to the ephemeral makeshift empires and irrational administrative schemes under which they live. And now we have found a flaw in their technology which we hope we can exploit."

He'd grabbed their attention. By the way they stared hungrily at him, he might have been some powdered ginger in front of a crowd of addicts. (He made himself put that problem out of his mind for now. He had to dwell on advantages, not problems.)

He said, "Our vehicles and aircraft are fueled by hydrogen and oxygen produced electrolytically from water with energy from the atomic engines of our starships. Getting all the fuel we need has never been a problem—if Tosev 3 possesses anything in excess, it is water. And, perhaps not surprisingly, we have evaluated the Big Uglies' capabilities in terms of our own. This evaluation has proved erroneous."

The shiplords murmured yet again. High-ranking members of the Race were usually less candid about admitting error, especially when it reflected discredit on them. Atvar would also have been less candid than he was, had the advantage he gained here not outweighed the damage he suffered for acknowledging previous wrong.

"Instead of hydrogen and oxygen, Tosevite aircraft and ground and sea vehicles run on one distillate of petroleum or another," he said. "This has disadvantages, not least among them the noxious fumes such vehicles emit while operating."

"That's true, by the Emperor," Straha said. "Go into one of the cities that we rule and your nictitating membranes will sizzle from all the garbage in the air."

"Indeed," Atvar said. "Pollutants aside, however, our engineers assure me there is no reason for petroleum-based engines to be less efficient than our own. In fact, they may even have certain minor advantages: because their fuels are liquids at ordinary temperatures, they don't require the extensive insulation around our vehicles' hydrogen tanks, and thus save weight."

Kirel said, "Still, it is criminal to waste petroleum by simply burning it when it may be put to so many more advantageous uses."

"Truth. When the conquest is complete, we shall phase out this profligate technology," Atvar said. "I might note, however, that our geologists believe Tosev 3 has more petroleum than any of the Empire's other planets, perhaps more than all three put together, in part due to its anomalously large percentage of water surface area. But this takes us away from the point on account of which I summoned today's assembly."

"What is that point?" Three shiplords said it together. In other circumstances, the blunt question would have come perilously close to insubordination. Now, though, Atvar was willing to forgive it.

"The point, assembled males, is that even on Tosev 3 petroleum is, as the shiplord Kirel said, a precious and relatively uncommon commodity," the fleetlord answered. "It is not found worldwide. The empire, or rather the not-empire, of Deutschland, for example, has but one primary source of petroleum, that being in the subordinate empire called Romania." He used a hologram to show the shiplords where Romania lay, and where inside its boundaries sat the underground petroleum pool.

"A question, Exalted Fleetlord?" called Shonar, a male of Kirel's faction. He waited for Atvar to recognize him, then said, "Shall we be required to occupy the petroleum-producing regions not already under our control? That could prove expensive in terms of both males and munitions."

"It will not be necessary," Atvar declared. "In some instances, we need not even attack the areas where petroleum comes from the ground. As I noted before, the Big Uglies burn not just petroleum in their vehicles, but rather distillates of petroleum. The facilities which produce those distillates are large and prominent. Identify and destroy them and we have destroyed the Tosevites' ability to resist. Is this clear?"

By the excited hisses and squeaks that came from the assembled shiplords, it was. Atvar wished the Race had found this strategy as soon as the conquest began. Wish as he would, though, he could not blame anyone too severely: Tosev 3 was simply so different from what the Race had expected to find that his technical staff had needed a while to figure out what was important and what wasn't. Now—he hoped—they had.

"By a year from now," he said, "Tosev 3 shall be under our claws." The males in the conference chamber gobbled and hooted. The Race's applause filled Atvar with a warm glow of pride. He might yet go down in the annals of his people as Atvar the Conqueror, subduer of Tosev 3.

The shiplords took up a chant: "May it be so! May it be so!" At first, Atvar took that as an expression of confident expectation. After a moment, though, he realized it could also have another meaning: if the Race hadn't conquered the Big Uglies within the coming year, how much trouble would it face by that year's end?

Grinding through the air high above the Isle of Wight, George Bagnall thought he could see forever. The day was, for once, brilliantly clear. As the Lancaster wheeled through another of its patrol circuits, the English Channel, France across it, and England were in turn spread out before him like successive examples of the cartographer's craft.

"Wonder how they ever made maps and got the shapes right before they could fly over them and *see* the way they were supposed to look," he said.

In the pilot's seat beside him, Ken Embry grunted. "I wonder what it looks like to the Lizards. They get up high enough to take in the whole world at a glance."

"Hadn't thought of that," the flight engineer said. "It would be something to see, wouldn't it?" He was filled with sudden anger that the Lizards had a privilege denied mankind. Under the anger, he realized, lay pure and simple envy.

"We'll just have to make the best of what we've got." Embry leaned forward against the restraint of his belts, pointed down toward the gray-blue waters of the Channel. "What do you make of that ship, for instance?"

"What do you think I am, a bloody spotter?" But Bagnall leaned forward, too. "It's a submarine, by God," he said in surprise. "Submarine on the surface in the Channel . . . one of ours?"

"I'd bet it is," Embry said. "Lizards or no Lizards, somehow I don't think Winnie is dead keen on having U-boats slide past the skirts of the home islands."

"Can't blame him for that." Bagnall took another look. "Westbound," he observed. "Wonder if it's carrying something interesting for the Yanks."

"There's a thought. Lizards aren't much when it comes to sea business, are they? I expect a sub'd be all the harder for them to take out." Embry leaned forward once more himself. "A bit of fun to guess, eh? Most days we'd be all swaddled in cotton batting up here and not have the sport of it."

"That's true enough." Now Bagnall twisted around in his chair to peer back into the bomb bay—which for some time had housed no bombs. "Most days Goldfarb has a better view of the world than we do. Radar cares nothing for clouds: it peers right through them."

"So it does," Embry said. "On the other hand, given the choice of jobs, I'd sooner peep out through the Perspex on a scene like this—or even on the usual clouds, come to that—than be stuck in the bowels of the aircraft watching electrons chase themselves."

"You get no arguments from me," Bagnall said. "None whatever. But then, I dare say Goldfarb's a bit of a queer bird all the way around. Fancy spending so long mooning after that barmaid Sylvia, finally getting her, and then throwing her aside bare days later."

The pilot laughed goatishly. "Maybe she wasn't as good as he'd hoped."

"I doubt that." Bagnall spoke from experience. "Never a dull moment there."

"I'd have thought as much from her looks, but one can't always judge by looks, enjoyable as it may be to try." Embry shrugged. "Well, it's not my affair, in either the literal or figurative sense of the word, and just as well, too. Speaking of Goldfarb, however . . ." He flicked the intercom switch. "Any sign of our scaly little chums, Radarman?"

"No, sir," Goldfarb said. "Dead quiet here."

"Dead quiet," Embry repeated. "Do you know, I quite like the ring of that."

"Yes, rather," Bagnall said. "One more mission from which we have some reasonable hope of landing." The flight engineer chuckled. "We've been living so long on borrowed time by now that I sometimes entertain hopes we shan't have to repay it one day."

"Disabuse yourselves of those, my friend. The day they took the limit off the number of missions an aircrew could be ordered to fly, they signed our death warrants, and no mistake. The trick lies in evading the inevitable as long as one can."

"After you got us down safe in France, I refuse to believe anything is impossible," Bagnall said.

"I was at least as surprised at surviving that as you, believe me: nothing like a bit of luck, what?" Embry laughed. "But if the Lizards choose not to stir about for another couple of hours, I concede we shall have had an easy time of it today. We are occasionally entitled to one such, don't you think?"

The Lizards did stay quiet. At the appointed hour, Embry gratefully swung the Lanc back toward Dover. The return descent and landing were so smooth that the pilot said, "Thank you for flying BOAC today," as the bulky bomber rolled to a stop. No commercial passengers, however, ever deplaned so rapidly as the men who flew with him.

As Bagnall scrambled out of the cockpit and down onto the tarmac, one of the groundcrew men gave him a cheeky grin. " 'Ere, you must've heard they've got the power on again, you're out an' 'eadin' for the barracks so quick."

"Have they?" The flight engineer stepped up his pace from quick to double-quick. All sorts of delightful visions danced in his head: light by which to read or play cards, an electric fire, a working hotplate on which to brew tea or heat water for a proper shave, a phonograph that spun . . . the possibilities seemed to stretch as far as the horizon had up in the Lancaster.

One that had entirely slipped his mind was listening to the BBC. Several weeks had gone by since the barracks last had power while the Beeb was on the air: the Lizards kept plastering the transmitter, trying to silence the human broadcast. Just hearing the newsreader made Bagnall once more feel part of a world larger than the airbase and its environs.

It had a different effect on David Goldfarb. "By God," he said, cocking his head toward the wireless set, "I wish I could talk like that."

Having a pretty fair public-school accent himself, Bagnall took the broadcaster's smooth tones for granted. When it was pointed out to him, though, he could see how they'd rouse jealousy in the heart of one from London's lower middle class: he was no Henry Higgins, but his ear pretty accurately placed Goldfarb.

The BBC man said, "We now present in its entirety a recording recently received in London from underground sources in Poland. The speaker is Mr. Moishe Russie, hitherto familiar to many as an apologist for the Lizards. A translation will follow."

The recording began. Bagnall had a little German, but found it didn't help much; unlike Russie's previous propaganda broadcasts, this one was in Yiddish. The flight engineer wondered if he should ask Goldfarb what Russie was saying. Perhaps not; the Jewish radarman was humiliated at having a quisling for a cousin. Goldfarb plainly had no trouble following Russie without translation. He stared at the wireless set as if he could see his relative there. Every so often, his right fist would come down thump on his thigh.

In the brief moment of silence that followed the end of Russie's statement, the radarman exclaimed, "Lies! I knew it was all lies!"

Before Bagnall could ask what was all lies, the BBC newsreader returned. "That was Mr. Moishe Russie," he said, his voice even more mellow than usual when heard hard on the heels of Yiddish gutturals. "And now, as promised, the translation. Here is our staffer, Mr. Nathan Jacobi."

A brief rustle of papers, then a new voice, just as cultured as the one that had gone before: "Mr. Russie spoke as follows: 'My last broadcast for the Lizards was a fraud from top to bottom. I was forced to speak with a gun to my head. Even then, the Lizards had to alter my words to force them into the meaning they desired. I categorically condemn their efforts to enslave mankind, and urge all possible resistance. Some may wonder why I ever spoke on their behalf. The answer is simple: their attack on Germany aided my people, whom the Nazis were murdering. When a folk is being slaughtered, even slavery seems a preferable alternative, and an enslaver can be looked upon with gratitude. But the Lizards have proved murderers, too, not just of Jews but of mankind in its entirety. God help each and every one of us find the strength and courage to resist them.'"

After more rustlings, the first BBC man came back on the air: "That was Mr. Nathan Jacobi, translating into English Mr. Moishe Russie's repudiation of recent statements he has made on behalf of the Lizards. This cannot fail to embarrass the alien invaders of our world, who see even their seemingly loyalest associates turn against their vicious and aggressive policies. The prime minister, Mr. Churchill, has expressed his admiration for the courage required of Mr. Russie in making this repudiation and his hope that Mr. Russie will succeed in escaping the Lizards' vengeance. In other news—"

David Goldfarb sighed deeply. "Nobody here has any notion of how fine that makes me feel," he announced to the barracks at large.

"Oh, I think we might," Ken Embry said. Bagnall had been about to say something along those lines himself, but decided the pilot's understatement did the job for both of them.

Goldfarb laughed. "The British way of speaking used to drive my father mad. He learned English quick enough after he got over here, but he never has fathomed how people can get along without screaming at each other now and again, whether they're angry or happy."

"What do you think we are, a pack of bloody fishwives?" Bagnall did his best to sound deeply offended. The restrained public-school accent didn't make it any easier.

"I was talking about him, not me," Goldfarb said. "I can read between the lines, you might say, and I know what you mean. You're a grand lot of chaps, every bloody one of you." He laughed again. "And I know that's more than a proper Englishman ought to say, but who says I'm proper? I wish I could get some leave; it's been too damned long since I got to go home and shout at my relations."

What a bizarre notion, Bagnall thought. Family ties were all very well, but the aircrew had largely replaced his relatives at the center of his life. Only after a few seconds did he think to wonder whether Goldfarb had something he lacked.

Through his interpreter, Adolf Hitler said, "Good day, *Herr* Foreign Commissar. I hope you slept well? Come in, come in; we have much of which to speak."

"Thank you, Chancellor." Vyacheslav Molotov followed Hitler into the small living room which had been part of the German leader's Berchtesgaden retreat before that was incorporated into the grander *Berghof* surrounding it.

Molotov supposed being ushered into Hitler's *sanctum sanctorum* was an honor. If so, he would willingly have forgone it. Everything in the room screamed *petit-bourgeois* at him: the overstuffed furniture with its old-German look, the rubber plants, the cactus—good heavens, the place even had a brass canary cage! Stalin would laugh when he heard about that.

Strewn here and there on the chairs and couches were embroidered pillows, most of them decorated with swastikas. Swastika-bedizened knickknacks crowded tables. Even Hitler looked embarrassed at their profusion. "I know they aren't what you'd call lovely," he said, waving at the display, "but the German women make them and send them to me, so I don't like to throw them away."

Petit-bourgeois *sentimentality, too,* Molotov thought scornfully. Stalin would also find that funny. The only sentiment Stalin had in him was a healthy regard for his own aggrandizement and that of the Soviet Union.

But the twisted romantic streak made Hitler more dangerous, not less, because it meant he acted in ways that could not be rationally calculated. His invasion of the USSR had sent Stalin into several days of shock before he began rallying Soviet resistance. Compared to German imperialism, that of the British and French was downright genteel.

Now, though, the whole world faced imperialism from aliens whose ancient economic and political systems were joined with a technology more than modern. Molotov had repeatedly gone through the words of

Marx and Engels to try to grasp how such an anomaly could be, but without success. What was clear was that advanced capitalist (even fascist) and socialist societies had to do everything in their power to resist being thrown catastrophically backward in their development.

Hitler said, "You may thank General Secretary Stalin for sharing with Germany the possible explosive materials which were obtained by the combined German-Soviet fighting team."

"I shall do so." Molotov inclined his head in a precise nod. As well he had long schooled his features to reveal nothing, for they did not show Hitler the consternation he felt. So that damned German tankman had got through after all! That was very bad. Stalin had intended proffering the image of cooperation, not its substance. He would not be pleased.

Hitler went on, "The government of the Soviet Union is to be commended for thinking this explosive too valuable to be flown to Germany and letting it come by the overland route where even you, *Herr* Foreign Commissar, traveled here by air."

The sarcasm there was enough to raise welts, not least because Molotov loathed flying of any sort and had been ordered by Stalin into the horrible little biplane that brought him to Germany. Pretending everything was serene, Molotov said, "Comrade Stalin solicited the advice of military experts and then followed it. He is of course delighted that your consignment reached you safely by the plan he devised." A thumping lie, but how was Hitler supposed to call him on it, especially since the courier had somehow beaten the odds of the journey?

But Hitler found a way: "Please tell *Herr* Stalin also that he would have done better to fly it here, as then we should not have had half of it hijacked by Jews."

"What's that?" Molotov said.

"Hijacked by Jews," Hitler repeated, as if to a backward child. Molotov concealed his irritation in the same way he concealed everything not immediately relevant to the business at hand. Hitler gestured violently; his voice rose to an angry shout. "As the good German major was traversing Poland, he was halted at gunpoint by Jewish bandits who forced him to divest himself of half the precious treasure he was bringing to German science."

This was news, and unsettling news, to Molotov. He could not resist a barb in return: "Had you not so tormented the Jews in the states your armies overcame, no doubt they would have been less eager to interfere with the courier."

"But the Jews are parasites on the body of mankind," Hitler said earnestly. "They have no culture of their own; the foundations of their situation of living are always taken from those around them. They completely lack the idealistic attitude, the will to contribute to the development of others. Look how they, more than anyone else, have cozied up to the Lizards' backsides."

"Look why they have," Molotov returned. His wife, Polina Zhemchuzhina, was of Jewish blood, though he did not think Hitler knew that. "Anyone drowning will grab for a spar, no matter where he finds it." *So the British joined us in the fight against you,* he thought. Aloud, he went on, "Besides, has not the Lizards' former chief spokesman among the Polish Jews repudiated them and gone into hiding?"

Hitler waved that aside. "Aliens themselves in Europe, they find their fit place toadying to the worse aliens who now torment us."

"What do you mean?" Molotov asked sharply. "Have they turned over to the Lizards the explosive metal they took from the courier? If so, I demand that you allow me to communicate with my government immediately." Stalin would have to know at once that the Lizards knew for certain human beings were working to duplicate their much greater weapons so he could apply yet another layer of secrecy to his project.

"No, not even they were so depraved as that," Hitler admitted; he sounded reluctant to make any concession, no matter how small.

"Well, what then? Did they keep it for themselves?" Molotov wondered what the Polish Jews would do if they had kept the explosive metal. Would they make a bomb and use it against the Lizards, or would they make one and use it against the *Reich*? That question would have been going through Hitler's mind, too.

But the German leader shook his head. "They did not keep it, either. They are going to try to smuggle it to the fellow Jews in the United States." Hitler's little toothbrush mustache quivered, as if he'd just smelled something rotten.

Molotov wondered how many of those Jews would have fled to the United States had the Nazis not forced them out of Germany and its allies. The tsars and their pogroms had done the same thing in pre-Communist Russia, and the present Soviet Union was the poorer for their shortsightedness. Molotov was too convinced an atheist to take any religion seriously as far as doctrine, but Jews tended to be both clever and well educated, valuable traits in any nation that aspired to build and grow.

With a scissorslike effort of will, the foreign minister snipped off those irrelevant threads of thought and returned to the matter at hand. He said, "I need to inform the General Secretary of the Communist Party of the Soviet Union of this development." It wasn't as urgent as if the Lizards had learned what Stalin was up to, but it was important news. America, after all, not Germany or Britain, was the most powerful capitalist state and so the most likely future opponent of the Soviet Union . . . assuming such concerns kept their meaning in a world with Lizards in it.

"Arrangements will be made for you to communicate," Hitler said.

"The telegraph through Scandinavia remains fairly reliable and fairly secure."

"That will have to do," Molotov said. Fairly reliable he could deal with; nothing could be expected to work perfectly. But fairly secure! The Nazis were bunglers indeed if they tolerated security that was only fair. Inside, where it did not show, the Soviet foreign minister smiled. The Germans had no idea how thoroughly agents of the USSR kept Stalin informed about everything they did.

"The nefarious Jews came close to preventing our brilliant Aryan scientists from having the amount of explosive metal with which they needed to work," Hitler said. Molotov made a mental note of that; it meant the Americans also probably had a marginal quantity of the material—and it meant the Soviet Union had plenty. Stalin had a right to expect results from his own researchers, then.

But Hitler wasn't thinking about that; what he had in mind was vengeance. "The Lizards must come first," he said. "I admit this. They are the greatest present danger to mankind. But after them, we shall punish the Jewish traitors who, true to their nature, aligned themselves with the alien against the Aryan essence of true creative humanity."

His voice rose almost to a screech in that last sentence. Now, abruptly, it turned low, conspiratorial: "And you Russians owe the Poles a little something, eh?"

"What's that?" Molotov said, caught off guard and stalling for time. Even though he needed the interpreter to follow Hitler's words, he could hear the control the German leader had over his tone. That made him a formidable orator—certainly more effective there than Stalin, who was not only pedantic but had never lost his Georgian accent.

"Come, come," Hitler said impatiently. "You must have heard the Lizards' Polish collaborators going on about the so-called massacre of their officers at Katyn, trying to discredit the Soviet Union in the same way the Jews paint the *Reich* with a big black brush."

"I do not trouble myself with the Lizards' propaganda broadcasts," Molotov said, which was true; he had underlings listen to them for him. As for Katyn, he thought, the Poles had little to fuss about. After the Soviets reannexed the eastern half of Poland (which had, after all, belonged to Russia for more than a century before the chaos of the Revolution broke it loose and let Pilsudski establish his fascist state there), what were they to do with the reactionary officers who had fallen into their hands? Turn them loose and let them foment rebellion? Not likely! By Soviet standards, getting rid of those few thousand unreliables was but a small purge.

Hitler said, "Both your government and mine have reason to be unhappy with those who dwell in the anomalous territory of Poland. We were wise to divide it between ourselves once. When the Lizards are dealt with, we can join in punishing the inhabitants of that land to the full extent they deserve."

"By which you mean with bombs of this explosive metal?" Molotov asked. Hitler nodded. Molotov said, "I cannot view this proposal favorably. Our scientists report the wind spreads poisons from these weapons over an area far broader than the site of the explosion itself. And since the prevailing winds are from west to east, the Soviet Union would be adversely affected by this devastation, however much the Poles may deserve it."

"Well, we can discuss it further at another time." Hitler sounded casual but looked unhappy. Had he expected Molotov to cooperate in devastating his own country? Maybe he had; the Germans had even less use for Russians than they did for Poles. But Russian scientists and engineers had already shown themselves better than the Nazis expected a great many times.

"No, let us discuss it now," Molotov said. Hitler looked unhappier yet, as he had back in 1940 when Molotov demanded specifics on the workings of the German-Soviet nonaggression treaty. No wonder he'd looked unhappy then; he was already plotting the Nazi attack on the USSR. What was he plotting now? The Soviet foreign minister repeated, "Let us discuss it now. Let us assume, for example, that we manage to defeat the Lizards completely. What then will be the proper relations, what then will be the proper boundaries, between the German *Reich* and the Soviet Union? Both I and General Secretary Stalin await your reply to this question with great interest."

The interpreter stumbled a couple of times in translating that; perhaps he tried to shade its bluntness. Hitler gave Molotov a baleful stare. His German toadies did not talk to him like that (for that matter, had Molotov talked to Stalin that way, he would have vanished within days, perhaps within minutes).

"If the Lizards are completely defeated, we will then review our relations with the Soviet Union, as with all nations of the world," the *Führer* answered. "How they are defeated will obviously have a great deal to do with the nature of that review."

Molotov started to complain that Hitler hadn't really said anything, but left those words unuttered. The Nazi leader had a point. Who did what to beat the Lizards would play a role in what the world looked like after they were beaten . . . if they were beaten.

Not a complaint, Molotov decided—*a warning.* "You must be aware of one thing," he told Hitler, who assumed an apprehensive expression, as if a dentist had just announced he needed more work. Molotov went on, "Your earlier remark indicated that you hoped to exploit Soviet ignorance of these explosive-metal bombs. This behavior is intolerable, and makes me understand how and why the Jews of Poland preferred the Lizards' yoke to yours. We have need of one another now, but Comrade Stalin will never again trust you, as he did after August 1939."

"I never trusted your pack of Jews and Bolsheviks," Hitler shouted. "Better to be under the hissing Lizards than the red flag." His whole body quivered. Molotov braced himself to endure a ranting speech like those that came hissing and popping out of the world's shortwave sets. But then, with an almost physical effort of will, Hitler made himself be calm. "Living alongside the red flag, however, may yet be possible. As you say, *Herr* Molotov, we have need of each other."

"*Da,*" Molotov said. He'd pushed Hitler hard, as Stalin had ordered, and the German still seemed to think cooperation—even if on his own terms wherever possible—a better gamble than any other.

"On one thing I think we can agree," Hitler persisted: "when all this is done, the map of Europe need no longer be stained by what has been miscalled the nation of Poland."

"Perhaps not. Its existence has sometimes been inconvenient for the Soviet Union as well as Germany," Molotov said. "Where would you place the boundary between German and Soviet control? On the line our two states established in 1939?"

Hitler looked pained. *Well he might,* Molotov thought with a frosty smile. The Nazis had overrun Soviet-occupied Poland in the first days of their treacherous attack; their line ran hundreds of kilometers to the east when the Lizards came. But if they were serious about working with the USSR, they would have to pay a price.

"As I said before, precise details can be worked out come the day," Hitler said. "For now, let me ask again if we agree in principle: first the Lizards, then the *Untermenschen* between us?"

"In principle, yes," Molotov said, "but as with all principles, details of implementation are critical. I might also note in passing—speaking of principles—that in times past German propaganda has frequently identified the people and Communist Party of the USSR as subhuman. This produces yet another difficulty in harmonious relations between our two nations."

"When we announce that you and I have conferred, we shall make no such statements," Hitler assured him. "You and I both know that what one advances for purposes of propaganda is often irrelevant to one's actual beliefs."

"That is certainly true," Molotov said. The example that flashed through his mind was all the pro-German material his own government had pumped out in the year and ten months before June 22, 1941. The converse also applied, but he had no doubts about where the Nazis' sincere feelings lay.

Hitler said, "You will of course take lunch with me."

"Thank you," Molotov said resignedly. The meal proved as abstemious as he'd expected: beef broth, a dry breast of pheasant (Hitler did not touch his portion), and a salad. The *Führer* kept his personal life simple. That did not, however, make him any more comfortable to deal with.

"I haven't ridden on a hay wagon since I got off the farm," Sam Yeager said as the wagon in question rolled west on U.S. 10 into the outskirts of Detroit Lakes, Minnesota. "And I haven't been through here since—was it '27? '28? something like that—when I was in the Northern League and we'd swing through on the way from Fargo to Duluth."

"Duluss I know, for we get off horrible boat thing there," said Ristin, who huddled in the wagon beside him, "but what is—Fargo?" The Lizard POW made the name sound like a Bronx cheer.

"Medium-sized town, maybe fifty miles west of where we are," Yeager answered.

Barbara Larssen rode in the wagon, too, though she sat as far away from him as she could. Still, her voice was casual as she asked, "Is there any place in the United States you haven't been, one time or another?"

"I haven't been up through the Northeast much—New York, New England. The towns there, they either belong to the International League or the bigs, and I never made it there." Yeager spoke without bitterness, simply stating a fact.

Barbara nodded. Yeager cautiously watched her. After those frenzied couple of minutes in her cabin on the *Caledonia*, he hadn't touched her, not even to help her in or out of a wagon. She hadn't spoken to him at all the first three days they were on the ship, and only in monosyllables the fourth. But since they'd unloaded at Duluth and started the slow plod west, she'd traveled in the same part of the wagon convoy as he did, and the last couple of days in the same wagon. Yesterday she'd talked more with Ullhass and Ristin than with him, but today everything seemed— well, not quite all right, but at least not too bad.

He looked around. The low, rolling hills were white with snow; it also covered the ice that sealed northern Minnesota's countless lakes. "It's not like this in summer," he said. "Everything's smooth and green, and the lakes sparkle like diamonds when the sun hits them at the right angle. The fishing is good around these parts—walleyes, pike, pickerel. I hear they fish here in the wintertime, too, cut holes in the ice and drop a line down. I don't see much sport in going out and freezing when you don't have to, myself."

"So much water," Ullhass said, turning one eye turret to the left and the other to the right. "It seems not natural."

"It seems not natural to me, too," Barbara said, "I'm from California, and the idea of fresh water just lying around all over the place strikes me as very strange. The ocean is all right, but fresh water? Forget it."

"Ocean is not natural, too," Ullhass insisted. "Have seen pictures of Tosev 3—this world—from—what do you say—outer space, yes? Looks all water, sometimes. Looks wrong." He emphasized the last word with the emphatic cough.

"Seeing Earth from space," Yeager said dreamily. How long would it have been before men managed that? In his lifetime? Maybe.

On the north shore of Detroit Lake, a little south of the actual town of Detroit Lakes, stood a tourist camp with cabins and picnic benches and a couple of bigger resort hotels, all looking much forlorn half a year out of the season for which they were built. "This place just buzzes in July," Yeager said. "They have themselves a summer carnival that won't quit, with floats and swimming and diving, races for canoes, races for speedboats, bathing beauties—"

"Yes, you'd like that," Barbara murmured.

Sam's ears got hot, but he gamely went on with what he'd been about to say: "—and all the beer a man could drink, even though it was still Prohibition when I went through here. I don't know if they brought it down from Canada or brewed it themselves, but the whole team got blitzed— 'course, we didn't call it that back then. Good thing the road back to Fargo ran straight and flat, or the bus driver would've killed us all, I expect."

Though the cabins were intended for summer use, several of them were open now, with wagons pulled up alongside. Barbara pointed. "Some of those aren't from our convoy; they're in the group that came by way of Highway 34."

"Good to see they've made it here," Yeager said. The refugees from the Met Lab hadn't traveled west across Minnesota all together, for fear such a large wagon train would bring Lizard aircraft down on them. In some places, though, the roads came together. Detroit Lakes was a scheduled layover point.

The wagon driver looked back from his team of plodding horses and said, "Look at all the firewood the people round about here got chopped for us. It's like, if they'd known we were coming, they'd've baked a cake."

When he got down from the wagon, Yeager discovered the locals *had* baked a cake. In fact, they'd baked a lot of cakes—though some, he noted, were made from potato flour, and none had any frosting. But such details were soon lost in a great profusion of eggs and turkey, steaks and fried chickens, legs of lamb . . . he lost track of what he was eating as he stuffed himself. "After so long living out of tin cans in Chicago, I almost forgot they made spreads like this," he said to a Detroit Lakes man who carried around yet another platter of drumsticks.

"We've got more than we know what to do with, when it comes to livestock," the fellow answered. "We used to ship all the way to the East Coast before the damned Lizards came. Now everything's just bottled up here. We'll run short of feed before too long, and have to really start slaughtering, but for now we're still fat. Happy to share with you folks. It's a Christian thing to do . . . even for those critters."

With undisguised curiosity, the local watched Ristin and Ullhass eat. The Lizards had manners, though not identical to those of Earthlings. Their technique for eating a drumstick was to stab it with a fork, hold it up to their snouts, and then nibble off bits. Every so often, their forked tongues would come out to clean grease off their hard, immobile lips.

Wagons kept coming into Detroit City every fifteen or twenty minutes; they'd been widely spread out to minimize damage from any air strikes that did descend on them (so far, none had, for which Yeager was heartily grateful—coming under air attack once was a thousand times too many). The natives greeted each one as if it held the Prodigal Son.

When shelters were assigned, Yeager found himself with a double cabin that had been altered in advance for use by him and his alien charges. Each of the two rooms had its own wood-burning stove and a bountiful supply of fuel—by now, Ullhass and Ristin knew how to keep a fire going. The windows on the Lizards' side had boards nailed across them to prevent escape (though Yeager was willing to bet they wouldn't have tried to run away from their heater). The connecting door between the rooms opened only from his side.

He got Ullhass and Ristin settled for the evening, then went back to his own half of the cabin. It wasn't luxuriously furnished: a table with a kerosene lantern, clothes tree, slop bucket (better that, he thought, than going to an outhouse in the middle of the night—it'd probably freeze right off), cot piled high with extra blankets. *So it isn't the Biltmore*, he thought. *It'll do.*

He sat down on the cot. He wished he had something to read—an *Astounding*, by choice. He wondered what had happened to *Astounding* since the Lizards came; the last issue he'd seen was the one he'd been reading the day the train down from Madison got shot up. But science fiction wouldn't be the same now that real live bug-eyed (or at least chameleon-eyed) monsters were loose on Earth and bent on conquest.

He bent down to untie his shoes, the only item of clothing he intended to take off tonight. He'd grown so used to sleeping in his uniform to stay warm that doing anything else was starting to seem unnatural.

He'd just grabbed a shoelace when someone scratched at the door. "Who's that?" Yeager wondered out loud. It had to be something to do with the Lizards, he thought, but whatever it was, couldn't it wait till morning? The scratching came again. Evidently it couldn't. Muttering under his breath, he got up and opened the door. "Oh," he said. It wasn't anything to do with the Lizards. It was Barbara Larssen.

"May I come in?" she asked.

"Oh," he said again, and then, "Sure. You'd better, in fact, or all the heat will get out."

There was no place to sit but the cot, so that was where she sat. After what had happened on the *Caledonia* and the way she'd acted since, Yeager didn't know if he ought to sit down beside her. With the instincts of a man who automatically moved back a few steps to prevent the extra-base hit in the late innings, he decided to play safe. He paced back and forth in front of the stove.

Barbara watched him for a few seconds, then said, "It's all right, Sam. I don't think you're going to molest me. That's what I wanted to talk about with you, anyway."

Yeager perched cautiously near the head of the cot, at the opposite end from Barbara. "What is there to talk about?" he said. "It was just one of those crazy things that happens sometimes. If you want to pretend it never did—" He started to finish with *that's all right*. But it wasn't, not quite. He tried a different phrase: "You can." That was better.

"No. I owe you an apology." She wasn't looking at him; she was looking at the worn, grayish-yellow boards of the floor. "I shouldn't have treated you the way I did afterward. I'm sorry. It's just that after we—did it, I really realized Jens is, is dead, he has to be dead, and that all came down on me at once. I am sorry." She covered her face with her hands. After a few seconds, he realized she was crying.

He slid down the cot toward her, put a hesitant hand on her shoulder. She stiffened at his touch, but then spun half around and buried her face against his chest. His arms could hardly help folding around her. "It's okay," he said, not knowing whether it was okay or not, not even knowing whether she heard him or not. "It's okay."

After a while, her sobs subsided to hiccups. She pushed herself away from him, then reached into her purse and dabbed at herself with a hanky. She ruefully shook her head. "I must look like hell."

Sam considered that. Tears still glistened on her cheeks and brimmed in her eyes. She wasn't wearing any mascara or shadow to streak and run. If her face was puffy from crying, it didn't show in the lantern light. But even if it had, so what? "Barbara, you look real good to me," he said slowly. "I've thought so for a long time."

"Have you?" she said. "You didn't really let on, not until—"

"Wasn't my place to," he answered, and stopped there.

"Not as long as there was any hope Jens was still alive, you mean," she said, filling it in for him. He nodded. Her face twisted, but she forced it back to steadiness. "You're a gentleman, Sam, do you know?"

"Me? I don't know anything about that. All I know is—" He stopped again. What had started to come out of his mouth was, *All I know is baseball, and I've spun my wheels there for too damn many years.* That was true, but it wasn't what Barbara needed to hear right now. He gave another try: "All I know is, I'll try to be good for you if that's what you want me to do."

"Yes, that's what I want," she said seriously. "Times like these, nobody can get through by himself. If we don't help each other, hold onto each other, what's the use of anything?"

"You've got me." He'd been on the road by himself for a lot of years. But he hadn't really been alone: he'd always had the team, the pennant race, the hope (though that had faded) of moving up—substitutes for family, goal, and dreams.

He shook his head. No matter how deeply baseball had dug its claws into his soul, this was not the time to be thinking about it. Still wary, still a little unsure, he put his arms around Barbara again. She looked at the floor and let out such a long sigh, he almost let go. But then she shook her head; he had a pretty good idea what she was telling herself to forget. She tilted her face up to his.

Later, he asked, "Do you want me to blow out the lamp?"

"Whichever way you'd like," she answered. She was probably less shy about undressing with it burning than he was; he reminded himself she was used to being with a man. They got under the covers together, not for modesty but for warmth.

Later still, after they'd warmed themselves enough to kick most of the blankets onto the floor, they lay with their arms wrapped around each other. The cot was so narrow, it gave them little choice about that. Yeager ran a hand down Barbara's back, learning the shape and feel of her. There hadn't been time for that aboard the *Caledonia*; there hadn't been time for anything except raw, driving lust. He'd never known anything to match that, maybe not even the night he lost his cherry, but this was pretty fine, too. It felt somehow more certain, as if he could be sure it would last.

Barbara's breasts slid against his chest as she leaned up on one elbow. She lay between him and the lamp, so her face was full of shadow. When she spoke, though, her words weren't quite what he thought of as romantic: "Do you want to see if you can buy some rubbers tomorrow, Sam? This place seems in good shape; the drugstore may still have a supply."

"Uh, okay," he said, taken aback. She was indeed used to being with a man, he thought. He did his best to sound matter-of-fact as he went on, "Probably a good idea."

"Certainly a good idea," she corrected. "We're all right about the first time—I know—and I don't mind taking a chance now and again, but if we're going to be making love a lot, we'd better be careful. I don't want to be expecting going cross-country in a wagon train."

"I don't blame you," he said. "I'll try and find some. Uh—what happens if I don't?" He wished he hadn't said that. It would make her think he only wanted to lay her. He did want to lay her, but he'd learned you seldom got anywhere treating a woman like a piece of meat, especially not a woman like this, who'd been married to a physicist and had plenty of brains herself.

He was in luck—she didn't get mad. Her hand wandered now, or rather moved, for she knew where it was going. It closed on him. "If you don't," she said, "we'll just have to figure out something else to do." She squeezed gently.

He couldn't decide whether he wanted some Detroit Lakes drugstore to have rubbers or not.

Behind Mutt Daniels, the Preemption House was burning. His heart felt like breaking for several reasons. It was always sad to see history go up in smoke, and the two-story Greek Revival frame building had been one of Naperville, Illinois', prides since 1834. More immediately, it was far from the only burning building in Naperville. Mutt didn't see how the Army could hold the town—and there wasn't a hell of a lot behind Naperville but Chicago itself.

And more immediately still, the Preemption House had been Naperville's leading saloon. Daniels hadn't been in town long, but he'd managed to liberate a fifth of good bourbon. He wore three stripes on his sleeves these days; just as kids had looked to him on how to be ballplayers, now he had to show them how to be soldiers. These days he borrowed his precepts from Sergeant Schneider instead of his own old managers.

Every half a minute or so, another liquor bottle inside the Preemption House would cook off, like a round inside a burning tank. Looking back, Mutt saw little blue alcohol flames flickering among the big lusty red ones from the burning timbers. He sighed and said, "Hell of a waste."

"You bet, Sarge," said the private beside him, a little four-eyed fellow named Kevin Donlan, who, by his looks, would probably start shaving one day fairly soon. Donlan went on, "That building must be more than a hundred years old."

Daniels sighed again. "I wasn't thinkin' so much about the building."

A whistling roar in the sky, growing fast, made both men dive for the nearest trench. The shell went off above ground level; fragments hissed through the air. So did other things that pattered and bounced off the hard ground like hailstones.

"You gotta watch where you put your feet now, son," Daniels said. "That bastard just spit out a bunch o' little bombs or mines or whatever you want to call 'em. First saw those out around Shabbona. You step on one, you'll walk like Peg-Leg Pete in the Disney cartoons the rest of your days."

More shells rained down; more of the little rolling mines scattered from them. A couple went off with short, unimpressive cracks, hardly louder than the screams that followed them. "They keep throwin' those at us, we ain't gonna be able to move around at all, Sergeant Daniels," Donlan said.

"That's the idea, son," Mutt said dryly. "They pound on us for a while, freeze us in place like this, then they bring in the tanks and take the ground away from us. If they had more tanks, they'd've finished kickin' our butts a long time ago."

Donlan hadn't seen close-up action yet; he'd joined the squad during the retreat from Aurora. He said, "How can those things beat on us like this? They ain't even human."

"One of the things you better understand right quick, kid, is that a bullet or a shell, it don't care who shot it or who gets in the way," Daniels said. "Besides, the Lizards got plenty o' balls of their own. I know the radio keeps callin' 'em 'push-button soldiers' to make it sound like all their gadgets is what's whuppin' us and keep the civilians cheerful, but don't let anybody tell you they can't fight."

The artillery barrage went on and on. Mutt endured it, as he'd endured similar poundings in France. In a way, France had been worse. Each of the Lizards' shells was a lot more deadly than the ones the *Boches* had thrown, but the Germans had thrown a *lot* of shells, so it sometimes seemed whole steel mills were falling out of the sky on top of the American trenches. Men would go mad from that—shell shock, they called it. This bombardment was more likely to kill you, but it probably wouldn't drive you nuts.

Through a pause in the shelling, Daniels heard running feet behind him. He swung around with his tommy gun—maybe the Lizards had used their whirligig flying machines to land troops behind human lines again.

But it wasn't a Lizard: it was a gray-haired colored fellow in blue jeans and a beat-up overcoat running along Chicago Avenue with a big wicker basket under one arm. A couple of shells burst perilously close to him. He yelped and jumped into the trench with Daniels and Donlan.

Mutt looked at him. "Boy, you are one crazy nigger, runnin' around in the open with that shit fallin' all around you."

He didn't mean anything particularly bad by his words; in Mississippi, he was used to talking to Negroes that way. But this wasn't Mississippi, and the colored man glared at him before answering, "I'm not a boy and I'm not a nigger, but I guess maybe I am crazy if I thought I could bring some soldiers fried chicken without getting myself called names."

Mutt opened his mouth, closed it again. He didn't know what to do. He'd hardly ever had a Negro talk back to him, not even up here in the North. Smart Negroes knew their place . . . but a smart Negro wouldn't have braved shellfire to bring him food. *Braved* was the word, too; Daniels didn't want to be anywhere but here under cover.

"I think maybe I'll shut the fuck up," he remarked to nobody in particular. He started to address the black man directly, but found himself brought up short—what did he call him? *Boy* wouldn't do it, and *Uncle* wasn't likely to improve matters, either. He couldn't bring himself to say *Mister*. He tried something else: "Friend, I do thank you."

"I'm no friend of yours," the Negro said. He might have added a couple of choice phrases himself, but he had an overcoat and his basket of chicken to set against Daniels' stripes and tommy gun. And Mutt had, after a fashion, apologized. The colored man sighed and shook his head. "What the hell's the use? Here, come on, feed yourselves."

The chicken was greasy, the baked potatoes that went with it cold and savorless without salt or butter. Daniels wolfed everything down anyhow. "You gotta eat when you get the chance," he told Kevin Donlan, "on account of you ain't gonna get the chance as often as you want to."

"You bet, Sarge." The kid wiped his mouth on his sleeve. He took his own tack in talking to the Negro: "That was great, Colonel. A real lifesaver."

"Colonel?" The colored fellow spat in the dirt of the trench. "You know damn well I'm not a colonel. Why don't you just call me by my name? I'm Charlie Sanders, and you could have found it out by askin'."

"Charlie, that was good chicken," Mutt said solemnly. "I'm obliged."

"Huh," Sanders said. Then he scrambled up out of the trench and dashed away toward the next couple of foxholes maybe thirty yards off.

"Watch out for them little mine things the Lizard shells throw around," Daniels yelled after him. He turned back to Donlan. "Hope he makes it. He keeps goin' all around like that, though, his number's gonna come up pretty damn quick."

"Yeah." Donlan peered over in the direction Charlie Sanders had run. "That takes guts. He doesn't even have a gun. I didn't think niggers had guts like that."

"You're under shellfire, son, it don't matter if you've got a gun," Mutt answered. But that wasn't the point, and he knew it. After a while, he went on, "One of my grandfathers, I misremember which one right now, he fought against colored troops one time in the States War. He said they weren't no different than any other damnyankees. Maybe he was right. Me, I don't know anything any more."

"But you're a sergeant," Donlan said, in exactly the same tone some of Daniels' ballplayers had used in exclaiming, *But you're the manager.*

Mutt sighed. "Just on account of I'm supposed to have all the answers, son, that don't mean I can pull 'em out from under my tin hat whenever you need 'em. Hell, come to that, it don't even mean they're really there. You get as old as I am, you ain't sure o' nothin' no more."

"Yes, Sergeant," Donlan said. By the way things were going, Mutt thought, the kid didn't have much chance of getting that old.

"No," General Patton said. "Hell, no."

"But, sir"—Jens Larssen spread his hands and assumed an injured expression—"all I want to do is get in touch with my wife, let her know I'm alive."

"No," Patton repeated. "No, repeat no, traffic about the Metallurgical Laboratory or any of its personnel save in direst emergency—from which personal matters of any sort are specifically excluded. Those are my direct orders from General Marshall, Dr. Larssen, and I have no intention of disobeying them. That is the most basic security precaution for any important project, let alone one of this magnitude. Marshall has told me next to nothing about the project, and I do not wish to acquire more information: I have not the need to know, and therefore should not—must not—know."

"But Barbara's not even with the Met Lab," Jens protested.

"Indeed not, but *you* are," Patton said. "Are you so soft that you would betray the hope of the United States to the Lizards for the sake of your own convenience? By God, sir, I hope you are not."

"I don't see how one message constitutes a betrayal," Larssen said. "Odds are the Lizards wouldn't even notice it."

"Possible," Patton admitted. He got up from behind his desk and stretched, which also gave him the advantage of staring down at Jens. "Possible, but not likely. If the Lizards' doctrine is at all like ours—and I've seen no reason to doubt that—they monitor as many of our signals as they can, and try to shape them into informative patterns. I speak from experience, sir, when I say that no one—*no* one—can know in advance which piece of the jigsaw puzzle will reveal enough for the enemy to form the entire picture in his mind."

Jens knew about security; the Met Lab had had large doses of it. But he'd never been subject to military discipline, so he kept arguing: "You could send a message without my name on it, just 'Your husband is alive and well' or something like that."

"No; your request is refused," Patton said. Then, as if reading Larssen's mind, he added, "Any attempt to ignore what I have just said and inveigle a signals officer into clandestinely sending such a message will result in your arrest and confinement, if not worse. I remind you I have military secrets of my own here, and I shall not permit you to compromise them. Do I make myself quite clear?"

"Yes, sir, you do," Larssen said dejectedly. He'd been all set to try to find a sympathetic radioman no matter what Patton said; he still didn't believe such an innocuous message would have blown the Met Lab's cover. But he couldn't gauge how much outgoing messages might endanger the offensive still building here in western Indiana. That had to succeed, too, or nothing that happened in Chicago would matter, because Chicago would belong to the Lizards.

"If it helps at all, Dr. Larssen, you have my sympathy," Patton said.

In a gruff sort of way, he probably even meant it, Jens thought. He said, "Thank you, General," and walked out of Patton's office.

Outside, the ground was mottled with melting snow and clumps of yellowish dead grass. Thick low yellow-gray clouds rolled by overhead. The wind came from out of the northwest, and carried a nip that quickly started to turn Jens' beaky nose to an icicle. It had all the makings of a winter storm, but no snow fell.

His thoughts as gloomy as the weather, Larssen walked on in Oxford, Indiana. *Potemkin village* ran through his mind. From the air, the little town undoubtedly seemed as quiet as any other gasoline-starved hamlet in the Midwest. But concealed by houses and garages, haystacks and wood-piles, gathered armored forces plenty, Jens thought, to give the Nazis pause. The only trouble was, they faced worse foes than mere Germans.

Larssen stepped into the Bluebird Cafe. A couple of locals and a couple of soldiers in civvies (nobody not in civvies was allowed on the streets of Oxford—*security again*, Jens thought) sat at the counter. Behind it, the cook made pancakes on a wood-burning griddle instead of his now useless gas range. The griddle wasn't vented; smoke filled the room. He looked over his shoulder at Larssen. "Waddaya want, mac?"

"I know what I *want*: how about a broiled lobster tail with drawn butter, asparagus in hollandaise sauce, and crisp green salad? Now, what do you have?"

"Good luck with the lobster, buddy," the cook said. "What I got is flapjacks here, powdered eggs, and canned pork and beans. You don't fancy that, go fishing."

"I'll take it," Jens said. It was what he'd been eating ever since that wonderful chicken dinner with General Patton. He wasn't as skinny as he had been when the Army scooped him up, but he'd long since sworn he'd never look a baked bean in the eye again if and when the war ever ended.

The only virtue he could find to the meal was that he didn't have to pay for it. Patton had taken over the handful of eateries in town and incorporated them into his commissary department. Larssen supposed that was fair; without the supplies they drew from the Army, they'd long since have closed down.

The better to conceal his soldiers, Patton had also billeted them on the townsfolk. As far as Jens knew, he hadn't asked anybody for permission before he did it, either. If Patton worried about that, he didn't let on. Maybe he had a point; the Founding Fathers hadn't anticipated an invasion from outer space.

But if you started fiddling with the Constitution and pleading military necessity, where would you stop? Jens wished he'd been in a better position to take that up with Patton. It might have made an interesting philosophical discussion if the general hadn't been steamed at him for trying to get a message to Barbara. As things were, Patton would either roar at him or ignore him, neither of which constituted an enlightened exchange of views.

"Anybody got a cigarette?" asked one of the soldiers in civvies.

The only answer Larssen expected to that was a horse laugh, and the soldier got one. Then a civilian, a leathery fellow in a hunting cap who had to be pushing seventy, looked the kid over and drawled, "Son, even if I did have one, you ain't pretty enough to give me what I'd want for it."

The young soldier turned the color of the fire under the griddle. The cook solemnly sketched a hash mark in the air. Larssen whistled. The old-timer let out a dry chuckle to show he wasn't all that impressed with his own wit, then returned to his cup of what the Army called, for lack of a suitable term of opprobrium, coffee.

High overhead, above the clouds, a Lizard jet flew by, its wail thin and fading with distance. Larssen's shiver had nothing to do with the weather. He wondered how well the aliens' sensors, whatever they were, could peer through the gray mass that shielded Oxford and the countryside around it from the sky . . . and how well Patton had managed to hide the carefully husbanded gear here. He'd know soon enough.

In one corner of the cafe stood a broken pinball machine, the mournful word TILT permanently on display. Since that constituted the place's entire potential for entertainment, Jens handed his plate and cutlery back to the cook and went out onto the street.

The wind had picked up while he ate. He was glad for his overcoat. His nose was also relieved at the fresh air. Full of soldiers as it was and without much working plumbing, Oxford had become an odorous place. If the buildup here went on a little longer, the Lizards wouldn't need visual reconnaissance to find their human foes: their noses would do the job for them.

Something stung Jens on the cheek. By reflex he brought up his hand, but felt only a tiny patch of moisture. Then he got stung again, this time on the wrist. He looked down, saw a fat white snowflake melting away to nothingness. More slipped and slid wildly through the air, jitterbug dancers made of ice.

For a moment, he just watched. The start of a snowfall always took him back to his Minnesota childhood, to snowmen and snow angels and snowballs knocking stocking caps off heads. Then the present rose up and smote nostalgia. This snow had nothing to do with childhood's pleasures. This snow meant attack.

Yi Min felt bigger than life, felt, in fact, as if he were the personification of Ho Tei, fat little god of luck. Who would have imagined so much profit was to be made from the coming of the little scaly devils? At first, when they'd raped him away from his home village and then taken him up into the plane that didn't land, the plane where he weighed nothing and his poor stomach even less, he'd thought them the worst catastrophe the world had ever known. Now, though . . . He smiled oleaginously. Now life was good.

True, he still lived in this camp, but he lived here like a warlord, almost like one of the vanished Manchu emperors. His dwelling was a hut in name only. Its wooden sides were proof against the worst winter winds. Brass braziers gave heat, soft carpets cushioned his every stride, fine pieces of jade and cloisonné delighted his eye wherever it happened to light. He ate duck and dog and other delicacies. When he wanted them, he enjoyed women who made Liu Han seem a diseased sow by comparison. One waited on his mattress now. He'd forgotten her name. What did it matter?

And all from a powder the scaly devils craved!

He laughed out loud. "What is it, man full of *yang*?" the pretty girl called from the other room. She sounded impatient for him to join her.

"Nothing—just a joke I heard this morning," he answered. However full of masculine essence he was, he still had too much hard sense to make a hired mattress partner privy to his thoughts. What one set of ears heard in the afternoon, a score would know by sunrise and the whole world by the next night.

Without false modesty (Yi Min had little modesty, false or otherwise), he knew he was far and away the biggest ginger dealer in the camp, probably in China, maybe in the whole world. Under him (the girl crossed his mind again, but only for a moment) were not only men who grew the spice and others who cured it with lime to make it particularly tasty to the scaly devils, but several dozen scaly devils who bought from him and sold to their fellows, either directly or through their own webs of secondary dealers. How the loot rolled in!

"Will you come soon, Tiger of the Floating World?" the girl said. She did her best to make herself alluring, but she was too much a businesswoman—and too little an actress—to keep a strident note from her voice. *What's keeping you?* she meant.

"Yes, I'll be there in a moment," he answered, but his tone suggested she wasn't worth hurrying over. Having a woman resent him for what he made her do fed his own excitement. He wasn't just taking pleasure that way, but also control.

What should we do when I finally go to her? he wondered: always an enjoyable contemplation. Something she wouldn't care for—she'd annoyed him. Maybe he'd use her as if she were a boy. He snapped his fingers in delight. The very thing! Women were so proud of the slit between their legs; ignoring it in favor of the other way never failed to irritate them. Besides, it would hurt her a little too, make her remember to treat him as the person of consequence he was.

Warmth flowed through him, tingled across his skin. He felt himself rising. He took one step toward the bedroom, then checked himself. Anticipation was also a pleasure. Besides, let her stew.

After a minute or two, she called, "Please hurry! Longing eats at me." She played the game, too, but her mah-jongg hand did not have the tiles to beat his.

When at last he judged the moment ripe, he started off to the back part of the dwelling. Before he'd gone three paces, though, a scratching noise came from the front door. He let out a long, angry hiss. That was a scaly devil. The girl's comeuppance would have to wait. No matter how thoroughly he controlled the devils who bought ginger from him, the illusion remained that he was servant and they masters.

He opened the door. Cold nipped at his fingers and face. A little scaly devil indeed, but not one he'd seen before—he'd grown skilled at telling them apart, even when, as now, the swaddlings they wore against winter hid their body paint. He'd also grown fluent in their speech. He bowed low, said, "Superior sir, you honor my humble hut. Enter, please, and warm yourself."

"I come." The little scaly devil skittered past Yi Min. He closed the door after it. He was pleased it had answered him in its own language. If he could do business in that tongue, he wouldn't have to send away the courtesan. Not only would she have longer to wait, she'd be impressed at how he dealt with the little devils on their terms.

The devil looked around his front room, its eye turrets swiveling independent of each other. That no longer unnerved Yi Min; he was used to it. He studied the scaly devil, the strong color inside its nostrils, the way its clawed hands had a slight quiver to them. Inside, he smiled. He might not know the devil, but he knew the signs. This one needed ginger, and needed it worse every second.

He bowed again. "Superior sir, will you tell me your name, that I may serve you better?"

The little scaly devil hissed, as if suddenly reminded of Yi Min's presence. "Yes. I am called Drefsab. You are thc Big Ugly Yi Min?"

"Yes, superior sir, I am Yi Min." The Race's insulting nickname for human beings didn't bother Yi Min. After all, he thought of its males as little scaly devils. He said, "How may I be of assistance to you, superior sir Drefsab?"

The scaly devil swung both eyes in his direction. "You are the Big Ugly who sells to the Race the powder known as ginger?"

"Yes, superior sir, I am that humble person. I have the honor and privilege to provide the Race with the pleasure the herb affords." Yi Min thought about asking the little scaly devil straight out whether it wanted ginger. He decided not to; though the devils were more direct about such matters than Chinese, they sometimes found direct questions rude. He did not want to offend a new customer.

"You have much of this herb?" Drefsab asked.

"Yes, superior sir." Yi Min was getting tired of saying that. "As much as any valiant male could desire. If I may say so, I think I have given more males bliss with powdered ginger than all but a handful of Tosevites." He used the little devils' less offensive name for his own kind. Now he did ask: "If the superior sir Drefsab desires a sample of the wares here, I would be honored to provide him with one without expecting anything in return." *This time,* he added to himself.

He thought Drefsab would leap at that; he'd hardly ever seen a scaly devil in more obvious need of his drug. But Drefsab still seemed to feel like talking. He said, "You are the Big Ugly whose machinations have turned males of the Race against their own kind, whose powders have spread corruption through the shining ships from Home?"

Yi Min stared; no matter how well he'd come to use the devils' language, he needed a moment to understand Drefsab's words, which were the opposite of what he'd expected to hear. But the pharmacist's reply came fast and smooth: "Superior sir, I do but try to give the valiant males of the Race what they seek." He wondered what game Drefsab was playing. If the little scaly devil thought to muscle in on his operation, he'd get a surprise. Ginger powder had bought Yi Min the adjutants to several high-ranking officers, and a couple of the officers themselves. They would clamp down on any scaly devil who got too bold with their supplier.

Drefsab said, "This ginger is a tumor eating at the vitality of the Race. This I know, for it has devoured me. Sometimes a tumor must be cut out."

Yi Min again had to struggle to make sense of that; he and the scaly devils with whom he'd conversed hadn't had any occasion to talk about tumors. He was still trying to figure out what the word meant when Drefsab reached inside his protective clothing and pulled out a gun. It spat fire, again and again and again. Inside Yi Min's hut, the shots rang incredibly loud. As the bullets clubbed him to the carpet, he heard through the reports the girl in the bedroom starting to scream.

At first Yi Min felt only the impacts, not the pain. Then it struck him. The world turned black, shot through with scarlet flames. He tried to scream himself, but managed only a bubbling moan through the blood that flooded into his mouth.

Dimly—ever more dimly—he watched Drefsab take the head off the plump Buddha that sat on a low lacquer table. The stinking little devil knew just where he stowed his ginger. Drefsab took a taste, hissed in delight, and poured the rest of the powder into a clear bag he'd also brought along inside his coat. Then he opened the door and left.

The courtesan kept screaming. Yi Min wanted to tell her to shut up and close the door; it was getting cold. The words would not come. He tried to crawl toward the door himself. The cold reached his heart. The scarlet flames faded, leaving only black.

Harbin was falling. Any day now, the Race would be in the city. It would be an important victory; Harbin anchored the Nipponese line. Teerts would have been gladder of it had the town not been falling around his head.

That was literally true. During the most recent raid on Harbin, bombs hit so close to his prison that chunks of plaster rained down from the ceiling and just missed knocking out what few brains he had left after so long in Tosevite captivity.

Outside, an antiaircraft gun began to hammer. Teerts didn't hear any planes; maybe the Big Ugly was just nervous. *Go ahead, waste ammunition,* Teerts thought. *Then you'll have less to fire off when my friends break in here, and then, dead Emperors willing, they won't have to suffer what I've gone through.*

He heard a commotion up the hall, orders barked in loud Nipponese too fast for him to follow. One of the guards came up to his cell. Teerts bowed; with this kind of Big Ugly, you couldn't go far wrong if you bowed and you could go disastrously wrong if you didn't. Better to bow, then.

The guard didn't bow back; Teerts was a prisoner, and so deserving only of contempt. Behind the armed man came Major Okamoto. Teerts bowed more deeply to his interrogator and interpreter. Okamoto didn't acknowledge him, either, not with a bow. He spoke in Teerts' language as he unlocked the cell door: "You will come with me. We leave this city now."

Teerts bowed again. "It shall be done, superior sir." He had no idea how it would be done, or if it could be done, but wondering about such things was not his responsibility. As a prisoner, as had been true in the days before he was captured, his duty was but to obey. Unlike his superiors of the Race, though, the Nipponese owed him no loyalty in return.

Major Okamoto threw at him a pair of black trousers and a baggy blue coat that could have held two males his size. Then Okamoto put a conical straw hat on his head and tied it under his jaws with a scratchy piece of cord. "Good," the Nipponese said in satisfaction. "Now if your people see you from the sky, they think you just another Tosevite."

They would, too, Teerts realized dismally. A gun camera, maybe even a satellite photo, might have picked him out from among the swarming masses of Big Uglies around him. Bundled up like this, though, he would be just one more grain of rice (a food he had come to loathe) among a million.

He thought about throwing off the clothes if one of the Race's aircraft came overhead. Reluctantly, he decided he'd better not. Major Okamoto would make his life not worth living if he tried it, and the Nipponese could spirit him away before his own folk, who were none too hasty, arranged a rescue effort.

Besides, Harbin was *cold*. The hat helped keep his head warm, and if he threw aside the coat, he was liable to turn into a lump of ice before either the Nipponese or the Race could do anything about it. Okamoto's hat and coat were made from the fur of Tosevite creatures. He understood why the beasts needed insulation from their truly beastly climate, and wondered why the Big Uglies themselves had so little hair that they needed to steal it from animals.

Outside the building in which Teerts had been confined, he saw more rubble than he ever had before. Some of the craters looked like meteor strikes on an airless moon. Teerts didn't get much of a chance to examine them; Major Okamoto hustled him onto a two-wheeled conveyance with a Big Ugly between the shafts instead of a beast of burden. Okamoto spoke to the puller in a language that wasn't Nipponese. The fellow seized the shafts, grunted, and started forward. The guard strode stolidly along beside the conveyance.

Tosevites streamed out of Harbin toward the east, fleeing the expected fall of the city. Disciplined columns of Nipponese soldiers contrasted with the squealing, squalling civilians all around them. Some of those, females hardly larger than Teerts, bore on their backs bundles of belongings almost as big as they were. Others carried burdens hung from poles balanced on one shoulder. It struck Teerts as a scene from out of the Race's prehistoric past, vanished a thousand centuries.

Before long, the guard got in front of the manhandled conveyance and started shouting to clear a path for it. When that failed, he laid about him with the butt end of his rifle. Squeals and squalls turned to screams. Teerts couldn't see that the brutality made much difference in how fast they went.

Eventually they reached the train station, which was noisier but less chaotic than the surrounding city. The Race had repeatedly bombed the station. It was more debris than building, but somehow still functioned. Machine-gun nests and tangles of wire with teeth kept everyone but soldiers away from the trains.

When a sentry challenged him, Major Okamoto flipped up Teerts' hat and said something in Nipponese. The sentry bowed low, answered apologetically. Okamoto turned to Teerts. "From here on, we walk. No one but Nipponese—and you—permitted in the station."

Teerts walked, Okamoto on one side of him and the guard on the other. For a little while, a surviving stretch of roof and wall protected them from the biting wind. Then they were picking their way through stone and bricks again, with snow sliding down from a gray, dreary sky.

Out past the station in the railroad yard, troops were filing onto a train. Again a sentry challenged Okamoto on his approach, again he used Teerts as his talisman to pass. He secured half a car for himself, the guard, and his prisoner. "You are more important than soldiers," he smugly told Teerts.

With a long, mournful blast from its whistle, the train jerked into motion. Teerts had shot up Tosevite trains when he was still free. The long plumes of black smoke they spat made them easy to pick out, and they could not flee, save on the rails they used for travel. They'd been easy, enjoyable targets. He hoped none of his fellow males would think the one he was riding a tempting target.

Major Okamoto said, "The farther from Harbin we go, the more likely we are to be safe. I do not mind losing my life for the emperor, but I am ordered to see that you safely reach the Home Islands."

Teerts was willing to lay down his life for *his* Emperor, *the* Emperor, but not for the parvenu Big Ugly who claimed the same title. Given a choice, he would have preferred not to lay down his life for anyone. He'd been given few choices lately.

The train rattled eastward. The ride was tooth-jarringly rough; the Race hit the rails themselves as well as the trains that rolled on them. But the Big Uglies, as they'd proved all over the planet, were resourceful beings. In spite of the bombs, the railroad kept working.

Or so Teerts thought until, some considerable time after the train had pulled out of Harbin, it shuddered to a stop. He hissed in dismay. He knew from experience what a lovely, tasty target a stopped train was. "What's wrong?" he asked Major Okamoto.

"Probably you males of the Race have broken the track again." Okamoto sounded more resigned than angry; that was part of war. "You are sitting by the window—tell me what you see."

Teerts peered through the dirty glass. "I see a whole swarm of Tosevites working at the curve ahead." How many Big Uglies labored there? Hundreds certainly, more likely thousands. No one carried anything more impressive than a pick, a shovel, or a crowbar. If one of the Race's aircraft spied them, a strafing run would leave great red steaming pools in the snow.

But if no aircraft came over, the Big Uglies could perform astonishing feats. Before he came to Tosev 3, Teerts had taken machinery for granted. He'd never imagined that masses of beings armed with hand tools could not only duplicate their results but also work nearly as fast as they did.

He said, "Forgive the ignorant question, superior sir, but how do you keep them from perishing of cold or from being injured at this hard, dangerous work?"

"They are only Chinese peasants," Major Okamoto said with chilling indifference. "As we use them up, we seize as many more as we need to do what must be done."

For some reason, Teerts had expected the Big Uglies to treat their own kind better than they did him. But to the Nipponese, the Tosevites here were not of their own kind, however much alike they seemed to a male of the Race. The reasons for distinction at a level lower than the species as a whole were lost on Teerts. Whatever they were, though, they let the Nipponese treat their laborers like pieces of the machines in whose place they were used, and with as little concern about their fate. That was something else Teerts hadn't imagined before he came to Tosev 3. This world was an education in all sorts of matters where he would have preferred continued ignorance.

The vast swarms of workers (Teerts thought not so much of people as of the little social hive-creatures that occasionally made nuisances of themselves back on Home) drew back from the railroad track after a surprisingly short time. The train rolled slowly forward.

Three or four laborers lay in the snow, too worn to move on to the next stretch of broken track. Nipponese guards—males dressed far more warmly than those in their charge—came up and kicked at the exhausted peasants. One managed to stagger to his feet and rejoin his comrades. The guards picked up crowbars and methodically broke in the heads of the others.

Teerts wished he hadn't seen that. He already knew the Nipponese had no compunctions about doing dreadful things to him if he failed to cooperate or even failed to be useful to them. Yet now he discovered that having knowledge confirmed before his eyes was ten times worse than merely knowing.

The train picked up speed after it passed the repaired curve. "Is this not a fine way to travel?" Okamoto said. "How swiftly we move!"

Teerts had crossed the gulf between the stars at half the speed of light—admittedly, in cold sleep. He ranged the air above this main landmass of Tosev 3 at speeds far greater than sound. How, then, was he supposed to be impressed with this wheezy train? The only conveyance next to which it seemed fast was the one in which the poor straining Tosevite had hauled him to the station.

But that latter sort of conveyance was what the Race had expected to find all over Tosev 3. Maybe the train, decrepit as it appeared to Teerts, was new enough to be marvelous to the Big Uglies. He knew better than to contradict Major Okamoto, anyhow. "Yes, very fast," he said with as much enthusiasm as he could feign.

Through the dirty window, Teerts watched more Tosevites—Chinese peasants, he supposed—struggling to build new defensive lines for the Nipponese. They were having a tough time; the miserable local weather had frozen the ground hard as stone.

He had no idea how sick he'd become of the train, of its endless shaking, of the seat that did not conform to his backside because it made no provision for a tailstump, of the endless jabber from the Nipponese troops in the back of the car, of the odor that rose from them and grew thicker as the journey went on. He even came to miss his cell, something he had not imagined possible.

The journey seemed to stretch endlessly, senselessly. How long could it take to traverse one small part of a planetary surface? Given fuel and maintenance for his killercraft, Teerts could have circumnavigated the whole miserable world several times in the interval he needed to crawl across this tiny portion of it.

He finally grew fed up—and incautious—enough to say that to Major Okamoto. The Big Ugly looked at him for a moment, then asked, "And how fast could you go if someone kept dropping bombs in front of your aircraft?"

After heading east for a day and a half, the train swung south. That puzzled Teerts, who said to his keeper, "I thought Nippon lay in this direction, across the sea."

"It does," Okamoto answered, "but the port Vladivostok, which is nearest to us, belongs to the Soviet Union, not to Nippon."

Teerts was neither a diplomat nor a particularly imaginative male. He'd never thought about the complications that might arise from having a planet divided up among many empires. Now, being forced to stay on the train because of one of those complications, he heaped mental scorn on the Big Uglies, though he realized the Race benefited from their disunity.

Even when the train came down close by the sea, it did not stop, but rumbled through a land Major Okamoto called Chosen. "*Wakarimasen,*" Teerts said, working on his villainous Nipponese: "I do not understand. Here is the ocean. Why do we not stop and get on a ship?"

"Not so simple," Okamoto answered. "We need a port, a place where ships can safely come into land, not be battered by storms." He leaned across Teerts, pointed out the window at the waves crashing against the shore. Home's lakes were surrounded by land, not the other way round; they seldom grew boisterous.

Shipwreck was another concept that hadn't crossed Teerts' mind till he watched this bruising ruffian of an ocean throwing its water about with muscular abandon. It was fascinating to see—certainly more interesting than the mountains that flanked the other side of the track—at least until Teerts had a really horrid thought: "We need to go across that ocean to get to Nippon, don't we?"

"Yes, of course," his captor answered blithely. "This disturbs you? Too bad."

Here in Chosen, farther from the fighting, damage to the railway net was less. The train made better time. It finally reached a port, a place called Fusan. Land ended there, running out into the sea. Teerts saw what Okamoto had meant by a port: ships lined up next to wooden sidewalks that ran out into the water on poles. Big Uglies and goods moved on and off.

Teerts realized that, primitive and smoky as this port was, a lot of business got done here. He was used to air and space transportation and the weight limits they imposed; one of these big, ugly Big Ugly ships could carry enormous numbers of soldiers and machines and sacks of bland, boring rice. And the Tosevites had many, many ships.

Back on the planets of the Empire, transportation by water was an unimportant sidelight; goods flowed along highways and railroads. All the interdiction missions Teerts had flown on Tosev 3 were against highways and railroads. Not once had he attacked shipping. But from what he saw in Fusan, the officers who gave him his targets had been missing a bet.

"Off," Okamoto said. Teerts obediently descended from the train, followed by the Nipponese officer and the stolid guard. After so long on the jouncing railway car, the ground seemed to sway beneath his feet.

At his captor's orders, he walked up a gangplank and onto one of the ships; the claws on his toes clicked against bare, cold metal. The floor (the Big Uglies had a special word for it, but he couldn't remember what the word was) shifted under his feet. He jumped into the air in alarm. "Earthquake!" he shouted in his own language.

That was not a word Major Okamoto knew. When Teerts explained it, the Nipponese let out a long string of the yips the Big Uglies used for laughter. Okamoto spoke to the guard in his own tongue. The guard, who had hardly said three words all the way down from Harbin through Chosen, laughed loudly, too. Teerts glared at one of them with each eye. He didn't see the joke.

Later, when out of sight of land the ship really started rolling and pitching, he understood why the Big Uglies had found his startlement at that first slight motion funny. He was, however, too busy wishing he was dead to be amused himself.

■

A rowboat took Colonel Leslie Groves across the Charles River toward the United States Navy Yard. The Charlestown Bridge, which had spanned the river and connected the yard with the rest of Boston on the southern bank, was nothing but a ruin. Engineers had repaired it a couple of times, but the Lizards kept knocking it down.

The ferryman pulled up under what had been the northern piers of the bridge. "Heah y'aah, friend," he said in broad New England accents, pointing to a set of rickety wooden stairs that led up to Main Street.

Groves scrambled out of the rowboat. The steps squeaked under his weight, though he, like most people, was a good deal lighter than he would have been had the Lizards stayed away. The fellow in the boat was backing oars, heading south across the river for his next ferry run.

As Groves turned right onto Chelsea Street, he reflected on how natural his ear found the Boston accent, though he'd not heard much of it since his days at MIT more than twenty years before. The country had been at war then, too, but with a foe safely across the ocean, not lodged all through the United States itself.

Naval ratings with rifles patrolled the long, high wall that separated the Navy Yard from the town behind it. Groves wondered how useful the fence was. If you stood on Breed's Hill (where, history books notwithstanding, the Americans and British had fought the Battle of Bunker Hill), you could look right down into the Yard. The colonel was, however, long used to security for security's sake. As he approached, he tapped the shiny eagle on the shoulders of his overcoat. The Navy guards saluted and stood aside to let him enter.

The Yard was not crowded with warships, as it had been before the Lizards came. The ships—those that survived—were dispersed up and down the coast, so as not to make any one target too attractive to bombardment from the air.

Still berthed in the Navy Yard was the USS *Constitution*. As always, seeing "Old Ironsides" gave Groves a thrill. In his MIT days, he'd toured the ship several times, and almost banged his head on the timbers belowdecks: any sailor much above five feet tall would have knocked himself silly running to his battle station. Glancing at the tall masts that probed the sky, Groves reflected that the Lizards had made the whole Navy as obsolete as the tough old frigate. It was not a cheery thought.

His own target lay a couple of piers beyond the *Constitution*. The boat tied up there was no longer than the graceful sailing ship, and much uglier: slabs of rust-stained iron could not compete against Old Ironsides' elegant flanks. *The only curves sweeter than a sailing ship's*, Groves thought, *are a woman's.*

The sentry who paced the pier wore Navy uniform, but not quite the one with which Groves was familiar. Nor was the flag that flapped from the submarine's conning tower the Stars and Stripes, but rather the Union Jack. Groves wondered if any Royal Navy vessels had used the Boston Navy Yard since the Revolution took Massachusetts off George III's hands.

"Ahoy the *Seanymph*!" he called as he strode up to the sentry. He was close enough now to see that the man carried a Lee-Enfield rifle, not the Springfields of his American counterparts.

"Ahoy yourself," the sentry answered; his vowels said London, not Back Bay. "Make yourself known, sir, if you'd be so kind."

"I am Colonel Leslie Groves, United States Army. Here are my identification documents." He waited while the Englishman inspected them, carefully comparing his photograph to his face. When the sentry nodded to show he was satisfied, Groves went on, "I am ordered to meet your Commander Stansfield here, to pick up the package he's brought to the United States."

"Wait here, sir." The sentry crossed the gangplank to the *Seanymph*'s deck, climbed the ladder to the conning tower, and disappeared below. He came out again a couple of minutes later. "You have permission to come aboard, sir. Watch your step, now."

The advice was not wasted; Groves did not pretend to be a sailor. As he carefully descended into the submarine, he was glad he'd lost some weight. As things were, the passage seemed alarmingly tight.

The long steel tube in which he found himself did nothing to ease that feeling. It was like peering down a dimly lit Thermos bottle. Even with the hatch open, the air was closed and dank; it smelled of metal and sweat and hot machine oil and, faintly in the background, full heads.

An officer with three gold stripes on the sleeves of his jacket came forward. "Colonel Groves? I'm Roger Stansfield, commanding the *Seanymph*. May I see your *bona fides*, please?" He examined Groves' papers with the same care the sentry had given them. Returning them, he said, "I hope you will forgive me, but it has been made quite clear that security is of the essence in this matter."

"Don't worry about it, Commander," Groves said easily. "The same point has been impressed upon me, I assure you."

"I don't even precisely know what it is I've ferried over to you Yanks," Stansfield said. "All I know is that I've been ordered to treat the stuff with the utmost respect, and have obeyed to the best of my ability."

"Good." Groves still wondered how he'd gotten roped into this atomic explosives project himself. Maybe the talk he'd had with the physicist—Larssen? was that the name?—had linked him and uranium in General Marshall's mind. Or maybe he'd complained once too often about fighting the war from behind a desk. He wasn't behind a desk any more, and wouldn't be for God only knew how long.

Stansfield said, "Having turned this—material—over to you, Colonel Groves, is there any way in which I can be of further assistance?"

"You'd have made my life a hell of a lot easier, Commander, if you could have sailed your *Seanymph* to Denver instead of Boston," Groves answered dryly.

"This is the port to which I was ordered to bring my boat," the Englishman said in a puzzled voice. "Had you wanted the material delivered elsewhere, your chaps upstairs should have told the Admiralty as much; I'm sure we would have done our best to oblige."

Groves shook his head. "I'm pulling your leg, I'm afraid." No reason for a Royal Navy man to be familiar with an American town that, to put it mildly, was not a port. "Colorado is a landlocked state."

"Oh. Quite." To Groves' relief, Stansfield didn't get mad. His grin showed pointed teeth that went well with his sharp, foxy features and hair that was somewhere between sandy and red. "They do say the new class of submarines was to have been capable of nearly everything, but that might have challenged it even had the advent of the Lizards not scuttled its development."

"Too bad," Groves said sincerely. "Now I have to transport the stuff myself."

"Perhaps we can make matters a bit easier," Stansfield said. One of the *Seanymph*'s ratings fetched up a canvas knapsack, which he presented to Groves with a flourish. Stansfield went on, "This arrangement should make rather easier transporting the saddlebag contained inside, which is, if you'll forgive the vulgarity, bloody heavy. I'd not be surprised to learn it was lined with lead, though I've been studiously encouraged not to enquire."

"Probably just as well." Groves knew the saddlebag was lined with lead. He didn't know how well the lead would shield him from the radioactive material inside; that was one of the things he'd have to find out the hard way. If this mission took years off his life but helped defeat the Lizards, the government had concluded that was a worthwhile price to pay. Having served that government his entire adult life, Groves accepted the estimation with as much equanimity as he could muster.

He shrugged on the knapsack. His shoulders and back did indeed feel the weight. If he had to haul it around for a while, he might even end up somewhere close to svelte. He hadn't been anything but portly—or worried about it—since his West Point days.

"I assume you have plans on how to reach, ah, Denver with your burden there," Stansfield said. "I do apologize for my limited ability to help you in that regard, but we are only a submarine, not a subterrene." He grinned again; he seemed taken with the idea of sailing to Colorado.

"Can't talk about that, I'm afraid," Groves said. "By rights, I shouldn't even have told you where I'm going."

Commander Stansfield nodded in understanding sympathy. He would have been even more sympathetic, Groves thought, had he known just how sketchy the American's plans were. He'd been ordered not to fly toward Denver; a plane was too likely to get knocked down. Not many trains were running, and even fewer cars. That left shank's mare, horseback, and luck—and as an engineer, Groves didn't take much stock in luck.

Complicating matters further was the stranglehold the Lizards had on the Midwest. Here on the coast, they were just raiders. But the farther inland you went, the more they seemed to have settled down to stay.

Groves wondered why the aliens didn't pay more attention to the ocean and to the land that lay alongside it. They hit land and air transportation all over the world, but ships still had a decent chance of getting through. Maybe that said something about the planet they came from. Groves shook his head. He had more immediate things to worry about.

Not least of them was the battle breaking out right around halfway between here and Denver. If that went wrong, not only would Chicago surely fall, but the United States would be hard-pressed to put up more than guerrilla resistance to the Lizards anywhere outside the East Coast. For that matter, getting to Denver might not matter if the battle went wrong, though Groves knew he'd keep going until he was either dead or ordered to turn aside.

He must have looked grim, for Commander Stansfield said, "Colonel, I've heard it said that your Navy bans alcohol aboard its vessels. Fortunately, the Royal Navy observes no such tiresome custom. Would you care for a tot of rum to fortify you for the journey ahead?"

"Commander, I'd be delighted, by God," Groves said. "Thank you."

"My pleasure—I thought it might do you some good. Wait here, if you please; I'll be back directly."

Stansfield hurried down the steel tube of the hull toward the rear of the submarine—*aft*, Groves supposed it was called in proper naval jargon. He watched the British officer lean into a little chamber off to the side of the main tube. *His cabin*, Groves realized. Stansfield didn't need to lean very far; the cabin had to be tiny. Bunks were stacked three deep, with bare inches between them. All things considered, the *Seanymph* was a claustrophobe's nightmare brought to clattering life.

The squat brown glass jug in Commander Stansfield's hand gurgled encouragingly. "Jamaican, than which there is none finer," he said, pulling the cork. Groves could almost taste the thick, heavy aroma that rose from it. Stansfield poured two healthy tots, handed one glass to Groves.

"Thanks." Groves took it with appropriate reverence. He raised it high—and almost barked his knuckles on a pipe that ran along the low ceiling. "His Majesty, the King!" he said gravely.

"His Majesty, the King!" Stansfield echoed. "Didn't think you Yanks knew to make that one."

"I read it somewhere." Groves knocked back the rum at a gulp. It was so smooth, his throat hardly knew he swallowed it, but it exploded in his stomach like a mortar round, throwing warmth in all directions. He looked at the empty glass with genuine respect. "That, Commander, is the straight goods."

"So it is." Stansfield sipped more sedately. He proffered the bottle once more. "Another?"

Groves shook his head. "One of those is medicinal. Two and I'd want to go to sleep. I appreciate the offer, though."

"You have a clear notion of what's best for you. I admire that." Stansfield turned so he faced west. The motion was quite deliberate; Groves imagined—as he was supposed to imagine—the Royal Navy man peering out through the sub's hull and across two thousand miles of dangerous country to the promised land of Denver, high in the Rockies. After a moment, Stansfield added, "I must say I don't envy you, Colonel."

Groves shrugged. With the heavy canvas knapsack on his shoulders, he felt like Atlas, trying to support the whole world. "The job has to be done, and I'm going to do it."

Rivka Russie scratched a match against the sole of her shoe. It flared into life. She used it to light first one *shabbas* candle, then the other. Bowing her head over them, she murmured the Sabbath blessing.

The puff of sulfurous smoke from the matchhead filled the little underground room and made Moishe Russie cough. The fat white candles were a sign he and his family had survived another week without the Lizards' finding them. They also helped light the bunker where the Russies sheltered.

Rivka lifted the ceremonial cloth cover from a braided loaf of *challah.* "I want some of that bread, Mama!" Reuven exclaimed.

"Let me slice it first, if you please," Rivka told her son. "Look: we even have some honey to spread on it."

All the comforts of home. The irony of the phrase echoed in Moishe's mind. Instead of their flat, they sheltered in this secret chamber buried under another Warsaw apartment block. In further irony, the bunker had been built to shelter Jews not from the Lizards but from the Nazis, yet here he used it to save himself from the creatures who had saved him from the Germans.

And yet the words were not entirely ironic. The vast majority of Warsaw's Jews lived far better under the Lizards than they had when Hitler's henchmen ruled the city. The wheat-flour *challah,* rich with eggs and dusted with poppy seeds, would have been unimaginable in the starving Warsaw ghetto—Russie remembered too well the chunk of fatty, sour pork for which he'd given a silver candlestick the night the Lizards came to Earth.

"When will I get to go out and play again?" Reuven asked. He looked from Rivka to Moishe and back again, hoping one of them would give him the answer he wanted.

They looked at each other, too. Moishe felt himself sag. "I don't know exactly," he told his son; he could not bring himself to lie to the boy. "I hope it will be soon, but more likely the day won't come for quite some time."

"Too bad," Reuven said.

"Don't you think we could—?" Rivka broke off, tried again: "I mean, who would betray a little boy to the Lizards?"

Moishe usually let his wife run their household, not least because she was better at it than he was. But now he said, "No," so sharply that Rivka stared at him in surprise. He went on, "We dare not let him go up above ground. Remember how many Jews were willing to betray their brethren to the Nazis for a crust of bread regardless of what the Nazis were doing to us? People have cause to *like* the Lizards, at least compared to the Germans. He wouldn't be safe where anybody could see him."

"All right," Rivka said. "If you think he'd be in danger up there, here he'll stay." Reuven let out a disappointed howl, but she ignored him.

"Anyone who has anything to do with me is in danger," Moishe answered bitterly. "Why do you think we never get to talk to the fighters who bring our supplies?" The door to the bunker was concealed by a sliding plasterboard panel; with the panel closed, the entranceway looked like a blank wall from the other side.

Russie wondered if the anonymous men who kept his family in food and candles even knew whom they were helping. He could easily imagine Mordechai Anielewicz ordering them to take their boxes down and leave them in the basement without telling them whom the things were for. Why not? What the men didn't know, they couldn't tell the Lizards.

He made a sour face: he was learning to think like a soldier. All he'd wanted to do was heal people and then, after the Lizards came like a sign from heaven, set people free. And the result? Here he was in hiding and thinking like a killer, not a healer.

Not too long after supper, Reuven yawned and went to bed without his usual fuss. In the dark, closed bunker, night and day no longer had much meaning for the little boy. Had the fighters not furnished the place with a clock, Moishe would have had no idea of the hour, either. One day he'd forget to wind it and slip into timelessness himself.

The *shabbas* candles were still burning. By their light, Moishe helped Rivka wash the supper dishes (though without electricity, the bunker had running water). She smiled at him. "The time you lived by yourself taught you some things. You're much better at that than you used to be."

"What you have to do, you learn to do," he answered philosophically. "Hand me that towel, would you?"

He'd just slid the last dish into its stack when he heard noise in the cellar next to the hidden bunker: men moving about in heavy shoes. He and Rivka froze. Her face was frightened; he was sure his was, too. Had their secret been betrayed? The Lizards wouldn't shout *"Juden heraus!"* but he didn't want to be caught by them any more than by the Nazis.

He wished he had a weapon. He wasn't altogether a soldier yet, or he'd have had the sense to ask for one before he sealed himself away here. Too late to worry about it now.

The footsteps came closer. Russie strained his ears, trying to pick out the skitters and clicks that would have meant Lizards were walking with the humans. He thought he did. Fear rose up in him like a smothering cloud.

The people—and aliens?—stopped just on the other side of the plaster-board barrier. Moishe's eyes flicked to the candlesticks that held the Sabbath lights. These were of pottery, not silver like the one he'd given up for food. But they were heavy, and of a length to serve as bludgeons. *I won't go down without a fight*, he promised himself.

Someone rapped on the barrier. Russie grabbed for a candlestick, then caught himself: two knocks, a pause, then another knock was the signal Anielewicz's men used when they brought him supplies. But they'd just done that a couple of days before, and the bunker still held plenty. They seemed to have a schedule of sorts, and even though the signal was right, the timing wasn't.

Rivka knew that, too. "What do we do?" she mouthed silently.

"I don't know," Moishe mouthed back. What he did know, though he didn't want to dishearten his wife by saying so, was that if the Lizards were out there, they were going to take him. But the footsteps receded. Had he really heard skitterings after all?

Rivka raised her voice to a whisper. "Are they gone?"

"I don't know," Russie said again. After a moment, he added, "Let's find out." If the Lizards knew he was here, they didn't need to wait for him to come out.

He picked up a candlestick, lit candle still inside (the cellar was as dark as the bunker would have been without light), unbarred the door, took half a step forward so he could slide aside the plasterboard panel. No box of food sat in front of it . . . but an envelope lay on the cement floor. He scooped it up, replaced the concealing panel, and went back into his hidey-hole.

"What is it?" Rivka asked when he was back inside.

"A note or letter of some sort," he answered, holding up the envelope. He tore it open, pulled out the folded sheet of paper inside, and held it close to the candlestick so he could see what it said. The one great curse of this underground life was never having either sunlight or electric light by which to read.

The candle sufficed for something short, though. He unfolded the paper. On it was a neatly typed paragraph in Polish. He read the words aloud for Rivka's benefit: "Just so you know, your latest message has been received elsewhere and widely circulated. Reaction is very much as we had hoped. Sympathy for us outside the area has increased, and certain parties would have red faces under other circumstances. They still would like to congratulate you for your wit. Suggest you let them continue to lavish their praises from a distance."

"That's all?" Rivka asked when he was through. "No signature or anything?"

"No," he answered. "I can make a pretty good guess about who sent it, though, and I expect you can, too."

"Anielewicz," she said.

"That's what I think," Moishe agreed. The note had all the hallmarks of the Jewish fighting leader. No wonder it was in Polish: he'd been thoroughly secular before the war. Being typewritten made it harder to trace if it fell into the wrong hands. So did its elliptical phrasing: someone who didn't know for whom it was intended would have trouble figuring out what it was supposed to mean. Anielewicz was careful every way he could think of. Moishe was sure he wouldn't know how the note had got down to the bunker.

Rivka said, "So the recording got abroad. Thank God for that. I wouldn't want you known as the Lizards' puppet."

"No; thank God I'm not." Moishe started to laugh. "I'd like to see Zolraag with his face all red." After what the Lizard governor had done to him, he wanted Zolraag both embarrassed and furious. From what the note said, he was getting his wish.

One of the things with which the bunker had been stocked was a bottle of *slivovitz.* Till now, Moishe had ignored it. He pulled it off the high shelf where it sat, yanked out the cork, and poured two shots. Handing one glass to Rivka, he raised the other himself.

"Confusion to the Lizards!" he said.

They both sipped the plum brandy. Fire ran down Moishe's throat. Rivka coughed several times. Then she lifted her glass. Quietly, she offered a toast of her own: "Freedom for our people, and even, one day, for us."

"Yes." Moishe finished the *slivovitz.* One of the Sabbath candles went out, filling the bunker with the smell of hot tallow—and cutting the light inside almost in half. New shadows swooped.

"The other one will go soon," Rivka said, watching that flame approach the candlestick, too.

"I know," Moishe answered gloomily. Up where Reuven could not knock them over, two little oil lamps burned. But for being made out of tin, they probably weren't much different from the ones the Maccabees had used when they took the Temple in Jerusalem away from Antiochus and his Greeks. The tiny amount of light they gave made Moishe think they were primitive, anyhow.

He carefully refilled them all the same. Waking up in absolute blackness in the crowded little underground room was a nightmare he'd suffered only once. The dreadful groping search for a box of matches made him vow never to go through it again. He'd lived up to the vow so far.

Reuven, Rivka, and he all shared one crowded bed. He gently rolled his son against the far wall. Reuven mumbled and thrashed, but didn't wake up. Moishe got into bed next to him, held up the covers so Rivka could slide in, too.

His hand brushed her hip as he let the blankets down over them. She turned toward him. The lamps gave just enough light to let him see the questioning look on her face. The touch had been as much an accident as a caress, but he drew her to him just the same. The questioning look turned to a smile.

Later, they lay nestled together like spoons, her backside warm against the bottom of his belly. It was a gentle way to make love, and one not likely to disturb their son. Moishe stroked Rivka's hair. She laughed quietly. "What's funny?" he asked. He could hear sleepiness blur his voice.

She laughed again. "We didn't do—this—so much when we were first married."

"Well, maybe not," he said. "I was just starting medical school and busy all the time, and then the baby came . . ."

And now, he thought, *what else is there to do? It's too dark to read much, we're both sleeping a lot—if we didn't take our pleasure from each other, we'd be as cross as a couple of bears cooped up down here.*

He didn't think saying he enjoyed Rivka's body because there wasn't anything else to do would endear him to her. Instead, he said with mock severity, "Most women, I hear, *kvetch* because their husbands don't pay them enough attention. Are you complaining because I pay you too much?"

"I didn't think I was complaining." She moved away from the edge of the bed, and against him. Pressed tight against her firm flesh, he felt himself begin to rise again. So did she. Without a word, she raised a leg enough to let him slip himself back into her. Her breath sighed out when he did.

No hurry, he thought. *We aren't going anywhere.* Unhurriedly, he tried to make the best of where they were.

The door to Bobby Fiore's cell hissed open. It wasn't the usual time for food, as well as he could judge without any clock. He looked around hopefully. Maybe the Lizards were bringing in Liu Han.

But no. It was only Lizards: the usual armed guards and another one, the latter with more elaborate body paint than the others. He'd figured out that was a mark of status among them, just as a man who wore a fancy suit was likely to be a bigger wheel than one in bib overalls and a straw hat.

The Lizard with the expensive paint job said something in his own language, too fast for Fiore to follow. He said as much, *I don't understand* being a phrase he'd found worth memorizing. The Lizard said, "Come—with," in English.

"It shall be done, superior sir," Fiore answered, trotting out a couple of other stock phrases. He got to his feet and approached the Lizard—not too close, though, because he'd learned that made the guards anxious. He didn't want anybody with a gun anxious about him.

The guards fell in around him, all of them too far away for him to try grabbing one of those guns. He wasn't feeling suicidal this morning—assuming it *was* morning; only God and the Lizards knew for sure—so he didn't try.

When the Lizards took him to Liu Han's cell, they turned right out the door. This time they turned left. He didn't know whether to be curious or apprehensive, and finally settled for a little of each: heading someplace out of the ordinary might be dangerous, but it gave him the chance to see something new. After being cooped up so long with essentially nothing to see, that counted for a good deal.

The trouble was, just because something was new didn't necessarily make it exciting. Corridors remained corridors, their ceilings unpleasantly close to his head. Some were bare metal, others painted a flat off-white. The Lizards who passed him in those corridors paid him no more attention than he would have given a dog walking down the street. He wanted to shout at them, just to make them jump. But that would have made the guards jumpy, too, and maybe earned him a bullet in the ribs, so he didn't.

Peering through open doorways was more interesting. He tried to figure out what the Lizards in those rooms that weren't cells were up to. Most of the time, he couldn't. A lot of the aliens just sat in front of what looked like little movie screens. Fiore couldn't see the pictures on them, just that they were in color: the bright squares stood out in the midst of silver and white.

Then came something new: an oddly curved stairway. But as he descended it, Fiore discovered that while his eyes saw the curve, his feet couldn't feel it, and when he got to the bottom, he seemed lighter than he had up at the top. He shifted his weight back and forth. No, he wasn't imagining it.

Boy, if I'd been this light on my feet, I'd've made the big leagues years ago, he thought. Then he shook his head. Maybe not. His bat had always been pretty light, too.

The Lizards took the weird stairs and the change in weight utterly for granted. They hustled him along the corridors on this level, which didn't seem any different from those up above. At last they took him into one of the rooms with the movie screens.

The Lizard who'd ordered him out of his own cell spoke to the one who waited in there. That one had an even spiffier paint job than the alien who'd come in with the guards. Fiore couldn't follow what the Lizards said as they talked back and forth, but he heard his own name several times. The Lizards massacred it worse than Liu Han did.

The alien who'd been in the room surprised him by speaking decent English: "You are the Tosevite male Bobby Fiore, the one mated to the female Liu Han in an exclusive"—the word came out as one long hiss—"arrangement?"

"Yes, superior sir," Fiore answered, also in English. He took a small chance by asking, "Who are you, superior sir?"

The Lizard didn't get mad. "I am Tessrek, senior psychologist." More hisses there. Tessrek went on, "I seek to learn more about this—arrangement."

"What do you want to know?" Fiore wondered if the Lizards had figured out Liu Han was pregnant yet. He or she would have to spell things out pretty soon if they kept on being dumb about it.

They knew more than he'd thought. Tessrek turned a knob on the desk behind which he was sitting. Out of thin air, Fiore heard himself saying, "Goddamn, who woulda thought my first kid would be half Chink?" Tessrek turned the knob again, then asked, "This mean the female Liu Han will lay eggs—no, will reproduce; you Big Uglies do not lay eggs—the female Liu Han will reproduce?"

"Uh, yeah," Fiore said.

"This is as a result of your matings?" Tessrek twiddled with another knob. The little screen behind him, which had been a blank blue square, started showing a picture.

Stag film, Fiore thought; he'd seen a few in his time. This one was in color good enough for Technicolor, not the grainy black-and-white typical of the breed. The color was what he noticed first; only half a heartbeat later did he realize the movie was of Liu Han and him.

He took a step forward. He wanted to squeeze Tessrek's neck until the Lizard's strange eyes popped from his head. The murder on his face must have shown even to the guards, because a couple of them hissed a sharp warning and trained their weapons on his midsection. Reluctantly, every muscle screaming to go on, he checked himself.

Tessrek seemed to have no notion of what had rattled his cage. The psychologist went on blithely, "This mating—this spawn, you would say—you and the female Liu Han will care for it?"

"I guess so," Bobby mumbled. Behind the Lizard, the dirty picture went on, Liu Han's face slack with ecstasy, his own intent above her. In a distant way, he wondered how the Lizards managed to show a movie in a lighted room with no projector visible. He made himself come back to the question. "Yeah, that's what we'll do if you"—*things*—"let us."

"This will be what you Big Uglies call a—family?" Tessrek pronounced the word with extra care, to make sure Fiore understood him.

"Yeah," he answered, "a family." He tried to look away from the screen, toward the Lizard, but his eyes kept sliding back. Some of his embarrassed anger spilled over into words: "What's the matter, don't you Lizards have families of your own? You gotta come to Earth to poke your snouts into ours?"

"No, we have none," Tessrek said, "not in your sense of word. With us, females lay eggs, raise hatchlings, males do other things."

Fiore gaped at him. More than his surroundings, more than the shamelessness with which the Lizards had filmed his lovemaking, the simple admission brought home how alien the invaders were. Men might build spaceships one day (Sam Yeager had read about that rockets-to-Mars stuff all the time; Bobby wondered if his roommate was still alive). Plenty of men were shameless, starting with Peeping Tom. But not knowing what a family was . . .

Oblivious to the turmoil he'd created, Tessrek went on, "The Race needs to learn how you Big Uglies live, so we rule you better, easier. Need to understand to—how do you say?—to control, that that word I want?"

"Yeah, that's it, all right," Fiore said dully. *Guinea pig* ran through his head, again and again. He'd had that thought before, but never so strong. The Lizards didn't care that he knew they were experimenting with him; what could he do about it? To them, he was just an animal in a cage. He wondered what guinea pigs thought of the scientists who worked on them. If it was nothing good, he couldn't blame them.

"When will the hatchling come out?" Tessrek asked.

"I don't know exactly," Fiore answered. "It takes nine months, but I don't know how long it's been since she caught. How am I supposed to tell you? You don't even turn off the lights in my room."

"Nine—months?" Tessrek fiddled with something on his desk. The dirty movie disappeared from the screen behind him, to be replaced by Lizard squiggles. Those changed as he did more fiddling. He turned one of his eye turrets back toward them. "This would be one and one-half years of the Race? One year of the Race, I tell you, is half a Tosev year, more or less."

Bobby Fiore hadn't juggled fractions in his head since high school. The trouble he'd had with them then had helped convince him he'd be better off playing ball for a living. He needed some painful mental work before he finally nodded. "Yeah, I think that's right, superior sir."

"Sstrange." Another word Tessrek turned into a hiss. "You Big Uglies take so long to give birth to your hatchlings. Why is this?"

"How the devil should I know?" Fiore answered; again he had the feeling of taking a test he hadn't studied for. "It's just the way we are. I'm not lying, superior sir. You can check that one with anybody."

"Check? This means confirm? Yes, I do that." The Lizard psychologist spoke Lizard talk into what looked like a little microphone. Different squiggles went up on the screen. Fiore wondered if it was somehow writing down what Tessrek said. Hell of a gadget if it could do that, he thought. The Lizard went on, "I do not think you lie. What is the advantage to you on this question? But I wonder why you Tosevites are so, not like Race and other species of the Empire."

"You oughta talk to a scientist or a doctor or somebody." Fiore scratched his head. "You say you Lizards lay eggs?"

"Of course." By his tone, Tessrek implied that was the only thing a right-thinking creature could possibly do.

Bobby thought back to the chickens that had squawked and clucked in a little coop behind his folks' house in Pittsburgh. Without those chickens and their eggs, he and his brothers and sisters would have gone hungry a lot more than they did, but that wasn't why they came to mind now. He said, "An egg can't get any bigger once you lay it. When the chick inside—or I guess the baby Lizard, too—is too big for the eggshell to hold it any more, it has to come out. But a baby inside a woman has more room to grow."

Tessrek brought both eyes to bear on him. He'd learned a Lizard did that only when you'd managed to get its full attention (he'd also learned its full attention wasn't always something you wanted to have). The psychologist said, "This may be worth more study." He made it sound like an accolade.

He leaned close to the microphone, went back into his language. Again, the screen showed fresh Lizard writing. It really was a note-taker, Fiore realized. He wondered what else it could do—besides showing movies that should never have been made.

Tessrek said, "You Big Uglies are of the kind of Tosevite creature where the female feeds the hatchling with a fluid that comes out of her body?" It wasn't exactly a question, even though he made the interrogative noise at the end: he already knew the answer.

Bobby Fiore had to take a mental step backward and work out what the Lizard was talking about. After a second, the light bulb went on. "With milk, you mean, superior sir? Yeah, we feed babies milk." He'd been a bottle baby himself, not nursed, but he didn't complicate the issue. Besides, what had the bottle held?

"Milk. Yes." Now Tessrek sounded as if Bobby had admitted humans picked their noses and fed babies on boogers, or else like a fastidious clubwoman who for some reason had to talk about syphilis. He paused, pulled himself together. "Only the females do this, am I correct? Not the males?"

"No, not the males, superior sir." Imagining a baby nursing at his flat, hairy tit made Fiore squeamish and also made him want to laugh. And it rammed home, just when he was starting to get used to the Lizards again, how alien they were. They didn't have a clue about what being human meant. Even though Liu Han and he had to use some Lizard words to talk with each other, they used them in a human context they both understood just because they were people, and probably used them in ways the Lizards would have found nonsensical.

That made him wonder how much Tessrek, in spite of his fluent English, truly grasped of the ideas he mouthed. Passing information back and forth was all very well; the Lizard psychologist's grasp of the language was good enough for that. But once he had the information, how badly would he misinterpret it just because it was different from anything he was used to?

Tessrek said, "If you males do not give—milk—to hatchlings, what point to staying by them and by females?"

"Men help women take care of babies," Fiore answered, "and they can feed babies, too, once the babies start eating real food. Besides, they usually make the money to keep families going."

"Understand *what* you Big Uglies do; not understand *why*," Tessrek said. "*Why* males want to stay with females? Why you have families, not males with females at random, like the Race and other species we know?"

In an abstract way, Bobby thought males with females at random sounded like fun. He'd enjoyed himself with the women with whom the Lizards had paired him before he'd ended up with Liu Han. But he enjoyed being with her, too, in a different and maybe deeper sense.

"Answer me," Tessrek said sharply.

"I'm sorry, superior sir. I was trying to figure out what to say. I guess part of the answer is that men fall in love with women, and the other way round, too."

"Love." Tessrek used the word with almost as much revulsion as he had when he said *milk*. "You Big Uglies talk loudly of this word. You do not ever make this a word with a meaning. You, Bobby Fiore, tell me what this *love* word means."

"Uh," Fiore said. That was a tall order for a poet, a philosopher, or even Cole Porter, let alone a minor-league second baseman. As he would have at the plate overmatched against Bob Feller, he gave it his best shot: "Love is when you care about somebody and want to take care of them and want them to be happy all the time."

"You say *what*. I want *why*," the Lizard psychologist said with a discontented hiss. "Is because you Big Uglies mate all the time, use mating as social bond, form families because of this mating bond?"

Fiore was anything but an introspective man. Nor had he ever spent much time contemplating the nature of the family: families were what you grew up in, and later what you started for yourself. Not only that, all the talk about sex, even with a Lizard, embarrassed him.

"I guess maybe you're right," he mumbled. When he thought about it, what Tessrek had to say did make some sense.

"I *am* right," Tessrek told him, and added the emphatic cough. "You help me show the disgusting habits of you Big Uglies are to blame for you being so strange, so—what is word?—so anomalous. Yes, anomalous. I prove this, yes I do." He spoke in his own language to the guards, who started marching Fiore back to his cell.

As he went, he reflected that while the Lizards were massively ignorant of humanity, they and people weren't so different in some ways: just like a lot of people he'd known, Tessrek was using his words to prop up an idea the Lizard had already had. If he'd said just the opposite, Tessrek would have found some way to use that, too.

20

Jens Larssen's neck muscles tensed under the unaccustomed weight of the tin hat on his head. He was developing a list to the right from the slung Springfield he'd been issued. Like most farm kids, he'd done some plinking with a .22, but the military rifle had a mass and heft to it unlike anything he'd ever known.

Technically, he still wasn't a soldier. General Patton hadn't impressed him into the Army—"Your civilian job is more important than anything you can do for me," he'd rumbled—but had insisted that he be armed: "We've got no time to coddle noncombatants." Jens knew an inconsistency when he heard one, but hadn't had any luck convincing the major general.

He looked at his watch. The greenly glowing hands showed it was just before four A.M. The night was dark and cloudy and full of blowing snow, but it was anything but peaceful. More engines added their roar and the stink of their exhaust to the air every moment. The second hand ticked round the dial. A minute before four . . . half a minute . . .

His watch was synchronized pretty well, but not perfectly. At—by his reckoning—3:59:34, what seemed like every cannon in the world cut loose. The low clouds glowed yellow for a few seconds from all the muzzle flashes packed together. The three-inch howitzers and the 90mm antiaircraft cannon pressed into service as field guns roared again and again, as fast as their crews could keep the shells coming.

As he'd been told, Jens yelled as loud as he could, to help equalize the pressure on his ears. The noise was lost in the overwhelming cacophony of the guns.

Lizard counterbattery fire began coming in a couple of minutes later. By then the tanks and men of Patton's force were already on the move. The American artillery barrage eased up as abruptly as it had begun. "Forward to the next firing position!" an officer near Larssen screamed. "The Lizards zero in on you fast if you stay in one place too long."

Some of the howitzers were on their own motorized chassis. Half-

463

tracks towed most of the rest of the artillery pieces. A few were either horse-drawn or pulled by teams of soldiers. If the advance went as Patton planned (*hoped*, Jens amended to himself), those would soon fall behind. For the moment, every shell counted.

"Come on, you lugs—get your butts in gear!" a sergeant yelled with the dulcet tones of sergeants all through history. "You think you're scared, just wait'll you see the goddamn Lizards when we hit 'em." That was the gospel according to Patton. Whether it was the gospel truth remained to be proved. Along with the men around him, Jens tramped off toward the west.

Airplanes roared low overhead, carefully husbanded against this day of need and now to be expended, win or die. Larssen waved at the planes as they darted past; he didn't think many of the pilots would be coming back. If attacking Lizard positions in the snowy dark wasn't a suicide mission, he didn't know what was.

Of course, he realized a few seconds later, that was what he was doing, too, even if he wasn't in a fighter. Off to one side, a soldier with a voice that still cracked exclaimed, "Ain't this exciting!"

"Now that you mention it, no," Larssen said.

Artillery Supervisor Svallah shouted into his field telephone: "What do you mean, you can't send me any more ammunition right now? The Big Uglies are *moving*, I tell you! We haven't faced large-scale combat like this since just after we landed on this miserable ball of muddy ice."

The voice that came out of the speaker was cold: "I am also receiving reports of heavy fighting on the northwestern flank of our thrust toward the major city by the lake. Supply officers are still evaluating priorities."

Had Svallah possessed hair like a Big Ugly, he would have pulled great clumps of it from his head. Supply still seemed to think they were back Home, where a delay of half a day never mattered and one of half a year wasn't always worth getting excited about, either. The Tosevites, worse luck, didn't operate that way.

"Listen," he yelled, "we're low on cluster bombs, our landcruisers are short of both high-explosive and antiarmor rounds, we don't have enough antilandcruiser missiles for the infantry . . . By the Emperor, though it's not my province, I hear we're even short on small-arms rounds!"

"Yours is not the only unit in this predicament," replied the maddeningly dispassionate voice on the other end of the line. "Every effort will be made to resupply to the best of our ability as quickly as possible. Shipments may not be full resupplies; shortages do exist, and expenditures have been too high for too long. I assure you, we shall do the best we can under the circumstances."

"You don't understand!" Svallah wasn't yelling any more—he was screaming. He had reason: Tosevite shells had started feeling for his position. "Do you hear those bursts? Do you hear them? May you be cursed with an Emperorless afterlife, those aren't *our* guns! The stinking Big Uglies have ammunition. It's not as good as ours, but if they're shooting and we're not, what difference does it make?"

"I assure you, Artillery Supervisor, resupply will reach you as expeditiously as is practicable," answered the male in Supply, who wasn't being shot at (*not yet*, Svallah thought bitterly). "I also assure you that yours is not the only unit urgently requesting munitions. We are making every effort to balance demands—"

The Tosevites' shells were walking closer; fragments of brass and steel rattled off tree trunks and branches. Svallah said, "Look, if you don't get me some shells pretty quick, my request won't matter, because I'm about to be overrun here. Is that plain enough for you? By the Emperor, it'd probably make you happy, because then you'd have one thing fewer to worry about."

"Your attitude is not constructive, Artillery Supervisor," the male safe in the rear said in hurt tones.

"Ask me if I care," Svallah retorted. "Just so you know, I'm going to order a retreat before I get chopped to pieces. Those are my only two choices, since you can't get me ammunition. I—"

A Tosevite round landed within a male's length of him. Between them, blast and fragments left him hardly more than a red rag splashed across the snow. By a freak of war, the field telephone was undamaged. It squawked, "Artillery Supervisor? Are you there, Artillery Supervisor? Respond, please. Artillery Supervisor . . . ?"

For the first couple of days, it was easier than Larssen would have imagined possible. Patton really had managed to catch the Lizards napping, and to hit them where their defenses were thin. How the soldiers cheered when they crossed from Indiana into Illinois! Instead of running or desperately holding on like a stunned boxer in a clinch, they were advancing. It made new men of them—*got their peckers up*, was the way one sergeant had put it.

All of a sudden, it wasn't easy any more. In the open fields in front of a grim little town called Cissna Park stood a Lizard tank. It was defiantly out in the open, with a view that reached for miles. In front of it, burning or by now burnt out, lay the hulks of at least half a dozen Lees and Shermans. Some had been killed at close to three miles. They didn't have a prayer of touching the Lizard tank at that range, let alone killing it.

The tank crew had high-explosive shells as well as armor-piercers. Larssen had been on the receiving end of bombardments back in Chicago. He preferred giving them out. He couldn't do anything about it, though, except throw himself flat when the big gun spoke again.

"That son of a whore's gonna hold up the whole brigade all by his lonesome," somebody said with sick dread in his voice. The soldiers' peckers might be up now, but how long would they stay that way if the onslaught failed?

A fellow who looked much too young to be wearing a major's gold oak leaves began ticking off men on his fingers. "You, you, you, you, and you, head off to the right flank and make that bastard notice you. I'm coming, too. We'll see what we can do about him."

Jens was the second of those *yous*. He opened his mouth to protest: he was supposed to be a valuable physicist, not a dogface. But he didn't have the nerve to finish squawking, not when the rest of the party was heading out, not when everybody was looking at them—and at him. Legs numb with fear, he lurched after the others.

The tank seemed almost naked out there. If it had any infantry support, the Lizards on the ground were holding their fire. Larssen watched the distant turret. It got less distant all the time, which meant it got more and more able to kill him. *If it swings this way, I know I'm going to run*, he thought. But he kept trotting forward.

One of the soldiers lay flat on the ground, opened up with a Browning automatic rifle. He had about as much chance of hurting the tank with it as a mosquito did blowing holes in an elephant. "Come on, keep moving!" the kid who was a major bawled. Jens kept moving. The farther he got from the brave maniac with the BAR, the better he liked it.

A couple of hundred yards farther on, another fellow, also armed with a BAR, took cover in some bushes that wouldn't have been there if the field had been tended since last summer. He too started firing short bursts at the Lizard tank. Now Larssen was close enough to see a couple of sparks as bullets spanged off its turret. Again, he couldn't see that they did any good.

"The rest of you, spread out, find what cover you can, and start shooting," the major said. "We are a diversion. We have to make that gunner pay attention to us."

Diversion indeed, Jens thought. The Lizard gunner ought to have extraordinarily good sport chewing up humans who couldn't do him any damage in return.

But there was another tall patch of snow-covered dead weeds just ahead. He dropped down behind them. Even through several layers of clothes, the snow chilled his belly. He drew a bead on the tank, squeezed the Springfield's trigger.

Nothing happened. Scowling, he checked the rifle. He'd left the safety on. "You idiot!" he snarled to himself as he clicked it off. He aimed again, fired. The kick hammered his shoulder, a lot harder than he remembered from when he'd fooled around with a .22.

The physicist part of him took over: *You're sending a heavier slug out at a higher velocity—of course it'll kick harder. Newton's Second Law, remember—good old* F = ma! He adjusted the sight for long range; his first shot, with it set for four hundred yards, couldn't have come close. He pulled the trigger again. This time he was better braced against the recoil. He still couldn't tell whether he hit it or not.

As he'd been ordered, he banged away. The rest of the detachment was making a lot of noise, too. If somebody got real lucky with a round, he might mess up a sight or a periscope. Past that, the major's diversion wasn't doing anything more than standing out in the open with a SHOOT ME sign would have accomplished.

After a while, though, the Lizard commanding the tank must have got tired of just sitting there in a target suit. The turret slewed toward one of the BAR men. Having seen American tank turrets in action, Larssen was appalled at how fast this one traversed.

Fire spurted from the turret, not the main armament—why swat flies with a sledgehammer?—but the coaxial machine gun by it. Snow and dirt spurted up all around the soldier with the automatic rifle. It wasn't a long burst—the gunner was firing for effect. After a few seconds' silence, the BAR man shifted his weapon on its bipod, sent back a few defiant rounds. *Here I am!* he seemed to be saying. *Nyaah, nyaah!*

The tank gunner squeezed off an answering burst, longer this time. Another silence fell after he stopped. The fellow with the Browning automatic rifle did not reply now. *Wounded or dead*, Larssen thought grimly. The tank turret turned on to the other BAR man.

He had a better spot from which to shoot back, and lasted quite a bit longer than the first gunner had. The firefight between him and the tank gunner went on through several exchanges. But the fellow with the BAR was under orders to keep the tank busy, and brave enough to carry out those orders with exactitude. That meant he had to keep exposing himself to fire . . . and in any case, the dirt and bushes behind which he lay were no match for the inches of armor that sheltered the Lizard in the tank turret.

When the second BAR fell silent, the tank turret traversed through another few degrees. Larssen watched it with fearful fascination—for now it bore on him. He was lying in what had been a plowed furrow. When the machine gun began to chatter again, he flattened himself out like a snake, hoping—praying—the hard earth would offer some protection. The second BAR man had lived a little while, after all.

Bullets lashed the ground all around him. Freezing dirt spattered onto his coat and the back of his neck. He could not force himself to get up and shoot back, not in the face of a machine gun behind armor. Did that make him a coward? He didn't know or care.

The burst from the tank broke off. He lifted his head out of the dirt. If by some miracle the turret had moved on to take up the hunt for someone else, he thought, he might start firing again, and then scoot for new cover. But no. The cannon—and, therefore, the machine gun, too—still bore on him.

He saw motion on the far side of the Lizard tank: more human soldiers, men who'd snuck close to the monster while he and his comrades occupied its attention. He wondered if they'd leap aboard and throw explosives into the turret through the cupola. Lizard tanks had died that way, but an awful lot more soldiers had died trying to kill them.

One of the Americans raised something to his shoulder. It wasn't a gun: it was longer and thicker. Flame spurted from its rear end. Trailing fire all the way, some kind of rocket round shot across the couple of hundred yards that separated the soldiers from the Lizard tank. It slammed into the engine compartment at the rear, right where the armor was thinnest.

More fire, some blue, some orange, spurted from the stricken vehicle. Hatches popped open in the turret; three Lizards bailed out. Now, yelling like a savage, Jens fired with ferocious glee. Suddenly the tables were turned, the tormentors all but helpless against those they had bedeviled. One Lizard fell, then another.

Then the tank brewed up as the fire reached the main fuel storage. Flame washed over the whole chassis; a smoke ring spurted up from the turret. Pops and booms marked ammunition starting to cook off. The last Lizard who'd made it out of the hatch went down under a fusillade of bullets.

The kid major was up on his feet, waving like a madman. Off to the east, the distant roar of engines marked new motion from the tanks and self-propelled guns the Lizard tank had stalled. Then the major ran back to see how the two BAR men were. Jens ran with him.

One of them was gruesomely dead, the top of his skull clipped off by a Lizard round and gray-red brains splashed in the snow. The other had a belly wound. He was unconscious but breathing. The major pulled aside clothes, dusted the bleeding wound with sulfa powder, slapped on a field dressing, and waved for a medic.

He turned to Larssen: "You know what? I think we're really gonna do this!"

"Maybe." Jens knew his voice wasn't everything it should be; he hadn't hardened himself against human beings' looking like selections from the butcher's. Trying not to think of that, he asked, "What did they use to take out the tank?" As if to punctuate his words, more rounds went up inside the blazing hulk.

"The rocket? Wasn't that great?" When the major grinned, he didn't look a day over seventeen. "The fancy name is 2.36-inch Rocket Launcher, but all the teams I know are calling it after that crazy instrument Bob Burns plays on the radio."

"A bazooka?" Larssen grinned, too. "I like that."

"So do I." The major's grin slipped a little. "I just wish we had a hell of a lot more of 'em. They were brand new last year, and of course we've had the devil's own time building 'em since the damned Lizards came. But what we've got, we're using." All at once, he went from informant back to officer. "Now we've got to get moving. Bust your hump, there."

"Shouldn't they go ahead, sir?" Jens pointed to the Lees and Shermans just now rattling past the carcass of the Lizard tank.

"They need us, too," the major answered. "They make the hole, we go through it and we support them. If the Lizards had had some infantry on the ground to support that vehicle, we couldn't have stalked it the way we did. Their machines are marvelous and you can't say they're not brave, but their tactical doctrine stinks."

Colonel Groves, Larssen remembered, had said the same thing. At the time, it hadn't seemed to matter; the aliens' machines were carrying everything before them. But it seemed they might be fought successfully after all.

The major was already moving west again. Jens trotted heavily after him, giving the pyre of the Lizard tank a wide berth.

Assault Force Commander Relhost said, "No, I can't send you more landcruisers up there in your sector."

On the radio, the voice of Zingiber, the Northern Flank Commander, was anguished. "But I need them! The Big Uglies have so much of their garbage coming at me that they're pushing me back. And it's not all garbage any more, either: I lost three landcruisers today to those stinking rockets they've started using. Our crews aren't trained to regard infantry as a tactical threat, and we can't pull them out for training sessions now."

"Hardly." Relhost didn't want to know whether Zingiber was serious or not. He might have been; some males still hadn't adjusted to the pace war required on Tosev 3. Relhost went on, "I say again, I have no more landcruisers to send. We've lost several on the southern flank as well, and the rocket threat is making us deploy them more cautiously there, too."

"But I need them," Zingiber repeated, as if his need would conjure landcruisers out of thin air. "*I* say again, superior sir, that as things stand we are losing ground. The two Big Ugly attacks may even succeed in joining."

"Yes, I know. I am also looking at a map screen." Relhost didn't like what he saw there, either. If the Big Uglies did manage to link their thrusts, they'd cut support for his principal assault force, which was finally pounding into the suburbs of Chicago. That was expensive, too; in the rubble of their towns, the Tosevites fought like *ssvapi* on Rabotev 2 protecting their burrows.

Zingiber said, "If you can't send landcruisers, send helicopters to help me take out some more of the Tosevites' armor."

Relhost made up his mind that if Zingiber made one more such idiotic request, he'd relieve him. He hissed angrily before he pressed the TRANSMIT button. "We have fewer helicopters than landcruisers to spare. The miserable Tosevites have learned something new." *They're faster at that than we are.* The thought worried him. He made himself continue: "They've brought their antiaircraft artillery as far forward as they can, towing it with light armor or sometimes even with soft-skinned vehicles. The helicopters are armored against rifle-caliber bullets. To armor them against these shells would make them too heavy to fly."

"Let them ship us landcruisers from elsewhere on this stinking planet, then," Zingiber said.

"The logistics!" Relhost cringed. "Landcruisers are so big and heavy only two will fit onto even our biggest hauler aircraft. And we brought few of those aircraft to Tosev 3, not anticipating so large a need. Besides, the haulers are unarmed and vulnerable to the upsurge in Tosevite air activity lately. It takes only one of those nasty little machines slipping through a killercraft screen to bring down the hauler and the landcruiser both."

"But if we don't get reinforcements from somewhere, we'll lose this battle," Zingiber said. "Let them put the landcruisers on a starship if they must, so long as we get them."

"Land a starship in the middle of a combat zone, vulnerable to artillery and the Emperor only knows what ingenious sabotage the Big Uglies can devise? You must be joking." Relhost made a bitter decision. "I'll pull a few landcruisers back from the principal assault force . . . maybe more than a few. They can return once they rectify the situation."

I hope, he thought. The landcruisers didn't run without fuel, and the Tosevites were doing everything they could to interfere with supply lines. No one loved logistics, but armies that ignored logistics died.

Of course, the Tosevites had fuel problems of their own. They'd stockpiled the noxious stuff their machines burned for this campaign, but the facilities that produced it were vulnerable to assault. Relhost looked at the map again. He hoped the Race would assault them soon.

A couple of Big Uglies in long black coats and wide-brimmed black hats pushed an ordnance cart toward the flight of killercraft. Gefron took no notice of them; Tosevites were doing a lot of menial work these days, to let males of the Race get on with the business of conquering Tosev 3.

Gefron gave Rolvar and Xarol, his fellow pilots in the flight, their last few instructions: "Remember, this one is important. We really have to plaster that Ploesti place; the Big Uglies of Deutschland draw much of their fuel from it."

"It shall be done," the other two males chorused together.

Gefron went on, "So much I have been ordered to tell you. But for myself, I would like to dedicate this mission to the spirit of my predecessor as head of this unit, Flight Leader Teerts. We shall aid in making it impossible for the Big Uglies to kill or capture—we still do not know his exact fate—any more brave males like Teerts. Thanks to us, the conquest of Tosev 3 shall grow nearer its completion."

"It shall be done," the pilots chorused again.

Mordechai Anielewicz walked along Nowolipie Street between closed armaments plants, listening to Nathan Brodsky. The Jewish fighting leader had long since grown used to taking promenades through Warsaw to listen to things he didn't want to take the chance of having the Lizards overhear. This was one of those things: Brodsky, who worked as a laborer at the airport, had picked up a lot of the Lizards' language.

"No doubt about it," Brodsky was saying. The hem of his coat flapped around his ankles as he walked beside Anielewicz. "Their destination is Ploesti; they were talking about knocking out all the Nazis' oil. *Nu*, I know that's important, so I told the Lizard boss I was sick and came straight to you."

"*Nu, nu*," Anielewicz answered. "You're not wrong; it is important. Now I have to figure out what to do about it." He stopped. "Let's head back toward my headquarters."

Brodsky obediently turned. Now Anielewicz walked with his head down, hands jammed into his pockets against the cold. He was thinking very hard indeed. Cooperating with the Germans in any way still left the worst of bad tastes in his mouth. He kept having second thoughts about letting that damned panzer major through with even half his saddlebag of explosive metal.

And now again. If the Lizards wrecked Ploesti, the Nazi war machine was liable to grind to a halt; the Germans, without oil of their own, desperately needed what they got from Romania. The Nazis were still fighting hard against the Lizards, and even hurting them now and again: no one could deny they turned out capable soldiers and clever engineers.

Suppose in the end the Germans won. Would they rest content inside their own borders? Anielewicz snorted. Not bloody likely! But suppose the Germans—suppose mankind—lost. Would the Lizards ever use human beings as anything but hewers of wood and drawers of water? That wasn't bloody likely, either.

The Jewish fighting leader came around the last corner before the office building his men occupied. Among many others, his bicycle stood out in front of it. Seeing it there helped him make up his mind. He slapped Brodsky on the back. "Thank you for letting me know, Nathan. I'll take care of it."

"What will you do?" Brodsky asked.

Anielewicz didn't answer; unlike Brodsky, he'd come to appreciate the need for tight security. What the other Jew didn't know, he couldn't tell.

Anielewicz hopped on his bicycle, rode rapidly to a house outside the ghetto. He knocked on the door. A Polish woman opened it. "May I use your telephone?" he said. "I'm sorry; I'm afraid it's quite urgent."

Her eyes went wide: few people who are part of contingency plans ever expect the contingencies to arrive. But after a moment she nodded. "Yes, of course. Come in. It's in the parlor."

Anielewicz knew where the phone was; his men had installed it. He cranked it, waited for an operator to answer. When she did, he said, "Give me Operator Three-Two-Seven, please."

"One moment." He heard clicks from the switchboard, then: "Three-Two-Seven speaking."

"Yes. This is Yitzhak Bauer. I need to place a call to my uncle Michael in Satu Mare, please. It's urgent."

The operator was one of his people. The false name was one for which she was supposed to be alert. And she was. Without a second's hesitation, she said, "I will try to put you through. It may take some time."

"As fast as you can, please." At full stretch from where he stood, Anielewicz could just reach a chair. He snagged it, sank into it. Polish long-distance phone service had been bad before the war started. It was worse now. He kept the receiver pressed to his ear. What he mostly heard was silence. Every so often, there would be more switchboard clicks or operators' voices at the very limit of hearing.

Time crawled by. The Polish woman brought him a cup of coffee, or rather the burnt-kasha brew that substituted for it. He'd long since grown used to the ersatz, and besides, it was warm. But if the call didn't get through pretty soon, he wouldn't have needed to bother making it: the Lizards would have bombed Ploesti and headed back.

How long to finish arming their planes? he wondered. That was the biggest variable; the flight from here to a little north of Bucharest wouldn't take long, especially not at the speeds the Lizards' aircraft used.

More clicks, more distant chatter, and then, sounding almost as clear as if she were sitting in his lap, Operator Three-Two-Seven said, "I am through to Satu Mare, sir." He heard another operator's voice, more distant, speaking oddly accented German rather than Polish or Yiddish: "Go ahead, Warsaw. To whom do you wish to speak?"

"My uncle Michael—Michael Spiegel, that is," Anielewicz said. "Tell him it's his nephew Yitzhak." Lieutenant-Colonel Michael Spiegel, he was given to understand, commanded the Nazi garrison at Satu Mare, the northernmost Romanian town still in German hands.

"I will connect you. Please wait," the distant operator said.

Anielewicz listened to still more clicks, and then at last a ringing phone. Someone picked it up; he heard a brisk male voice say, *"Bitte?"* The operator explained who he claimed to be. A long pause followed, and then, "Yitzhak? Is that you? I hadn't expected to hear from you."

I hadn't expected to call, either, you Nazi bastard, Anielewicz thought; Spiegel's clear German set his teeth on edge by conditioned reflex. But he made himself say, "Yes, it's me, Uncle Michael. I thought you ought to know that our friends will want some cooking grease from your family—as much as you can spare."

He felt how crude the improvised code was. Spiegel, fortunately, proved quick on the uptake. Hardly missing a beat, the German said, "We'll have to get it ready for them. Do you know when they're coming?"

"I shouldn't be surprised if they'd already left," Anielewicz answered. "I'm sorry, but I just found out they felt like getting it myself."

"Such is life. We'll do what we can. *Hei—* Good-bye." The line went dead.

He started to say Heil Hitler, Anielewicz thought. *Damn good thing he caught himself, in case the Lizards are listening in.*

As soon as he replaced the receiver, the Polish woman stuck her head into the parlor. "Is everything all right?" she asked anxiously.

"I—hope so," he answered, but felt he had to add, "If you have relatives you can stay with, that might be a good idea."

Her pale blue eyes went wide. She nodded. "I'll arrange to have someone get word to my husband," she said. "Now you'd better go."

Anielewicz left in a hurry. He felt bad about endangering a noncombatant family, and even worse about endangering them to benefit the Nazis. *I hope I did the right thing*, he thought as he climbed onto his bicycle. *I wonder if I'll ever be sure.*

Blips appeared on the head-up display that reflected into Gefron's eyes from the inside of the killercraft's windscreen. "Some of the Big Uglies on the ground must have spotted us," the flight leader said. "They're sending aircraft up to try to keep us away from Ploesti." His mouth fell open in amusement at the absurdity of the idea.

The other two pilots in the flight confirmed that their electronics saw the Tosevite aircraft, too. Xarol observed, "They're sending up a lot of aircraft."

"This fuel is important to them," Gefron answered. "They know they have to try to protect it. What they don't know is that they can't. We'll have to show them."

He studied the velocity vectors of the planes the Big Uglies were flying. A couple were the new jets the Deutsche had started throwing into the air. They were fast enough to have been troublesome if they were equipped with radar. As it was, he knew they were there while they still groped for him.

"I'll take the jets," he told the other males. "You two handle the ones with the revolving airfoils. Knock down a few and keep going; we haven't any time to waste toying with them."

He chose targets for his missiles, gave them to the computer. When the tone from the speaker taped to his hearing diaphragm told him the computer had acquired them, he touched the firing button. The killercraft bucked slightly as the wingtip missiles leapt away.

One of the jets never knew what hit it. He watched electronically as a missile swatted it out of the air. The other Tosevite pilot must have spotted the missile meant for him. He tried to dive away from it, but his aircraft wasn't fast enough for that. He went down, too.

Gefron's wingmales salvoed all their missiles, wingtip and pylon both, at the Deutsche aircraft. That blasted a gaping hole in their formation, through which the killercraft flew. Rolvar and Xarol shouted excitedly; they hadn't seen so much opposition since the war was new.

Gefron was pleased, too, but also a little worried. The Big Ugly pilots weren't fleeing; they were trying to regroup in the wake of the killercraft. Returning to base, only he would have missiles left to fire at them.

It shouldn't matter, Gefron told himself. *If we can't get by them with our speed, altitude, radar, and cannon, we don't deserve to conquer this planet.* But it was one more thing to worry about.

He studied the radar display. "Approaching target," he said. "Remember, the Deutsche have set up a dummy target north of the real installation. If you bomb that one by mistake, I promise that you'll never get your tailstumps into a killercraft again as long as you live."

The real Ploesti lay in a little vale. Gefron had it on his radar set. He peered through the windscreen, ready to paint the assigned refineries with his laser to guide the bombs in. But instead of the towers of the refineries and petroleum wells, the big squat cylinders that stored refined hydrocarbons, all he saw was a spreading, thickening cloud of gray-black smoke. He hissed. The Deutsche weren't playing fair.

His wingmales noticed the problem at the same time he did. "What are we supposed to do now?" Rolvar asked. "How can we light up the targets through all that junk?"

Gefron wanted to abort the mission and fly back to base. But, because he was the flight leader, anything that went wrong would get blamed on him. "We'll bomb anyway," he declared. "Whatever in the smoke we hit will hurt the Deutsche somehow."

"Truth," Xarol declared. The flight went on. Gefron turned on the laser targeting system in the hope it would penetrate the smoke or find some clear patches through which to acquire accurate targets for the bombs his killercraft carried under its wings. No luck—instead of the steady tone he wanted to hear, all he got was the complaining warble of a system that couldn't lock on.

The Deutsch antiaircraft guns that lined the ridges on either side of the petroleum wells and refineries opened up with everything they had. More smoke dotted the sky, now in big black puffs around and mostly behind the flight of killercraft: the Big Uglies at the guns weren't leading the Race's aircraft quite enough.

Even so, the display of firepower was impressive. The bursts from exploding Tosevite shells seemed close enough together for Gefron to get out of his aircraft and walk across them. Once or twice he heard sharp rattles, like gravel bouncing off sheet metal. It wasn't gravel, though; it was fragments of shell casing punching holes in his fuselage and wing. He anxiously scanned the instrument panel for damage lights. None came on.

The Deutsche were defending Ploesti every way they knew how. Above the clotted smoke floated balloons tethered to stout cables that might wreck an aircraft that ran into them. More antiaircraft guns, some cannons like those on the high ground to either side, others mere machine guns that spat glowing tracers, fired out of the smoke. They had no radar control and so could not see what they hoped to hit, but they added more metal to an already crowded sky.

"Does anyone have laser lock-on?" Gefron asked hopefully. Both wingmales denied it. Gefron sighed. The results would not be what his superiors had hoped for. "Proceed on purely visual bombing run."

"It shall be done, Flight Leader," Xarol and Rolvar chorused.

Then they were over the billowing smoke. Gefron poised a claw at the bomb-release button. The killercraft lost both weight and drag as the ordnance fell away. All at once it seemed a much better performer.

"We *did* hurt them, by the spirits of departed Emperors!" Xarol said exultantly.

The wingmale was right. Sudden new angry clouds of black, greasy smoke roiled up through the screen the Deutsche had stretched above Ploesti. Through new smoke and old, Gefron saw sullen orange fireballs blooming like so many huge, terrible flowers.

"The Big Uglies will be a long time repairing that," the flight leader agreed happily. He radioed a report of success to the base from which he'd set out, then returned to the intraflight frequency: "Now we go home."

"As if we had any real home on this cold ball of mud," Rolvar said.

"Part of it—the more southerly latitudes—can be quite pleasant," Gefron replied. "And even this area's not too bad in local summer. Present conditions, of course, are something else again—I assure you, I find frozen water as revolting as does any other male in his right mind."

He brought his killercraft onto the reciprocal of the course he'd flown to Ploesti. As he did so, his radar picked up the Big Ugly aircraft through which his flight had barreled on the way to the refinery complex. They hadn't come straight after the killercraft; instead, they'd loitered along the likely return route and used the time while he and his wingmales were making their bombing run to gain altitude.

Gefron would have been just as glad to scoot past unnoticed, but one of the Big Uglies spotted him and his comrades. They might have been radarless, but they had radios. What one of them saw, the others learned in moments. Their aircraft turned toward the flight for an attack run.

The range closed frighteningly fast. The Big Uglies flew inadequate aircraft, but they flew them with panache and courage, darting straight at Gefron and his wingmales. The flight leader fired his next-to-last missile and then, a moment later, his last one. Two Tosevite planes tumbled in ruins. The rest kept coming.

On the head-up display, Gefron saw another enemy aircraft break up, and yet another: Rolvar and Xarol were using their cannon to good effect. But the Big Uglies were firing, too; through the windscreen, past the head-up display, the flight leader watched the pale flashes from their guns. He turned the nose of his killercraft toward the nearest Big Ugly, fired a short burst. Smoke poured from the enemy's engine; the plane began to fall.

Then the flight was through the horde of Tosevites. Gefron let out a long sigh of relief: the Big Uglies could not hope to pursue. He keyed his radio: "All well, wingmales?"

"All well, Flight Leader," Rolvar answered. But Xarol said, "Not all well, superior sir. I took several hits as we mixed it up with the Big Uglies. I've lost electrical power to some of my control surfaces, and I'm losing hydraulic pressure in the backup system. I am not certain I will be able to complete return to base."

"I will inspect visually." Gefron gained altitude and lost speed, letting Xarol pull ahead of him. What he saw made him hiss in dismay: part of the tail surface of his wingmale's killercraft had been shot away, and two lines of dismayingly large holes stitched the right wing and fuselage. "You didn't just take several hits; you got yourself chewed up. Can you keep it flying?"

"For the time being, superior sir, but altitude control grows increasingly difficult."

"Do the best you can. If you are able to set down on one of our airstrips, the Race will have the opportunity to repair your aircraft rather than writing it off."

"I understand, superior sir."

The Race had lost far more equipment on Tosev 3 than even the most pessimistic forecasts allowed for. Keeping what was left operational was a priority that grew higher every day.

But luck was not with Xarol. He did manage to keep his killercraft airborne until the flight reached territory the Race controlled. Gefron had just radioed the nearest landing strip of his wingmale's predicament when Xarol announced, "I regret, superior sir, that I have no choice but to abandon the aircraft." Moments later, a blue-white fireball marked the machine's impact point.

When Gefron landed back at Warsaw, he learned his wingmale had ejected safely and been rescued. That pleased him—but the next time Xarol needed to fly, what aircraft would he use?

Small-arms fire rattled through Naperville. Mutt Daniels crouched in the trench in front of the ruins of the Preemption House. Every so often, when the firing slackened, he'd stick his tommy gun up over the forward rim of the trench, squeeze off a short burst in the direction of the Lizards, and then yank it back down again.

"Kinda quiet today, isn't it, Sarge?" Kevin Donlan said just as one such burst was answered by a storm of fire from the aliens, whose forward outposts were only a few hundred yards to the east.

Mutt pressed his face against the dirt wall of the trench as bullets whined just overhead. "You call this here quiet?" he said, thinking he'd chill the kid with sarcasm.

But Donlan wouldn't chill. "Yeah, Sarge. I mean, it is, isn't it. Just rifle fire right now—just rifle fire all day long, pretty much. I don't miss the artillery one little bit, let me tell you."

"Me neither. Rifles are bad enough, but that other stuff, that's what slaughters you." Daniels paused, played back the day's action in his head. "You know, you're right, and I didn't even notice. They ain't done much with their big guns today, have they?"

"I didn't think so. What do you suppose it means?"

"Damfino." Mutt wished he had a cigarette or a chew or even a pipe. "I ain't sorry not to be on this end of it either, though; don't get me wrong about that. But why they're off with it . . . son, I couldn't begin to tell you."

The more he thought about it, the more it worried him. The Lizards didn't have numbers going for them; their strength had always lain in their guns: their tanks and self-propelled pieces. If they were easing off with those . . .

"Maybe our offensive really is putting the screws to them, making them pull back," Donlan said.

"Mebbe." Daniels remained unconvinced. He'd been falling back before the invaders ever since he got strafed out of his train. The idea that other troops could move forward against them was galling; it seemed to say nothing he'd done, nothing Sergeant Schneider—as fine a soldier as ever lived—had done, was good enough. He didn't like believing that.

Behind him, back toward Chicago, an American artillery barrage opened up on the Lizard position. It was an odd, pawky sort of shelling, on again, off again, nothing like the endless rains of projectiles that had punctuated combat in France. If you kept a gun in the same place for more than two or three rounds, the Lizards would figure out where it was and blast it. Mutt didn't know how they did it, but he knew they did. He'd seen too many dead artillerymen and wrecked guns to have any doubt left.

He waited for counterbattery fire to start. With the cynical sense of self-preservation soldiers soon develop, he would sooner have had the Lizards shelling positions miles behind him than lobbing their presents into his trench.

American shells kept falling on the Lizards. When half an hour went by without reply, Daniels said, "You know, kid, you might just be right. Feels mighty damn good to give it to 'em instead of taking it, don't you reckon?"

"Hell yes, Sergeant," Donlan said happily.

A runner came down heavily into the trench where the two men sheltered. He said, "Check your watches, Sergeant, soldier. We're advancing against their lines in"—he glanced at his own watch—"nineteen minutes." He ran down the trench toward the next knot of men.

"You got a watch?" Donlan asked.

"Yeah," Mutt answered absently. Advancing against the Lizards! He hadn't heard orders like that since outside Shabbona, halfway across the state. That had been a disaster. This time, though . . . "Maybe we really are hurting 'em out there. God damn, I hope we are."

General Patton's personal vehicle was a big, ungainly Dodge command and reconnaissance car, one of the kind that had been nicknamed jeeps until the squarish little Willys vehicles took the name away from them. This one had been altered with a .50 caliber machine-gun mount that let Patton blaze away as well as command.

To Jens Larssen, who munched on crackers in the backseat and tried to stay inconspicuous, the gun seemed excessive. No one had asked his opinion. As far as he could see, no one ever asked anyone's opinion in the Army. You either gave orders or you went out and did what you were told.

Patton turned to him and said, "I do regret that you were thrust into the front line, Dr. Larssen. You bear too much value to your country for you to have been so cavalierly risked."

"It's all right," Larssen said. "I lived through it." *Somehow*, he added to himself. "Where are we now, anyhow?"

"D'you see that hill there, the one with the tall building sprouting from it?" Patton asked, pointing through the Dodge jeep's windshield. On the flat prairie country of central Illinois, any rise, no matter how slight, stood out. Patton went on, "The building is the State Farm Insurance headquarters, and the town"—he paused for dramatic effect—"the town, Dr. Larssen, is Bloomington."

"The objective." Larssen hoped General Patton would not take offense at the surprise in his voice. The Lizards had seemed so nearly invincible ever since they came to Earth. He hadn't dared believe Patton could not only force a breakthrough but exploit it once made.

"The objective," Patton agreed proudly. As if answering the thought

Jens hadn't spoken, he added, "Once we broke through their crust, they were hollow behind it. No doubt we were confused and scared, attacking such a formidable foe. But they showed confusion and fright themselves, sir, not least because they were being attacked."

The bulky radio console set into the space behind the rear seat of the Dodge jeep let out a squawk. Patton grabbed for the earphones and mike. He listened for a minute or so, then softly breathed one word: "Outstanding." He stowed the radio gear, gave his attention back to Larssen: "Our scouts, sir, have met advance parties from General Bradley's army north of Bloomington. We now have the force which was attacking Chicago trapped within our ring of steel."

"That's—wonderful," Larssen said. "But will they stay trapped?"

"A legitimate question," Patton said. "We will learn soon: reports indicated that the armor they had been using to spearhead their advance into Chicago has now reversed its direction."

"It's bearing down on us?" Jens felt some of the bladder-loosening fear he'd known while diverting the Lizard tank so the fellow with the bazooka could stalk and kill it. He remembered the gaggle of American tanks the monster had taken out, and the wrecked fighting vehicles that littered the snowy plains of Indiana and Illinois. If lots of those tanks were heading this way, how was Second Armor supposed to stop them?

Patton said, "I understand your concern, Dr. Larssen, but fighting aggressively while holding the strategic defensive should let us inflict heavy losses on them. And infantry teams firing antitank rockets from ambush will present a challenge they have not previously experienced."

"I sure hope so," Larssen said. He went on, "If they're coming from Chicago, sir, when will I be able to go into the city to find out what's become of the Metallurgical Laboratory?" *And, even more important, what's become of Barbara,* he thought. But he'd learned he was more likely to get what he wanted from Patton by leaving personal concerns out of the equation.

"As soon as we have destroyed the Lizard tank forces, of course," Patton said grandly. "We'll do to them what Rommel did to the British time and again in the desert: make them charge down lines of fire we'll already have preregistered. Not only that, our forces farther east have gone over to the attack and are pursuing them out of Chicago. It should be a slaughter."

Of whom? Jens wondered. The Lizard tanks were not the slow, balky, unreliable machines England used. Would any defenses be enough to hold them back when they wanted to go somewhere?

As if to underscore his concern, half a mile ahead a helicopter skimmed low over the ground like a mechanized shark. A rocket lanced out to obliterate an American halftrack and however many men it was carrying. Patton swore and started hammering away with his heavy machine gun. The noise was overpowering, like standing next to a triphammer. Tracers showed he was scoring hits, but the tough machine ignored them.

Then, without warning, something heavier than a .50 caliber slug must have hit it. It heeled awkwardly in the air; Patton almost shot off his driver's ear as he tried to keep a bead on it. The helicopter scurried away, back toward the west where the Lizards still held the countryside.

Maybe another shell found it then. Maybe the cumulative damage from all the bullets Patton and every other American in range poured into it took a toll. Or maybe the Lizard pilot, fleeing under heavy fire, just made a mistake. The helicopter's rotor clipped a tree. The machine did a twisting somersault straight into the ground.

Patton yelled like a madman. So did Jens and the jeep driver. Patton pounded the physicist on the back. "Do you see, Dr. Larssen? Do you see?" he shouted. "They're not invulnerable, not even slightly."

"So they're not," Jens admitted. Lizard tanks, though, carried more firepower and more armor than their helicopters. They might not be invulnerable, but they sure had seemed close to it until that crazy bazooka thing took one out. Even then, the rocket round hadn't wrecked it with a frontal hit, but with one to the less heavily protected engine compartment.

"Yes, sir, Larssen, it won't be long before you can head into Chicago as a conqueror," Patton boomed. "If you're going to do, by God, do it with style!"

Jens didn't care anything about style. He would gladly have gone into Chicago naked and in blackface if that was the only way to get there. And if Patton insisted on holding him away much longer, he'd damn well take French leave and head into town on his own. *Why not?* he thought. *It's not like I'm really a soldier.*

Atvar increased the magnification on the situation map. The Race's movements appeared in red arrows, those of the Big Uglies in rather fuzzier white ones that reflected the uncertainties of reconnaissance. The fleetlord hissed in discontent. "I don't know whether we're going to be able to extricate our forces there or not."'

Kirel peered at the situation map, too. "This is the pocket in which the Tosevites on the lesser continental map have trapped our assault units, Exalted Fleetlord?"

"Yes," Atvar said. "They have taught us a lesson here: never be so concerned about the point of an attack as to neglect the flanks."

"Indeed." Kirel left one eye on the map, turned the other toward Atvar. "Forgive me, Exalted Fleetlord, but I had not looked for you to be so, ah, sanguine over our misfortunes in the, ah, not-empire called the United States."

"You mistake me, Shiplord," Atvar said sharply, and Kirel lowered his eyes in apology. Atvar went on, "I do not enjoy seeing our brave males endangered by the Big Uglies under any circumstances. Moreover, I have hope we shall still be able to get many of them out. If the beastly weather would let up, our aircraft ought to be able to blast an escape corridor through which we could conduct our retreat. Failing that, the landcruisers will have to do the job."

"Landcruiser losses have been unusually heavy in this action," Kirel said.

"I know." That did pain Atvar; without those landcruisers, his ground-based forces were going to have ever more trouble conducting needed operations. He said, "The Big Uglies have come up with something new again."

"So they have." The disgust with which Kirel freighted his words made it sound as if he were cursing the Tosevites for their ingenuity. The Race had had plenty of cause to do that; had the Big Uglies been less fiendishly ingenious, all of Tosev 3 would long since have been incorporated into the Empire.

Atvar said, "As with most of their innovations, we will need a certain amount of time to develop appropriate countermeasures." *They should be in place about the time the Big Uglies invent their next new weapon,* he thought. *And, of course, they won't work against that.* Aloud, he continued, "Still, considering how different this world is from what our probe predicted, we should count ourselves lucky that we've not got our tailstumps pinched in the doorway more often."

"As you say, Exalted Fleetlord." But Kirel sounded anything but convinced.

Atvar let his mouth fall open. "In case you're wondering, Shiplord, I've not started tasting ginger; I don't suffer from the insane self-confidence the drug induces. I have reason for being sanguine, as you termed it. Observe."

He poked a control with a claw. The situation map vanished from the screen, to be replaced by images from a killercraft's gun cameras. On the screen, bombs arced down into drifting, blowing smoke. Moments later, fireballs and more smoke mushroomed into the sky. The angle of the tape jerked sharply as the killercraft dodged through desperate Tosevite efforts to shoot it down.

"That, Shiplord," Atvar declared, "is a Tosevite petroleum refinery going up in flames. It happens to be the one that supplies Deutschland, but we have struck several in recent days. If we continue on that pattern, the embarrassments we have suffered around this town of Chicago should soon fade into insignificance as the Big Uglies run low on fuel."

"How massive is this destruction when compared to the overall production of the facility?" Kirel asked.

Atvar replayed the tape. He enjoyed watching the enemy's petroleum stocks going up in flames. "Do the images not speak for themselves? Smoke has shrouded this, ah, Ploesti place ever since our attack, which means the Big Uglies have yet to suppress the blazes we started."

"But there was smoke around the facility before," Kirel persisted. "Is this not part of the Tosevites' ongoing camouflage efforts?"

"Infrared imaging indicates otherwise," Atvar said. "Some of these hot spots have remained in place since our bombs ignited them."

"That is good news," Kirel admitted.

"It is the best possible news, and the story at other refineries is similar," the fleetlord said. "They have gone down to destruction more easily even than I anticipated when I began this series of strikes against them. The war for Tosev 3 may have hung in the balance up until this time, but now we are tilting the balance decisively in our favor."

"May it be so." Ever cautious, Kirel accepted nothing new until it was proved overwhelmingly. "The future of the Race here depends on its being so. The colony ships are behind us, after all."

"So they are." Atvar played the tape of the burning refinery yet again. "We shall be ready for them, by the Emperor." He cast his eyes to the floor in reverence for his sovereign. So did Kirel.

George Patton aimed the jeep's machine gun up in the air, squeezed the triggers. As the gun roared, he tried to outyell it. After a few seconds, he stopped firing and turned to Jens Larssen. He pummeled the physicist with his fists. "We've done it, by God!" he bawled. "We've held the sons of bitches."

"We really have, haven't we?" Larssen knew he sounded more amazed than overjoyed, but he couldn't help it—that was how he felt.

Patton didn't get angry; nothing, Jens thought, would have angered Patton this morning. He said, "This is the greatest victory in the war against the Lizards." (It was also, for all practical purposes, the first and only victory in the war against the alien invaders, but Jens didn't want to cut into Patton's ebullience by pointing that out.) "Now that we know it can be done and how to do it, we'll beat them again and again."

If confidence had anything to do with anything, Patton would, too. He looked as if he'd just stepped off a recruiting poster. His chin, as usual, was naked of stubble, his uniform clean, his boots shiny. He smelled of Ivory soap and aftershave.

How he managed that right through a hard-driving campaign was beyond Larssen, whose own face was like a wire brush, whose splotched and spotted overcoat (he devoutly hoped) helped camouflage him, and whose shoes had broken laces and no finish whatsoever. Patton insisted spruced-up soldiers had better morale. Seeing the spruced-up Patton beside him only reminded Jens how grubby he was himself.

But victory kicked morale harder and higher than mere cleanliness ever could. Larssen said, "It's a damn shame any of the Lizards broke out."

"It is indeed," Patton said. "I console myself by remembering that perfection is an attribute belonging only to God. This consolation comes easier because we closed off the breakout after the tanks punched through. Few foot soldiers managed to follow them." He pointed to a burnt-out Lizard tank not far away. "And more of their armor ended up like that."

Larssen remembered the murdered Lees and Shermans in the front of the Lizard tank he'd helped stalk. "A lot of ours ended up that way, too, sir. Do you know what the ratio was?"

"About a dozen to one," Patton answered easily. Jens' mouth fell open in dismay; he hadn't thought the butcher's bill as high as that. Patton held up a hand. "Before you expostulate, Dr. Larssen, let me remind you: that is far and away the best ratio we have yet achieved in combat with the Lizards. If we can maintain it, the ultimate triumph will be ours."

"But—" A Lizard tank had a crew of three. A Sherman carried five men, a Lee six; the casualty ratio had to be even worse than the one for vehicles.

"I know, I know." Patton cut off his objection before it could get started. "We are still manufacturing tanks, so far as we know, the Lizards cannot make good their losses. The same applies to crews: our pool replenishes itself, while theirs does not."

A couple of men with technical sergeants' stripes climbed onto the dead Lizard tank. One peered down into the turret through the open cupola. He called to his companion, who scrambled over to take his own look.

Patton beamed at them. "And, you see, with every vehicle of theirs we examine, we learn more about how to defeat them. I tell you, Dr. Larssen, we are tilting the balance in our favor."

"I hope you're right." Jens decided to strike while the iron was hot: "Since we've won this battle, sir, may I finally have permission to go into Chicago and see what's become of the Metallurgical Laboratory?"

The general frowned; he looked like a poker player deciding whether to play a hand or throw it in. At last he said, "I don't suppose I can in justice object, Dr. Larssen, and no doubt your country needs your services with that project." He wouldn't say what the Met Lab was about, even with only his driver listening. *Security*, Jens thought. Patton went on, "I also want to thank you for the good nature with which you have borne your stay with us."

Larssen nodded politely, though there hadn't been anything good-natured about it, not from his end. He'd simply had to yield to superior force. Whining about it afterward would only have put him further into the doghouse.

"I will provide you with an escort to take you into the city," Patton said. "Lizard holdouts still infest the territory through which you'll have to pass."

"Sir, if it's all the same to you, that's an honor I'd really like to decline," Larssen said. "Wouldn't traveling with an escort just make me a likelier target rather than safer? I'd sooner hunt up a bicycle and go by myself."

"You are a national resource, Dr. Larssen, which in some measure gives me continued responsibility for your well-being." Patton chewed on his lower lip. "You may be right, though; who can say? Will you also decline help in the form of, ah, hunting up a bicycle and a letter of *laissez-passer* from me?"

"No, sir," Jens answered at once. "I'd be very grateful for both those things."

"Good." Patton smiled his wintry smile. Then he waved to draw the attention of some soldiers not far away. They came trotting over to find out what he wanted. When he'd explained, they grinned and scattered in all directions to do his bidding. While he waited for them to return, he pulled out a sheet of stationery embossed with two gold stars (Jens marveled that he'd still have a supply of such a thing) and a fountain pen. Shielding the paper from blowing snow with his free hand, he wrote rapidly, then handed the sheet to Larssen. "Will this suffice?"

Jens' eyebrows rose. It was more than a *laissez-passer*: it not only ordered the military to feed him, but nearly conferred on him the power to bind and to loose. Larssen wouldn't have cared to be a soldier who ignored it and had word of that get back to Patton. He folded it, stuck it in a trouser pocket. "Thank you, sir. That's very generous."

"I've given you a hard time since you turned up on my doorstep. I don't apologize for it; military necessity took precedence over your needs. But I will make such amends for it as I can."

Inside half an hour, the soldiers had come up with four or five bikes for Jens to choose from. Nobody said anything about giving back the Springfield he'd been issued, so he kept it. He swung onto a sturdy Schwinn and pedaled off toward the northeast.

"Chicago," he said under his breath as he rolled along. But the grin he wore at being at last free of the army soon fell from his lips. The country between Bloomington and Chicago had been fought over twice, first when the Lizards pushed toward Lake Michigan and then when they tried to break back through the ring Patton and Bradley had thrown around them. Larssen found out firsthand how ugly the aftermath of war could be.

The only thing he'd known about Pontiac, Illinois, was that the phrase "out at Pontiac" meant somebody was at the state penitentiary on the southern edge of town. The penitentiary was a bombed-out ruin now. The wreckage of an American fighter plane lay just outside the prison gates, the upright tail the only piece intact. It was also probably the only cross the pilot who'd been inside would ever get.

The rest of the town was in no better shape. Machine-gun bullet scars pocked the soot-stained walls of the county courthouse. Larssen almost rode over a crumpled bronze tablet lying in the street. He stopped to read it. It had, he found, been mounted on a cairn of glacial stones as a monument to the Indian chief who'd given Pontiac its name. He looked at the courthouse lawn. No cairn stood, only scattered and broken stones. He pedaled out of town as fast as he could.

Every so often he'd hear gunfire. From a distance, it sounded absurdly cheerful, like firecrackers on the Fourth of July. Now that he'd been on the receiving end of it, though, it made the hair on the back of his neck rise. Those little popping noises meant somebody was trying to kill someone else.

The next day he came to Gardner, a little town dominated by slag piles. Gardner couldn't have been lovely before war raked it coming and going; it was a lot less lovely now. But the Stars and Stripes fluttered from atop one of the piles. When Larssen saw soldiers moving around up there, he decided to test Patton's letter.

It worked like a charm. The men fed him a big bowl of the mulligan stew they were eating, gave him a slug of what he presumed to be highly unofficial whiskey to wash it down, and plied him with questions about the general whose signature he flourished.

The squad leader, a worn-looking, chunky sergeant whose thinning gray hair said he was surely a First World War veteran, summed up the soldiers' view of Patton by declaring, "Shitfire there, pal, sure is fine to see somebody goin' for'ards instead o' back. We done went back too much." His drawl was thick and rich as coffee heavily laced with chicory; he seemed to go by the name Mutt.

"It cost us a lot," Larssen said quietly.

"Goin' back toward Chicago wasn't what you'd call cheap, neither," the sergeant said, to which Jens could only nod.

He got into Joliet just before dark. Joliet had had a prison, too, with thick corbeled limestone walls. It was just rubble; it had been made into a fortress to try to halt the Lizards—the twisted barrel of a field gun still stuck out through a window—and then bombed and shelled into oblivion. Jens wondered what had become of the prisoners.

As he had so often in his wandering through war-torn America, he found a ruined, empty house in which to sleep. Only after he'd already unrolled his sleeping bag did he notice the bones scattered across the floor. A caved-in skull left no doubt they were human. Before the Lizards came, he wouldn't have stayed there for a minute. Now he just shrugged. He'd seen worse than bones lately. Thinking again of the prisoners, he made sure his Springfield had a round in the chamber and the safety off when he set it beside the sleeping bag.

No one murdered him in the night. When he woke up, he flipped on the safety but left the round chambered. Chicago lay straight ahead.

He took longer to get there than he'd expected. The heaviest, most sustained fighting had been in the suburbs right on the edge of town. He'd never seen devastation like that, nor had to try to pick his way through it. Long stretches were impassable by bike; he had to lug the two-wheeler along with him, which also made him slower afoot.

Scavengers were out poking through the ruins. Some, who wore Army uniform, were busy examining disabled Lizard vehicles and aircraft to see what they could learn from them, or else salvaging as much American gear from the field as they could. Others were in no uniform at all, and plainly out for whatever they could get their hands on. Jens flipped the Springfield's safety off again.

Once he actually got into Chicago, the going improved. Rubble still spilled onto roads, but on the whole you could tell where the roads were. Some of the buildings had signs painted across them: WHEN SHELLS COME IN, THIS SIDE OF THE STREET IS SAFER. A lot of shells had come in.

Along with rubble, the streets also had people in them. Except for soldiers, Jens hadn't seen so many people in a long time. Where there'd been fighting, the civilians were mostly either dead or fled. Many were dead or fled in Chicago, too, but the town had had three million to start out with, and a good many were left, too.

They were skinny and ragged and dirty; a lot of them had haunted eyes. They didn't look like the Americans Larssen was used to seeing. They looked like people you'd see in a newsreel, people who'd been through a war. He'd never expected to come across that in the United States, but here it was, like a kick in the teeth.

A girl leaned against a streetcorner lamppost. Her dress was too short for the chilly weather. She twitched her hips at Jens as he rode by. No matter how long he'd been celibate, he kept riding—her face was as hard and merciless as any combat veteran's.

"Cheap bastard!" she yelled after him. "Lousy fairy! I hope it rots off!" He wondered how she treated men who actually bought from her. Better than that, he hoped.

If possible, the Negroes in the Bronzeville district looked even more miserable than the whites in the rest of town. Jens felt the glances he was drawing as he pedaled along, but no one seemed inclined to do more than glance at a man who wore an Army overcoat and carried an Army rifle.

The apartment building where he'd lived with Barbara was on the edge of Bronzeville. He rounded the last corner, used the hand brake to slide to a stop . . . in front of a pile of bricks and tiles and broken glass that wasn't a building any more. Sometime after he'd left, it had taken a direct hit. A couple of colored kids were pawing through the ruins. One of them exclaimed in triumph over a foot-long board. He stuck it into a burlap bag.

"Do you know what happened to Mrs. Larssen, the white lady who used to live here?" Jens called to the boys. Fear rose up in him like a choking cloud; he wasn't sure he wanted the answer.

But both kids just shook their heads. "Never heard of her, mistuh," one of them said. They went back to looking for fuel.

Larssen rode east, to the University of Chicago campus. If he couldn't find Barbara, the Met Lab crew was the next best bet—they might even know what had happened to her.

Though bare of students, the university didn't seem as badly battered as the city around it, perhaps because its buildings were more widely scattered. Jens rode up Fifty-eighth and then across the lawns in the center of campus. They had been a lot more pleasant before they were pocked with bomb and shell craters.

Off to the right, Swift Hall was a burnt-out ruin; God hadn't spared the university's divinity school. But Eckhart Hall still stood, and, but for broken windows, looked pretty much intact. Worn as he was, hope made Jens all but sprint the bike toward the entrance.

He started to leave it outside, then thought better of that and brought it in—no use giving looters temptation they didn't need. "Where is everybody?" he called down the hallway. Only echoes answered. *It's after quitting time,* he told himself, but hope flickered all the same.

He walked to the stairway, took the steps two at a time. No matter when the secretaries and such went home, the Met Lab scientists were busy almost around the clock. But the halls upstairs were empty and silent, the offices and labs not only vacant but methodically stripped. Wherever the Metallurgical Laboratory was, it didn't live at the University of Chicago any more.

He trudged downstairs much more slowly than he'd gone up. Somebody was standing by his bicycle. He started to snatch his rifle off his shoulder, then recognized the man. "Andy!" he exclaimed.

The gray-haired custodian whirled in surprise. "Jesus and Mary, it's you, Dr. Larssen," he said, his voice still flavored with the Auld Sod though he'd been born in Chicago. "I tell you true, I never thought I'd see you again."

"Plenty of times I never thought I'd get here," Jens answered. "Where the devil has the Met Lab gone?"

Instead of answering directly, Reilly fumbled in his shirt pocket, pulled out a creased and stained envelope. "Your wife gave me this to give to you if ever you came back. Like I said, I had my doubts you would, but I always hung on to it, just on the off chance—"

"Andy, you're a wonder." Jens tore open the envelope. He let out a soft exclamation of delight as he recognized Barbara's handwriting. The note was stained and blurry—probably from the janitor's sweat—but the gist was still clear. Larssen shook his head in tired dismay. He'd come so far, been through so much.

"Denver?" he said aloud. "How the devil am I supposed to get to Denver?" Like the war, his journey had a long way to go.

ABOUT THE AUTHOR

HARRY TURTLEDOVE has lived in Southern California all his life. He has a Ph.D. in history from UCLA and has taught at UCLA, California State Fullerton, and California State University, Los Angeles. He has published in both history and speculative fiction. He is married to novelist Laura Frankos. They have three daughters: Alison, Rachel, and Rebecca.